THE COMPLETE ILLUSTRATED STORIES OF
THE BROTHERS GRIMM

THE COMPLETE ILLUSTRATED STORIES OF
THE BROTHERS GRIMM

WITH TWO HUNDRED ILLUSTRATIONS BY E. H. WEHNERT

CHANCELLOR
PRESS

First published in Great Britain in 1853 by
George Routledge & Sons Ltd under the title
Grimm's Household Stories
This redesigned edition published in 1984 by
Chancellor Press
59 Grosvenor Street
London W1
Reprinted 1985, 1986

Arrangement and design © 1984 Octopus Books Ltd

ISBN 0 907 486 63 0

Printed in Hungary
50562

The story now called 'The Thief among Thorns'
was originally entitled 'The Jew among Thorns'.

CONTENTS

CHILDREN'S LEGENDS

The Frog Prince

In the olden time, when wishing was having, there lived a King, whose daughters were all beautiful; but the youngest was so exceedingly beautiful that the Sun himself, although he saw her very often, was enchanted every time she came out into the sunshine.

Near the castle of this King was a large and gloomy forest, and in the midst stood an old lime-tree, beneath whose branches splashed a little fountain; so, whenever it was very hot, the King's youngest daughter ran off into this wood, and sat down by the side of this fountain; and, when she felt dull, would often divert herself by throwing a golden ball up in the air and catching it. And this was her favourite amusement.

Now, one day it happened, that this golden ball, when the King's daughter threw it into the air, did not fall down into her hand, but on the grass; and then it rolled past her into the fountain. The King's daughter followed the ball with her eyes, but it disappeared beneath the water, which was so deep that no one could see to the bottom. Then she began to lament, and to cry louder and louder; and, as she cried, a voice called out, "Why weepest thou, O King's daughter? thy tears would melt even a stone to pity." And she looked around to the spot whence the voice came, and saw a Frog stretching his thick ugly head out of the water. "Ah! you old water-paddler," said she, "was it you that spoke? I am weeping for my golden ball which has slipped away from me into the water."

"Be quiet, and do not cry," answered the Frog; "I can give thee good advice. But what wilt thou give me if I fetch thy plaything up again?"

"What will you have, dear Frog?" said she. "My dresses, my pearls and jewels, or the golden crown which I wear?"

The Frog answered, "Dresses, or jewels, or golden crowns, are not for me; but if thou wilt love me, and let me be thy companion and playfellow, and sit at thy table, and eat from thy little golden plate, and drink out of thy cup, and sleep in thy little bed, – if thou wilt promise me all these, then will I dive down and fetch up thy golden ball."

"Oh, I will promise you all," said she, "if you will only get me my ball." But she thought to herself, "What is the silly Frog chattering about? Let him remain in the water with his equals; he cannot mix in society." But the Frog, as soon as he had received her promise, drew his head under the water and dived down. Presently he swam up again with the ball in his mouth, and threw it on the grass. The King's daughter was full of joy when she again saw her beautiful plaything; and, taking it up, she ran off immediately. "Stop! stop!" cried the Frog; "take me with thee. I cannot run as thou canst." But all his croaking was useless; although it was loud enough, the King's daughter did not hear it, but, hastening home, soon forgot the poor Frog, who was obliged to leap back into the fountain.

The next day, when the King's daughter was sitting at table with her father and all his courtiers, and was eating from her own little golden plate, something was heard coming up the marble stairs, splish-splash, splish-splash; and when it arrived at the top, it knocked at the door, and a voice said, "Open the door, thou youngest daughter of the King!" So she rose and went to see who it was that called her; but when she opened the door and caught sight of the Frog, she shut it again with great vehemence, and sat down at the table, looking very pale. But the King perceived that her heart was beating violently, and asked her whether it were a giant who had come to fetch her away who stood at the door. "Oh, no!" answered she; "it is no giant, but an ugly Frog."

"What does the Frog want with you?" said the King.

"Oh, dear father, when I was sitting yesterday playing by the fountain, my golden ball fell into the water, and this Frog fetched it up again because I cried so much: but first, I must tell you, he pressed me so much, that I promised him he should be my companion. I never thought that he could come out of the water, but somehow he has jumped out, and now he wants to come in here."

At that moment there was another knock, and a voice said,—

> "King's daughter, youngest,
>   Open the door.
> Hast thou forgotten
> Thy promises made
> At the fountain so clear
> 'Neath the lime-tree's shade
> King's daughter, youngest,
>   Open the door."

Then the King said, "What you have promised, that you must perform; go and let him in." So the King's daughter went and opened the door, and the Frog hopped in after her right up to her chair: and as soon as she was seated, the Frog said, "Take me up;" but she hesitated so long that at last the King ordered her to obey. And as soon as the Frog sat on the chair he jumped on to the table and said, "Now push thy plate near me, that we may eat together." And she did so, but as every one saw, very unwillingly. The Frog seemed to relish his dinner much, but every bit that the King's daughter ate nearly choked her, till at last the Frog said, "I have satisfied my hunger and feel very tired; wilt thou carry me upstairs now into thy chamber, and make thy bed ready that we may sleep together?" At this speech the King's daughter began to cry, for she was afraid of the cold Frog, and dared not touch him; and besides, he actually wanted to sleep in her own beautiful, clean bed.

But her tears only made the King very angry, and he said, "He who helped you in the time of your trouble, must not now be despised!" So she took the Frog up with two fingers, and put him in a corner of her chamber. But as she lay in her bed, he crept up to it, and said, "I am so very tired that I shall sleep well; do take me up or I will tell thy father." This speech put the King's daughter in a terrible passion, and catching the Frog up, she threw him with all her strength against the wall, saying, "Now, will you be quiet, you ugly Frog!"

But as he fell he was changed from a frog into a handsome Prince with beautiful eyes, who after a little while became, with her father's consent, her dear companion and betrothed. Then he told her how he had been transformed by an evil witch, and that no one but herself could have had the power to take him out of the fountain; and that on the morrow they would go together into his own kingdom.

The next morning, as soon as the sun rose, a carriage drawn by eight white horses, with ostrich feathers on their heads, and golden bridles, drove up to the door of the palace, and behind the carriage stood the trusty Henry, the servant of the young Prince. When his master was changed into a frog, trusty Henry had grieved so much that he had bound three iron bands round his heart, for fear it should break with grief and sorrow. But now that the carriage was ready to carry the young Prince to his own country, the faithful Henry helped in the bride and bridegroom, and placed himself in the seat behind, full of joy at his master's release. They had not proceeded far when the Prince heard a crack as if something had broken behind the carriage; so he put his head out of the window and asked Henry what was broken, and Henry answered, "It was not the carriage, my master, but a band which I bound round my heart when it was in such grief because you were changed into a frog."

Twice afterwards on the journey there was the same noise, and each time the Prince thought that it was some part of the carriage that had given way; but it was only the breaking of the bands which bound the heart of the trusty Henry, who was thenceforward free and happy.

The Cat and the Mouse in Partnership

A CAT having made the acquaintance of a Mouse, told her so much of the great love and affection that he had for her, that the Mouse at last consented to live in the same house with the Cat, and to have their domestic affairs in common. "But we must provide for the winter," said the Cat, "or we shall be starved: you little Mouse cannot go anywhere, or you will meet with an accident." This advice was followed, and a pot was brought with some grease in it. However, when they had got it, they could not imagine where it should be put; at last, after a long consideration, the Cat said, "I know no better place to put it than in the church, for there no one dares to steal anything: we will set it beneath the organ, and not touch it till we really want it." So the pot was put away in safety; but not a long while afterwards the Cat began to wish for it again, so he spoke to the Mouse and said, "I have to tell you that I am asked by my aunt to stand godfather to a little son, white with brown marks, whom she has just brought into the world, and so I must go to the christening. Let me go out to-day, and do you stop at home and keep house." "Certainly," answered the Mouse; "pray, go; and if you eat anything nice, think of me: I would also willingly drink a little of the sweet red christening-wine." But it was all a story; for the Cat had no aunt, and had not been asked to stand godfather. He went straight to the church, crept up to the grease-pot, and licked it till he had eaten off the top; then he took a walk on the roofs of the houses in the town, thinking over his situation, and now and then stretching himself in the sun and stroking his whiskers as often as he thought of the pot of fat. When it was evening he went home again, and the Mouse said, "So you have come at last: what a charming day you must have had!"

"Yes," answered the Cat; "it went off very well!"

"What have you named the kitten?" asked the Mouse.

"*Top-off!*" said the Cat, very quickly.

"*Top-off!*" replied the Mouse; "that is a curious and remarkable name: is it common in your family?"

"What does that matter?" said the Cat; "it is not worse than Crumb-stealer, as you children are called."

Not long afterwards the Cat felt the same longing as before, and said to the Mouse, "You must oblige me by taking care of the house once more by yourself; I am again asked to stand godfather, and, since the youngster has a white ring round his neck, I cannot get off the invitation." So the good little Mouse consented, and the Cat crept away behind the wall to the church again, and ate half the contents of the grease-pot. "Nothing tastes better than what one eats by oneself," said he, quite contented with his day's work; and when he came home the Mouse asked how this child was named.

"*Half-out,*" answered the Cat.

"*Half-out!* What do you mean? I never heard such a name before in my life: I will wager anything it is not in the calendar."

The Cat's mouth now began to water again at the recollection of the feasting. "All good things come in threes," said he to the Mouse. "I am again required to be godfather; this child is quite black and has little white claws, but not a single white hair on his body; such a thing only happens once in two years, so pray excuse me this time."

"*Top-off! Half-out!*" answered the Mouse; "these are such curious names, they make me a bit suspicious."

"Ah!" replied the Cat, "there you sit in your grey coat and long tail, thinking nonsense. That comes of never going out."

The Mouse busied herself during the Cat's absence in putting the house in order, but meanwhile greedy Puss licked the grease-pot clean out. "When it is all done one will rest in peace," thought he to himself, and as soon as night came he went home fat and tired. The Mouse, however, again asked what name the third child had received. "It will not please you any better," answered the Cat, "for he is called *All-out.*"

"*All-out!*" exclaimed the Mouse; "well, that is certainly the most curious name by far. I have never yet seen it in print. *All-out!* What can that mean?" and, shaking her head, she rolled herself up and went to sleep.

After that nobody else asked the Cat to stand godfather; but the winter had arrived, and nothing more was to be picked up out-of-doors; so the Mouse bethought herself of their store of provision, and said, "Come, friend Cat, we will go to our grease-pot which we laid by; it will taste well now."

"Yes, indeed," replied the Cat; "it will taste as well as if you stroked your tongue against the window."

So they set out on their journey, and when they arrived at the church the pot stood in its old place – but it was empty! "Ah," said the Mouse, "I see what has happend; now I know you are indeed a faithful friend. You have eaten the whole as you stood godfather; first *Top-off*, then *Half-out*, then——"

"Will you be quiet?" cried the Cat. "Not a word, or I'll eat you."

But the poor Mouse had "*All-out*" at her tongue's end, and had scarcely uttered it when the Cat made a spring, seized her in his mouth, and swallowed her.

This happens every day in the world.

The Three Spinsters

THERE was once a lazy girl who would not spin, and let her mother say what she would she could not get her to work. At last the mother, getting both angry and impatient, gave her a blow, which made the girl cry very loud. Just then the Queen passing by, heard the noise, and stopping the carriage, she stepped into the house and asked the mother why she beat her daughter in such a way that the passers-by in the street heard her shrieks. The mother, however, was ashamed that her daughter's laziness should be known, and said, "I cannot make her leave off spinning; she will spin for ever and ever, and I am so poor that I cannot procure the flax." The Queen replied, "I never heard anything I like better than spinning, and I am never more pleased than when the wheels are whirring. Let your daughter go with me to the castle; I have flax enough, and she may spin as much as she pleases." The mother was very glad at heart, and the Queen took the girl home with her. As soon as they entered the castle she led her up into three rooms, which were all full of the finest flax from top to bottom. "Now, spin this flax for me," said the Queen; "and, when you have prepared it all, you shall have my eldest son for a husband. Although you are poor, I do not despise you on that account; your unwearied industry is dowry enough." The girl, however, was inwardly frightened, for she could not have spun the flax had she sat there from morning to night until she was three hundred years old. When she was left alone she began to cry, and thus she sat three days without stirring a hand. On the third day the Queen came, and when she saw that nothing was yet spun she wondered; and the maiden excused herself by saying that she had not been able to begin yet, on account of her great sorrow at leaving her mother's house. So the Queen was satisfied; but on leaving she said, "You must begin to work for me to-morrow."

As soon as the girl was again alone, she knew not how to act or help herself, and in her vexation she went and looked out of the window. She saw three women passing by; the first of whom had a broad, flat foot, the second such a large under-lip that it reached nearly to her chin, and the third a very big thumb. They stopped before the window, and, looking up, asked the girl what she wanted. She told them her trouble, and they offered her their help, saying, "Will you invite us to the wedding, and not be ashamed of us, but call us your aunts, and let us sit at your table? If you do all these, we will spin the flax in a very short time for you."

"With all my heart," replied the girl; "come in, and begin at once." Then she let in these three women and, making a clear place in the first room, they sat themselves down and began spinning. One drew the thread and trod the wheel, the other moistened the thread, and the third pressed it and beat with her fingers on the table; and as often as she did so a pile of thread fell on the ground, which was spun in the finest manner. The girl hid the three spinsters, however, from the Queen, and showed her, as often as she came, the heaps of spun yarn; so that she received no end of praise. When the first room was empty, the three women went to the second, and at length to the third, so that soon all was cleared out. Now the three spinsters took leave, saying to the girl, "Do not forget what you promised us; it will make your fortune."

When the girl showed the Queen the empty rooms and the great pile of thread, the wedding was performed, and the bridegroom was glad that he had such a clever and industrious wife, and praised her exceedingly.

"I have three aunts," said the girl, "who have done me much service; so I would not willingly forget them in my good fortune. Allow me, therefore, to invite them to the wedding, and to sit with me at table." The Queen and the bridegroom asked, "Why should we not allow it?"

When the feast was begun, the three old maids entered in great splendour, and the bride said, "You are welcome, dear aunts."

"Ah," said the bridegroom, "how do you come by such ugly friends?" And, going up to the one with the big foot, he asked, "Why have you such a broad foot?" "From treading, from treading," she replied. Then he went to the second, and asked, "Why have you such an overhanging lip?" "From licking," she answered, "from licking." Then he asked the third, "Why have you such a broad thumb?" "From pressing the thread," she replied, "from pressing the thread." At this the Prince was frightened, and said, "Therefore my bride shall never touch a spinning-wheel again."

And so she was set free from the unlucky flax-spinning.

The Woodcutter's Child

ONCE upon a time, near a large forest, there dwelt a woodcutter and his wife, who had only one child, a little girl three years old; but they were so poor that they had scarcely food sufficient for every day in the week, and often they were puzzled to know what they should get to eat. One morning the woodcutter, his heart full of care, went into the wood to work; and, as he chopped the trees, there stood before him a tall and beautiful woman, having a crown of shining stars upon her head, who thus addressed him: "I am the Guardian Angel of every Christian child; thou art poor and needy; bring me thy child, and I will take her with me. I will be her mother, and henceforth she shall be under my care." The woodcutter consented, and calling his child, gave her to the Angel, who carried her to the land of Happiness. There everything went happily; she ate sweet bread, and drank pure milk; her clothes were gold, and her playfellows were beautiful children. When she attained her fourteenth year, the Guardian Angel called her to her side, and said, "My dear child, I have a long journey for thee. Take these keys of the thirteen doors of the land of Happiness: twelve of them thou mayest open, and behold the glories therein; but the thirteenth, to which this little key belongs, thou art forbidden to open. Beware! if thou dost disobey, harm will befall thee."

The maiden promised to be obedient, and, when the Guardian Angel was gone, began her visits to the mansions of Happiness. Every day one door was unclosed, until she had seen all the twelve. In each mansion there sat an angel, surrounded by a bright light. The maiden rejoiced at the glory, and the child who accompanied her rejoiced with her. Now the forbidden door alone remained. A great desire possessed the maiden to know what was hidden there; and she said to the child, "I will not quite open it, nor will I go in, but I will only unlock the door, so that we may peep through the chink." "No, no," said the child; "that will be a sin. The Guardian Angel has forbidden it, and misfortune would soon fall upon us."

At this the maiden was silent, but the desire still remained in her heart, and tormented her continually, so that she had no peace. One day, however, all the children were away, and she thought, "Now I am alone and can peep in, no one will know what I do;" so she found the keys, and, taking them in her hand, placed the right one in the lock and turned it around. Then the door sprang open, and she saw three angels sitting on a throne, surrounded by a great light. The maiden remained a little while standing in astonishment; and then, putting her finger in the light, she drew it back, and found it covered with gold. Then great alarm seized her, and, shutting the door hastily, she ran away. But her fear only increased more and more, and her heart beat so violently that she thought it would burst; the gold also on her finger would not come off, although she washed it and rubbed it with all her strength.

Not long afterwards the Guardian Angel came back from her journey, and, calling the maiden to her, demanded the keys of the mansion. As she delivered them up, the Angel looked in her face, and asked, "Hast thou opened the thirteenth door?" "No," answered the maiden.

Then the Angel laid her hand upon the maiden's heart, and felt how violently it was beating; and she knew that her command had been disregarded, and that the child had opened the door. Then she asked again, "Hast thou opened the thirteenth door?" "No," said the maiden, for the second time.

Then the Angel perceived that the child's finger had become golden from touching the light, and she knew that the child was guilty; and she asked her for the third time, "Hast thou opened the thirteenth door?" "No," said the maiden again.

Then the Guardian Angel replied, "Thou hast not obeyed me, nor done my bidding; therefore thou art no longer worthy to remain among good children."

And the maiden sank down into a deep sleep, and when she awoke she found herself in the midst of a wilderness. She wished to call out, but she had lost her voice. Then she sprang up, and tried to run away; but wherever she turned thick bushes held her back, so that she could not escape. In the deserted spot in which she was now inclosed, there stood an old hollow tree; this was her dwelling-place. In this place she slept by night; and when it rained and blew she found shelter within it. Roots and wild berries were her food, and she sought for them as far as she could reach. In the autumn she collected the leaves of the trees, and laid them in her hole; and when the frost and snow of the winter came, she clothed herself with them, for her clothes had dropped into rags. But during the sunshine she sat outside the tree, and her long hair fell down on all sides and covered her like a mantle. Thus she remained a long time, experiencing the misery and poverty of the world.

But, once, when the trees had become green again, the King of the country was hunting in the forest, and, as a bird flew into the bushes which surrounded the wood, he dismounted, and, tearing the brushwood aside, cut a path for himself with his sword. When he had at last made his way through, he saw a beautiful maiden, who was clothed from head to foot with her own golden locks, sitting under the tree. He stood in silence, and looked at her for some time in astonishment; at last he said, "Child, how came you into this wilderness?" But the maiden answered not, for she had become dumb. Then the King asked, "Will you go with me to my castle?" At that she nodded her head, and the King, taking her in his arms, put her on his horse and rode away home. Then he gave her beautiful clothing, and everything in abundance. Still she could not speak; but her beauty was so great, and so won upon the King's heart, that after a little while he married her.

When about a year had passed away the Queen brought a son into the world, and the same night, while lying alone in her bed, the Guardian Angel appeared to her, and said—

"Wilt thou tell the truth, and confess that thou didst unlock the forbidden door? For then will I open thy mouth, and give thee again the power of speech; but if thou remainest obstinate in thy sin, then will I take from thee thy new-born babe."

And the power to answer was given to her, but her heart was hardened, and she said, "No, I did not open the door;" and at these words the Guardian Angel took the child out of her arms and disappeared with him.

The next morning, when the child was not to be seen, a murmur arose among the people that their Queen was a murderess, who had destroyed her only son; but, although she heard everything, she could say nothing. But the King did not believe the ill report, because of his great love for her.

About a year afterwards another son was born, and on the night of his birth the Guardian Angel again appeared, and asked, "Wilt thou confess that thou didst open the forbidden door? Then will I restore to thee thy son, and give thee the power of speech; but if thou hardenest thyself in thy sin, then will I take this new-born babe also with me."

Then the Queen answered again, "No, I did not open the door;" so the Angel took the second child out of her arms and bore him away. On the morrow, when the infant could not be found, the people said openly that the Queen had slain him, and the King's councillors advised that she should be brought to trial. But the King's affection was still so great that he would not believe it, and he commanded his councillors never again to mention the report on pain of death.

The next year a beautiful little girl was born, and for the third time the Guardian Angel appeared and said to the Queen, "Follow me;" and taking her by the hand, she led her to the kingdom of Happiness, and showed to her the two other children, who were playing merrily. The Queen rejoiced at the sight, and the Angel said, "Is thy heart not yet softened? If thou wilt confess that thou didst unlock the forbidden door, then will I restore to thee both thy sons." But the Queen again answered, "No, I did not open it;" and at these words she sank upon the earth, and her third child was taken from her.

When this was rumoured abroad the next day, all the people exclaimed, "The Queen is a murderess! she must be condemned!" and the King could not this time repulse his councillors. Thereupon a trial was held, and since the Queen could make no good answer or defence, she was condemned to die upon a funeral pile. The wood was collected, she was bound to the stake, and the fire was lighted all around her. Then the iron pride of her heart began to soften, and she was moved to repentance, and she thought, "Could I but now, before my death, confess that I opened the door!" And her tongue was loosened, and she cried aloud, "Thou good Angel, I confess." At these words the rain descended from heaven and extinguished the fire; then a great light shone above, and the Angel appeared and descended upon the earth, and by her side were the Queen's two sons, one on her right hand and the other on her left, and in her arms she bore the new-born babe. Then the Angel restored to the Queen her three children, and loosening her tongue, promised her a happy future, and said, "Whoever will repent and confess their sins, they shall be forgiven."

A Tale of One Who Travelled to Learn What Shivering Meant

A FATHER had two sons, the elder of whom was forward and clever enough to do almost anything; but the younger was so stupid that he could learn nothing, and when the people saw him, they said, "Will thy father still keep thee as a burden to him?" So if anything was to be done, the elder had at all times to do it; but sometimes the father would call him to fetch something in the dead of night, and perhaps the way led through the churchyard or by a dismal place, and then he used to answer, "No, father, I cannot go there, I am afraid," for he was a coward. Or sometimes of an evening, tales were told by the fireside which made one shudder, and the listeners exclaimed, "Oh, it makes us shiver!" In a corner, meanwhile, sat the younger son, listening, but he could not comprehend what was said, and he thought "They say continually, 'Oh, it makes us shiver, it makes us

shiver!' but perhaps shivering is an art which I cannot understand."
One day, however, his father said to him, "Do you hear, you there in
the corner? You are growing stout and big; you must learn some
trade to get your living by. Do you see how your brother works? But
as for you, you are not worth malt and hops."

"Ah, father!" answered he, "I would willingly learn something.
What shall I begin? I want to know what shivering means, for of that
I can understand nothing."

The elder brother laughed when he heard this speech, and thought
to himself, "Ah! my brother is such a simpleton, that he cannot earn
his own living. He who would make a good hedge, must learn
betimes to bend." But the father sighed and said, "What shivering
means you may learn soon enough, but you will never get your bread
by that."

Soon after the parish sexton came in for a gossip, so the father told
him his troubles, and how that his younger son was such a
simpleton, that he knew nothing and could learn nothing. "Just
fancy, when I asked him how he intended to earn his bread, he
desired to learn what shivering meant!" "Oh, if that be all,"
answered the sexton, "he can learn that soon enough with me; just
send him to my place, and I will soon teach him." The father was
very glad, because he thought that it would do the boy good; so the
sexton took him home to ring the bells. About two days afterwards
he called him up at midnight to go into the church-tower to toll the
bell. "You shall soon learn what shivering means," thought the
sexton, and getting up he went out too. As soon as the boy reached
the belfry, and turned himself round to seize the rope, he saw upon
the stairs, near the sounding-hole, a white figure. "Who's there?" he
called out; but the figure gave no answer, and neither stirred nor
spoke. "Answer," said the boy, "or make haste off; you have no
business here to-night." But the sexton did not stir, so that the boy
might think it was a ghost.

The boy called out a second time, "What are you doing here?
Speak, if you are an honest fellow, or else I will throw you
downstairs."

The sexton said to himself, "That is not a bad thought;" but he remained quiet as if he were a stone. Then the boy called out for the third time, but it produced no effect; so, making a spring, he threw the ghost down the stairs, so that it rolled ten steps, and then lay motionless in a corner. Thereupon he rang the bell, and then going home he went to bed without saying a word, and fell fast asleep. The sexton's wife waited some time for her husband, but he did not come; so at last she became anxious, woke the boy, and asked him if he knew where her husband was, who had gone before him to the belfry.

"No," answered the boy; "but there was some one standing on the steps who would not give any answer, nor go away, so I took him for a thief and threw him downstairs. Go now and see where he is; perhaps it may be he, but I should be sorry for it." The wife ran off and found her husband lying in a corner, groaning, with one of his ribs broken.

She took him up and ran with loud outcries to the boy's father, and told him, "Your son has brought a great misfortune on us; he has thrown my husband down and broken his bones. Take the good-for-nothing fellow from our house."

The terrified father came in haste and scolded the boy. "What do these wicked tricks mean? They will only bring misfortune upon you."

"Father," answered the lad, "hear me! I am quite innocent. He stood there at midnight like one who had done some evil; I did not know who it was, and cried three times, 'Speak, of be off!' "

"Ah!" said the father, "everything goes badly with you. Get out of my sight; I do not wish to see you again!"

"Yes, father, willingly; wait but one day, then I will go out and learn what shivering means, that I may at least understand one business which will support me."

"Learn what you will," replied the father, "all is the same to me. Here are fifty dollars; go forth with them into the world, and tell no man whence you came or who your father is, for I am ashamed of you."

"Yes, father, as you wish; but if you desire nothing else, I shall esteem that very lightly."

As soon as day broke the youth put his fifty dollars into a knapsack and went out upon the highroad, saying continually, "Oh, if I could but shiver!"

Presently a man came up, who heard the boy talking to himself; and, as they were just passing the place where the gallows stood, the man said, "Do you see? There is the tree where seven fellows have married the hempen maid, and now swing to and fro. Sit yourself down there and wait till midnight, and then you will know what it is to shiver!"

"Oh, if that be all," answered the boy, "I can very easily do that! But if I learn so speedily what shivering is, then you shall have my fifty dollars if you come again in the morning."

Then the boy went to the gallows, sat down, and waited for evening, and as he felt cold he made a fire. But about midnight the wind blew so sharp, that, in spite of the fire, he could not keep himself warm. The wind blew the bodies against one another, so that they swung backwards and forwards, and he thought, "If I am cold here below by the fire, how must they freeze above!" So his compassion was excited, and, contriving a ladder, he mounted, and, unloosening them one after another, he brought down all seven. Then he poked and blew the fire, and set them round that they might warm themselves; but as they sat still without moving their clothing caught fire. So he said, "Take care of yourselves, or I will hang all of you up again." The dead heard not, and silently allowed their rags to burn. This made him so angry that he said, "If you will not hear I cannot help you; but I will not burn with you." So he hung them up again in a row, and sitting down by the fire he soon went to sleep. The next morning the man came, expecting to receive his fifty dollars, and asked, "Now do you know what shivering means?" "No," he answered; "how should I know? Those fellows up there have not opened their mouths, and were so stupid that they let the old rags on their bodies be burnt." Then the man saw that he should not carry away the fifty dollars that day, so he went away saying, "I never met with such a one before."

The boy also went on his way and began again to say, "Ah, if only I could but shiver – if I could but shiver!" A waggoner walking behind overheard him, and asked, "Who are you?"

"I do not know," answered the boy.

The waggoner asked again, "What do you here?"

"I know not."

"Who is your father?"

"I dare not say."

"What is it you are continually grumbling about?"

"Oh," replied the youth, "I wish to learn what shivering is, but nobody can teach me."

"Cease your silly talk," said the waggoner. "Come with me, and I will see what I can do for you." So the boy went with the waggoner and about evening time they arrived at an inn where they put up for the night, and while they were going into the parlour he said, quite aloud, "Oh, if could but shiver – if I could but shiver!" The host overheard him and said, laughingly, "Oh, if that is all you wish, you shall soon have the opportunity." "Hold your tongue," said his wife; "so many imprudent people have already lost their lives, it were a shame and sin to such beautiful eyes that they should not see the light again." But the youth said, "If it were ever so difficult I would at once learn it; for that reason I left home;" and he never let the host have any peace till he told him that not far off stood an enchanted castle, where any one might soon learn to shiver if he would watch there three nights. The King had promised his daughter in marriage to whom ever would venture, and she was the most beautiful young lady that the sun ever shone upon. And he further told him that inside the castle there was an immense amount of treasure guarded by evil spirits; enough to make any one free, and turn a poor man into a very rich one. Many had, he added, already ventured into this castle, but no one had ever come out again.

The next morning this youth went to the King, and said, "If you will allow me, I wish to watch three nights in the enchanted castle." The King looked at him, and because his appearance pleased him, he said, "You may make three requests, but they must be inanimate things you ask for, and such as you can take with you into the castle." So the youth asked for a fire, a lathe, and a cutting-board.

The King let him take these things by day into the castle, and when it was evening the youth went in and made himself a bright fire in one of the rooms, and, placing his cutting-board and knife near it, he sat down upon his lathe. "Ah, if I could but shiver!" said he. "But even here I shall never learn." At midnight he got up to stir the fire, and, as he poked it, there shrieked suddenly in one corner, "Miau, miau! how cold I am!" "You simpleton!" he exclaimed, "what are you shrieking for? if you are so cold, come and sit down by the fire and warm yourself!" As he was speaking, two great black cats sprang up to him with an immense jump and sat down one on each side, looking at him quite wildly with their fiery eyes. When they had warmed themselves for a little while they said, "Comrade, shall we have a game of cards?" "Certainly," he replied; "but let me see your paws first." So they stretched out their claws, and he said, "Ah, what long nails you have got; wait a bit, I must cut them off first;" and so saying he caught them up by the necks, and put them on his board and screwed their feet down. "Since I have seen what you are about I have lost my relish for a game at cards," said he; and, instantly killing them, threw them away into the water. But no sooner had he quieted these two and thought of sitting down again by his fire, than there came out of every hole and corner black cats and black dogs with glowing chains, continually more and more, so that he could not hide himself. They howled fearfully, and jumped upon his fire, and scattered it about as if they would extinguish it. He looked on quietly for some time, but at last, getting angry, he took up his knife and called out, "Away with you, you vagabonds!" and chasing them about a part ran off, and the rest he killed and threw into the pond. As soon as he returned he blew up the sparks of his fire again and warmed himself, and while he sat, his eyes began to feel very heavy and he wished to go to sleep. So looking around he saw a great bed in one corner, in which he lay down; but no sooner had he closed his eyes, than the bed began to move of itself and travelled all round the castle. "Just so," said he, "only better still;" whereupon the bed galloped away as if six horses pulled it up and down steps and stairs, until at last all at once it overset, bottom upwards, and lay upon him like a mountain; but up he got, threw pillows and mattresses into the air, and saying, "Now, he who wishes may travel," laid himself down by the fire and slept till day broke. In the morning the King came, and, seeing the youth lying on the ground, he thought that the spectres had killed him, and that he was dead; so he said, "It is a great misfortune that the finest men are thus killed;" but the youth, hearing this, sprang up, saying, "It is not come to that with me yet!" The King was much astonished, but still very glad, and asked him how he had fared. "Very well," replied he; "as one night has passed, so also may the other two." Soon after he met his landlord, who opened his eyes when he saw him. "I never thought to see you alive again," said he; "have you learnt now what shivering means?" "No," said he; "it is all of no use. Oh, if anyone would but tell me!"

The second night he went up again into the castle, and sitting down by the fire, began his old song, "If I could but shiver!" When midnight came, a ringing and a rattling noise was heard, gentle at first and louder and louder by degrees; then there was a pause, and presently with a loud outcry half a man's body came down the chimney and fell at his feet. "Holloa;" he exclaimed, "only half a man answered that ringing; that is too little." Then the ringing began afresh, and a roaring and howling was heard, and the other half fell down. "Wait a bit," said he; "I will poke up the fire first." When he had done so and looked round again, the two pieces had joined themselves together, and an ugly man was sitting in his place. "I did not bargain for that," said the youth; "the bench is mine." The man tried to push him away, but the youth would not let him, and giving him a violent push sat himself down in his old place. Presently more men fell down the chimney, one after the other, who brought nine thigh-bones and two skulls, which they set up, and then they began to play at ninepins. At this the youth wished also to play, so he asked whether he might join them. "Yes, if you have money!" "Money enough," he replied, "but your balls are not quite round;" so saying he took up the skulls, and, placing them on his lathe, turned them round. "Ah, now you will roll well," said he. "Holloa! now we will go at it merrily." So he played with them and lost some of his money, but as it struck twelve everything disappeared. Then he lay down and went to sleep quietly. On the morrow the King came for news, and asked him how he had fared this time. "I have been playing ninepins," he replied, "and lost a couple of dollars." "Have you not shivered?" "No! I have enjoyed myself very much; but I wish someone would teach me that!"

On the third night he sat down again on his bench, saying in great vexation, "Oh, if I could only shiver!" When it grew late, six tall men came in bearing a coffin between them. "Ah, ah," said he, "that is surely my little cousin, who died two days ago;" and beckoning with his finger he called, "Come, little cousin, come!" The men set down the coffin upon the ground, and he went up and took off the lid, and there lay a dead man within, and as he felt the face it was as cold as ice. "Stop a moment," he cried; "I will warm it in a trice;" and stepping up to the fire he warmed his hands, and then laid them upon the face, but it remained cold. So he took up the body, and sitting down by the fire, he laid it on his lap and rubbed the arms that the blood might circulate again. But all this was to no avail, and he thought to himself if two lie in a bed together they warm each other; so he put the body in the bed, and covering it up laid himself down by its side. After a little while the body became warm and began to move about. "See, my cousin," he exclaimed, "have I not warmed you?" But the body got up and exclaimed, "Now I will strangle you." "Is that your gratitude?" cried the youth. "Then you shall get into your coffin again;" and taking it up, he threw the body in, and made the lid fast. Then the six men came in again and bore it away. "Oh, deary me," said he, "I shall never be able to shiver if I stop here all my lifetime!" At these words in came a man who was taller than all the others, and looked more horrible; but he was very old and had a long white beard. "Oh, you wretch," he exclaimed, "now thou shalt learn what shivering means, for thou shalt die!"

"Not so quick," answered the youth; "if I die I must be brought to it first."

"I will quickly seize you," replied the ugly one.

"Softly, softly; be not too sure. I am as strong as you, and perhaps stronger."

"That we will see," said the ugly man. "If you are stronger than I, I will let you go; come, let us try;" and he led him away through a dark passage to a smith's forge. Then taking up an axe he cut through the anvil at one blow down to the ground. "I can do that still better," said the youth, and went to another anvil, while the old man followed him and watched him with his long beard hanging down. Then the youth took up an axe, and, splitting the anvil at one blow, wedged the old man's beard in it. "Now I have you; now death comes upon you!" and, taking up an iron bar, he beat the old man until he groaned, and begged him to stop, and he would give him great riches. So the youth drew out the axe, and let him loose. Then the old man, leading him back into the castle, showed him three chests full of gold in a cellar. "One share of this," said he, "belongs to the poor, another to the King, and a third to yourself." And just then it struck twelve and the old man vanished, leaving the youth in the dark. "I must help myself out here," said he, and groping round he found his way back to his room and went to sleep by the fire.

The next morning the King came and inquired, "Now have you learnt to shiver?" "No," replied the youth; "what is it? My dead cousin came here, and a bearded man, who showed me a lot of gold down below; but what shivering means, no one has showed me!" Then the King said, "You have won the castle, and shall marry my daughter."

"That is all very fine," replied the youth, "but still I don't know what shivering means."

So the gold was fetched, and the wedding was celebrated, but the young Prince (for the youth was a Prince now), notwithstanding his love for his bride, and his great contentment, was still continually crying, "If I could but shiver! if I could but shiver!" At last it fell out in this wise: one of the chambermaids said to the Princess, "Let me bring in my aid to teach him what shivering is." So she went to the brook which flowed through the garden, and drew up a pail of water full of little fish; and, at night, when the young Prince was asleep, his bride drew away the covering and poured the pail of cold water and the little fishes over him, so that they slipped all about him. Then the Prince woke up directly, calling out, "Oh! that makes me shiver! dear wife, that makes me shiver! Yes, now I know what shivering means!"

The Wolf and the Seven Little Goats

ONCE upon a time there lived an old Goat who had seven young ones whom she loved as every mother loves her children. One day she wanted to go into the forest to fetch some food, so, calling her seven young ones together, she said, "Dear children, I am going away into the wood; be on your guard against the Wolf, for if he comes here, he will eat you all up – skin, hair and all. He often disguises himself, but you may know him by his rough voice and his black feet." The little Goats replied, "Dear mother, we will pay great attention to what you say; you may go away without any anxiety." So the old one bleated and ran off, quite contented, upon her road.

Not long afterwards, somebody knocked at the hut-door, and called out, "Open, my dear children; your mother is here and has brought you each something." But the little Goats perceived from the rough voice that it was a Wolf, and so they said, "We will not undo the door; you are not our mother; she has a gentle and loving voice; but yours is gruff; you are a Wolf." So the Wolf went to a shop and bought a great piece of chalk, which he ate, and by that means rendered his voice more gentle. Then he came back, knocked at the hut-door, and called out, "Open, my dear children; your mother has come home, and has brought you each something." But the Wolf had placed his black paws upon the window-sill, so the Goats saw them, and replied, "No, we will not open the door; our mother has not black feet; you are a Wolf." So the Wolf went to a baker and said, "I have hurt my foot, put some dough on it." And when the baker had done so, he ran to the miller, saying, "Strew some white flour upon my feet." But the miller, thinking he was going to deceive somebody, hesitated, till the Wolf said, "If you do not do it at once, I will eat you." This made the miller afraid, so he powdered his feet with flour. Such is mankind!

Now, the villain went for the third time to the hut, and, knocking at the door, called out, "Open to me, my children; your dear mother is come, and has brought with her something for each of you out of the forest." The little Goats exclaimed, "Show us first your feet, that we may see whether you are our mother." So the Wolf put his feet up on the window-sill, and when they saw that they were white, they thought it was all right, and undid the door. But who should come in? The Wolf. They were terribly frightened, and tried to hide themselves. One ran under the table, the second got into the bed, the third into the cupboard, the fourth into the kitchen, the fifth into the oven, the sixth into the wash-tub, and the seventh into the clock-case. But the Wolf found them all out, and did not delay, but swallowed them all up one after another; only the youngest one, hid in the clock-case, he did not discover. When the Wolf had satisfied his appetite, he dragged himself out, and lying down upon the green meadow under a tree, went fast asleep.

Soon after the old Goat came home out of the forest. Ah, what a sight she saw! The hut-door stood wide open; the table, stools and benches were overturned; the wash-tub was broken to pieces, and the sheets and pillows pulled off the bed. She sought her children, but could find them nowhere. She called them by name, one after the other; but no one answered. At last, when she came to the name of the youngest, a little voice replied, "Here I am, dear mother, in the clock-case." She took her out, and heard how the Wolf had come and swallowed all the others. You cannot think how she wept for her poor little ones.

At last she went out all in her misery, and the young Goat ran by her side; and when they came to the meadow, there lay the Wolf under the tree, snoring so that the boughs quivered. She viewed him on all sides, and perceived that something moved and stirred about in his body. "Ah, mercy!" thought she, "should my poor children, whom he has swallowed for his dinner, be yet alive!" So saying, she ran home and fetched a pair of scissors and a needle and thread. Then she cut open the monster's hairy coat, and had scarcely made one slit, before one little Goat put his head out, and, as she cut further, out jumped one after another, all six, still alive, and without any injury; for the monster, in his eagerness, had gulped them down quite whole. There was a joy! They hugged their dear mother, and jumped about like tailors keeping their wedding day. But the old mother said, "Go and pick up at once some large stones, that we may fill the monster's stomach, while he lies fast asleep.' So the seven little Goats dragged up in great haste a pile of stones and put them in the Wolf's stomach, as many as they could bring; and then the old mother went, and, looking at him in a great hurry, saw that he was still insensible, and did not stir, and so she sewed up the slit.

When the Wolf at last woke up, he raised himself upon his legs, and because the stones which were lying in his stomach made him feel thirsty, he went to a brook in order to drink. But as he went along, rolling from side to side, the stones began to tumble about in his body, and he called out,—

"What rattles, what rattles
Against my poor bones?
Not little goats, I think,
But only big stones!"

And when the Wolf came to the brook he stooped down to drink and the heavy stones made him lose his balance, so that he fell, and sank beneath the water.

As soon as the seven little Goats saw this, they came running up, singing aloud, "The Wolf is dead! the Wolf is dead!" and they danced for joy around their mother by the side of the brook.

The Pack of Ragamuffins

A COCK once addressed his Hen thus, "It is now the time when the nuts are ripe, let us go together to the hills, and eat all we can, before the squirrels carry them away." "Yes," answered the Hen, "let us go and enjoy ourselves." So they went together to the hills, and as it was a bright day they stopped till evening. Now I do not know whether they had eaten too much, or whether they had become proud, but the Hen would not go home on foot, and the Cock had to build a little carriage out of the nutshells. As soon as it was ready the Hen sat herself in it and said to the Cock, "You can harness yourself to it." "You are very kind," said he, "but I would rather walk home than harness my own self; – no! we did not agree to that. I will willingly be coachman and sit on the box; but drag it myself I never will."

While they were quarrelling a Duck called out hard by, "You thieving folk, who asked you to come to my nut-hill? Wait a bit and it shall cost you dearly;" and she rushed up to the Cock with outstretched beak. But the Cock was not idle either, and attacked the Duck valiantly, and at last wounded her so badly with his spur that she begged for mercy, and willingly undertook to draw the carriage as a punishment. The Cock set himself on the box as coachman, and off they started at a great rate, crying out, "Quick, Duck! quick!" When they had gone a portion of the way they met two walkers, a Pin and a Needle, who called out to them to stop, and said it had become too dark to stitch, and they could not go another step; that it was very dirty upon the road, and might they get in for a little way. They had been stopping at the door of the tailor's house drinking beer and had been delayed. The Cock, seeing they were thin people, who would not take much room, let them both get up, but not till they had promised not to tread on the toes of himself or his Hen. Later in the evening they came to an inn, and because they could not travel further that evening, and because the Duck had hurt her foot very much, and staggered from side to side, they turned in. The landlord at first made many objections, saying his house was already full; he thought, too, that they were nobody of any consequence; but at last, after they had made many fine speeches, and promised that he should have the egg which the Hen had laid on the road, and the one which the Duck laid every day, he said at last that they might remain over night. So when they had refreshed themselves they held a great revel and tumult; but early in the morning, when everybody was asleep, and it was still dark, the Cock awoke the Hen, and fetching the egg they broke it, and ate it together, throwing the shell away into the hearth. Then they went to the Needle, who was still asleep, and, taking him by the head, stuck him in the cushion of the landlord's chair, and the Pin they put in his towel, and then they flew off over the fields and away. The Duck, who had gone to sleep in the open air, and had stopped in the yard, heard them fly past, and, getting up quickly, found a pond, into which she waddled, and in which she swam much faster than she walked when she had to pull the carriage. A couple of hours later the landlord rose up from his feather-bed, washed himself, and took up the towel to wipe himself dry; then the Pin, in passing over his face, made a red scratch from one ear to the other; so he went into the kitchen to light his pipe, but just as he stepped on the hearth the eggshells sprang into his eyes. "This morning everything happens unlucky to me," said he, sitting down in vexation in his grandfather's chair; but he quickly jumped up again, crying, "Woe's me!" for the Needle had pricked him very badly. This drove him completely wild, and he laid the mischief on the guests, who had arrived so late the evening before, and when he went out to look after them they were gone. So he swore that he would never again take such a pack of ragamuffins into his house, who destroyed so much, paid no reckoning, and played mischievous tricks in the place of thanks.

Faithful John

ONCE upon a time there lived an old King, who fell very sick, and thought he was lying upon his death-bed; so he said, "Let faithful John come to me." This faithful John was his affectionate servant, and was so called because he had been true to him all his lifetime. As soon as John came to the bedside, the King said, "My faithful John, I feel that my end approaches, and I have no other care than about my son, who is still so young that he cannot always guide himself aright. If you do not promise to instruct him in everything he ought to know, and to be his guardian, I cannot close my eyes in peace." Then John answered, "I will never leave him; I will always serve him truly, even if it costs me my life." So the old King was comforted, and said, "Now I can die in peace. After my death you must show him all the chambers, halls, and vaults in the castle, and all the treasures which are in them; but the last room in the long corridor you must not show him, for in it hangs the portrait of the daughter of the King of the Golden Palace; if he sees her picture, he will conceive a great love for her, and will fall down in a swoon, and on her account undergo great perils, therefore you must keep him away." The faithful John pressed his master's hand again in token of assent, and soon after the King laid his head upon the pillow and expired.

After the old King had been borne to his grave, the faithful John related to the young King all that his father had said upon his deathbed, and declared, "All this I will certainly fulfil; I will be as true to you as I was to him, if it cost me my life." When the time of mourning was passed, John said to the young King, "It is now time for you to see your inheritance; I will show you your paternal castle." So he led the King all over it, up stairs and down stairs, and showed him all the riches, and all the splendid chambers; only one room he did not open, containing the perilous portrait, which was so placed that one saw it directly the door was opened, and, moreover, it was so beautifully painted, that one thought it breathed and moved; nothing in all the world could be more lifelike or more beautiful. The young King remarked, however, that the faithful John always passed by one door, so he asked, "Why do you not open that one?" "There is something in it," he replied, "which will frighten you."

But the King said, "I have seen all the rest of the castle, and I will know what is in there;" and he went and tried to open the door by force. The faithful John pulled him back, and said, "I promised your father before he died that you should not see the contents of that room, it would bring great misfortunes both upon you and me."

"Oh, no," replied the young King, "if I do not go in, it will be my certain ruin; I should have no peace night nor day until I had seen it with my own eyes. Now I will not stir from the place till you unlock the door."

Then the faithful John saw that it was of no use talking; so, with a heavy heart and many sighs, he picked the key out of the great bunch. When he had opened the door, he went in first, and thought he would cover up the picture, that the King should not see it; but it was of no use, for the King stepped upon tiptoes and looked over his shoulder; and as soon as he saw the portrait of the maiden, which was so beautiful and glittered with precious stones, he fell down on the ground insensible. The faithful John lifted him up and carried him to his bed, and thought with great concern, "Mercy on us! the misfortune has happened; what will come of it?" and he gave the young King wine until he came to himself. The first words he spoke were, "Who does that beautiful picture represent?" "That is the daughter of the King of the Golden Palace," was the reply.

"Then," said the King, "my love for her is so great, that if all the leaves on the trees had tongues, they should not gainsay it; my life is set upon the search for her. You are my faithful John, you must accompany me."

The trusty servant deliberated for a long while how to set about this business, for it was very difficult to get into the presence of the King's daughter. At last he bethought himself of a way, and said to the King, "Everything which she has around her is of gold, – chairs, tables, dishes, bowls, and all the household utensils. Among your treasures are five tons of gold; let one of the goldsmiths of your kingdom manufacture vessels and utensils of all kinds therefrom – all kinds of birds, and wild and wonderful beasts, such as will please her; then we will travel with these, and try our luck." Then the King summoned all his goldsmiths, who worked day and night until many very beautiful things were ready. When all had been placed on board a ship, the faithful John put on merchant's clothes, and the King likewise, so that they might travel quite unknown. Then they sailed over the wide sea, and sailed away until they came to the city where dwelt the daughter of the King of the Golden Palace.

The faithful John told the King to remain in the ship, and wait for him. "Perhaps," said he, "I shall bring the King's daughter with me, therefore take care that all is in order, and set out the golden vessels and adorn the whole ship." Thereupon John placed in a napkin some of the golden cups, stepped upon land, and went straight to the King's palace. When he came into the castle-yard, a beautiful maid stood by the brook, who had two golden pails in her hand, drawing water; and when she had filled them and had turned round, she saw a strange man, and asked who he was. Then John answered, "I am a merchant," and opening his napkin, he showed her its contents. Then she exclaimed, "Oh, what beautiful golden things!" and, setting the pails down, she looked at the cups one after another, and said, "The King's daughter must see these; she is so pleased with anything made of gold that she will buy all these." And taking him by the hand, she led him in; for she was the lady's maid. When the King's daughter saw the golden cups, she was much pleased, and said, "They are so finely worked, that I will purchase them all." But the faithful John replied, "I am only the servant of a rich merchant; what I have here is nothing in comparison to those which my master has in his ship, than which nothing more delicate or costly has ever been worked in gold." Then the King's daughter wished to have them all brought; but he said, "It would take many days, and so great is the quantity, that your palace has not halls enough in it to place them around." Then her curiosity and desire were still more excited, and at last she said, "Take me to the ship; I will go myself and look at your master's treasure."

The faithful John conducted her to the ship with great joy, and the King, when he beheld her, saw that her beauty was still greater than the picture had represented, and thought nothing else but that his heart would jump out of his mouth. Presently she stepped on board, and the King conducted her below; but the faithful John remained on deck by the steersman, and told him to unmoor the ship and put on all the sail he could, that it might fly as a bird through the air. Meanwhile the King showed the Princess all the golden treasures, – the dishes, cups, bowls, the birds, the wild and wonderful beasts. Many hours passed away while she looked at everything, and in her joy she did not remark that the ship sailed on and on. As soon as she had looked at the last, and thanked the merchant, she wished to depart. But when she came on deck, she perceived that they were upon the high sea, far from the shore, and were hastening on with all sail. "Ah," she exclaimed in affright, "I am betrayed; I am carried off and taken away in the power of a strange merchant. I would rather die!"

But the King, taking her by the hand, said, "I am not a merchant, but a king, thine equal in birth. It is true that I have carried thee off; but that is because of my overwhelming love for thee. Dost thou know that when I first saw the portrait of thy beauteous face, that I fell down in a swoon before it?" When the King's daughter heard these words, she was reassured, and her heart was inclined towards him, so that she willingly became his bride. While they thus went on their voyage on the high sea, it happened that the faithful John, as he sat on the deck of the ship, playing music, saw three crows in the air, who came flying towards them. He stopped playing, and listened to what they were saying to each other, for he understood them perfectly. The first one exclaimed, "There he is, carrying home the daughter of the King of the Golden Palace." "But he is not home yet," replied the second. "But he has her," said the third; "she is sitting by him in the ship." Then the first began again, and exclaimed, "What matters that? When they go on shore, a fox-coloured horse will spring towards them, on which he will mount; and as soon as he is on it, it will jump up with him into the air, so that he will never again see his bride." The second one asked, "Is there no escape?" "Oh yes, if another mounts behind quickly, and takes out the firearms which are in the holster, and with them shoots the horse dead, then the young King will be saved. But who knows that? And if any one does know it, and tells him, such a one will be turned to stone from the toe to the knee." Then the second spoke again, "I know still more; if the horse should be killed, the young King will not then retain his bride; for when they come into the castle, a beautiful bridal shirt will lie there upon a dish, and seem to be woven of gold and silver, but it is nothing but sulphur and pitch; and if he puts it on, it will burn him to his marrow and bones." Then the third Crow asked, "Is there no escape?" "Oh yes," answered the second; "if some one takes up the shirt with his gloves on, and throws it into the fire, so that it is burnt, the young King will be saved. But what does that signify? Whoever knows it, and tells him, will be turned to stone from his knee to his heart." Then the third Crow spoke: "I know still more: even if the bridal shirt be consumed, still the young King will not retain his bride. For if, after the wedding, a dance is held, while the young Queen dances, she will suddenly turn pale, and fall down as if dead; and if some one does not raise her up, and take three drops of blood from her right breast and throw them away, she will die. But whoever knows that, and tells it, will have his whole body turned to stone, from the crown of his head to the toes of his feet."

After the Crows had thus talked with one another, they flew away, and the trusty John, who had perfectly understood all they had said, was from that time very quiet and sad; for if he concealed from his master what he had heard, misfortune would happen to him, and if he told him all he must give up his own life. But at last he thought, "I will save my master, even if I destroy myself."

As soon as they came on shore, it happened just as the Crow had foretold, and an immense fox-red horse sprang up. "Capital!" said the King; "this shall carry me to my castle," and he tried to mount; but the faithful John came straight up, and swinging himself quickly on, drew the firearms out of the holster and shot the horse dead. Then the other servants of the King, who were not on good terms with the faithful John, exclaimed, "How shameful to kill the beautiful creature, which might have borne the King to the castle!" But the King replied, "Be silent, and let him go; he is my very faithful John – who knows the good he may have done?" Now they went into the castle, and there stood a dish in the hall, and the splendid bridal shirt lay in it, and seemed nothing else than gold and silver. The young King went up to it and wished to take it up, but the faithful John pushed him away, and taking it up with his gloves on, bore it quickly to the fire and let it burn. The other servants thereupon began to murmur, saying, "See, now he is burning the King's bridal shirt!" But the young King replied, "Who knows what good he has done? Let him alone – he is my faithful John."

Soon after, the wedding was celebrated, and a grand ball was given, and the bride began to dance. So the faithful John paid great attention, and watched her countenance; all at once she grew pale, and fell as if dead to the ground. Then he sprang up hastily, raised her up and bore her to a chamber, where he laid her down, kneeled beside her, and drawing the three drops of blood out of her right breast, threw them away. As soon as she breathed again, she raised herself up; but the young King had witnessed everything, and not knowing why the faithful John had done this, was very angry, and called out, "Throw him into prison!" The next morning the trusty John was brought up for trial, and led to the gallows; and as he stood upon them, and was about to be executed, he said, "Every one condemned to die may once before his death speak. Shall I also have that privilege?" "Yes," answered the King, "it shall be granted you." Then the faithful John replied, "I have been unrighteously judged, and have always been true to you;" and he narrated the conversation of the Crows which he heard at sea; and how, in order to save his master, he was obliged to do all he had done. Then the King cried out, "Oh, my most trusty John, pardon, pardon; lead him away!" But the trusty John had fallen down at the last word and was turned into stone.

At this event both the King and the Queen were in great grief, and the King thought, "Ah, how wickedly have I rewarded his great fidelity!" and he had the stone statue raised up and placed in his sleeping-chamber, near his bed; and as often as he looked at it, he wept and said, "Ah, could I bring you back to life again, my faithful John!"

After some time had passed, the Queen bore twins, two little sons, who were her great joy. Once when the Queen was in church, and the two children at home playing by their father's side, he looked up at the stone statue full of sorrow, and exclaimed with a sigh, "Ah, could I restore you to life, my faithful John!" At these words the statue began to speak, saying, "Yes, you can make me alive again, if you will bestow on me that which is dearest to you." The King replied, "All that I have in the world I will give up for you." The statue spoke again: "If you, with your own hand, cut off the heads of both your children and sprinkle me with their blood, I shall be brought to life again." The King was terrified when he heard that he must himself kill his two dear children; but he remembered his servant's great fidelity, and how the faithful John had died for him, and drawing his sword he cut off the heads of both his children with his own hand. And as soon as he had sprinkled the statue with blood, life came back to it, and the trusty John stood again alive and well before him, and said, "Your faith shall not go unrewarded;" and taking the heads of the two children, he set them on again, and anointed their wounds with their blood, and thereupon they healed again in a moment, and the children sprang away and played as if nothing had happened.

Now the King was full of happiness, and as soon as he saw the Queen coming, he hid the faithful John and both the children in a great closet. As soon as she came in he said to her, "Have you prayed in the church?" "Yes," she answered; "but I thought continually of the faithful John, who has come to such misfortune through us." Then he replied, "My dear wife, we can restore his life again to him, but it will cost us both our little sons, whom he must sacrifice." The Queen became pale and was terrified at heart, but she said, "We are guilty of his life on account of his great fidelity." Then he was very glad that she thought as he did, and going up to the closet, he unlocked it, brought out the children and the faithful John, saying, "God be praised! he is saved, and we have still our little sons:" and then he told her all that happened. Afterwards they lived happily together to the end of their days.

A Good Bargain

A COUNTRYMAN drove his cow to market, and sold it for seven dollars. On the way home he had to pass by a pond, where he heard from a distance the Frogs croaking. "Ack, ack, ack, ack!"* "Yes," said he, "they cry out so even in their owner's field; but it is seven which I have got, not eight." As he came up to the water he exclaimed, "Stupid creatures that you are, do you not know better? Here are seven dollars, and not eight!" But the Frogs still continued their "Ack, ack!" "Now, if you will not believe it I will count them out to you;" and, taking the money from his pocket, he counted out the seven dollars, four-and-twenty groschen in each. The Frogs, however, paid no attention to his reckoning, and kept calling out, "Ack, ack, ack!" "Ah!" exclaimed the Countryman, quite angry, "if

* "Acht" is the German word for eight.

you know better than I, count it yourself!" and, one by one, he threw the pieces of money into the water. He stopped and waited till they should be ready to bring him his own again, but the Frogs were obstinate in their opinion, and cried continually, "Ack, ack, ack!" neither did they throw the money back. So the man waited a long while, until evening approached and it was time to go home; then he began to abuse the Frogs, shouting out, "You water-paddlers, you thick-heads, you blind-eyes! you have indeed great mouths, and can make noise enough to stun one's ears, but you cannot count seven dollars! do you think I am going to wait here till you are ready?" And thereupon he went away, but the Frogs cried still behind his back, "Ack, ack, ack!" so that he reached home in a very savage mood!

After a little time he again bargained for a cow, which he killed, and then he made a calculation that, if he sold the flesh well, he should gain as much as both the cows were worth, and should have the skin beside. As he came to town with the flesh, a great troop of dogs was collected before the gate, and in front was a large greyhound, who sprang around the flesh, snapping and barking, "Was, was, was!"* As he did not cease, the Countryman said to him, "I know well you say, 'Was, was!' because you wish for some of the flesh, but I ought to receive something as good if I should give it you." The dog replied only, "Was, was!"

"Will you not let your comrades there eat with you?" "Was, was!" said the Dog.

"If you stick to that I will let you have it. I know you well, and to whom you belong; but this I tell you, in three days I must have my money, or it will go ill with you. You can bring it to me."

Thereupon he unloaded the flesh and turned homewards again, and the dogs gathering around it, barked loudly, "Was, was!" The Peasant, who heard them at a distance, said, "Mind, you may share it among you, but the big one must answer for you to me."

When three days were passed, the Countryman thought to himself, "This evening I shall have my money in my pocket," and so

---

*That, that.

made himself happy. But nobody came to pay the reckoning. "There is no faith in any one," said he at last, losing all patience, and he went into the town to the butcher and demanded his money. The butcher thought it was a joke, but the Countryman said, "Joking aside I will have my money; did not the great dog, three days ago, bring you home a whole slaughtered cow?" This put the butcher in a passion, and, taking up a broomstick, he hunted the Countryman out of his doors.

"Wait a bit," said the Countryman; "justice is to be had in the world;" and he went to the King's palace and requested an audience. So he was led before the King, who sat there with his daughter, and asked, "What misfortune has befallen you?"

"Ah," said he, "frogs and the dogs have taken away my property, and the butcher has repaid me with a stick;" and he narrated at length all that had happened. The King's daughter laughed aloud at his tale, and the King said to him, "I cannot give you justice here; but, nevertheless, you shall have my daughter for a wife: all her lifetime she has not laughed except before you, and I have promised her to that man who should make her laugh. You may thank God for your luck."

"O dear!" replied the Countryman, "I do not wish it at all; I have one wife at home, who is already too much for me." This made the King angry, and he said, "You are an ill-bred fellow."

"Ah, my lord the King," answered the Countryman, "what can you expect from an ox except beef?"

"Wait a bit," replied the King, "you shall have another reward. Now be off at once, and return in three days, and you shall receive five hundred."

As the Countryman came to the gate, the sentinel said to him, "Since you have made the King's daughter laugh, no doubt you have received a great reward." "Yes, I think so," answered the Peasant; "five hundred are to be counted out for me."

"Indeed!" said the soldier; "give me some of it; what will you do with all that money?"

"Since you ask me," replied the Countryman, "you shall have two hundred: apply to the King in three days, and they will be counted out to you." A Jew, who stood near, and heard their conversation, ran after the Countryman, and catching him by his coat, cried out, "O wonderful! what a child of fortune are you! I will change, I will change with you in small coins! What will you do with the hard dollars?"

"You, Jew!" said the Countryman, "you can yet have the three hundred; give me the same amount in small coins, and in three days after to-day it shall be counted out to you by the King." The Jew rejoiced at his profit, and brought the sum in worn-out farthings, three of which were equal to two good ones.

After the lapse of three days, the Countryman went before the King, according to his command. The King called out, "Pull off his coat; he shall have his five hundred!" "Oh!" replied the Country-man, "they do not belong to me now: I have presented two hundred to the sentinel, and the Jew has changed with me for three hundred, so that rightly nothing at all belongs to me."

Meanwhile the soldier and the Jew came in, desiring their shares for which they had bargained with the Countryman, but, instead of dollars, each received his stripes justly measured out. The soldier bore his patiently, having already known how they tasted; but the Jew behaved very badly, crying out, "Ah, woe is me, these *are* hard dollars!" The King was forced to laugh at the Countryman, and, when all his anger had passed away, he said to him, "Since you lost your reward before you received it, I will give you compensation; so go into my treasure-chamber, and take as much money as you wish for." The Countryman did not stop to be told twice, but filled his deep pockets as full as they would hold, and immediately after went to an inn, and told out the money. The Jew sneaked after him, and overheard him muttering to himself, "Now, that thief of a King has again deceived me. Could he not have given me the money, and then I should have known what I had got; but now, how can I tell what I have by good luck put into my pocket is just?"

"Heaven preserve us!" said the Jew to himself, "he has spoken disrespectfully of his Majesty; I will run and inform against him, and then I shall get a reward, and he will be punished." When the King heard the speech of the Countryman his anger was excited, and he bade the Jew go and fetch the offender. So the Jew, running back to the Countryman, said to him, 'You must go before his Majesty the King, just as you are."

"I know better what is becoming," replied the Countryman; "I must first have a new coat made. Do you think a man who has so much money in his pocket ought to go in this old rag of a coat?" The Jew, perceiving that the Countryman would not stir without another coat, and fearing, if the King's anger should evaporate, he would not get his reward nor the other his punishment, said to him, "Out of pure friendship, I will lend you a beautiful coat for a short time. What will one not do out of pure love?"

The Countryman, well pleased, took the coat from the Jew, and went off straight to the King, who charged him with the speech which the Jew had informed about.

"Oh," said the Countryman, "what a Jew says is nothing, for not a true word comes out of his mouth; that rascal there is able to assert, and does assert, that I have his coat on!"

"What is that?" screamed the Jew; "is not the coat mine? Have I not lent it to you out of pure friendship, that you might step in it before his Majesty the King?" As soon as the King heard this he said, "The Jew has deceived one of us;" and then he had counted out to him some more of the *hard* dollars.

Meanwhile the Countryman went off home in the good coat, and with the good gold in his pocket, singing to himself, "This time I have hit it!"

The Wonderful Musician

ONCE upon a time a wonderful Fiddler was travelling through a wood, thinking of all sorts of things as he went along, and presently he said to himself, "I have plenty of time and space in this forest, so I will fetch a good companion;" and, taking the fiddle from his back, he fiddled till the trees re-echoed. Presently a wolf came crashing through the brushwood.

"Ah! a wolf comes, for whom I have no desire," said the Fiddler; but the Wolf, approaching nearer, said, "Oh, you dear Musician, how beautifully you play! might I learn how?"

"It is soon learnt; you have only to do exactly as I tell you." Then the Wolf replied, "I will mind you just as a schoolboy does his master." So the Musician told the Wolf to come with him; and when they had gone a little distance together they came to an old oak-tree, which was hollow within and split in the middle. "See here," said the

Musician, "if you wish to learn how to fiddle, put your fore-foot in this cleft." The Wolf obeyed; but the Fiddler, snatching up a stone, quickly wedged both his feet so fast with one blow that the Wolf was stuck fast, and obliged to remain where he was. "Wait there till I come again," said the Fiddler, and went on his way.

After a while he said to himself a second time, "I have plenty of time and space in the forest, so I will fetch another companion;" and taking his fiddle, he played away in the wood. Presently a fox came sneaking through the trees.

"Ah!" said the Musician, "here comes a fox, whom I did not desire."

The Fox, running up, said, "Ah, you dear Mister Musician, how is it you fiddle so beautifully? might I learn too?"

"It is soon learnt," answered he; "but you must do all I tell you." I will obey you as a schoolboy does his master," answered the Fox and he followed the Musician. After they had walked a little distance he came to a footpath, with high hedges on each side. The Musician stopped, and pulling the bough of a hazel-tree down to the ground on one side, he put his foot upon it, and then bent another down on the other side, saying, "Come, little Fox, if you wish to learn something, reach me here your left forefoot." The Fox obeyed, and the Musician bound the foot to the left bough. "Now reach me the other, little Fox," said he, and he bound that to the right bough. And as soon as he saw that the knots were fast he let go, and the boughs sprang back into the air, carrying the Fox, shaking and quivering, up with them. "Wait there till I come again," said the Musician, and went on his way.

After a little while he said again to himself, "Time and space are not wanting to me in this forest; I will fetch another companion;" and, taking his fiddle, he made the sound re-echo in the woods.

"Aha!" said he, "a hare! I won't have him."

"Oh, you dear Musician!" said the Hare, "how do you fiddle so beautifully? Could I learn it too?"

"It is soon learnt," replied the Musician, "only do all I tell you."
The little Hare replied, "I will obey you as a schoolboy does his

master;" and they went on together till they came to a clear space in the forest where an aspen-tree stood. The Musician bound a long twine round the neck of the Hare, and knotted the other end to a tree. "Now, my lively little Hare, jump twenty times round the tree," exclaimed the Musician. The Hare obeyed; and as he jumped round the twentieth time the twine had wound itself round the tree twenty times also, and made the Hare prisoner; and pull and tug as much as he would, the cord only cut the deeper into his neck. "Wait there till I come again," said the Musician, and went on further.

The Wolf, meanwhile, had been pulling, dragging, and biting at the stone, and worked at it so long that at last he set his feet at liberty, and drew them again out of the cleft. Then, full of rage and anger, he hastened after the Musician, intending to tear him into pieces. As the Fox saw him running past he began to groan, and shouted with all his power, "Brother Wolf, come and help me; the Musician has deceived me!" So the Wolf, pulling the branches down, bit the knot to pieces, and freed the Fox, who went on with him in order to take revenge on the Musician. On their way they found the Hare tied, and setting him at liberty, all three set out in pursuit of their enemy.

The Musician, however, had once more played his fiddle, and this time had been very lucky, for the notes came to the ears of a poor woodcutter, who left off his work directly, whether he wished or not, and with his axe under his arm, came up to hear the music.

"At last the right companion has come," said the Musician; "for I desired a man, and not a wild beast." And beginning to play, he played so beautifully and delightfully, that the poor man was as if enchanted, and his heart beat for joy. While he thus stood, the Wolf, the Fox, and the Hare came up, and he observed directly that they had some bad design, so raising his bright axe he placed himself before the Musician, as if he would say, "Who wishes to attack must take care of himself." His looks made the animals afraid, and they ran back into the forest; but the Musician, after playing one more tune out of gratitude to the woodcutter, went on his journey.

The Twelve Brothers

ONCE upon a time there lived happily together a Queen and a King, who had twelve children – all boys. One day the King said to his consort, "If the thirteenth child, whom you are about to bring into the world, should be a girl, then shall the twelve boys die, that her riches may be great, and that the kingdom may fall to her alone." He then ordered twelve coffins to be made, which were filled with shavings, and in each a pillow was placed, and, all of them having been locked up in a room, he gave the key thereof to the Queen, and bade her tell nobody about the matter.

But the mother sat crying the whole day long, so that her youngest child, who was always with her, and whom she had named Benjamin, said to her, "Mother dear, why are you so sorrowful?" "My dearest child," she replied, "I dare not tell you!" But he let her have no peace until she went and unlocked the room, and showed him the twelve coffins filled with shavings. Then she said, "My dearest Benjamin, these coffins your father has had prepared for yourself and your eleven brothers, for, if I bring a little girl into the world, you will all be killed together and buried in them." And as she wept while she spoke these words, the son comforted her, saying, "Do not cry, dear mother; we will help ourselves, and go away." But she said, "Go with your eleven brothers into the wood, and let one of you climb into the highest tree which is to be found, and keep watch, looking towards the tower of the castle here. If I bear a little son, I will hang out a white flag, and you may venture home again; but if I bear a little daughter, I will hang out a red flag; and then flee away as quickly as you can, and God preserve you! Every night I will arise and pray for you: in winter, that you may have a fire to warm yourselves; and in summer, that you may not be melted with the heat."

Soon after she gave her blessing to all her sons, and they went away into the forest. Each kept watch in turn, sitting upon the highest oak-tree, and looking towards the tower. When eleven days had passed by, and it came to Benjamin's turn, he perceived a flag hung out; but it was not the white but the red flag, which announced that they must all die. As the brothers heard this, they became very angry, and said, "Shall we suffer death on account of a maiden? Let us swear that we will avenge ourselves; wherever we find a maiden, her blood shall flow."

Thereupon they went deeper into the forest, and in the middle, where it was most gloomy, they found a little charmed cottage standing empty, and they said, "Here we will dwell, and you, Benjamin, as you are the youngest and the weakest, shall stop here and keep house while we go out to fetch meat." So they set forth into the forest, and shot hares, wild fawns, birds, and pigeons, and what else they could find. These they brought home to Benjamin, who cooked and dressed them for their different meals. In this little cottage they lived ten years together, and the time passed very quickly.

The little daughter, whom their mother, the Queen, had borne, was now grown up: she had a kind heart, was very beautiful, and always wore a golden star upon her brow. Once, when there was a great wash, she saw twelve boys' shirts hanging up, and she asked her mother, "To whom do these twelve shirts belong, for they are much too small for my father?" Then she answered with a heavy heart, "My dear child, they belong to your twelve brothers!" The maiden replied, "Where are my twelve brothers? I have never yet heard of them." The Queen answered, "God only knows where they are; they have wandered into the wide world." Then she took the maiden, and, unlocking the room, showed her twelve coffins with the shavings and pillows. "These coffins," said she, "were ordered for your brothers, but they went away secretly before you were born;" and she told her how everything had happened. Then the maiden said, "Do not cry, dear mother, I will go forth and seek my brothers;" and, taking the twelve shirts, she set out at once straight into the great forest. All day long she walked on and on, and in the evening she came to the charmed house, into which she stepped. There she found a young lad, who asked her, "Whence dost thou come, and whither goest thou?" and he stood astonished to see how beautiful she was, and at the queenly robes she wore, and the star upon her brow. Then she answered, "I am a King's daughter, and am seeking my twelve brothers, and will go as far as heaven is blue until I find them;" and she showed him the twelve shirts that belonged to them. Benjamin perceived at once that it was his sister, and he said, "I am Benjamin, thy youngest brother." At his words, she began to weep for joy, and Benjamin wept also, and they kissed and embraced one another with the greatest affection. Presently he said, "Dear sister, there is one terrible condition; we have agreed together that every maiden whom we meet shall die, because we were obliged to leave our kingdom on account of a maiden."

Then the maiden replied, "I will willingly die, if I can by that means release my twelve brothers."

"No," answered he, "thou shalt not die; hide thyself under this tub until our eleven brothers come home, with whom I shall then be united." She did so; and when night came the others returned from hunting, and their dinner was made ready, and as they sat at the table eating, they asked, "What is the news?" Benjamin said, "Do you not know?"

"No," they answered. Then he spoke again: "You have been in the forest, and I have stopped at home, yet I know more than you."

"Tell us directly!" they exclaimed. He answered, "First promise me that you will not kill the first maiden who shall meet us." "Yes, we promise!" they exclaimed, "she shall have pardon; now tell us at once." Then he said, "Our sister is here;" and, lifting up the tub, the King's daughter came from beneath, looking most beautiful, delicate, and gentle in her royal robes, and with the golden star upon her brow. The sight gladdened them all; and, falling upon her neck, they kissed her, and loved her with all their hearts.

Now she stopped at home with Benjamin, and helped him in his work, while the eleven others went into the wood, and caught wild animals, deer, birds, and pigeons, for their eating, which their sister and brother took care to make ready. The sister sought for wood for the fire, and for the vegetables, which she dressed, and put the pots on the fire, so that their dinner was always ready when the eleven came home. She also kept order in the cottage, and covered the beds with beautiful white and clean sheets, and the brothers were always contented, and they all lived in great unity.

One day, when the brother and sister had made ready a most excellent meal, and the others had come in, they sat down and ate and drank, and were full of happiness. But there was a little garden belonging to the charmed house, in which stood twelve lilies (which one calls also African marigolds), and the sister, thinking to give her twelve brothers a pleasure, broke off the twelve flowers, intending to give each of them one. But as she broke off each flower the twelve brothers were changed, one by one, into twelve Crows, and flew off into the forest, and at the same moment the house and garden both disappeared.

Thus the poor maiden was left alone in the wild forest, and as she looked round an old woman stood near, who said, "My child, what hast thou done? Why didst thou not leave the twelve white flowers? They were thy brothers, who are now changed into crows!" Then the maiden asked with tears, "Is there no means of saving them?" "There is but one way in the whole world," said the old woman, "but that is so difficult that thou canst not free them. Thou must be dumb for seven years, – thou mayest not speak, nor laugh, and if thou speakest but a single word, even if it wants but one hour of the seven years, all will be in vain, and thy brothers will die at that single word."

Then the maiden said in her heart, "I know for certain that I shall free my brothers;" and she went and found a tall tree, into the branches of which she climbed and passed her time spinning, without ever speaking or laughing.

Now it happened once that a King was hunting in the forest, who had a large greyhound, which ran to the tree on which the maiden sat, and, springing round, barked furiously. So the King came up and saw the beautiful girl with the golden star upon her brow, and was so enchanted with her beauty, that he asked her if she would become his bride. To this she gave no answer, but slightly nodded with her head; so the King, mounting the tree himself, brought her down, and placing her upon his horse carried her home.

Then the wedding was celebrated with great pomp and joy, but the bride neither spoke nor laughed.

After they had lived contentedly together two years, the King's mother, who was a wicked woman, began to slander the young Queen, and said to her son, "This is a common beggar girl whom you have brought home with you: who knows what impish tricks she practised at home? If she be dumb and not able to speak, she might still laugh once; but they who do not laugh have a bad conscience." The King would not at first believe it, but the old woman persisted in it so long, and accused the Queen of so many wicked things, that the King at last let himself be persuaded, and she was condemned to die.

Now a great fire was kindled in the courtyard in which she was to be burnt; and the King standing above at the window, looked on with tearful eyes, because he still loved her so much. And now she was bound to the stake, and the fire began to lick her clothing with its red tongues, and just at that time the last moment of the seven years expired. Then a whirring was heard in the air, and twelve Crows came flying by, and sank down to the earth, and as they alighted on the ground they became her twelve brothers whom she had freed. They tore away the fire from around her, and, extinguishing the flames, set their sister free, and kissed and embraced her. And now, as she could open her mouth and speak, she told the King why she was dumb, and why she never laughed.

And the King was highly pleased when he heard she was innocent and they all lived together in great happiness to the end of their lives.

The Three Little Men in the Wood

ONCE upon a time there lived a man, whose wife had died; and a woman, also, who had lost her husband: and this man and this woman had each a daughter. These two maidens were friendly with each other, and used to walk together, and one day they came by the widow's house. Then the widow said to the man's daughter, "Do you hear, tell your father I wish to marry him, and you shall every morning wash in milk and drink wine, but my daughter shall wash in water and drink water." So the girl went home and told her father what the woman had said, and he replied, "What shall I do? marriage is a comfort, but it is also a torment." At last, as he could come to no conclusion, he drew off his boot and said: "Take this boot, which has a hole in the sole, and go with it out-of-doors and hang it on the great nail, and then pour water into it. If it holds the water, I will again take a wife; but if it runs through, I will not have her." The girl did as he bid her but the water drew the hole together and the boot became full to overflowing. So she told her father how it had happened, and he, getting up, saw it was quite true; and going to the widow he settled the matter, and the wedding was celebrated.

The next morning, when the two girls arose, milk to wash in and wine to drink were set for the man's daughter, but only water, both for washing and drinking, for the woman's daughter. The second morning, water for washing and drinking stood before both the man's daughter and the woman's; and on the third morning, water to wash in and water to drink were set before the man's daughter, and milk to wash in and wine to drink before the woman's daughter, and so it continued.

Soon the woman conceived a deadly hatred for her step-daughter and knew not how to behave badly enough to her, from day to day. She was envious too, because her step-daughter was beautiful and lovely, and her own daughter was ugly and hateful.

Once, in the winter time, when the river was frozen as hard as a stone, and hill and valley were covered with snow, the woman made a cloak of paper, and called the maiden to her and said, "Put on this cloak, and go away into the wood to fetch me a little basketful of strawberries, for I have a wish for some."

"Mercy on us!" said the maiden, "in winter there are no strawberries growing; the ground is frozen, and the snow, too, has covered everything. And why must I go in that paper cloak? It is so cold out-of-doors that it freezes one's breath even, and if the wind does not blow off this cloak, the thorns will tear it from my body."

"Will you dare to contradict me?" said the stepmother. "Make haste off, and let me not see you again until you have found me a basket of strawberries." Then she gave her a small piece of dry bread, saying, "On that you must subsist the whole day." But she thought – out-of-doors she will be frozen and starved, so that my eyes will never see her again!

So the girl did as she was told, and put on the paper cloak, and went away with the basket. Far and near there was nothing but snow, and not a green blade was to be seen. When she came to the forest she discovered a little cottage, out of which three little Dwarfs were peeping. The girl wished them good morning, and knocked gently at the door. They called her in, and entering the room, she sat down on a bench by the fire to warm herself, and eat her breakfast. The Dwarfs called out, "Give us some of it!" "Willingly," she replied, and, dividing her bread in two, she gave them half. They asked, "What do you here in the forest, in the winter time, in this thin cloak?"

"Ah!" she answered, "I must seek a basketful of strawberries, and I dare not return home until I can take them with me." When she had eaten her bread, they gave her a broom, saying, "Sweep away the snow with this from the back door." But when she was gone out-of-doors the three Dwarfs said one to another, "What shall we give her, because she is so gentle and good, and has shared her bread with us?" Then said the first, "I grant to her that she shall become more beautiful every day." The second said, "I grant that a piece of gold shall fall out of her mouth for every word she speaks." The third said, "I grant that a King shall come and make her his bride."

Meanwhile, the girl had done as the Dwarfs had bidden her, and had swept away the snow from behind the house. And what do you think she found there? Actually, ripe strawberries! which came quite red and sweet up under the snow. So filling her basket in great glee, she thanked the little men and gave them each her hand, and then ran home to take her stepmother what she wished for. As she went in and said, "Good evening," a piece of gold fell from her mouth. Thereupon she related what had happened to her in the forest; but at every word she spoke a piece of gold fell, so that the whole floor was covered.

"Just see her arrogance," said the step-sister, "to throw away money in that way!" but in her heart she was jealous, and wished to go into the forest too, to seek strawberries. Her mother said, "No, my dear daughter; it is too cold, you will be frozen!" but as her girl let her have no peace, she at last consented, and made her a beautiful fur cloak to put on; she also gave her buttered bread and cooked meat to eat on her way.

The girl went into the forest and came straight to the little cottage. The three Dwarfs were peeping out again, but she did not greet them; and, stumbling on without looking at them or speaking, she entered the room, and, seating herself by the fire, began to eat the bread and butter and meat. "Give us some of that," exclaimed the Dwarfs; but she answered, "I have not got enough for myself, so how can I give any away?" When she had finished they said, "You have a broom there, go and sweep the back door clean." "Oh, sweep it yourself," she replied; "I am not your servant." When she saw that they would not give her anything she went out at the door, and the three Dwarfs said to each other, "What shall we give her? she is so ill-behaved, and has such a bad and envious disposition, that nobody can wish well to her." The first said, "I grant that she becomes more ugly every day." The second said, "I grant that at every word she speaks a toad shall spring out of her mouth." The third said, "I grant that she shall die a miserable death." Meanwhile the girl had been looking for strawberries out-of-doors, but as she could find none she went home very peevish. When she opened her mouth to tell her mother what had happened to her in the forest, a toad jumped out of her mouth at each word, so that every one fled away from her in horror.

The stepmother was now still more vexed, and was always thinking how she could do the most harm to her husband's daughter, who every day became more beautiful. At last she took a kettle, set it on fire, and boiled a net therein. When it was sodden she hung it on the shoulder of the poor girl, and gave her an axe, that she might go upon the frozen pond and cut a hole in the ice to drag the net. She obeyed, and went away and cut an ice-hole; and while she was cutting, an elegant carriage came by, in which the King sat. The carriage stopped, and the King asked, "My child, who are you? and what do you here?" "I am a poor girl, and I am dragging a net," said she. Then the King pitied her, and saw how beautiful she was, and said, "Will you go with me?" "Yes, indeed, with all my heart," she replied, for she was glad to get out of the sight of her mother and sister.

So she was handed into the carriage, and driven away with the King; and as soon as they arrived at his castle the wedding was celebrated with great splendour, as the Dwarfs had granted to the maiden. After a year the young Queen bore a son; and when the stepmother heard of her great good fortune, she came to the castle with her daughter, and behaved as if she had come on a visit. But one day, when the King had gone out, and no one was present, this bad woman seized the Queen by the head, and her daughter caught hold of her feet, and raising her out of bed, they threw her out of the window into the river which ran past. Then, laying her ugly daughter in the bed, the old woman covered her up, even over her head; and when the King came back he wished to speak to his wife, but the old woman exclaimed, "Softly! softly! do not go near her; she is lying in a beautiful sleep, and must be kept quiet to-day." The King, not thinking of any evil design, came again the next morning the first thing; and when he spoke to his wife, and she answered, a toad sprang out of her mouth at every word, as a piece of gold had done before. So he asked what had happened, and the old woman said, "That is produced by her weakness, she will soon lose it again."

But in the night the kitchen-boy saw a Duck swimming through the brook, and the Duck asked,

> "King, King, what are you doing?
> Are you sleeping, or are you waking?"

And as he gave no answer the Duck said,

"What are my guests a-doing?"

Then the boy answered,

"They all sleep sound."

And she asked him,

"How fares my child?"

And he replied,

"In his cradle he sleeps."

Then she came up in the form of the Queen to the cradle, and gave the child drink, shook up his bed, and covered him up, and then swam again away as a duck through the brook. The second night she came again; and on the third she said to the kitchen-boy, "Go and tell the King to take his sword, and swing it thrice over me, on the threshold." Then the boy ran and told the King, who came with his sword, and swung it thrice over the Duck; and at the third time his bride stood before him, bright, living, and healthful, as she had been before.

Now the King was in great happiness, but he hid the Queen in a chamber until the Sunday when the child was to be christened; and when all was finished he asked, "What ought to be done to one who takes another out of a bed and throws her into the river?" "Nothing could be more proper," said the old woman, "than to put such a one into a cask, stuck round with nails, and to roll it down the hill into the water." Then the King said, "You have spoken your own sentence;" and ordering a cask to be fetched, he caused the old woman and her daughter to be put into it, and the bottom being nailed up, the cask was rolled down the hill until it fell into the water.

The Little Brother and Sister

THERE was once a little Brother who took his Sister by the hand, and said, "Since our own dear mother's death we have not had one happy hour; our stepmother beats us every day, and, if we come near her, kicks us away with her foot. Our food is the hard crusts of bread which are left, and even the dog under the table fares better than we, for he often gets a nice morsel. Come, let us wander forth into the wide world." So the whole day long they travelled over meadows, fields, and stony roads, and when it rained the Sister said, "It is heaven crying in sympathy." By evening they came into a large forest, and were so wearied with grief, hunger, and their long walk, that they laid themselves down in a hollow tree, and went to sleep. When they awoke the next morning, the sun had already risen high in the heavens, and its beams made the trees so hot, that the little boy said to his Sister, "I am so thirsty, if I knew where there was a brook I

THE LITTLE BROTHER AND SISTER

would go and drink. Ah! I think I hear one running;" and so saying, he got up, and taking his Sister's hand, they went in search of the brook.

The wicked stepmother, however, was a witch, and had witnessed the departure of the two children; so, sneaking after them secretly, as is the habit of witches, she had enchanted all the springs in the forest.

Presently they found a brook which ran trippingly over the pebbles, and the Brother would have drunk out of it, but the Sister heard how it said as it ran along, "Who drinks of me will become a tiger!" So the Sister exclaimed, "I pray you, Brother, drink not, or you will become a tiger, and tear me to pieces!" So the Brother did not drink, although his thirst was so great, and he said, "I will wait till the next brook." As they came to the second, the Sister heard it say, "Who drinks of me becomes a wolf!" The Sister ran up crying, "Brother, do not, pray do not, drink, or you will become a wolf and eat me up!" Then the Brother did not drink, saying, "I will wait until we come to the next spring, but then I must drink, you may say what you will; my thirst is much too great." Just as they reached the third brook, the Sister heard the voice saying, "Who drinks of me will become a fawn, – who drinks of me will become a fawn!" So the Sister said, "O, my Brother! do not drink, or you will be changed to a fawn, and run away from me!" But he had already kneeled down, and drunk of the water, and, as the first drops passed his lips, his shape became that of a fawn.

At first the Sister cried over her little changed Brother, and he wept too, and knelt by her very sorrowful; but at last the maiden said, "Be still, dear little Fawn, and I will never forsake you;" and, undoing her golden garter, she put it round his neck, and weaving rushes made a white girdle to lead him with. This she tied to him, and, taking the other end in her hand, she led him away, and they travelled deeper and deeper into the forest. After they had walked a long distance they came to a little hut, and the Maiden, peeping in, found it empty, and thought, "Here we can stay and dwell." Then she looked for leaves and moss to make a soft couch for the Fawn, and every morning she went out and collected roots and berries and nuts for herself, and tender grass for the Fawn, which he ate out of her hand, and played happily around her. In the evening, when the Sister was tired, and had said her prayers, she laid her head upon the back of the Fawn, which served for a pillow, on which she slept soundly. Had but the Brother regained his own proper form, their life would have been happy indeed.

Thus they dwelt in this wilderness, and some time had elapsed, when it happened that the King of the country held a great hunt in the forest; and now resounded through the trees the blowing of horns, the barking of dogs, and the lusty cries of the hunters, so that the little Fawn heard them, and wanted very much to join. "Ah!" said he to his Sister, "let me go to the hunt, I cannot restrain myself any longer;" and he begged so hard that at last she consented. "But," said she to him, "return again in the evening, for I shall shut my door against the wild huntsmen, and, that I may know you, do you knock, and say, 'Sister, let me in,' and if you do not speak I shall not open the door." As soon as she had said this, the little Fawn sprang off, quite glad and merry in the fresh breeze. The King and his huntsmen perceived the beautiful animal, and pursued him; but they could not catch him, and when they thought they had him for certain, he sprang away over the bushes, and got out of sight. Just as it was getting dark, he ran up to the hut, and, knocking, said, "Sister mine, let me in." Then she undid the little door, and he went in, and rested all night long upon his soft couch. The next morning the hunt was commenced again, and as soon as the little Fawn heard the horns and the tally-ho of the sportsmen he could not rest, and said, "Sister dear, open the door, I must be off." The Sister opened it, saying, "Return at evening, mind, and say the words as before." When the King and his huntsmen saw again the Fawn with the golden necklace, they followed him close, but he was too nimble and quick for them. The whole day long they kept up with him, but towards evening the huntsmen made a circle round him, and one wounded him slightly in the foot behind, so that he could only run slowly. Then one of them slipped after him to the little hut, and heard him say, "Sister dear, open the door," and saw that the door was opened and immediately shut behind. The huntsman, having observed all this, went and told the King what he had seen and heard, and he said, "On the morrow I will once more pursue him."

The Sister, however, was terribly frightened when she saw that her Fawn was wounded, and, washing off the blood, she put herbs upon the foot, and said, "Go and rest upon your bed, dear Fawn, that the wound may heal." It was so slight, that the next morning he felt nothing of it, and when he heard the hunting cries outside, he exclaimed, "I cannot stop away – I must be there, and none shall catch me so easily again!" The Sister wept very much, and told him, "Soon they will kill you, and I shall be here all alone in this forest, forsaken by all the world: I cannot let you go."

"I shall die here in vexation," answered the Fawn, "if you do not: for when I hear the horn, I think I shall jump out of my skin." The Sister, finding she could not prevent him, opened the door with a heavy heart, and the Fawn jumped out, quite delighted, into the forest. As soon as the King perceived him, he said to his huntsmen, "Follow him all day long till the evening, but let no one do him an injury." When the sun had set the King asked his huntsmen to show him the hut; and as they came to it, he knocked at the door, and said, "Let me in, dear Sister." Then the door was opened, and, stepping in, the King saw a maiden more beautiful than he had ever before seen. She was frightened when she saw not her Fawn, but a man step in, who had a golden crown upon his head. But the King, looking at her with a friendly glance, reached her his hand saying, "Will you go with me to my castle, and be my dear wife?" "Oh, yes," replied the maiden; "but the Fawn must go too: him I will never forsake." The King replied, "He shall remain with you as long as you live, and shall want for nothing." In the meantime the Fawn had come in, and the Sister, binding the girdle to him, again took it in her hand, and led him away with her out of the hut.

The King took the beautiful maiden upon his horse, and rode to his castle, where the wedding was celebrated with great splendour, and she became Queen, and they lived together a long time; while the Fawn was taken care of and lived well, playing about the castle garden. The wicked stepmother, however, on whose account the children had wandered forth into the world, supposed that long ago the Sister had been torn in pieces by the wild beasts, and the little Brother hunted to death in his Fawn's shape by the hunters. As soon, therefore, as she heard how happy they had become, and how everything prospered with them, envy and jealousy were roused in her heart, and left her no peace; and she was always thinking in what way she could work misfortune to them. Her own daughter, who was as ugly as night, and had but one eye, for which she was continually reproached, said, "The luck of being a Queen has never yet happened to me." "Be quiet now," said the old woman, "and make yourself contented: when the time comes, I shall be at hand." As soon, then, as the time came when the Queen brought into the world a beautiful little boy, which happened when the King was out hunting, the old witch took the form of a chambermaid, and got into the room where the Queen was lying, and said to her, "The bath is ready, which will restore you, and give you fresh strength; be quick, before it gets cold." Her daughter being at hand, they carried the weak Queen between them into the room, and laid her in the bath, and then, shutting the door to, they ran off; but first they had made up an immense fire in the stove, which must soon suffocate the young Queen.

When this was done, the old woman took her daughter, and, putting a cap on her, laid her in the bed in the Queen's place. She gave her, too, the form and appearance of the real Queen, as far as she could; but she could not restore the lost eye, and, so that the King might not notice it, she turned upon that side where there was no eye. When he came home at evening, and heard that a son was born to him, he was much delighted, and prepared to go to his wife's bedside, to see how she did. So the old woman called out in a great hurry, "For your life, do not undraw the curtains; the Queen must not yet see the light, and must be kept quiet." So the King went away, and did not discover that a false Queen was laid in the bed.

When midnight came, and every one was asleep, the nurse, who sat by herself, wide awake, near the cradle, in the nursery, saw the door open and the true Queen come in. She took the child in her arms, and rocked it a while, and then, shaking up its pillow, laid it down in its cradle, and covered it over again. She did not forget the Fawn either, but, going to the corner where he was, stroked his back, and then went silently out at the door. The nurse asked in the morning of the guards, if any one had passed into the castle during the night; but they answered, "No, we have seen nobody." For many nights afterwards she came constantly, and never spoke a word; and the nurse saw her always, but she would not trust herself to speak about it to any one.

When some time had passed away, the Queen one night began to speak, and said,—

> "How fares my child, how fares my fawn?
> Twice more will I come, but never again."

The nurse made no reply; but, when she had disappeared, went to the King, and told him all. The King exclaimed, "Oh, heavens! what does this mean? – the next night I will watch myself by the child." In the evening he went into the nursury, and about midnight the Queen appeared, and said,—

> "How fares my child, how fares my fawn?
> Once more will I come, but never again."

And she nursed the child, as she was used to do, and then disappeared. The King dared not speak; but he watched the following night, and this time she said,—

> "How fares my child, how fares my fawn?
> This time have I come, but never again."

At these words, the King could hold back no longer, but sprang up and said, "You can be no other than my dear wife!" Then she answered, "Yes, I am your dear wife;" and at that moment her life was restored by God's mercy, and she was again as beautiful and charming as ever. She told the King the fraud which the witch and her daughter had practised upon him, and he had them both tried and sentence pronounced against them. The daughter was taken into the forest, where the wild beasts tore her in pieces, but the old witch was led to the fire and miserably burnt. And as soon as she was reduced to ashes, the little Fawn was unbewitched, and received again his human form; and the Brother and Sister lived happily together to the end of their days.

Hansel and Grethel

ONCE upon a time there dwelt near a large wood a poor woodcutter, with his wife and two children by his former marriage, a little boy called Hansel, and a girl named Grethel. He had little enough to break or bite; and once, when there was a great famine in the land, he could not procure even his daily bread; and as he lay thinking in his bed one evening, rolling about for trouble, he sighed, and said to his wife, "What will become of us? How can we feed our children, when we have no more than we can eat ourselves?"

"Know, then, my husband," answered she, "we will lead them away, quite early in the morning, into the thickest part of the wood, and there make them a fire, and give them each a little piece of bread; then we will go to our work, and leave them alone, so they will not find the way home again, and we shall be freed from them." "No, wife," replied he, "that I can never do; how can you bring your heart to leave my children all alone in the wood; for the wild beasts will soon come and tear them to pieces?"

"Oh, you simpleton!" said she, "then we must all four die of hunger; you had better plane the coffins for us." But she left him no peace till he consented, saying, "Ah, but I shall regret the poor children."

The two children, however, had not gone to sleep for very hunger, and so they overheard what the stepmother said to their father. Grethel wept bitterly, and said to Hansel, "What will become of us?" "Be quiet, Grethel," said he; "do not cry – I will soon help you." And as soon as their parents had fallen asleep, he got up, put on his coat, and, unbarring the back door, slipped out. The moon shone brightly, and the white pebbles which lay before the door seemed like silver pieces, they glittered so brightly. Hansel stooped down, and put as many into his pocket as it would hold; and then going back, he said to Grethel, "Be comforted, dear sister, and sleep in peace; God will not forsake us." And so saying, he went to bed again.

The next morning, before the sun arose, the wife went and awoke the two children. "Get up, you lazy things; we are going into the forest to chop wood." Then she gave them each a piece of bread, saying, "There is something for your dinner; do not eat it before the time, for you will get nothing else." Grethel took the bread in her apron, for Hansel's pocket was full of pebbles; and so they all set out upon their way. When they had gone a little distance, Hansel stood still, and peeped back at the house; and this he repeated several times, till his father said, "Hansel, what are you peeping at, and why do you lag behind? Take care, and remember your legs."

"Ah, father," said Hansel, "I am looking at my white cat sitting upon the roof of the house, and trying to say good-bye." "You simpleton!" said the wife, "that is not a cat; it is only the sun shining on the white chimney." But in reality Hansel was not looking at a cat; but every time he stopped, he dropped a pebble out of his pocket upon the path.

When they came to the middle of the wood, the father told the children to collect wood, and he would make them a fire, so that they should not be cold. So Hansel and Grethel gathered together quite a little mountain of twigs. Then they set fire to them; and as the flame burnt up high, the wife said, "Now, you children, lie down near the fire, and rest yourselves, whilst we go into the forest and chop wood; when we are ready, I will come and call you."

Hansel and Grethel sat down by the fire, and when it was noon, each ate the piece of bread; and because they could hear the blows of an axe, they thought their father was near: but it was not an axe, but a branch which he had bound to a withered tree, so as to be blown to and fro by the wind. They waited so long, that at last their eyes closed from weariness, and they fell fast asleep. When they awoke, it was quite dark, and Grethel began to cry, "How shall we get out of the wood?" But Hansel tried to comfort her by saying, "Wait a little while till the moon rises, and then we will quickly find the way." The moon soon shone forth, and Hansel, taking his sister's hand, followed the pebbles, which glittered like new-coined silver pieces, and showed them the path. All night long they walked on, and as day broke they came to their father's house. They knocked at the door, and when the wife opened it, and saw Hansel and Grethel, she exclaimed, "You wicked children! why did you sleep so long in the wood? We thought you were never coming home again." But their father was very glad, for it had grieved his heart to leave them all alone.

Not long afterwards there was again great scarcity in every corner of the land; and one night the children overheard their mother saying to their father, "Everything is again consumed; we have only half a loaf left, and then the song is ended: the children must be sent away. We will take them deeper into the wood, so that they may not find the way out again; it is the only means of escape for us."

But her husband felt heavy at heart, and thought, "It were better to share the last crust with the children." His wife, however, would listen to nothing that he said, and scolded and reproached him without end.

He who says A must say B too; and he who consents the first time must also the second.

The children, however, had heard the conversation as they lay awake, and as soon as the old people went to sleep Hansel got up, intending to pick up some pebbles as before; but the wife had locked the door, so that he could not get out. Nevertheless he comforted Grethel, saying, "Do not cry; sleep in quiet; the good God will not forsake us."

Early in the morning the stepmother came and pulled them out of bed, and gave them each a slice of bread, which was still smaller than the former piece. On the way, Hansel broke his in his pocket, and, stooping every now and then, dropped a crumb upon the path. "Hansel, why do you stop and look about?" said the father, "keep in the path." "I am looking at my little dove," answered Hansel, "nodding a good-bye to me." "Simpleton!" said the wife, "that is no dove, but only the sun shining on the chimney." But Hansel kept still dropping crumbs as he went along.

The mother led the children deep into the wood, where they had never been before, and there making an immense fire, she said to them, "Sit down here and rest, and when you feel tired you can sleep for a little while. We are going into the forest to hew wood, and in the evening, when we are ready, we will come and fetch you."

When noon came Grethel shared her bread with Hansel, who had strewn his on the path. Then they went to sleep; but the evening arrived and no one came to visit the poor children, and in the dark night they awoke, and Hansel comforted his sister by saying, "Only wait, Grethel, till the moon comes out, then we shall see the crumbs of bread which I have dropped, and they will show us the way home." The moon shone and they got up, but they could not see any crumbs, for the thousands of birds which had been flying about in the woods and fields had picked them all up. Hansel kept saying to Grethel, "We will soon find the way;" but they did not, and they walked the whole night long and the next day, but still they did not come out of the wood; and they got so hungry, for they had nothing to eat but the berries which they found upon the bushes. Soon they got so tired that they could not drag themselves along, so they lay down under a tree and went to sleep.

It was now the third morning since they had left their father's house, and they still walked on; but they only got deeper and deeper into the wood, and Hansel saw that if help did not come very soon they would die of hunger. As soon as it was noon they saw a beautiful snow-white bird sitting upon a bough, which sang so sweetly that they stood still and listened to it. It soon left off, and spreading its wings flew off; and they followed it until it arrived at a cottage, upon the roof of which it perched; and when they went close up to it they saw that the cottage was made of bread and cakes, and the window-panes were of clear sugar.

"We will go in there," said Hansel, "and have a glorious feast. I will eat a piece of the roof, and you can eat the window. Will they not be sweet?" So Hansel reached up and broke a piece off the roof, in order to see how it tasted; while Grethel stepped up to the window and began to bite it. Then a sweet voice called out in the room, "Tip-tap, tip-tap, who raps at my door?" and the children answered, "The wind, the wind, the child of heaven;" and they went on eating without interruption. Hansel thought the roof tasted very nice, and so he tore off a great piece; while Grethel broke a large round pane out of the window, and sat down quite contentedly. Just then the door opened, and a very old woman, walking up on crutches, came out. Hansel and Grethel were so frightened that they let fall what they had in their hands; but the old woman, nodding her head, said, "Ah, you dear children, what has brought you here? Come in and stop with me, and no harm shall befall you;" and so saying she took them both by the hand, and led them into her cottage. A good meal of milk and pancakes, with sugar, apples and nuts, was spread on the table, and in the back room were two nice little beds, covered with white, where Hansel and Grethel laid themselves down, and thought themselves in heaven. The old woman behaved very kindly to them, but in reality she was a wicked witch who waylaid children, and built the bread-house in order to entice them in; but as soon as they were in her power she killed them, cooked and ate them, and made a great festival of the day. Witches have red eyes, and cannot see very far; but they have a fine sense of smelling, like wild beasts, so that they know when children approach them. When Hansel and Grethel came near the witch's house she laughed wickedly, saying, "Here come two who shall not escape me." And early in the morning, before they awoke, she went up to them, and saw how lovingly they lay sleeping, with their chubby red cheeks; and she mumbled to herself, "That will be a good bite." Then she took up Hansel with her rough hand, and shut him up in a little cage with a lattice-door; and although he screamed loudly it was of no use. Grethel came next, and, shaking her till she awoke, she said, "Get up, you lazy thing, and fetch some water to cook something good for your brother who must remain in that stall and get fat; when he is fat enough I shall eat him." Grethel began to cry, but it was all useless, for the old witch made her do as she wished. So a nice meal was cooked for Hansel, but Grethel got nothing else but a crab's claw.

Every morning the old witch came to the cage and said, "Hansel, stretch out your finger that I may feel whether you are getting fat." But Hansel used to stretch out a bone, and the old woman, having very bad sight, thought it was his finger, and wondered very much that he did not get more fat. When four weeks had passed, and Hansel still kept quite lean, she lost all her patience, and would not wait any longer. "Grethel," she called out in a passion, "get some water quickly; be Hansel fat or lean, this morning I will kill and cook him." Oh, how the poor little sister grieved, as she was forced to fetch the water, and fast the tears ran down her cheeks. "Dear good God, help us now!" she exclaimed. "Had we only been eaten by the wild beasts in the wood, then we should have died together." But the old witch called out, "Leave off that noise; it will not help you a bit."

So early in the morning Grethel was forced to go out and fill the kettle, and make a fire. "First, we will bake, however," said the old woman; "I have already heated the oven and kneaded the dough;" and so saying, she pushed poor Grethel up to the oven, out of which the flames were burning fiercely. "Creep in," said the witch, "and see if it is hot enough, and then we will put in the bread; but she intended when Grethel got in to shut up the oven and let her bake, so that she might eat her as well as Hansel. Grethel perceived what her thoughts were, and said, "I do not know how to do it; how shall I get in?" "You stupid goose," said she, "the opening is big enough. See, I could even get in myself!" and she got up, and put her head into the oven. Then Grethel gave her a push, so that she fell right in, and then shutting the iron door she bolted it. Oh! how horribly she howled; but Grethel ran away, and left the ungodly witch to burn to ashes.

Now she ran to Hansel, and, opening his door, called out, "Hansel, we are saved; the old witch is dead!" So he sprang out, like a bird out of his cage when the door is opened; and they were so glad that they fell upon each other's neck, and kissed each other over and over again. And now, as there was nothing to fear, they went into the witch's house, where in every corner were caskets full of pearls and precious stones. "These are better than pebbles," said Hansel, putting as many into his pocket as it would hold; while Grethel thought, "I will take some home too," and filled her apron full. "We must be off now," said Hansel, "and get out of this enchanted forest;" but when they had walked for two hours they came to a large piece of water. "We cannot get over," said Hansel; "I can see no bridge at all." "And there is no boat either," said Grethel, "but there swims a white duck, I will ask her to help us over," and she sang,

> "Little Duck, good little Duck,
>   Grethel and Hansel, here we stand;
> There is neither stile nor bridge,
>   Take us on your back to land."

So the Duck came to them, and Hansel sat himself on, and bade his sister sit behind him. "No," answered Grethel, "that will be too much for the Duck, she shall take us over one at a time." This the good little bird did, and when both were happily arrived on the other side, and had gone a little way, they came to a well-known wood, which they knew the better every step they went, and at last they perceived their father's house. Then they began to run, and, bursting into the house, they fell on their father's neck. He had not had one happy hour since he had left the children in the forest: and his wife was dead. Grethel shook her apron, and the pearls and precious stones rolled out upon the floor, and Hansel threw down one handful after the other out of his pocket. Then all their sorrows were ended, and they lived together in great happiness.

My tale is done. There runs a mouse; whoever catches her may make a great, great cap out of her fur.

The Three Snake-Leaves

THERE was once a poor man who was unable to feed his only son any longer; so the son said, "My dear father, everything goes badly with you, and I am a burden to you; I would rather go away and try to earn my own bread." So the father gave him his blessing, and took leave of him with great grief. At that time the King of a powerful empire was at war, and the youth taking service under him, went with him to the field. When he came in sight of the enemy, battle was given and he was in great peril, and the arrows flew so fast that his comrades fell around him on all sides. And when the captain was killed the rest would have taken to flight; but the youth, stepping forward, spoke to them courageously, exclaiming, "We will not let our fatherland be ruined!" Then the others followed him, and pressed on so furiously, that they routed the enemy. As soon as the King heard that he had to thank the youth for the victory, he raised him above all the others, gave him great treasures, and made him first in his kingdom.

Now the King had a daughter who was very beautiful, but she was also very whimsical. She had made a vow never to take a lord and husband who would not promise, if she should die first, to let himself be buried alive with her. "Does he love me with all his heart?" said she: "what use to him, then, can his life be afterwards?" At the same time she was prepared to do the same thing, and if her husband should die first to descend with him to the grave. This vow had hitherto frightened away all suitors, but the youth was so taken with her beauty that he waited for nothing, but immediately asked her in marriage of her father.

"Do you know," said the King, "what you must promise?"

"I must go with her into the grave," he replied, "if I survive her; but my love is so great that I mind not the danger." Then the King consented, and the wedding was celebrated with great splendour.

For a long time they lived happily and contented with one another, until it happened that the young Queen fell grievously sick, so that no physician could cure her. When she died the young Prince remembered his forced promise, and shuddered at the thought of laying himself alive in the grave; but there was no escape, for the King had set watchers at all the doors, and it was not possible to avoid his fate. When the day came that the body should be laid in the royal vault, he was led away with it, and the door closed and locked behind him. Near the coffin stood a table, having upon it four lights, four loaves of bread, and four bottles of wine: as soon as this supply came to an end he must die of hunger. Full of bitterness and sorrow, he sat down, eating each day but a little morsel of bread, and taking but one draught of wine: every day he saw death approaching nearer and nearer. Whilst he thus sat gazing before him he saw a snake creeping out of the corner of the vault, which approached the dead body. Thinking that it came to feed on the body, he drew his sword, and exclaiming, "So long as I live you shall not touch her!" he cut it in three pieces. After a while another snake crawled out of the corner; but when it saw the other lying dead it went back, and returned soon with three green leaves in its mouth. Then it took the three pieces of the snake, and, laying them together so as to join, it put one leaf on each wound. As soon as the divided parts were joined the snake moved and was alive again, and both snakes hastened away together. The leaves remained lying on the ground, and the unfortunate man, who had seen all, bethought himself whether the miraculous power of the leaves, which had restored a snake to life, might not help him. So he picked up the leaves, and laid one on the mouth of the corpse of his wife, and the other two on her eyes; and he had scarcely done so when the blood circulated again in the veins, and mounting into the pale countenance, flushed it with colour. Then she drew her breath, opened her eyes, and said, "Ah, where am I?" "You are with me, dear wife," he replied, and told her how everything had happened, and how he had brought her to life. Then he helped her to some wine and bread; and, when her strength had returned, she raised herself up, and they went to the door, and knocked and shouted so loudly, that the watchers heard them and told the King. The King came down himself and opened the door, and there found them both alive and well, and he rejoiced with them that their trouble had passed away. But the young Prince took away the three snake-leaves, and gave them to his servant, saying, "Preserve them carefully for me, and carry them with you at all times. Who knows in what necessity they may not help us?"

A change, however, had come over the wife after she was restored to life, and it was as if all love for her husband had passed out of her heart. And when, some little time after, he wished to make a voyage over the sea to his old father, and they had gone on board the ship, she forgot the great love and fidelity which he had shown, and through which he had saved her life, and disclosed a wicked plan to the Captain. When the young Prince lay asleep, she called up the Captain, and, taking the sleeper by the head, while he carried the feet, they threw the Prince into the sea. And as soon as the evil deed was done she said to the Captain, "Now let us return home, and say he died on the voyage. I will so praise and commend you to my father that he shall give you to me in marriage, and you shall sit as his heir."

But the faithful servant, who had seen all unremarked, let loose a little boat from the ship, and getting in it himself, rowed after his master, and let the betrayers sail away. He fished the dead body up again, and, by the help of the three snake-leaves, which he carried with him, he brought it happily to life again. Then they both rowed away with all their strength day and night, and their little boat glided on so fast that they arrived before the others at the old King's palace. He marvelled to see them return alone, and asked what had happened. When he heard of the wickedness of his daughter, he said, "I can scarcely believe that she has done such evil; but the truth will soon come to light." Then he bade them both go into a secret chamber, and keep themselves private from everybody. Soon afterwards the great vessel came sailing up, and the godless wife appeared before her father with a sorrowful countenance. "Why are you returned alone?" he asked. "Where is your husband?" "Alas! dear father," she replied, "I return home with great grief, for my husband was suddenly taken ill during the voyage and died; and if the good Captain had not given me his assistance it would have gone terribly with me; he was present at my husband's death, and can tell you all about it." The King said, "I will bring the dead to life," and opening the chamber, he bade the Prince and his servant both to come forth. As soon as the wife perceived her husband she was struck as if by lightning, and, falling on her knees, she begged his pardon. But the King answered, "For you there is no pardon. He was ready to die with you, and gave you life again; but you have conspired against him in his sleep, and shall receive your due reward." Then she was put, with her companion in crime, on board a ship which was pierced with holes, and drawn out into the sea; and they soon sank beneath the waves.

Rapunzel

ONCE upon a time there lived a man and his wife, who much wished to have a child, but for a long time in vain. These people had a little window in the back part of their house, out of which one could see into a beautiful garden which was full of fine flowers and vegetables; but it was surrounded by a high wall, and no one dared to go in, because it belonged to a Witch, who possessed great power, and who was feared by the whole world. One day the woman stood at this window looking into the garden, and there she saw a bed which was filled with the most beautiful radishes, and which seemed so fresh and green that she felt quite glad, and a great desire seized her to eat of these radishes. This wish tormented her daily, and as she knew that she could not have them she fell ill, and looked very pale and miserable. This frightened her husband, who asked her, "What ails you, my dear wife?"

"Ah!" she replied, "if I cannot get any of those radishes to eat out of the garden behind the house I shall die!" The husband, loving her very much, thought, "Rather than let my wife die, I must fetch her some radishes, cost what they may." So, in the gloom of the evening, he climbed the wall of the Witch's garden, and, snatching a handful of radishes in great haste, brought them to his wife, who made herself a salad with them, which she relished extremely. However, they were so nice and so well-flavoured, that the next day after she felt the same desire for the third time, and could not get any rest, so that her husband was obliged to promise her some more. So, in the evening, he made himself ready, and began clambering up the wall; but, oh! how terribly frightened he was, for there he saw the old Witch standing before him. "How dare you," – she began, looking at him with a frightful scowl, – "how dare you climb over into my garden to take away my radishes like a thief? Evil shall happen to you for this."

"Ah!" replied he, "let pardon be granted before justice; I have only done this from a great necessity; my wife saw your radishes from her window, and took such a fancy to them that she would have died if she had not eaten of them." Then the Witch ran after him in a passion, saying, "If she behave as you say, I will let you take away all the radishes you please, but I make one condition; you must give me the child which your wife will bring into the world. All shall go well with it, and I will care for it like a mother." In his anxiety the man consented, and when the child was born the Witch appeared at the same time, gave the child the name "Rapunzel," and took it away with her.

Rapunzel grew to be the most beautiful child under the sun, and when she was twelve years old the Witch shut her up in a tower,

RAPUNZEL

which stood in a forest, and had neither stairs nor door, and only one little window just at the top. When the Witch wished to enter, she stood beneath, and called out,—

> "Rapunzel! Rapunzel!
> Let down your hair."

For Rapunzel had long and beautiful hair, as fine as spun gold; and as soon as she heard the Witch's voice she unbound her tresses, opened the window, and then the hair fell down twenty ells, and the Witch mounted up by it.

After a couple of years had passed away it happended that the King's son was riding through the wood, and came by the tower. There he heard a song so beautiful that he stood still and listened. It was Rapunzel, who, to pass the time of her loneliness away, was exercising her sweet voice. The King's son wished to ascend to her, and looked for a door in the tower, but he could not find one. So he rode home, but the song had touched his heart so much that he went every day to the forest and listened to it; and as he thus stood one day behind a tree, he saw the Witch come up and hear her call out,—

> "Rapunzel! Rapunzel!
> Let down your hair."

Then Rapunzel let down her tresses, and the Witch mounted up. "Is that the ladder on which one must climb? Then I will try my luck too," said the Prince; and the following day, as he felt quite lonely, he went to the tower, and said,—

> "Rapunzel! Rapunzel!
> Let down your hair."

Then the tresses fell down, and he climbed up. Rapunzel was much frightened at first when a man came in, for she had never seen one before; but the King's son talked in a loving way to her, and told how his heart had been so moved by her singing that he had no peace until he had seen her himself. So Rapunzel lost her terror, and when he asked her if she would have him for a husband, and she saw that he was young and handsome, she thought, "Any one may have me rather than the old woman:" so, saying "Yes," she put her hand within his: "I will willingly go with you, but I know not how I am to descend. When you come, bring with you a skein of silk each time, out of which I will weave a ladder, and when it is ready I will come down by it, and you must take me upon your horse." Then they agreed that they should never meet till the evening, as the Witch came in the day time. The old woman remarked nothing about it, until one day Rapunzel innocently said, "Tell me, mother, how it happens you find it more difficult to come up to me than the young King's son, who is with me in a moment!"

"Oh, you wicked child!" exclaimed the Witch; "what do I hear? I thought I had separated you from all the world, and yet you have deceived me." And, seizing Rapunzel's beautiful hair in a fury, she gave her a couple of blows with her left hand, and, taking a pair of scissors in her right, snip, snap, she cut off all her beautiful tresses, and they fell upon the ground. Then she was so hard-hearted that she took the poor maiden into a great desert, and left her to die in great misery and grief.

But the same day when the old Witch had carried Rapunzel off, in the evening she made the tresses fast above to the window-latch, and when the King's son came, and called out,—

"Rapunzel! Rapunzel!
Let down your hair."

she let them down. The Prince mounted; but when he got to the top he found, not his dear Rapunzel, but the Witch, who looked at him with furious and wicked eyes. "Aha!" she exclaimed, scornfully, "you would fetch your dear wife; but the beautiful bird sits no longer in her nest, singing; the cat has taken her away, and will now scratch out your eyes. To you Rapunzel is lost; you will never see her again."

The Prince lost his senses with grief at these words, and sprang out of the window of the tower in his bewilderment. His life he escaped with, but the thorns into which he fell put out his eyes. So he wandered blind, in the forest, eating nothing but roots and berries, and doing nothing but weep and lament for the loss of his dear wife. He wandered about thus, in great misery, for some few years, and at last arrived at the desert where Rapunzel, with her twins, a boy and a girl which had been born, lived in great sorrow. Hearing a voice which he thought he knew he followed in its direction; and, as he approached, Rapunzel recognised him, and fell upon his neck and wept. Two of her tears moistened his eyes, and they became clear again, so that he could see as well as formerly.

Then he led her away to his kingdom, where he was received with great demonstrations of joy, and where they lived long, contented and happy.

What became of the old Witch no one ever knew.

The White Snake

A LONG while ago there lived a King whose wisdom was world-renowned. Nothing remained unknown to him, and it seemed as if the tidings of the most hidden things were borne to him through the air. But he had one strange custom: every noontime, when the table was quite cleared, and no one was present, his trusty servant had to bring him a dish, which was covered up, and the servant himself did not know what lay in it, and no man knew, for the King never uncovered it nor ate thereof until he was quite alone. This went on for a long time, until one day such a violent curiosity seized the servant, who as usual carried the dish, that he could not resist the temptation, and took the dish into his chamber. As soon as he had carefully locked the door, he raised the cover, and there lay before him a White Snake. At the sight he could not restrain the desire to taste it, so he cut a piece off and put it in his mouth. But scarcely had his tongue touched it, when he heard before his window a curious whispering of low voices. He went and listened, and found out that it was the Sparrows who were conversing with one another, and relating what each had seen in field or wood. The morsel of the Snake had given him the power to understand the speech of animals. Now it happened just on this day that the Queen lost her finest ring, and suspicion fell on this faithful servant, who had the care of all her jewels, that he had stolen it. The King ordered him to appear before him, and threatened in angry words that he should be taken up and tried if he did not know before the morrow whom to name as the guilty person. He protested his innocence in vain, and was sent away without any mitigation of the sentence. In his anxiety and trouble he went away into the courtyard, thinking how he might help himself. There, on a running stream of water, the Ducks were congregated familiarly together, and smoothing themselves down with their beaks while they held a confidential conversation. The servant stood still and listened to them as they narrated to each other whereabouts they had waddled, and what nice food they had found; and one said in a vexed tone, "Something very hard is in my stomach, for in my haste I swallowed a ring which lay under the Queen's window." Then the servant caught the speaker up by her neck, and carried her to the cook, saying, "Just kill this fowl, it is finely fat." "Yes," said the cook, weighing it in her hand, "it has spared no trouble in cramming itself; it ought to have been roasted long ago." So saying, she chopped off its head, and, when she cut it open, in its stomach was found the Queen's ring. Now, the servant was able to prove easily his innocence to the Queen, and, as she wished to repair her injustic, she granted him her pardon, and promised him the greatest place of honour which he wished for at court. The servant refused everything, and only requested a horse and money, for he had a desire to see the world, and to travel about it for a while. As soon as his request was granted, he set off on his tour and came one day by a pond, in which he remarked three fishes which were caught in the reeds, and lay gasping for water. Although men say Fishes are dumb, yet he understood their complaint, that they must soon die so miserably. Having a compassionate heart, he dismounted and put the three prisoners again into the water. They splashed about for joy, and putting their heads above water said to him, "We shall be grateful, and repay you for saving us." He rode onwards, and, after a while, it happened that he heard, as it were, a voice in the sand at his feet. He listened, and perceived that an Ant King was complaining thus: "If these men could but keep away with their great fat beasts! Here comes an awkward horse treading my people under foot unmercifully." So he rode on to a side path, and the Ant King called to him, "We will be grateful and reward you." His way led him into a forest, and there he saw a male and female Crow, standing by their nest, and dragging their young out. "Off with you, you gallows birds!" they exclaimed, "we can feed you no longer, you are big enough now to help yourselves." The poor young ones lay on the ground fluttering and beating their wings, and crying, "We, helpless children, we must feed ourselves, we who cannot fly yet! what is left to us but to die here of hunger?" Then the Servant dismounted, and, killing his horse with his sword, left it for the young Crows to feed upon. They soon hopped upon it, and when they were satisfied they exclaimed, "We will be grateful, and reward you in time of need!"

He was obliged now to use his own legs, and after he had gone a long way he came to a large town, where in the streets there was a great crowd and shouting, and a man upon horseback riding along, who proclaimed, "The Princess seeks a husband; but he who would win her must perform a difficult task, and, if he should not luckily complete it, his life will be forfeited." Many had tried already, but in vain; their life had been forfeited. But the youth, when he had seen the Princess, was so blinded by her beauty, that he forgot all danger, and stepping before the King, offered himself as a suitor. Immediately he was conducted to the sea, and a golden ring thrown in before his eyes. Then the King bade him fetch this ring up again from the bottom of the sea, adding, "If you rise without the ring, you shall be thrown in again and again, until you perish in the waves." Everyone pitied the handsome Youth, and then left him alone on the seashore. There he stood considering what he should do, and presently he saw three Fishes at once swimming towards him, and they were no others than the three whose lives he had saved. The middle one bore a mussel-shell in its mouth, which it laid on the shore at the feet of the Youth, who, taking it up and opening it, found the gold ring within. Full of joy, he brought it to the King, expecting that he should receive his promised reward. But the proud Princess, when she saw that he was not her equal in birth, was ashamed of him, and desired that he should undertake a second task. She went into the garden, and stewed there ten bags of millet-seed in the grass, "These he must pick up by the morning, before the sun rise, and let him not venture to miss one grain." The Youth sat himself down in the garden, thinking how it was possible to perform this task, but he could imagine no way, so he sat there sorrowfully awaiting at the dawn of day to be conducted to death. But, as soon as the first rays of the sun fell on the garden, he saw that the ten sacks were all filled, and standing by him, while not a single grain remained in the grass. The Ant King had come in the night with his thousands and thousands of men and the grateful insects had collected the millet with great industry, and put it into the sacks. The Princess herself came into the garden, and saw with wonder that the Youth had performed what was required of him. But still she could not bend her proud heart, and she said, "Although he may have done these two tasks, yet he shall not be my husband until he has brought me an apple from the tree of life." The Youth did not know where the tree of life stood; he got up, indeed, and was willing to go so long as his legs bore him, but he had no hope of finding it. After he had wandered through three kingdoms, he came by evening into a forest, and sitting down under a tree, he wished to sleep; when he heard a rustling in the branches, and a golden apple fell into his hand. At the same time three Ravens flew down, and settled on his knee saying, "We are the three young ravens whom you saved from dying of hunger; when we were grown up, and heard that you sought the golden apple, then we flew over the sea, even to the end of the world where stands the tree of life, and we have fetched you the apple."

Full of joy, the Youth set out homewards, and presented the golden apple to the beautiful Princess, who now had no more excuses. So they divided the apple of life, and ate it between them; then her heart was filled with love towards him, and they lived to a great age in undisturbed tranquillity.

The Fisherman and his Wife

THERE was once upon a time a fisherman and his wife, who lived together in a little hut near the sea, and every day he went down to fish. There he sat with his rod, and looked out upon the blank water; and this he did for many a long day. One morning the line went to the bottom, and when he drew it up a great Flounder was hooked at the end. The Flounder said, "Let me go, I pray you, fisherman; I am not a real fish, but an enchanted Prince. What good shall I do you if you pull me up? I should not taste well; put me back into the water, and let me swim."

"Ah," said the man, "you need not make such a palaver, a fish which can speak I would rather let swim;" and so saying, he put the fish into the water, and as it sank to the bottom it left a long streak of blood behind it. Then the fisherman got up, and went back to his wife in their hut.

"Have you caught nothing to-day, husband?" said she. "Oh!" he replied, "I caught a Flounder, who said he was an enchanted Prince; so I threw him again into the sea to swim."

"Did you not wish first?" she inquired. "No," said he.

"Ah," said the wife, "that is very unlucky; is one to remain in this hovel for ever? you might have wished for a better hut, at least. Go again and call him; tell him we choose to have a better hut, and for certain you'll get it."

"Ah!" replied he, "how shall I manage that?" "Why," said his wife, "you must catch him again, and before you let him swim away he will grant what you ask: be quick." The man was not much pleased, and wished his wife further; but, nevertheless, he went down to the sea. When he came to the water, it was green and yellow, and looked still more blank; he stood by it and said,—

> "Flounder, Flounder, in the sea,
> Hither quickly come to me;
> For my wife, dame Isabel,
> Wishes what I dare not tell."

Then the Fish came swimming up, and said, "What do you want with me?" "Oh!" said the man, "I was to catch you again; for my wife says I ought to have wished before. She won't stay any longer in her hovel, and desires a cottage."

"Go home again," said the Flounder, "she has it already." So the fisherman departed, and there was his wife, no longer in the dirty hovel, for in its place stood a clean cottage, before whose door she sat upon a bench. She took him by the hand, saying, "Come in now and see: is not this much better?" So in they went, and in the cottage there was a beautiful parlour, and a fine fireplace, and a chamber where a bed stood; there were also a kitchen and a store-room, with nice earthenware, all of the best; tinware and copper vessels, and everything very clean and neat. At the back was a large yard, with hens and chickens, as well as a nice garden, full of fruit-trees and vegetables. "See," said the wife, "is not this charming?"

"Yes," said her husband, "so long as it blooms you will be very well content with it."

"We will consider about that," she replied, and they went to bed.

Thus eight to fourteen days passed on, when the wife said, "Husband, the hut is far too narrow for me, and the yard and garden are so small; the Flounder may very well give us a larger house. I wish to live in a large stone palace; go, then, to the Flounder, and ask him to give us a castle."

"Ah, wife!" said he, "the cottage is good enough; why should you choose to have a castle?"

"Go along," she replied, "the Flounder will soon give you that."

"Nay, wife," he said, "the Flounder gave us the cottage at first, but when I go again he will perhaps be angry."

"Never you mind," said she, "he can do what I wish for very easily and willingly; go and try." The husband was vexed at heart, and did not like going, and said to himself, "This is not right." But at last he set off.

When he came to the sea, the water was quite clouded and deep blue coloured, and black and thick: it looked green no longer, yet it was calm. So he went and said,—

> "Flounder, Flounder, in the sea,
> Hither quickly come to me,
> For my wife, dame Isabel,
> Wishes what I scarce dare tell."

"Now, then, what do you want?" said the Flounder. "Oh," said the man, half-frightened, "she wants to live in a great stone castle." "Go home, and see it at your door," replied the Fish.

The fisherman went away, and lo! where formerly his house stood, there was a great stone castle; and his wife called to him from the steps to come in, and, taking him by the hand, she said, "Now let us look about." So they walked about, and in the castle there was a great hall, with marble tables, and there were ever so many servants, who ushered them through folding-doors into rooms hung all round with tapestry, and filled with fine golden stools and chairs, with crystal looking-glasses on the walls; and all the rooms were similarly fitted up. Outside the house were large courtyards with horse and cow-stalls, and waggons, all of the best, and besides a beautiful garden filled with magnificent flowers and fruit-trees, and a meadow full a mile long, covered with deer, and oxen, and sheep, as many as one could wish for. "Is not this pretty?" said the wife. "Ah," said her husband, "so long as the humour lasts you will be content with this, and then you will want something else."

"We will think about that," said she, and with that they went to bed.

The next morning the wife woke up just as it was day, and looked out over the fine country which lay before her. Her husband did not get up, and there she stood with her arms akimbo, and called out, "Get up, and come and look here at the window; see, shall I not be Queen over all the land? Go, and say to the Flounder, we choose to be King and Queen." "Ah, wife," said he, "why should I wish to be King?" "No," she replied, "you do not wish, so I will be Queen. Go, tell the Flounder so."

"Oh, why do you wish this? I cannot say it."

"Why not? go off at once; I *must* be Queen." The husband set out quite stupified, but she would have her way, and when he came to the sea it was quite black-looking, and the water splashed up and smelled very disagreeably. But he stood still, and repeated,—

> "Flounder, Flounder, in the sea,
> Hither quickly come to me;
> For my wife, dame Isabel,
> Wishes what I scarce dare tell."

"What does she want now?" asked the Flounder. "Ah!" said he, "she would be Queen." "Go home, she is so already," replied the Fish. So he departed, and when he came near the palace he saw it had become much larger, with a great tower and gateway in front of it; and before the gate stood a herald, and there were many soldiers, with kettledrums and trumpets. When he came into the house he found everything made of the purest marble and gold; with magnificent curtains fringed with gold. Through the hall he went in at the doors where the great court apartment was, and there sat his wife upon a high throne of gold and diamonds; having a crown of gold upon her head, and a sceptre of precious stones in her hand; and upon each side stood six pages, in a row, each one a head taller than the other. Then he went up, and said, "Ah, wife, are you Queen now?" "Yes," said she, "now I am Queen!" There he stood looking for a long time. At last he said, "Ah, wife, how do you like being Queen? now we have nothing else to choose." "No, indeed!" she replied, "I am very dissatisfied; time and tide do not wait for me; I can bear it no longer. Go then to the Flounder: Queen I am; now I must be Pope." "Ah, wife! what would you? Pope thou canst not be, the Pope is the head of Christendom, the Flounder cannot make you that."

"I *will* be Pope," replied the wife, and he was obliged to go, and, when he came to the shore, the sea was running mountains high, and the sky was so black that he was quite terrified, and began to say in a great fright,—

> "Flounder, Flounder, in the sea,
> Quickly, quickly, come to me,
> For my wife, dame Isabel,
> Wishes what I dare not tell."

"What now?" asked the Flounder. "She wants to be Pope," said he. "Go home, and find her so," was the reply.

So he went back, and found a great church, in which she was sitting upon a much higher throne, with two rows of candles on each side, some as thick as towers, down to those no bigger than rushlights, and before her footstool were Kings and Queens kneeling. "Wife," said he, "now be contented: since you are Pope, you cannot be anything else." "That I will consider about," she replied, and so they went to bed; but she could not sleep for thinking that she should be next. Very early she rose, and looked out of the window, and as she saw the sun rising, she thought to herself, "Why should I not do that?" and so she shook her husband, and called out to him, "Go, tell the Flounder I want to make the sun rise." Her husband was so frightened that he tumbled out of bed, but she would hear nothing, and he was obliged to go.

When he got down to the sea a tremendous storm was raging, and the ships and boats were tossing about in all directions. Then he shouted out, though he could not hear his own words,—

> "Flounder, Flounder, in the sea,
> Quickly, quickly, come to me;
> For my wife, dame Isabel,
> Wishes what I dare not tell."

"What would she have now?" said the Fish. "Ah!" he replied, "she wants to be Ruler of the Universe."

"Return, and find her back in her hovel," replied the Flounder.

And there the fisherman and his wife remained for the rest of their days.

The Seven Crows

THERE was a man who had seven sons, but never a daughter, although he wished very much for one; at last his wife promised him another child, and when it was born, lo! it was a daughter. Their happiness was great, but the child was so weak and small that, on account of its delicate health, it had to be baptized immediately. The father sent one of his sons hastily to a spring in order to fetch some water, but the other six would run as well; and as each strove to be first to fill the pitcher, between them all it fell into the water. They stood by, not knowing what to do, and none of them dared to go home. As they did not come back, the father became impatient, saying, "They have forgotten all about it in a game of play, the godless youths." Soon he became anxious lest the child should die unbaptized, and in his haste he exclaimed, "I would they were all changed into Crows!" Scarcely were the words out of his mouth, when he heard a whirring over his head, and looking up he saw seven coal-black Crows flying over the house.

The parents could not recall their curse, and grieved very much for their lost sons; but they comforted themselves in some measure with their dear daughter, who soon grew strong, and became more and more beautiful every day. For a long time she did not know she had any brothers, for her parents were careful not to mention them; but one day accidentally she overheard some people talking about her, and saying, "She is certainly very beautiful; but still the guilt of her seven brothers rests on her head." This made her very sad, and she went to her parents and asked whether she had any brothers, and whither they were gone. The old people durst no longer keep their secret, but said it was the decree of heaven, and her birth had been the unhappy cause. Now the maiden daily accused herself, and thought how she could again deliver her brothers. She had neither rest nor quiet, until she at last set out secretly, and journeyed into the wide world to seek out her brothers, and to free them, wherever they were, cost what it might. She took nothing with her but a ring of her parents' for a remembrance, a loaf of bread for hunger's sake, a bottle of water for thirst's sake, and a little stool for weariness.

Now on and on went the maiden, further and further, even to the world's end. Then she came to the Sun, but he was too hot and fearful, and burnt up little children. So she ran hastily away to the Moon, but she was too cold, and even wicked-looking, and said, "I smell, I smell man's flesh!" So she ran away quickly, and went to the Stars, who were friendly and kind to her, each one sitting upon his own little seat. But the Morning-star was standing up, and gave her a crooked bone, saying, "If you have not this bone you cannot unlock the glass castle, where your brothers are."

The maiden took the bone, and wrapped it well up in a handkerchief, and then on she went again till she came at last to the glass castle. The door was closed, and she looked therefore for the little bone; but when she unwrapped her handkerchief it was empty – she had lost the present of the good Star. What was she to do now?

She wished to save her brothers, and she had no key to the glass castle. The good little sister bent her little finger, and put it in the door, and luckily it unlocked it. As soon as she entered a little Dwarf came towards her, who said, "My child, what do you seek?"

"I seek my brothers, the seven Crows," she replied.

The Dwarf answered, "My Lord Crows are not at home; but if you wish to wait their return, come in and sit down."

Thereupon the little Dwarf carried in the food of the seven Crows upon seven dishes and in seven cups, and the maiden ate a little piece off each dish, and drank a little out of every cup; but in the last cup she dropped the ring which she had brought with her.

All at once she heard a whirring and cawing in the air, and the Dwarf said, "My Lord Crows are now flying home."

Presently they came in and prepared to eat and drink; each seeking his own dish and cup. Then one said to the other, "Who has been eating off my dish? Who has been drinking out of my cup? There has been a human mouth here!"

When the seventh came to the bottom of his cup, the little ring rolled out. He looked at it, and recognised it as a ring of his parents and said, "God grant that our sister be here; then are we saved?"

As the maiden, who had stood behind the door watching, heard these words, she came forward, and immediately all the Crows received again their human forms, and embraced and kissed their sister, and then they all went joyfully home together.

The Valiant Little Tailor

ONE summer's morning a Tailor was sitting on his bench by the
window in very good spirits, sewing away with all his might, and
presently up the street came a peasant woman, crying, "Good
preserves for sale! Good preserves for sale!" This cry sounded nice in
the Tailor's ears, and, sticking his diminutive head out of the
window, he called out, "Here, my good woman, just bring your
wares here!" The woman mounted the three steps up to the Tailor's
house with her heavy basket, and began to unpack all the pots
together before him. He looked at them all, held them up to the light,
put his nose to them, and at last said, "These preserves appear to me
to be very nice, so you may weigh me out four half-ounces, my good
woman; I don't mind even if you make it a quarter of a pound." The
woman, who expected to have met with a good customer, gave him
what he wished, and went away grumbling, very much dissatisfied.

"Now!" exclaimed the Tailor, "Heaven will send me a blessing on this preserve, and give me fresh strength and vigour;" and, taking the bread out of the cupboard, he cut himself a slice the size of the whole loaf, and spread the preserve upon it. "That will taste by no means badly," said he; "but, before I have a bite, I will just get this waistcoat finished." So he laid the bread down near him and stitched away, making larger and larger stitches every time for joy. Meanwhile the smell of the preserve mounted to the ceiling, where flies were sitting in great numbers, and enticed them down, so that soon a regular swarm of them had settled on the bread. "Holloa! who invited you?" exclaimed the Tailor, hunting away the unbidden guests; but the flies, not understanding his language, would not be driven off, and came again in greater numbers than before. This put the little man in a boiling passion, and, snatching up in his rage a bag of cloth, he brought it down with an unmerciful swoop upon them. When he raised it again he counted no less than seven lying dead before him with outstretched legs. "What a fellow you are!" said he to himself, wondering at his own bravery. "The whole town shall know of this." In great haste he cut himself out a band, hemmed it, and then put on it in large characters, "SEVEN AT ONE BLOW!" "Ah," said he, "not one city alone, the whole world shall know it!" and his heart fluttered with joy, like a lambkin's tail.

The little Tailor bound the belt round his body, and prepared to travel forth into the wide world, thinking the workshop too small for his valiant deeds. Before he set out, however, he looked round his house to see if there was anything he could take with him; but he found only an old cheese, which he pocketed, and remarking a bird before the door which was entangled in the bushes, he caught it, and put that in his pocket also. Directly after he set out bravely on his travels; and, as he was light and active, he felt no weariness. His road led him up a hill, and when he reached the highest point of it he found a great Giant sitting there, who was looking about him very composedly.

The little Tailor, however, went boldly up, and said, "Good day, comrade; in faith you sit there and see the whole world stretched

below you. I am also on my road thither to try my luck. Have you a
mind to go with me?"

The Giant looked contemptuously at the little Tailor, and said,
"You vagabond! you miserable fellow!"

"That may be," replied the Tailor; "but here you may read what
sort of a man I am;" and, unbuttoning his coat, he showed the Giant
his belt. The Giant read, "Seven at one blow;" and thinking they
were men whom the Tailor had slain, he conceived a little respect for
him. Still he wished to prove him first; so taking up a stone, he
squeezed it in his hand, so that water dropped out of it. "Do that
after me," said he to the other, "if you have any strength."

"If it be nothing worse than that," said the Tailor, "that's play to
me." And, diving into his pocket, he brought out the cheese, and
squeezed it till the whey ran out of it, and said, "Now, I think, that's
a little better."

The Giant did not know what to say, and could not believe it of
the little man; so taking up another stone, he threw it so high that
one could scarcely see it with the eye, saying, "There, you mannikin,
do that after me."

"Well done," said the Tailor; "but your stone must fall down
again to the ground. I will throw one up which shall not come back:"
and, dipping into his pocket, he took out the bird and threw it into
the air. The bird, rejoicing in its freedom, flew straight up, and then
far away, and did not return. "How does that little affair please you,
comrade?" asked the Tailor.

"You can throw well, certainly," replied the Giant; "now let us see
if you are in trim to carry something out of the common." So saying
he led him to a huge oak-tree, which lay upon the ground, and said,
"If you are strong enough, just help me to carry this tree out of the
forest."

"With all my heart," replied the Tailor; "do you take the trunk
upon your shoulder, and I will raise the boughs and branches, which
are the heaviest, and carry them."

The Giant took the trunk upon his shoulder, but the Tailor placed
himself on the branch, so that the Giant, who was not able to look

round, was forced to carry the whole tree and the Tailor besides. He, being behind, was very merry, and chuckled at the trick, and presently began to whistle the song, "There rode three tailors out at the gate," as if the carrying of trees were child's play. The Giant, after he had staggered along a short distance with his heavy burden, could go no further, and shouted out, "Do you hear? I must let the tree fall." The Tailor, springing down, quickly embraced the tree with both arms, as if he had been carrying it, and said to the Giant, "Are you such a big fellow, and yet cannot you carry this tree by yourself?"

Then they journeyed on further, and as they came to a cherry-tree, the Giant seized the top of the tree where the ripest fruits hung, and, bending it down, gave it to the Tailor to hold, bidding him eat. But the Tailor was much too weak to hold the tree down, and when the Giant let go the tree flew up into the air, and the Tailor was carried with it. He came down on the other side, however, without injury, and the Giant said. "What does that mean? Have you not strength enough to hold that twig?" "My strength did not fail me," replied the Tailor; "do you suppose that that was any hard thing for one who has killed seven at one blow? I have sprung over the tree because the hunters were shooting below there in the thicket. Spring after me if you can." The Giant made the attempt, but could not clear the tree, and stuck fast in the branches; so that in this affair, too, the Tailor was the better man.

After this the Giant said, "Since you are such a valiant fellow, come with me to our house, and stop a night with us." The Tailor consented, and followed him; and when they entered the cave, there sat by the fire two other Giants, each having a roast sheep in his hand, of which he was eating. The Tailor sat down thinking, "Ah, this is much more like the world than is my workshop." And soon the Giant showed him a bed where he might lie down and go to sleep. The bed, however, was too big for him, so he slipt out of it, and crept into a corner. When midnight came, and the Giant thought the Tailor would be in a deep sleep, he got up, and, taking a great iron bar, beat the bed right through at one stroke, and supposed he had thereby given the Tailor his death-blow. At the earliest dawn of morning the Giants went forth into the forest, quite forgetting the Tailor, when presently up he came, quite merry, and showed himself before them. The Giants were terrified, and fearing he would kill them all, they ran away in great haste.

The Tailor journeyed on, always following his nose, and after he had wandered some long distance, he came into the courtyard of a royal palace; and as he felt rather tired he laid himself down on the grass and went to sleep. Whilst he lay there the people came and viewed him on all sides, and read upon his belt, "Seven at one blow." "Ah," said they, "what does this great warrior here in time of peace? This must be some mighty hero." So they went and told the King, thinking that, should war break out, here was an important and useful man, whom one ought not to part with at any price. The King took counsel, and sent one of his courtiers to the Tailor to ask for his fighting services, if he should be awake. The messenger stopped at the sleeper's side, and waited till he stretched out his limbs and opened his eyes, and then he laid before him his message. "Solely on that account did I come here," was the reply; "I am quite ready to enter into the King's service." Then he was conducted away with great honour, and a fine house was appointed him to dwell in.

The courtiers, however, became jealous of the Tailor, and wished he were a thousand miles away. "What will happen?" said they to one another. "If we go to battle with him, when he strikes out seven will fall at one blow, and nothing will be left for us to do." In their rage they came to the resolution to resign, and they went all together to the King, and asked his permission, saying, "We are not prepared to keep company with a man who kills seven at one blow." The King was grieved to lose all his faithful servants for the sake of one, and wished that he had never seen the Tailor, and would willingly have now been rid of him. He dared not, however, dismiss him, because he feared the Tailor would kill him and all his subjects, and place himself upon the throne. For a long time he deliberated, till at last he came to a decision; and, sending for the Tailor, he told him that, seeing he was so great a hero, he wished to ask a favour of him. "In a certain forest in my kingdom," said the King, "there live two Giants, who, by murder, rapine, fire, and robbery, have committed great havoc, and no one dares to approach them without perilling his own life. If you overcome and kill both these Giants, I will give you my only daughter in marriage, and the half of my kingdom for a dowry: a hundred knights shall accompany you, too, in order to render you assistance."

"Ah, that is something for such a man as I," thought the Tailor to himself; "a beautiful Princess and half a kingdom are not offered to one every day." "Oh, yes," he replied, "I will soon manage these two Giants, and a hundred horsemen are not necessary for that purpose; he who kills seven at one blow need not fear two."

Thus talking the little Tailor set out, followed by the hundred knights, to whom he said, as soon as they came to the borders of the forest, "Do you stay here; I would rather meet these Giants alone." Then he sprang off into the forest, peering about him right and left; and after a while he saw the two Giants lying asleep under a tree, snorning so loudly, that the branches above them shook violently. The Tailor, full of courage, filled both his pockets with stones and clambered up the tree. When he got to the middle of it he crept along a bough, so that he sat just above the sleepers, and then he let fall one stone after another upon the breast of one of them. For some time the Giant did not stir, until, at last awaking, he pushed his companion, and said, "Why are you beating me?"

"You are dreaming," he replied; "I never hit you." They laid themselves down again to sleep, and presently the Tailor threw a stone down upon the other. "What is that?" he exclaimed. "What are you knocking me for?"

"I did not touch you; you must dream," replied the first. So they wrangled for a few minutes; but, being both very tired with their day's work, they soon fell asleep again. Then the Tailor began his sport again, and, picking out the biggest stone, threw it with all his force upon the breast of the first Giant. "That is too bad!" he exclaimed; and, springing up like a madman, he fell upon his companion, who, feeling himself equally aggrieved, they set to in such good earnest, that they rooted up trees and beat one another about until they both fell dead upon the ground. Now the Tailor jumped down, saying, "What a piece of luck they did not uproot the tree on which I sat, or else I must have jumped on another like a squirrel, for I am not given to flying." Then he drew his sword, and, cutting a deep wound in the breast of each, he went to the horsemen and said, "The deed is done; I have given each his death-stroke; but it was a hard job, for in their necessity they uprooted trees to defend themselves with; still, all that is of no use when such a one as I come, who killed seven at one stroke."

"Are you not wounded, then?" asked they.

"That is not to be expected: they have not touched a hair of my head," replied the little man. The knights could scarcely believe him, till, riding away into the forest, they found the Giants lying in their blood and the uprooted trees around them.

Now the Tailor demanded his promised reward of the King; but he repented of his promise, and began to think of some new scheme to get rid of the hero. "Before you receive my daughter and the half of my kingdom," said he to him, "you must perform one other heroic deed. In the forest there runs wild a unicorn, which commits great havoc, and which you must first of all catch."

"I fear still less for a unicorn than I do for two Giants! Seven at one blow! that is my motto," said the Tailor. Then he took with him a rope and an axe and went away to the forest, bidding those who were ordered to accompany him to wait on the outskirts. He had not to search long, for presently the unicorn came near and prepared to rush at him as if it would pierce him on the spot. "Softly, softly!" he exclaimed; "that is not done so easily;" and, waiting till the animal was close upon him, he sprang nimbly behind a tree. The unicorn, rushing with all its force against the tree, fixed its horn so fast in the trunk, that it could not draw it out again, and so it was made prisoner. "Now I have got my bird," said the Tailor; and, coming from behind the tree, he first bound the rope around its neck, and then, cutting the horn out of the tree with his axe, he put all in order, and, leading the animal, brought it before the King.

The King, however, would not yet deliver up the promised reward, and made a third request, that, before the wedding, the Tailor should catch a wild boar which did much injury, and he should have the huntsmen to help him. "With pleasure," was the reply; "it is mere child's play." The huntsmen, however, he left behind, to their entire content, for this wild boar had already so often hunted them, that they had no pleasure in hunting it. As soon as the boar perceived the Tailor, it ran at him with gaping mouth and glistening teeth, and tried to throw him on the ground; but our flying hero sprang into a little chapel which was near, and out again at a window on the other side in a trice. The boar ran after him, but he, skipping round, shut the door behind it, and there the raging beast was caught, for it was much too unwieldy and heavy to jump out of the window. The Tailor now called the huntsmen up, that they might see his prisoner with their own eyes; but our hero presented himself before the King, who was compelled now, whether he would or no, to keep his promise, and surrender his daughter and the half of his kingdom.

Had he known that it was no warrior, but only a Tailor, who stood before him, it would have gone to his heart still more!

So the wedding was celebrated with great splendour, though with little rejoicing, and out of a Tailor was made a King.

Some little while afterwards the young Queen heard her husband talking in his sleep, and saying, "Boy, make me a waistcoat, and stitch up these trousers, or I will lay the yard-measure over your ears!" Then she remarked of what condition her lord was, and complained in the morning to her father, and begged he would deliver her from her husband, who was nothing else than a tailor. The King comforted her by saying, "This night leave your chamber door open; my servants shall stand without, and when he is asleep they shall enter, bind him, and bear him away to a ship, which shall carry him forth into the wide world." The wife was contented with his proposal; but the King's armour-bearer, who had overheard all, went to the young King and disclosed the whole plot. "I will shoot a bolt upon this affair," said the brave Tailor. In the evening at their usual time they went to bed, and when his wife believed he slept she got up, opened the door, and laid herself down again. The Tailor, however, only feigned to be asleep, and began to exclaim in a loud voice, "Boy, make me this waistcoat, and stitch up these trousers, or I will beat the yard-measure about your ears! Seven have I killed with one blow, two Giants have I slain, a unicorn have I led captive, and a wild boar have I caught, and shall I be afraid of those who stand without my chamber?" When the men heard these words spoken by the Tailor, a great fear overcame them, and they ran away as if the wild huntsmen were behind them; neither afterwards durst any man venture to oppose him. Thus became the Tailor a King, and so he remained the rest of his days.

The Straw, the Coal, and the Bean

IN a certain village there dwelt a poor old woman, who had gathered a dish of beans, which she wished to cook. So she made a fire upon the hearth, and, that it might burn the quicker, she lighted it with a handful of straw. And as she shook the beans up in the saucepan, one fell out unperceived, and came down upon the ground near a straw; soon after a glowing coal burst out of the fire, and fell just by these two. Then the Straw began to say, "My dear friend, whence do you come?" The Coal replied, "By good luck I have sprung out of the fire, and, if I had not jumped away by force, my death had been certain, and I should have been reduced to ashes." The Bean continued, "I also have got away with a whole skin, but, had the old woman put me in the pot with the others, I should have been boiled to pieces, as my comrades are." "Would a better fate have fallen to my share?" said the Straw; "for the old woman has suffocated in fire and smoke all my brothers; sixty has she put on at once, and deprived of life; happily, I slipped between her fingers."

"But what shall we do now?" asked the Coal.

"I think," answered the Bean, "since we have so luckily escaped death, we will join in partnership, and keep together like good companions: lest a new misfortune overtake us, let us wander forth, and travel into a strange country."

This proposition pleased the two others, and they set out together on their travels. Presently they came to a little stream, over which there was no bridge nor path, and they did not know how they should get over. The Straw gave good advice, and said, "I will lay myself across, so that you may cross over upon me, as upon a bridge." So the Straw stretched itself from one bank to the other, and the Coal, which was of a fiery nature, tripped lightly upon the newly-built bridge. But when it came to the middle of it, and heard the water running along beneath, it was frightened, and stood still, not daring to go further. The Straw, however, beginning to burn, broke in two and fell into the stream, and the Coal slipping after, hissed as it reached the water, and gave up the ghost. The Bean, which had prudently remained upon the shore, was forced to laugh at this accident, and, the joke being so good, it laughed so immoderately that it burst itself. Now they would all have been done for alike, if a tailor, who was out on his wanderings, had not just then, by great good luck, sat himself down near the stream. Having a commiserating heart, he took out needle and thread, and sewed the Bean together. The Bean thanked him exceedingly; but as the tailor used black thread it has happened since that time, every Bean has a black seam.

Little Red-Cap

ONCE upon a time there lived a sweet little girl, who was beloved by every one who saw her; but her grandmother was so excessively fond of her that she never knew when she had thought and done enough for her.

One day the grandmother presented the little girl with a red velvet cap; and as it fitted her very well, she would never wear anything else; and so she was called Little Red-Cap. One day her mother said to her, "Come, Red-Cap, here is a piece of nice meat, and a bottle of wine: take these to your grandmother; she is ill and weak, and will relish them. Make haste before she gets up; go quietly and carefully; and do not run, lest you should fall and break the bottle, and then your grandmother will get nothing. When you go into her room, do not forget to say 'Good-morning;' and do not look about in all the corners." "I will do everything as you wish," replied Red-Cap, taking her mother's hand.

The grandmother dwelt far away in the wood, half an hour's walk from the village, and as Little Red-Cap entered among the trees, she met a wolf; but she did not know what a malicious beast it was, and so she was not at all afraid. "Good day, Little Red-Cap," he said.

"Many thanks, Wolf," said she.

"Whither away so early, Little Red-Cap?"

"To my grandmother's," she replied.

"What are you carrying under your apron?"

"Meat and wine," she answered. "Yesterday we baked the meat, that grandmother, who is ill and weak, might have something nice and strengthening."

"Where does your grandmother live?" asked the Wolf.

"A good quarter of an hour's walk further in the forest. The cottage stands under three great oak-trees; near it are some nut bushes, by which you will easily know it."

But the Wolf thought to himself, "She is a nice tender thing, and will taste better than the old woman: I must act craftily, that I may snap them both up."

Presently he came up again to Little Red-Cap, and said, "Just look at the beautiful flowers which grow around you; why do you not look about you? I believe you don't hear how beautifully the birds sing. You walk on as if you were going to school; see how merry everything is around you in the forest."

So Little Red-Cap opened her eyes; and when she saw how the sunbeams glanced and danced through the trees, and what splendid flowers were blooming in her path, she thought, "If I take my grandmother a fresh nosegay she will be very pleased; and it is so very early that I can, even then, get there in good time;" and running into the forest she looked about for flowers. But when she had once begun she did not know how to leave off, and kept going deeper and deeper among the trees in search of some more beautiful flower. The

Wolf, however, ran straight to the house of the old grandmother, and knocked at the door.

"Who's there?" asked the old lady.

"Only Little Red-Cap, bringing you some meat and wine: please open the door," replied the Wolf.

"Lift up the latch," cried the grandmother; "I am too weak to get up."

So the Wolf lifted the latch, and the door flew open; and jumping without a word on the bed, he gobbled up the poor old lady. Then he put on her clothes, and tied her cap over his head; got into the bed, and drew the blankets over him. All this time Red-Cap was still gathering flowers; and when she had plucked as many as she could carry, she remembered her grandmother, and made haste to the cottage. She wondered very much to see the door wide open; and when she got into the room, she began to feel very ill, and exclaimed, "How sad I feel! I wish I had not come to-day." Then she said, "Good morning," but received no answer; so she went up to the bed, and drew back the curtains, and there lay her grandmother, as she thought, with the cap drawn half over her eyes, looking very fierce.

"Oh, grandmother, what great ears you have!"

"The better to hear with," was the reply.

"And what great eyes you have!"

"The better to see with."

"And what great hands you have!"

"The better to touch you with."

"But, grandmother, what great teeth you have!"

"The better to eat you with;" and scarcely were the words out of his mouth, when the Wolf made a spring out of bed, and swallowed up poor Little Red-Cap.

As soon as the Wolf had thus satisfied his appetite, he laid himself down again in the bed, and began to snore very loudly. A huntsman passing by overheard him, and thought, "How loudly the old woman snores! I must see if she wants anything."

So he stepped into the cottage; and when he came to the bed, he saw the Wolf lying in it. "What! do I find you here, you old sinner? I have long sought you," exclaimed he; and taking aim with his gun, he shot the old Wolf dead.

Some folks say that the last story is not the true one, but that one day, when Red-Cap was taking some baked meats to her grandmother's, a Wolf met her, and wanted to mislead her; but she went straight on, and told her grandmother that she had met a Wolf, who wished her good-day; but he looked so wickedly out of his great eyes, as if he would have eaten her had she not been on the highroad.

So the grandmother said, "Let us shut the door, that he may not enter."

Soon afterwards came the Wolf, who knocked, and exclaimed, "I am Red-Cap, grandmother; I bring you some roast meat." But they kept quite still, and did not open the door; so the Wolf, creeping several times round the house, at last jumped on the roof, intending to wait till Red-Cap went home in the evening, and then to sneak after her and devour her in the darkness. The old woman, however, saw all that the rascal intended; and as there stood before the door a great stone trough, she said to Little Red-Cap, "Take this pail, child: yesterday I boiled some sausages in this water, so pour it into that stone trough." Red-Cap poured many times, until the huge trough was quite full. Then the Wolf sniffed the smell of the sausages, and smacked his lips, and wished very much to taste; and at last he stretched his neck too far over, so that he lost his balance, and slipped quite off the roof, right into the great trough beneath, wherein he was drowned; and Little Red-Cap ran home in high glee, but no one sorrowed for Mr Wolf!

Old Mother Frost

THERE was once a widow who had two daughters, one of whom was beautiful and industrious, and the other ugly and lazy. She behaved most kindly, however, to the ugly one, because she was her own daughter; and made the other do all the hard work, and live like a kitchen maid. The poor maiden was forced out daily on the highroad, and had to sit by a well and spin so much that the blood ran from her fingers. Once it happened that her spindle became quite covered with blood, so, kneeling down by the well, she tried to wash it off, but, unhappily, it fell out of her hands into the water. She ran crying to her stepmother, and told her misfortune: but she scolded her terribly, and behaved very cruelly, and at last said, "Since you have let your spindle fall in, you must yourself fetch it out again!" Then the maiden went back to the well, not knowing what to do, and, in her distress of mind, she jumped into the well to fetch the spindle out. As she fell she lost all consciousness, and when she came to herself again she found herself in a beautiful meadow, where the sun was shining, and many thousands of flowers blooming around her. She got up and walked along till she came to a baker's, where the oven was full of bread, which cried out, "Draw me, draw me, or I shall be burnt. I have been baked long enough." So she went up, and, taking the bread-peel, drew out one loaf after the other. Then she walked on further, and came to an apple tree, whose fruit hung very thick, and which exclaimed, "Shake us, shake us; we apples are all ripe!" So she shook the tree till the apples fell down like rain, and, when none were left on, she gathered them all together in a heap, and went further. At last she came to a cottage, out of which an old woman was peeping, who had such very large teeth that the maiden was frightened and ran away. The old woman, however, called her back, saying, "What are you afraid of, my child? Stop with me; if you will put all things in order in my house, then shall all go well with you; only you must take care that you make my bed well, and shake it tremendously, so that the feathers fly; then it snows upon earth. I am 'Old Mother Frost.'" As the old woman spoke so kindly, the maiden took courage, and consented to engage in her service. Now, everything made her very contented, and she always shook the bed so industriously that the feathers blew down like flakes of snow; therefore her life was a happy one, and there were no evil words; and she had roast and baked meat every day.

For some time she remained with the old woman; but, all at once, she became very sad, and did not herself know what was the matter. At last she found she was home-sick; and, although she fared a thousand times better than when she was at home, still she longed to go. So she told her mistress, "I wish to go home, and if it does not go so well with me below as up here, I must return." The mistress replied, "It appeared to me that you wanted to go home, and, since you have served me so truly, I will fetch you up again myself." So saying, she took her by the hand and led her before a great door, which she undid; and, when the maiden was just beneath it, a great shower of gold fell, and a great deal stuck to her, so that she was covered over and over with gold. "That you must have for your industry," said the old woman, giving her the spindle which had fallen into the well. Thereupon the door was closed, and the maiden found herself upon the earth, not far from her mother's house; and, as she came into the court, the cock sat upon the house, and called,—

"Cock-a-doodle-doo!
Our golden maid's come home again."

Then she went in to her mother, and, because she was so covered with gold, she was well received.

The maiden related all that had happened; and, when the mother heard how she had come by these great riches, she wished her ugly, lazy daughter to try her luck. So she was forced to sit down by the well and spin; and, in order that her spindle might become bloody, she pricked her finger by running a thorn into it; and then, throwing the spindle into the well, she jumped in after it. Then, like the other, she came upon the beautiful meadow, and travelled on the same path. When she arrived at the baker's, the bread called out, "Draw me out, draw me out or I shall be burnt. I have been baked long enough." But she answered, "I have no wish to make myself dirty about you," and so went on. Soon she came to the apple tree, which called out, "Shake me, shake me; my apples are all quite ripe." But she answered, "You do well to come to me; perhaps one will fall on my head;" and so she went on further. When she came to "Old Mother Frost's" house she was not afraid of the teeth, for she had been warned; and so she engaged herself to her. The first day she set to work in earnest, was very industrious, and obeyed her mistress in all she said to her, for she thought about the gold which she would present to her. On the second day however, she began to idle; on the third, still more so; and then she would not get up of a morning. She did not make the beds, either, as she ought, and the feathers did not fly. So the old woman got tired, and dismissed her from her service, which pleased the lazy one very well, for she thought, "Now the gold-shower will come." Her mistress led her to the door; but, when she was beneath it, instead of gold, a tubful of pitch was poured down upon her. "That is the reward of your service," said "Old Mother Frost," and shut the door to. Then came Lazy-bones home, but she was quite covered with pitch; and the cock upon the house when he saw her, cried—

"Cock-a-doodle doo!
Our dirty maid's come home again."

But the pitch stuck to her, and, as long as she lived, would never come off again.

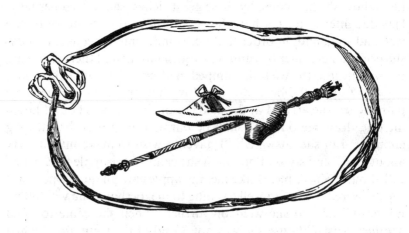

Cinderella

ONCE upon a time the wife of a certain rich man fell very ill, and as she felt her end drawing nigh she called her only daughter to her bedside, and said, "My dear child, be pious and good, and then the good God will always protect you, and I will look down upon you from heaven and think of you." Soon afterwards she closed her eyes and died. Every day the maiden went to her mother's grave and wept over it, and she continued to be good and pious; but when the winter came, the snow made a white covering over the grave, and in the spring-time, when the sun had withdrawn this covering, the father took to himself another wife.

The wife brought home with her two daughters, who were beautiful and fair in the face, but treacherous and wicked at heart. Then an unfortunate era began in the poor step-child's life. "Shall the stupid goose sit in the parlour with us?" said the two daughters. "They who would eat bread must earn it; out with the kitchen-maid!" So they took off her fine clothes, and put upon her an old grey cloak, and gave her wooden shoes for her feet. "See how the once proud princess is decked out now," said they, and they led her mockingly into the kitchen. Then she was obliged to work hard from morning to night, and to go out early to fetch water, to make the fire, and cook and scour. The sisters treated her besides with every possible insult, derided her, and shook the peas and beans into the ashes, so that she had to pick them out again. At night, when she was tired, she had no bed to lie on, but was forced to sit in the ashes on the hearth; and because she looked dirty through this, they named her CINDERELLA.

One day it happened that the father wanted to go to the fair, so he asked his two daughters what he should bring them. "Some beautiful dresses," said one; "Pearls and precious stones," replied the other, "But you, Cinderella," said he, "what will you have?" "The first bough, father, that knocks against your hat on your way homewards, break it off for me," she replied. So he bought the fine dresses, and the pearls and precious stones, for his two step-daughters; and on his return, as he rode through a green thicket, a hazel-bough touched his hat, which he broke off and took with him. As soon as he got home, he gave his step-daughters what they had wished for; and to Cinderella he gave the hazel-branch. She thanked him very much, and going to her mother's grave she planted the branch on it, and wept so long that her tears fell and watered it, so that it grew and became a beautiful tree. Thrice a day Cinderella went beneath it to weep and pray; and each time a little white Bird flew on the tree, and if she wished aloud, then the little Bird threw down to her whatever she wished for.

After a time it fell out that the King appointed a festival, which was to last three days, and to which all the beautiful maidens in the country were invited, from whom his son was to choose a bride. When the two step-daughters heard that they might also appear, they were very glad, and calling Cinderella, they said, "Comb our hair, brush our shoes, and fasten our buckles, for we are going to the festival at the King's palace." Cinderella obeyed, crying, because she wished to go with them to the dance; so she asked her stepmother whether she would allow her.

"You, Cinderella!" said she; "you are covered with dust and dirt – will you go to the festival? You have no clothes or shoes, and how can you dance?" But, as she urged her request, the mother said at last, "I have now shaken into the ashes a tubful of beans; if you have picked them up again in two hours, you shall go."

Then the maiden left the room, and went out at the back-door into the garden, and called out, "You tame pigeons, and doves, and all you birds of heaven, come and help me to gather the good beans into the tub, and the bad ones you may eat." Presently, in at the kitchen-window came two white pigeons, and after them the doves, and soon all the birds under heaven flew chirping in down upon the ashes. They then began, pick, pick, pick, and gathered all the good seeds into the tub; and scarcely an hour had passed when all was completed, and the birds flew away again. Then the maiden took the tub to the stepmother, rejoicing at the thought that she might now go to the festival; but the stepmother said, "No Cinderella, you have no clothes, and cannot dance; you will only be laughed at." As she began to cry, the stepmother said, "If you can pick up quite clean two tubs of beans which I throw amongst the ashes in one hour, you shall accompany them;" and she thought to herself, "She will never manage it." As soon as the two tubs had been shot into the ashes, Cinderella went out at the back door into the garden, and called out as before, "You tame pigeons, and doves, and all you birds under heaven, come and help me to gather the good ones into the tubs, and the bad ones you may eat." Presently, in at the kitchen-window came two white pigeons, and soon after them the doves, and soon all the birds under heaven flew chirping in down upon the ashes. They then began, pick, pick, pick, and gathered all the seeds into the tub; and scarcely had half-an-hour passed before all was picked up, and off they flew again. The maiden now took the tubs to the stepmother, rejoicing at the thought that she could go to the festival. But the mother said, "It does not help you a bit; you cannot go with us, for you have no clothes, and cannot dance; we should be ashamed of you." Thereupon she turned her back upon the maiden, and hastened away with her two proud daughters.

As there was no one at home, Cinderella went to her mother's grave, under the hazel-tree, and said,—

"Rustle and shake yourself, dear tree,
  And silver and gold throw down to me."

Then the Bird threw down a dress of gold and silver, and silken slippers ornamented with silver. These Cinderella put on in great haste, and then she went to the ball. Her sisters and stepmother did not know her at all and took her for some foreign princess as she looked so beautiful in her golden dress; for of Cinderella they thought not but that she was sitting at home picking the beans out of the ashes. Presently the Prince came up to her, and, taking her by the hand, led her to the dance. He would not dance with any one else, and even would not let go her hand; so that when any one else asked her to dance, he said, "She is my partner." They danced till evening, when she wished to go home; but the Prince said, "I will go with you, and see you safe," for he wanted to see to whom the maiden belonged. She flew away from him, however, and sprang into the pigeon-house; so the Prince waited till the father came, whom he told that the strange maiden had run into the pigeon-house. Then the stepmother thought, "Could it be Cinderella?" And they brought an axe wherewith the Prince might cut open the door, but no one was found within. And when they came into the house, there lay Cinderella in her dirty clothes among the ashes, and an oil-lamp was burning in the chimney; for she had jumped quickly out on the other side of the pigeon-house, and had run to the hazel-tree, where she had taken off her fine clothes, and laid them on the grave, and the Bird had taken them again, and afterwards she had put on her little grey cloak, and seated herself among the ashes in the kitchen.

The next day, when the festival was renewed, and her stepmother and her sisters had set out again, Cinderella went to the hazel-tree and sang as before:—

> "Rustle and shake yourself, dear tree,
> And silver and gold throw down to me."

Then the Bird threw down a much more splendid dress than the former, and when the maiden appeared at the ball every one was astonished at her beauty. The Prince, however, who had waited till she came, took her hand, and would dance with no one else; and if others came and asked, he replied as before, "She is my partner." As soon as evening came she wished to depart, and the Prince followed her, wanting to see into whose house she went; but she sprang away from him, and ran into the garden behind the house. Therein stood a fine large tree, on which hung the most beautiful pears, and the boughs rustled as though a squirrel was among them; but the Prince could not see whence the noise proceeded. He waited, however, till the father came, and told him, "The strange maiden has escaped from me, and I think she has climbed up into this tree." The father thought to himself, "Can it be Cinderella?" and taking an axe he chopped down the tree, but there was no one on it. When they went into the kitchen, there lay Cinderella among the ashes, as before, for she had sprung down on the other side of the tree, and, having taken her beautiful clothes again to the Bird upon the hazel-tree, she had put on once more her old grey cloak.

The third day, when her stepmother and her sisters had set out, Cinderella went again to her mother's grave, and said,—

"Rustle and shake yourself, dear tree,
And silver and gold throw down to me."

Then the Bird threw down to her a dress which was more splendid and glittering than she had ever had before, and the slippers were of pure gold. When she arrived at the ball they knew not what to say for wonderment, and the Prince danced with her alone as at first, and replied to every one who asked her hand, "She is my partner." As soon as evening came she wished to go, and as the Prince followed her she ran away so quickly that he could not overtake her. But he had contrived a stratagem, and spread the whole way with pitch, so that it happened as the maiden ran that her left slipper came off. The Prince took it up, and saw it was small and graceful, and of pure gold; so the following morning he went with it to the father, and said, "My bride shall be no other than she whose foot this golden slipper fits." The two sisters were glad of this, for they had beautiful feet, and the elder went with it to her chamber to try it on, while her mother stood by. She could not, however, get her great toe into it, and the shoe was much too small; but the mother, reaching a knife, said, "Cut off your toe, for if you are queen, you need not go any longer on foot." The maiden cut it off, and squeezed her foot into the shoe, and, concealing the pain she felt, went down to the Prince. Then he placed her as his bride upon his horse, and rode off; and as they passed by the grave, there sat two little doves upon the hazel-tree, singing,—

"Backwards peep, backwards peep,
There's blood upon the shoe;
The shoe's too small, and she behind
Is not the bride for you."

Then the Prince looked behind, and saw the blood flowing; so he turned his horse back, and took the false bride home again, saying she was not the right one. Then the other sister must needs fit on the shoe, so she went to the chamber and got her toes nicely into the shoe, but the heel was too large. The mother, reaching a knife, said,

"Cut a piece off your heel, for when you become queen you need not go any longer on foot." She cut a piece off her heel, squeezed her foot into the shoe, and, concealing the pain she felt, went down to the Prince. Then he put her upon his horse as his bride, and rode off; and as they passed the hazel-tree, there sat two little doves, who sang,—

> "Backwards peep, backwards peep,
> There's blood upon the shoe;
> The shoe's too small, and she behind
> Is not the bride for you."

Then he looked behind, and saw the blood trickling from her shoe, and that the stocking was dyed quite red; so he turned his horse back, and took the false bride home again, saying, "Neither is this one the right maiden; have you no other daughter?" "No," replied the father, "except little Cinderella, daughter of my deceased wife, who cannot possibly be the bride." The Prince asked that she might be fetched; but the stepmother said, "Oh, no! she is much too dirty; I dare not let her be seen." But the Prince would have his way; so Cinderella was called, and she, first washing her hands and face, went in and curtseyed to the Prince, who gave her the golden shoe. Cinderella sat down on a stool, and taking off her heavy wooden shoes, put on the slipper, which fitted her to a shade; and as she stood up, the Prince looked in her face, and recognising the beautiful maiden with whom he had danced, exclaimed, "This is my true bride." The stepmother and the two sisters were amazed and white with rage, but the Prince took Cinderella upon his horse, and rode away; and as they came up to the hazel-tree the two little white doves sang,—

> "Backwards peep, backwards peep,
> There's no blood on the shoe;
> It fits so nice, and she behind
> Is the true bride for you."

And as they finished they flew down and lighted upon Cinderella's shoulders, and there they remained; and the wedding was celebrated with great festivities, and the two sisters were smitten with blindness as a punishment for their wickedness.

The Riddle

ONCE upon a time there was a King's son, who had a mind to see the world; so he set forth, and took no one with him but a faithful servant. One day he came into a great forest, and when evening drew on he could find no shelter, and did not know where to pass the night. Just then he perceived a maiden who was going towards a little cottage, and as he approached he saw that she was young and beautiful, so he asked her whether he and his servant could find a welcome in the cottage for the night. "Yes, certainly," replied the maiden in a sorrowful voice, "you can; but I advise you not to enter." "Why not?" asked the Prince. The maiden sighed, and answered, "My stepmother practises wicked arts; she acts not hospitably to strangers." He perceived now that he was come to a

Witch's cottage; but because it was very dark, and he could go no further, he went in, for he was not at all afraid. The old woman was sitting in an arm-chair by the fire, and looked at the strangers out of her red eyes. "Good evening," she muttered, appearing very friendly; "sit yourselves down and rest." Then she poked up the fire on which a little pot was boiling. The daughter warned them both to be cautious, and neither to eat nor drink anything, for the old woman brewed bad drinks; so they slept quietly till morning. As they made ready for their departure, and the Prince was already mounted on horseback, the old Witch said, "Wait a bit, I will bring you a parting draught." While she went for it the Prince rode away; but the servant, who had to buckle his saddle, was left alone when she came with the draught. "Take that to thy master," she said, but at the same moment the glass cracked, and the poison spirted on the horse, and so strong was it that the poor animal fell backwards dead. The servant ran after his master, and told him what had occurred; but as he would not leave the saddle behind, he went back to fetch it. As he came to the dead horse he saw a crow perched upon it feeding himself. "Who knows whether we shall meet with anything better to-day?" said the servant, and killing the crow he took it with him. The whole day long they journeyed on in the forest, but could not get out of it; and at the approach of night, finding an inn, they entered it. The servant gave the crow to the host, that he might cook it for their supper; but they had fallen into a den of thieves, and in the gloom of night twelve ruffians came, intending to rob and murder the strangers. Before they began, however, they sat down to table, and the host and the Witch joined them, and then they all partook of a dish of pottage, in which the flesh of the crow was boiled. Scarcely had they eaten two morsels apiece when they all fell down dead; for the poison which had killed the horse had impregnated the flesh of the crow. There was now no one left in the house but the daughter of the host, who seemed to be honest, and had had no share in the wicked deeds. She opened all the doors to the Prince, and showed him the heaped-up treasure; but the Prince said she might keep it all, for he would have none of it, and so rode on further with his servant.

After they had wandered a long way in the world, they came to a city where dwelt a beautiful but haughty Princess, who had declared that whoever propounded to her riddle which she could not solve should be her husband; but if she solved it he must have his head cut off. Three days was the time given to consider, but she was always so sharp that she discovered the proposed riddle before the appointed time. Nine suitors had been sacrificed in this way, when the Prince arrived, and being blinded with her great beauty, resolved to stake his life upon her. So he went before her and proposed his riddle; namely, "What is this? One killed no one, and yet killed twelve." She knew not what it was, and thought and thought, but she could not make it out; and, although she searched through all her riddle books she could find nothing to help her; in short, her wisdom was quite at fault. At last at her wits' ends how to help herself, she bade her maid slip into the sleeping-room of the Prince and there listen to his dreams, thinking perhaps he might talk in his sleep and unfold the riddle. The bold servant, however, had put himself instead of his master into the bed; and when the servant came into the room he tore off the cloak in which she had wrapped herself, and hunted her out with a rod. The second night the Princess sent her chambermaid to see if she could be more fortunate in listening; but the servant snatched her mantle away, and hunted her away with a rod. The third night the Prince himself thought he should be safe, and so he lay in his own bed; and the Princess herself came, having on a dark grey cloak, and sat herself down by him. When she thought he was asleep and dreaming she spoke to him, hoping he would answer, as many do; but he was awake, and heard and understood everything very well. First she asked, "One kills none; what is that?" He answered, "A crow which ate of a dead and poisoned horse, and died of it," Further she asked, "And yet killed twelve; what is that?" "Twelve robbers who partook of the crow, and died from eating it."

As soon as she knew the riddle she tried to slip away, but he held her mantle so fast that she left it behind. The following morning the Princess announced that she had discovered the riddle, and bade the twelve judges come and she would solve it before them. The Prince, however, requested a hearing for himself, and said, "She has stolen in upon me at night and asked me, or she would never have found it out." The judges said, "Bring us a witness." Then the servant brought up the three mantles; and when the judges saw the dark grey cloak which the Princess used to wear, they said, "Let the cloak be adorned with gold and silver, that it may be a wedding garment."

The Spider and the Flea

A Spider and a Flea dwelt together in one house, and brewed their beer in an egg-shell. One day, when the Spider was stirring it up, she fell in and scalded herself. Thereupon the Flea began to scream. And then the Door asked, "Why are you screaming, Flea?"

"Because little Spider has scalded herself in the beer-tub," replied she.

Thereupon the Door began to creak as if it were in pain; and a

Broom which stood in the corner, asked, "What are you creaking for, Door?"

"May I not creak?" it replied:

> "The little Spider's scalt herself,
> And the Flea weeps."

So the Broom began to sweep industriously, and presently a little Cart came by, and asked the reason. "May I not sweep?" replied the Broom—

> "The little Spider's scalt herself,
> And the Flea weeps;
> The little Door creaks with the pain."

Thereupon the little Cart said, "So will I run," and began to run very fast past a heap of Ashes, which cried out, "Why do you run, little Cart?"

"Because," replied the Cart,

> "The little Spider's scalt herself,
> And the Flea weeps;
> The little Door creaks with the pain,
> And the Broom sweeps."

"Then," said the Ashes, "I will burn furiously." Now, next the Ashes there grew a Tree, which asked, "Little heap, why do you burn?"

"Because," was the reply,

> "The little Spider's scalt herself,
> And the Flea weeps;
> The little Door creaks with the pain,
> . And the Broom sweeps;
> The little Cart runs on so fast."

Thereupon the Tree cried, "I will shake myself!" and went on shaking till all its leaves fell off.

A little girl passing by with a water-pitcher saw it shaking, and asked, "Why do you shake yourself, little Tree?"

"Why may I not?" said the Tree—

> "The little Spider's scalt herself,
>   And the Flea weeps;
> The little Door creaks with the pain,
>   And the Broom sweeps;
> The little Cart runs on so fast,
>   And the Ashes burn."

Then the Maiden said, "If so, I will break my pitcher;" and she threw it down and broke it.

At this the Streamlet, from which she drew the water, asked, "Why do you break your pitcher, my little Girl?"

"Why may I not?" she replied; for

> "The little Spider's scalt herself,
>   And the Flea weeps;
> The little Door creaks with the pain,
>   And the Broom sweeps;
> The little Cart runs on so fast,
>   And the Ashes burn;
> The little Tree shakes down its leaves –
>   Now it is my turn!"

"Ah, then," said the Streamlet, "now must I begin to flow." And it flowed and flowed along, in a great stream, which kept getting bigger and bigger, until at last it swallowed up the little Girl, the little Tree, the Ashes, the Cart, the Broom, the Door, the Flea, and, last of all, the Spider, all together.

The Little Mouse, the Little Bird, and the Sausage

ONCE upon a time a Mouse, a Bird, and a Sausage, went to housekeeping together, and agreed so well that they accumulated wealth fast. It was the duty of the Bird to fetch wood, of the Mouse to draw water and make the fire, and of the Sausage to cook.

They who are prosperous are for ever hankering after something new, and thus one day the Bird, meeting another bird on her way home, told him of her condition in a very boastful way. The other bird, however, blamed her for her great labours for the two who lived at ease at home; for when the Mouse had made the fire and drawn the water she could retire to her chamber, and rest till she was called to lay the table; while the Sausage remained by the fire, and saw that the food was well cooked, and when dinner-time approached dressed it with the gravy and vegetables, and made it ready with butter and salt. As soon, then, as the Bird returned and laid down her burden, they sat down to table, and after their meal was finished they slept till the next morning, and this life was a very happy one. The next day the Bird would not go for the wood, saying she had been slave long enough; for once they must change about and try another plan. And although the Mouse and the Sausage protested earnestly against it, the Bird was unconvinced; it must be tried. And so they tossed up, and it fell to the lot of the Sausage to fetch wood, while the Mouse had to cook, and the Bird to procure water.

What happened? The Sausage went forth into the forest, the Bird made the fire, the Mouse put on the pot, and waited alone until the Sausage should come home, bringing wood for the next day. But it remained away such a long time that they suspected some misfortune, and the Bird flew round a little way to see, and met near their house a Dog, which, having met the Sausage, had seized upon it and devoured it. The Bird complained bitterly against the Dog as a public robber, but it availed nothing; for the Dog declared he had found forged letters upon the Sausage, for which its life was forfeited.

The Bird, full of grief, took the wood upon her back, and flew home to relate what she had seen and heard. Both she and the Mouse were very sad, but agreed to do their best, and remain with one another. Now the Bird laid the table and the Mouse prepared their meal; and in order to make it quite fit she got into the pot to stir the vegetables up, and flavour them as the Sausage had been used to do; but alas! before she had scarcely got in, her skin and hair came off, and her life was sacrificed.

When the Bird came, and wished to sit down to dinner, no cook was to be found! so, throwing away in a pet the sticks she had gathered, she called and searched high and low; but no cook could she discover. From her carelessness the fire reached the wood, and a grand conflagration commenced; so that the poor Bird hastened to the brook for water but her pail falling in, she was carried with it, and not being able to extricate herself in time, she sank to the bottom.

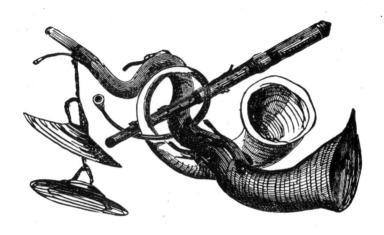

The Musicians of Bremen

A CERTAIN man had a Donkey, which had served him faithfully for many long years, but whose strength was so far gone that at last it was quite unfit for work. So his master was thinking how much he could make of the skin, but the Donkey perceiving that no good wind was blowing, ran away along the road to Bremen. "There," thought he, "I can be town musician." When he had run some way, he found a Hound lying by the road-side, yawning like one who was very tired. "What are you yawning for now, you big fellow?" asked the Ass.

"Ah," replied the Hound, "because every day I grow older and weaker; I cannot go any more to the hunt, and my master has wellnigh beaten me to death, so that I took to flight; and now I do not know how to earn my bread."

"Well! do you know," said the Ass, 'I am going to Bremen, to be town-musician there; suppose you go with me and take a share in the

music. I will play on the lute, and you shall beat the kettle-drums."
The Dog was satisfied, and off they set.

Presently they came to a Cat, sitting in the middle of the path, with
a face like three rainy days! "Now then, old shaver, what has crossed
you?" asked the Ass.

"How can one be merry when one's neck has been pinched like
mine?" answered the Cat. "Because I am growing old, and my teeth
are all worn to stumps, and because I would rather sit by the fire and
spin, than run after mice, my mistress wanted to drown me; and so I
ran away. But now good advice is dear, and I do not know what to
do."

"Go with us to Bremen. You understand nocturnal music, so you
can be town musician." The Cat consented, and went with them.
The three vagabonds soon came near a Farm-yard, where upon the
barn-door, the Cock was sitting crowing with all his might. "You
crow through marrow and bone," said the Ass, "what do you do
that for?"

"That is the way I prophesy fine weather," said the Cock; "but,
because grand guests are coming for the Sunday, the housewife has
no pity, and has told the cookmaid to make me into soup for the
morrow; and this evening my head will be cut off. Now I am crowing
with a full throat as long as I can."

"Ah, but you, Red-comb," replied the Ass, "rather come away
with us. We are going to Bremen, to find there something better than
death; you have a good voice, and if we make music together it will
have full play."

The Cock consented to this plan, and so all four travelled on
together. They could not, however, reach Bremen in one day, and at
evening they came into a forest, here they meant to pass the night.
The Ass and the Dog laid themselves down under a large tree, the
Cat and the Cock climbed up into the branches, but the latter flew
right to the top, where he was most safe. Before he went to sleep he
looked all round the four quarters, and soon thought he saw a little
spark in the distance; so, calling his companions, he said they were
not far from a house, for he saw a light. The Ass said, "If it is so, we

THE MUSICIANS OF BREMEN

had better get up and go further, for the pasturage here is very bad;" and the Dog continued, "Yes, indeed! a couple of bones with some meat on would also be very acceptable!" So they made haste towards the spot where the light was, and which shone now brighter and brighter, until they came to a well-lighted robber's cottage. The Ass, as the biggest, went to the window and peeped in. "What do you see, Gray-horse?" asked the Cock. "What do I see?" replied the Ass; "a table laid out with savoury meats and drinks, with robbers sitting around enjoying themselves."

"That were the right sort of thing for us," said the Cock.

"Yes, yes, I wish we were there," replied the Ass. Then these animals took counsel together how they should contrive to drive away the robbers, and at last they thought of a way. The Ass placed his fore feet upon the window ledge, the Hound got on his back, the Cat climbed up upon the Dog, and lastly the Cock flew up and perched upon the head of the Cat. When this was accomplished, at a given signal they commenced together to perform their music: the Ass brayed, the Dog barked, the Cat mewed, and the Cock crew; and they made such a tremendous noise, and so loud, that the panes of the window were shivered! Terrified at these unearthly sounds, the robbers got up with great precipitation, thinking nothing less than that some spirits had come, and fled off into the forest. The Four companions immediately sat down at the table, and quickly ate up all that was left, as if they had been fasting for six weeks.

As soon as the four players had finished, they extinguished the light, and each sought for himself a sleeping place, according to his nature and custom. The Ass laid himself down upon some straw, the Hound behind the door, the Cat upon the hearth, near the warm ashes, and the Cock flew up upon a beam which ran across the room. Weary with their long walk, they soon went to sleep.   .

At midnight, the robbers perceived from their retreat that no light was burning in their house, and all appeared quiet; so the captain said, "We need not to have been frightened into fits;" and, calling one of the band, he sent him forward to reconnoitre. The messenger, finding all still, went into the kitchen to strike a light, and, taking the glistening fiery eyes of the Cat for live coals, he held a lucifer-match to them, expecting it to take fire. But the Cat, not understanding the joke, flew in his face, spitting and scratching, which dreadfully frightened him, so that he made for the back door; but the Dog, who laid there, sprang up and bit his leg; and as he limped upon the straw where the Ass was stretched out, it gave him a powerful kick with its hind foot. This was not all, for the Cock, awaking at the noise, clapped his wings, and cried from the beam, "Cock-a-doodle-doo, cock-a-doodle-doo!"

Then the robber ran back as well as he could to his captain, and said, "Ah, my master, there dwells a horrible witch in the house, who spat on me and scratched my face with her long nails; and then before the door stands a man with a knife, who chopped at my leg; and in the yard there lies a black monster, who beat me with a great wooden club; and besides all, upon the roof sits a judge, who called out, 'Bring the knave up, do!' so I ran away as fast as I could."

After this the robbers dared not again go near their house; but everything prospered so well with the four town musicians of Bremen, that they did not forsake their situation! And there they are to this day, for anything I know.

The Giant with the Three Golden Hairs

THERE was once upon a time a poor woman whose son was born with a caul, and so it was foretold of him that in his fourteenth year he should marry the King's daughter. As it happened the King soon after came into the village, quite unknown to any one, and when he asked the people what news there was, they answered, "A few days since a child with a caul was born, which is a sure sign that he will be very lucky; and, indeed, it has been foretold of him that in his fourteenth year he will marry the King's daughter."

The King had a wicked heart, and was disturbed concerning this prophecy, so he went to the parents, and said to them in a most friendly manner, "Give me up your child and I will care of him." At first they refused, but the stranger begged for it with much gold, and so at last they consented and gave him the child, thinking, "It is a luck-child, and, therefore, everything must go on well with it."

The King laid the child in a box and rode away till he came to a deep water, into which he threw the box, saying to himself, "From this unsought-for bridegroom have I now freed my daughter."

The box, however, did not sink, but floated along like a boat, and not one drop of water penetrated it. It floated at last down to a mill two miles from the king's palace, and in the mill-dam it stuck fast. The miller's boy, who was fortunately standing there, observed it, and drew it ashore with a hook, expecting to find a great treasure. When, however, he opened the box, he saw a beautiful child alive and merry. He took it to the people at the mill, who, having no children, adopted it for their own saying, "God has sent it to us." They took good care of the child, and it grew up a steady, good lad.

It happened one day that the King went into the mill for shelter during a thunderstorm, and asked the people whether the boy was their child. "No," they answered; "he is a foundling, who, fourteen years ago, floated into our dam in a box, which the miller's boy drew out of the water." The King observed at once, that it was no other than the luck-child whom he had thrown into the water, and so said to them, "Good people, could not the youth carry a letter to my wife the Queen? If so I will give him two pieces of gold for a reward."

"As my lord the King commands," they replied, and bade the youth get ready.

Then the King wrote a letter to the Queen, wherein he said, "So soon as this boy arrives with this letter, let him be killed and buried, and let all be done before I return."

The youth set out on his journey with the letter, but he lost himself, and at evening came into a great forest. In the gloom he saw a little light, and going up to it he found a cottage, into which he went, and perceived an old woman sitting by the fire. As soon as she saw the lad she was terrified, and exclaimed, "Why do you come here; and what would you do?"

"I am come from the mill," he answered, "and am going to my lady the Queen to carry a letter; but because I have lost my way in this forest, I wish to pass the night here."

"Poor boy!" said the woman, "you have come to a den of robbers, who, when they return, will murder you."

"Let who will come," he replied, "I am not afraid; I am so weary that I can go no further;" and, stretching himself upon a bench, he went to sleep. Presently the robbers entered, and asked in a rage what strange lad was lying there. "Ah," said the old woman, "it is an innocent youth, who has lost himself in the forest, and whom I have taken in out of compassion. He carries with him a letter to the Queen."

The robbers seized the letter and read it, and understood that as soon as the youth arrived he was to be put to death. Then the robbers also took compassion on him, and the captain tore up the letter and wrote another, wherein he declared that the youth upon his arrival was to be married to the Princess. They let him sleep quietly on his bench till the morning, and as soon as he awoke they gave him the letter and showed him the right road.

When the Queen received the letter she did as it commanded, and caused a splendid marriage feast to be prepared, and the Princess was given in marriage to the luck-child, who, since he was both young and handsome, pleased her well, and they were all very happy. Some little time afterwards the King returned to his palace and found the prophecy fulfilled, and his daughter married to the luck-child. "How did this happen?" he asked. "In my letter I gave quite another command."

"Then the Queen handed him the letter, that he might read for himself what it stated. The king perceived directly that it had been forged by another person, and he asked the youth what he had done with the original letter that had been entrusted to him. "I know nothing about it," he replied; "it must have been changed in the forest where I passed the night."

Inflamed with rage the King answered, "Thou shalt not escape so easily; he who would have my daughter must fetch for me three golden hairs from the head of the Giant; bring thou to me what I desire, then shalt thou receive my daughter."

The King hoped by this means to get rid of him, but he answered, "The three Golden hairs I will fetch, for I fear not the Giant;" and so he took leave and began his wanderings.

The road led him by a large town, where the watchman at the gate asked him what trade he understood, and what he knew. "I know everything," replied the youth.

"Then you can do us a kindness," said the watch, "if you tell us the reason why the fountain in our market-place, out of which wine used to flow, now, all at once, does not even give water."

"That you shall know," was the answer; "but you must wait till I return."

Then he went on further and came to a rather large city; where the watchman asked him, as before, what trade he understood, and what he knew. "I know everything," he replied.

"Then you can do us a kindness, if you tell us the reason why a tree growing in our town, which used to bear golden apples, does not now even have any leaves."

"That you shall know," replied the youth, "if you wait till I return;" and so saying he went on further till he came to a great lake, over which it was necessary that he should pass. The ferryman asked him what trade he understood, and what he knew. "I know everything," he replied.

"Then," said the ferryman, "you can do me a kindness, if you tell me why, for ever and ever, I am obliged to row backwards and forwards, and am never to be released." "You shall learn the reason why," replied the youth; "but wait till I return."

As soon as he got over the water he found the entrance into the Giant's kingdom. It was black and gloomy, and the Giant was not at home; but his old grandmother was sitting there in an immense armchair. "What do you want?" said she, looking at him fixedly. "I want three Golden hairs from the head of the King of these regions," replied the youth, "else I cannot obtain my bride." "That is a bold request," said the woman; "for if he comes home and finds you here it will be a bad thing for you; but still you can remain, and I will see if I can help you."

Then she changed him into an ant, and told him to creep within the fold of her gown, where he would be quite safe.

"Yes," he said, "that is all very well; but there are three things I am desirous of knowing: – Why a fountain, which used to spout wine, is now dry, and does not even give water. – Why a tree, which used to bear golden apples, does not now have leaves. – And why a ferryman is always rowing backwards and forwards and never gets released."

"Those are difficult questions," replied the old woman; "but do you keep quiet, and pay attention to what the King says when I pluck each of the three golden hairs."

As soon as evening came the Giant returned, and scarcely had he entered, when he remarked that the air was not quite pure. "I smell! I smell the flesh of man!" he exclaimed; "all is not right." Then he peeped into every corner and looked about, but could find nothing. Presently his old grandmother began to scold, screaming, "There now, just as I have dusted and put everything in order, you are pulling them all about again: you are for ever having man's flesh in your nose! Sit down and eat your supper."

When he had finished he felt tired, and the old woman took his head in her lap, and said she would comb his hair a bit. Presently he yawned, then winked, and at last snored. Then she plucked out a golden hair and laid it down beside her.

"Bah!" cried the King, "what are you about?"

"I have had a bad dream," answered the old woman, "and so I plucked one of your hairs."

"What did you dream, then?" asked he.

"I dreamt that a market-fountain, which used to spout wine, is dried up, and does not even give water: what is the matter with it, pray?"

"Why, if you must know," answered he, "there sits a toad under a stone in the spring, which, if any one kills, the wine will gush out as before."

Then the old woman went on combing till he went to sleep again, and snored so that the windows shook. Presently she pulled out a second hair.

"Confound it! what are you about?" exclaimed the King in a passion.

"Don't be angry," said she; "I did it in a dream."

"What did you dream about this time?" he asked.

"I dreamt that in a certain royal city there grew a fruit-tree, which formerly bore golden apples, but now has not a leaf upon it: what is the cause of it?"

"Why," replied the King, "at the root a mouse is gnawing. But if they kill it golden apples will grow again; if not, the mouse will gnaw till the tree dies altogether. However, let me go to sleep in peace now; for if you disturb me again you will catch a box on the ears."

Nevertheless the old woman, when she had rocked him again to sleep, plucked out a third golden hair. Up jumped the King in a fury and would have ill-treated her, but she pacified him and said, "Who can help bad dreams?"

"What did you dream this time?" he asked, still curious to know.

"I dreamt of a ferryman, who is forever compelled to row backwards and forwards, and will never be released. What is the reason thereof?"

"Oh, you simpleton!" answered the Giant. "When one comes who wants to cross over, he must give the oar into his hand; then will the other be obliged to go to and fro, and he will be free."

Now, since the old woman had plucked the three golden hairs, and had received answers to the three questions, she let the Giant lie in peace, and he slept on till daybreak.

As soon as he went out in the morning the old woman took the ant out of the fold of her gown, and restored him again to his human form.

"There you have the three golden hairs from the King's head, and what he replied to the three questions you have just heard."

"Yes, I have heard, and will well remember," said the luck-child; and, thanking the old woman for her assistance in his trouble, he left those regions, well pleased that he had been so lucky in everything. When he came to the ferryman he had to give him the promised answer. But he said, "First row me over, and then I will tell you how you may be freed;" and as soon as they reached the opposite side he gave him the advice, "When another comes this way, and wants to pass over, give him the oar in his hand."

Then he went on to the first city, where stood the barren tree, and where the watchman waited for the answer. So he said to him, "Kill the mouse which gnaws at the root of the tree, and then it will again bear golden apples." The watchman thanked him, and gave him for a reward two asses laden with gold, which followed him. Next he came to the other city, where the dry fountain was, and he told the watchman as the Giant had said, – "Under a stone in the spring there sits a toad, which you must uncover and kill, and then wine will flow again as before."

The watchman thanked him, and gave to him, as the other had done, two asses laden with gold.

Now the lucky youth soon reached home, and his dear bride was very glad when she saw him return, and heard how capitally everything had gone with him. He brought the King what he had desired – the three golden hairs from the head of the Giant – and when his Majesty saw the four asses laden with gold he was quite pleased, and said, "Now are the conditions fulfilled, and you may have my daughter: but tell me, dear son-in-law, whence comes all this gold? This is, indeed, bountiful treasure."

"I was ferried over a river," he replied, "and there I picked it up, for it lies upon the shore like sand."

"Can I not fetch some as well?" asked the King, feeling quite covetous.

"As much as you like; there is a ferryman who will row you across, and then you can fill your sacks on the other side."

The covetous King set out in great haste upon his journey, and as soon as he came to the river beckoned to the ferryman to take him over. The man came and bade him step into his boat; and as soon as they reached the opposite shore, the ferryman put the oar into his hand and sprang on shore himself.

So the King was obliged to take his place, and there he is obliged to row to and fro forever for his sins.

And there he still rows, for no-one has yet come to take the oar from him.

The Three Languages

IN Switzerland there lived an old Count, who had an only son, who was quite stupid and never learned anything. One day the father said, "My son, listen to what I have to say; do all I may, I can knock nothing into your head. Now you shall go away, and an eminent master shall try his hand with you."

So the youth was sent to a foreign city, and remained a whole year with his master, and at the end of that time he returned home. His father asked him at once what he had learned, and he replied, "My father, I have learned what the dogs bark."

"Mercy on us!" exclaimed the father, "is this all you have learned? I will send you to some other city, to another master." So the youth went away a second time, and after he had remained a year with this master, came home again. His father asked him, as before, what he had learned, and he replied, "I have learned what the birds sing." This answer put the father in a passion, and he exclaimed, "Oh, you prodigal! Has all this precious time passed, and have you learned nothing? Are you not ashamed to come into my presence? Once more, I will send you to a third master; but if you learn nothing this time I will no longer be a father to you."

With this third master the boy remained, as before, a twelve-month; and when he came back to his father, he told him that he had learned the language that the frogs croak. At this the father flew into a great rage, and, calling his people together, said, "This youth is no longer my son; I cast him off, and command that you lead him into the forest and take away his life."

The servants led him away into the forest, but they had not the heart to kill him, and so they let him go. They cut out, however, the eyes and the tongue of a fawn, and took them for a token to the old Count.

The young man wandered along, and after some time came to a castle, where he asked for a night's lodging. The Lord of the castle said, "Yes, if you will sleep down below. There is the tower; you may go, but I warn you it is very perilous, for it is full of wild dogs, which bark and howl at every one, and, at certain hours, a man must be thrown to them, whom they devour."

Now, on account of these dogs the whole country round was in terror and sorrow, for no one could prevent their ravages; but the youth, being afraid of nothing, said, "Only let me in to these barking hounds, and give me something to throw to them; they will not harm me."

Since he himself wished it, they gave him some meat for the wild hounds, and let him into the tower. As soon as he entered, the dogs ran about him quite in a friendly way, wagging their tails, and never once barking; they ate, also, the meat he brought, and did not attempt to do him the least injury. The next morning, to the astonishment of every one, he came forth unharmed, and told the Lord of the castle, "The hounds have informed me, in their language, why they thus waste and bring destruction upon the land. They have the guardianship of a large treasure beneath the tower, and till that is raised, they have no rest. In what way and manner this is to be done I have also understood from them."

At these words every one began rejoicing, and the Lord promised him his daughter in marriage, if he could raise the treasure. This task he happily accomplished, and the wild hounds thereupon disappeared, and the country was freed from that plague. Then the beautiful maiden was married to him, and they lived happily together.

After some time, he one day got into a carriage with his wife and set out on the road to Rome. On their way thither, they passed a swamp, where the frogs sat croaking. The young Count listened, and when he heard what they said, he became quite thoughtful and sad, but he did not tell his wife the reason. At last they arrived at Rome, and found the Pope was just dead, and there was a great contention among the Cardinals as to who should be his successor. They at length resolved, that he on whom some miraculous sign should be shown should be elected. Just as they had thus resolved, at the same moment the young Count stepped into the church, and suddenly two snow-white doves flew down, one on each of his shoulders, and remained perched there. The clergy recognised in this circumstance the sign they required, and asked him on the spot whether he would be Pope. The young Count was undecided, and knew not whether he were worthy; but the Doves whispered to him that he might take the honour, and so he consented. Then he was anointed and consecrated; and so was fulfilled what the Frogs had prophesied – and which had so disturbed him, – that he should become the Pope. Upon his election he had to sing a mass, of which he knew nothing; but the two Doves sitting upon his shoulder told him all that he required.

The Handless Maiden

A CERTAIN Miller had fallen by degrees into great poverty, until he had nothing left but his mill and a large apple-tree. One day, when he was going into the forest to cut wood, an old man, whom he had never seen before, stepped up to him, and said, "Why do you trouble yourself with chopping wood? I will make you rich, if you will promise me what stands behind your mill."

The Miller thought to himself that it could be nothing but his apple-tree, so he said "Yes," and concluded the bargain with the strange man. The other, however, laughed derisively, and said, "After three years I will come and fetch what belongs to me;" and then he went away.

As soon as the Miller reached home, his wife came to him, and said, "Tell me, husband, whence comes this sudden flow of gold into our house? All at once every chest and cupboard is filled, and yet no man has brought any in; I cannot tell how it has happened."

The Miller, in reply, told her, "It comes from a strange lord, whom I met in the forest, who offered me great treasure, and I promised him in return, what stands behind the mill, for we can very well spare the great apple-tree."

"Ah, my husband," exclaimed his wife, "it is the Evil Spirit whom you have seen; he did not mean the apple-tree, but our daughter, who was behind the mill sweeping the yard."

This Miller's daughter was a beautiful and pious maiden, and during all the three years lived in the fear of God without sin. When the time was up, and the day came when the Evil One was to fetch her, she washed herself quite clean and made a circle around herself with chalk. Quite early came the Evil One, but he could not approach her; so, in a rage, he said to the Miller, "Take away from her all water, that she may not be able to wash herself, else have I no power over her." The Miller did so, for he was afraid. The next morning came the Evil One again, but she had wept upon her hands so that they were quite clean. Then he was baffled again, and in his anger said to the Miller, "Cut off both her hands, or else I cannot now obtain her." The Miller was horrified, and said, "How can I cut off the hands of my own child?" But the Evil One pressed him, saying, "If you do not, you are mine, and I will take you yourself away!" At last the Miller promised, and he went to the maiden, and said, "My child, if I do not cut off both your hands, the Evil One will carry me away, and in my terror I have promised him. Now help me in my trouble, and forgive me for the wickedness I am about to do you."

She replied, "Dear father, do with me what you will; I am your daughter."

Thereupon she laid down both her hands, and her father cut them off. For the third time now the Evil One came, but the maiden had let fall so many tears upon her arms, that they were both quite clean. So he was obliged to give her up, and after this lost all power over her.

The Miller now said to her, "I have received so much good through you, my daughter, that I will care for you most dearly all your life long."

But she answered, "Here I cannot remain; I will wander forth into the world, where compassionate men will give me as much as I require."

Then she had her arms bound behind her back, and at sunrise departed on her journey, and walked the whole day long till night fell. At that time she arrived at a royal garden, and by the light of the moon she saw a tree standing there bearing most beautiful fruits, but she could not enter, for there was water all round. Since, however, she had walked the whole day without tasting a morsel, she was tormented by hunger, and said to herself, "Ah, would I were there, that I might eat of the fruit, else shall I perish with hunger." So she kneeled and prayed to God, and all at once an angel came down, who made a passage through the water, so that the ground was dry for her to pass over. Then she went into the garden, and the angel with her. There she saw a tree full of beautiful pears, but they were all numbered; so she stepped up and ate one to appease her hunger, but no more. The gardener perceived her do it, but because the angel stood by he was afraid, and thought the maiden was a spirit; so he remained quiet and did not address her. As soon as she had eaten the pear she was satisfied, and went and hid herself under the bushes.

The next morning the King to whom the garden belonged came down and counting the pears found that one was missing; and he asked the gardener whither it was gone. The gardener replied, "Last night a spirit came, who had no hands, and ate the pear with her mouth." The King then asked, "How did the spirit come through the water? and whither did it go after it had eaten the pear?"

The gardener answered, "One clothed in snow-white garments came down from heaven and made a passage through the waters, so that the spirit walked through on dry land. And because it must have been an angel, I was afraid, and neither called out nor questioned it; and as soon as the spirit had finished the fruit, she returned as she came."

The King said, "If it be as you say, I will this night watch with you."

As soon as it was dark the King came into the garden, bringing with him a priest, who was to address the spirit, and all three sat down under the tree. About midnight the maiden crept out from under the bushes and again ate with her mouth a pear off the tree, whilst the angel clothed in white stood by her. Then the priest went towards her, and said, "Art thou come from God or from earth? Art thou a spirit of a human being?" She replied, "I am no spirit, but a poor maiden, deserted by all, save God alone."

The King said, "If you are forsaken by all the world, yet will I not forsake you;" and he took her with him to his royal palace, and, because she was so beautiful and pious, he loved her with all his heart, and ordered silver hands to be made for her, and made her his bride.

After a year had passed by, the King was obliged to go to war, so he commended the young Queen to the care of his mother, and told her to write him word if she had a child born, and to pay her especial attention. Soon afterwards the Queen bore a fine boy; so the old mother wrote a letter to her son, containing the joyful news. The messenger, however, rested on his way by a brook, and, being weary with his long journey, fell asleep. Then came the Evil One, who had always been trying to do some evil to the Queen, and changed the letter for another, wherein it was said that the Queen had brought a changeling into the world. As soon as the King had read this letter, he was frightened and much troubled; nevertheless, he wrote an answer to his mother, that she should take great care of the Queen until his arrival. The messenger went back with this letter, but on his way rested at the same spot, and went to sleep. Then the Evil One came a second time, and put another letter in his pocket, wherein it was said the Queen and her child should be killed. When the old mother received this letter, she was struck with horror, and could not believe it; so she wrote another letter to the King; but she received no other answer, for the Evil One again placed a false letter in the messenger's pocket; and in this last it said that she should preserve the tongue and eyes of the Queen for a sign that she had fulfilled the order.

The old mother was sorely grieved to shed innocent blood, so she caused a calf to be fetched by night, and cut out its tongue and eyes. Then she said to the Queen, "I cannot let you be killed, as the King commands; but you must remain here no longer. Go forth with your child into the wide world, and never return here again."

Thus saying, she bound the child upon the young Queen's back, and the poor wife went away weeping bitterly. Soon she entered a large wild forest, and there she fell upon her knees and prayed to God; and the angel appeared, and led her to a little cottage, and over the door was a shield inscribed with the words, "Here may every one live freely." Out of the house came a snow-white maiden, who said, "Welcome, Lady Queen!" and led her in. Then she took the little child from the Queen's back, and gave it some nourishment, and laid it on a beautifully covered bed. Presently the Queen asked, "How do you know that I am a queen?" and the maiden answered, "I am an angel sent from God to tend you and your child;" and in this cottage she lived seven years, and was well cared for, and through God's mercy to her, on account of her piety, her hands grew again as before.

Meanwhile the King had come home again, and his first thought was to see his wife and child. Then his mother began to weep, and said, "You wicked husband, why did you write to me that I should put to death two innocent souls!" and, showing him the two letters which the Evil One had forged, she continued, "I have done as you commanded;" and she brought him the tokens, the two eyes and the tongue. Then the King began to weep so bitterly for his dear wife and son that the old mother pitied him, and said, "Be comforted, she lives yet! I caused a calf to be slain, from whom I took these tokens; but the child I bound on your wife's back, and I bade them go forth into the wide world; and she promised never to return here, because you were so wrathful against her."

"So far as heaven is blue," exclaimed the King, "I will go; and neither will I eat nor drink until I have found again my dear wife and child, if they have not perished of hunger by this time."

Thereupon the King set out, and for seven long years sought his wife in every stony cleft and rocky cave, but found her not; and he began to think she must have perished. And all this time he neither ate nor drank, but God sustained him.

At last he came into a large forest, and found there the little cottage whereon the shield was the words, "Here may every one live freely." Out of the house came the white maiden, and she took him by the hand; and, leading him in, said, "Be welcome, Great King! Whence comest thou?"

He replied, "For seven long years I have sought everywhere for my wife and child; but I have not succeeded."

Then the angel offered him meat and drink, but he refused both, and would only rest a little while. So he lay down to sleep, and covered his face with a napkin.

Now went the angel into the chamber where sat the Queen, with her son, whom she usually called "SORROWFUL," and said to her, "Come down, with your child: you husband is here." So she went to where he lay, and the napkin fell from off his face; so the Queen said, "SORROWFUL, pick up the napkin, and cover again your father's face." The child did as he was bid; and the King, who heard in his slumber what passed, let the napkin again fall from off his face. At this the boy became impatient, and said, "Dear mother, how can I cover my father's face? Have I indeed a father on the earth? I have learnt the prayer, 'Our Father which art in heaven;' and you have told me my father was in heaven, – the good God: how can I talk to this wild man; he is not my father."

As the King heard this he raised himself up, and asked the Queen who she was. The Queen replied: "I am your wife, and this is your son, SORROWFUL." But when he saw her human hands, he said "My wife had silver hands." "The merciful God," said the Queen, "has caused my hands to grow again;" and the angel, going into the chamber, brought out the silver hands, and showed them to him.

Now he perceived that they were certainly his dear wife and child; and he kissed them gladly, saying, "A heavy stone is taken from my heart;" and, after eating a meal together with the angel, they went home to the King's mother.

Their arrival caused great rejoicings everywhere: and the King

and Queen celebrated their marriage again, and ever afterwards
lived happily together to the end of their lives.

The Singing Bone

ONCE upon a time great complaints were made in a certain country
of a Wild Boar, which laid waste the fields of the peasants, killed the
cattle, and often tore to pieces the inhabitants. The King promised a
great reward to whomever should free the land of this plague; but the
beast was so big and strong that no one durst venture in the
neighbourhood of the forest where it raged. At last the King allowed
it to be proclaimed that whoever should take or kill the Wild Boar,
should have his only daughter in marriage.

Now, there lived in this country two brothers, the sons of a poor
man, and they each wished to undertake the adventure; the elder,
who was bold and brave, out of pride; the younger, who was
innocent and ignorant, from a good heart. They agreed, that they

might the sooner find the boar, that they should enter the forest on opposite sides; so the elder departed in the evening, and the other on the following morning. When the younger had gone a short way, a little Dwarf stepped up to him, holding a black spear in his hand, and said, "I give you this spear, because your heart is innocent and good; with it you may boldly attack the Boar, who can do you no harm."

He thanked the Dwarf, and, taking the spear, went forward bravely. In a little while he perceived the Wild Boar, which ran straight at him; but he held the spear in front of his body, so that, in its blind fury, it rushed on so rashly that its heart was pierced quite through. Then he took the beast upon his shoulder, and went home to show it to the King.

However, just as he came out on the other side of the forest, there stood on the outskirts a house, where the people were making merry, dancing and drinking. His elder brother was amongst them, exciting his courage by wine, and never thinking at all that the Boar might be killed by any other than himself. As soon, therefore, as he saw his younger brother coming out of the forest laden with his booty, his envious and ill-natured heart had no rest. Still he called to him, "Come in here, my dear brother, and rest, and strengthen yourself with a cup of wine." The younger brother, suspecting no evil, went in and related his story of the good little Dwarf, who had given him the spear wherewith he had killed the boar. The elder brother detained him till evening, and then they went away together. But when they came in the darkness to a bridge over a stream, the elder, letting his brother pass on before till he came to the middle of the bridge, gave him a blow which felled him dead. Then he buried him in the sand below the bridge, and taking the Boar brought it to the King, representing that he had killed it, and so received in marriage the Princess. He declared, moreover, that the Boar had torn in pieces the body of his younger brother, and, as he did not come back, every one believed the tale to be true.

But, since nothing is hidden from God's sight, so also this black deed at last came to light. Many years after, as a peasant was driving his herd across the brook, he saw lying in the sand below a snow-white bone, which he thought would make a good mouth-piece. So he stepped down, took it up, and fashioned it into a mouth-piece for his horn. But as soon as he blew through it for the first time, to the great astonishment of the herdsman, the bone began to sing of itself—

"My brother slew me, and buried my bones,
Under the sand and under the stones:
I killed the boar as he came from his lair,
But *he* won the prize of the lady fair."

"What a wonderful little bone!" exclaimed the herdsman; "it sings of itself! I must take it to the King."

As soon as he came before the King it began again to repeat its song, and the King understood it perfectly. So he caused the earth below the bridge to be dug up, and there all the bones of the younger brother came to light. The wicked brother could not deny the deed, and, for his punishment, he was sewed up in a sack and drowned.

And the bones of the other brother were placed in a splendid tomb in the churchyard.

The Discreet Hans

Hans's mother asked, "Whither are you going, Hans?" "To Grethel's," replied he. "Behave well, Hans." "I will take care: good bye, mother." "Good bye, Hans."

Hans came to Grethel. "Good day," said he. "Good day," replied Grethel. "What treasure do you bring to-day?" "I bring nothing. Have you anything to give?" Grethel presented Hans with a needle. "Good bye," said he. "Good bye, Hans." Hans took the needle, stuck it in a load of hay, and walked home behind the waggon.

"Good evening, mother." "Good evening Hans. Where have you been?" "To Grethel's." "And what have you given her?" "Nothing: she has given me something." "What has Grethel given you?" "A needle," said Hans. "And where have you put it?" "In the load of hay." "Then you have behaved stupidly, Hans; you should put needles on your coat-sleeve." "To behave better, do nothing at all," thought Hans.

"Whither are you going, Hans?" "To Grethel's, mother."

"Behave well, Hans." "I will take care: good bye, mother." "Good bye, Hans."

Hans came to Grethel. "Good day," said he. "Good day, Hans. What treasure do you bring?" "I bring nothing. Have you anything to give?" Grethel gave Hans a knife. "Good bye, Grethel." "Good bye, Hans." Hans took the knife, put it in his sleeve, and went home.

"Good evening, mother." "Good evening, Hans. Where have you been?" "To Grethel's." "And what did you take to her?" "I took nothing: she has given to me." "And what did she give you?" "A knife," said Hans. "And where have you put it?" "In my sleeve." "Then you have behaved foolishly again, Hans: you should put knives in your pocket." "To behave better, do nothing at all," thought Hans.

"Whither are you going, Hans?" "To Grethel's, mother." "Behave well, Hans." "I will take care: good bye, mother." "Good bye, Hans."

Hans came to Grethel. "Good day, Grethel." "Good day, Hans. What treasure do you bring?" "I bring nothing. Have you anything to give?" Grethel gave Hans a young goat. "Good bye, Grethel." "Good bye, Hans." Hans took the goat, tied its legs, and put it in his pocket.

Just as he reached home it was suffocated. "Good evening, mother." "Good evening, Hans." "Where have you been?" "To Grethel's." "And what did you take to her?" "I took nothing; she gave to me." "And what did Grethel give you?" "A goat." "Where did you put it, Hans?" "In my pocket." "There you acted stupidly, Hans; you should have tied the goat with a rope." "To behave better, do nothing," thought Hans.

"Whither away, Hans?" "To Grethel's, mother." "Behave well, Hans." "I'll take care: good bye, mother." "Good bye, Hans."

Hans came to Grethel. "Good day," said he. "Good day, Hans. What treasure do you bring?" "I bring nothing. Have you anything to give?" Grethel gave Hans a piece of bacon. "Good bye, Grethel." "Good bye, Hans." Hans took the bacon, tied it with a rope, and swung it to and fro so that the dogs came and ate it up. When he reached home he held the rope in his hand, but there was nothing on it.

"Good evening, mother," said he. "Good evening, Hans. Where have you been?" To Grethel's, mother." "What did you take there?" "I took nothing: she gave to me." "And what did Grethel give you?" "A piece of bacon," said Hans. "And where have you put it?" I tied it with a rope, swung it about, and the dogs came and ate it up." "There you acted stupidly, Hans; you should have carried the bacon on your head." "To behave better, do nothing," thought Hans.

"Whither away, Hans?" "To Grethel's mother." Behave well, Hans." "I'll take care: good bye, mother." "Good bye, Hans."

Hans came to Grethel. "Good day," said he. "Good day, Hans. What treasure do you bring?" "I bring nothing. Have you anything to give?" Grethel gave Hans a calf. "Good bye," said Hans. "Good bye." Hans took the calf, set it on his head, and the calf scratched his face.

"Good evening, mother." "Good evening, Hans. Where have you been?" "To Grethel's." "What did you take her?" "I took nothing: she gave to me." "And what did Grethel give you?" "A calf," said Hans. "And what did you do with it?" "I set it on my head, and it kicked my face." "Then you acted stupidly, Hans; you should have led the calf home, and put it in the stall." "To behave better, do nothing," thought Hans.

"Whither away, Hans?" "To Grethel's, mother." "Behave well, Hans." "I'll take care: good bye, mother." "Good bye, Hans."

Hans came to Grethel. "Good day," said he. "Good day, Hans. What treasure do you bring?" "I bring nothing. Have you anything to give?" Grethel said, "I will go with you, Hans." Hans tied a rope round Grethel, led her home, put her in the stall, and made the rope fast; and then he went to his mother.

"Good evening, mother." "Good evening, Hans. Where have you been?" "To Grethel's" "What did you take her?" "I took nothing." "What did Grethel give you?" "She gave nothing; she came with me." "And where have you left her, then?" "I tied her with a rope, put her in the stall, and threw in some grass." "Then you acted

stupidly, Hans; you should have looked at her with friendly eyes."
"To behave better, do nothing," thought Hans; and then he went
into the stall, and made sheep's eyes at Grethel.

And after that Grethel became Hans's wife.

Clever Alice

ONCE upon a time there was a man who had a daughter, who was
called "Clever Alice;" and when she was grown up, her father said,
"We must see about her marrying," "Yes," replied her mother,
"when one comes who shall be worthy of her."

At last a certain youth, by name Hans, came from a distance to
make a proposal for her, but he put in one condition, that the Clever
Alice should also be very prudent. "Oh," said her father, "she has
got a head full of brains;" and the mother added, "Ah, she can see
the wind blow up the street, and hear the flies cough!"

"Very well," replied Hans, "but if she is not very prudent, I will not have her." Soon afterwards they sat down to dinner, and her mother said, "Alice, go down into the cellar and draw some beer."

So Clever Alice took the jug down from the wall, and went into the cellar, jerking the lid up and down on her way to pass away the time. As soon as she got downstairs, she drew a stool and placed it before the cask, in order that she might not have to stoop, whereby she might do some injury to her back, and give it an undesirable bend. Then she placed the can before her and turned the tap, and while the beer was running, as she did not wish her eyes to be idle, she looked about upon the wall above and below, and presently perceived, after much peeping into this and that corner, a hatchet, which the bricklayers had left behind, sticking out of the ceiling right above her. At the sight of this the Clever Alice began to cry, saying, "Oh, if I marry Hans, and we have a child, and he grows up, and we send him into the cellar to draw beer, the hatchet will fall upon his head and kill him;" and so saying, she sat there weeping with all her might over the impending misfortune.

Meanwhile the good folks upstairs were waiting for the beer, but as Clever Alice did not come, her mother told the maid to go and see what she was stopping for. The maid went down into the cellar, and found Alice sitting before the cask crying heartily, and she asked, "Alice, what are you weeping about?" "Ah," she replied, "have I not cause? If I marry Hans, and we have a child, and he grow up, and we send him here to draw beer, that hatchet will fall upon his head and kill him."

"Oh," said the maid, "what a clever Alice we have!" And, sitting down, she began to weep, too, for the misfortune that was to happen.

After a while, and the maid did not return, the good folks above began to feel very thirsty; so the husband told the boy to go down into the cellar, and see what had become of Alice and the maid. The boy went down, and there sat Clever Alice and the maid both crying, so he asked the reason; and Alice told him the same tale of the hatchet that was to fall on her child, as she had told the maid. When she had finished, the boy exclaimed, "What a clever Alice we have!"

CLEVER ALICE

and fell weeping and howling with the others.

Upstairs they were still waiting, and the husband said, when the boy did not return, "Do you go down, wife, into the cellar and see why Alice stops." So she went down, and finding all three sitting there crying, asked the reason, and Alice told her about the hatchet which must inevitably fall upon the head of her son. Then the mother likewise exclaimed, "Oh, what a clever Alice we have!" and, sitting down, began to weep with the others. Meanwhile the husband waited for the wife's return; but at last he felt so very thirsty that he said, "I must go myself down into the cellar and see what Alice stops for." As soon as he entered the cellar, there he found the four sitting and crying together, and when he heard the reason, he also exclaimed, "Oh, what a clever Alice we have!" and sat down to cry with the others. All this time the bridegroom above sat waiting, but when nobody returned, he thought they must be waiting for him, so he went down to see what was the matter. When he entered, there sat the five crying and groaning, each one in a louder key than his neighbour. "What misfortune has happened?" he asked. "Ah, dear Hans!" cried Alice, "if we should marry one another, and have a child, and he grow up, and we, perhaps, send him down here to tap the beer, the hatchet which has been left sticking there may fall on his head, and so kill him; and do you not think that enough to weep about?"

"Now," said Hans, "more prudence than this is not necessary for my housekeeping; because you are such a clever Alice I will have you for my wife." And, taking her hand, he led her home, and celebrated the wedding directly.

After they had been married a little while, Hans said one morning, "Wife, I will go out to work and earn some money; do you go into the field and gather some corn wherewith to make bread."

"Yes," she answered, "I will do so, dear Hans." And when he was gone, she cooked herself a nice mess of pottage to take with her. As she came to the field, she said to herself, "What shall I do? Shall I cut first, or eat first? Ay, I will eat first!" Then she ate up the contents of her pot, and when it was finished, she thought to herself, "Now, shall

I reap first or sleep first? Well, I think I will have a nap!" and so she laid herself down amongst the corn, and went to sleep. Meanwhile Hans returned home, but Alice did not come, and so he said, "Oh, what a prudent Alice I have! she is so industrious that she does not even come home to eat anything." By-and-by, however, evening came on, and still she did not return; so Hans went out to see how much she had reaped; but, behold, nothing at all, and there lay Alice fast asleep among the corn! So home he ran very fast, and brought a net with little bells hanging on it, which he threw over her head while she still slept on. When he had done this, he went back again and shut to the house door, and, seating himself on his stool, began working very industriously.

At last, when it was quite dark, the Clever Alice awoke, and as soon as she stood up, the net fell all over her hair, and the bells jingled at every step she took. This quite frightened her, and she began to doubt whether she were really Clever Alice, and said to herself, "Am I she, or am I not?" This question she could not answer, and she stood still a long while considering. At last she thought she would go home and ask whether she were really herself – supposing they would be able to tell. When she came to the house-door it was shut; so she tapped at the window, and asked, "Hans, is Alice within?" "Yes," he replied, "she is." Now she was really terrified, and exclaiming, "Ah, heaven, then I am not Alice!" she ran up to another house; but as soon as the folks within heard the jingling of the bells they would not open their doors, and so nobody would receive her. Then she ran straight away from the village, and no one has ever seen her since.

The Wedding of Mrs Fox

FIRST TALE

THERE was once upon a time a Fox with nine tails, who thought his wife was not faithful to him, and determined to put it to the proof. So he stretched himself along under a bench, and keeping his legs perfectly still, he appeared as if quite dead. Mrs Fox, meanwhile, had ascended to her room, and shut herself in; and her maid, the young Cat, stood near the hearth cooking. As soon as it was known that Mr Fox was dead, several suitors came to pay their respects to his widow. The maid, hearing some one knocking at the front door, went and looked out, and saw a young Fox, who asked,

"How do you do, Miss Kitten?
Is she asleep or awake?"

The maid replied—

"I neither sleep nor wake;
Would you know my business?
Beer and butter both I make;
Come and be my guest."

"I am obliged, Miss Kitten," said the young Fox; "but how is Mrs Fox?"

"She sits in her chamber,
Weeping so sore;
Her eyes red with crying –
Mr Fox is no more."

"Tell her then, my maiden, that a young Fox is here, who wishes to marry her," said he. So the Cat went pit-pat, pit-a-pat up the stairs, and tapped gently at the door, saying, "Are you there, Madam Fox?" "Yes, my good little Cat," was the reply. "There is a suitor below." "What does he look like?" asked her mistress. "Has he nine as beautiful tails as my late husband?" "Oh, no," answered the maid, "he has only one." "Then I will not have him," said the mistress. The young Cat went down and sent away the suitor; and soon after there came a second knock at the door from another Fox, with *two* tails, who wished to marry the widow; he fared, however, no better than the former one. After wards came six more, one after the other, each having one tail more than he who preceded him; but these were all turned away. At last there arrived a Fox with nine tails, like the deceased husband; and when the widow heard of it, she said, full of joy, to the Cat, "Now you may open all the windows and doors, and turn the old Fox out of the house." But just as the wedding was about to be celebrated, the old Fox roused himself from his sleep beneath the bench, and drubbed the whole rabble, together with his wife, out of the house, and hunted them far away.

A SECOND ACCOUNT

Narrates that when the old Fox appeared dead, the Wolf came as a suitor, and knocked at the door; and the Cat, who served as a

THE WEDDING OF MRS FOX

servant to the Widow, got up to see who was there.

"Good day, Miss Cat; how does it happen that you are sitting all alone? What good are you about?"

The Cat answered, "I have been making some bread and milk. Will my lord be my guest?"

"Thanks, many thanks!" replied the Wolf; "is Madam Fox not at home?"

The Cat sang,

> "She sits in her chamber,
> Weeping so sore;
> Her eyes red with crying –
> Mr Fox is no more."

Then the Wolf said, "If she wishes for another husband she had better come down to me."

So the Cat ran up the stairs, her tail trailing behind, and when she got to the chamber door, she knocked five times, and asked, "Is Madam Fox at home? If so, and she wishes to have another husband, she must come downstairs."

Mrs Fox asked, "Does the gentleman wear red stockings, and has he a pointed mouth?" "No," replied the Cat. "Then he will not do for me," said Mrs Fox, and shut the door.

After the Wolf had been turned away, there came a Dog, a Stag, a Hare, a Bear, a Lion, and all the beasts of the forest, one after another. But each one was deficient of the particular qualities which the old Fox had possessed, and the Cat was obliged therefore to turn away every suitor. At last came a young Fox; and when the question was asked whether he had red stockings and a pointed mouth, the Cat replied, "Yes;" and she was bid to call him up and prepare for the wedding. Then they threw the old Fox out of the window, and the Cat caught and ate as many mice as she could, in celebration of the happy event.

And after the marriage they had a grand ball, and, as I have never heard to the contrary, perhaps they are dancing still.

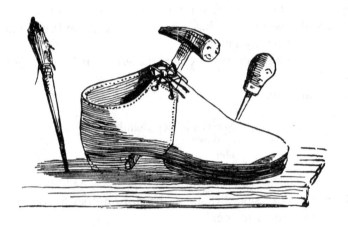

The Little Elves

FIRST STORY

THERE was once a Shoemaker, who, from no fault of his own, had become so poor that at last he had nothing left, but just sufficient leather for one pair of shoes. In the evening he cut out the leather, intending to make it up in the morning; and, as he had a good conscience, he lay quietly down to sleep, first commending himself to God. In the morning he said his prayers, and then sat down to work; but, behold, the pair of shoes were already made, and there they stood upon his board. The poor man was amazed, and knew not what to think; but he took the shoes into his hand to look at them more closely, and they were so neatly worked, that not a stitch was wrong; just as if they had been made for a prize. Presently a customer came in; and as the shoes pleased him very much, he paid down more than was usual; and so much that the Shoemaker was able to buy with it leather for two pairs. By the evening he had got his leather shaped out; and when he arose the next morning, he prepared to work with fresh spirit; but there was no need – for the shoes stood all perfect on his board. He did not want either for customers; for two came who paid him so liberally for the shoes that he bought with the money material for four pairs more. These also – when he awoke – he found all ready-made, and so it continued; what he cut out overnight was, in the morning, turned into the neatest shoes possible. This went on until he had regained his former appearance, and was even becoming a prosperous man.

One evening – not long before Christmas – as he had cut out the usual quantity, he said to his wife before going to bed, "What say you to stopping up this night, to see who it is that helps us so kindly?" His wife was satisfied, and fastened up a light; and then they hid themselves in the corner of the room, where hung some clothes which concealed them. As soon as it was midnight in came two little mannikins, who squatted down on the board; and, taking up the prepared work, set to with their little fingers, stitching and sewing, and hammering so swiftly and lightly, that the Shoemaker could not take his eyes off them for astonishment. They did not cease until all was brought to an end, and the shoes stood ready on the table; and then they sprang quickly away.

The following morning the wife said, "The little men have made us rich, and we must show our gratitude to them; for although they run about they must be cold, for they have nothing on their bodies. I will make a little shirt, coat, waistcoat, trousers, and stockings for each, and do you make a pair of shoes for each."

The husband assented; and one evening, when all was ready, they laid presents, instead of the usual work, on the board, and hid themselves to see the result.

At midnight in came the Elves, jumping about, and soon prepared to work; but when they saw no leather, but the natty little clothes, they at first were astonished, but soon showed their rapturous glee. They drew on their coats, and smoothing them down, sang—

> "Smart and natty boys are we;
> Cobblers we'll no longer be;"

and so they went on hopping and jumping over the stools and chairs, and at last out at the door. After that evening they did not come again; but the Shoemaker prospered in all he undertook, and lived happily to the end of his days.

SECOND STORY

Once upon a time there was a poor servant girl, who was both industrious and cleanly, for every day she dusted the house and shook out the sweepings on a great heap before the door. One morning, just as she was going to throw them away, she saw a letter lying among them, and, as she could not read, she put her broom by in a corner, and took it to her master. It contained an invitation from the Elves, asking the girl to stand godmother to one of their children. The girl did not know what to do, but at last, after much consideration, she consented, for the little men will not easily take a refusal. So there came three Elves, who conducted her to a hollow mountain where they lived. Everything was very small of course, but all more neat and elegant than I can tell you. The mother lay in a bed of ebony studded with pearls, and the coverings were all wrought with gold; the cradle was made of ivory and the bath was of gold. The girl stood godmother, and afterwards wished to return home, but the little Elves pressed her earnestly to stay three days longer. So she remained, passing the time in pleasure and play, for the elves behaved very kindly to her. At the end of the time she prepared to return home, but first they filled her pockets full of gold, and then led her out of the hill. As soon as she reached the house, she took the broom, which still stood in the corner, and went on with her sweeping; and presently out of the house came some strange people, who asked her who she was, and what she was doing there. Then she found out that it was not three days, as she had supposed, but seven years, that she had passed with the little Elves in the hill, and that her former master had died in her absence.

THIRD STORY

The little Elves once stole a child out of its cradle, and put in its place a changeling, with a clumsy head and red eyes, who would neither eat nor drink. The mother, in great trouble, went to a neighbour to ask her advice, and she advised her to carry the changeling into the kitchen, set it on the hearth, and boil water in two egg-shells. If the changeling was made to laugh, then its fate was sealed. The woman did all the neighbour said; and as she set the egg-shells over the fire, the creature sang out,—

> "Though I am as old as the oldest tree,
> Cooking in an egg-shell never did I see."

and then it burst into a horse-laugh. While it was laughing, a number of little Elves entered, bringing the real child, whom they placed on the hearth, and then took away the changeling with them.

Thumbling

ONCE upon a time there lived a poor peasant, who used to sit every evening by the hearth, poking the fire, while his wife spun. One night, he said, "How sad it is that we have no children! everything is so quiet here, while in other houses it is so noisy and merry."

"Ah!" sighed his wife, "if we had but only one, and were he no bigger than my thumb, I should still be content, and love him with all my heart." A little while after the wife fell ill; and after seven months a child was born, who, although he was perfectly formed in all his limbs, was not actually bigger than one's thumb. So they said to one another that it had happened just as they wished; and they called the child "Thumbling." Every day they gave him all the food he could eat; still he did not grow a bit, but remained exactly the height he was when first born; he looked about him, however, very knowingly, and showed himself to be a bold and clever fellow, who would prosper in everything he undertook.

One morning the peasant was making ready to go into the forest to fell wood, and said, "Now I wish I had some one who could follow me with the cart."

"Oh, father!" exclaimed Thumbling, "I will bring the cart; don't you trouble yourself; it shall be there at the right time."

The father laughed at this speech, and said, "How shall that be? You are much too small to lead the horse by the bridle."

"That matters not, father. If mother will harness the horse, I can sit in his ear, and tell him which way to take."

"Well, we will try for once," said the father; and so, when the hour came, the mother harnessed the horse, and placed Thumbling in its ear, and told him how to guide it. Then he set out quite like a man, and the cart went on the right road to the forest; and just as it turned a corner, and Thumbling called out, "Steady, steady!" two strange men met it; and one said to the other, "My goodness! what is this? Here comes a cart, and the driver keeps calling to the horse, but I can see no one." "That cannot be right," said the other: "let us follow and see where the cart stops."

The cart went on safely deep into the forest, and straight to the place where the wood was cut. As soon as Thumbling saw his father, he called to him, "Here, father; here I am, you see, with the cart: just take me down." The peasant caught the bridle of the horse with his left hand, and with his right took his little son out of its ear, and he sat himself down merrily on a straw. When the two strangers saw the little fellow, they knew not what to say for astonishment; and one of them took his companion aside, and said, "This little fellow might make our fortune, if we could exhibit him in the towns. Let us buy him." They went up to the peasant, and asked, "Will you sell us your son? We will treat him well." "No," replied the man; "he is my heart's delight, and not to be bought for all the money in the world!" But Thumbling, when he heard what was said, climbed up by his father's skirt, and sat himself on his shoulder, and whispered in his ear, "Let me go now, and I will soon come back again." So his father gave him to the two men for a fine piece of gold, and they asked him where he would sit. "Oh," replied he, "put me on the rim of your hat, and then I can walk round and survey the country. I will not fall off." They did as he wished; and when he had taken leave of his father, they set out. Just as it was getting dark he asked to be lifted down; and, after some demur, the man on whose hat he was took him off and placed him on the ground. In an instant Thumbling ran off, and crept into a mouse-hole, where they could not see him. "Good evening, masters," said he, "you can go home without me;" and, with a quiet laugh, he crept into his hole still further. The two men poked their sticks into the hole, but all in vain, for Thumbling only went down further; and when it had grown quite dark, they were obliged to return home full of vexation and with empty pockets.

As soon as Thumbling perceived that they were off, he crawled out of his hiding-place, and said, "How dangerous it is to walk in this field in the dark: one might soon break one's head or legs!" and so saying he looked round, and by great good luck he saw an empty snail-shell. "God be praised!" he exclaimed, "here I can sleep securely;" and in he went. Just as he was about to fall asleep he heard two men coming by, one of whom said to the other, "How shall we manage to get at the parson's gold and silver?"

"That I can tell you," interrupted Thumbling.

"What was that?" exclaimed the thief, frightened. "I heard some one speak." They stood still and listened; and then Thumbling said,

"Take me with you, and I will help you."

"Where are you?" asked the thieves.

"Search on the ground, and mark where my voice comes from," replied he. The thief looked about, and at last found him; and lifted him up in the air, "What! will you help us, you little wight?" said they.

"Do you see, I can creep between the iron bars into the chamber of the parson, and reach out to you whatever you require."

"Very well; we will see what you can do," said the thief.

When they came to the house, Thumbling crept into the chamber, and cried out, with all his might, "Will you have all that is here?" The thieves were terrified, and said, "Speak gently, or some one will awake."

But Thumbling feigned not to understand, and exclaimed, louder still, "Will you have all that is here?"

This awoke the cook, who slept in the room, and sitting up in her bed she listened. The thieves, however, had run back a little way, quite frightened; but, taking courage again, and thinking the little fellow wished to tease them, they came and whispered to him to make haste and hand them out something. At this, Thumbling cried out still more loudly, "I will give you it all, only put your hands in." The listening maid heard this clearly, and, springing out of bed, hurried out at the door. The thieves ran off as if they were pursued by the wild huntsman, but the maid, as she could see nothing, went to strike a light. When she returned, Thumbling escaped without being seen into the barn, and the maid, after she had looked round, and searched in every corner, without finding anything, went to bed again, believing she had been dreaming with her eyes open. Meanwhile Thumbling had crept in amongst the hay, and found a beautiful place to sleep, where he intended to rest till daybreak, and then to go home to his parents.

Other things, however, was he to experience, for there is much tribulation and trouble going on in this world.

The maid got up at dawn of day to feed the cow. Her first walk was to the barn, where she took an armful of hay, and just the bundle where poor Thumbling lay asleep. He slept so soundly, however, that he was not conscious, and only awoke when he was in the cow's mouth. "Ah, goodness!" exclaimed he, "how ever came I into this mill!" but soon he saw where he really was. Then he took care not to come between the teeth, but presently slipped quite down the cow's throat. "There are no windows in this room," said he to himself, "and no sunshine, and I brought no light with me." Overhead his quarters seemed still worse, and, more than all, he felt his room growing narrower, as the cow swallowed more hay. So he began to call out in terror, as loudly as he could, "Bring me no more food! I do not want any more food!" Just then the maid was milking the cow, and when she heard the voice without seeing anything, and knew it was the same she had listened to in the night, she was so frightened that she slipped off her stool and overturned the milk. In great haste she ran to her master, saying, "Oh, Mr Parson, the cow has been speaking."

"You are crazy," he replied; but still he went himself into the stable to see what was the matter, and scarcely had he stepped in when Thumbling began to shout out again, "Bring me no more food, bring me no more food." This terrified the parson himself, and he thought an evil spirit had entered into his cow, and so ordered her to be killed. As soon as that was done, and they were dividing the carcass, a fresh accident befell Thumbling, for a wolf, who was passing at the time, made a snatch at the cow, and tore away the part where he was stuck fast. However, he did not lose courage, but as soon as the wolf had swallowed him, he called out from inside, "Oh, Mr Wolf, I know of a capital meal for you." "Where is it to be found?" asked the Wolf. "In the house by the meadow; you must creep through the gutter, and there you will find cakes, and bacon, and sausages, as many as you can eat," replied Thumbling, describing exactly his father's house.

The wolf did not wait to be told twice, but in the night crept in, and ate away in the larder to his heart's content. When he had finished he tried to escape by the way he entered, but the hole was not large enough. Thereupon Thumbling, who had reckoned on this, began to make a tremendous noise inside the poor wolf, screaming and shouting as loud as he could. "Will you be quiet?" said the Wolf; "you will awake the people." "Eh, what!" cried the little man, "since you have satisfied yourself, it is my turn now to make merry;" and he set up a louder howling than before. At last his father and mother awoke, and came to the room and looked through the chinks of the door; and as soon as they perceived the ravages the wolf had committed, they ran and brought, the man his axe, and the woman the scythe. "Stop you behind," said the man, as they entered the room; "if my blow does not kill him, you must give him a cut with your weapon, and chop off his head if you can."

When Thumbling heard his father's voice, he called out, "Father dear, I am here, in the wolf's body." "Heaven be praised!" said the man, full of joy, "our dear child is found again;" and he bade his wife take away the scythe, lest it should do any harm to his son. Then he raised his axe, and gave the wolf, such a blow on its head that it fell dead, and, taking a knife, he cut it open, and released the little fellow his son. "Ah," said his father, "what trouble we have had about you!" "Yes, father," replied Thumbling, "I have been travelling a great deal about the world. Heaven be praised! I breathe fresh air again."

"Where have you been, my son?" he inquired.

"Once I was in a mouse's hole, once inside a cow, and lastly inside that wolf; and now I will stop here with you," said Thumbling.

"Yes," said the old people, "we will not sell you again for all the riches of the world;" and they embraced and kissed him with great affection. Then they gave him plenty to eat and drink, and had new clothes made for him, for his old ones were worn out with travelling.

The Table, the Ass, and the Stick

A LONG while ago there lived a Tailor who had three sons, but only a
single Goat, which, as it had to furnish milk for all, was obliged to
have good fodder every day, and to be led into the meadow for it.
This the sons had to do by turns; and one morning the eldest took
the Goat into the churchyard, where grew the finest herbs, which he
let it eat, and then it frisked about undisturbed till the evening, when
it was time to return; and then he asked, "Goat, are you satisfied?"
The Goat replied,—

> "I am satisfied, quite;
> No more can I bite."

"Then come home," said the youth; and, catching hold of the
rope, he led it to the stall and made it fast. "Now," said the old

Tailor, "has the Goat had its proper food?" "Yes," replied the son, "it has eaten all it can." The father, however, would see for himself; and so, going into the stall, he stroked the Goat, and asked it whether it was satisfied. The Goat replied,—

> "Whereof should I be satisfied?
> I only jumped about the graves,
> And found not a single leaf."

"What do I hear?" exclaimed the Tailor; and ran up to his son and said, "Oh, you bad boy! you said the Goat was satisfied, and then brought it away hungry!" and, taking the yard-measure down from the wall, he hunted his son out of the house in a rage.

The following morning was the second son's turn, and he picked out a place in the garden-hedge, where some very fine herbs grew, which the Goat ate up entirely. When, in the evening, he wanted to return, he asked the Goat first whether it were satisfied, and it replied as before,—

> "I am satisfied, quite;
> No more can I bite."

"Then come home," said the youth, and drove it to its stall, and tied it fast. Soon after the old Tailor asked, "Has the Goat had its usual food?" "Oh, yes!" answered his son; "it ate up all the leaves." But the Tailor would see for himself, and so he went into the stall, and asked the Goat whether it had had enough.

> "Whereof should I be satisfied?
> I only jumped about the hedge,
> And found not a single leaf."

replied the animal.

"The wicked scamp!" exclaimed the Tailor, "to let such a capital animal starve!" and running in-doors, he drove his second son out of the house with his yard-measure.

It was now the third son's turn, and he, willing to make a good beginning, sought some bushes full of beautifully tender leaves, of which he let the Goat partake plentifully; and at evening-time, when he wished to go home, he asked the Goat the same question as the others had done, and received the same answer,—

> "I am satisfied, quite;
> No more can I bite."

So then he led it home, and tied it up in its stall; and presently the old man came and asked whether the Goat had had its regular food, and the youth replied, "Yes." But he would go and see for himself, and then the wicked beast told him, as it had done before,—

> "Whereof should I be satisfied?
> I only jumped about the bush,
> And found not a single leaf."

"Oh, the scoundrel!" exclaimed the Tailor, in a rage; "he is just as careless and forgetful as the others; he shall no longer eat my bread," and rushing into the house, he dealt his youngest son such tremendous blows with the yard-measure, that the boy ran quite away.

The old Tailor was now left alone with his Goat, and the following morning he went to the stall, and fondled the animal, saying, "Come, my dear little creature, I will lead you myself into the meadow;" and, taking the rope, he brought it to some green lettuces, and let it feed to its heart's content. When evening arrived he asked it, as his sons had done before, whether it were satisfied, and it replied,—

> "I am satisfied, quite;
> No more can I bite."

So he led it home, and tied it up in its stall; but, before he left it, he turned round and asked once more, "Are you quite satisfied?" The malicious brute answered in the same manner as before,—

"Whereof should I be satisfied?
I only jumped about the green,
And found not a single leaf."

As soon as the Tailor heard this he was thunderstruck, and perceived directly that he had driven away his three sons without cause. "Stop a bit, you ungrateful beast!" he exclaimed. "To drive you away will be too little punishment; I will mark you so that you shall no more dare to show youself among honourable tailors." So saying, he sprang up with great speed, and, fetching a razor, shaved the Goat's head as bare as the palm of his hand; and, because the yard-measure was too honourable for such service, he laid hold of a whip, and gave the animal such hearty cuts with it, that it ran off as fast as possible.

When the old man sat down again in his house he fell into great grief, and would only have been too happy to have had his three sons back; but no one knew whither they had wandered.

The eldest, however, had gone apprentice to a joiner, with whom he worked industriously and cheerfully; and when his time was out, his master presented him with a table, which had certainly a very ordinary appearance, and was made of common wood; but it had one excellent quality: – If its owner placed it before him, and said, "Table, cover thyself," the good table was at once covered with a fine cloth, and plates, and knives and forks, and dishes of roast and baked meat took their places on it, and a great glass filled with red wine, which gladdened one's heart. Our young fellow thought, "Herewith you have enough for your lifetime," and went, full of glee, about the world, never troubling himself whether the inn were good or bad, or whether it contained anything or nothing. Whenever he pleased he went to no inn at all, but in the field, or wood, or any meadow; in fact, just where he liked to take the table off his back, and set it before him, saying, "Table, cover thyself," he had all he could desire to eat and drink.

At last it came into his head that he would return to his father, whose anger, he thought, would be abated by time, and with whom he might live very comfortably with his excellent table. It fell out that, on his journey home, he one evening arrived at an inn which was full of people, who made him welcome, and invited him to come in and eat with them, or he would get nothing at all. But our Joiner replied, "No; I will not take a couple of bites with you; you must rather be my guests." At this the others laughed, and thought he was making game of them; but he placed his wooden table in the middle of the room, and said, "Table, cover thyself;" and in the twinkling of an eye it was set out with meats as good as any that the host could have furnished, and the smell of which mounted very savoury into the noses of the guests. "Be welcome, good friends," said the Joiner; and the guests, when they saw he was in earnest, waited not to be asked twice, but, quickly seating themselves, set to valiantly with their knives. What made them most wonder, however, was that, when any dish became empty, another full one instantly took its place; and the landlord, who stood in a corner looking on, thought to himself, "You could make good use of such a cook as that in your trade;" but he said nothing. The Joiner and his companions sat making merry till late at night; but at last they went to bed, and the Joiner too, who placed his wishing-table against the wall before going to sleep. The landlord, however, could not get to sleep, for his thoughts troubled him, and, suddenly remembering that there stood in his lumber room an old table which was useless, he went and fetched it, and put it in the place of the wishing-table. The next morning the Joiner counted out his lodging-money, and placed the table on his back, ignorant that it had been changed, and went his way. At noon-day he reached his father's house, and was received with great joy.

"Now, my dear son," said the old man, "what have you learned?"

"I have become a joiner, father."

"A capital trade, too. But what have you brought home with you from your travels?"

"The best thing I have brought," said the youth, "is this table."

The father looked at it on every side, and said, "You have made a very bad hand of that; it is an old worthless table."

"But," interrupted his son, "it is one which covers itself; and when I place it before me and say, 'Table, cover thyself,' it is instantly filled with the most savoury meats and wine, which will make your heart sing. Just invite your friends and acquaintances, and you shall soon see how they will be refreshed and revived."

As soon, then, as the company was arrived he placed his table in the middle of the room, and called out to it to cover itself. But the table did not stir, and remained as empty as any other table which does not understand what is spoken; and the poor Joiner at once perceived that the table was changed, and he was ashamed to appear thus like an impostor before the guests, who laughed at him, and were obliged to go home without eating or drinking. So the father took up his mending again, and stitched away as fast as ever, and the son was obliged to go and work for a master carpenter.

Meanwhile the second son had been living with a miller, and learning his trade, and as soon as his time was up, his master said to him, "Because you have served me so well, I present you with this ass, which has a wonderful gift, although it can neither draw a waggon nor carry a sack." "For what, then, is it useful?" asked the youth. "It speaks gold," replied the miller. "If you tie a pocket under his chin and cry 'Bricklebrit,' then the good beast will pour out gold coin like hail." "That is a very fine thing," thought the youth; and, thanking the master, he went off upon his journey. Now, whenever he needed money, he had only to say to his ass "Bricklebrit," and it rained down gold pieces, so that he had no other trouble than to pick them up again from the ground. Wherever he went, the best only was good enough for him, and the dearer it was the better, for he had always a full purse. When he had looked about him for some time in the world, he thought he would go and visit his father, whose anger he supposed had abated, and, moreover, since he brought with him an ass of gold, he would no doubt receive him gladly. It so happened that he came to the very same inn where his brother's table had been changed, and as he came up, leading his ass by the hand, the landlord would have taken it and tied it up, but our young master said to him, "You need not trouble yourself; I will lead my grey beast myself into the stable and tie him, for I must know where he stands." The landlord wondered at this, and he thought that one who looked after his own beast would not spend much; but presently our friend, dipping into his pocket and taking out two pieces of gold, gave them to him, and bid him fetch the best he could. This made the landlord open his eyes, and he ran and fetched, in a great hurry, the best he could get. When he had finished his meal, the youth asked what further he was indebted, and the landlord, having no mind to spare him, said that a couple of gold pieces more was due. The youth felt in his pocket, but his money was just at an end; so he exclaimed, "Wait a bit, my landlord; I will go and fetch some gold," and, taking the table-cloth with him, he went out. The landlord knew not what to think; but, being covetous, he slunk out after the youth, and, as he bolted the stable-door, the landlord peeped through a hole in the wall. The youth spread the cloth beneath the ass, and then called out "Bricklebrit," and in a moment the beast began to speak out gold, as if rain were falling. "By the powers!" exclaimed the landlord, "ducats are soon coined so: that is not a bad sort of purse!" The youth now paid his bill and laid down to sleep; but in the middle of the night the landlord slipped into the stable and led away the mint-master, and tied up a different ass in its place.

In the morning early, the youth drove away with his ass, thinking it was his own, and at noon-day he arrived at his father's, who was very glad to see him return, and received him kindly. "What trade have you become?" asked the father. "A miller," was the reply. "And what have you brought home with you from your wander-ings?" "Nothing but an ass." "Oh, there are plenty of that sort here now; it had far better been a goat," said the old man. "Yes," replied the son, "but this is no common animal, but one which, when I say 'Bricklebrit,' speaks gold right and left. Just call your friends here, and I will make them all rich in a twinkling." "Well," exclaimed the Tailor, "that would please me very well, and so I need not use my needle any more;" and running out, he called together all his acquaintances. As soon as they were assembled, the young Miller bade them make a circle, and, spreading out a cloth, he brought the ass into the middle of the room. "Now, pay attention," said he to them, and called out "Bricklebrit!" but not a single gold piece fell, and it soon appeared that the ass understood not coining, for it is not every one that can be so taught. The poor young man began to make a long face, when he saw that he had been deceived; and he was obliged to beg pardon of the guests, who were forced to return as poor as they came. So it happened that the old man had to take to his needle again, and the youth to bind himself to another master.

Meanwhile, the third brother had gone to a turner to learn his trade; but he got on very slowly, as it was a very difficult art to acquire. And while he was there, his brothers sent him word how badly things had gone with them, and how the landlord had robbed them of their wishing-gifts on their return home. When the time came round that he had learnt everything and wished to leave, his master presented him with a sack, saying, "In it there lies a stick."

"I will take the sack readily, for it may do me good service," replied the youth. "But what is the stick for? it only makes the sack heavier to carry."

"That I will tell you:– if any one does you an injury, you have only to say, 'Stick, out of the sack!' and instantly the stick will spring out, and dance about on the people's backs in such a style that they will not be able to stir a finger for a week afterwards; and, moreover, it will not leave off till you say, 'Stick, get back into the sack.'"

The youth thanked him, and hung the sack over his shoulders; and when any one came too near, and wished to meddle with him, he said "Stick, come out of the sack," and immediately it sprang out and began laying about it; and when he called it back, it disappeared so quickly that no one could tell where it came from.

One evening he arrived at the inn where his brothers had been basely robbed, and, laying his knapsack on the table, he began to talk of all the wonderful things he had seen in the world. "Yes," said he, "one may find, indeed, a table which supplies itself, and a golden ass, and suchlike things – all very good in their place, and I do not despise them; but they shrink into nothing beside the treasure which I carry with me in this sack."

The landlord pricked up his ears, saying, "What on earth can it be?" but he thought to himself, "The sack is certainly full of precious stones, and I must manage to get hold of them; for all good things come in threes."

As soon as it was bedtime our youth stretched himself upon a bench, and laid his sack down for a pillow; and, when he appeared to be in a deep sleep, the landlord crept softly to him, and began to pull very gently and cautiously at the sack, to see if he could manage to draw it away, and put another in its place. The young Turner, however, had been waiting for him to do this, and, just as the man gave a good pull, he exclaimed, "Stick, out of the sack with you!" Immediately out it jumped, and thumped about on the landlord's back and ribs with a good will.

The landlord began to cry for mercy; but the louder he cried, the more forcibly did the stick beat time on his back, until at last he fell exhausted to the ground.

Then the Turner said, "If you do not give up the table which feeds itself and the golden ass, that dance will commence again."

"No, no!" cried the landlord, in a weak voice; "I will give them up with pleasure, but just let your horrible hobgoblin get back into his sack."

"I will give you pardon, if you do right; but take care what you are about," replied the Turner; and he let him rest, and bade the stick return.

On the following morning the Turner accordingly went away with the table and the ass, on his road home to his father, who, as soon as he saw him, felt very glad, and asked what he had learned in foreign parts.

"Dear father," replied he, "I have become a turner."

"A difficult business that; but what have you brought back with you from your travels?"

"A precious stick," replied the son; "a stick in this sack."

"What!" exclaimed the old man, "a stick! Well, that is worth the trouble! Why, you can cut one from every tree!"

"But not such a stick as this; for, if I say, 'Stick, out of the sack,' it instantly jumps out and executes such a dance upon the back of any one who would injure me, that at last he is beaten to the ground, crying for mercy. Do you see, with this stick I have got back again the wonderful table and the golden ass of which the thievish landlord robbed my brothers? Now, let them both be summoned home, and invite all your acquaintances, and I will not only give them plenty to eat and drink, but pocketsful of money."

The old Tailor would scarcely believe him; but, nevertheless, he called in his friends. Then the young Turner placed a tablecloth in the middle of the room, and led in the ass, saying to his brother, "Now, speak to him."

The Miller called out "Bricklebrit!" and in a moment the gold pieces dropped down on the floor in a pelting shower; and so it continued, until they had all so much that they could carry no more. (I fancy my readers would have been very happy to have been there too!)

After this the table was fetched in, and the Joiner said, "Table, cover thyself;" and it was at once filled with the choicest dishes. Then they began such a meal as the Tailor had never had before in his house; and the whole company remained till late at night merry and jovial.

The next day the Tailor forsook needle and thread, and put them all away, with his measures and goose, in a cupboard, and for ever after lived happily and contentedly with his three sons.

But now I must tell you what became of the Goat, whose fault it was that the three brothers were driven away. It was so ashamed of its bald head that it ran into a Fox's hole and hid itself. When the Fox came home he saw a pair of great eyes looking at him in the darkness, which so frightened him that he ran back, and presently met a Bear, who perceiving how terrified Reynard appeared, said to him, "What is the matter, Brother Fox, that you make such a face?"

"Ah!" he replied, "in my hole sits a horrible beast, who glared at me with most fiery eyes."

"Oh! we will soon drive it out," said the Bear; and going up to the hole he peeped in himself; but as soon as he saw the fiery eyes, he also turned tail, and would have nothing to do with the terrible beast, and so took to flight. On his way a Bee met him, and soon saw he could not feel much through his thick coat; and so she said, "You are making a very rueful face, Mr Bear; pray, where have you left your merry one?"

"Why," answered Bruin, "a great horrible beast has laid himself down in Reynard's house, and glares there with such fearful eyes, we cannot drive him out."

"Well, Mr Bear," said the Bee, "I am sorry for you; I am a poor creature whom you never notice, but yet I believe I can help you."

So saying, she flew into the Fox's hole, and settling on the clean shaved head of the Goat, stung it so dreadfully that the poor animal sprang up and ran madly off; and nobody knows to this hour where it ran to.

The Golden Bird

A LONG, long while ago there was a King who had, adjoining his palace, a fine pleasure-garden, in which stood a tree, which bore golden apples, and as soon as the apples were ripe they were counted, but the next day one was missing. This vexed the King very much, and he ordered that watch should be kept every night beneath the tree; and having three sons he sent the eldest, when evening set in, into the garden; but about midnight the youth fell into a deep sleep, and in the morning another apple was missing. The next night the second son had to watch, but he also fared no better; for about midnight he fell fast asleep, and another apple was wanting in the morning. The turn came now to the third son, who was eager to go; but the King hesitated for a long time, thinking he would be even less wakeful than his brothers, but at last he consented. The youth lay down under the tree and watched steadily, without letting sleep be his master; and just as twelve o'clock struck something rustled in the air, and, looking up, he saw a bird flying by, whose feathers were of bright gold. The bird lighted upon the tree, and had just picked off one of the apples, when the youth shot a bolt at it, which did not prevent its flying away, but one of its golden feathers dropped off. The youth took the feather up, and, showing it the next morning to the King, told him what he had seen during the night. Thereupon the King assembled his council, and every one declared that a single feather like this was worth a kingdom. "Well, then," said the King, "if this feather is so costly, I must and will have the whole bird, for one feather is of no use to me." The eldest son was now sent out on his travels, and, relying on his own prudence, he doubted not that he should find the Golden Bird. When he had walked about a mile he saw sitting at the edge of a forest a Fox, at which he levelled his gun; but it cried out, "Do not shoot me, and I will give you a piece of good advice! You are now on the road to the Golden Bird, and this evening you will come into a village where two inns stand opposite to each other: one will be brightly lit up and much merriment will be going on inside, but turn not in there; enter rather into the other, though it seem a poor place to you."

The young man, however, thought to himself, "How can such a silly beast give me rational advice?" and, going nearer, he shot at the Fox; but he missed, and the Fox ran away with its tail in the air.

THE GOLDEN BIRD

After this adventure he walked on, and towards evening he came to the village where stood the two public-houses, in one of which singing and dancing were going on; while the other looked a very ill-conditioned house. "I should be a simpleton," said he to himself, "if I were to go into this dirty inn while that capital one stood opposite." So he entered the dancing-room, and there, living in feasting and rioting, he forgot the Golden Bird, his father, and all good manners.

As time passed by and the eldest son did not return home, the second son set out also on his travels to seek the Golden Bird. The Fox met him as it had its brother, and gave him good counsel, which he did not follow. He likewise arrived at the two inns, and out of the window of the riotous house his brother leaned, and invited him in. He could not resist, and entered, and lived there only to gratify his pleasures.

Again a long time elapsed with no news of either brother, and the youngest wished to go and try his luck; but his father would not consent. "It is useless," said he; "you are still less likely than your brothers to find the Golden Bird, and, if a misfortune should happen to you, you cannot help yourself, for you are not very quick." The King at last, however, was forced to consent, for he had no rest while he refused.

On the edge of the forest the Fox was again sitting, and again it offered in return for its life the same piece of good advice. The youth was good-hearted, and said, "Be not afraid, little Fox; I will do you no harm."

"You shall not repent of your goodness," replied the Fox; "but that you may travel quicker, get up behind on my tail."

Scarcely had he seated himself when away they went, over hedges and ditches, uphill and downhill, so fast that their hair whistled in the wind.

As soon as they arrived at the village the youth dismounted, and, following the advice he had received, turned, without looking round, into the mean-looking house, where he passed the night comfortably. The next morning, when he went into the fields, he found the Fox already there, who said, "I will tell you what further you must do. Go straight forwards, and you will come to a castle, before which a whole troop of soldiers will be sleeping and snoring; be not frightened at them, but go right through the middle of the troop into the castle, and through all the rooms, till you come into a chamber where a Golden Bird hangs in a wooden cage. Near by stands an empty golden cage for show, but take care you do not take the bird out of its ugly cage to place it in the golden one, or you will fare badly." With these words the Fox again stretched out its tail, and the King's son mounting as before, away they went over hill and valley, while their hair whistled in the wind from the pace they travelled at. When they arrived at the castle the youth found everything as the Fox had said. He soon discovered the room where the Golden Bird sat in its wooden cage, and by it stood the golden one, and three golden apples were lying around. The youth thought it would be a pity to take the bird in such an ugly and dirty cage, and, opening the door, he put it in the splendid one. At the moment he did this the bird set up a piercing shriek, which woke the soldiers, who started up and made him a prisoner. The next morning he was brought to trial, and when he confessed all he was condemned to death. Still the King said he would spare his life under one condition; namely, if he brought to him the Golden Horse, which travelled faster than the wind, and then for a reward he should also receive the Golden Bird.

The young Prince walked out, sighing and sorrowful, for where was he to find the Golden Horse? All at once he saw his old friend the Fox, who said, "There, you see what has happened, because you did not mind what I said. But be of good courage; I will protect you, and tell you where you may find the horse. You must follow this road straight till you come to a castle: in the stable there this horse stands. Before the door a boy will lie fast asleep and snoring, so you must lead away the horse quietly; but there is one thing you must mind: put on his back the old saddle of wood and leather, and not the golden one which hangs close by, for if you do it will be very unlucky." So saying the Fox stretched out its tail, and again, they went as fast as the wind. Everything was as the Fox had said, and the youth went into the stall where the Golden Horse was; but, as he was about to put on the dirty saddle, he thought it would be a shame if he did not put on such a fine animal the saddle which appeared to belong to him, and so he took up the golden saddle. Scarcely had it touched the back of the horse when it set up a loud neigh, which awoke the stable-boys, who put our hero into confinement. The next morning he was condemned to death; but the King promised to give him his life and the horse, if he would bring the Beautiful Daughter of the King of the Golden Castle.

With a heavy heart the youth set out, and by great good fortune soon met the Fox. "I should have left you in your misfortune," it said; "but I felt compassion for you, and I am willing once more to help you out of your trouble. Your road to the palace lies straight before you, and when you arrive there, about evening, wait till night, when the Princess goes to take a bath. As soon as she enters the bath-house, do you spring up and give her a kiss, and she will follow you wheresoever you will; only take care that she does not take leave of her parents first, or all will be lost."

With these words the Fox again stretched out its tail, and the King's son seating himself thereon, away they went over hill and valley like the wind. When they arrived at the Golden Palace, the youth found everything as the Fox had foretold, and he waited till midnight when everybody was in a deep sleep, and at that hour the beautiful Princess went to her bath, and he sprang up instantly and kissed her. The Princess said she was willing to go with him, but begged him earnestly, with tears in her eyes, to permit her first to take leave of her parents. At first he withstood her prayers; but, when she wept still more, and even fell at his feet, he at last consented. Scarcely had the maiden stepped up to her father's bedside, when he awoke, and all the others who were asleep awakening too, the poor youth was captured and put in prison.

The next morning the King said to him, "Thy life is forfeited, and thou canst only find mercy if thou clearest away the mountain which lies before my window, and over which I cannot see; but thou must remove it within eight days. If thou accomplish this, then thou shalt have my daughter as a reward."

The King's son at once began digging and shovelling away; but when, after seven days, he saw how little was effected and that all his work went for nothing, he fell into great grief and gave up all hope. But on the evening of the seventh day the Fox appeared and said, "You do not deserve that I should notice you again, but go away and sleep while I work for you."

When he awoke the next morning, and looked out of the window, the hill had disappeared, and he hastened to the King full of joy, and told him the conditions were fulfilled; and now, whether he liked it or not, the King was obliged to keep his word, and give up his daughter.

Away then went these two together, and no long time had passed before they met the faithful Fox. "You have the best certainly," said he, "but to the Maid of the Golden Castle belongs also the Golden Horse."

"How shall I obtain it?" inquired the youth.

"That I will tell you," answered the Fox; "first take to the King who sent you to the Golden Castle the beautiful Princess. Then there will be unheard-of joy, and they will readily show you the Golden Horse and give it to you. Do you mount it, and then give your hand to each for a parting shake, and last of all to the Princess, whom you must keep tight hold of, and pull her up behind you, and as soon as that is done ride off, and no one can pursue you, for the horse goes as fast as the wind." All this was happily accomplished, and the King's son led away the beautiful Princess in triumph on the Golden Horse. The Fox did not remain behind, and said to the Prince, "Now I will help you to the Golden Bird. When you come near the castle where it is, let the maiden get down, and I will take her into my cave. Then do you ride into the castle-yard, and at the sight of you there will be such joy that they will readily give you the bird; and as soon as you hold the cage in your hand ride back to us, and fetch again the maiden."

As soon as this deed was done, and the Prince had ridden back with his treasure, the Fox said, "Now you must reward me for my services."

"What do you desire?" asked the youth.

"When we come into yonder wood, shoot me dead and cut off my head and feet."

"That were a curious gratitude," said the Prince; "I cannot possibly do that."

"If you will not do it, I must leave you," replied the Fox; "but before I depart I will give you one piece of counsel. Beware of these two points: buy no gallows-flesh, and sit not on the brink of a spring!" With these words it ran into the forest.

The young Prince thought, "Ah, that is a wonderful animal, with some curious fancies! Who would buy gallows-flesh? and I don't see the pleasure of sitting on the brink of a spring!" Onwards he rode with his beautiful companion, and by chance the way led him through the village where his two brothers had stopped. There he found a great uproar and lamentation; and when he asked the reason, he was told that two persons were about to be hanged. When he came nearer, he saw that they were his two brothers, who had done some villanous deeds, besides spending all their money. He inquired if they could not be freed, and was told by the people that he might buy them off if he would, but they were not worth his gold, and deserved nothing but hanging. Nevertheless, he did not hesitate, but paid down the money and his two brothers were released.

After this they all four set out in company, and soon came to the forest where they had first met the Fox; and as it was cool and pleasant beneath the trees, for the sun was very hot, the two brothers said, "Come, let us rest awhile here by this spring, and eat and drink." The youngest consented, forgetting in the heat of conversation the warning he had received, and feeling no anxiety; but all at once the brothers threw him backwards into the water, and taking the maiden, the horse, and the bird, went home to their father. "We bring you," said they to him, "not only the Golden Bird, but also the Golden Horse and the Princess of the Golden Castle." At their arrival there was great joy; but the Horse would not eat, the Bird would not sing, and the Maiden would not speak, but wept bitterly from morning to night.

The youngest brother, however, was not dead. The spring, by

great good luck, was dry, and he fell upon soft moss without any injury; but he could not get out again. Even in this necessity the faithful Fox did not leave him, but soon came up, and scolded him for not following its advice. "Still I cannot forsake you," it said; "but I will again help you to escape. Hold fast upon my tail, and I will draw you up to the top." When this was done, the Fox said, "You are not yet out of danger, for your brothers are not confident of your death, and have set spies all round the forest, who are to kill you if they should see you."

The youth thereupon changed clothes with a poor old man who was sitting near, and in that guise went to the King's palace. Nobody knew him; but instantly the Bird began to sing, the Horse began to eat, and the beautiful Maiden ceased weeping. Bewildered at this change, the King asked what it meant. "I know not," replied the Maiden; "but I who was sad am now gay, for I feel as if my true husband were returned." Then she told him all that had happened; although the other brothers had threatened her with death if she disclosed anything. The King summoned before him all the people who were in the castle, and among them came the poor youth, dressed as a beggar, in his rags; but the Maiden knew him, and fell upon his neck. The wicked brothers were seized and tried; but the youngest married the Princess, and succeeded to the King's inheritance.

But what happened to the poor Fox? Long after, the Prince went once again into the wood, and there met the Fox, who said, "You have now everything that you can desire, but to my misfortunes there is no end, although it lies in your power to release me." And, with tears, it begged the Prince to cut off its head and feet. At last he did so; and scarcely was it accomplished when the Fox became a man, who was no other than the brother of the Princess, delivered at length from the charm which bound him. From that day nothing was ever wanting to the happiness of the Hero of the Golden Bird.

The Travels of Thumbling

A CERTAIN Tailor had a son who was so very diminutive in stature
that he went by the nickname of Thumbling; but the little fellow had
a great deal of courage in his soul, and one day he said to his father,
"I must and will travel a little." "You are very right, my son,"
replied his father; "take a long darning-needle with you, and stick a
lump of sealing-wax on the end of it, and then you will have a sword
to travel with."

Now, the Tailor would eat once more with his son, and so he
skipped into the kitchen to see what his wife had cooked for their last
meal. It was just ready, however, and the dish stood upon the hearth,
and he asked his wife what it was.

"You can see for yourself," replied she.

Just then Thumbling jumped on the fender and peeped into the
pot; but, happening to stretch his neck too far over the edge of it, the

smoke of the hot meat carried him up the chimney. For a little distance he rode on the smoke in the air; but at last he sank down on the earth. The little tailor was now embarked in the wide world, and went and engaged with a master in his trade; but with him the eating was not good, so Thumbling said to the mistress, "If you do not give us better food, I shall leave you, and early tomorrow morning write on your door with chalk, 'Too many potatoes, too little meat; adieu, my lord potato-king.'" "What do you think you will do, grasshopper?" replied the mistress, and in a passion she snatched up a piece of cloth, and would have given him a thrashing; but the little fellow crept nimbly under a thimble, and peeped out beneath at the mistress, and made faces at her. So she took up the thimble and tried to catch him; but Thumbling skipped into the cloth, and as she threw it away to look for him he slipped into the crevice of the table. "He, he, he, old mistress!" laughed he, putting his head up; and when she would have hit him, he dropped down into the drawer beneath. At last however, she did catch him, and hunted him out of the house.

The little tailor wandered about till he came to a great forest, where he met a band of robbers who were going to steal the King's treasure. As soon as they saw the tailor, they thought to themselves, "Ah, such a little fellow as that can creep through the keyhole and serve us as a picklock!" "Hilloa!" cried one, "you Goliath, will you go with us to the treasure chamber? You can easily slip in, and hand us out the gold and silver."

Thumbling considered for a while, and at last consented and went with them to the palace. Then he looked all over the doors to see if there were any chinks, and presently discovered one which was just wide enough for him to get through. Just as he was about to creep in one of the watchmen at the door saw him, and said to the other, "What ugly spider is that crawling there? I will crush it."

"Oh, let the poor thing be," said the other; "he has done nothing to you." So Thumbling got luckily through the chink into the chamber, and, opening the window beneath which the robbers stood, threw out, one by one, the silver dollars. Just as the tailor was in the heat of his work, he heard the King coming to visit his treasure-chamber, and in a great hurry he hid himself. The King observed that many dollars were gone; but he could not imagine who could have stolen them, for the locks and bolts were all fast, and everything appeared quite safe. So he went away again, and said to the watchmen, "Have a care! there is some one at my gold." Presently Thumbling began his work again, and the watchmen heard the gold moving, chinking, and falling down with a ring; so they sprang in, and would have seized the thief. But the tailor, when he heard them coming, was still quicker, and ran into a corner and covered himself over with a dollar, so that nothing of him could be seen. Then he called to the watchmen, "Here I am!" and they went up to the place; but before they could search he was in another corner, crying, "Ha, ha! here I am!" The watchmen turned there, but he was off again in a third corner, crying, "He, he, he! here I am!" So it went on, Thumbling making fools of them each time; and they ran here and there so often about the chamber, that at last they were wearied out and went away. Then he threw the dollars out as before; and, when he came to the last, he gave it a tremendous jerk, and, jumping out after it, flew down upon it to the ground. The robbers praised him very highly, saying, "You are a mighty hero; will you be our captain?" Thumbling refused, as he wished first to see the world. So they shared the booty among them; but the little tailor only took a farthing, because he could not carry any more.

After this deed he buckled his sword again round his body, and, bidding the robbers good day, set out further on his travels. He went to several masters seeking work; but none of them would have him, and at last he engaged himself as waiter at an inn. The maids, however, could not bear him, for he could see them without their seeing him, and he gave information to the master of what they took secretly from the larder, and how they helped themselves out of the cellar. So the servants determined among themselves to serve him out by playing him some trick. Not long afterwards one of them was mowing grass in the garden, and saw Thumbling skipping about from daisy to daisy, so she mowed down in a great hurry the grass where he was, and tying it in a bundle together threw it slily into the cows' stall. A great black cow instantly swallowed it up, and Thumbling, too, without injuring him; but he was not at all pleased, for it was a very dark place, and no light to be seen at all! While the cow was being milked, Thumbling called out, "Holloa! when will that pail be full?" but the noise of the running milk prevented his being heard. By-and-bye the master came into the stable and said, "This cow must be killed to-morrow!" This speech made Thumbling tremble, and he shouted out in a shrill tone, "Let me out first, I say; let me out!"

The master heard him but could not tell where the voice came from, and he asked, "Where are you?"

"In the dark," replied Thumbling; but this the master could not understand, so he went away.

The next morning the cow was killed. Happily Thumbling escaped without a wound from all the cutting and carving, and was sent away in the sausage-meat. As soon as the butcher began his work, he cried with all his might, "Don't chop too deep! don't chop too deep!" But the whirring of the cleaver again prevented his being heard. Necessity is the mother of invention, and so Thumbling set his wits to work, and jumped so cleverly out between the cuts, that he came off with a whole skin. He was not able to get away very far, but fell into the basin where the fragments were, and presently he was rolled up in a skin for a sausage. He found his quarters here very narrow, but afterwards, when he was hung up in the chimney to be smoked, the time appeared dreadfully long to him. At last, one day he was taken down, for a guest was to be entertained with a sausage. When the good wife cut the sausage in half, he took care not to stretch out his neck too far, lest it should be cut through. Then, seizing his opportunity, he made a jump, and sprang quite out.

In this house, however, where thing had gone so badly, the little tailor would not stop any longer; so he set out again on his travels. His liberty did not last very long. In the open fields he met a Fox, who snapped him up in a twinkling. "Ah, Mr Fox," called Thumbling, "I don't want to stick here in your throat; let me out again."

"You are right," replied the Fox, "you are no use there; but if you will promise me all the hens in your father's farmyard, I will let you off scot-free."

"With all my heart," said Thumbling; "you shall have all the fowls, I promise you."

Then the Fox let him out, and carried him home; and as soon as the farmer saw his dear son again, he gave all the hens instantly to the Fox as his promised reward. Thereupon Thumbling pulled out the farthing which he had earned upon his wanderings, and said, "See I have brought home with me a beautiful piece of gold."

"But why did they give the Fox the poor little hens to gobble up?"

"Why, you simpleton, don't you think your father would rather have his dear child than all the fowls in his farmyard!"

The Godfather Death

A CERTAIN poor man had twelve children, and was obliged to work day and night to find them bread to eat; but when the thirteenth child was born, he ran out in despair on the highroad to ask the first person he should meet to stand godfather to it.

Presently he met Death striding along on his withered legs, who said, "Take me for godfather." The man asked him who he was, and received for reply, "I am Death, who make all things equal." "Then," answered the man, "you are the right person – you make no difference between the rich and poor; you shall be godfather to my boy."

Death replied, "I will make your child rich and famous; he who has me for a friend can need nought." Then the man told him the christening was fixed for the following Sunday, and invited him to come; and at the right time he did appear, and acted very becomingly on the occasion.

When the boy arrived at years of discretion, the godfather came and took him away with him, and leading him into a forest showed him a herb which grew there. "Now," said Death, "you shall receive your christening gift. I will make you a famous physician. Every time you are called to a sick person I will appear to you. If I stand at the head of your patient, you may speak confidently that you can restore him, and if you give him a morsel of that vegetable he will speedily get well, but if I stand at the feet of the sick he is mine, and you may say all medicine is in vain, for the best physician in the world could not cure him. Dare not, however, use the herb against my will, for then it will go ill with you."

In a very short space of time the youth became the most renowned physician in the world. "He only wants just to see the sick person, and he knows instantly whether he will live or die," said every one to his neighbour; and so it came to pass, that from far and near people came to him, bringing him the sick, and giving him so much money that he soon became a very rich man. Once it happened that the King fell sick, and our Physician was called in to say if recovery were possible. When he came to the bedside, he saw that Death stood at the feet of the King. "Ah," thought he, "if I might this once cheat Death; he will certainly take offence; but then I am his godchild, and perhaps he will shut his eyes to it, – I will venture."

So saying he took up the sick man, and turned him round, so that Death stood at the head of the King; then he gave the King some of the herb, and he instantly rose up quite refreshed.

Soon afterwards Death, with an angry and gloomy face, came to the Physician, and pressed him on the arm, saying, "You have put my light out, but this time I will excuse you, because you are my godchild; however, do not dare to act so again, for it will cost you your life, and I shall come and take you away."

Soon after this event the daughter of the King fell into a serious illness, and, as she was his only child, he wept day and night until his eyes were almost blinded. He also caused to be made known, that whoever saved her life should receive her for a bride, and inherit his crown. When the Physician came to the bedside of the sick, he perceived Death at her feet, and he remembered the warning of his god-father; but the great beauty of the Princess, and the fortune which her husband would receive, so influenced him that he cast all other thoughts to the wind. He would not see that Death cast angry looks at him, and threatened him with his fist; but he raised up his patient, and laid her head where her feet had been. Then he gave her a portion of the wonderful herb, and soon her cheeks regained their colour, and her blood circulated freely.

When Death thus saw his kingdom a second time invaded, and his power mocked, he strode up swiftly to the side of the Physician and said, "Now is your turn come;" and he struck him with his icy-cold hand so hard, that the Physician was unable to resist, and was obliged to follow Death to his underground abode. There the Physician saw thousands upon thousands of lamps burning in immeasurable rows, some large, others small, and others yet smaller. Every moment some were extinguished, but others in the same instant blazed out, so that the flames appeared to dance up here and there in continual variation.

"Do you see?" said Death. "These are the lamps of men's lives. The larger ones belong to children, the next to those in the flower of their age, and the smallest to the aged and grey-headed. Yet some of the children and youth in the world have but the smallest lamps."

The Physician begged to be shown his own lamp, and Death pointed to one almost expiring, saying, "There, that is thine."

"Ah, my dear godfather," exclaimed the Physician, frightened, "kindle a new one for me; for your love of me do it, that I may enjoy some years of life, marry the Princess, and come to the crown."

"I cannot," answered Death; "one lamp must be extinguished before another can be lighted."

"Then place the old one over a new lamp, that its dying fire may kindle a fresh blaze," said the Physician, entreatingly.

Death made as if he would perform his wish, and prepared a large and fresh lamp; but he did it very slowly, in order to revenge himself, and the little flame died before he finished. Then the Physician sank to the earth, and fell forever into the hands of Death!

The Robber-Bridegroom

THERE was once a Miller who had a beautiful daughter, whom he much wished to see well married. Not long after there came a man who appeared very rich, and the Miller, not knowing anything to his disadvantage, promised his daughter to him. The maiden, however, did not take a fancy to this suitor, nor could she love him as a bride should; and, moreover, she had no confidence in him, but as often as she looked at him, or thought about him, her heart sank within her. Once he said to her, "You are my bride, yet you never visit me." The maiden answered "I do not know where your house is." "It is deep in the shades of the forest," said the man. Then the maiden tried to excuse herself by saying she should not be able to find it; but the Bridegroom said, "Next Sunday you must come and visit me; I have already invited guests, and, in order that you may find your way through the forest, I will strew the path with ashes."

When Sunday came, the maiden prepared to set out; but she felt very anxious and knew not why, and, in order that she might know her way back, she filled her pockets with beans and peas. These she threw to the right and left of the path of ashes, which she followed till it led her into the thickest part of the forest; there she came to a solitary house, which looked so gloomy and desolate that she felt quite miserable. She went in, but no one was there, and the most profound quiet reigned throughout. Suddenly a voice said—

"Return, fair maid, return to your home;
'Tis to a murderer's den you've come."

The maiden looked round, and perceived that it was a bird in a cage against the wall which sang the words. Once more it uttered them—

"Return, fair maid, return to your home;
'Tis to a murderer's den you've come."

The maiden went from one room to the other, through the whole house, but all were empty, and not a human being was to be seen anywhere. At last she went into the cellar, and there sat a withered old woman, shaking her head. "Can you tell me," asked the maiden, "whether my bridegroom lives in this house?"

"Ah, poor girl," said the old woman, "when are you to be

married? You are in a murderer's den. You think to be a bride, and to celebrate your wedding, but you will only wed with Death! See here, I have a great cauldron filled with water, and if you fall into their power they will kill you without mercy, cook, and eat you, for they are cannibals. If I do not have compassion and save you, you are lost."

So saying, the old woman led her behind a great cask, where no one could see her. "Be as still as a mouse," said she, "and don't move hand or foot, or all is lost. At night, when the robbers are asleep, we will escape; I have long sought an opportunity." She had scarcely finished speaking when the wicked band returned, dragging with them a poor girl, to whose shrieks and cries they paid no attention. They gave her some wine to drink, three glasses, one white, one red, and one yellow, and at the last she fell down in a swoon. Meanwhile the poor Bride behind the cask trembled and shuddered to see what a fate would have been hers. Presently one of the robbers remarked a gold ring on the finger of the girl, and, as he could not draw it off easily, he took a hatchet and chopped off the finger. But the finger, with the force of the blow, flew up and fell behind the cask, right into the lap of the Bride; and the robber, taking a light, went to seek it, but could not find it. Then one of the others asked, "Have you looked behind the cask?"

"Oh! do come and eat," cried the old woman in fright; "come and eat, and leave your search till the morning: the finger will not run away."

"The old woman is right," said the robbers, and, desisting from their search, they sat down to their meal; and the old woman mixed with their drink a sleeping draught, so that presently they lay down to sleep on the floor and snored away. As soon as the Bride heard them, she came from behind the cask and stepped carefully over the sleepers, who lay side by side, fearing to awake any of them. Heaven helped her in her trouble, and she got over this difficulty well; and the old woman started up too and opened the door, and then they made as much haste as they could out of the murderers' den. The wind had blown away the ashes, but the beans and peas the Bride had scattered in the morning had sprouted up, and now showed the path in the moonlight. All night long they walked on, and by sunrise they came to the mill, and the poor girl narrated her adventures to her father the Miller.

Now, when the day came that the wedding was to be celebrated, the Bridegroom appeared, and the Miller gathered together all his relations and friends. While they sat at table each kept telling some tale, but the Bride sat silent, listening. Presently the Bridegroom said, "Can you not tell us something, my heart; do not you know of anything to tell?"

"Yes," she replied, "I will tell you a dream of mine. I thought I went through a wood, and by-and-bye I arrived at a house wherein there was not a human being, but on the wall there hung a bird in a cage, which sang—

'Return, fair maid, return to your home;
'Tis to a murderer's den you've come.'

And it sang this twice. – My treasure, thus dreamed I. – Then I went through all the rooms, and every one was empty and desolate, and at last I stepped down into the cellar, and there sat a very old woman, shaking her head from side to side. I asked her, 'Does my Bridegroom dwell in this house?' and she replied, 'Ah, dear child, you have fallen into a murderer's den; thy lover does dwell here, but he will kill you.' – My treasure, thus dreamed I. – Then I thought that the old woman hid me behind a great cask, and scarcely had she done so when the robbers came home, dragging a maiden with them, to whom they gave three glasses of wine, one red, one white, and one yellow; and at the third her heart snapped. – My treasure, thus dreamed I. – Then one of the robbers saw a gold ring on her finger, and because he could not draw it off he took up a hatchet and hewed at it, and the finger flew up, and fell behind the cask into my lap. And there is the finger with the ring!"

With these words she threw it down before him, and showed it to all present.

The Robber, who during her narration had become pale as death, now sprang up, and would have escaped; but the guests held him, and delivered him up to the judges.

And soon afterwards he and his whole band were condemned to death for their wicked deeds.

The Old Witch

THERE was once a little girl who was very obstinate and wilful, and who never obeyed when her elders spoke to her; and so how could she be happy? One day she said to her parents, "I have heard so much of the old Witch, that I will go and see her. People say she is a wonderful old woman, and has many marvellous things in her house; and I am very curious to see them."

Her parents, however, forbade her going, saying, "The Witch is a wicked old woman, who performs many godless deeds; and if you go near her, you are no longer a child of ours."

The girl, however, would not turn back at her parents' command, but went to the Witch's house. When she arrived there the woman asked her, "Why are you so pale?"

"Ah," replied she, trembling all over, "I have frightened myself so with what I have just seen."

"And what did you see?" inquired the old Witch.

"I saw a black man on your steps."

"That was a collier," replied she.

"Then I saw a grey man."

"That was a sportsman," said the old woman.

"After him I saw a blood-red man."

"That was a butcher," replied the woman.

"But oh, I was most terrified," continued the girl, "when I peeped through your window, and saw not you, but a creature with a fiery head."

"Then you have seen the Witch in her proper dress," said the old woman; "for you I have long waited, and now you shall give me light." So saying, she changed the girl into a block of wood, and then threw it into the fire; and when it was fully alight she sat down on the hearth, warmed herself, and said, "Ah, now for once it burns brightly!"

Herr Korbes

THERE once lived a Cock and a Hen, who agreed to set out on their travels together. The Cock, therefore, bought a smart carriage, which had four red wheels, and to which he harnessed four little Mice; and then the Hen got inside along with him, and they set off together. They had not gone far, when they met a Cat, who asked them where they were going. The Cock answered, "To Herr Korbes." "Will you take me with you?" said the Cat. "Oh, yes, willingly; but get up behind, for you might fall out in front, and take care that you do not dirty my red wheels," replied the Cock; and then he cried, "Now, turn away, little Wheels, and hurry on, little Mice, or we shall be too late to find Herr Korbes at home."

On the road there afterwards came a Grindstone, a Pin, an Egg, a Duck, and, last of all, a Needle, and every one mounted into the carriage and went on with it. When they arrived at the house, Herr Korbes was not at home, so the mice drew the carriage into the barn, the Cock and Hen flew on to a perch, the Cat seated herself on the hearth, the Duck perched on a water-butt, the Egg wrapped itself up in the towel, the Pin hid itself in the cushion of a chair, the Needle jumped on to the bed and buried itself in the pillow, and the Grindstone placed itself just over the door. Soon afterwards Herr Korbes returned, and going to the hearth poked the fire; then the Cat threw the ashes in his face. He ran into the kitchen to wash himself, and the Duck spirted the water in his eyes; so he took up the towel to wipe them, and the Egg broke and ran about over his chin. All these mishaps made him feel tired, and he dropped into a chair to rest himself; but the Pin was there before him, and made him jump up in a rage and throw himself on the bed; where the Needle in the pillow pricked him so that he shouted with pain, and ran in terrible wrath out of the room. Just as he got to the door, the Stone fell down on his head, and knocked him down on the spot.

So we conclude that this Herr Korbes must have been a very bad man.

The Feather Bird

ONCE upon a time there lived a Sorcerer, who used to take the form of a beggar, and go begging before the houses, and stealing little girls, and nobody knew where he took them. One day he appeared before the house of a man who had three pretty daughters, disguised as a poor, weak, old cripple, carrying a sack on his back to put all his alms in. He begged for something to eat, and when the eldest girl came out and offered him a piece of bread, he only touched her and she was compelled to jump into his sack. Then he hurried away with great strides, and carried her through a dark forest to his house, in which everything was very splendid. There he gave her what she wished, and told her, "All will be well with you, for you will have all your heart can desire." This lasted two days, and he then said, "I must be off and leave you for a short time alone: these are the house-keeping keys, you can look over everything; but into one room which this little key unlocks, I forbid you to enter on pain of death." He gave her also an egg, saying, "Preserve this carefully for me, and always carry it about with you; for if it be lost, a great misfortune will happen."

She took the key and the egg and promised all he required; but as soon as he was gone her curiosity overmastered her, and after she had looked over the whole house, from attic to cellar, she unlocked the forbidden door and went in. She was terribly frightened when she entered the room, for in the middle there stood a large basin, wherein was some blood. In her terror the egg fell from her hand, and rolled into the basin; and although she fished it out again directly, and wiped it, it was of no use, for, scrub and wash all she might, the blood appeared as fresh as ever. The next day the Sorcerer came home, and demanded the key and the egg. She handed them to him with trembling; and he instantly perceived that she had been into the forbidden chamber. "Have you then dared to enter that room against my will?" said he; "then now you enter it again against yours. Your life is forfeited." So saying he drew her in by the hair and locked her up.

"Now I will fetch the second one," said the Sorcerer to himself: and, assuming the disguise of a begger, he went and begged before the house. Then the second girl brought him a piece of bread, and he seized her, as the first, and bore her away. It happened to her as it had to her eldest sister, curiosity led her astray, and on the Sorcerer's return she was locked up for having opened the forbidden door.

He went now and fetched the third sister; but she was prudent and cunning. As soon as he had given her his directions and had ridden away, she first carefully laid by the egg, and then went and opened the forbidden chamber. Ah, what a scene! She saw her two dear sisters lying there half starved. She raised them, however, and gave them food, and soon they got well and were very happy, and kissed and embraced one another.

On his return the Sorcerer demanded the key and the egg; and when he could find no spot of blood on them, he said to the maiden, "You have withstood temptation; you shall be my bride, and whatever you desire, that will I do."

"Very well," she replied; then first you must take my father and mother a sackful of gold, and you must carry it yourself on your back; in the meantime I will arrange the wedding." Then she ran to her sisters, whom she had concealed in a chamber, and said, "The moment has arrived when I can save you; the Sorcerer himself shall carry you away; and as soon as you arrive at our home, send me help." Then she placed them both in a sack, and covered them over with gold, so that nothing of them could be seen; and then, calling the Sorcerer in, she said, "Now, carry away the sack; but I shall peep through my window, and keep a sharp look-out that you do not rest at all on your journey."

The Sorcerer raised the sack on his shoulder, and went away with it; but it weighed so heavily that the perspiration ran down his face. Presently he wished to rest a minute, but a voice called to him out of the sack, "I am looking through my window, and see that you are stopping: will you go on?" He thought it was his Bride calling to him, so he instantly got up again. A little further he would have rested again; but the same voice called, "I am looking through my window, and see that you are stopping; will you go on again?" And as often as he stopped he heard the same words; and so he was obliged to keep on, until he at last arrived, exhausted and out of breath, with the sack of gold at the house of the father and mother.

Meanwhile, at home the Bride prepared the wedding-feast, and invited the friends of the Sorcerer to come. Then she took a turnip and cut out places for the eyes and teeth, and put a head-dress on it and a crown of flowers, and set it at the topmost window, and left it there peeping down. As soon as all was ready she dipped herself in a cask full of honey, and then ripping up the bed, she rolled herself among the feathers until she looked like marvellous bird, whom no one could possibly recognise. After this she went out of the house; and on the way some of the wedding-guests met her, and asked her whence she came; and she replied, "I come from the house of the Feather King."

"How does the young Bride?" asked they.

"She has taken herself to the top of the house, and is peeping out of the window."

Soon after the Bridegroom met her as he was slowly travelling back, and asked exactly the same questions as the others, and received the same answers. Then the Bridegroom looked up and saw the decorated turnip, and he thought it was his Bride, and nodded to it and kissed his hand lovingly. But just as he was gone into the house with his guests, the brothers and relations of the Bride, who had been sent to her rescue, arrived. They immediately closed up all the doors of the house, so that no one could escape, and then set fire to it; and the Sorcerer and all his accomplices were burnt to ashes.

The Godfather

A CERTAIN poor man had so many children that he had already
asked all the world and his wife to stand godfathers and godmothers
to them; and when yet another child was born, he knew not where to
find any one to ask. In great perplexity he went to sleep, and
dreamed that he should go out of his door and ask the first person he
met to be godfather. As soon as he awoke the next morning he
resolved to follow out his dream; so he went out and asked the first
person he met. This was a man who gave him a little glass of water,
saying, "This is a miraculous water, with which you can restore the
sick to health; only you must observe where the disease lies. If it is
near the head, give the patient some of the water, and he will become
well again; but if it is near the feet, all your labour will be in vain, the
sick person must die."

The man was now able to say at any time whether such a one
would recover, and through this ability he became famous and

earned much money. Once he was summoned to the child of the King, and as soon as he entered he saw the disease was situated near the head, and so he healed it with the water. This happened a second time also, but at the third time the malady affected the feet, and he knew at once the child would die.

Not long after this event the man determined to visit the Godfather, and tell him all his adventures with the water. But when he came to the house, behold most wonderful doings were going on within! On the first stair were a Dustpan and a Broom quarrelling and beating one another, and he asked them where the master lived. The Broom replied, "A stair higher." On the second stair he saw a number of Fingers lying, and he asked them where the master lived. One of the Fingers replied, "A stair higher." On the third stair lay a heap of Bowls, who showed him up a stair higher yet; and on this fourth stair he found some Fish frying themselves in a pan over the fire, who told him to go a stair higher yet. When he had mounted this fifth stair, he came to a room and peeped through the keyhole of the door, and saw the Godfather there with a pair of long horns on. As soon as the poor man opened the door and went in, the Godfather got very quickly into a bed and covered himself up. Then the man said, "Ah, Mr Godfather, what wonderful doings are these I see in your house? When I mounted the first stair there were a Broom and a Dustpan quarrelling and beating one another."

"How very simple you are!" replied the Godfather; they were my boy and maid talking to one another."

"But on the second stair I saw some Fingers lying."

"Why, how absurd you are!" said the other; "those were roots of plants."

"But on the third stair I found a heap of Bowls," said the man.

"Why, you silly fellow," replied the Godfather; "those were cabbages."

"But on the fourth stair I saw Fish frying themselves in a pan;" and as the man spoke the Fish came and served up themselves on a dish.

"And when I mounted the fifth stair, I peeped through the keyhole of a door, and there I saw *you*, O Godfather, and you wore two very long horns."

"Holloa! that is not true!" exclaimed the Godfather; which so frightened the man that he ran straight off, or nobody knows what the Godfather would have done to him!

The Six Swans

A KING was once hunting in a large wood, and pursued his game so hotly, that none of his courtiers could follow him. But when evening approached he stopped, and looking around him perceived that he had lost himself. He sought a path out of the forest, but could not find one, and presently he saw an old woman with a nodding head, who came up to him. "My good woman," said he to her, "can you not show me the way out of the forest?" "Oh, yes, my lord King," she replied; "I can do that very well, but upon one condition, which, if you do not fulfil, you will never again get out of the wood, but will die of hunger."

"What, then, is this condition?" asked the King.

"I have a daughter," said the old woman, "who is as beautiful as any one you can find in the whole world, and well deserves to be your bride. Now, if you will make her your Queen, I will show you your way out of the wood." In the anxiety of his heart, the King consented, and the old woman led him to her cottage, where the daughter was sitting by the fire. She received the King as if she had expected him, and he saw at once that she was very beautiful, but yet she did not quite please him, for he could not look at her without a secret shuddering. However, after all he took the maiden up on his horse, and the old woman showed him the way, and the King arrived safely at his palace, where the wedding was to be celebrated.

The King had been married once before, and had seven children by his first wife, six boys and a girl, whom he loved above everything else in the world. He became afraid, soon, that the stepmother might not treat them very well, and might even do them some great injury, so he took them away to a lonely castle which stood in the midst of a forest. This castle was so hidden, and the way to it so difficult to discover, that he himself could not have found it if a wise woman had not given him a ball of cotton which had the wonderful property, when he threw it before him, of unrolling itself and showing him the right path. The King went, however, so often to see his dear children, that the Queen noticed his absence, became inquisitive, and wished to know what he went to fetch out of the forest. So she gave his servants a great quantity of money, and they disclosed to her the secret, and also told her of the ball of cotton which alone could show her the way. She had now no peace until she discovered where this ball was concealed, and then she made some fine silken shirts, and, as she had learnt of her mother, she sewed within each one a charm. One day soon after, when the King was gone out hunting, she took the little shirts and went into the forest, and the cotton showed her the path. The children, seeing someone coming in the distance, thought it was their dear father, and ran out towards her full of joy.

Then she threw over each of them a shirt, which, as it touched their bodies, changed them into Swans, which flew away over the forest. The Queen then went home quite contented, and thought she was free of her stepchildren; but the little girl had not met her with the brothers, and the Queen did not know of her.

The following day the King went to visit his children, but he found only the maiden. "Where are your brothers?" asked he. "Ah, dear father," she replied, "they are gone away and have left me alone;" and she told him how she had looked out of the window and seen them changed into Swans, which had flown over the forest; and then she showed him the feathers which they had dropped in the courtyard, and which she had collected together. The King was much grieved, but he did not think that his wife could have done this wicked deed, and, as he feared the girl might also be stolen away, he took her with him. She was, however, so much afraid of the stepmother, that she begged him not to stop more than one night in the castle.

The poor Maiden thought to herself, "This is no longer my place, I will go and seek my brothers;" and when night came she escaped and went quite deep into the wood. She walked all night long and great part of the next day, until she could go no further from weariness. Just then she saw a rude hut, and walking in she found a room with six little beds, but she dared not get into one, but crept under, and, lying herself upon the hard earth, prepared to pass the night there. Just as the sun was setting, she heard a rustling, and saw six white Swans come flying in at the window. They settled on the ground and began blowing one another until they had blown all their feathers off, and their swan's down stripped off like a shirt. Then the maiden knew them at once for her brothers, and gladly crept out from under the bed, and the brothers were not less glad to see their sister, but their joy was of short duration. "Here you must not stay," said they to her; "this is a robbers' hiding-place; if they should return and find you here, they will murder you." "Can you not protect me, then?" inquired the sister.

"No," they replied; "for we can only lay aside our swan's feathers for a quarter of an hour each evening, and for that time we regain our human form, but afterwards we resume our changed appearance."

Their sister then asked them with tears, "Can you not be restored again?"

"Oh, no," replied they; "the conditions are too difficult. For six long years you must neither speak nor laugh, and during that time you must sew together for us six little shirts of star-flowers, and should there fall a single word from your lips, then all your labour will be vain." Just as the brother finished speaking, the quarter of an hour elapsed, and they all flew out of the window again like Swans.

The little sister, however, made a solemn resolution to rescue her brothers, or die in the attempt; and she left the cottage, and, penetrating deep into the forest, passed the night amid the branches of a tree. The next morning she went out and collected the star-flowers to sew together. She had no one to converse with, and for laughing she had no spirits, so there up in the tree she sat, intent upon her work. After she had passed some time there, it happened that the King of the country was hunting in the forest, and his huntsmen came beneath the tree on which the Maiden sat. They called to her and asked, "Who art thou?" But she gave no answer. "Come down to us," continued they; "we will do thee no harm." She simply shook her head, and, when they pressed her further with questions, she threw down to them her gold necklace, hoping therewith to satisfy them. They did not, however, leave her, and she threw down her girdle, but in vain; and even her rich dress did not make them desist. At last the hunter himself climbed the tree and brought down the maiden, and took her before the King. The King asked her, "Who art thou? What dost thou upon that tree?" But she did not answer; and then he asked her in all the languages that he knew, but she remained dumb to all as a fish. Since, however, she was so beautiful, the King's heart was touched, and he conceived for her a strong affection. Then he put around her his cloak, and, placing her before him on his horse, took her to his castle. There he ordered rich clothing to be made for her, and, although her beauty shone as the sunbeams, not a word escaped her. The King placed her by his side at table, and there her dignified mien and manners so won upon him, that he said, "This Maiden will I marry, and no other in the world;" and after some days he was united to her.

Now, the King had a wicked stepmother who was discontented with his marriage, and spoke evil of the young Queen. "Who knows whence the wench comes?" said she. "She who cannot speak is not worthy of a King." A year after, when the Queen brought her first-born into the world, the old woman took him away. Then she went to the King and complained that the Queen was a murderess. The King, however, would not believe it, and suffered no one to do any injury to his wife, who sat composedly sewing at her shirts and paying attention to nothing else. When a second child was born, the false stepmother used the same deceit, but the King again would not listen to her words, but said, "She is too pious and good to act so: could she but speak and defend herself, her innocence would come to light." But when again, the third time, the old woman stole away the child, and then accused the Queen, who answered not a word to the accusation, the King was obliged to give her up to be tried, and she was condemned to suffer death by fire.

When the time had elapsed, and the sentence was to be carried out, it happened that the very day had come round when her dear brothers should be made free; the six shirts were also ready, all but the last, which yet wanted the left sleeve. As she was led to the scaffold, she placed the shirts upon her arm, and just as she had mounted it, and the fire was about to be kindled, she looked round, and saw six Swans come flying through the air. Her heart leapt for joy as she perceived her deliverers approaching, and soon the Swans, flying towards her, alighted so near that she was enabled to throw over them the shirts, and as soon as she had so done their feathers fell off and the brothers stood up alive and well; but the youngest wanted his left arm, instead of which he had a swan's wing. They embraced and kissed each other, and the Queen, going to the King, who was thunderstruck, began to say, "Now may I speak, my dear husband, and prove to you that I am innocent and falsely accused;"

and then she told him how the wicked woman had stolen away and hidden her three children. When she had concluded, the King was overcome with joy, and the wicked stepmother was led to the scaffold and bound to the stake and burnt to ashes.

The King and the Queen for ever after lived in peace and prosperity with their six brothers.

Old Sultan

A CERTAIN Peasant had a trusty dog called Sultan, who had grown quite old in his service, and had lost all his teeth, so that he could not hold anything fast. One day the Peasant stood with his wife at the house door, and said, "This morning I shall shoot old Sultan, for he is no longer of any use." His Wife, however, compassionating the poor animal, replied, "Well, since he has served us so long and so faithfully, I think we may very well afford him food for the rest of his life." "Eh, what?" replied her husband; "you are not very clever; he has not a tooth in his head, and never a thief is afraid of him, so he must trot off. If he has served us, he has also received every day his dinner."

The poor Dog, lying stretched out in the sun not far from his master, heard all he said, and was much troubled at learning that the morrow would be his last day. He had one good friend, the Wolf in the forest, to whom he slipt at evening, and complained of the sad fate which awaited him. "Be of good courage, my father," said the Wolf; "I will help you out of your trouble. I have just thought of something. Early to-morrow morning your master goes haymaking with his wife, and they will take with them their child, because no one will be left in the house. And while they are at work they will put him behind the hedge in the shade, and set you by to watch him. I will then spring out of the wood and steal away the child, and you must run after me hotly as if you were pursuing me. I will let it fall, and you shall take it back to its parents, who will then believe you have saved it, and they will be too thankful to do you any injury; and so you will come into great favour, and they will never let you want again."

This plan pleased the Dog, and it was carried out exactly as proposed. The father cried when he saw the Wolf running off with the child, but as old Sultan brought it back he was highly pleased, and stroked him, and said, "Not a hair of your head shall be touched; you shall eat your meals in comfort to the end of your days." He then told his wife to go home and cook old Sultan some bread and broth, which would not need biting, and also to bring the pillow out of his bed, that he might give it to him for a resting-place. Henceforth old Sultan had as much as he could wish for himself; and soon afterwards the Wolf visited him and congratulated him on his prosperous circumstances. "But, my father," said he slily, "you will close your eyes if I by accident steal away a fat sheep from your master." "Reckon not on that," replied the Dog; "my master believes me faithful; I dare not give you what you ask." The Wolf, however, thought he was not in earnest, and by night came slinking into the yard to fetch away the sheep. But the Peasant, to whom the

Dog had communicated the design of the Wolf, caught him and gave him a sound thrashing with the flail. The Wolf was obliged to scamper off, but he cried out to the Dog, "Wait a bit, you rascal, you shall pay for this!"

The next morning the Wolf sent the Boar to challenge the Dog, that they might settle their affair in the forest. Old Sultan, however, could find no other second than a Cat, who had only three legs, and, as they went out together, the poor Cat limped along, holding her tail high in the air from pain. The Wolf and his second were already on the spot selected, but as they saw their opponent coming they thought he was bringing a great sabre with him, because they saw in front the erect tail of the Cat; and, whenever the poor animal hopped on its three legs, they thought nothing else than he was going to take up a great stone to throw at them. Both of them, thereupon, became very nervous, and the Boar crept into a heap of dead leaves, and the Wolf climbed up a tree. As soon as the Dog and Cat arrived on the spot they wondered what had become of their adversary. The wild Boar, however, had not quite concealed himself, for his ears were sticking out; and, while the Cat was considering them attentively, the Boar twitched one of his ears, and the Cat took it for a mouse, and, making a spring, gave it a good bite. At this the Boar shook himself with a great cry, and ran away, calling out, "There sits the guilty one, up in the tree!" The Dog and the Cat looked up and saw the Wolf, who was ashamed at himself for being so fearful, and, begging the Dog's pardon, entered into treaty with him.

The Almond-Tree

LONG, long ago, perhaps two thousand years, there was a rich man who had a beautiful and pious wife; and they were very fond of one another, but had no children. Still they wished for some very much, and the wife prayed for them day and night; still they had none.

Before their house was a yard; in it stood an almond-tree, under which the woman stood once in the winter peeling an apple; and as she peeled the apple she cut her finger, and the blood dropped on to the snow. "Ah," said the woman, with a deep sigh, and she looked at the blood before her, and was very sad; "had I but a child as red as blood and as white as snow!" and as she said that, her heart grew light; and it seemed to her as if something would come of her wish. Then she went into the house; and a month passed, the snow disappeared; and two months, then all was green; and three months, then came the flowers out of the ground; and four months, then all the trees in the wood squeezed up against one another, and the green boughs all grew twisted together, and the little birds sang, so that the whole wood resounded, and the blossoms fell from the trees. When the fifth month had gone, and she stood under the almond-tree, it smelt so sweet, that her heart leaped for joy, and she could not help falling down on her knees; and when the sixth month had passed, the fruits were large, and she felt very happy; at the end of the seventh month, she snatched the almonds and ate them so greedily, that she was dreadfully ill; then the eighth month passed away, and she called her husband and cried, and said, "If I die, bury me under the almond-tree;" then she was quite easy, and was glad, till the next month was gone; then she had a child as white as snow, and as red as blood; and when she saw it, she was so delighted that she died.

Then her husband buried her under the almond-tree and began to grieve most violently: a little time and he was easier; and when he had sorrowed a little longer he left off; and a little time longer and he took another wife.

With the second wife he had a daughter; but the child by the first wife was a little son, and was as red as blood, and as white as snow. When the woman looked at her daughter, she loved her so much; but then she looked at the little boy, and it seemed to go right through her heart; and it seemed as if he always stood in her way, and then she was always thinking how she could get all the fortune for her daughter; and it was the Evil One who suggested it to her, so that she couldn't bear the sight of the little boy, and poked him about from one corner to another, and buffeted him here, and cuffed him there, so that the poor child was always in fear; and when he came from school he had no peace.

Once the woman had gone into the store-room, and the little daughter came up and said, "Mother, give me an apple." "Yes, my child," said the woman, and gave her a beautiful apple out of the box: the box had a great heavy lid, with a great, sharp iron lock. "Mother," said the little daughter, "shall not brother have one too?" That annoyed the woman; but she said, "Yes, when he comes from school." And as she saw out of the window that he was coming, it

THE ALMOND-TREE

was just as if the Evil One came over her, and she snatched the apple away from her daughter again, and said, "You shall not have one before your brother!" She threw the apple into the box and shut it. Then the little boy came in at the door; and the Evil One made her say, in a friendly manner, "My son, will you have an apple?" and she looked at him wickedly. "Mother," said the little boy, "how horribly you look! yes, give me an apple." Then she thought she must pacify him. "Come with me," she said, and opened the lid; "reach out an apple;" and as the little boy bent into the box, the Evil One whispered to her – bang! she slammed the lid to, so that his head flew off and fell amongst the red apples. Then in the fright she thought, "Could I get that off my mind!" Then she went up into her room to the chest of drawers, and got out a white cloth from the top drawer, and she set the head on the throat again and tied the handkerchief round, so that nothing could be seen; and placed him outside the door on a chair, and gave him the apple in his hand. After a while little Marline came in the kitchen to her mother, who stood by the fire and had a kettle with hot water before her, which she kept stirring round. "Mother," said little Marline, "brother is sitting outside the door, and looks quite white, and has got an apple in his hand. I asked him to give me the apple, but he didn't answer me; then I was quite frightened." "Go again," said the Mother, "and if he will not answer you, give him a box on the ear." Then Marline went to her brother, and said, "Give me the apple;" but he was silent. Then she gave him a box on the ear, and the head tumbled off, at which she was frightened, and began to cry and sob. Then she ran to her mother, and said, "Oh, mother, I have knocked my brother's head off!" and she cried and cried, and would not be pacified. "Marline," said the Mother, "what have you done? But be quiet, so that nobody may notice it; it can't be helped now; we'll bury him under the almond-tree."

Then the mother took the little boy and put him into a box, and put it under the almond-tree; but little Marline stood by, and cried and cried, and the tears all fell into the box.

Soon the father came home and sat down to table, and said,

"Where is my son?" Then the mother brought in a great big dish of stew; and little Marline cried, and could not leave off. Then said the father again, "Where is my son?" "Oh," said the mother, "he has gone across the country to Mütten; he is going to stop there a bit!" "What is he doing there? and why did he not say good-bye to me?" "Oh, he wanted to go, and asked me if he might stop there six weeks, he will be taken care of there!" "Ah," said the man, "I feel very sorry; that was not right; he ought to have wished me good-bye." With that he began to eat, and said to Marline, "What are you crying for? your brother will soon come back." "Oh, wife," said he then, "how delicious this tastes; give me some more!" And he ate till all the broth was done.

Little Marline went to her box and took from the bottom drawer her best silk handkerchief, and carried it outside the door, and cried bitter tears. Then she laid herself under the almond-tree on the green grass; and when she had laid herself there, all at once she felt quite light and happy, and cried no more. Then the almond-tree began to move, and the boughs spread out quite wide, and then went back again; just as when one is very much pleased and claps with the hands. At the same time a sort of mist rose from the tree; in the middle of the mist it burned like a fire; and out of the fire there flew a beautiful bird that sang very sweetly, and flew high up in the air: and when it had flown away, the almond-tree was as it had been before. The little Marline was as light and happy as if her brother were alive still and went into the house to dinner.

The bird flew away and perched upon a Goldsmith's house, and began to sing,—

> "My mother killed me;
> My father grieved for me;
> My sister, little Marline,
> Wept under the almond-tree;
> Kywitt, kywitt, what a beautiful bird am I!"

The Goldsmith sat in his workshop and was making a gold chain when he heard the bird that sat upon his roof and sang, and it seemed to him so beautiful. Then he got up, and as he stepped over the sill of the door he lost one of his slippers; but he went straight up the middle of the street with one slipper and one sock on. He had his leather apron on, and in the one hand he had the gold chain, and in the other the pincers, and the sun shone brightly up the street. He went and stood and looked at the bird. "Bird," said he then, "how beautifully you can sing! Sing me that song again." "Nay," said the Bird, "I don't sing twice for nothing. Give me the gold chain and I will sing it you again." "There," said the Goldsmith, "take the gold chain; now sing me that again." Then the bird came and took the gold chain in the right claw, and sat before the Goldsmith, and sang,—

> "My mother killed me;
> My father grieved for me;
> My sister, little Marline,
> Wept under the almond-tree:
> Kywitt, kywitt, what a beautiful bird am I!"

Then the bird flew off to a Shoemaker, and perched upon the roof of his house, and sang,—

> "My mother killed me;
> My father grieved for me;
> My sister, little Marline,
> Wept under the almond-tree:
> Kywitt, kywitt, what a beautiful bird am I!"

The Shoemaker heard it, and ran outside the door in his shirt sleeves and looked up at the roof, and was obliged to hold his hand before his eyes to prevent the sun from blinding him. "Bird," said he, "how beautifully you sing!" Then he called in at the door, "Wife, come out, here's a bird; look at the bird; he just can sing beautifully." Then he called his daughter, and children, and apprentices, servant-boy, and maid; and they all came up the street and looked at the bird: oh, how beautiful he was, and he had such red and green feathers, and round about the throat was all like gold, and the eyes sparkled in his head like stars! "Bird," said the Shoemaker, "now sing me that piece again." "Nay," said the Bird, "I don't sing twice for nothing; you must make me a present of something." "Wife," said the man, "go into the shop; on the top shelf there stands a pair of red shoes, fetch them down." The wife went and fetched the shoes. "There, Bird," said the man; "now sing me that song again." Then the bird came and took the shoes in the left claw, and flew up on to the roof again, and sang,—

> "My mother killed me;
> My father grieved for me;
> My sister, little Marline,
> Wept under the almond-tree:
> Kywitt, kywitt, what a beautiful bird am I!"

And when he had done singing he flew away. The chain he had in the right claw, and the shoes in the left claw; and he flew far away to a mill; and the mill went clipp-clapp, clipp-clapp, clipp-clapp. And in the mill there sat twenty miller's men; they were shaping a stone, and chipped away, hick-hack, hick-hack, hick-hack; and the mill went clipp-clapp, clipp-clapp, clipp-clapp. Then the bird flew and sat on a lime-tree that stood before the mill, and sang,—

> "My mother killed me;"

then one left off;

> "My father grieved for me;"

then two more left off and heard it;

> "My sister,"

then again four left off;

> "little Marline,"

now there were only eight chipping away;

"Wept under"

now only five;

"the almond-tree:"

now only one:

"Kywitt, kywitt, what a beautiful bird am I!"

Then the last left off, when he heard the last word. "Bird," said he, "how beautifully you sing! let me, too, hear that; sing me that again." "Nay," said the Bird, "I don't sing twice for nothing. Give me the millstone and I will sing it again." "Ay," said he, "if it belonged to me alone, you should have it." "Yes," said the others, "if he sings again he shall have it." The the bird came down, and all the twenty millers caught hold of a pole, and raised the stone up, hu, uh, upp! hu, uh, upp! And the bird stuck his head through the hole, and took it round his neck like a collar, and flew back to the tree, and sang,—

"My mother killed me;
My father grieved for me;
My sister, little Marline,
Wept under the almond-tree:
Kywitt, kywitt, what a beautiful bird am I!"

And when he had done singing he spread his wings, and had in his right claw the gold chain, in his left the shoes, and round his neck the millstone, and he flew far away to his father's house.

In the room sat the father, the mother, and little Marline at dinner; and the father said, "Oh, dear, how light and happy I feel!" "Nay," said the mother, 'I am all of a tremble, just as if there were going to be a heavy thunderstorm." But little Marline sat and cried and cried, and the bird came flying and as he perched on the roof the father said, "I feel so cheerful, and the sun shines so deliciously outside, it's exactly as if I were going to see some old acquaintance again." "Nay," said the wife, "I am so frightened, my teeth chatter, and it's like fire in my veins;" and she tore open her stays; but little Marline sat in a corner and cried, and held her plate before her eyes and cried it quite wet. Then the bird perched on the almond-tree, and sang, —

"My mother killed me;"

Then the mother held her ears and shut her eyes, and would neither see nor hear; but it rumbled in her ears like the most terrible storm, and her eyes burned and twittered like lighting.

"My father grieved for me;"

"Oh, mother," said the man, "there is a beautiful bird that sings so splendidly; the sun shines so warm, and everything smells all like cinnamon!"

"My sister, little Marline,"

Then Marline laid her head on her knees and cried away; but the man said, "I shall go out, I must see the bird close." "Oh, do not go," said the woman; "it seems as if the whole house shook and were on fire!" But the man went out and looked at the bird.

"Wept under the almond-tree:
Kywitt, kywitt, what a beautiful bird am I!"

And the bird let the gold chain fall, and it fell just round the man's neck, and fitted beautifully. Then he went in and said, "See what an excellent bird it is; it has given me such a beautiful gold chain, and it looks so splendid." But the woman was so frightened that she fell her whole length on the floor, and her cap tumbled off her head. Then the bird sang again, —

"My mother killed me;"

"Oh, that I were a thousand fathoms under the earth, not to hear that!"

"My father grieved for me;"

Then the woman fainted.

"My sister, little Marline,"

"Ah," said Marline, "I will go out too, and see if the bird will give me something!" and she went out. Then the bird threw the shoes down.

"Wept under the almond-tree:
Kywitt, kywitt, what a beautiful bird am I!"

Then, she was so happy and lively, she put the new red shoes on, and danced and jumped back again. "Oh," said she, "I was so dull when I went out, and now I am so happy. That is a splendid bird: he has given me a pair of shoes."

"Well," said the woman, and jumped up, and her hair stood on end like flames of fire, "I feel as if the world were coming to an end; I will go out too, and see if it will make me easier." And as she stepped outside the door – bang! the bird threw the millstone on to her head, so that she was completely overwhelmed. The father and little Marline heard it and went out. Then a smoke, and flames, and fire rose from the place, and when that had passed there stood the little brother; and he took his father and little Marline by the hand, and all three embraced one another heartily, and went into the house to dinner.

Briar Rose

IN olden times there lived a King and Queen, who lamented day by day that they had no children, and yet never a one was born. One day, as the Queen was bathing and thinking of her wishes, a Frog skipped out of the water, and said to her, "Your wish shall be fulfilled, – before a year passes you shall have a daughter."

As the Frog had said, so it happened, and a little girl was born who was so beautiful that the King almost lost his senses, but he ordered a great feast to be held, and invited to it not only his relatives, friends, and acquaintances, but also all the wise women who are kind and affectionate to children. There happened to be thirteen in his dominions, but, since he had only twelve golden plates out of which they could eat, one had to stop at home. The fête was celebrated with all the magnificence possible, and, as soon as it was over, the wise women presented the infant with their wonderful gifts: one with virtue, another with beauty, a third with riches, and so on,

BRIAR ROSE

so that the child had everything that is to be desired in the world. Just as eleven had given their presents, the thirteenth old lady stepped in suddenly. She was in a tremendous passion because she had not been invited, and, without greeting or looking at any one, she exclaimed loudly, "The Princess shall prick herself with a spindle on her fifteenth birthday and die!" and without a word further she turned her back and left the hall. All were terrified, but the twelfth fairy, who had not yet given her wish, then stepped up, but because she could not take away the evil wish, but only soften it, she said, "She shall not die, but shall fall into a sleep of a hundred years' duration."

Then the King, who naturally wished to protect his child from this misfortune, issued a decree commanding that every spindle in the kingdom should be burnt. Meanwhile all the gifts of the wise women were fulfilled, and the maiden became so beautiful, gentle, virtuous, and clever, that every one who saw her fell in love with her. It happened on the day when she was just fifteen years old that the Queen and the King were not at home, and so she was left alone in the castle. The maiden looked about in every place, going through all the rooms and chambers just as she pleased, until she came at last to an old tower. Up the narrow winding staircase she tripped until she arrived at a door, in the lock of which was a rusty key. This she turned, and the door sprang open, and there in the little room sat an old woman with a spindle spinning flax. "Good day, my good old lady," said the Princess, "what are you doing here?"

"I am spinning," said the old woman, nodding her head.

"What thing is that which twists round so merrily?" inquired the maiden, and she took the spindle to try her hand at spinning. Scarcely had she done so when the prophecy was fulfilled, for she pricked her finger; and at the very same moment she fell back upon a bed which stood near in a deep sleep. This sleep was extended over the whole palace. The King and Queen, who had just come in, fell asleep in the hall, and all their courtiers with them – the horses in the stables, the doves upon the eaves, the flies upon the walls, and even the fire upon the hearth, all ceased to stir – the meat which was cooking ceased to frizzle, and the cook at the instant of pulling the hair of the kitchen-boy lost his hold and began to snore too. The wind also fell entirely, and not a leaf rustled on the trees round the castle.

Now around the palace a thick hedge of briars began growing, which every year grew higher and higher, till the castle was quite hid from view, so that one could not even see the flag upon the tower. Then there went a legend through the land of the beautiful maiden Briar Rose, for so was the sleeping Princess named, and from time to time Princes came endeavouring to penetrate through the hedge into the castle; but it was not possible, for the thorns held them, as if by hands, and the youths were unable to release themselves, and so perished miserably.

After the lapse of many years, there came another King's son into the country, and heard an old man tell the legend of the hedge of briars, how that behind it stood a castle where slept a wondrously beauteous Princess called Briar Rose, who had slumbered nearly a hundred years, and with her the Queen and King and all their court. The old man further related what he had heard from his grandfather, that many Princes had come and tried to penetrate the hedge, and had died a miserable death. But the youth was not to be daunted, and however much the old man tried to dissuade him, he would not listen, but cried out, "I fear not, I will see this hedge of briars!"

Just at that time came the last day of the hundred years when Briar Rose was to awake again. As the young Prince approached the hedge, the thorns turned to fine large flowers, which of their own accord made a way for him to pass through, and again closed up behind him. In the courtyard he saw the horses and dogs lying fast asleep, and on the eaves were the doves with their heads beneath their wings. As soon as he went into the house, there were the flies asleep upon the wall, the cook still stood with his hand on the hair of the kitchen-boy, the maid at the board with the unplucked fowl in her hand. He went on, and in the hall he found the courtiers lying asleep, and above, by the throne, were the King and Queen. He went on further, and all was so quiet that he could hear himself breathe, and at last he came to the tower and opened the door of the little room where slept Briar Rose. There she lay, looking so beautiful that he could not turn away his eyes, and he bent over her and kissed her. Just as he did so she opened her eyes, awoke, and greeted him with smiles. Then they went down together, and immediately the King and Queen awoke, and the whole court, and all stared at each other wondrously. Now the horses in the stable got up and shook themselves – the dogs wagged their tails – the doves upon the eaves drew their heads from under their wings, looked around, and flew away – and flies upon the walls began to crawl, the fire to burn brightly and to cook the meat – the meat began again to fizzle – the cook gave his lad a box upon the ear which made him call out – and the maid began to pluck the fowl furiously. The whole palace was once more in motion as if nothing had occurred, for the hundred years' sleep had made no change in any one.

By-and-by the wedding of the Prince with Briar Rose was celebrated with great splendour, and to the end of their lives they lived happy and contented.

King Thrush-Beard

A CERTAIN King had a daughter who was beautiful above all belief, but withal so proud and haughty, that no suitor was good enough for her, and she not only turned back every one who came, but also made game of them all. Once the King proclaimed a great festival, and invited thereto from far and near all the marriageable young men. When they arrived they were all set in a row, according to their rank and standing: first the Kings, then the Princes, the Dukes, the Marquesses, the Earls, and last of all the Barons. Then the King's daughter was led down the rows, but she found something to make game of in all. One was too fat. "The wine-tub!" said she. Another was too tall. "Long and lanky has no grace," she remarked. A third was too short and fat. "Too stout to have any wits," said she. A fourth was too pale. "Like Death himself," was her remark; and a fifth who had a great deal of colour she called "a cockatoo." The sixth was not straight enough, and him she called "a green log scorched in the oven!" And so she went on, nicknaming every one of the suitors, but she made particularly merry with a good young King whose chin had grown rather crooked. "Ha, ha!" laughed she, "he has a chin like a thrush's beak;" and after that day he went by the name of Thrush-beard.

The old King, however, when he saw that his daughter did nothing but mock at and make sport of all the suitors who were collected, became very angry, and swore that she should take the first decent beggar for a husband who came to the gate.

A couple of days after this a player came beneath the windows to sing and earn some bounty if he could. As soon as the King saw him he ordered him to be called up, and presently he came into the room in all his dirty ragged clothes, and sang before the King and Princess, and when he had finished he begged for a slight recompense. The King said, "Thy song has pleased so much that I will give thee my daughter for a wife."

The Princess was terribly frightened, but the King said, "I have taken an oath, and mean to perform it, that I will give you to the first beggar." All her remonstrances were in vain, the priest was called, and the Princess was married in earnest to the player. When the ceremony was performed, the King said, "Now it cannot be suffered that you should stop here with your husband, in my house; no! you must travel about the country with him."

So the beggarman led her away with him, and she was forced to trudge along with him on foot. As they came to a large forest she asked—

"To whom belongs this beautiful wood?"

The echo replied—

"King Thrush-beard the good!
Had you taken him, so was it thine."

"Ah, silly," said she,

"What a lot had been mine
Had I happily married King Thrush-beard!"

Next they came to a meadow, and she asked,
"To whom belongs this meadow so green?"
"To King Thrush-beard," was again the reply.
Then they came to a great city, and she asked,
"To whom does this beautiful town belong?"
"To King Thrush-beard," said one.

"Ah, what a simpleton was I that I did not marry him when I had the chance!" exclaimed the poor Princess.

"Come," broke in the Player, "it does not please me, I can tell you, that you are always wishing for another husband: am I not good enough for you?"

By-and-by they came to a very small hut, and she said, "Ah, heavens, to whom can this miserable, wretched hovel belong?"

The Player replied, "That is my house, where we shall live together."

The Princess was obliged to stoop to get in at the door, and when she was inside, she asked, "Where are the servants?" "What servants?" exclaimed her husband, "you must yourself do all that you want done. Now make a fire and put on some water, that you may cook my dinner, for I am quite tired."

The Princess, however, understood nothing about making fires or cooking, and the beggar had to set to work himself, and as soon as they had finished their scanty meal they went to bed. In the morning the husband woke up his wife very early, that she might set the house to rights, and for a couple of days they lived on in this way, and made an end of their store. Then the husband said, "Wife, we must not go on in this way any longer, stopping here, doing nothing: you must weave some baskets." So he went out and cut some osiers and brought them home, but when his wife attempted to bend them the hard twigs wounded her hands and made them bleed. "I see that won't suit," said the husband; "you had better spin, perhaps that will do better."

So she sat down to spin, but the harsh thread cut her tender fingers very badly, so that the blood flowed freely. "Do you see," said the husband, "how you are spoiling your work? I made a bad bargain in taking you! Now I must try and make a business in pots and earthen vessels: you shall sit in the market and sell them."

"Oh, if anybody out of my father's dominions should come and see me in the market selling pots," thought the Princess to herself, "how they will laugh at me!"

However, all her excuses were in vain: she must either do that or die of hunger.

The first time all went well, for the people bought of the Princess, because she was so pretty-looking, and not only gave her what she asked, but some even laid down their money and left the pots behind. On her earnings this day they lived for some time as long as they lasted; and then the husband purchased a fresh stock of pots. With these she placed her stall at a corner of the market, offering them for sale. All at once a drunken hussar came plunging down the street on his horse, and rode right into the midst of her earthenware, and shattered it into a thousand pieces. The accident, as well it might, set her a-weeping, and in her trouble, not knowing what to do, she ran home crying, "Ah, what will become of me, what will my good man say?" When she had told her husband he cried out, "Who ever would have thought of sitting at the corner of the market to sell earthenware? but well, I see you are not accustomed to any ordinary work. There, leave off crying; I have been to the King's palace, and asked if they were not in want of a kitchenmaid, and they have agreed to take you, and there you will live free of cost."

Now the Princess became a kitchenmaid, and was obliged to do as the cook bade her, and wash up the dirty things. Then she put a jar into each of her pockets, and in them she took home what was left of what fell to her share of the good things, and of these she and her husband made their meals. Not many days afterwards it happened that the wedding of the King's eldest son was to be celebrated, and the poor wife placed herself near the door of the saloon to look on. As the lamps were lit and guests more and more beautiful entered the room, and all dressed most sumptuously, she reflected on her fate with a saddened heart, and repented of the pride and haughtiness which had so humiliated and impoverished her. Every now and then the servants threw her out of the dishes morsels of rich delicacies which they carried in, and whose fragrant smells increased her regrets, and these pieces she put into her pockets to carry home. Presently the King entered, clothed in silk and velvet, and having a golden chain round his neck. As soon as he saw the beautiful maiden standing at the door, he seized her by the hand and would dance with her, but she, terribly frightened, refused; for she saw it was King Thrush-beard, who had wooed her, and whom she had laughed at. Her struggles were of no avail, he drew her into the ballroom, and there tore off the band to which the pots were attached, so that they fell down and the soup ran over the floor, while the pieces of meat, etc. skipped about in all directions. When the fine folks saw this sight they burst into one universal shout of laughter and derision, and the poor girl was so ashamed that she wished herself a thousand fathoms below the earth. She ran out at the door and would have escaped; but on the steps she met a man, who took her back, and when she looked at him, lo! it was King Thrush-beard again. He spake kindly to her, and said, "Be not afraid; I and the musician, who dwelt with you in the wretched hut, are one; for love of you I have acted thus; and the hussar who rode in among the pots was also myself. All this has taken place in order to humble your haughty disposition, and to punish you for your pride, which led you to mock me."

At these words she wept bitterly, and said, "I am not worthy to be your wife, I have done you so great a wrong." But he replied, "Those evil days are passed: we will now celebrate our marriage."

Immediately after came the bridesmaids, and put on her the most magnificent dresses: and then her father and his whole court arrived, and wished her happiness on her wedding-day; and now commenced her true joy as Queen of the country of King Thrush-beard.

Rumpelstiltskin

THERE was once a poor Miller who had a beautiful daughter; and
one day, having to go to speak with the King, he said, in order to
make himself appear of consequence, that he had a daughter who
could spin straw into gold. The King was very fond of gold, and
thought to himself, "That is an art which would please me very
well;" and so he said to the Miller, "If your daughter is so very
clever, bring her to the castle in the morning, and I will put her to the
proof."

As soon as she arrived the King led her into a chamber which was
full of straw; and, giving her a wheel and a reel, he said, "Now set
yourself to work, and if you have not spun this straw into gold by an
early hour to-morrow, you must die." With these words he shut the
room door, and left the maiden alone.

There she sat for a long time, thinking how to save her life; for she
understood nothing of the art whereby straw might be spun into

gold; and her perplexity increased more and more, till at last she began to weep. All at once the door opened and in stepped a little Man, who, said, "Good evening, fair maiden; why do you weep so sore?" "Ah," she replied, "I must spin this straw into gold, and I am sure I do not know how."

The little Man asked, "What will you give me if I spin it for you?"

"My necklace," said the maiden.

The Dwarf took it, placed himself in front of the wheel, and whirr, whirr, whirr, three times round, and the bobbin was full. Then he set up another, and whirr, whirr, whirr, thrice round again, and a second bobbin was full; and so he went all night long, until all the straw was spun, and the bobbins were full of gold. At sunrise the King came, very much astonished to see the gold; the sight of which gladdened him, but did not make his heart less covetous. He caused the maiden to be led into another room, still larger, full of straw; and then he bade here spin it into gold during the night if she valued her life. The maiden was again quite at a loss what to do; but while she cried the door opened suddenly, as before, and the Dwarf appeared and asked her what she would give him in return for his assistance. "The ring off my finger," she replied. The little Man took the ring and began to spin at once, and by the morning all the straw was changed to glistening gold. The King was rejoiced above measure at the sight of this, but still he was not satisfied; but, leading the maiden into another still larger room, full of straw as the others, he said, "This you must spin during the night; but if you accomplish it you shall be my bride." "For," thought he to himself, "a richer wife thou canst not have in all the world."

When the maiden was left alone, the Dwarf again appeared, and asked for the third time, "What will you give me to do this for you?"

"I have nothing left that I can give you," replied the maiden.

"Then promise me your first-born child if you become Queen," said he.

The Miller's daughter thought, "Who can tell if that will ever happen?" and, ignorant how else to help herself out of her trouble, she promised the Dwarf what he desired; and he immediately set about and finished the spinning. When morning came, and the King found all he had wished for done, he celebrated his wedding, and the fair Miller's daughter became Queen.

About a year after the marriage, when she had ceased to think about the little Dwarf, she brought a fine child into the world; and, suddenly, soon after its birth, the very man appeared and demanded what she had promised. The frightened Queen offered him all the riches of the kingdom if he would leave her her child; but the Dwarf answered, "No; something human is dearer to me than all the wealth of the world."

The Queen began to weep and groan so much, that the Dwarf compassionated her, and said, "I will leave you three days to consider; if you in that time discover my name you shall keep your child."

All night long the Queen racked her brains for all the names she could think of, and sent a messenger through the country to collect far and wide any new names. The following morning came the Dwarf, and she began with "Caspar," "Melchior," "Balthassar," and all the odd names she knew; but at each the little Man exclaimed, "That is not my name." The second day the Queen inquired of all her people for uncommon and curious names, and called the Dwarf "Ribs-of-Beef," "Sheep-shank," "Whalebone;" but at each he said, "This is not my name." The third day the messenger came back and said, "I have not found a single name; but as I came to a high mountain near the edge of a forest, where foxes and hares say good night to each other, I saw there a little house, and before the door a fire was burning, and round this fire a very curious little Man was dancing on one leg, and shouting,—

> " 'To-day I stew, and then I'll bake,
> To-morrow I shall the Queen's child take;
> Ah! how famous it is that nobody knows
> 'That my name is Rumpelstiltskin.' "

When the Queen heard this she was very glad, for now she knew the name; and soon after came the Dwarf, and asked, "Now, my lady Queen, what is my name?"

First she said, "Are you called Conrade?" "No."
"Are you called Hal?" "No."
"Are you called Rumpelstiltskin?"

"A witch has told you! a witch has told you!" shrieked the little Man, and stamped his right foot so hard in the ground with rage that he could not draw it out again. Then he took hold of his left leg with both his hands, and pulled away so hard that his right came off in the struggle, and he hopped away howling terribly. And from that day to this the Queen has heard no more of her troublesome visitor.

Little Snow-White

ONCE upon a time in the depth of winter, when the flakes of snow were falling like feathers from the clouds, a Queen sat at her palace window, which had an ebony black frame, stitching her husband's shirts. While she was thus engaged and looking out at the snow she pricked her finger, and three drops of blood fell upon the snow. Because the red looked so well upon the white, she thought to herself, "Had I now but a child as white as this snow, as red as this blood, and as black as the wood of this frame!" Soon afterwards a little daughter was born to her, who was as white as snow, and red as blood, and with hair as black as ebony, and thence she was named "Snow-White," and when the child was born the mother died.

About a year afterwards the King married another wife, who was very beautiful, but so proud and haughty that she could not bear any one to be better-looking than herself. She possessed a wonderful mirror, and when she stepped before it and said,—

> "Oh, mirror, mirror on the wall,
> Who is the fairest of us all?"

it replied,—

> "Thou art the fairest, lady Queen."

Then she was pleased, for she knew that the mirror spoke truly.

Little Snow-White, however, grew up, and became pretty and prettier, and when she was seven years old her complexion was as clear as the noon-day, and more beautiful than the Queen herself. When the Queen now asked her mirror,—

> "Oh, mirror, mirror on the wall,
> Who is the fairest of us all?"

it replied,—

> "Thou wert the fairest, lady Queen,
> Snow-White is fairest now, I ween."

This answer so frightened the Queen that she became quite yellow with envy. From that hour, whenever she perceived Snow-White, her heart was hardened against her, and she hated the maiden. Her envy and jealousy increased so that she had no rest day nor night, and she said to a Huntsman, "Take the child away into the forest, I will never look upon her again. You must kill her, and bring me her heart and tongue for a token."

The Huntsman listened and took the maiden away, but when he drew out his knife to kill her, she began to cry, saying, "Ah, dear Huntsman, give me my life! I will run into the wild forest, and never come home again."

This speech softened the Hunter's heart, and her beauty so touched him that he had pity on her and said, "Well, run away then, poor child;" but he thought to himself, "The wild beasts will soon devour you." Still he felt as if a stone had been taken from his heart, because her death was not by his hand. Just at that moment a young boar came roaring along to the spot, and as soon as he clapt eyes upon it the Huntsman caught it, and, killing it, took its tongue and heart, and carried them to the Queen for a token of his deed.

But now the poor Snow-White was left motherless and alone, and overcome with grief, she was bewildered at the sight of so many trees, and knew not which way to turn. Presently she set off running, and ran over stones and through thorns, and wild beasts sprang up as she passed them, but they did her no harm. She ran on till her feet refused to go farther, and as it was getting dark, and she saw a little house near, she entered in to rest. In this cottage everything was very small, but more neat and elegant than I can tell you. In the middle stood a little table with a white cloth over it, and seven little plates upon it, each plate having a spoon and a knife and fork, and there were also seven little mugs. Against the wall were seven little beds ranged in a row, each covered with snow-white sheets. Little Snow-White, being both hungry and thirsty, ate a little morsel of porridge out of each plate, and drank a drop or two of wine out of each glass, for she did not wish to take away the whole share of any one. After that, because she was so tired, she laid herself down on one bed, but it did not suit; she tried another, but that was too long; a fourth was too short, a fifth too hard, but the seventh was just the thing, and tucking herself up in it she went to sleep, first commending herself to God.

When it became quite dark the lords of the cottage came home, seven Dwarfs, who dug and delved for ore in the mountains. They first lighted seven little lamps, and perceived at once – for they illumined the whole apartment – that somebody had been in, for everything was not in the order in which they had left it. The first asked, "Who has been sitting on my chair?" The second, "Who has been eating off my plate?" The third said, "Who has been nibbling at my bread?" The fourth, "Who has been at my porridge?" The fifth, "Who has been meddling with my fork?" The sixth grumbled out, "Who has been cutting with my knife?" The seventh said, "Who has been drinking out of my glass?" Then the first looking round began again. "Who has been lying on my bed?" he asked, for he saw that the sheets were tumbled. At these words the others came, and looking at their beds cried out too, "Someone has been lying in our beds!" But the seventh little man, running up to his, saw Snow-White sleeping in it; so he called his companions, who shouted with wonder and held up their seven torches, so that the light fell on the maiden. "Oh heavens! oh heavens!" said they, "what a beauty she is!" and they were so much delighted that they would not awaken her, but left her to her repose, and the seventh Dwarf, in whose bed she was, slept with each of his fellows one hour, and so passed the night.

As soon as morning dawned Snow-White awoke, and was quite frightened when she saw the seven little men; but they were very friendly, and asked her what she was called. "My name is Snow-White," was her reply. "Why have you entered our cottage?" they asked. Then she told them how her stepmother would have had her killed, but the Huntsman had spared her life, and how she had wandered about the whole day until at last she had found their house. When her tale was finished the Dwarfs said, "Will you see after our household; be our cook, make the beds, wash, sew, and knit for us, and keep everything in neat order? if so, we will keep you here, and you shall want for nothing."

And Snow-White answered, "Yes, with all my heart and will;" and so she remained with them, and kept their house in order. In the morning the Dwarfs went into the mountains and searched for ore and gold, and in the evenings they came home and found their meals ready for them. During the day the maiden was left alone, and therefore the good Dwarfs warned her and said, "Be careful of your stepmother, who will soon know of your being here; therefore let nobody enter the cottage."

The Queen meanwhile, supposing that she had eaten the heart and tongue of her daughter-in-law, did not think but that she was above all comparison the most beautiful of every one around. One day she stepped before her mirror, and said,—

> "Oh, mirror, mirror on the wall,
> Who is the fairest of us all?"

and it replied,—

> "Thou wert the fairest, lady Queen;
> Snow-White is fairest now, I ween.
> Amid the forest, darkly green,
> She lives with Dwarfs – the hills between."

This reply frightened her, for she knew that the mirror spoke the truth, and she perceived that the Huntsman had deceived her, and that Snow-White was still alive. Now she thought and thought how she should accomplish her purpose, for so long as she was not the fairest in the whole country, jealousy left her no rest. At last a thought struck her, and she dyed her face and clothed herself as a pedlar woman, so that no one could recognise her. In this disguise she went over the seven hills to the seven Dwarfs, knocked at the door of the hut, and called out, "Fine goods for sale! beautiful goods for sale!" Snow-White peeped out of the window and said, "Good day, my good woman, what have you to sell?" "Fine goods, beautiful goods!" she replied, "stays of all colours;" and she held up a pair which was made of variegated silks. "I may let in this honest woman," thought Snow-White; and she unbolted the door and bargained for one pair of stays. "You can't think, my dear, how it becomes you!" exclaimed the old woman, "Come, let me lace it up for you." Snow-White suspected nothing, and let her do as she wished, but the old woman laced her up so quickly and so tightly that all her breath went, and she fell down like one dead. "Now," thought the old woman to herself, hastening away, "now am I once more the most beautiful of all!"

Not long after her departure, at eventide, the seven Dwarfs came home, and were much frightened at seeing their dear little maid lying on the ground, and neither moving nor breathing, as if she were dead. They raised her up, and when they saw she was laced too tight they cut the stays in pieces, and presently she began to breathe again, and by little and little she revived. When the Dwarfs now heard what had taken place, they said, "The old pedlar woman was no other than your wicked stepmother, take more care of yourself, and let no one enter when we are not with you."

Meanwhile the old Queen had reached home, and, going before her mirror, she repeated her usual words,—

> "Oh, mirror, mirror on the wall,
> Who is the fairest of us all?"

and it replied as before,—

> "Thou wert the fairest, lady Queen;
> Snow-White is fairest now, I ween.
> Amid the forest, darkly green,
> She lives with Dwarfs – the hills between."

As soon as it had finished, all her blood rushed to her heart, for she was so frightened to hear that Snow-White was yet living. "But now," thought she to herself, "will I contrive something which shall destroy her completely." Thus saying, she made a poisoned comb, by arts which she understood, and, then disguising herself, she took the form of an old widow. She went over the seven hills to the house of the seven Dwarfs, and, knocking at the door, called out, "Good wares to sell to-day!" Snow-White peeped out and said, "You must go further, for I dare not let you in."

"But still you may look," said the old woman, drawing out her poisoned comb and holding it up. The sight of this pleased the maiden so much, that she allowed herself to be persuaded, and opened the door. As soon as she had made a purchase the old woman said, "Now let me for once comb you properly," and Snow-White consented, but scarcely was the comb drawn through the hair when the poison began to work, and the maiden soon fell down senseless. "You pattern of beauty," cried the wicked old Queen, "it is now all over with you," and so saying she departed.

Fortunately, evening soon came, and the seven Dwarfs returned, and as soon as they saw Snow-White lying, like dead, upon the ground, they suspected the old Queen, and soon discovering the poisoned comb, they immediately drew it out, and the maiden very soon revived and related all that had happened. Then they warned her again against the wicked stepmother, and bade her to open the door to nobody.

Meanwhile the Queen, on her arrival home, had again consulted her mirror, and received the same answer as twice before. This made her tremble and foam with rage and jealousy, and she swore Snow-White should die if it cost her her own life. Thereupon she went into an inner secret chamber where no one could enter, and there made an apple of the most deep and subtle poison. Outwardly it looked nice enough, and had rosy cheeks which would make the mouth of every one who looked at it water; but whoever ate the smallest piece of it would surely die. As soon as the apple was ready, the old Queen again dyed her face, and clothed herself like a peasant's wife, and then over the seven mountains to the seven Dwarfs she made her way. She knocked at the door, and Snow-White stretched out her head and said, "I dare not let any one enter; the seven Dwarfs have forbidden me."

"That is hard for me," said the old woman; "for I must take back my apples: but there is one which I will give you."

"Now," answered Snow-White, "no, I dare not take it."

"What! are you afraid of it?" cried the old woman; "there, see, will cut the apple in halves; do you eat the red cheeks, and I will eat the core." (The apple was so artfully made that the red cheeks alone were poisoned.) Snow-White very much wished for the beautiful apple, and when she saw the woman eating the core she could no longer resist, but, stretching out her hand, took the poisoned part. Scarcely had she placed a piece in her mouth when she fell down dead upon the ground. Then the Queen, looking at her with glittering eyes, and laughing bitterly, exclaimed, "White as snow, red as blood, black as ebony! This time the Dwarfs cannot re-awaken you."

When she reached home and consulted her mirror—

"Oh, mirror, mirror on the wall,
Who is the fairest of us all?"

it answered—

"Thou art the fairest, lady Queen."

Then her envious heart was at rest, as peacefully as an envious heart can rest.

When the little Dwarfs returned home in the evening, they found Snow-White lying on the ground, and there appeared to be no life in her body; she seemed to be quite dead. They raised her up, and searched if they could find anything poisonous; unlaced her, and even uncombed her hair, and washed her with water and with wine; but nothing availed: the dear child was really and truly dead. Then they laid her upon a bier, and all seven placed themselves around it, and wept and wept for three days without ceasing. Afterwards they would bury her, but she looked still fresh and lifelike, and even her red cheeks had not deserted her, so they said to one another, "We cannot bury her in the black ground," and they ordered a case to be made of transparent glass. In this one could view the body on all sides, and the Dwarfs wrote her name with golden letters upon the glass, saying that she was a King's daughter. Now they placed the glass-case upon the ledge of a rock, and one of them always remained by it watching. Even the beasts bewailed the loss of Snow-

White; first came an owl, then a raven, and last of all a dove.

For a long time Snow-White lay peacefully in her case, and changed not, but looked as if she were only asleep, for she was still white as snow, red as blood, and black-haired as ebony. By-and-bye it happened that a King's son was travelling in the forest, and came to the Dwarf's house to pass the night. He soon perceived the glass-case upon the rock, and the beautiful maiden lying within, and he read also the golden inscription.

When he had examined it, he said to the Dwarfs, "Let me have this case, and I will pay what you like for it."

But the Dwarfs replied, "We will not sell it for all the gold in the world."

"Then give it to me," said the Prince; "for I cannot live without Snow-White. I will honour and protect her so long as I live."

When the Dwarfs saw he was so much in earnest, they pitied him, and at last gave him the case, and the Prince ordered it to be carried away on the shoulders of one of his attendants. Presently it happened that they stumbled over a rut, and with the shock the piece of poisoned apple which lay in Snow-White's mouth fell out. Very soon she opened her eyes, and, raising the lid of the glass-case, she rose up and asked, "Where am I?"

Full of joy, the Prince answered, "You are safe with me;" and he related to her what she had suffered, and how he would rather have her than any other for his wife, and he asked her to accompany him home to the castle of the King his father. Snow-White consented, and when they arrived there the wedding between them was celebrated as speedily as possible, with all the splendour and magnificence proportionate to the happy event.

By chance the old stepmother of Snow-White was also invited to the wedding, and when she was dressed in all her finery to go, she first stepped in front of her mirror, and asked,—

> "Oh, mirror, mirror on the wall,
> Who is fairest of us all?"

and it replied,—

"Thou wert the fairest, oh lady Queen;
The Prince's bride is more fair, I ween."

At these words the old Queen was in a fury, and was so terribly mortified that she knew not what to do with herself. At first she resolved not to go to the wedding, but she could not resist the wish for a sight of the young Queen, and as soon as she entered she recognised Snow-White, and was so terrified with rage and astonishment that she remained rooted to the ground. Just then a pair of red-hot iron shoes were brought in with a pair of tongs and set before her, and these she was forced to put on and to dance in them till she fell down dead.

The Dog and the Sparrow

THERE was once a Shepherd's Dog, which had a very bad master, who never gave him food enough for his services; and one day, having made up his mind to endure such treatment no longer, the

Dog left the man's service and took his way, though with much sorrow. On the road the Dog met a Sparrow, who said "Brother Dog, why are you so glum?"

The Dog replied, "I am hungry and have nothing to eat."

"Oh," replied the Sparrow, "come with me, and I will soon satisfy you."

So they went together to the town, and, when they came to a butcher's shop, the bird said, "Wait a bit here, I will peck you down a piece of meat;" and flying into the shop, and looking round to see that no one observed her, she pecked and pulled at a joint which hung just over the window till it fell down. The Dog instantly snatched it, and, running into a corner, soon devoured it. When he had done, the Sparrow took him to another shop and pecked down a second piece of meat, and, when the Dog had finished this, the Sparrow asked, "Are you satisfied now, Brother Dog?"

"Yes," he replied, "with flesh; but I have touched no bread at all yet."

So the Sparrow, saying, "That you shall have if you will come with me," led him to a baker's, and pushed down a couple of loaves, and, when the Dog had finished them, she took him to another shop and pushed down more. As soon as these were consumed the Sparrow asked again if he were satisfied, and the Dog replied, "Yes; and now we'll walk awhile round the town."

Off they started now upon the highroad; but it being very warm weather, they had not walked far, when, as they came to a corner, the Dog said, "I am tired and must go to sleep."

"Very well," replied the Sparrow; "meanwhile I will sit on this twig." So the Dog laid down in the middle of the road and was soon fast asleep.

Presently a Carrier came up the road driving a waggon with three horses, laden with two casks of wine, and as the Sparrow saw that the man did not turn aside, but kept in the middle of the road where the Dog lay, she called out, "Carrier, take care what you do, or I will make you poor!"

But the Carrier, grumbling to himself, "You make me poor,

indeed!" cracked his whip and drove the waggon straight on, so that the wheels passed over the Dog and killed him. "You have killed my brother the Dog, and that shall cost you your horses and your cart!"

"Horses and cart, indeed!" said the Carrier; "what harm can you do me?" and he drove on.

Then the Sparrow, hopping under the wagon-covering, pecked at the bunghole of one of the casks until she worked out the cork, so that all the wine ran out without its being perceived by the Carrier; but all at once the man looked behind him and saw the wine dropping from the cart, and, trying the casks, found that one of them was empty. "Ah," cried he, "now I am a poor man!" "Yet not poor enough!" said the Sparrow, and, flying on to the head of one of the horses, she pecked out one of its eyes. When the Carrier saw this he drew out his hatchet and tried to hit the bird, but she flew up, and, instead, he cut his own horse's head, so that it fell down dead. "Ah," cried he, "now I am a poor man!"

"Still not poor enough!" said the Sparrow; and, while the Carrier drove further on with his two horses, she crept again under the covering of the waggon and pecked out the bung of the second cask, so that all the wine dripped out. When the man found this he exclaimed again, "Ah, now I am a poor man!" but the Bird replied, "Not poor enough yet!" and, settling on the head of the second horse, she pecked out its eyes also. Again the driver lifted his axe and made a cut at the Sparrow which flew away, so that the blow fell on his horse and killed it. "Ah, now I am poorer still!" cried the man; but the Bird replied, "Not yet poor enough!" and, perching on the third horse, she pecked out its eyes also. In a terrible passion the driver aimed a blow with his axe as before at the Sparrow, but, unfortunately missing, hit his own horse instead, and so killed his third and last animal. "Ah me! poorer and poorer!" exclaimed the Carrier.

"Not yet poor enough!" reiterated the Sparrow; "now I will make you poor at home;" and so flew away.

The Carrier was forced to leave his waggon in the road, and went home full of rage and passion. "Oh," said he to his wife, "what misfortunes I have had to endure! my wine has all run out, and my horses are all three dead! woe's me!"

"Ah, my husband!" she replied, "and what a wicked bird has come to this house: she has brought with her all the birds in the world, and there they sit among our corn and are eating every ear of it!"

The man stepped out, and, behold, thousands on thousands of birds had alighted upon the ground and had eaten up all the corn, and among them sat the Sparrow. "Ah me, I am poorer than ever!" he cried. "Still not poor enough, Carrier; it shall cost you your life!" replied the Bird, as she flew away.

Thus the Carrier lost all his property, and, now entering the kitchen, he sat down behind the stove and became quite morose and savage. The Sparrow, however, remained outside on the window-sill, calling out, "Carrier, it shall cost you your life!"

At this the man seized his axe and threw it at the Sparrow, but he only cut the window-frame in two, without hurting the bird. Now the Sparrow hopped in, and, perching on the stove, said again, "Carrier, it shall cost you your life!" Blinded with rage and fury he only cut the stove with his axe, and, as the Bird hopped about from one place to another, he pursued her, and hacked through all his furniture, glasses, seats, tables, and lastly, the walls even of his house, without once touching the Bird. However, he at length caught her with his hand, while his wife asked whether she should kill her. "No," said he, "that were too merciful: she shall die much more horribly, for I will eat her." So saying he swallowed her whole, but she began to flutter about in his stomach, and presently came again into his mouth, and called out, "Carrier, it shall cost you your life!"

Thereupon the man handed his wife the axe, saying, "Kill the wretch for me dead in my mouth!" His wife took it and aimed a blow, but, missing her mark, she struck her husband on the head and killed him. Then the Sparrow flew away and was never seen there again.

Roland

ONCE upon a time there lived a real old Witch who had two daughters, one ugly and wicked, whom she loved very much, because she was her own child; and the other fair and good, whom she hated, because she was her stepdaughter. One day the stepchild wore a very pretty apron, which so pleased the other that she turned jealous, and told her mother she must and would have the apron. "Be quiet, my child," said she, "you shall have it; your sister has long deserved death. To-night, when she is asleep, I will come and cut off her head; but take care that you lie nearest the wall, and push her quite to the side of the bed."

Luckily the poor maiden, hid in a corner, heard this speech, or she would have been murdered; but all day long she dared not go out of doors, and when bedtime came she was forced to lie in the place fixed for her: but happily the other sister soon went to sleep, and then she contrived to change places and get quite close to the wall. At midnight the old Witch sneaked in, holding in her right hand an axe, while with her left she felt for her intended victim; and then raising the axe in both her hands, she chopped off the head of her own daughter.

As soon as she went away, the maiden got up and went to her sweetheart, who was called Roland, and knocked at his door. When he came out she said to him, "Dearest Roland, we must flee at once; my stepmother would have killed me, but in the dark she has murdered her own child: if day comes, and she discovers what she has done, we are lost!"

"But I advise you," said Roland, "first to take away her magic wand, or we cannot save ourselves if she should follow and catch us."

So the maiden stole away the wand, and taking up the head dropped three drops of blood upon the ground: one before the bed, one in the kitchen, and one upon the step: this done, she hurried away with her lover.

When the morning came and the old Witch had dressed herself, she called to her daughter and would have given her the apron, but no one came. "Where are you?" she called. "Here upon the step," answered one of the drops of blood. The old woman went out, but seeing nobody on the step, she called a second time, "Where are you?" "Hi, hi, here in the kitchen; I am warming myself," replied the second drop of blood. She went into the kitchen, but could see nobody; and once again she cried, "Where are you?"

"Ah! here I sleep in the bed," said the third drop; and she entered the room, but what a sight met her eyes! There lay her own child covered with blood, for she herself had cut off her head.

The old Witch flew into a terrible passion, sprang out of the window, and looking far and near, presently spied out her stepdaughter, who was hurrying away with Roland. "That won't help you!" she shouted; "were you twice as far, you should not escape me." So saying, she drew on her boots, in which she went an hour's walk with every stride, and before long she overtook the fugitives. But the maiden, as soon as she saw the Witch in sight, changed her dear Roland into a lake with the magic wand, and herself into a duck, who could swim upon its surface. When the old Witch arrived at the shore, she threw in bread-crumbs, and tried all sorts of means to entice the duck; but it was all of no use, and she was obliged to go away at evening without accomplishing her ends. When she was gone the maiden took her natural form, and Roland also, and all night long till daybreak they travelled onwards. Then the maiden changed herself into a rose, which grew amid a very thorny hedge, and Roland became a fiddler. Soon after up came the old Witch, and said to him, "Good player, may I break off your flower?" "Oh! yes," he replied, "and I will accompany you with a tune." In great haste she climbed up the bank to reach the flower, and as soon as she was in the hedge he began to play, and whether she liked it or not she was obliged to dance to the music, for it was a bewitched tune. The quicker he played, the higher was she obliged to jump, till the thorns tore all the clothes off her body, and scratched and wounded her so much that at last she fell down dead.

Then Roland, when he saw they were saved, said, "Now I will go to my father, and arrange the wedding."

"Yes," said the maiden, "and meanwhile I will rest here, and wait for your return, and, that on one may know me, I will change myself into a red stone."

Roland went away and left her there, but when he reached home he fell into the snares laid for him by another maiden, and forgot his true love, who for a long time waited his coming; but at last, in sorrow and despair of ever seeing him again, she changed herself into a beautiful flower, and thought that perhaps someone might pluck her and carry her to his home.

A day or two after a shepherd who was tending his flock in the field chanced to see the enchanted flower; and because it was so very beautiful he broke it off, took it with him, and laid it by in his chest. From that day everything prospered in the shepherd's house, and marvellous things happened. When he arose in the morning he found all the work already done: the room was swept, the chairs and tables dusted, the fire lighted upon the hearth, and the water fetched; when he came home at noonday the table was laid, and a good meal prepared for him. He could not imagine how it was all done, for he could find nobody ever in his house when he returned, and there was no place for any one to conceal himself. The good arrangements certainly pleased him well enough, but he became so anxious at last to know who it was, that he went and asked the advice of a wise woman. The woman said, "There is some witchery in the business; listen one morning if you can hear anything moving in the room, and if you do and can see anything, be it what it will, throw a white napkin over it, and the charm will be dispelled."

The shepherd did as he was bid, and the next morning, just as day broke, he saw his chest open and the flower come out of it. He instantly sprang up and threw a white napkin over it, and immediately the spell was broken, and a beautiful maiden stood before him, who acknowledged that she was the handmaid who, as a flower, had put his house in order. She told him her tale, and she pleased the shepherd so much, that he asked her if she would marry him, but she said, "No," for she would still keep true to her dear Roland, although he had left her; nevertheless, she promised still to remain with the shepherd, and see after his cottage.

Meanwhile, the time had arrived for the celebration of Roland's wedding, and, according to the old custom, it was proclaimed through all the country round, that every maiden might assemble to sing in honour of the bridal pair. When the poor girl heard this, she was so grieved that it seemed as if her heart would break, and she would not have gone to the wedding if others had not come and taken her with them.

When it came to her turn to sing, she stepped back till she was quite by herself, and as soon as she began, Roland jumped up, exclaiming, "I know the voice! that is my true bride! no other will I have!" All that he had hitherto forgotten and neglected to think of was suddenly brought back to his heart's remembrance, and he would not again let her go.

And now the wedding of the faithful maiden to her dear Roland was celebrated with great magnificence; and their sorrows and troubles being over, happiness became their lot.

The Knapsack, the Hat, and the Horn

ONCE upon a time there were three brothers, who every day sank deeper and deeper in poverty, until at last their need was so great that they were in danger of death from starvation, having nothing to bite or break. So they said to one another, "We cannot go on in this way; we had better go forth into the wide world and seek our fortunes." With these words they got up and set out, and travelled many a long mile over green fields and meadows without happening with any luck. One day they arrived in a large forest, and in the middle of it they found a hill, which, on their nearer approach, they saw was all silver. At this sight the eldest brother said, "Now I have met with my expected good fortune, and I desire nothing better."

And, so saying, he took as much of the silver as he could carry, and turned back again to his house.

The others, however, said, "We desire something better than mere silver;" and they would not touch it, but went on further. After they had travelled a couple of days longer, the came to another hill, which was all gold. There the second brother stopped, and soon became quite dazzled with the sight. "What shall I do?" said he to himself; "shall I take as much gold as I can, that I may have enough to live upon, or, shall I go further still?" At last he came to a conclusion, and, putting what he could in his pockets, he bade his brother good-bye and returned home. The third brother said, however, "Silver and gold will I not touch; I will seek my fortune yet; perhaps something better than all will happen to me."

So he travelled along for three days alone, and at the end of the third he came to a great forest, which was a great deal more extensive than the former, and so much so that he could not find the end: and, moreover, he was almost perished with hunger and thirst. He climbed up a high tree to discover if he could by chance find an outlet to the forest; but so far as his eyes could reach there was nothing but tree-tops to be seen. His hunger now began to trouble him very much, and he though to himself, "Could I now only for this once have a good meal, I might get on." Scarcely were the words out of his mouth when he saw, to his great astonishment, a napkin under the tree, spread over with all kings of good food, very grateful to his senses. "Ah, this time," thought he, "my wish is fulfilled at the very nick:" and, without any consideration as to who brought or who cooked the dishes, he sat himself down and ate to his heart's content. When he had finished, he thought it would be a shame to leave such a fine napkin in the wood, so he packed it up as small as he could, and carried it away in his pocket. After this he went on again, and as he felt hungry towards evening, he wished to try his napkin; and, spreading it out, he said aloud, "I should like to see you again spread with cheer;" and scarcely had he spoke when as many dishes as there was room for stood upon the napkin. At the sight he exclaimed, "Now you are dearer to me than a mountain of silver and gold, for I

THE KNAPSACK, THE HAT, AND THE HORN

perceive you are a wishing-cloth;" but, however, he was not yet satisfied, but would go farther and seek his fortune.

The next evening he came up with a Charcoal-burner, who was busy with his coals, and who was roasting some potatoes at his fire for his supper. "Good evening, my black fellow," said our hero; "how do you find yourself in your solitude?" "One day is like another," replied he, "and every night potatoes: have you a mind for some? if so, by my guest."

"Many thanks," replied the traveller; "but I will not deprive you of your meal; you did not reckon on having a guest; but, if you have no objection, you shall yourself have an invitation to supper." "Who will invite me?" asked the Charcoal-burner; "I do not see that you have got anything with you, and there is no one in the circuit of two hours' walk who could give you anything."

"And yet there shall be a meal," returned the other, "better than you have ever seen."

So saying, he took out his napkin, and, spreading it on the ground, said, "Cloth, cover thyself!" and immediately meats boiled and baked, as hot as if just out of the kitchen, were spread about. The Charcoal-burner opened his eyes wide, but did not stare long, but soon began to eat away, cramming his black mouth as full as he could. When they had finished, the man, smacking his lips, said, "Come, your cloth pleases me; it would be very convenient for me here in the wood, where I have no one to cook. I will strike a bargain with you. There hangs a soldier's knapsack, which is certainly both old and shabby; but it possesses a wonderful virtue, and, as I have no more use for it, I will give it you in exchange for your cloth."

"But first I must know in what this wonderful virtue consists," said the traveller.

"I will tell you," replied the other. "If you tap thrice with your fingers upon it, out will come a corporal and six men, armed from head to foot, who will do whatsoever you command them."

"In faith," cried our hero, "I do not think I can do better; let us change;" and, giving the man his wishing-cloth, he took the knapsack off its hook, and strode away with it on his back.

He had not gone very far before he wished to try the virtue of his bargain; so he tapped upon it, and immediately the seven warriors stepped before him, and the leader asked his commands. "What does my lord and master desire?"

"March back quickly to the Charcoal-burner, and demand my wishing-cloth again," said our hero.

The soldiers wheeled round to the left, and before very long they brought what he desired, having taken it from the Collier without so much as asking his leave. This done, he dismissed them, and travelled on again, hoping his luck might shine brighter yet. At sunset he came to another Charcoal-burner, who was also preparing his supper at the fire, and asked, "Will you sup with me? Potatoes and salt, without butter, is all I have; sit down if you choose."

"No," replied the traveller; "this time you shall be my guest;" and he unfolded his cloth, which was at once spread with the most delicate fare. They ate and drank together, and soon got very merry; and when their meal was done, the Charcoal-burner said, "Up above there on that board lies an old worn-out hat, which possesses the wonderful power, if one puts it on and presses it down on his head, of causing, as it were, twelve field-pieces to go off, one after the other, and shoot down all that comes in their way. The hat is of no use to me in that way, and therefore I should like to exchange it for your cloth."

"Oh! I have no objection to that," replied the other; and, taking the hat, he left his wishing-cloth behind him; but he had not gone very far before he tapped on his knapsack, and bade the soldiers who appeared to fetch it back from his guest.

"Ah," thought he to himself, "one thing happens so soon upon another, that it seems as if my luck would have no end." And his thoughts did not deceive him; for he had scarcely gone another day's journey when he met with a third Charcoal-burner, who invited him, as the others had, to a potato-supper. However, he spread out his wishing-cloth, and the feast pleased the Charcoal-burner so well, that he offered him, in return for his cloth, a horn, which had still more wonderful properties than either the knapsack or hat; for, when one blew it, every wall and fortification fell down before its blast, and even whole villages and towns were overturned. For this horn he gladly gave his cloth, but he soon sent his soldiers back for it; and now he had not only that, but also the knapsack, the hat, and the horn.

"Now," said he, "I am a made man, and it is high time that I should return home and see how my brothers get on."

When he arrived at the old place, he found his brothers had built a splendid palace with their gold and silver, and were living in clover. He entered their house; but because he came in with a coat torn to rags, the shabby hat upon his head, and the old knapsack on his back, his brothers would not own him. They mocked him, saying, "You pretend to be our brother; why, he despised silver and gold, and sought better luck for himself; he would come accompanied like a mighty king, not as a beggar!" and they hunted him out of doors.

This treatment put the poor man in such a rage, that he knocked upon the knapsack so many times till a hundred and fifty men stood before him in rank and file. He commanded them to surround his brothers' house, and two of them to take hazel-sticks and thrash them both until they knew who he was. They set up a tremendous howling, so that the people ran to the spot and tried to assist the two brothers; but they could do nothing against the soldiers. By-and-by the King himself heard the noise, and he ordered out a captain and troop to drive the disturber of the peace out of the city; but the man with his knapsack soon gathered together a greater company, who beat back the captain and his men, and sent them home with bleeding noses. At this the King said, "This vagabond fellow shall be driven away;" and the next day he sent a larger troop against him; but they fared no better than the first. The beggar, as he was called, soon ranged more men in opposition, and, in order to do the work quicker, he pressed his hat down upon his head a couple of times; and immediately the heavy guns began to play, and soon beat down all the King's people, and put the rest to flight. "Now," said our hero, "I will never make peace till the King gives me his daughter to wife, and he places me upon the throne as ruler of his whole dominion." This vow which he had taken he caused to be communicated to the King, who said to his daughter "Must is a hard nut to crack: what is there left to me but that I do as this man desires? If I wish for peace, and to keep the crown upon my head, I must yield."

So the wedding was celebrated; but the Princess was terribly vexed that her husband was such a common man, and wore not only a very shabby hat, but also carried about with him everywhere a dirty old knapsack. She determined to get rid of them; and day and night she was always thinking how to manage it. It struck her suddenly that perhaps his wonderful power lay in the knapsack; so she flattered, caressed him, saying, "I wish you would lay aside that dirty knapsack; it becomes you so ill that I am almost ashamed of you."

"Dear child," he replied, "this knapsack is my greatest treasure; as long as I possess it I do not fear the greatest power on earth;" and he further told her all its wonderful powers. When he had finished, the Princess fell on his neck as if she would kiss him; but she craftily untied the knapsack, and, loosening it from his shoulders, ran away with it. As soon as she was alone she tapped upon it, and ordered the warriors who appeared to bind fast her husband and lead him out of the royal palace. They obeyed; and the false wife caused other soldiers to march behind, who were instructed to hunt the poor man out of the kingdom. It would have been all over with him had he not still possessed the hat, which he pressed down on his head as soon as his hands were free, and immediately the cannons began to go off, and demolished all before them. The Princess herself was at last obliged to go and beg pardon of her husband. He at last consented to make peace, being moved by her supplications and promises to behave better in future; and she acted so lovingly, and treated him so well for some time after, that he entrusted her with the secret, that although he might be deprived of the knapsack, yet so long as he had the hat no one could overcome him. As soon as she knew this, she waited until he was asleep and then stole away the hat, and caused her husband to be thrown into a ditch. The horn, however, was still left to him; and in a great passion, he blew upon it such a blast that in a minute down came tumbling the walls, forts, houses, and palaces, and buried the King and his daughter in the ruins. Luckily he ceased to blow for want of breath; for had he kept it up any longer all the houses would have been overturned, and not one stone left upon another. After this feat nobody dared to oppose him, and he set himself up as King over the whole country.

The Little Farmer

THERE was a certain village, wherein several rich farmers were settled, and only one poor one, who was therefore called "The Little Farmer." He had not even a cow, nor money to buy it, though he and his wife would have been only too happy to have had one. One day he said to her, "A good thought has just struck me: our father-in-law, the carver, can make us a calf out of wood and paint it brown, so that it will look like any other; in time, perhaps, it will grow big and become a cow." This proposal pleased his wife, and the carver was instructed accordingly, and he cut out the calf, painted it as it should be, and so made it that its head was bent down as if eating.

When, the next morning, the cows were driven out to pasture, the Farmer called the Shepherd in and said, "See, I have here a little calf, but it is so small that it must as yet be carried." The Shepherd said, "Very well;" and, taking it under his arm, carried it down to the meadow and set it among the grass. All day the calf stood there as if eating, and the Shepherd said, "It will soon grow big and go alone: only see how it is eating!" At evening time, when he wanted to drive his flocks home, he said to the calf, "Since you can stand there to satisfy your hunger, you must also be able to walk upon your four legs, and I shall not carry you home in my arms." The Little Farmer stood before his house-door waiting for his calf, and as the Shepherd drove his herd through the village he asked after it. The Shepherd replied, "It is still standing there eating: it would not listen and come with me." The Farmer exclaimed, "Eh, what? I must have my calf!" and so they both went together down to the meadow, but some one had stolen the calf, and it was gone. The Shepherd said, "Perhaps it has run away itself;" but the Farmer replied, "Not so – that won't do for me;" and dragging him before the Mayor, he was condemned for his negligence to give the Little Farmer a cow in the place of the lost calf.

Now the Farmer and his wife possessed the long-desired cow, and were very glad; but having no fodder they could give her nothing to eat, so that very soon they were obliged to kill her. The flesh they salted down, and the skin the Little Farmer took to the next town to sell, to buy another calf with what he got for it. On the way he passed a mill, where a raven was sitting with a broken wing, and out of compassion he took the bird up and wrapped it in the skin he was carrying. But the weather being just then very bad, a great storm of wind and rain falling, he was unable to go further, and, turning into the mill, begged for shelter. The Miller's wife was at home alone, and said to the Farmer, "Lie down on that straw," and give him a piece of bread and cheese. The Farmer ate it and lay down, with his skin near him, and the Miller's wife thought he was asleep. Presently in came a man, whom she received very cordially, and invited to sup with her; but the Farmer, when he heard talk of the feast, was vexed that he should have been treated only to bread and cheese. So the woman went down into the cellar and brought up four dishes, – roast meat, salad, boiled meat, and wine. As they were sitting down to eat there was a knock outside, and the woman exclaimed, "Oh, gracious! there is my husband!" In a great hurry she stuck the roast meat in the oven, the wine under the pillow, the salad upon the bed, and the boiled meat under it, while her guest stepped into a closet where she kept the linen. This done she let in her husband, and said, "God be praised you are returned again! what weather it is, as if the world were coming to an end!"

The Miller remarked the man lying on the straw, and asked what the fellow did there. His Wife said, "Ah, the poor fellow came in the wind and rain and begged for shelter, so I gave him some bread and cheese and showed him the straw!"

The husband said he had no objection, but bade her bring him quickly something to eat. The wife said, "I have nothing but bread and cheese," and her husband told her with that he should be contented, and asked the Farmer to come and share his meal. The Farmer did not let himself be twice asked, but got up and ate away. Presently the Miller remarked the skin lying upon the ground, in which was the raven, and asked, "What have you there!" The Farmer replied, "I have a truth-teller therein." "Can it tell me the truth too?" inquired the Miller.

"Why not?" said the other; "but he will only say four things, and the fifth he keeps to himself." The Miller was curious, and wished to hear it speak, and the Farmer squeezed the raven's head, so that it squeaked out. The Miller then asked, "What did he say?" and the Farmer replied, "The first thing·is, under the pillow lies wine." "That is a rare tell-tale!" cried the Miller, and went and found the wine. "Now again," said he. The Farmer made the raven croak again, and said, "Secondly, he declares there is roast meat in the oven." "That is a good tell-tale!" again cried the Miller, and, opening the oven, he took out the roast meat. Then the Farmer made the raven croak again, and said, "For the third thing, he declares there is salad on the bed."

"That is a good tell-tale!" cried the Miller, and went and found the salad. Then the Farmer made his bird croak once more, and said, "For the fourth thing, he declares there is boiled meat under the bed."

"That is a capital tell-tale!" cried the Miller, while he went and found as it said.

The worthy pair now sat down together at the table, but the Miller's wife felt terribly anxious, and went to bed, taking all the keys with her. The Miller was very anxious to know the fifth thing, but the Man said, "First let us eat quietly these four things, for the other is somewhat dreadful."

After they had finished their meal, the Miller bargained as to how much he should give for the fifth thing, and at last he agreed for three hundred dollars. Then the Farmer once more made the raven croak, and when the Miller asked what it said, he told him, "He declares that in the cupboard where the linen is there is an evil spirit."

The Miller said, "The evil spirit must walk out!" and tried the door, but it was locked, and the woman had to give up the key to the Farmer, who unlocked it. The unbidden guest at once bolted out, and ran out of the house, while the Miller said, "Ah, I saw the black fellow, that was all right!" Soon they went to sleep; but at daybreak the Farmer took his three hundred dollars and made himself scarce.

The Farmer was now quite rich at home, and built himself a fine house, so that his fellows said, "The Little Farmer has certainly found the golden snow, of which he has brought away a basketful;" and they summoned him before the Mayor, that he might be made to say whence his riches came. The man replied, "I have sold my cow's skin in the city for three hundred dollars." And as soon as the others heard this they desired also to make a similar profit. The farmers ran home, killed all their cows, and, taking their skins off, took them to the city to sell them for so good a price. The Mayor, however, said, "My maid must go first;" and when she arrived at the city she went to the merchant, but he gave her only three dollars for her skin. And when the rest came he would not give them so much, saying, "What should I do with all these skins?"

The farmers were much vexed at being outwitted by their poor neighbour, and, bent on revenge, they complained to the Mayor of his deceit. The innocent Little Farmer was condemned to death unanimously, and was to be rolled in a cask full of holes into the sea. He was led away, and a priest sent for who should say for him the mass for the dead. Every one else was obliged to remove to a distance, and when the Farmer looked at the priest he recognised the guest whom he had met at the mill. So he said to him, "I have delivered you out of the cupboard, now deliver me from this cask." Just at that moment the Shepherd passed by with a flock of sheep, and the Farmer, knowing that for a long time the man had desired to be mayor, cried out with all his might, "No, no! I will not do it; if all the world asked me I would not be it! No, I will not!"

When the Shepherd heard this he came up and said, "What are you doing here? What will you not do?"

The Farmer replied, "They will make me mayor if I keep in this cask; but no, I will not be here!"

"Oh," said the Shepherd, "if nothing more is wanting to be mayor I am willing to put myself in the cask!"

"Yes, you will be mayor if you do that," said the Farmer; and, getting out of the cask, the other got in, and the Farmer nailed the lid down again. Now he took the Shepherd's flock and drove it away, while the parson went to the Judge and told him he had said the prayers for the dead. Then they went and rolled the cask down to the water, and while it rolled the Shepherd called out, "Yes, I should like to be mayor!" They thought it was the Little Farmer who spoke; and saying, "Yes, we mean it; only you must first go below there;" and they sent the cask right into the sea.

That done the farmers returned home; and as they came into the village, so came also the Little Farmer, driving a flock of sheep quietly and cheerfully. The sight astounded the others, and they asked, "Whence comest thou? dost thou come out of the water?" "Certainly," answered he; "I sank deeper and deeper till I got to the bottom, where I pushed up the head of the cask, and, getting out, there were beautiful meadows, upon which many lambs were pasturing, and I brought this flock of them up with me."

"Are there any more?" inquired the farmers. "Oh, yes," replied he, "more than you know what to do with!"

Then the farmers agreed that they would go and each fetch up a flock for himself; but the Mayor said, "I must go first." So they went together down to the water, and there happened to be a fine blue sky with plenty of fleecy clouds over it, which were mirrored in the water and looked like little lambs. The farmers called one to another, "Look there! we can see the sheep already on the ground below the water!" and the Mayor, pressing quite forward, said, "I will go first and look about me, and see if it is a good place, and then call you."

So saying, he jumped in plump, and, as he splashed the water about, the others thought he was calling "Come along!" and so one after another the whole assemblage plunged in in a grand hurry. Thus was the whole village cleared out, and the "Little Farmer," as their only heir, became a very rich man.

Jorinde and Joringel

ONCE upon a time, in a castle in the midst of a large thick wood, there lived an old Witch all by herself. By day she changed herself into a cat or an owl; but in the evening she resumed her right form. She was able also to allure to her the wild animals and birds, whom she killed, cooked, and ate, for whoever ventured within a hundred steps of her castle was obliged to stand still, and could not stir from the spot until she allowed it; but if a pretty maiden came into the circle the Witch changed her into a bird, and then put her into a basket, which she carried into one of the rooms in the castle; and in this room were already many thousand such baskets of rare birds.

Now there was a young maiden called Jorinde, who was exceedingly pretty, and she was betrothed to a youth named Joringel, and just at the time that the events which I am about to relate happened, they were passing the days together in a round of pleasure. One day they went into the forest for a walk, and Joringel said, "Take care that you do not go too near the castle." It was a beautiful evening; the sun shining between the stems of the trees, and brightening up the dark green leaves and the turtle-doves cooing softly upon the may-bushes. Jorinde began to cry, and sat down in the sunshine with Joringel, who cried too, for they were quite frightened, and thought they should die, when they looked round and saw how far they had wandered, and that there was no house in sight. The sun was yet half above the hills and half below, and Joringel, looking through the brushwood, saw the old walls of the castle close by them, which frightened him terribly, so that he fell off his seat. Then Jorinde sang,—

> "My little bird, with his ring so red,
>   Sings sorrow, and sorrow and woe;
> For he sings that the turtle-dove soon will be dead,
>   Oh sorrow, and sorrow – jug, jug, jug."

Joringel lifted up his head, and saw Jorinde was changed into a nightingale, which was singing, "Jug, jug, jug," and presently an owl flew round thrice, with his eyes glistening, and crying, "Tu wit, tu woo." Joringel could not stir; there he stood like a stone, and could not weep, nor speak, nor move hand or foot. Meanwhile the sun set, and, the owl flying into a bush, out came an ugly old woman, thin and yellow, with great red eyes, and a crooked nose which reached down to her chin. She muttered, and seized the nightingale, and carried it away in her hand, while Joringel remained there incapable of moving or speaking. At last the Witch returned, and said, with a hollow voice, "Greet you, Zachiel! if the moon shines on your side, release this one at once." Then Joringel became free, and fell down on his knees before the Witch, and begged her to give him back Jorinde; but she refused, and said he should never again have her, and went away. He cried, and wept, and groaned after her, but all to no purpose; and at length he rose and went into a strange village, where for some time he tended sheep. He often went round about the

JORINDE AND JORINGEL

enchanted castle, but never too near, and one night, after so walking, he dreamt that he found a blood-red flower, in the middle of which lay a fine pearl. This flower, he thought he broke off, and, going therewith to the castle, all he touched with it was free from enchantment, and thus he regained his Jorinde.

When he awoke next morning he began his search over hill and valley to find such a flower, but nine days had passed away. At length, early one morning he discovered it, and in its middle was a large dewdrop, like a beautiful pearl. Then he carried the flower day and night, till he came to the castle; and, although he ventured within the enchanted circle, he was not stopped, but walked on quite to the door. Joringel was now in high spirits, and touching the door with his flower it flew open. He entered, and passed through the hall, listening for the sound of the birds, which at last he heard. He found the room, and went in, and there was the Enchantress feeding the birds in the seven thousand baskets. As soon as she saw Joringel, she became frightfully enraged, and spat out poison and gall at him, but she dared not come too close. He would not turn back for her, but looked at the baskets of birds; but, alas! there were many hundreds of nightingales, and how was he to know his Jorinde? While he was examining them he perceived the old woman secretly taking away one of the baskets, and slipping out of the door. Joringel flew after her, and touched the basket with his flower, and also the old woman, so that she could no longer bewitch; and at once Jorinde stood before him, and fell upon his neck, as beautiful as she ever was. Afterwards he disenchanted all the other birds, and then returned home with his Jorinde, and for many years they lived together happily and contentedly.

Fir-Apple

ONCE on a time as a forester was going into the wood he heard a cry like that of a child, and walking in the direction of the sound he came to a fir-tree on which sat a little boy. A mother had gone to sleep under the tree with her child in her lap, and while she slept a golden eagle had seized it, and borne it away to the topmost bough in his beak. So the forester mounted and fetched the child down, and took it home to be brought up with his daughter Helen; and the two grew up together. The boy whom he had rescued he named Fir-Apple, in remembrance of his adventure, and Helen and the boy loved each other so fondly, that they were quite unhappy whenever they were separated. This forester had also an old Cook, who one evening took two pails and went to fetch water; but she did not go once only, but many times to the spring. Little Helen, seeing her, asked, "Why do you carry in so much water, old Sarah?"

"If you will promise not to tell any one, I will let you know," replied the Cook.

Little Helen promised not to tell, and the Cook said, "Early in the morning, when the forester is away to the chase, I shall heat the water, and when it boils I shall throw in Fir-Apple and stew him."

The next day the forester arose with the sun and went out, while the children were still in bed. Then Helen said to Fir-Apple, "Forsake me not, and so I will never leave you;" and he replied, "Now and for ever I will stay with you."

"Do you know," continued Helen, "yesterday the old Cook fetched ever so many pails of water, and I asked her why she did so, and she said to me, 'If you do not say anything I will tell you;' and, as I promised not to tell, she said, early this morning, when father has gone out, she should boil the copper full of water and stew you in it. But let us get up very quickly, and escape while there is time." So saying, they both arose, and dressing themselves very hastily, ran away as quickly as they could. When the water had become boiling hot the old Cook went into the sleeping-room to fetch Fir-Apple; but lo! as soon as she entered and stepped up to the beds, she perceived that both the children were off, and at the sight she grew very anxious, saying to herself, "What shall I say if the forester comes home and finds both the children gone? I must send after them and fetch them back."

Thus thinking, she sent after them three slaves, bidding them overtake the children as quickly as possible and bring them home. But the children saw the slaves running towards them, and little Helen said, "Forsake me not, and so I will never leave you."

"Now and always I will keep by you," replied Fir-Apple.

"Do you then become a rose-stock, and I will be the bud upon it," said Helen.

So, when the slaves came up, the children were nowhere to be found, and only a rose-tree, with a single bud thereon, to be seen, and the three agreed there was nothing to do, and went home and told the old Cook they had seen nothing at all in the world but a rose-tree with a single flower upon it. At their tale the old Cook began to scold terribly, and said, "You stupid simpletons, you should have cut the rose-bush in two, and broken off the flower and brought it home to me: make haste now and do so." For a second time they had to go out and search, and the children seeing them at a distance, little Helen asked her companion the same question as the first time, and when he gave the same reply, she said, "Do you then become a church and I will be the crown therein."

When now the three slaves approached, they found nothing but a church and a crown inside, so they said to one another, "What can we do here? let us go home." As soon as they reached the house, the Cook inquired what they had found; and when they had told their tale she was very angry, and told them they ought to have pulled down the church and brought the crown home with them. When she had finished scolding, she set out herself, walking with the three slaves, after the children, who espied her coming from a distance. This time little Helen proposed that she should become a pond, and Fir-Apple a duck, who should swim about on it, and so they changed into these immediately. When the old woman came up and saw the pond, she lay down by it and began to drink it up, but the Duck swam very quickly toward her, and without her knowledge struck his beak into her cap and drew her into the water, where, after vainly endeavouring to save herself, she sank to the bottom.

After this the children returned home together and were very happy; and, if they are not dead, I suppose they are still alive and merry.

Catherine and Frederick

ONCE upon a time there was a youth named Frederick, and a girl called Catherine, who had married and lived together as a young couple. One day Fred said, "I am now going into the fields, dear Catherine, and by the time I return let there be something hot upon the table, for I shall be hungry, and something to drink too, for I shall be thirsty."

"Very well, dear Fred," said she, "go at once, and I will make all right for you."

As soon, then, as dinner-time approached, she took down a sausage out of the chimney, and putting it in a frying-pan with batter set it over the fire. Soon the sausage began to frizzle and spit while Catherine stood by holding the handle of the pan and thinking; and among other things she thought that while the sausage was getting ready she might go into the cellar and draw some beer. So she took a can and went down into the cellar to draw the beer, and while it ran into the can, she bethought herself that perhaps the dog might steal the sausage out of the pan, and so up the cellar stairs she ran, but too late, for the rogue had already got the meat in his mouth and was sneaking off. Catherine, however, pursued the dog for a long way over the fields, but the heart was quicker than she, and would not let the sausage go, but bolted off at a great rate. "Off is off!" said Catherine, and turned round, and being very tired and hot, she went home slowly to cool herself. All this while the beer was running out of the cask, for Catherine had forgotten to turn the tap off, and so as soon as the can was full the liquor ran over the floor of the cellar until it was all out. Catherine saw the misfortune at the top of the steps. "My gracious!" she exclaimed, "what shall I do that Fred may not find this out?" She considered for some time till she remembered that a sack of fine malt yet remained from the last brewing, in one corner, which she would fetch down and strew about in the beer. "Yes," said she, "it was spared at the right time to be useful to me now in my necessity;" and down she pulled the sack so hastily that she overturned the can of beer for Fred, and away it mixed with the rest on the floor. "It is all right," said she, "where one is, the other should be;" and she strewed the malt over the whole cellar. When it was done she was quite overjoyed at her work, and said, "How clean and neat it does look to be sure!"

At noontime Fred returned. "Now, wife, what have you ready for me?" said he. "Ah, my dear Fred," she replied, "I would have fried you a sausage, but while I drew the beer the dog stole it out of the pan, and while I hunted the dog the beer all ran out, and as I was about to dry up the beer with the malt, I overturned your can; but be contented, the cellar is quite dry again now."

"Oh, Catherine, Catherine!" said Fred, "you should not have done so! to let the sausage be stolen! and the beer run out! and over all to shoot our best sack of malt!!!"

"Well, Fred," said she, "I did not know that; you should have told me."

But the husband thought to himself, if one's wife acts so, one must look after things one's self. Now, he had collected a tolerable sum of silver dollars, which he changed into gold, and then he told his wife, "Do you see, these are yellow counters, which I will put in a pot and bury in the stable under the cow's stall; but mind that you do not meddle with it, or you will come to some harm."

, Catherine promised to mind what he said, but, as soon as Fred was gone, some hawkers came into the village with earthenware for sale, and amongst others they asked her if she would purchase anything. "Ah, good people," said Catherine, "I have no money, and cannot buy anything, but if you can make use of yellow counters I will buy them."

"Yellow counters! ah! why not? let us look at them," said they.

"Go into the stable," she replied, "and dig under the cow's stall, and there you will find the yellow counters. I dare not go myself."

The rogues went at once, and soon dug up the shining gold, which they quickly pocketed, and then they ran off, leaving behind them their pots and dishes in the house. Catherine thought she might as well make use of the new pottery, and since she had no need of anything in the kitchen, she set out each pot on the ground, and then put others on the top of the palings round the house for ornament. When Fred returned, and saw the fresh decorations, he asked Catherine what she had done. "I have bought them, Fred," said she, "with the yellow counters which lay under the cow's stall; but I did not dig them up myself; the pedlars did that."

"Ah, wife, what have you done?" replied Fred, "they were not counters, but bright gold, which was all the property we possessed: you should not have done so."

"Well, dear Fred," replied his wife, "you should have told me so before. I did not know that."

Catherine stood considering for a while, and presently she began, "Come, Fred, we will soon get the gold back again; let us pursue the thieves."

"Well, come along," said Fred; "we will try at all events; but take butter and cheese with you, that we may have something to eat on our journey."

"Yes, Fred," said she, and soon made herself ready; but, her husband being a good walker, she lagged behind. "Ah!" said she, "this is my luck, for when we turn back I shall be a good bit forward." Presently she came to a hill, on both sides of which there were very deep ruts. "Oh, see!" said she, "how the poor earth is torn, flayed, and wounded: it will never be well again all its life!" And out of compassion she took out her butter, and greased the ruts over right and left, so that the wheels might run more easily through them, and, while she stooped in doing this, a cheese rolled out of her pocket down the mountain. Catherine said when she saw it, "I have already once made the journey up, and I am not coming down after you: another shall run and fetch you." So saying, she took another cheese out of her pocket, and rolled it down; but, as it did not return, she thought, "Perhaps they are waiting for a companion, and don't like to come alone;" and down she bowled a third cheese. Still all three stayed, and she said, "I cannot think what was this means; perhaps it is that the third cheese has missed his way: I will send a fourth, that he may call him as he goes by." But this one acted no better than the others, and Catherine became so anxious that she threw down a fifth and a sixth cheese also, and they were the last. For a long time after this she waited, expecting they would come, but when she found they did not she cried out, "You are nice fellows to send after a dead man! you stop a fine time! but do you think I shall wait for you? Oh, no! I shall go on; you can follow me; you have younger legs than I."

So saying, Catherine walked on and came up with Fred, who was waiting for her, because he needed something to eat. "Now," said he, "give me quickly what you brought." She handed him the dry bread. "Where are the butter and cheese?" cried her husband. "Oh, Fred, dear," she replied, "with the butter I have smeared the ruts, and the cheeses will soon come, but one ran away, and I sent the others after it to call it back!"

"It was silly of you to do so," said Fred, "to grease the roads with butter, and to roll cheeses down the hill!"

"If you had but told me so," said Catherine, vexatiously.

So they ate the dry bread together, and presently Fred said, "Catherine, did you make things fast at home before you came out?"

"No, Fred," said she, "you did not tell me."

"Then go back and lock up the house before we go further; bring something to eat with you, and I will stop here for you."

Back went Catherine, thinking, "Ah! Fred will like something else to eat. Butter and cheese will not please; I will bring with me a bag of dried apples and a mug of vinegar to drink." When she had put these things together she bolted the upper half of the door, but the under door she raised up and carried away on her shoulder, thinking that certainly the house was well protected if she took such good care of the door! Catherine walked along now very leisurely, for said she to herself, "Fred will have all the longer rest!" and as soon as she reached him she gave him the door, saying, "There, Fred, now you have the house door, you can take care of the house yourself."

"Oh! my goodness," exclaimed the husband, "what a clever wife I have! she has bolted the top door, but brought away the bottom part, where any one can creep through! Now it is too late to go back to the house, but since you brought the door here you may carry it onwards."

"The door I will willingly carry," replied Catherine, "but the apples and the vinegar will be too heavy, so I shall hang them on the door, and make that carry them!"

Soon after they came into a wood, and looked about for the thieves, but they could not find them, and when it became dark they climbed up into a tree to pass the night. But scarcely had they done this when up came the fellows who carried away what should not go with them, and find things before they are lost. They laid themselves down right under the tree upon which Fred and Catherine were, and making a fire prepared to share their booty. Then Fred slipped down on the other side, and collected stones, with which he climbed the tree again to beat the thieves with. The stones, however, did them no harm, for the fellows called out, "Ah! it will soon be morning, for the wind is shaking down the chestnuts." All this while Catherine still had the door upon her shoulder, and, as it pressed very heavily, she thought the dried apples were in fault, and said to Fred, "I must throw down these apples." "No, Catherine," said he, "not now, they might discover us." "Ah, I must though, they are so heavy."

"Well, then, do it in the hangman's name!" cried Fred.

As they fell down the rogues said, "Ah! the birds are pulling off the leaves."

A little while after Catherine said again, "Oh! Fred, I must pour out the vinegar, it is so heavy."

"No, no!" said he, "it will discover us."

"Ah! but I must, Fred, it is very heavy," said Catherine.

"Well, then, do it in the hangman's name!" cried Fred.

So she poured out the vinegar, and as it dropped on them the thieves said, "Ah! the dew is beginning to fall."

Not many minutes after Catherine found the door was still quite as heavy, and said again to Fred, "Now I must throw down this door."

"No, Catherine," said he, "that would certainly discover us."

"Ah! Fred, but I must; it presses me so terribly."

"No, Catherine dear! do hold it fast," said Fred.

"There – it is gone!" said she.

"Then let it go in the hangman's name!" cried Fred, while it fell crashing through the branches. The rogues below thought the Evil One was descending the tree, and ran off, leaving everything behind them. And early in the morning Fred and his wife descended, and found all their gold under the tree.

As soon as they got home again, Fred said, "Now, Catherine, you must be very industrious and work hard."

"Yes, my dear husband," said she; "I will go into the fields to cut corn." When she was come into the field she said to herself, "Shall I eat before I cut, or sleep first before I cut?" She determined to eat, and soon became so sleepy over her meal, that when she began to cut she knew not what she was doing, and cut off half her clothes, gown, petticoat, and all. When after a long sleep Catherine awoke, she got up half stripped, and said to herself, "Am I myself! or am I not? Ah! I am not myself." By-and-by night came on, and Catherine ran into the village and, knocking at her husband's window, called, "Fred!"

"What is the matter?" cried he.

"I want to know if Catherine is indoors!" said she.

"Yes, yes!" answered Fred, "she is certainly within, fast asleep."

"Then I am at home," said she, and ran away.

Standing outside Catherine found some thieves, wanting to steal, and going up to them she said, "I will help you."

At this the thieves were very glad, not doubting but that she knew where to light on what they sought. But Catherine, stepping in front of the houses, called out, "Good people, what have you that we can steal?" At this the thieves said, "You will do for us with a vengeance!" and they wished they had never come near her; but in order to rid themselves of her they said, "Just before the village the parson has some roots lying in his field; go and fetch some."

Catherine went as she was bid, and began to grub for them, and soon made herself very dirty with the earth. Presently a man came by and saw her, and stood still, for he thought it was the Evil One who was grovelling so among the roots. Away he ran into the village to the parson, and told him the Evil One was in his field, rooting up the turnips. "Ah! heavens!" said the parson, "I have a lame foot, and I cannot go out to exorcise him."

"Then I will carry you a pick-a-back," said the man, and took him up.

Just as they arrived in the field, Catherine got up and drew herself up to her full height.

"Oh! it is the Evil One!" cried the parson, and both he and the man hurried away; and, behold! the parson ran faster with his lame legs, through fear and terror, than the countryman could with his sound legs.

The Two Brothers

ONCE upon a time there were two brothers, the one rich and the other poor. The rich man was a Goldsmith, and of an evil disposition; but the poor brother maintained himself by mending brooms, and withal was honest and pious. He had two children – twins, as like one another as two drops of water – who used often to go into their rich uncle's house and receive a meal of the fragments which he left. One day it happened when the poor man had gone into the wood for twigs that he saw a bird, which was of gold, and more beautiful than he had ever before set eyes on. He picked up a stone and flung it at the bird, and luckily hit it, but so slightly that only a single feather dropped off. This feather he took to his brother, who looked at it and said, "It is of pure gold!" and gave him a good sum of money for it. The next day he climbed up a birch-tree to lop off a bough or two, when the same bird flew out of the branches, and as he looked round he found a nest which contained an egg, also of gold. This he took home as before to his brother, who said it was of pure gold, and gave him what it was worth, but said that he must have the bird itself. For the third time now the poor brother went into the forest, and saw the Golden Bird sitting again upon the tree, and taking up a stone he threw it at it, and, securing it, took it to his brother, who gave him for it a large pile of gold. With this the man thought he might return, and went home light-hearted.

But the Goldsmith was crafty and bold, knowing very well what sort of a bird it was. He called his wife and said to her, "Roast this bird for me, and take care of whatever falls from it, for I have a mind to eat it by myself." Now, the bird was not an ordinary one, certainly, for it possessed this wonderful power, that whoever should eat its heart and liver would find henceforth every morning a gold piece under his pillow. The wife made the bird ready, and putting it on the spit, set it down to roast. Now it happened that while it was at the fire, and the woman had gone out of the kitchen on some other necessary work, the two children of the poor Broom-mender ran in, and began to turn the spit round at the fire for amusement. Presently two little titbits fell down into the pan out of the bird, and one of the boys said, "Let us eat these two little pieces, I am so hungry, and nobody will find it out." So they quickly despatched the two morsels, and presently the woman came back, and, seeing at once that they had eaten something, asked them what it was. "Two little bits which fell down out of the bird," was the reply. "They were the heart and liver!" exclaimed the woman quite frightened; and, in order that her husband might not miss them and be in a passion, she quickly killed a little chicken, and, taking out its liver and heart, put it inside the Golden Bird. As soon as it was done enough she carried it to the Goldsmith, who devoured it quite alone, and left nothing at all on the plate. The next morning, however, when he looked under his pillow, expecting to find the gold pieces, there was not the smallest one possible to be seen.

The two children did not know what good luck had fallen upon them, and, when they got up the next morning, something fell ringing upon the ground, and as they picked it up they found it was two gold pieces. They took them to their father, who wondered very much, and considered what he should do with them; but as the next morning the same thing happened, and so on every day, he went to his brother, and narrated to him the whole story. The Goldsmith perceived at once what had happened, that the children had eaten the heart and liver of his bird; and in order to revenge himself, and because he was so covetous and hard-hearted, he persuaded the father that his children were in league with the devil, and warned him not to take the gold, but to turn them out of the house, for the Evil One had them in his power, and would make them do some mischief. Their father feared the Evil One, and, although it cost him a severe pang, he led his children out into the forest and left them there with a sad heart.

Now, the two children ran about the wood, seeking the road home, but could not find it, so that they only wandered further away. At last they met a Huntsman, who asked them to whom they belonged. "We are the children of the poor Broom-mender," they replied, and told him that their father could no longer keep them at home, because a gold piece lay under their pillows every morning. "Well," replied the Huntsman, "that does not seem right, if you are honest and not idle." And the good man, having no children of his own, took home with him the twins, because they pleased him, and told them he would be their father and bring them up. With him they learnt all kinds of hunting, and the gold pieces, which each one found at his uprising, they laid aside against a rainy day.

When now they became quite young men the Huntsman took them into the forest, and said, "To-day you must perform your shooting trial, that I may make you free huntsmen like myself." So they went with him, and waited a long time, but no wild beast approached, and the Huntsman, looking up, saw a flock of wild geese flying over in the form of a triangle. "Shoot one from each corner," said he to the twins, and when they had done this, another flock came flying over in the form of a figure of two, and from these they were also bid to shoot one at each corner. When they had likewise performed this deed successfully, their foster-father said, "I now make you free; for you are capital marksmen."

Thereupon the two brothers went together into the forest, laying plans and consulting with each other; and, when at evening-time they sat down to their meal, they said to their foster-father, "We shall not touch the least morsel of food till you have granted our request."

He asked them what it was, and they replied,—

"We have now learned everything: let us go into the world, and see what we can do there, and let us set out at once."

"You have spoken like brave huntsmen," cried the old man, overjoyed; "what you have asked is just what I wished; you can set out as soon as you like, for you will be prosperous."

Then they ate and drank together once more in great joy and hilarity.

When the appointed day arrived, the old Huntsman gave to each youth a good rifle and a dog, and let them take from the gold pieces as many as they liked. Then he accompanied them a part of their way, and at leaving gave them a bare knife, saying, "If you should separate, stick this knife in a tree by the roadside, and then, if one returns to the same point, he can tell how his absent brother fares; for the side upon which there is a mark will, if he die, rust; but as long as he lives it will be as bright as ever."

The two brothers now journeyed on till they came to a forest so large that they could not possibly get out of it in one day, so there they passed the night, and ate what they had in their hunters' pockets. The second day they still walked on, but came to no opening, and having nothing to eat, one said, "We must shoot something, or we shall die of hunger;" and he loaded his gun and looked around. Just then an old Hare came running up, at which he aimed, but it cried out,—

> "Dear huntsman, pray now let me live,
> And I will two young lev'rets give."

So saying, it ran back into the brushwood and brought out two hares, but they played about so prettily and actively that the Hunters could not make up their minds to kill them. So they took them with them, and the two leverets followed in their footsteps. Presently a Fox came up with them, and, as they were about to shoot it, it cried out,—

> "Dear hunters, pray now let me live,
> And I will two young foxes give."

These it brought; and the brothers, instead of killing them, put them with the young hares, and all four followed. In a little while a Wolf came out of the brushwood, whom the Hunters also aimed at, but he cried out as the others,—

> "Dear hunters, pray now let me live,
> Two young ones, in return, I'll give.

The Hunters placed the two wolves with the other animals, who still followed them; and soon they met a Bear, who also begged for his life, saying,—

> "Dear hunters, pray now let me live,
> Two young ones, in return, I'll give."

These two bears were added to the others; they made eight; and now who came last? A Lion, shaking his mane. The two brothers were not frightened, but aimed at him, and he cried,—

> "Dear hunters, pray now let me live,
> Two young ones, in return, I'll give."

The Lion then fetched his two young cubs, and now the Huntsmen had two lions, two bears, two wolves, two foxes, and two hares following and waiting upon them. Meanwhile their hunger had received no satisfaction, and they said to the Foxes, "Here, you slinks, get us something to eat, for you are both sly and crafty."

The Foxes replied, "Not far from here lies a village, where we can procure many fowls, and thither we will show you the way."

So they went into the village, and bought something to eat for themselves and their animals, and then went on further, for the Foxes were well acquainted with the country where the hen-roosts were, and so could direct the Huntsmen well.

For some little way they walked on without finding any situations where they could live together; so they said to one another, "It cannot be otherwise, we must separate." Then the two brothers divided the beasts, so that each one had a lion, a bear, a wolf, a fox, and a hare; and then they took leave of each other, promising to love one another till death; and the knife which their foster-father gave them they stuck in a tree, so that one side pointed to the east, and the other to the west.

The younger brother came afterwards with his animals to a town which was completely hung with black crape. He went into an inn and inquired if he could lodge his beasts, and the landlord gave him a stable, and in the wall was a hole through which the hare crept and seized upon a cabbage; the fox fetched himself a hen, and when he had eaten it he stole the cock also; but the lion, the bear, and the wolf, being too big for the hole, could get nothing. The master, therefore, made the host fetch an ox for them on which they regaled themselves merrily, and so, having seen after his beasts, he asked the landlord why the town was all hung in mourning. The Landlord replied, it was because the next day the King's only daughter was to die. "Is she then sick unto death?" inquired the Huntsman.

"No," replied the other, "she is well enough; but still she must die."

"How is that?" asked the Huntsman.

"Out there before the town," said the Landlord, "is a high mountain on which lives a Dragon, who must every year have a pure maiden, or he would lay waste all the country. Now, all the maidens have been given up, and there is but one left, the King's daughter, who must also be given up, for there is no other escape, and to-morrow morning it is to happen."

The Huntsman asked, "Why is the Dragon not killed?"

"Ah!" replied the Landlord, "many knights have tried, but every one has lost his life; and the King has promised his own daughter to him who conquers the Dragon, and after his death the inheritance of his kingdom."

The Huntsman said nothing further at that time, but the next morning, taking with him his beasts, he climbed the Dragon's mountain. A little way up stood a chapel, and upon an altar therein were three cups, and by them was written, "Whoever drinks the contents of these cups will be the strongest man on earth, and may take the sword which lies buried beneath the threshold." Without drinking, the Huntsman sought and found the sword in the ground, but he could not move it from its place; so he entered, and drank out the cups, and then he easily pulled out the sword, and was so strong that he waved it about like a feather.

When the hour arrived that the maiden should be delivered over to the Dragon, the King and his Marshal accompanied her with all the court. From a distance they perceived the Huntsman upon the mountain, and took him for the Dragon waiting for them, and so would not ascend; but at last, because the whole city must otherwise have been sacrificed, the Princess was forced to make the dreadful ascent. The King and his courtiers returned home full of grief, but the Marshal had to stop and watch it all from a distance.

As the King's daughter reached the top of the hill, she found there, not the Dragon, but the young Hunter, who comforted her, saying, he would save her, and, leading her into the chapel, shut her up therein. In a short time the seven-headed Dragon came roaring up with a tremendous noise, and, as soon as he perceived the Hunter, he was amazed, and asked, "What do you here on my mountain?"

The Hunter replied that he came to fight him, and the Dragon said, breathing out fire as he spoke from his seven jaws, "Many a knight has already left his life behind him, and you I will soon kill as dead as they." The fire from his throat set the grass in a blaze, and would have suffocated the Hunter with the smoke, had not his beasts come running up and stamped it out. Then the Dragon made a dart at the Hunter, but he swung his sword round so that it whistled in the air, and cut off three of the beast's heads. The Dragon now became furious, and raised himself in the air, spitting out fire over his enemy, and trying to overthrow him; but the Hunter, springing on one side, raised his sword again, and cut off three more of his heads. The beast was half killed with this, and sank down, but tried once more to catch the Hunter, but he beat him off, and, with his last strength, cut off his tail; and then, being unable to fight longer, he called his beasts, who came and tore the Dragon in pieces.

As soon as the battle was over, he went to the chapel and unlocked the door, and found the Princess lying on the floor; for, from anguish and terror, she had fainted away while the contest was going on. The Hunter carried her out, and when she came to herself and opened her eyes, he showed her the Dragon torn to pieces, and said she was now safe for ever. The sight made her quite happy, and she said, "Now you will be my husband, for my father has promised me to him who should kill the Dragon." So saying, she took off her necklace of coral and divided it among the beasts for a reward, the Lion receiving the gold snap for his share. But her handkerchief, on which her name was marked, she presented to the Huntsman, who went and cut out the tongues of the Dragon's seven mouths, and, wrapping them in the handkerchief, preserved them carefully.

All this being done, the poor fellow felt so weary with the battle with the Dragon and the fire, that he said to the Princess, "Since we are both so tired, let us sleep awhile." She consented, and they lay down on the ground, and the Hunter bid the Lion watch that nobody surprise them. Soon they began to snore, and the Lion sat down near them to watch; but he was also weary with fighting, and he said to the Bear, "Do you lie down near me, for I must sleep a bit; but wake me up if any one comes." So the Bear did as he was bid; but soon getting tired, he asked the Wolf to watch for him. The Wolf consented, but before long he called the Fox, and said, "Do watch for me a little while, I want to have a nap, and you can wake me if any one comes." The Fox lay down by his side, but soon felt so tired himself that he called the Hare, and asked him to take his place and watch while he slept a little. The Hare came, and lying down too, soon felt very sleepy; but he had no one to call in his place, so by degrees he dropped off himself, and began to snore. Here, then, were sleeping, the Princess, the Huntsman, the Lion, the Bear, the Wolf, the Fox, and the Hare; and all were very sound asleep.

Meanwhile the Marshal, who had been set to watch below, not seeing the Dragon fly away with the Princess, and all appearing very quiet, took heart and climbed up the mountain. There lay the Dragon dead and torn to pieces on the ground, and not far off the King's daughter and a Huntsman with his beasts, all reposing in a deep sleep. Now, the Marshal was very wickedly disposed, and, taking his sword, he cut off the head of the Huntsman, and then, taking the maiden under his arm, carried her down the mountain. At this she awoke, terrified, and the Marshal cried to her, "You are in my hands: you must say that it was I who have killed the Dragon."

"That I cannot," she replied, "for a hunter and his animals did it." Then he drew his sword, and threatened her with death if she did not obey, till at last she was forced to consent. Thereupon he brought her before the King, who went almost beside himself with joy at seeing again his dear daughter, whom he supposed had been torn in pieces by the monster. The Marshal told the King that he had killed the Dragon, and freed the Princess and the whole kingdom, and therefore he demanded her for a wife, as it had been promised. The King inquired of his daughter if it were true? "Ah, yes," she replied, "it must be so; but I make a condition, that the wedding shall not take place for a year and a day;" for she thought to herself that perhaps in that time she might hear some news of her dear Huntsman.

But up the Dragon's mountain the animals still laid asleep beside their dead master, when presently a great Bee came and settled on the Hare's nose, but he lifted his paw and brushed it off. The Bee came a second time, but the Hare brushed it off again, and went to sleep. For the third time the Bee settled, and stung the Hare's nose so that he woke quite up. As soon as he had risen and shaken himself he awoke the Fox, and the Fox awoke the Wolf, the Wolf awoke the

Bear, and the Bear awoke the Lion. As soon as the Lion got up and saw that the maiden was gone and his dear master dead, he began to roar fearfully, and asked, "Who has done this? Bear, why did you not wake me?" The Bear asked the Wolf, "Why did you not wake me?" The Wolf asked the Fox, "Why did you not wake me?" and the Fox asked the Hare, "Why did you not wake me?" The poor Hare alone had nothing to answer, and the blame was attached to him, and the others would have fallen upon him, but he begged for his life, saying, "Do not kill me, and I will restore our dear master to life. I know a hill where grows a root, and he who puts it in his mouth is healed immediately from all diseases or wounds; but this mountain lies two hundred hours' journey from hence."

The Lion said, "In four-and-twenty hours you must go and return here bringing the root with you."

The Hare immediately ran off, and in four-and-twenty hours returned with the root in his mouth. Now the Lion put the Huntsman's head again to his body while the Hare applied the root to the wound, and immediately the Huntsman began to revive, and his heart beat and life returned. The Huntsman now awoke, and was frightened to see the maiden no longer with him, and he thought to himself, "Perhaps she ran away while I slept, to get rid of me." But, in his haste, the Lion had unluckily set his master's head on the wrong way, but the Hunter did not find it out till midday, when he wanted to eat, being so occupied with thinking about the Princess. Then, when he wished to help himself, he discovered his head was turned to his back, and, unable to imagine the cause, he asked the animals what had happened to him in his sleep. The Lion told him that from weariness they had all gone to sleep, and, on awaking, they had found him dead, with his head cut off; that the Hare had fetched the life-root, but in his great haste he had turned his head the wrong way, but that he would make it all right again in no time. So saying, he cut off the Huntsman's head and turned it round, while the Hare healed the wound with the root.

After this the Hunter became very mopish, and went about from place to place, letting his animals dance to the people for show. It chanced, after a year's time, that he came again to the same town where he had rescued the Princess from the Dragon; and this time it was hung all over with scarlet cloth. He asked the Landlord of the inn, "What means this? a year ago the city was hung with black crape, and to-day it is all in red!" The Landlord replied, "A year ago our King's daughter was delivered to the Dragon, but our Marshal fought with it and slew it, and this day their marriage is to be celebrated; before the town was hung with crape in token of grief and lamentation, but to-day with scarlet cloth, to show our joy."

The next day, when the wedding was to take place, the Huntsman said to the Landlord, "Believe it or not, mine host, but to-day I will eat bread at the same table with the King!"

"Well," said he, "I will wager you a hundred pieces that that doesn't come true."

The Huntsman took the bet, and laid down his money; and then, calling the Hare, he said, "Go, dear Jumper, and fetch me a bit of bread such as the King eats."

Now, the Hare was the smallest and therefore could not intrust his business to any one else, but was obliged to make himself ready to go. "Oh!" thought he, "if I jump along the streets alone, the butchers' dogs will come out after me."

While he stood considering it happened as he thought; for the dogs came behind and were about to seize him for a choice morsel, but he made a spring (had you but seen it!), and escaped into a sentry-box without the soldier knowing it. The dogs came and tried to hunt him out, but the soldier, not understanding their sport, beat them off with a club so that they ran howling and barking away. As soon as the Hare saw the coast was clear, he ran up to the castle and into the room where the Princess was; and, getting under her stool, began to scratch her foot. The Princess said, "Will you be quiet?" thinking it was her dog. Then the Hare scratched her foot a second time, and she said again, "Will you be quiet?" but the Hare would not leave off, and a third time scratched her foot; and now she peeped down and recognised the Hare by his necklace. She took him up in her arms, and carried him into her chamber, "Dear Hare, what do you want?" The Hare replied, "My master, who killed the Dragon, is here, and sent me: I am come for a piece of bread such as the King eats."

At these words she became very glad, and bade her servant bring her a piece of bread such as the King was accustomed to have. When it was brought, the Hare said, "The Baker must carry it for me, or the butchers' dogs will seize it." So the Baker carried it to the door of the inn, where the Hare got upon his hind legs, and, taking the bread in his forepaws, carried it to his master. Then the Huntsman said, "See here, my host: the hundred gold pieces are mine."

The Landlord wondered very much, but the Huntsman said further, "Yes, I have got the King's bread, and now I will have some of his meat." To this the Landlord demurred, but would not bet again; and his guest, calling the Fox, said, "My dear Fox, go and fetch me some of the meat which the King is to eat to-day."

The Fox was more cunning than the Hare, and went through the lanes and alleys, without seeing a dog, straight to the royal palace, and into the room of the Princess, under whose stool he crept. Presently he scratched her foot, and the Princess, looking down, recognised the Fox with her necklace, and, taking him into her room, she asked, "What do you want, dear Fox?" He replied, "My master who killed the Dragon is here, and sent me to beg a piece of the meat such as the King will eat to-day."

The Princess summoned the cook, and made her prepare a dish of meat like the King's; and, when it was ready, carry it for the Fox to the door of the inn. Then the Fox took the dish himself; and, first driving the flies away with a whisk of his tail, carried it in to the Hunter.

"See here, master Landlord," said he; "here are the bread and meat: now I will have the same vegetables as the King eats."

He called the Wolf, and said, "Dear Wolf, go and fetch me some vegetables the same as the King eats to-day."

The Wolf went straight to the castle like a person who feared nobody, and, when he came into the Princess's chamber, he plucked at her clothes behind so that she looked round. The maiden knew the

Wolf by his necklace, and took him with her into her room, and said, "Dear Wolf, what do you want?"

The beast replied, "My master who killed the Dragon is here, and has sent me for some vegetables like those the King eats to-day."

Then she bade the cook prepare a dish of vegetables the same as the King's, and carry it to the inn-door for the Wolf, who took it off her and bore it in to his master. The Hunter said, "See here, my host: now I have bread, meat and vegetables the same as the King's, but I will also have the same sweetmeats." Then he called to the Bear, "Dear Bear, go and fetch me some sweetmeats like those the King has for his dinner to-day, for you like sweet things." The Bear rolled along up to the castle, while every one got out of his way; but, when he came to the guard, he pointed his gun at him and would not let him pass into the royal apartments. The Bear, however, got up on his hind legs, and gave the guard right and left a box on the ears with his paw, which knocked him down; and thereupon he went straight to the room of the Princess, and, getting behind her, growled slightly. She looked round, and perceived the Bear, whom she took into her own chamber, and asked him what he came for. "My master who slew the Dragon is here," said he, "and has sent me for some sweetmeats such as the King eats." The Princess let the sugar-baker be called, and bade him prepare sweetmeats like those the King had, and carry them for the Bear to the inn. There the Bear took charge of them; and, first licking off the sugar which had boiled over, he took them in to his master.

"See here, friend Landlord," said the Huntsman; "now I have bread, meat, vegetables and sweetmeats from the table of the King, but I mean also to drink his wine."

He called the Lion, and said, "Dear Lion, I should be glad to have a draught: go and fetch me some wine like the King drinks."

The Lion strode through the town, where all the people made way for him, and soon came to the castle, where the watchmen attempted to stop him at the gates; but, just giving a little bit of a roar, they were so frightened that they all ran away. He walked on to the royal apartments, and knocked with his tail at the door; and, when the

Princess opened it, she was at first frightened to see a Lion; but, soon recognising him by the gold snap of her necklace which he wore, she took him into her room, and asked, "Dear Lion, what do you wish?"

The Lion replied, "My master who killed the Dragon is here, and has sent me to fetch him wine like that the King drinks at his own table." The Princess summoned the butler, and told him to give the Lion wine such as the King drank. But the Lion said, "I will go down with you and see that I have the right." So he went with the butler; and, as they were come below, he was about to draw the ordinary wine such as was drunk by the King's servants, but the Lion cried, "Hold! I will first taste the wine;" and, drawing for himself half a cupful, he drank it, and said, "No! that is not the real wine." The butler looked at him askance, and went to draw from another cask which was made for the King's Marshal. Then the Lion cried, "Hold! first I must taste;" and, drawing half a flagon full, he drank it off, and said, "This is better; but still not the right wine." At these words the butler put himself in a passion, and said, "What does such a stupid calf as you know about wine?" The Lion gave him a blow behind the ear, so that he fell down upon the ground; and, as soon as he came to himself, he led the Lion quite submissively into a peculiar little cellar where the King's wine was kept, of which no one ever dared to taste. But the Lion, first drawing for himself half a cupful, tried the wine, and saying, "This must be the real stuff," bade the butler fill six bottles with it. When this was done they mounted the steps again, and as the Lion came out of the cellar into the fresh air he reeled about, being a little elevated; so that the butler had to carry the wine-basket for him to the inn, where the Lion, taking it again in his mouth, carried it in to his master. The Hunter called the Landlord and said, "See here: now I have bread, meat, vegetables, sweetmeats, and wine, the very same as the King will himself eat to-day, and so I will make my dinner with my animals." They sat down and ate and drank away, for he gave the Hare, the Fox, the Wolf, the Bear, and the Lion, their share of the good things, and was very happy, for he felt the King's daughter still loved him. When he had finished his meal he said to the Landlord, "Now, as I have eaten and drunk the same things as the King, I will even go to the royal palace and marry the Princess."

The Landlord said, "How can that be, for she is already betrothed, and to-day the wedding is to be celebrated?"

Then the Hunter drew out the handkerchief which the King's daughter had given him on the Dragon's mountain, and wherein the seven tongues of the Dragon's seven heads were wrapped, and said, "This shall help me to do it."

The Landlord looked at the handkerchief and said, "If I believe all that has been done, still I cannot believe that, and will wager my house and garden upon it."

Thereupon the Huntsman took out a purse with a thousand gold pieces in it, and said, "I will bet you that against your house and garden."

Meanwhile the King asked his daughter, "What do all these wild beasts mean who have come to you to-day, and passed and repassed in and out of my castle?"

She replied, "I dare not tell you, but send and let the master of these beasts be fetched, and you will do well."

The King sent a servant to the inn to invite the strange man to come, and arrived just as the Hunter had concluded his wager with the Landlord. So he said, "See, mine host, the King even sends a servant to invite me to come, but I do not go yet." And to the servant he said, "I beg that the King will send me royal clothes, and a carriage with six horses, and servants to wait on me."

When the King heard this answer, he said to his daughter, "What shall I do?" "Do as he desires, and you will do well," she replied. So the King sent a suit of royal clothes, a carriage and six horses, and some servants to wait upon the man. As the Hunter saw them coming, he said to the Landlord, "See here, I am fetched just as I desired," and, putting on the royal clothes, he took the handkerchief with him and drove to the King. When the King saw him coming he asked his daughter how he should receive him, and she said, "Go out to meet him, and you will do well." So the King met him and led him into the palace, the animals following. The King showed him a seat near himself and his daughter, and the Marshal sat upon the other side as the bridegroom. Now, against the walls was the the seven-headed Dragon placed, stuffed as if it were yet alive; and the King said, "The seven heads of that Dragon were cut off by our Marshal, to whom this day I give my daughter in marriage."

Then the Hunter rose up, and, opening the seven jaws of the Dragon, asked where were the seven tongues. This frightened the Marshal, and he turned pale as death, but at last, not knowing what else to say, he stammered out, "Dragons have no tongues."

The Hunter replied, "*Liars* should have none, but the Dragon's tongues are the trophies of the Dragon-slayer;" and so saying he unwrapped the handkerchief, and there lay all seven, and he put one into each mouth of the monster, and they fitted exactly. Then he took the handkerchief upon which her name was marked and showed it to the maiden, and asked her to whom she had given it, and she replied, "To him who slew the Dragon." Then he called his beasts, and taking from each the necklace, and from the Lion the golden snap, he put them together and showing them to the Princess too, asked to whom they belonged. The Princess said, "The necklace and the snap were mine, and I shared it among the animals who helped to conquer the Dragon." Then the Huntsman said, "When I was weary and rested after the fight, the Marshal came and cut off my head, and then took away the Princess, and gave out that it was he who had conquered the Dragon. Now that he has lied, I show these tongues, this necklace, and this handkerchiefs for proofs." And then he related how the beasts had cured him with a wonderful root, and that for a year he had wandered, and at last had come hither again, where he had discovered the deceit of the Marshal through the innkeeper's tale. Then the King asked his daughter, "Is it true that this man killed the Dragon?"

"Yes," she replied, "it is true; for I dared not disclose the treachery of the Marshal, because he threatened me with instant death. But now it is known without my mention, and for this reason have I delayed the wedding a year and a day."

After these words the King ordered twelve councillors to be

summoned who should judge the Marshal, and these condemned him to be torn in pieces by four oxen. So the Marshal was executed, and the King gave his daughter to the Huntsman, and named him Stadtholder over all his kingdom. The wedding was celebrated with great joy, and the young King caused his father and foster-father to be brought to him, and loaded them with presents. He did not forget either the Landlord, but bade him welcome, and said to him, "See you here, my host: I have married the daughter of the King, and thy house and garden are mine." The Landlord said that was according to right; but the young King said, "It shall be according to mercy;" and he gave him back not only his house and garden, but also presented him with the thousand gold pieces he had wagered.

Now the young King and Queen were very happy, and lived together in contentment. He often went out hunting, because he delighted in it; and the faithful animals always accompanied him.

In the neighbourhood there was a forest which it was said was haunted, and that if one entered it he did not easily get out again. The young King, however, took a great fancy to hunt in it, and he let the old King have no peace till he consented to let him. Away then he rode with a great company; and, as he approached the forest, he saw a snow-white hind going into it; so, telling his companions to await his return, he rode off among the trees, and only his faithful beasts accompanied him. The courtiers waited and waited till evening, but he did not return; so they rode home, and told the young Queen that her husband had ridden into the forest after a white doe, and had not again come out. The news made her very anxious about him. He, however, had ridden farther and farther into the wood after the beautiful animal without catching it; and, when he thought it was within range of his gun, with one spring it got away, till at last it disappeared altogether. Then he remarked for the first time how deeply he had plunged into the thickets; and, taking his horn, he gave a blast, but there was no answer, for his people could not hear it. Presently night began to close in; and, making a fire, prepared to pass the night. While he sat by the fire, with his beasts lying near all around him, he thought he heard a human voice, but on looking

round, he could see noblody. Soon after he heard again a groan, as if
from a box; and, looking up, he saw an old Woman sitting upon the
tree, who was groaning and crying, "Oh, oh, oh, how I do freeze!"
He called out, "Come down and warm yourself if you freeze." But
she said, "No; your beasts will bite me." He replied, "They will not
harm you, my good lady, if you like to come down." But she was a
Witch, and said, "I will throw you down a twig, which if you beat
upon their backs they will then do nothing to me." He did as was
requested; and immediately they laid down quietly enough, for they
were changed into stones. Now, when the old woman was safe from
the animals, she sprang down, and, touching the King too with a
twig, coverted him also into a stone. Thereupon she laughed to
herself, and buried him and his beasts in a grave where already were
many more stones.

Meanwhile the young Queen was becoming more and more
anxious and sad when her husband did not return; and, just then it
happened that the other brother, who had travelled towards the east
when they separated, came into the territory. He had been seeking
and had found no service to enter, and was, therefore, travelling
through the country, and making his animals dance for a living.
Once he thought he would go and look at the knife which they had
stuck in a tree at their separation, in order to see how his brother
fared. When he looked at it, lo! his brother's side was half rusty and
half bright! At this he was frightened, and thought his brother had
fallen into some great misfortune; but he hoped yet to save him, for
one-half of the knife was bright. He, therefore, went with his beasts
towards the west; and, as he came to the capital city, the watch went
out to him, and asked if he should mention his arrival to his bride,
for the young Queen had for two days been in great sorrow and
distress at his absence, and feared he had been killed in the
enchanted wood. The watchman thought certainly he was no one
else than the young King, for he was so much like him, and had also
the same wild beasts returning after him. The Huntsman perceived
he was speaking of his brother, and thought it was all for the best
that he should give himself out as his brother, for so, perhaps, he

might more easily save him. So he let himself be conducted by the watchman into the castle, and was there received with great joy, for the young Queen took him for her husband also, and asked him where he had stopped so long. He told her he had lost his way in a wood, and could not find his way out earlier.

For a couple of days he rested at home, but was always asking about the enchanted wood; and at last he said, "I must hunt there once more." The King and the young Queen tried to dissuade him, but he was resolved, and went out with a great number of attendants. As soon as he got into the wood, it happened to him as to his brother: he saw a white hind, and told his people to wait his return where they were, while he hunted the wild animal, and immediately rode off, his beasts following his footsteps. But he could not catch the hind any more than his brother; and he went so deep into the wood that he was forced to pass the night there. As soon as he had made a fire, he heard some one groaning above him, and saying, "Oh, oh, oh, how I do freeze!" The he looked up, and there sat the same old Witch in the tree, and he said to her, "If you freeze, old Woman, why don't you come down and warm yourself?" She replied, "No, your beasts would bite me; but if you will beat them with a twig which I will throw down to you they can do me no harm." When the Hunter heard this, he doubted the old Woman, and said to her, "I do not beat my beasts; so come down, or I will fetch you." But she called out, "What are you thinking if, you can do nothing to me?" He answered, "Come down, or I will shoot you." The old Woman laughed, and said, "Shoot away! I am not afraid of your bullets!"

He knelt down and shot, but she was bullet proof; and, laughing till she yelled, called out, "You cannot catch me!" However, the Hunter knew a trick or two, and tearing three silver buttons from his coat, he loaded his gun with them; and, while he was ramming them down, the old Witch threw herself from the tree with a loud shriek, for she was not proof against such shot. He placed his foot upon her neck, and said, "Old Witch, if you do not quickly tell me where my brother is, I will tie your hands together, and throw you into the fire!"

She was in great anguish, begged for mercy, and said, "He lies with his beasts in a grave, turned into stone." Then he forced her to go with him, threatening her, and saying, "You old cat, now turn my brother and all the creatures which lie here into their proper forms, or I will throw you into the fire!"

The old Witch took a twig, and changed the stones back to what they were, and immediately his brother and the beasts stood before the Huntsman, as well as many merchants, work-people, and shepherds, who, delighted with their freedom, returned home; but the twin brothers, when they saw each other again, kissed and embraced, and were very glad. They seized the old Witch, bound her, and laid her on the fire; and, when she was consumed, the forest itself disappeared, and all was clear and free from trees, so that one could see the royal palace three miles off.

Now the two brothers went together home; and on the way told each other their adventures. And when the younger one said he was lord over the whole land in place of the King, the other one said, "All that I was well aware of; for, when I went into the city, I was taken for you. And all kingly honour was paid to me, the young Queen even mistaking me for her true husband, and making me sit at her table, and sleep in her room." When the first one heard this, he became very angry, and so jealous and passionate, that, drawing his sword, he cut off the head of his brother. But as soon as he had done so, and saw the red blood flowing from the dead body, he repented sorely, and said, "My brother has saved me, and I have killed him for so doing;" and he groaned pitifully. Just then the Hare came, and offered to fetch the healing root, and then, running off, brought it just at the right time, so that the dead man was restored to life again, and not even the mark of the wound was to be seen.

After this adventure they went on, and the younger brother said, "You see that we have both got on royal robes, and have both the same beasts following us; we will, therefore, enter the city at opposite gates, and arrive from the two quarters the same time before the King."

So they separated; and at the same moment the watchman from

each gate came to the King, and informed him that the young Prince with the beasts had returned from the hunt. The King said, "It is not possible, for your two gates are a mile asunder!" But in the meantime the two brothers had arrived in the castle-yard, and began to mount the stairs. When they entered, the King said to his daughter, "Tell me which is your husband, for one appears to me the same as the other, and I cannot tell." The Princess was in great trouble, and could not tell which was which; but at last she bethought herself of the necklace which she had given to the beasts, and she looked and found on one of the Lions her golden snap, and then she cried exultingly, "He to whom this Lion belongs is my rightful husband." Then the young King laughed, and said, "Yes, that is right;" and they sat down together at table, and ate, and drank, and were merry. At night when the young King went to bed his wife asked him why he had placed on the two previous nights a sword in the bed, for she thought it was to kill her. Then the young King knew how faithful his brother had been.

The Golden Goose

THERE was once a man who had three sons, the youngest of whom was named Dummling, and on that account was despised and slighted, and put back on every occasion. It happened that the eldest wished to go into the forest to hew wood, and before he went his mother gave him a fine large pancake and a bottle of wine to take with him. Just as he got into the forest, he met a grey old man, who bade him good-day, and said, "Give me a piece of your pancake and a sip of your wine, for I am very hungry and thirsty." The prudent youth, however, would not, saying, "If I should give you my cake and wine, I shall have nothing left for myself; no, pack off!" and he left the man there and went onwards. He now began to hew down a tree, but he had not made many strokes before he missed his aim, and the axe cut into his arm so deeply, that he was forced to go home and have it bound up. But this wound came from the little old man.

Afterwards the second son went into the forest, and the mother gave him, as she had given the eldest, a pancake and a bottle of wine. The same little old man met him also, and requested a piece of his cake and a draught from his bottle. But he likewise refused, and said, "What I give to you I cannot have for myself; go, take yourself off!" and, so speaking, he left the old man there and went onwards. His reward, however, soon came for when he had made two strokes at the tree he cut his own leg, so that he was obliged to return home.

Then Dummling asked his father to let him go and hew wood; but his father said, "No; your brothers have harmed themselves in so doing, and so will you, for you do not understand anything about it." But Dummling begged and prayed so long, that his father at length said, "Well then, go, and you will become prudent through experience." His mother gave him only a cake which had been baked in the ashes, and a bottle of sour beer. As he entered the forest the same grey old man greeted him, and asked, "Give me a piece of your cake and a draught out of your bottle, for I am hungry and thirsty."

Dummling answered, "I have only a cake baked in the ashes, and a bottle of sour beer; but, if they will suit you, let us sit down and eat."

They sat down, and as soon as Dummling took out his cake, lo! it was changed into a nice pancake, and the sour beer had become wine. They ate and drank, and when they had done the little man said, "Because you have a good heart, and have willingly shared what you had, I will make you lucky. There stands an old tree, cut it down, and you will find something at the roots." Thereupon the little man took leave.

Dummling went directly and cut down the tree, and when it fell, there sat amongst the roots a Goose, which had feathers of pure gold. He took it up and carried it with him to an inn, where he intended to pass the night. The landlord had three daughters, who, as soon as they saw the Goose, were very covetous of such a wonderful bird, even to have but one of its feathers. The eldest girl thought she would watch an opportunity to pluck out one, and, just as Dummling was going out, she caught hold of one of the wings, but her finger and thumb stuck there, and she could not move. Soon

319 THE GOLDEN GOOSE

after came the second, desiring also to pluck out a feather; but scarcely had she touched her sister, when she was bound fast to her. At last the third came also, with like intention, and the others exclaimed, "Keep away! for heaven's sake keep away!" But she did not see why she should, and thought, "The others are there, why should I not be too?" and springing up to them, she touched her sister, and at once was made fast, so they had to pass the night with the Goose.

The next morning Dummling took the Goose under his arm and went out, without troubling himself about the three girls, who were still hanging on, and who were obliged to keep on the run behind him, now to the left, and now to the right, just as he thought proper. In the middle of a field the Parson met them, and when he saw the procession he cried out, "For shame, you good-for-nothing wenches! what are you running after that young man across the fields for? Come, pray leave off that sport!" So saying he took the youngest by the hand and tried to pull her away; but as soon as he touched her he also stuck fast, and was forced to follow in the train. Soon after came the Clerk, and saw his master the Parson following in the footsteps of the three maidens. The sight astonished him much, and he called, "Holloa, master! where are you going so quickly? have you forgotten that there is a christening to-day?" and he ran up to him and caught him by the gown. The Clerk also could not release himself, and so there tramped the five, one behind another, till they met two countrymen returning with their hatchets in their hands. The Parson called out to them, and begged them to come and release him and the Clerk; but no sooner had they touched the Clerk, than they stuck fast to him, and so now there were seven all in a line following behind Dummling and the golden Goose. By-and-by he came into a city, where a King ruled, who had a daughter so seriously inclined that no one could make her laugh; so he had made a law that whoever should cause her to laugh, should have her to wife.

Now, when Dummling heard this, he went with his Goose and all his train before the Princess, and, as soon as she saw these seven poor creatures continually on the trot behind one another, she began to laugh so heartily, as if she were never going to cease. Dummling thereupon demanded his bride; but his intended son-in-law did not please the King, who, after a variety of excuses, at last said he must bring him a man who could drink a cellar-full of wine. Dummling bethought himself of the grey little man, who would, no doubt, be able to help him; and, going into the forest, on the same spot where he had felled the tree, he saw a man sitting with a very melancholy countenance. Dummling asked him what he was taking to heart so sorely, and he answered, "I have such a great thirst and cannot quench it; for cold water I cannot bear, and a cask of wine I soon empty; for what good is such a drop as that to a hot stone?"

"There I can help you," said Dummling; "come with me, and you shall be satisfied."

He led him into the King's cellar, and the man drank and drank away at the cask till his veins swelled; but before the day was out he had emptied all the wine-barrels. Dummling now demanded his bride again, but the King was vexed that such an ugly fellow, whom every one called Dummling, should take away his daughter, and he made a new condition that he must first find a man who could eat a whole mountain of bread. Dummling did not consider long, but set off into the forest, where, on the same spot as before, there sat a man, who was strapping his body round with a leather strap, and all the while making a horrible face, and saying, "I have eaten a whole oven full of rolls; but what use is that when one has such a hunger as I? My stomach remains empty still, and I must strap myself to prevent my dying of hunger!"

At these words Dummling was glad, and said, "Get up and come with me, and you shall eat enough to satisfy you."

He led him to the Royal Palace, where the King had collected all the meal in his whole kingdom, and had caused a huge mountain of bread to be baked with it. The man out of the wood, standing before it, began to eat, and in the course of the day the whole mountain had vanished.

Dummling then, for the third time, demanded his bride, but the

King began again to make fresh excuses, and desired a ship which could travel both on land and water.

"So soon as you return blessed with that," said the King, "you shall have my daughter for your bride." ·

Dummling went, as before, straight into the forest, and there he found the little old grey man to whom he had given the cake. When Dummling had said what he wanted, the old man gave him the vessel which could travel both on land and water, with these words, "Since I have eaten and drunk with you, I give you the ship, and all this I do because you were good-natured."

As soon now as the King saw the ship, he could not any longer keep back his daughter, and the wedding was celebrated, and after the King's death Dummling inherited the kingdom, and lived for a long time contentedly with his bride.

The Three Feathers

ONCE upon a time there was a King who had three sons, two of whom were bold and decided, but the third was a simpleton, and, having nothing to say for himself, was called Dummling. When the King became old and weak, and thought his end was approaching, he knew not which of his sons to appoint to succeed him. So he said to them, "Go out upon your travels, and whoever brings me back the finest carpet shall be king at my death." Then, to prevent their quarrelling, he led them out before the castle, and, blowing three feathers into the air, said, "As they fly, so shall you go."

One feather flew towards the east, another towards the west, but the third went in a straight direction, and soon fell to the ground. So one brother went right, another left, laughing at poor Dummling, who had to remain where the third feather had fallen.

Dummling sat himself down, and was sad at heart; but presently he remarked that near the feather was a trap-door. He raised it, and, finding steps, descended below the ground. He came to another door, and knocking, heard a voice singing—

"Frog, with the crooked leg,
Small and light green,
See who 'tis that knocks,
Be quick; let him in!"

The door was opened, and, going in, he saw a large Frog, and round her were squatted several smaller ones. The big one asked what he desired? and he replied, "I seek the finest and most beautiful carpet." The big Frog then called a young one, and said, "Bring me hither the great box." So the young Frog fetched it; and the old one, opening it, took out and gave to Dummling a carpet more beautiful than any one could make. Dummling thanked her for the gift and came up the steps again.

His two brothers, meanwhile, thinking their youngest brother so simple, believed that he would not bring home anything at all, and said to each other, "Let us take the best shawl we can from the back of some shepherd's wife." So they stole the first they met with, and carried it to the King. At the same time Dummling arrived, bringing his fine and beautiful carpet, and as soon as the King saw it he was astonished, and said, "By right this kingdom belongs to the youngest of you."

But the two others let the King have no peace, saying, "It is impossible that Dummling should have the kingdom, for he lacks common understanding." So the King then decreed that whoever brought him the most beautiful ring should be his heir; and, taking the three brothers out, he blew, as before, three feathers into the air, for them to follow. The two eldest went east and west, but Dummling's feather flew again as far as the trap-door, and there settled down. He descended a second time to the fat old Frog, and told her he needed the most beautiful ring in the world. The Frog ordered her jewel-casket to be brought, and gave him out of it a ring which sparkled with diamonds, and was finer than any goldsmith in the world could have made. The two eldest brothers gave themselves no further trouble than the beating of a nail, which they carried to the King. But as soon as Dummling displayed his gold ring, the father said, "The Kingdom belongs to him." The two eldest brothers, however, would not let the King be at peace until he appointed a third condition, which was, that whoever brought him the prettiest woman should have the kingdom. A third time he blew the feathers into the air, and they flew, as before, east and west, and one straight out.

Now Dummling went again down to the fat Frog, and said, "I have to take home the most beautiful bride I can find." "Ah," said the Frog, "the most beautiful bride! that is not easy for every one, but you shall have her;" and, so saying, she gave him a hollow carrot, to which six little mice were harnessed. Dummling asked sadly what he was to do with them, and the Frog told him to place in the carriage one of her little handmaids. He took up one Frog at random out of the circle, and placed her in the carrot; but no sooner was she seated than she became a beautiful maiden, and the carrot and the six mice were changed into a fine carriage and horses. Dummling kissed the maiden, and drove away from the place to the King's palace. His brothers came afterwards, having given themselves no trouble to find a pretty girl, but taking the first peasants they met. When the King had seen them all, he said, "At my death, the kingdom belongs to my youngest son."

But the two elder brothers again besieged the ears of the King with their cries, saying, "We cannot allow that Dummling should be King;" and they requested that there should be a trial for the superiority, to see whose wife could best jump through a ring which hung in the hall; for they thought to themselves, "These peasant girls will be strong enough, but that tender thing will kill herself in the attempt." At last the King consented. The two peasant girls sprang easily through the ring, but they were so plump that they fell down and broke their arms and legs. Then the beautiful bride of Dummling sprang through as lightly and gracefully as a fawn, and all opposition was put an end to. So Dummling, after all, received the crown, and ruled a long time happily and wisely.

The Queen Bee

ONCE upon a time two King's sons set out to seek adventures, and fell into such a wild kind of life that they did not return home. So their youngest brother, Dummling, went forth to seek them; but when he found them they mocked him, because of his simplicity. Nevertheless they journeyed on, all three together, till they came to an ant-hill, which the two eldest brothers would have overturned, to see how the little ants would run in their terror, carrying away their eggs; but Dummling said, "Let the little creatures be in peace; I will not suffer them to be overturned." Then they went further, till they came to a lake, on which ducks were swimming in myriads. The two brothers wanted to catch a pair and roast them; but Dummling would not allow it, saying, "Let these fowls alone; I will not suffer them to be killed!" At last they came to a bees' nest, in which was so much honey that it was running out at the mouth of the nest. The two brothers would have laid down under the tree and caught the bees as they passed, for the sake of their honey; but Dummling again held them back, saying, "Leave the creatures alone; I will not suffer them to be touched!"

After this the three brothers came to a castle, where in the stable stood several stone horses, but no man was to be seen; and they went through all the rooms, until they came to a door quite at the end on which hung three locks, and in the middle of the door was a hole through which one could see into the room. Peeping through this hole, they saw a fierce looking man sitting at the table. They called him once, twice, but he heard not; but as they called the third time he got up, opened the door and came out. Not a word did he speak, but led them to a well-supplied table, and when they had eaten and drunk, he took each of them into a sleeping chamber. The next morning the man came to the eldest, and beckoning him up, led him to a stone table on which were written three sentences. The first was that under the moss in the wood lay the pearls of the King's daughter, a thousand in number, which must be sought for, and if at sunset even one was wanting, he who had searched for them would be changed to stone. The eldest brother went off and searched the whole day, but only found a hundred, so that it happened to him as the table had said – he was changed into stone. The next day the second brother undertook the adventure, but he fared no better than the other, for he found but two hundred pearls, and he, therefore, was turned into stone. Then the turn came to Dummling, who searched the moss, but it was very difficult to find the pearls, and the work went on but slowly. Then he sat himself down on a stone, and wept, and while he did so, the Ant-King whose life he had formerly saved came up with five thousand companions, and before very long they searched for, and found, and piled in a heap, the whole thousand pearls. But the second sentence was to fetch the key of the Princess's sleeping chamber out of a lake which, by chance, the brothers had passed. When Dummling came to the lake, the Ducks whose lives he had before saved seam up to him, and diving below the water, quickly brought up the key. The third sentence, however, was the most difficult of all: of the three daughters of the King, to pick out the youngest and prettiest. They were all asleep, and appeared all the same, without a single mark of difference, except that before they fell asleep they had eaten different sweetmeats – the eldest a piece of sugar, the second a little syrup, and the youngest a spoonful of honey. Presently in came the Queen Bee of all the bees, who had been saved by Dummling from the fire, and tried the mouths of the three. At last she settled on the mouth which had eaten the honey, and thus the King's son soon knew which was the right Princess. Then the spell was broken; everyone was delivered from the sleep, and those who had been changed into stone received their human form again. Now Dummling was married to the youngest and prettiest Princess, and became King at his father's death; but his two brothers were obliged to be content with the two other sisters.

Allerleirauh

(THE COAT OF ALL COLOURS)

THERE was once a King, whose wife had golden hair, and was altogether so beautiful, that her equal was not to be found in the world. It happened that she fell ill, and when she felt she must soon die she called the King, and said, "If you marry again after my death, take no one who is not as beautiful as I have been, nor who has not golden hair like mine, and this you must promise me." After the King had promised she closed her eyes and soon died.

For a long time the King would not be comforted, and thought not of taking a second wife, but his councillors said at last that he must marry again. Then messengers were sent far and wide to seek such a bride as should be as beautiful as the late Queen, but there was no one to be found in the whole world so beautiful, and with such

golden hair. So the messengers returned home without accomplishing anything.

Now the King had a daughter, who was just as beautiful as her
dead mother, and had also the same golden hair, and as she grew up,
the King saw how like she was to his lost wife. He told the
councillors that he wished to marry his daughter to his oldest
councillor, and that she should be as Queen. When the oldest
councillor heard this he was delighted. But the daughter was
frightened at the resolve of the King, but hoped yet to turn him from
his intention. So she said to him, "Before I fulfil your wish, I must
have three dresses: one as golden as the sun, another as silver as the
moon, and a third as shining as the stars; further, I desire a cloak
composed of thousands of skins and hides, and to which every beast
in your kingdom must contribute a portion of his skin."

The Princess thought this would be impossible to do, and so she
should reclaim her father from his intention. But the King would not
give it up, and the cleverest maidens in his kingdom had to weave the
three dresses – one as golden as the sun, a second as silver as the
moon, and a third as shining as the stars; while his Huntsmen had to
catch all the beasts in the whole kingdom, and from each take a piece
of his skin, wherewith a mantle of a thousand pieces was made. At
length, when all was ready, the King let the mantle be fetched, and,
spreading it before him, said, "To-morrow shall the wedding be."

When the King's daughter now saw that there was no hope left of
turning her father from his resolve, she determined to flee away. In
the night, while all slept, she got up and took three of her treasures –
a golden ring, a gold spinning-wheel, and a gold reel; she put also in a
nutshell the three dresses of the sun, moon, and stars, and, putting
on the mantle of all skins, she dyed her hands and face black with
soot. Then, commending herself to God, she set off and travelled the
whole night till she came to a large wood, where, feeling very tired,
she took refuge in a hollow tree and went to sleep. The sun arose, and
she still slept and slept on till it was again far into the morning. Then
it happened that the King who owned this forest came to hunt in it.
As soon as his dogs ran to the tree they snapped about it, barked,

and growled, so that the King said to his Huntsmen, "See what wild animal it is that is concealed there." The Hunters obeyed his orders, and, when they returned, they said, "In that hollow lies a wonderful creature, whose like we have never before seen; its skin is composed of a thousand different colours, but it lies quite quiet and asleep." The King said, "Try if you can catch it alive, and then bind it to the carriage, and we will take it with us."

As soon as the Hunters caught hold of the Maiden, she awoke full of terror, and called out to them, "I am a poor child, forsaken by both father and mother! pray pity me, and take me with you!" They named her "Allerleirauh," because of her mantle, and took her home with them to serve in the kitchen, and rake out the ashes. They went to the Royal Palace, and there they showed her a little stable under the step, where no daylight could enter, and told her she could live and sleep there. Afterwards she went into the kitchen, and there she had to carry water and wood to make the fire, to pluck the fowls, to peel the vegetables, to rake out the ashes, and to do all manner of dirty work.

Here, for a length of time, Allerleirauh lived wretchedly; but it happened once that a feast was held in the palace, and she asked the Cook, "May I go and look on for a little while? I will place myself just outside the door." The Cook said, "Yes; but in half-an-hour's time you must return and rake out the ashes."

Allerleirauh took an oil-lamp, and, going to her stable, put off the gown of skins, and washed the soot from her face and hands, so that her real beauty was displayed. Then she opened her nut, and took out the dress which shone as the sun, and as soon as she was ready she went up to the ball-room, where every one made way for her, supposing that she was certainly some Princess. The King himself soon came up to her and taking her hand, danced with her, thinking the while in his heart that he had never seen any one like her. As soon as the dance was finished she curtsied, and, before the King could look round, she had disappeared, and nobody knew whither. The Watchmen also at the gates were called and questioned, but they had not seen her.

She had run back to her stable, and, having quickly taken off her dress, had again blackened her face and hands, and put on the dress of all skins, and became "Allerleirauh" once more. As soon as she went into the kitchen to do her work, in sweeping up the ashes, the Cook said, "Let that be for once till the morning, and cook the King's supper for me instead, while I go upstairs to have a peep; but mind you do not let one of your hairs fall in, or you will get nothing to eat for the future."

So saying, she went away, and Allerleirauh cooked the King's supper, making some soup as good as she possibly could, and when it was ready she went into the stable and fetched her gold ring, and laid it in the dish. When the dance was at an end the King ordered his supper to be brought, which, when he had tasted, he thought he had never eaten anything so nice before. Just as he nearly finished it he saw a gold ring at the bottom, and not being able to imagine how it came there, he commanded the Cook to be brought before him. The Cook was terrified when he heard this order, and said to Allerleirauh, "Are you certain you did not let a hair fall into the soup, for if it is so, you will catch a beating?"

Then he came before the King, who asked who had cooked the supper, and he answered, "I did." But the King said, "That is not true; for it is of a much better kind and much better cooked than usual." Then the Cook said, "I must confess that not I, but Allerleirauh, cooked it." So the King commanded that she should be brought up.

When Allerleirauh came the King asked,—

"Who are you?"

"I am a poor child, without father or mother," replied she.

"Why did you come into my palace?" then inquired the King.

"I am good for nothing else but to have the boots thrown at my head," said she.

The King asked again, "Where did you get this ring, then, which was in the soup?"

Allerleirauh said, "I know nothing of it." And, as she would say no more, she was at last sent away.

After a time there was another ball, and Allerleirauh asked the Cook's permission to go again and look on, and he consented, and told her, "Return here in half an hour to cook the King again the same soup which he liked so much before."

Allerleirauh ran into the stable, and, washing herself quickly, took out of the shell the dress which was silver as the moon, and put it on. Then she went up to the ball-room and appeared like a Princess, and the King, stepping up to her, was very glad to see her again; and, as the dancing was just begun, they joined it. But as soon as it was over, his partner disappeared so quickly, that the King did not notice where she went. She ran to her stable and changed her garments again, and then went into the kitchen to make the soup. While the Cook was upstairs, she fetched the golden spinning-wheel and put it in the tureen, so that the soup was served up with it. Afterwards it was brought before the King, who ate it, and found it taste as good as the former; and the Cook was called, who was obliged to confess again that Allerleirauh had made it. Allerleirauh was accordingly taken before the King, but she repeated what she had before said, that she was of no use but to have boots thrown at her, and that she knew nothing of the gold spinning-wheel.

Not long afterwards a third fête was given by the King, at which everything went as before. The Cook said to Allerleirauh when she asked leave to go, "You are certainly a witch, and always put something in the soup which makes it taste better than mine. Still, since you beg so hard, you shall go at the usual time." This time she put on the dress shining as the stars, and stepped with it into the ball-room. The King danced again with her, and thought he had never seen any maiden so beautiful; and while the dance went on he slipped the gold ring on to her finger without her perceiving it, and told the musicians to prolong the tune. When at last it ended, he would have kept fast hold of her hand, but she tore herself away, and sprang so quickly in among the people that she disappeared from his sight. Allerleirauh ran as well as she could back to her stable; but she had stayed over and above the half hour, and she had not time to pull off her beautiful dress, but was obliged to throw over it her cloak of skins. She did not either quite finish the blacking of her skin, but left one finger white. Then she ran into the kitchen, cooked the soup for the King, and put in it the reel, while the Cook stayed upstairs. Afterwards, when the King found the reel at the bottom of the soup, he summoned Allerleirauh, and perceived at once her white finger, and the ring which he had put on it during the dance. He took her by the hand and held it fast, and when she tried to force herself from him and run away, her cloak of skins fell partly off, and the starry dress was displayed to view. The King then pulled the cloak wholly off, and down came her golden hair, and there she stood in all her beauty, and could no longer conceal herself. As soon, then, as the soot and ashes were washed off her face, she stood up and appeared more beautiful than anyone could conceive possible on earth. But the King said to her, "You are my dear bride, and we will never separate from each other." Thereupon was the wedding celebrated, and they lived happily to the end of their lives.

The Twelve Hunters

A CERTAIN King's son, unknown to his father, was betrothed to a Maiden whom he loved very much, and once while he was sitting by

THE TWELVE HUNTERS

her side, happy and contented, news came that his father was very ill, and desired to see him before his end. So the Prince said to his beloved, "I must go away and leave you; I will give you this ring for a memorial. When I become King, I will return and take you home with me."

So saying, he rode off; and when he arrived, he found his father at the point of death. The old King said to him, "My dearest son, I have desired to see you once more before I died, that I may have your promise to marry according to my wishes;" and he named to him a certain Princess whom he was to make his bride. The young King was so grieved that he did not know what he was saying, and so promised his father that he would fulfil his wish. Soon afterwards the old King closed his eyes in death.

When the time of mourning for the late King was over, the young Prince, who had succeeded to the throne, was called upon to fulfil the promise which he had given to his father, and the Princess was betrothed to him accordingly. By chance the Maiden heard of this, and grieved so much about the faithlessness of her beloved that she fast faded away. Then her father said to her, "My dear child, why are you sad? whatever you wish for you shall have."

For a few minutes she considered, and at last said, "Dear father, I wish for eleven maidens exactly like myself in figure and stature."

Her father told her that if it were possible her wish should be carried out, and he ordered a search to be made in his country until eleven maidens were found resembling exactly his daughter in figure and stature. When they came to the Maiden she had twelve hunters' dresses made all exactly alike, and each of the maidens had to put on one, while she herself drew on the twelfth. Thereupon she took leave of her father and rode away with her companions to the court of her former betrothed, whom she loved so much. There she inquired if he needed any Huntsmen, and if he would not take them all into his service. The King looked at her without recognising her, and as they were such handsome people he consented to take them, and so they became the twelve royal Huntsmen.

The King, however, possessed a Lion who was such a wonderful beast that he knew all hidden and secret affairs. So one evening he said to the King, "Do you suppose that you have got twelve Huntsmen?" "Yes," replied he, "twelve Huntsmen." "You are mistaken there," replied the Lion; "they are twelve maidens."

"That can never be true," said the King; "how will you prove it to me?"

"Order some peas to be strewn in your ante-room," said the Lion, "and you will at once see; for men have a firm tread when walking on peas, and do not slip; but maidens trip, and stumble, and slide, and make the peas roll about."

This advice pleased the King, and he ordered peas to be strewn.

Now, there was a servant of the King's who was kind to the Huntsmen; and, as he heard that they were to be put to this trial, he went and told them all that had passed, and that the Lion wished to show the King that they were maidens. The Maiden thanked him and told her companions to compel themselves to tread firmly on the peas. When, therefore, the next morning the King summoned the twelve Hunters, and they came into the ante-room, they trod firmly upon the peas with so sturdy a step that not one rolled or moved in the least. Afterwards, when they had left the room, the King said to the Lion, "You have deceived me; they walk like men!"

The Lion replied, "They knew that they were to be put to the proof, and so summoned all their strength. Let twelve spinning-wheels be now brought into the ante-room, and, when they come to pass them, they will be pleased at the sight thereof as no man would be."

This advice also pleased the King, and he caused the twelve spinning-wheels to be placed in the room.

But the servant who was kind to the Hunters went and disclosed the plan to the Maiden, who instructed her eleven attendants to take no notice whatever of the spinning-wheels. The following morning the King summoned his Hunters, and they passed through the ante-room without once looking round at the spinning-wheels. So the King said to the Lion again, "You have deceived me; these are men, for they have not noticed the wheels."

The Lion replied as before, "They knew that they would be put on trial, and they have behaved accordingly;" but the King would believe the Lion no more.

After this the twelve Hunters followed the King customarily in his sporting, and the longer he had them the more he seemed to like them. Now it happened that once, as they were going out to the hunt, news came that the Princess who had been betrothed to the young King was on her way to his court. As soon as the true betrothed heard this, she was so overcome that all her strength forsook her, and she fell heavily to the ground. The King soon perceived that something had happened to his best Huntsman, and ran up to help him just as his glove was drawn off. He then saw upon one finger the ring which he had given to his first love, and, as he looked in the face of the supposed Huntsman, he recognised her. At the sight his heart was so touched that he kissed her, and, as she opened her eyes he said, "You are mine, and I am thine, and no power on earth shall make it otherwise."

The King then sent a messenger to the Princess, begging her to return to her own country, for he had already a bride.

Soon afterwards the wedding was celebrated, and the Lion came again into favour, because, after all, he had spoken the truth.

The Rogue and his Master

A CERTAIN man, named John, was desirous that his son should learn some trade, and he went into the church to ask the Priest's opinion what would be most desirable. Just then the Clerk was standing near the altar, and he cried out, "The rogue, the rogue!" At these words the man went away, and told his son he must learn to be a rogue, for so the Priest had said. So they set out, and asked one man and another whether he was a rogue, till, at the end of the day, they entered a large forest, and there found a little hut with an old woman in it.

John asked the old woman, "Do you know any man who can teach roguery?" "Here," said the old Woman, "here you may learn, for my son is a master of the art." Then John asked the son whether he could teach it perfectly? and the rogue replied, "I will teach your son well; return in four years, and if you know your son then I will not ask any recompense; but if you do not, then you must give me two hundred dollars."

John now went home, and left his son to learn roguery and witchcraft. When the time was up, the father set out to see his son, considering as he went along by what he should know him. On his way he met a little man, who stopped him, and asked, "Why are you grieving and looking so mournful?" "Oh," replied John, "four years ago I left my son to learn roguery, and the master said, if I returned in that time and knew my son, I should have nothing to pay; but if I did not know him, I must give him two hundred dollars; and, since I have no means of recognising him, I am troubled where to procure the money."

Then the little man told him to take a basket of bread with him, and when he came to the Rogue's house to put the basket under a hollow tree which stood there, and the little Bird which should peep out would be his son.

John went and did as he was told, and out came a little Bird to peck at the bread. "Holloa, my son! are you here?" said John. The son was very glad to hear his father's voice, and said, "Father, let us go!" but first the Rogue-master called out, "The Evil One must have told you where to find your son!"

So the father and son returned home, and on their way they met a coach, and the son said to his father, "I will change myself into a fine greyhound, and then you can earn some money by me."

The Lord who was riding in the coach called out, "Man, will you sell your dog?"

"Yes," replied the father.

"How much do you want for him?"

"Thirty dollars," was the reply.

"That is too much, my man," said the Lord, "but on account of his very beautiful skin I will buy him off you."

The bargain concluded, the dog was put inside the coach; but when they had travelled a mile or two the greyhound jumped right out through the glass, and rejoined his father.

After this adventure they went home together, and the following day they went to the next village to market. On their way the son said, "Father, I will change myself into a Horse, and then you can sell me; but first untie my bridle, and then I can change myself into the form of a man."

The father drove his horse to market, and thither came the Rogue-master and bought him for a hundred dollars, but the father forgot to untie the bridle.   .

The Rogue rode his horse home, and put him in the stable, and, when the maid came with the corn, the Horse said to her, "Undo my bridle, undo my bridle!"

"Ah, can you speak?" said she, terrified, and untied the horse directly. The Horse thereupon became a sparrow, and flew away out at the door, pursued by the Rogue, who changed himself also into a bird. When they came up with each other, the Rogue changed himself into water, and the other into a fish. But the Rogue could not catch him so, and he changed himself into a cock, but the other instantly became a fox, and bit his master's head off, so that he died.

And he lies there to this very day.

The Wolf and the Fox

A WOLF, once upon a time, caught a Fox. It happened one day that they were both going through the forest, and the Wolf said to his companion, "Get me some food, or I will eat you up."

The Fox replied, "I know a farmyard where there are a couple of young lambs, which, if you wish, we will fetch."

This proposal pleased the Wolf, so they went, and the Fox, stealing first one of the lambs, brought it to the Wolf, and then ran away. The Wolf devoured it quickly, but was not contented, and went to fetch the other lamb by himself, but he did it so awkwardly that he aroused the attention of the mother, who began to cry and bleat loudly, so that the peasants ran up. There they found the Wolf, and beat him so unmercifully that he ran, howling and limping, to the Fox, and said, "You have led me to a nice place, for, when I went to fetch the other lamb, the peasants came and beat me terribly!"

"Why are you such a glutton?" asked the Fox.

The next day they went again into the fields, and the covetous Wolf said to the Fox, "Get me something to eat now, or I will devour you!"

The Fox said he knew a country house where the cook was going that evening to make some pancakes, and thither they went. When they arrived, the Fox sneaked and crept round the house, until he at last discovered where the dish was standing, out of which he took six pancakes, and took them to the Wolf, saying, "There is something for you to eat!" and then ran away. The Wolf dispatched these in a minute or two, and, wishing to taste some more, he went and seized the dish, but took it away so hurriedly that it broke in pieces. The noise of its fall brought out the woman, who, as soon as she saw the Wolf, called her people, who, hastening up, beat him with such a good will that he ran home to the Fox, howling, with two lame legs! "What a dirty place have you drawn me into now," cried he, "the peasants have caught me, and dressed my skin finely!"

"Why, then, are you such a glutton?" said the Fox.

When they went out again the third day, the Wolf limping along with weariness, he said to the Fox, "Get me something to eat now, or I will devour you!"

The Fox said he knew a man who had just killed a pig, and salted the meat down in a cask in his cellar, and that they could get at it. The Wolf replied that he would go with him on condition that he helped him if he could not escape. "Oh, of course I will, on mine own account!" said the Fox, and showed him the tricks and ways by which they could get into the cellar. When they went in there was meat in abundance, and the Wolf was enraptured at the sight. The Fox, too, had a taste, but kept looking round while eating, and ran frequently to the hole by which they had entered, to see if his body would slip through it easily. Presently the Wolf asked, "Why are you running about so, you Fox, jumping in and out?" "I want to see if any one is coming," replied the Fox, cunningly; "but mind you do not eat too much!"

The Wolf said he would not leave till the cask was quite empty;

and meanwhile the peasant, who had heard the noise made by the Fox, entered the cellar. The Fox, as soon as he saw him, made a spring, and was through the hole in a jiffy; and the Wolf tried to follow his example, but he had eaten so much that his body was too big for the hole, and he stuck fast. Then came the peasant with a cudgel, and beat him to death; but the Fox leapt away into the forest, very glad to get rid of the old glutton.

The Fox and Godmother-Wolf

A CERTAIN She-Wolf had brought a whelp into the world, and invited the Fox to stand godfather, for, said she, "He is, a near relative, and possesses a good understanding and much cleverness, so that he can instruct my son, and help him on in the world." The Fox appeared to be very honourable, and said to the Wolf, "My worthy fellow god-parent, I thank you much for the honour you show me, and I will so conduct myself that you shall be quite satisfied." At the feast he made himself very sociable and merry; and when it was over he said to the Wolf, "My dear lady, it is our duty to care for the child, and therefore he must have good food, that he may grow strong. I know a sheepfold whence we can easily fetch somewhat."

This speech pleased the Wolf, and she went with the Fox to the farmyard, and there he showed her the place, and said, "You can creep in there unseen, and meanwhile I will go round to the other side, and see if I can pick up a hen."

The Fox, however, did not go as he said, but ran away and stretched himself upon the ground, near the edge of the forest, to rest. The Wolf crept into the stall, where lay a dog, who began to bark, so that the labourers ran in, and, surprising the Wolf, poured a panful of burning coals over her skin. At last she escaped, and slipped away out of the stall, and found the Fox lying near the forest. The Fox made a very wry face, and said, "Ah, my dear godmother, how badly I have fared! The peasants fell upon me, and have nearly broken all my bones, and, if you do not wish me to perish here where I lie, you must carry me away!"

The poor Wolf could scarcely move herself; but yet, out of her great concern for the Fox, she took him upon her back, and carried home, slowly enough, the really strong and unhurt godfather. When they reached home, the Fox cried out to the Wolf, "Farewell, my dear godmother; may you relish your scorching!" and, so saying, he laughed in her face, and quickly bolted off!

The Fox and The Cat

ONCE upon a time it fell out that a Cat met a Fox in a wood; and thinking him clever and well experienced in the ways of the world, she spoke friendly to him, and said, "Good day, dear master Fox; how do you do, how do you get on, and how do you find your living in these dear times?"

The Fox considered the Cat from head to foot with all the pride in his nature, and doubted for a time whether to answer or not. At last he said, "Oh, you wretched shaver! you pied simpleton! you hungry mouse-hunter! what has put it into your head to ask me how I fare? what have you learnt? how many arts do you understand?"

"I understand but a single one," replied the Cat, decisively.

"And what sort of an art is that?" inquired the Fox.

"When the dogs pursue me, to climb up a tree, and so save myself," said the Cat.

"Oh, is that all?" returned the Fox; "why, I understand a hundred arts; and have, moreover, a sackful of cunning! I pity you! Come with me, and I will show you how to escape the hounds."

Presently a Hunter came riding along with four dogs. The Cat ran nimbly up a tree, and perched herself upon his highest point, where the branches and leaves completely concealed her, and then called to the Fox, "Open your sack, my Fox! open your sack?" But the hounds had already seized poor Reynard, and held him tight. "Oh, Mr Fox," cried the Cat, when she saw the end, "you are come to a standstill in spite of your hundred arts. Now, could you have crept up a tree like me, your life would not have been sacrificed!"

The Three Luck-Children

THERE was once upon a time a father, who called his three sons to him, and gave the first a cock, the second a scythe, and the third a cat, and then addressed them thus: – "I am very old, and my end draweth nigh, but I wish to show my care for you before I die. Money I have not, and what I now give you appears of little worth; but do not think that, for if each of you use his gift carefully, and seek some country where such a thing is not known, your fortunes will be made."

Soon after, the father died, and the eldest son set out on his travels with his cock, but wherever he came, such a creature was already well known. In the towns he saw it from afar, sitting upon the church-steeples, and turning itself round with the wind; and in the villages he heard more than one crow, and nobody troubled himself about another, so that it did not seem as if he would ever make his fortune by it. At last, however, it fell out that he arrived on an island where the people knew nothing about cocks, nor even how to divide their time. They knew, certainly, when it was evening and morning, but at night, if they did not sleep through it, they could not comprehend the time. "See," said he to them, "what a proud creature it is, what a fine red crown it wears on its head, and it has spurs like a knight! Thrice during the night it will crow at certain hours, and the third time it calls you may know the sun will soon rise; but, if it crows by day, you may prepare then for a change of weather."

The good people were well pleased, and the whole night they laid awake and listened to the cock, which crowed loudly and clearly at two, four, and six o'clock. The next day they asked if the creature were not for sale, and how much he asked, and he replied, "As much gold as an ass can bear." "A ridiculously small sum," said they, "for such a marvellous creature!" and gave him readily what he asked.

When he returned home with his money, his brothers were astonished and the second said he would also go out and see what luck his scythe would bring him. But at first it did not seem likely that fortune would favour him, for all the countrymen he met carried equally good scythes upon their shoulders. At last, however, he also came to an island whose people were ignorant of the use of scythes; for when a field of corn was ripe, they planted great cannons and shot it down! In this way, it was no uncommon thing that many of them shot quite over it; others hit the ears instead of the stalks, and shot them quite away, so that a great quantity was always ruined, and the most doleful lamentations ensued. But our hero, when he arrived, mowed away so silently and quickly, that the people held their breath and noses with wonder, and willingly gave him what he desired, which was a horse laden with as much gold as it could carry.

On his return the third brother set out with his cat to try his luck, and it happened to him exactly as it had done to the others: so long as he kept on the old roads he met with no place which did not already boast its cat; indeed, so many were there that the new-born kittens were usually drowned. At last he voyaged to an island where, luckily for him, cats were unknown animals; and yet, the mice were so numerous that they danced upon the tables and chairs, whether the master of the house were at home or not. These people complained continually of the plague, and the King himself knew not how to deliver them from it; for in every corner the mice were swarming, and destroyed what they could not carry away in their teeth. The cat, however, on its arrival, commenced a grand hunt; and so soon cleared a couple of rooms of the troublesome visitors, that the people begged the King to buy it for the use of his kingdom. The King gave willingly the price that was asked for the wonderful animal, and the third brother returned home with a still larger treasure, in the shape of a mule laden with gold.

Meanwhile the cat was having capital sport in the royal palace with the mice, and bit so many that the dead were not to be numbered. At last she became very thirsty with the hot work, and stopped, and, raising its head, cried, "Miau, miau!" At the unusual sound, the King, together with all his courtiers, were much frightened, and in terror they ran out of the castle. There the King held a council what it were best to do, and at length it was resolved to send a herald to the cat, to demand that it should quit the castle, or force would be used to make it. "For," said the councillors, "we would rather be plagued by the mice, to which we are accustomed, than surrender ourselves a prey to this beast." A page was accordingly sent to the cat to ask whether it would quit the castle in peace; but the cat, whose thirst had all the while been increasing, replied nothing but "Miau, miau!" The page understood it to say,

"No, no!" and brought the King word accordingly. The councillors agreed then that it should feel their power, and cannons were brought out and fired, so that the castle was presently in flames. When the fire reached the room where the cat was, it sprang out of the window, but the besiegers ceased not until the whole was levelled with the ground.

How Six Travelled through the World

THERE was once a man who understood a variety of arts; he had served in the army, where he had behaved very bravely, but when the war came to an end he received his discharge, and three dollars only for his services. "Wait a bit! this does not please me," said he; "if I find the right people, I will make the King give me the treasures of the whole kingdom." Thereupon, inflamed with anger, he went into a forest, where he found a man who had just uprooted six trees, as if they were straw, and he asked him whether he would be his servant, and travel with him. "Yes" replied the man; "but I will first take home to my mother this bundle of firewood;" and, taking up one of the trees, he wound it round the other five, and, raising the bundle upon his shoulder, bore it away. Soon he returned, and said to his master, "We two shall travel well through the world!" They had not gone far before they came up with a hunter who was kneeling upon one knee, and preparing to take aim with his gun. The master asked what he was going to shoot, and he replied, "Two miles from hence sits a fly upon the branch of an oak-tree, whose left eye I wish to shoot out."

"Oh, go with me!" said the man; "for, if we three are together, we must pass easily through the world."

The huntsman consented, and went with him, and soon they arrived at seven windmills, whose sails were going round at a rattling pace, although right or left there was no wind and not a leaf stirring. At this sight the man said, "I wonder what drives these mills, for there is no breeze!" and they went on: but they had not proceeded more than two miles when they saw a man sitting upon a tree, who held one nostril while he blew out of the other. "My good fellow," said our hero, "what are you driving up there?"

"Did you not see," replied the man, "two miles from hence, seven windmills? it is those which I am blowing, that the sails may go round."

"Oh, then come with me," said our hero; "for, if four people like us travel together, we shall soon get through the world."

So the blower got up and accompanied him, and in a short while they met with another man standing upon one leg, with the other leg unbuckled and lying by his side. The leader of the others said, "You have done this, no doubt, to rest yourself?" "Yes," replied the man, "I am a runner, and in order that I may not spring along too quickly I have unbuckled one of my legs, for when I wear both I go as fast as a bird can fly."

"Well, then, come with me," said our hero; "five such fellows as we are will soon get through the world."

The five heroes went on together, and soon met a man who had a

HOW SIX TRAVELLED THROUGH THE WORLD

hat on, which he wore quite over one ear. The captain of the others said to him, "Manners! manners! don't hang your hat on one side like that; you look like a simpleton!"

"I dare not do so," replied the other; "for, if I set my hat straight, there will come so sharp a frost that the birds in the sky will freeze and fall dead upon the ground."

"Then come with me," said our hero, "for it is odd if six fellows like us cannot travel quickly through the world."

These six new companions went into a city where the King had proclaimed, that whoever should run a race with his daughter, and bear away the prize, should become her husband; but if he lost the race he should also lose his head. This was mentioned to our hero, who said that he would have his servant run for him; but the King told him that in that case he must agree that his servant's life, as well as his own, should be sacrificed if the wager were lost. To this he agreed and swore, and then he bade his runner buckle on his other leg, and told him to be careful and to make sure of winning. The wager was, that whoever first brought back water from a distant spring should be victor. Accordingly the runner and the princess both received a cup, and they both began to run at the same moment. But the princess had not proceeded many steps before the runner was quite out of sight, and it seemed as if but a puff of wind had passed. In a short time he came to the spring, and filling his cup, he turned back again, but had not gone very far, before, feeling tired he set his cup down again, and laid down to take a nap. He made his pillow of a horse's skull which lay upon the ground; thinking, from its being hard, that he would soon awake. Meantime, the princess, who was a better runner than many of the men at court, had arrived at the spring, and was returning with her cup of water, when she perceived her opponent lying asleep. In great joy, she exclaimed, "My enemy is given into my own hands!" and, emptying his cup, she ran on faster still. All would now have been lost, if, by good luck, the huntsman had not been standing on the castle, looking on with his sharp eyes. When he saw the princess was gaining the advantage, he loaded his gun and shot so cleverly that he carried away the horse's skull under the runner's head, without doing the man any injury. This awoke him, and, jumping up, he found his cup empty and the princess far in advance. However, he did not lose courage, but ran back again to the spring, and, filling his cup, returned home ten minutes earlier than his opponent. "See, you," said he, "now I have used my legs, the former was not worth calling running."

The King was disgusted, and his daughter not less, that a common soldier should carry off the prize, and they consulted together how they should get rid of him and his companions. At last the King said, "Do not distress yourself, my dear: I have found a way to prevent their return." Then he called to the six travellers, and, saying to them, "You must now eat and drink and be merry," he led them into a room with a floor of iron, doors of iron, and the windows guarded with iron bars. In the room was a table set out with choice delicacies, and the King invited them to enter and refresh themselves, and as soon as they were inside he locked and bolted all the doors. That done, he summoned the Cook, and commanded him to keep a fire lighted beneath till the iron was red-hot. The Cook obeyed, and the six champions, sitting at table, soon began to feel warm, and at first thought it arose from eating; but as it kept getting warmer and warmer, they rose to leave the room, and found the doors and windows all fast. Then they perceived that the King had some wicked design in hand, and wished to suffocate them. "But he shall not succeed!" cried the man with the hat; "I will summon such a frost as shall put to shame and crush this fire;" and, so saying, he put his hat on straight, and immediately such a frost fell, that all the heat disappeared, and even the meats upon the dishes began to freeze. When two hours had passed, the King thought they would be stifled, and he caused the door to be opened, and went in himself to see after them. But, as soon as the door was opened, there stood all six fresh and lively, and requested to come out to warm themselves, for the cold in the room had been so intense that all the dishes were frozen! In a great passion the King went down to the Cook and scolded him, and asked why he had not obeyed his instructions. The Cook, however, pointing to the fire, said, "There is heat enough there, I should think;" and the King was obliged to own there was, and he saw clearly that he should not be able to get rid of his visitors in that way.

The King now began to think afresh how he could free himself, and he caused the master to be summoned, and said, "Will you not take money, and give up your right to my daughter? If so, you shall have as much as you wish."

"Well, my lord King," replied the man, "just give me as much as my servant can carry, and you are welcome to keep your daughter."

This answer pleased the King very much, and our hero said that he would come and fetch the sum in fourteen days. During that time he collected all the tailors in the kingdom, and made them sew him a sack, which took up all that time. As soon as it was ready, the Strong Man, who had uprooted the trees, took the sack upon his shoulder, and carried it to the King. At the sight of him, the King said, "What a powerful fellow this must be, carrying this great sack upon his shoulders!" and sorely frightened, he wondered how much gold he would slip in. The King, first of all, caused a ton of gold to be brought, which required sixteen ordinary men to lift; but the Strong Man, taking it up with one hand shoved it into the sack, saying, "Why do you not bring more at a time? – this scarcely covers the bottom of the sack." Then by degrees the King caused all his treasures to be brought, which the Strong Man put in, and yet they did not half fill his sack. "Bring more, more!" said he; "these are only a couple of crumbs." Then they were obliged to bring seven thousand waggons, oxen, and all. Still it was not full, and the Strong Man offered to take whatever they brought, if they would but fill his sack. When everything that they could find was put in, the man said, "Well, I must make and end to this; and, besides, if one's sack is not quite full, why it can be tied up so much the easier!" and, so saying, he hoisted it upon his back, and went away, and his companions with him.

When the King saw this one man bearing away all the riches of his kingdom, he got into a tremendous passion, and ordered his cavalry to pursue the six men, and at all risks to bring back the Strong Man with the sack. Two regiments accordingly pursued them quickly, and shouted out to them, "You are our prisoners! lay down the sack of gold, or you will be hewn to pieces!"

"What is that you are saying?" asked the Blower; "you will make us prisoners! but first you shall have a dance in the air!" So saying, he held one nostril, and blew with the other the two regiments right away into the blue sky, so that one flew over the hills on the right side and the other on the left. One sergeant begged for mercy: he had nine wounds, and was a brave fellow undeserving of such disgrace. So the Blower sent after him a gentle puff which brought him back without harming him, and then sent him back to the King with a message that, whatever number of knights he might yet send, all would be blown into the air like the first lot. When the King heard this message, he said, "Let the fellows go! they will meet with their deserts!" So the six companions took home all the wealth of that kingdom, and, sharing it with one another, lived contentedly all the rest of their days.

The Clever Grethel

ONCE upon a time there was a Cook who wore shoes with red knots, and when she went out with them on she used to figure her feet about here and there, and then say to herself, quite complacently, "Ah, you are still a pretty girl!" And when she came home she drank a glass of wine for joy, and, as the wine made her wish to eat, she used to look out the best she had, and excuse herself by saying, "The Cook ought to know how her cooking tastes."

One day it happened that her master said to her, "Grethel, this evening a guest is coming, so cook me two fowls." "I will do it directly, master," replied Grethel. She soon killed the fowls, plucked, dressed, and spitted them, and, as evening came on, she put them down to the fire to roast. They soon began to brown and warm through, but still the guest was not come, and Grethel said to the master, "If your guest does not come soon I shall have to take the fowls from the fire, but it will be a great shame not to eat them soon, when they are just in the gravy."

The master agreed, therefore, to run out himself and bring home his guest; and, as soon as he had turned his back, Grethel laid aside the spit, with its two fowls, and thought to herself, "Ah, I have stood so long before the fire, I am quite hot and thirsty; who knows when he will come? Meanwhile I will run down into the cellar and have a draught."

Grethel ran down the stairs and filled a jug, and, saying "God bless you, Grethel!" took a good pull at the beer, and when that was down she had another draught. Then she went up again, and placed the fowls before the fire, and turned the spit round quite merrily, first spreading some butter over their skins. However, the roasting fowls smelt so well that Grethel thought she had better try how they tasted; and so she dipped her finger into the gravy, and said, "Ah, how good these fowls are! it is a sin and shame that they should not be eaten at once!" She ran to the window, therefore, to see if her master was yet coming with his guests, but there was nobody, and she turned again to the fowls. "Ah, one wing is burnt!" said she, "I had better eat that!" and, cutting it off, she ate it. But then she thought, "Master will see that something is wanting, I had better take the other!" When she had finished the two wings, she went again to see whether her master was coming, but without success. "Who knows," said she, "whether they will come or not! and perhaps they are stopping where they are. Come, Grethel, be of good courage! the one is begun, have another drink, and then eat it up completely, for when it is all done you will be at rest; and besides, why should the good things be spoiled?" So thinking, Grethel ran once more into the cellar, took a capital drink, and then ate up one fowl with great pleasure. As soon as it was down, and the master still had not returned, Grethel looked at the other fowl, and said, "Where the one is, the other ought to be also; the two belong to one another; what is right for the one is right for the other; I believe if I take another draught it will not hurt me." So saying, she took a hearty drink, and let the second fowl slip down after the other.

Just as she was in the best of the eating, the master came running up, and called, "Make haste, Grethel! the guest is coming directly!"

"Yes, master," said she, "it will soon be ready."

The master went in to see if the table were properly laid, and, taking up the great knife wherewith he was to carve the fowls, he went to sharpen it upon the stones. Meantime came the guest, and knocked politely at the door. Grethel ran to see who it was; and, when she perceived the guest, she held her finger to her mouth to enjoin silence, and said, "Make haste quickly away! if my master discovers you here, you are lost; he certainly did invite you here to supper, but he has it in his mind to cut off your ears; just listen how he is sharpening his knife!"

The guest listened to the sound, and then hurried down the steps as fast as he could, while Grethel ran screaming to her master, and said to him, "You have invited a fine guest!"

"Eh! what?" said he, "what do you mean?"

"Why," replied Grethel, "just as I was about to serve them up, your guest has taken the two fowls from off the dish, and bolted away with them!"

"That is fine manners, certainly!" said the master, grieved for his fine fowls; "if he had but left me one at the least, that I might have had something to eat!" Then he called after his guest, who pretended not to hear him, and so he pursued him, knife in hand, calling out, "Only one! only one!" meaning that his guest should leave one fowl behind him; but the latter supposed that his host meant that he would only cut off one ear, and so he ran faster and faster, as if fire were at his heels, that he might reach home safe and sound.

The Pink

ONCE upon a time there lived a Queen who had been denied children for many years, but every morning she went into the garden and prayed to God that he would grant her a son or a daughter. And once an Angel came down and said to her, "Be satisfied, you shall have a son gifted with this power: whatsoever he wishes for in this world shall be given unto him."

The Queen went directly to the King, and told him the joyful message; and when the time arrived she bore a son, and the King rejoiced exceedingly.

Now, the Queen went every morning into the park with her child, and washed it at a clear spring which flowed there. One day she fell asleep with the child in her lap, and the old Cook, who knew that the child possessed wishing powers, took it from her; and, killing a fowl, sprinkled the blood upon the Queen's apron and clothes. Then he carried the child away to a secret place, where a nurse took charge of it, and then ran to the King, and stated that the Queen had allowed her son to be torn from her by the wild beasts. The King, when he saw the blood upon her apron, believed the tale, and fell into such a rage that he caused a high tower to be built, into which neither sun nor moon shone, and therein he shut up his wife, to stay there for seven years without meat or drink, and so perish. But two white doves flew daily twice to her with food during the whole seven years.

But the Cook thought to himself, "Since this child has the gift of wishing, it may bring me into misfortune if I stop here;" and so he left the castle and went to the child, who had already grown so much that he could speak. He told the child to wish for a noble house, with a garden, and all appurtenances; and scarcely were the words out of his mouth before all appeared. After a time had elapsed the Cook said to the boy, "It is not good for you to be so alone; therefore wish for a beautiful maiden to bear you company." This also the boy did, and immediately there stood before him one more beautiful than any painter could depict. The two children played together, and grew to love each other much, while the old Cook went daily to hunt like any gentleman. By-and-bye, however, the thought occurred to him that perhaps the young Prince might wish to be with his father, and so bring him into great trouble, and to prevent that he took the maiden aside one day, and said to her, "To-night, when the boy sleeps, stick this dagger into his heart, and cut out his tongue; and if you do not do it your own life shall be sacrificed."

So saying, he went out as usual, and when he returned the next day she had not done it, and excused herself by saying, "What! shall I take the life of an innocent youth who has never yet injured any one?"

"If you do not," said the Cook, "your own life shall pay the forfeit!"

Afterwards, when he was gone out, the maiden had a little calf fetched, and killed, and its heart and tongue taken out, which she laid upon a plate, and when she saw the old Cook return, she told the youth to get into bed and draw the covering over him.

Soon the old wretch came in, and asked, "Where are the heart and tongue of the boy?" The maiden reached him the plate, but the Prince threw off the covering and cried, "You old sinner! why would you have killed me? now I will pronounce your sentence. You shall become a black poodle-dog, and wear a golden chain round your neck, and swallow live coals, so that you shall breathe out fire."

As soon as he had spoken these words, the Cook took the form of a poodle-dog, and had a golden chain round his neck, and when he ate live coals, a flame burst out of his mouth. The King's son remained in the palace a short time, but soon remembered his mother, and wondered if she were yet alive. And at last he said to the maiden, "I must go home to my father, and if you will go with me I will take care of you."

"Alas!" she replied, "the way is too far, and what shall I do in a strange land where I am unknown?"

But the young Prince would not depart without her, and when he found her inflexible, he wished her into a beautiful pink, and carried her away in that form. The dog had to run behind, and so they travelled to their native land. There he went to the tower where his mother dwelt, and as it was so lofty, he wished for a ladder, which reached to the top. Then he mounted, and, looking in, called, "Dearest mother, lady Queen, are you yet alive, or are you dead?"

The Queen replied, "I have just eaten, and am satisfied;" for she thought it was the dove who spoke.

But the Prince said, "I am your dear son, whom the wild beasts were said to have stolen from your lap, but I am yet alive, and will soon rescue you."

So saying, he went down, and came to his father's palace, and caused himself to be announced as a huntsman who desired to enter the King's service. The King answered that he might do so if he could procure any venison, but he himself had not been able to find any in any part of his territories. Then the huntsman promised to procure him as many deer as he could use for the royal table, and caused all the others to be summoned to accompany him. So they went out, and the young Prince bade them enclose a large circle, open at one end, in the middle of which he placed himself, and began to wish. Soon two hundred and odd head of game ran into the circle, at which the huntsmen began to shoot. All these were heaped upon sixty carts, and driven home to the King, who once more, after a long interval, was enabled to garnish his table with venison.

The King, therefore, received the game with great satisfaction, and ordered that on the following day his whole court should dine with him at a great festival. When they were assembled, he said to the young huntsman, "Since you are so clever you must sit next me;" but he replied, "May it please your majesty to excuse me, I am but a poor huntsman."

The King, however, resolved, and said, "You must sit next me;" and as the Prince did so, he thought of his dear mother, and wished that one of the King's courtiers might inquire whether the Queen were yet alive, or had perished in the tower. Scarcely had he so wished, when the marshal began to speak, saying, "May it please your majesty, here are we living in great happiness, but how fares our lady the Queen, in the tower? is she still alive, or dead?"

But the King said, "She suffered my beloved son to be torn away by wild beasts, and I will hear nothing of her."

At these words, the huntsman got up and said, "My dear and gracious father, she is still alive, and I am her son, for the wild beasts did not take me away, but that wretch the Cook took me out of her lap when she was asleep, and sprinkled the blood of a hen over her apron."

Thereupon he took up the dog with the golden necklace, and said, "This is the wretch!" and he ordered live coals to be brought, which he was forced to eat in the presence of all, so that the flames burst out of his mouth. Then he changed him back into his right form again, and there stood the Cook with his white apron on, and his knife by his side. As soon as the King recognised him, he became terribly angry, and ordered him to be thrown into the deepest dungeon of the castle. Then the young Prince asked his father whether he would see the maiden who had treated him so tenderly, and had saved his life at the peril of her own; and the King replied, "Yes, most willingly." "I will show you her first in the form of a flower," said the Prince; and searching in his bosom he took out the pink, and placed it upon the royal table, and all confessed they had never seen so beautiful a flower. "Now I will show you the real maiden," said the Prince; and, wishing again, she stood before all, and appeared more beautiful than any artist could have painted.

After this, the King sent two men of the household, and two attendants, up into the tower, to fetch the Queen, and bring her to the royal table. But as soon as she was led in she ceased to eat, and murmured, "The all-gracious and all-merciful God who preserved me in the tower will soon release me!" For three days after this, she lingered, and then she died happily; and, when she was buried, two white doves followed her, which were those which had brought her food in the tower, and after her burial, they hovered about her grave in the form of two angels from heaven.

But the old King grieved at heart for her for some time, and at length died, and the young King then married the beautiful maiden whom he had cherished in his bosom as a flower; but whether they yet live is not known to me.

The Old Man and his Grandson

ONCE upon a time there was a very old, old Man, whose eyes were dim, his ears useless for hearing, and his knees trembled. When he sat at table he could scarcely hold his spoon, and often he spilled his food over the tablecloth and sometimes down his clothes. His son and daughter-in-law were much vexed about this, and at last they made the old Man sit behind the oven in a corner, and gave him his meals in an earthen dish, and not enough either; so that the poor man grew sad, and his eyes were moistened with tears. Once his hands trembled so much that he could not hold the dish, and it fell on the ground and broke all to pieces, so that the young Wife scolded him, but he made no reply, and only sighed. After that they bought him a wooden dish, for a couple of pence, and out of that he had now to feed; and one day, as he was sitting in his usual place, he saw his little Grandson, of four years old, upon the ground, fitting together some pieces of wood. "What are you making?" asked the old Man.

"I am making a wooden trough," replied the child, "for father and mother to feed out of when I grow big."

At these words the Man looked at his Wife a little while, and presently they began to cry, and henceforth they let the old Grandfather sit at table with them, and always take his meals there, and they did not even say anything if he spilled a little upon the cloth.

The Wolf and the Man

A CERTAIN Fox once told to a Wolf many tales of the wonderful strength that men were possessed of, so that no beasts could stand against them, but were therefore obliged to use cunning. The Wolf replied, "If I ever happen to meet a man I will fly at him."

"Well," replied the Fox, "I can help you to that; only come with me early to-morrow morning, and I will show you one."

Early the next day, accordingly, the Wolf appeared, and the Fox took him to the road which the hunters passed every day. First came an old discharged soldier.

"Is that a man?" asked the Wolf.

"No," replied the Fox; "he has been one."

Next came a little boy going to school.

"Is that a man?" asked the Wolf.

"No," said the Fox; "he will be one."

Then came a forester, his double-barrelled gun upon his back, and his wood-knife by his side. On his approach the Fox said to the Wolf, "See, here comes a man upon whom you must spring; but I will first take myself off into my hole."

The Wolf made a spring at the Hunter, who, when he saw it, said to himself, "It is a pity I did not load with ball;" but he took aim, and discharged his shot at the beast's head. The Wolf made a very wry face, but still went boldly forward, and the Hunter gave it the contents of the second barrel. The Wolf, suppressing the pain, now rushed on the Hunter, who drew his long sharp wood-knife, and gave the beast a couple of cuts right and left, so that it fell over and over covered with blood, and laid howling on the ground.

Presently the Fox came. "Now, brother Wolf," said the Fox, "how have you fared with a man?"

"Oh," replied the Wolf, "it is not their strength I have suffered from; for first this Hunter took a stick from his shoulder and blew into it, and out flew something in my face, which ticked it dreadfully. Then he puffed again into this stick, and there came in my face a shower like hail and lightning; and as I approached quite near, he drew out a naked bone from his body, and beat me with it till I fell, as it were, dead before him."

"Ah, do you not see," said the Fox, "what a boaster you are! You throw the hatchet so far that you cannot catch it again."

The Gold Children

ONCE upon a time there was a poor Man and his Wife, who had nothing in the world but their hut, and they lived from hand to mouth by catching fish. But once it happened that the man, sitting by the water's edge, threw in his net and drew out a Golden Fish. And while he was looking at the fish with great wonderment, it exclaimed, "Do you hear, Fisherman? throw me back into the water, and I will change your hut into a fine castle." But the Fisherman replied, "What use is a castle to me if I have nothing to eat?" "That is taken care about," rejoined the Fish, "for in the castle you will find a cupboard, which, on opening, you will see full of dishes of the most delicate food, and as much as you like."

"Well, if that be so," said the Man, "you shall soon have your wish."

"Yes," said the Fish, "but there is one condition: that you disclose

THE GOLD CHILDREN

to nobody in the world, whoever he may be, from whence your luck comes, for if you speak a single word about it, all will be lost."

The Man threw the wonderful Fish back into the water and went home, and where formerly stood his hut was a large castle. The sight made him open his eyes, and stepping in, he found his Wife dressed out in costly clothes, sitting in a magnificent room. She appeared very much pleased, and said, "Husband, how has all this happened? this is very nice!"

"Yes," replied her Husband, "it pleases me also; but now I am tremendously hungry, so give me something to eat."

His Wife said, "I have got nothing, and I am sure I do not know where to find any food in this new house!"

"Oh! there is a great cupboard; open that," said the Husband; and, as soon as she did so, behold! there were cakes, meat, fruit, and wine. At the sight of these the Wife laughed exultingly, and cried, "What else can you wish for now, my dear?" and she and he commenced eating and drinking at once. But, when they had had enough, the Wife asked, "Now, my husband, whence comes all this?" "Ah," he replied, "do not ask me! I dare not tell you, for if I let out the secret to any one our fortune will fly." "Well, if I may not know, I am sure I do not want," replied she; but she was not in earnest, and let him have no peace night or day, teasing and tormenting him so long, till at last, in a fit of impatience, he let out that all their fortune came from a Golden Fish which he had caught and set at liberty again. Scarcely were the words out of his mouth, when all the fine castle, with its cupboard, disappeared, and they found themselves again in their old hut.

Now was the Man obliged to take up with his old trade of fishing, and fortune so favoured him that he pulled out a second time the Golden Fish. "Alas!" said the Fish, "let me go again, and I will give you back your castle, with the cupboard of meat and wine; only keep it secret, and reveal not on any account from whence they spring, or again you will lose all."

"I will take care," replied the Fisherman, and threw the Fish into the water. At home immediately everything was in its former splendour, and the wife rejoiced at her good fortune; but her curiosity could not rest, and after a couple of days she began to plague her husband again to tell her the source of their prosperity. For a long time the man held his tongue, but at length he got into such a passion, that he broke out and told the secret. At the same moment the castle disappeared, and they found themselves in the old hut. "There, are you satisfied now?" said the Man to his Wife; "now we may feel the pangs of hunger again." "Ah," she replied, "I would rather not have wealth at all than not know whence it comes; for then I have no peace of mind."

The Man went fishing again, and in a few days he was lucky enough to pull up the Golden Fish for the third time. "Well, well," said the Fish, "I see I am fated to fall into your hands, so take me home and cut me into six pieces; two of which you must give to your wife to eat, two to your horse, and two you must put in the ground, and then you will be blessed."

The Man took home the Fish, and did as it had said, and it happened that from the two pieces which he sowed in the ground two golden lilies grew up; from the eating of the two pieces by the mare, two golden folds were born; and from the wife's eating of her share, she brought forth two golden children.

The children grew up beautiful and fair, and with them the two lilies and the two foals; and one day the children said to their father, "We will mount our golden steeds and travel in the world."

But he replied sorrowfully, "How shall I manage, when you are out, to know how you are getting on?"

"The two golden lilies," said they, "will remain here, and by them you can see how we prosper; are they fresh, so are we well; do they droop, so are we ill; do they die, so are we dead."

With these words they rode away, and soon came to an inn wherein were many people, who, when they saw the two golden children, laughed at them mockingly. One of them, when he heard the jeers, was ashamed, and would not go onward, but turned round and went home to his father; while the other rode on till he came to a large forest. Just as he was about to ride into it, the people said to him, "You had better not go there, for the forest is full of robbers, who will act badly to you, and certainly when they see you are golden, and your horse too, they will kill you."

But the youth would not be frightened, and said, "I must and will go."

Then he took bears' skins, and covered with them himself and his horse, so that nothing golden could be seen, and this done, he rode confidently into the wood. When he had ridden a little way he heard a rustling among the bushes, and soon distinguished voices talking to one another. One said, "Here comes one!" but another said, "Let him alone; he's only a bear-hunter, and as poor and cold as a church-mouse. What should we do with him?"

So the Gold Child rode without danger through the forest, and came to no harm. Next it happened that he came to a village, wherein he saw a maiden so beautiful that he thought there could be no one more so in the world. He conceived a great love for her, and went to her and asked her whether she would be his wife. The maiden was very much pleased, and consented, saying, "Yes, I will become your wife, and be faithful to you all your life." Then they celebrated the wedding together, and just as they were in the middle of their festivities the father of the bride returned, and, when he saw that his daughter was married, he asked, in great astonishment, where the bridegroom was? They showed him the Golden Child, who still wore his bear-skins around him, and the father exclaimed, "Never shall a bear-hunter marry my daughter!" and he would have murdered him. The bride begged for his life, saying, "He is my husband, and I love him with all my heart;" and she begged so piteously that her father at last spared him.

The father, however, was always thinking about this man, and one morning he rose early in order to look at his daughter's husband, and see whether he were a common and ragged beggar or no. But when he looked, behold there was a magnificent Golden Man in the bed, while the thrown-off bear's skin laid upon the ground. So the father went away, thinking, "What a good thing it was I restrained my passion, or I should have made a great mistake."

The same night the Gold Child dreamt that he hunted a fine stag, and when he awoke in the morning, he said to his bride, "I must be off to the hunt!" She was grieved, and begged him to stay, and said, "A great misfortune may easily happen to you;" but he answered, "I must and will go!" So he rode away into the forest, and soon met a proud stag, just as he had dreamed. He aimed at it, and would have shot, but the stag sprang off. Then he followed it over hedges and ditches without wearying the whole day, and at evening it disappeared from his sight. When now the Gold Child looked round, he stood before a little house, wherein dwelt a Witch. He knocked at the door, and a little old woman came, and asked, "What are you doing so late in the midst of this forest?"

"Have you not seen a stag?" he inquired.

"Yes," she replied; "I know the stag well:" and just then a little dog which was in-doors barked loudly at the stranger. "Will you be quiet, you rascally dog?" he cried; "or I will shoot you dead." At this the Witch exclaimed in a great passion, "What! will you kill my dog?" and bewitched him at once, so that he lay there like a stone. His poor wife meanwhile waited for him in vain, and soon she thought, "Ah! what I feared in the anguish of my heavy heart has fallen upon him."

But at home the other brother stood by the golden lilies, and suddenly one of them fell off. "Ah, heaven!" said he, "some great misfortune has happened to my brother! I must be off, and see if, haply, I can save him."

But the father said, "Stop here. If I lose you too, what will become of me?"

"I must and will go," said the youth. So he mounted his golden horse, and rode away till he came to the large forest where his brother lay in the form of a stone. Out of her house came the old Witch, called to him, and would have enchanted him too, but he went not near her, but said, "I will shoot you down if you do not restore to me my brother."

She was frightened, but still she acted very unwillingly, and, touching the stone with her fingers, the Gold Child took again his human form. The two Gold Children were overjoyed when they saw one another again, and kissed and embraced, and rode together out of the forest. There they parted – the one returned to his bride, and the other to his father. When the latter arrived, his father said to him, "I knew that you had saved your brother, for the golden lily all at once revived, and now flourishes again."

After this time they lived contentedly and happily, and all went well with them till the end of their lives.

The Soaring Lark

THERE was once a man who had to go a very long journey, and on his departure he asked his three daughters what he should bring them. The eldest chose pearls, the second diamonds, but the third said, "Dear father, I wish for a singing, soaring lark." The father promised her she should have it if he could meet with one; and then, kissing all three, he set out.

When the time came round for his return, he had bought the pearls and the diamonds for the two elder sisters, but the lark he had sought in vain everywhere; and this grieved him very much, for the youngest daughter was his dearest child. By chance his road led through a forest, in the middle of which stood a noble castle, and near that a tree, upon whose topmost bough he saw a singing, soaring lark. "Ah! I happen with you in the very nick of time!" he exclaimed, and bade his servant climb the tree and catch the bird. But as soon as he stepped up to the tree a Lion sprang from behind, shaking his mane, and roaring so that the leaves upon the branches trembled. "Who will steal my singing, soaring lark?" cried the beast; "I will eat you up!"

"I did not know," replied the man, "that the bird belonged to you; I will repair the intended injury, and buy myself off with gold; only let me have my life."

"Nothing can save you," said the Lion, "except you promise me the first person who meets you on your return home; if you do that, I will give you not only your life, but also the bird for your daughter."

This condition the man refused, saying, "That might be my youngest daughter, who is dearest to me, and will most likely run to meet me on my return." But the servant was anxious, and said, "It does not follow that your daughter will come; it may be a cat or a dog." At length the man let himself be persuaded, and, taking the singing, soaring lark, he promised the Lion whatever should first meet him.

Soon he arrived at home, and on entering his house the first who greeted him was no other than his dearest daughter, who came running up, kissed and embraced him, and when she saw the lark in his hand was almost beside herself with joy. The poor father, however, could not rejoice, but began to weep, and said, "My dearest child, this bird I have bought very dear; I was forced to promise you for it to a wild Lion, and when he gets you he will tear you in pieces and eat you." Then he told her all that had passed, and begged her not to go away, let what might be the consequences. But his daughter consoled him and said, "My dear father, what you have

THE SOARING LARK

promised you must perform; I will go and soften the heart of this Lion, so that I shall soon return to you."

The next morning she had the way shown to her, and, taking leave, she went boldly into the forest. But the Lion was an enchanted Prince, who by day, with all his attendants, had the forms of lions, and by night they resumed their natural human figure. On her arrival, therefore, the maiden was received kindly, and led into the castle; and when night came on, and the Lion took his natural form, the wedding was celebrated with great splendour. Here they lived contented with each other, sleeping by day and watching by night. One day the Prince said to his wife, "To-morrow is a feast-day in your father's house, because your eldest sister is to be married, and if you wish to go, my lions shall accompany you."

She replied that she should like very much to see her father again, and went, accompanied by the lions. On her arrival there was great rejoicing, for all had believed that she had been torn in pieces by the lions, and killed long ago. But she told them what a handsome husband she had, and how well she fared, and stopped with them so long as the wedding lasted; after which she went back into the forest.

Not many weeks afterwards the second daughter was to be married, and the youngest was again invited to the wedding; but she said to the Lion, "This time I will not go alone, for you must accompany me." But the Lion said it would be dangerous for him; for, should a ray from a burning light touch him, then he would instantly be changed into a pigeon, and in that form fly about for seven long years.

"Oh! do go with me!" entreated his bride; "I will protect you and ward off all light."

So at last they went away together, taking their little child with them; and the Princess caused a room to be built, strong and thick, so that no ray could pierce through, wherein her husband, was to sit when the bridal lights were put up. But the door was made of green wood, which split, and left a little chink which no one perceived. Now the marriage was performed, but, as the train returned from church with its multitude of torches and lights passing by the door, a ray pierced through the chink and fell like a hair line upon the Prince, who, in the same instant that it touched him, was changed into a Dove. When, then, the Princess entered the room she found only a white Dove, who said to her, "For seven years must I fly about in the world, but at every seventh mile I will let fall a drop of red blood and a white feather, which shall show you the way; and, if you follow in their track, ultimately you may save me."

With these words the Dove flew out of the doors, and she followed it; and at every seventh mile it let fall a drop of blood and a feather, over the world, without looking about or resting, so that the seven years were at length almost spent; and the prospect cheered her heart, thinking that so soon they would be saved; and yet were they far enough off it. Once while she walked on no feather fell, and not even a drop of blood, and when she cast her eyes upwards the Dove had disappeared. Then she thought to herself, "No man can help you now;" so she mounted up to the Sun, and asked, "Hast thou seen a white Dove on the wing, for thou shinest into every chasm and over every peak?"

"No, I have not seen one," replied the Sun; "but I will give you this little casket; open it if you stand in need of help."

She thanked the Sun and walked on till evening, when the Moon shone out, and then she asked it, "Hast thou seen a white Dove on the wing, for thou shinest over every field and through every wood all night long?"

"No, I have not seen one," replied the Moon; but I will give you this egg; break it if ever you fall into trouble."

She thanked the Moon and walked on till the North Wind passed by, and she asked again, "Hast thou not seen a white Dove, for thou passeth through all the boughs, and shakest every leaf under Heaven?"

"No, I have not seen one," replied the North Wind; "but I will ask the three other Winds, who may, perhaps, have seen him you seek."

So the East and West Winds were asked, but they had seen nothing; but the South Wind said, "I have seen the white Dove; it has flown to the Red Sea, where it has again become a Lion, for the seven years are up; and the Lion stands there in combat with a caterpillar, who is really an enchanted Princess."

At these words the North Wind said to her, "I will advise you; go to the Red Sea; on the right shore thereof stand great reeds; count them, and cut off the eleventh, and beat the caterpillar therewith. The Lion will then vanquish it, and both will take again their human forms. This done, look round, and you will see the griffin which sits on the Red Sea, and upon its back leap with your beloved Prince, and the bird will bear you safely to your home. There, I give you a nut to let fall when you are in the midst of the sea; for a large nut-tree will then grow out of the water, upon which the griffin will rest; and if it cannot rest there you will then know that it is not strong enough to carry you over; but if you forget to let the nut drop, you will both fall into the sea."

So the Princess set out, and found everything as the North Wind had said. She counted the reeds on the shore, and cut off the eleventh one, wherewith she beat the caterpillar till it was conquered by the lion, and immediately both took their human forms. But, as soon as the Princess who had been a caterpillar regained her nature, she seized the Prince, and leapt with him on to the back of a griffin, and so flew away. Thus the poor wanderer was again forsaken, and sat down to weep, but soon she recovered herself and said, "So far as the wind blows, and so long as the cock crows, I will travel, until I find my husband again!"

With this resolve she travelled on further and further, till she at length arrived at the place where they had lived together. Here she heard that a festival would soon be held, when the marriage of her husband and the Princess would be performed, and in her distress she opened the casket which the Sun had given her, and found a dress in it as glittering as the Sun himself. She took it out, and, putting it on, went up to the castle, and everybody, the Princess included, regarded her with wonderment. The dress pleased the intended bride so much that she thought it would make a magnificent bridal garment, and inquired if it were for sale.

"Not for gold or silver," was the reply, "but for flesh and blood!"

The Princess asked the stranger what she meant, and she replied, "Let me for one night sleep in the chamber of the bridegroom!"

To this request the bride would not at first accede, but for love of the dress she consented, and ordered her servant to give the Prince a sleeping-draught. Then when night came the stranger was led into the room where the Prince was already fast asleep. There she sat herself down upon the bed, and said, "For seven long years have I followed you, the Sun and the Moon have I visited and inquired after you, and at the Red Sea I helped you against the caterpillar: will you, then, quite forget me?"

But the Prince slept so soundly that her words appeared only like the rushing of the wind through the fir-trees; and so at daybreak she was conducted out of the chamber, and had to give up the golden dress. Then thinking how little it had helped her, she became very sad, and going away to a meadow, sat down there and wept. While she did so she suddenly bethought herself of the egg which the Moon had given her, and on cracking it there came out a hen with twelve chickens, all of gold, which ran about to peck, and crept under the old hen's wing, so that nothing in the world could be prettier. She got up and drove them before her on the meadow, till the bride saw them out of her window, and they pleased her so much that she even came down and asked if they were not for sale. "Not for gold or silver, but for flesh and blood," replied the stranger: "let me sleep once more in the chamber where the Bridegroom sleeps."

The bride consented, and would have deceived her as the night before, but the Prince, on going to bed, asked his servant what the rustling and murmuring he had heard the previous night had been caused by. The servant told him all that had happened, and that he had given him a sleeping-draught, because a poor maiden had slept that night in his room, and would again do so. The Prince bade him pour out the sleeping-draught, and when the maiden came at night, and began to tell her sorrowful tale as she had done before, he recognised the voice of his true wife, and sprang up exclaiming, "Now am I saved! all this has passed to me like a dream, for the strange Princess has bewitched me, so that I must have forgotten everything, had not you been sent at the right time to deliver me."

Then as quickly as possible they both went out of the palace, for they were afraid of the father of the Princess, who was an enchanter. They set themselves upon the griffin, who carried them over the Red Sea, and as soon as they were in the middle of it, the Princess let drop her nut. Thereupon a great nut-tree grew up, whereon the bird rested, and then it carried them straight to their home, where they found their child grown tall and handsome, and with him they ever afterwards lived happily to the end of their lives.

The Rabbit's Bride

ONCE there was a woman and her daughter who lived in a garden full of fine cabbages, but a Rabbit came in and ate them up. The woman said one day to her daughter, "Go into the garden and hunt that Rabbit."

Mary said to the Rabbit, "There, there, little Rabbit! do not eat all the cabbages."

"Come with me, Mary," it said, "and sit upon my bushy tail, and go with me to my bushy house."

Mary would not; and the next day the Rabbit came again, and ate the cabbages, and the woman said to the daughter, "Go into the garden, and hunt the Rabbit."

Mary said to the Rabbit, "There, there, little Rabbit! do not eat all the cabbages."

"Come with me, then, Mary," said the Rabbit; "sit upon my bushy tail, and come with me to my bushy house."

Mary would not; and the third day the Rabbit came again, and ate the cabbages, and the woman said again to her daughter, "Go into the garden, and hunt the Rabbit."

Mary said to the Rabbit, "There, there, little Rabbit! eat not all our cabbages."

"Come with me, then, Mary," said the Rabbit; "sit upon my bushy tail, and come with me to my bushy house."

So Mary this time sat herself upon the Rabbit's tail, and he carried her out to his hut, and said, "Now cook me green lettuces and bran, while I will ask the wedding guests." Soon all the visitors came. (Who, then, were the wedding guests? That I cannot tell you, except as another has told me: they were all Rabbits, and the Crow was there as the parson to marry the bride and bridegroom, and the Fox as the Clerk, and the altar was under a rainbow.)

But Mary was sad, because she was alone; and the little Rabbit came and said, "Get up, get up! the wedding folks are merry and pleased."

Mary said, "No," and wept; and the little Rabbit went away, but soon returned, and said, "Get up, get up! the wedding folks are hungry."

The Bride said "No!" again, and the little Rabbit went away; but she made a doll of straw with her own clothes, and gave it a red lip, and set it on the kettle with bran, and went home to her mother. Once more came the little Rabbit, and said, "Get up, get up!" and, going towards the doll, he knocked it on the head, so that it fell over on one side.

Then the little Rabbit thought his bride was dead, and went away very sad and sorrowful.

The Death of the Cock

ONCE upon a time a Cock and a Hen lived together in a nut-grove, and made an agreement that whichever found a nut-kernel should share it with the other. Now the Cock once found a kernel, an extremely fine one, but he said nothing about it to the Hen, intending to eat it all himself. But it was so big that it would not pass down his throat, and there it stuck, so that soon he was in danger of being suffocated. Then he cried to the Hen, "Run quickly, I pray you, and fetch me some water, or I shall be stifled." She ran as fast as she could to the spring, and said, "Spring, you must give me some water, the Cock lies in the nut-grove, and is nearly suffocated from having swallowed too large a kernel." "Run first to the Bride, and get me some red silk," replied the Brook. The Hen ran and said, "Bride, please give me some red silk; red silk must I give to the Brook, that the Brook may give me water to take to my husband, who lies in the nut-grove half-suffocated with a big nut." The Bride said, "Run and fetch me, first, my garland, which hangs upon yonder meadow." So the Hen ran and fetched the garland from the bough where it hung and brought it to the Bride, who gave her red silk for it, which she took to the Brook, which then gave her water, which she took home to her husband; but meanwhile, alas! he had died, and there he lay motionless. The Hen was very sad at the sight, and shrieked aloud, so that all the other animals came and mourned for the Cock, and six little mice built a little coach, whereon to carry him to his grave, and, as soon as it was ready, they harnessed themselves to it, and the Hen followed as chief mourner. On the road they met the Fox, who asked what was the matter, and the Hen told him, "I am going to bury my husband." "May I go with you?" asked the Fox. "Yes," replied she; "but place yourself behind the carriage, for my horses do not allow any one in front of them." The Fox went behind and followed, and so did the Wolf, the Bear, the Goat, the Lion, and all the beasts of the forest. The train had not gone very far when it came to a stream. "Now, how shall we get over here?" said the Hen. "I will lay myself across," said a Straw, which was near them, "and you can pass over me." But as soon as the six mice went upon the bridge it broke down, and they were thrown into the stream and soon drowned. There was need now for another bridge, and a Coal came up, and said, "I am big enough, I will lay myself across and you shall pass over me." So the Coal set himself in the water, but, unluckily, he went in too deep, and all his fire was extinguished, so that he died! Then a Stone took pity upon the poor Hen, and laid himself across the water, and the Hen, drawing the wagon, got safely over to the other side. But then the others had to cross, and the wagon was sent back for them; but, alas! there were too many of them, and the waggon overturned, and threw them all into the water, where they sank to rise no more. Now the poor Hen was left alone with the dead Cock; and, digging a grave she laid him in, and threw up a heap of earth over him, on which she sat and mourned so long till she also died.

And so all of them quitted this life.

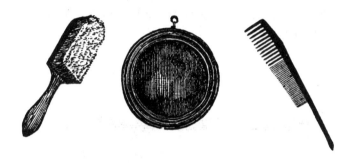

The Water-Sprite

A LITTLE Boy and his Sister were once playing upon the edge of a stream, and both fell in. Under the water was a Sprite, who took them, saying, "Now I have got you I will make you work for me." She gave the Maiden dirty and tangled flax to spin, and water to drink out of a hollow jar; while the Boy had to hew down a tree with a blunt axe, and received nothing to eat but stony lumps of sand. This treatment made the children so impatient, that they waited till one Sunday when the Water-Sprite was gone to church, and then they ran away. When the Sprite came out of church, therefore, she saw that her birds were flown, and set out after them with great leaps. But the little girl threw behind her a large brush, with thousands and thousands of bristles, over which the Sprite could glide only with great difficulty, but at last she did so.

As soon as the children saw her again the Boy threw behind him a large comb, with thousands and thousands of teeth; but over this the

Sprite glided at last, as she knew how to save herself from the points.

Then the little Girl threw behind a mirror, which seemed like a glass mountain, and was so very smooth that she could not possibly get over it.

The Water-Sprite thought she would go home quickly, and fetch an axe, to cut in halves this glass rock; but when she returned the children had swum far enough away, and so the Sprite had to amuse herself as best she could.

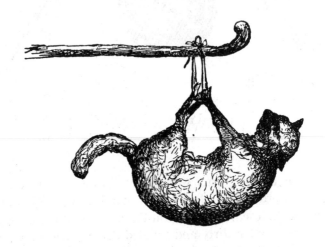

Brother Lustig

ONCE there was a great war, which at last came to an end, and then many soldiers received their discharge, and amongst others was Brother Lustig, who was sent away with nothing else but a small loaf of ammunition-bread and four farthings in money. Now, a holy Saint dressed himself as a poor beggar and sat by the roadside, where Brother Lustig passed, and begged an alms of him. – "My good beggar," said the Soldier in reply, "what shall I give you? I have been in the army, and have just received my discharge with no other reward than a loaf of ammunition-bread and four farthings; and when those are done, I also must beg; still, what I have, that will I share with you." So saying Brother Lustig divided the loaf into four parts, and gave one to the beggar, and also one farthing. The Saint thanked him, and, going further, sat himself down in the form of another beggar by the roadside. And when the Soldier came up he asked him as before for a gift. Brother Lustig replied just as he had to the first beggar, and gave again a fourth part of his bread and a farthing. The Saint thanked him, and, going still further, took the form of a third beggar, and asked for an alms; and Brother Lustig gave him the third share of his bread and one of his two remaining farthings. The Saint thanked him and left him to pursue his way in peace with his one portion of bread and single piece of money. With these he entered an inn, ate his bread, and with his farthing procured some beer. When he had done his meal he went on again, and presently the Saint, in the form of a discharged soldier, like himself, came up to him, and said, "Good day, comrade; can you not give me a bit of bread and a farthing to buy some beer?" "Where shall I get them?" said Lustig; "I have just received my discharge, and nothing with it but a loaf of ammunition-bread and four farthings, and those I have shared with three beggars whom I have met by the way. The last farthing I have spent for a draught of beer to wash down my own share of the loaf, and so I am empty in purse; and, if you have no more, we may as well go begging together."

"No," replied the Saint, "that is not yet necessary, for I understand a little of the healing art, and with that I can earn as much as I require."

"Ah, well!" replied Brother Lustig, "then I must go alone since I am quite ignorant of that science."

"You can come with me," said the Saint, "and of what I earn you shall have the half."

"That is all right," replied Brother Lustig; and they walked on together.

Soon they came to a farm-house, and heard within a great crying and groaning. So they entered, and found the master lying on his bed, very ill, and nigh unto death, while his wife sat by weeping and howling. "Cease your tears and groans," said the Saint to the woman, "I will make your husband well!" and he took out of his pocket an ointment, with which he anointed him, and in a minute the farmer stood up quite recovered. In their joy and satisfaction the man and his wife asked the Saint, "How can we reward you, or what shall we give you?" The Saint, however, would take nothing, and the more they begged him the more earnestly he refused; but Brother Lustig nudged him, and said, "Do take something, we shall want it." At last the countrywoman brought a lamb and asked the Saint to take it, but he still refused, till Lustig, nudging him again, and saying, "Pray take it, we shall certainly want it," he consented, saying to Brother Lustig, "I will take this lamb, but I cannot carry it; you must do that, since you wish for it." "Oh, as to that matter," said Lustig, "I will readily take it;" and he tied its legs to a stick and put it upon his shoulder. Now they went on till they came to a forest, where the lamb would soon have become a burden to Lustig, but he was hungry, and said to the Saint, "See, here is a beautiful place to cook and eat the lamb."

"Very well," replied his companion; "but I cannot stay here while you cook: do you see to that – here's a kettle. Meanwhile I will walk about till it is ready; but mind, you must not begin to eat until I return, which will be at the right time." "You can go if you please," said Lustig; "I understand cooking well, and all will soon be ready." And so saying, he killed the lamb, made a fire, and threw the flesh into the pot to boil. The meat was soon done enough, but still the Saint did not return; and Brother Lustig at length took it out of the pot, and, cutting it up, found the heart. "This is the best part," said he, as he ate it; and just then the Saint returned, and said to him, "You can eat the whole lamb by yourself, but give me the heart." Brother Lustig took up his knife and fork, and pretended to search very eagerly among the flesh for the heart, without success. "There is none," said he, at length. "No! where should it be, then?" asked the

Saint. "That I do not know," replied the other; "but what simpletons we both are to expect to find a lamb's heart, when it has none!"

"Eh!" said the Apostle, "that is something new; every animal has a heart, and why should not a lamb have one?" "No, certainly, comrade," said Lustig, "a lamb has no heart; just think for a minute, and you will readily allow it has not."

"Well, then," rejoined the Saint, "since there is no heart, I need none of the flesh; you may eat it all yourself."

"And what I cannot eat I shall put in my knapsack," said the Soldier; and as he ate but half, he disposed of the other as he said.

This over, they travelled on farther, and soon came to a stream which they were obliged to pass. "Go you first," said the Saint to his companion; but he refused, thinking, if the other went before, he should know whether the water were deep or no. The holy Saint walked through, and the water was only up to his knees; and then Brother Lustig followed, but the water had become deeper, and covered him up to the neck, so that he called, "Help me, comrade!" But the Saint said, "Will you confess that you ate the heart of the lamb?"

"No," he replied, "I have not eaten it;" and immediately the water rose still more, till it reached his mouth. "Help me, comrade!" cried the Soldier again; but the Saint asked a second time, "Will you confess that you ate the lamb's heart?" "No, I have not eaten it," said Lustig; but, nevertheless, the Saint would not drown him, but took him by the hand and pulled him out. Now they walked on again, and came to a country where they heard that the King's daughter lay deadly sick. "Halloa, comrade!" said the Soldier to the Saint, "here is a windfall for us; if we can restore her to life, our fortune is made for ever." But the holy Saint would not hurry, and Lustig said, "Pray make haste, comrade, and lift your legs quicker, or we shall not arrive in time." Still the Saint went on slowly, slowly, although his companion tried to push him along, until they at last heard that the Princess was dead. "There," said the Soldier, "this comes of your sleepy walking."

But the Saint said, "Be quiet! I can do more than make the sick well, for I can also restore the dead to life."

"Well, if that be so," said Brother Lustig, "that will please; but you must ask the half of the kingdom for a reward." Thereupon they went into the royal palace, where all were in great grief; and the Saint said to the King, "I will restore your daughter to life." So he was led to her, and he asked for a kettle of water; and as soon as it was brought, he caused every one to go out of the room, and only Brother Lustig to remain. Then he cut all the limbs of the dead Princess one from another, and threw them into the water; and, making a fire beneath the kettle, waited till nothing was left but the bones. Then he took out the white bones and laid them upon a table, and arranged them in their natural order; and when that was done, he stepped in front of them, and said, "Stand up, oh dead!"

At the third repeating of these words, the Princess arose, in full enjoyment of health and vigour; and the King was so rejoiced, that he said to the Saint, "Ask your recompense, and whatever it is I will give it you, even to the half of my kingdom."

But the Saint answered, "I desire nothing." "Oh, you simple fellow!" thought the Soldier to himself, and taking his comrade aside, he whispered to him, "Be not so foolish; if you desire nothing, still I have need." But the Saint would ask nothing. The King, however, seeing that the other wished for some recompense, caused his knapsack to be filled with gold by the treasurer.

After this, they travelled on farther; and as they entered a wood, Brother Lustig said to the Saint, "Let us now share the gold," "Yes," replied the Saint, "now is the time;" and he divided the gold into three portions. Brother Lustig thought, "Why, what crotchet had he got in his head now, to make three portions, while we are only two?"

The Saint said, "I have now divided it; one share for me, one for you, and one for him who ate the lamb's heart."

"Oh, I ate that!" replied Brother Lustig quickly, and snatched at the gold; "you may believe me."

"But how can that be true?" asked the Saint; "lambs have no hearts!"

"Eh, what!" replied the Soldier; "why, what are you thinking of? A lamb has a heart as well as any other animal. Why should a lamb alone have no heart?"

"Ah!" said the Saint, "now you may keep the gold yourself; I will travel no longer with such a man, but will go my own path."

"As you like, comrade," replied the Soldier; "as you like. Farewell!"

So the holy Saint went another road, and Brother Lustig thought, "It is well that he is gone; he is certainly a wonderful man."

The Soldier had gold enough now; but what with visiting, giving presents, feasting, and such like, before many months had elapsed he was again quite poor. At that time he came into a country where he heard that the King's daughter had just died. "Ah!" thought he, "here is a good thing! I will restore her to life again, and I will have such a sum counted out as the importance of my art warrants!" So he went to the King, and offered to bring the dead to life. Now, this King had heard that a discharged Soldier was travelling about, who had raised the dead, and he supposed our Brother Lustig to be the man. Nevertheless, as he did not feel certain, he first asked the advice of his councillors, who decided that there was no harm in trying the man, as the Princess was really dead. So Brother Lustig caused water to be brought to him in a kettle, and, when every one had left the room, he cut the limbs asunder, and put them into the water, and made a fire beneath, just as he had seen the Saint do. Then when the water boiled, and nothing was left but the bones, he took them out and laid them on a table; but he knew not in what order to put them, and so placed them the wrong way. This done, he rose up, and said thrice, "Arise, oh dead!" but the bones did not move. "You shining fellows, get up, or it will be the worse for you!" said he; and just as he spoke the Saint came in, in his former disguise as a discharged Soldier, and said, "You impious man! what are you about? how can the dead rise, when you have placed the limbs all wrong?"

"Comrade, I did it as well as I could," said he. "This time," continued the Saint, "I will help you out of your trouble; but do not undertake anything of this sort again, or it will be your ruin.

Likewise I warn you, you are not to take or desire the least thing of the King for this service."

Thereupon the Saint laid the bones in their right order, and said thrice aloud, "Arise, oh dead!" and immediately the Princess arose as well as ever, and as beautiful. Then the Saint disappeared through the window, and left Brother Lustig rejoicing at the miracle, but vexed that he must not take any reward for the deed. "I should like to know," said he, "what whim now he has taken into his head; for what he gives with one hand he takes with the other, and there is no understanding him." And so thinking, when the King asked him what he wished for, he dared not take anything; but, through artifice and cunning, he managed to get his knapsack filled with gold. Then he took his leave with many thanks; and as he went out of the door, the Saint stood there, and said, "What sort of a man are you? I forbade you to take anything, and yet you have your knapsack filled with gold."

"How can I help it, if it is put in for me?" replied Brother Lustig.

"Well, this I tell you," continued the Saint, "if you undertake such things in future, you will suffer."

"Oh, comrade, what care I! now I have money, what do I want with bone-boiling?" said Brother Lustig.

"Ah!" said the Saint, "the gold will last long, will it not? but, that you may not tread again in forbidden paths, I will give your knapsack this power, – whatever you wish, that you shall see within it. Farewell! you will not now see me again."

"Heaven be praised!" exclaimed Brother Lustig, "I am glad that you are gone, you strange fellow; I certainly will not follow you." But of the wonderful power of his knapsack he did not then think.

On again he travelled and travelled, spending and wasting his money as at first, till at length he had but four farthings left, with which sum he arrived at an inn on his road. "The money must go," thought he, and he laid it out in three farthings' worth of wine, and one of bread. As he sat eating, the smell of roast goose tickled his nose, and he got up and peeped about, and presently discovered that the Landlord had put two geese into the oven to bake. Just then it

occurred to him to try the wonderful power of his knapsack, and he
went out at the door, and wished that two roast geese were safe
within it. As soon as he had said the words, he unbuckled and looked
in, and there they both lay snug enough! "Ah! all's right," said he; "I
am a made man:" and he turned into a meadow, and pulled out his
prize. Just as he was in the best of his eating, two working men came
by, and looked at the goose which was yet untouched with hungry
eyes.

Brother Lustig, thinking when he saw them that he had quite
enough with one, called up the two fellows, and said, "There, take
this goose, and eat it to my health and happiness." They thanked
him, and went on to the inn, and ordered some wine and bread, and
then, pulling out their present, began to eat. The Landlady looked at
them, and then at her husband, and said to him, "They are eating a
goose; just see if it is not one of ours out of the oven."

The Landlord ran to look, and behold, there was the oven empty;
and, coming back, he cried out, "You thieving rascals! weld you eat
goose so cheaply? Pay me for it quickly, or I will beat you with the
thickest stick I can find!"

But the two cried together, "We are not thieves! A discharged
Soldier out there on the meadow gave us this goose." "Tell me no
lies," said the Landlord; "the Soldier has been here, certainly; but he
has gone out at the door like an honest man: I have no suspicion of
him. You are thieves, and must pay the reckoning." But as they
would not pay, he took a stick and flogged them out of the house.
Meanwhile, Brother Lustig walked on till he came to a village, on
one side of which stood a noble castle, and on the other a mean little
inn, into which he went, and asked for a night's lodging; but the host
refused, saying, "There is no room; my house is full of excellent
guests." "It is a wonder to me, then," replied the Soldier, "that they
come to you instead of going into that fine castle."

"Ah! that would be worth while, surely," said the Landlord.
"Why, no one who has tried to sleep there one night has ever yet
come out alive."

"I will try it, then, as others have," replied Brother Lustig.

"You had better not," said the Landlord; "you will lose your life." "We shall see – we shall see!" rejoined the Soldier. "Give me the key, and something substantial to eat and drink."

The Landlord, therefore, gave him the key, and some meat and beer, and Brother Lustig took them into the castle and ate a hearty meal, after which, feeling sleepy, he laid down upon the ground, for there was no bed. He soon went to sleep, but in the middle of the night he was awakened by a great screeching, and when he aroused himself he saw nine ugly evil spirits, who had joined hands in a circle, and were dancing round him. When Brother Lustig saw them he said, "Dance as long as you like, but don't come too near!" But the spirits did not pay any attention to him, and kept approaching nearer and nearer till they almost kicked their feet in his face. "Be quiet, you wretched spirits!" said the Soldier again; but still they came nearer and nearer, so that he grew quite angry and called out, "Then I will make you still!" and, taking up the leg of a chair, he made an attack upon them. The evil spirits, however, were rather too many against one Soldier, and, even if he knocked one down, another instantly flew at his hair and tore it out unmercifully. "You pack of evils!" cried he, "this is too much for me; but wait. All nine into my knapsack!" No sooner had he said the words than in they tumbled, and, buckling up the knapsack instantly, he threw it into the corner. Then everything was quiet at once, and Brother Lustig laid himself down and slept till broad daylight. At that time the landlord and the nobleman to whom the castle belonged entered it, to see how he had passed the night, and as soon as they saw him alive and well, they were astonished, and inquired, "What! have the spirits done nothing to you?"

"No; and for a good reason," replied Brother Lustig. "I have them all nine in my knapsack. You may live in your castle again in quiet: henceforth nothing of this sort will happen."

The nobleman thanked him, and rewarded him liberally, and begged him to remain in his service, and he would take care of him all his lifetime. But the Soldier refused, saying he was used to wandering about, and wished to proceed further. So Brother Lustig travelled on, and, coming to a smithy, he laid the knapsack wherein were the nine evil spirits upon the anvil, and bade the smith and his companions beat it, and they beat it with their heavy hammers with all their strength, so that the evil spirits received an unmerciful crushing, and when he opened the knapsack eight were dead; but one who had crept into a corner was still living, and slipping out, ran away to his old place.

After this Brother Lustig travelled about still more, the whole world through, and whoever knows them might tell many tales of his wanderings. At length he began to grow old, and bethought himself of his end; so he went to a pilgrim who was known as a very pious man, and said to him, "I am weary of wandering, and wish now to tread in a holy path."

The Pilgrim said to him, "There are two roads, the one broad and smooth, and leading to the abode of evil spirits; the other narrow and rugged, which leads to the abode of angels." "I should be a simpleton," thought Brother Lustig within himself, "if I should walk in the narrow and rugged road;" and, getting up, he chose the broad and smooth path, along which he travelled till he came to a large black gate, which was the entrance to the abode of evil. At this he knocked, and the door-porter peeped out to see who it was, and as soon as he saw Brother Lustig he was frightened, for he was the same ninth evil spirit who had been shut up in the knapsack, and had escaped with a black eye. He pushed the bolt in quicker than before, and ran to the chief evil spirit and said, "There is a fellow outside with a knapsack who wants to enter; but let him not get his body inside or he will wish the whole place in his knapsack, as he once did to me."

So Brother Lustig was told that he must go away again, for he could not enter, and he resolved, therefore, to try if he could find a welcome in the abode of angels, for somewhere he must go. So he turned and travelled on till he came to the door, at which he knocked, and there sat by the door at watch the same Saint who had travelled with him. Brother Lustig recognised him at once, and thought, "Since I find an old friend here, it will be more lucky for me."

But the holy Saint said, "I suppose you wish to enter this abode?"

"Yes; let me in, comrade," said he.

"No," said the Saint, "you cannot enter."

"Well then, since you will not let me in, take back your knapsack, for I will have nothing of yours."

"Give it me here," said the Saint; and he reached it through the bars of the gate, and the Saint hung it up near his seat. Then Brother Lustig said, "Now I wish myself inside the knapsack," and in a moment he was there, and so outwitted the Saint, who was thus compelled to let him enter the abode of the angels.

Hans in Luck

HANS had served his master seven years, and at the end of that time he said to him, "Master, since my time is up, I should like to go home to my mother; so give me my wages, if you please."

His Master replied, "You have served me truly and honestly, Hans, and such as your service was, such shall be your reward;" and with these words he gave him a lump of gold as big as his head. Hans thereupon took his handkerchief out of his pocket, and, wrapping the gold up in it, threw it over his shoulder and set out on the road towards his native village. As he went along, carefully setting one foot to the ground before the other, a horseman came in sight, trotting gaily and briskly along upon a capital animal. "Ah," said Hans aloud, "what a fine thing that riding is! one is seated, as it were, upon a stool, kicks against no stones, spars one's shoes, and gets along without any trouble!"

The Rider, overhearing Hans making these reflections, stopped and said, "Why, then, do you travel on foot, my fine fellow?"

"Because I am forced," replied Hans, "for I have got a bit of a lump to carry home; it certainly is gold, but then I can't carry my head straight, and it hurts my shoulder."

"If you like we will exchange," said the Rider; "I will give you my horse, and you can give me your lump of gold."

"With all my heart," cried Hans; "but I tell you fairly you undertake a very heavy burden."

The man dismounted, took the gold, and helped Hans on to the horse, and, giving him the reins into his hands, said, "Now, when you want to go faster, you must chuckle with your tongue and cry, 'Gee up! gee up!'"

Hans was delighted indeed when he found himself on the top of a horse, and riding along so freely and gaily. After awhile he thought he should like to go rather quicker, and so he cried, "Gee up! gee up!" as the man had told him. The horse soon set off at a hard trot, and, before Hans knew what he was about, he was thrown over head and heels into a ditch which divided the fields from the road. The horse, having accomplished this feat, would have bolted off if he had not been stopped by a Peasant who was coming that way, driving a cow before him. Hans soon picked himself up on his legs, but he was terribly put out, and said to the countryman, "That is bad sport, that riding, especially when on mounts such a beast as that, which stumbles and throws one off so as to nearly break one's neck: I will never ride on that animal again. Commend me to your cow: one may walk behind her without any discomfort, and besides one has, every day for certain, milk, butter, and cheese. Ah! what would I not give for such a cow!"

"Well," said the Peasant, "such an advantage you may soon enjoy I will exchange my cow for your horse."

To this Hans consented with a thousand thanks, and the Peasant swinging himself upon the horse, rode off in a hurry.

Hans now drove his cow off steadily before him, thinking of his lucky bargain in this wise: "I have a bit of bread, and I can, as often as I please, eat with it butter and cheese; and when I am thirsty I can milk my cow and have a draught: and what more can I desire?"

As soon, then, as he came to an inn he halted, and ate with great satisfaction all the bread he had brought with him for his noonday and evening meals, and washed it down with a glass of beer, to buy which he spent his two last farthings. This over, he drove his cow further, but still in the direction of his mother's village. The heat meantime became more and more oppressive as noontime approached, and just then Hans came to a common which was an hour's journey across. Here he got into such a state of heat that his tongue clave to the roof of his mouth and he thought to himself, "This won't do; I will just milk my cow, and refresh myself." Hans, therefore, tied her to a stump of a tree, and, having no pail, placed his leathern cap below, and set to work, but not a drop of milk could he squeeze out. He had placed himself, too, very awkwardly, and at last the impatient cow gave him such a kick on the head that he tumbled over on the ground, and for a long time knew not where he was. Fortunately, not many hours after, a Butcher passed by, trundling a young pig along upon a wheelbarrow. "What trick is this!" exclaimed he, helping up poor Hans; and Hans told him all that had passed. The Butcher then handed him his flask, and said, "There, take a drink; it will revive you. Your cow might well give no milk: she is an old beast, and worth nothing at the best but for the plough or the butcher!"

"Eh! eh!" said Hans, pulling his hair over his eyes, "who would have thought it? It is all very well when one can kill a beast like that at home, and make a profit of the flesh; but for my part I have no relish for cow's flesh; it is too tough for me! Ah! a young pig like yours is the thing that tastes something like, let alone the sausages!"

"Well now, for love of you," said the Butcher, "I will make an exchange, and let you have my pig for your cow."

"Heaven reward you for your kindness!" cried Hans; and, giving up the cow, he untied the pig from the barrow, and took into his hand the string with which it was tied.

Hans walked on again, considering how everything had happened just as he wished, and how all his vexations had turned out for the best after all! Presently a Boy overtook him, carrying a fine white goose under his arm, and after they had said "Good day" to each other, Hans began to talk about his luck, and what profitable exchanges he had made. The Boy on his part told him that he was carrying the goose to a christening-feast. "Just lift it," said he to Hans, holding it up by its wings, "just feel how heavy it is; why, it has been fattened up for the last eight weeks, and whoever bites it when it is cooked will have to wipe the grease from each side of his mouth!"

"Yes," said Hans, weighing it with one hand, "it is weighty, but my pig is no trifle either."

While he was speaking the Boy kept looking about on all sides, and shaking his head suspiciously, and at length he broke out, "I am afraid it is not all right about your pig. In the village, through which I have just come, one has been stolen out of the sty of the mayor himself; and I am afraid, very much afraid, you have it now in your hand! They have sent out several people, and it would be a very bad job for you if they found you with the pig; the best thing you can do is to hide it in some dark corner!"

Honest Hans was thunderstruck, and exclaimed, "Ah, Heaven help me in this fresh trouble! you know the neighbourhood better than I; do you take my pig and let me have your goose," said he to the boy.

"I shall have to hazard something at that game," replied the Boy, and, so saying, he took the rope into his own hand, and drove the pig off quickly by a side path, while Hans, lightened of his cares, walked on homewards with the goose under his arm. "If I judge rightly," thought he to himself, "I have gained even by this exchange: first there is the good roast; then the quantity of fat which will drip out will make goose broth for a quarter of a year; and then there are the fine white feathers, which when once I have put into my pillow I warrant I shall sleep without rocking. What pleasure my mother will have!"

As he came to the last village on his road there stood a Knife-grinder, with his barrow by the hedge, whirling his wheel round, and singing –

> "Scissors and razors and such-like I grind,
>   And gaily my rags are flying behind."

Hans stopped and looked at him, and at last he said, "You appear to have a good business, if I may judge by your merry song?"

"Yes," answered the Grinder, "this business has a golden bottom! A true knife-grinder is a man who as often as he puts his hand into his pocket feels money in it! But what a fine goose you have got; where did you buy it?"

"I did not buy it at all," said Hans, "but took it in exchange for my pig." "And the pig?" "I exchanged for my cow." "And the cow?" "I exchanged a horse for her." "And the horse?" "For him I gave a lump of gold as big as my head." "And the gold?" "That was my wages for a seven years' servitude." "And I see you have known how to benefit yourself each time," said the Grinder; "but, could you now manage that you heard the money rattling in your pocket as you walked, your fortune would be made." "Well! how shall I manage that?" asked Hans.

"You must become a grinder like me; to this trade nothing peculiar belongs but a grindstone, and other necessaries find themselves. Here is one which is a little worn, certainly, and so I will not ask anything more for it than your goose; are you agreeable?"

"How can you ask me?" said Hans; "why, I shall be the luckiest man in the world; having money as often as I dip my hand into my pocket, what have I to care about any longer?"

So saying, he handed over the goose, and received the grindstone in exchange.

"Now," said the Grinder, picking up an ordinary big flint stone which lay near, "now, there you have a capital stone, upon which only beat them long enough and you may straighten all your old nails! Take it, and use if carefully!"

Hans took the stone and walked on with a satisfied heart, his heys glistening with joy. "I must have been born," said he, "to a heap of luck; everything happens just as I wish, as if I were a Sunday-child."

Soon, however, having been on his legs since daybreak, he began to feel very tired, and was plagued too with hunger, since he had eaten all his provision at once in his joy about the cow bargain. At last he felt quite unable to go farther, and was forced, too, to halt every minute, for the stones encumbered him very much. Just then the thought overcame him, what a good thing it were if he had no need to carry them any longer, and at the same moment he came up to a stream. Here he resolved to rest and refresh himself with a drink, and so that the stones might not hurt him in kneeling he laid them carefully down by his side on the bank. This done, he stooped down to scoop up some water in his hand, and then it happened that he pushed one stone a little too far, so that both presently went plump into the water. Hans, as soon as he saw them sinking to the bottom, jumped up for joy, and then kneeled down and returned thanks, with tears in his eyes, that so mercifully, and with out any act on his part, and in so nice a way, he had been delivered from the heavy stones, which alone hindered him from getting on.

"So lucky as I am," exclaimed Hans, "is no other man under the sun!"

Then with a light heart, and free from every burden, he leaped gaily along till he reached his mother's house.

The Fox and the Geese

THE Fox one day came to a meadow where a flock of fine fat Geese were feeding, and he said, with a grin, "I am come just as if I had been invited; you sit together so charmingly, I can eat you one after the other." The Geese cackled for terror, and sprang on their feet, and began to groan and beg pitifully for their lives; but the Fox would hear nothing, and said, "There is no mercy – you must die!" At length one of them took heart, and said, "If we poor Geese must at once lose our young lives, show us yet one single grace, and permit us to say our prayers, that we may not die in our sins. Afterwards we will all stand in a row, and you can then pick out the fattest as you want us."

"Well," said the Fox, "that is a just and pious request. Pray away! I will wait for you."

So the first one began a long prayer, and, because it would not cease, the second also commenced before his time, and cried, "Ga! ga! ga!" The third and fourth soon followed, and in a few minutes they were all cackling together their prayers.

When they have done praying, this tale shall be continued; but meanwhile, as I suppose, they are praying still.

The Goose Girl

ONCE upon a time there lived an old Queen, whose husband had been dead some years, and left her with one child, a beautiful daughter. When this daughter grew up she was betrothed to a King's son, who lived far away; and when the time arrived that she should be married, and as she had to travel into a strange country, the old lady packed up for her use much costly furniture, utensils of gold and silver, cups and jars; in short, all that belonged to a royal bridal treasure, for she loved her child dearly. She sent also a maid to wait upon her and to give her away to the bridegroom, and two horses for the journey; and the horse of the Princess called Falada, could speak. As soon as the hour of departure arrived, the mother took her daughter into a chamber, and there with a knife she cut her finger with it so that it bled; then she held a napkin beneath, and let three drops of blood fall into it which she gave to her daughter, saying, "Dear child, preserve this well, and it will help you out of trouble."

Afterwards the mother and daughter took a sorrowful leave of each other, and the Princess placed the napkin in her bosom, mounted her horse, and rode away to her intended bridegroom. After she had ridden on foot for about an hour she became very thirsty, and said to her servant, "Dismount, and procure me some water from yonder stream in the cup which you carry with you, for I am thirsty."

"If you are thirsty," replied the servant, "dismount yourself, and stoop down to drink the water, for I will not be your maid!"

The Princess, on account of her great thirst, did as she was bid, and bending over the brook she drank of its water, without daring to use her golden cup. While she did so the three Drops of Blood said, "Ah! if thy mother knew this, her heart would break." And the Princess felt humbled, but said nothing, and remounted her horse. Then she rode several miles further, but the day was so hot and the sun so scorching that she felt thirsty again; and as soon as she reached a stream she called her handmaiden again, and bade her take the golden cup and fill it with water, for she had forgotten all the saucy words which before had passed. The maiden, however, replied more haughtily than before, "If you wish to drink, help yourself! I will not be your maid!"

The Princess thereupon got off her horse, and helped herself at the stream, while she wept and cried, "Ah! woe's me!" and the three Drops of Blood said again, "If your mother knew this, her heart would break." As she leaned over the water, the napkin wherein were the three drops of blood fell out of her bosom and floated down the stream without her perceiving it, because of her great anguish. But her servant had seen what happened, and she was glad, for now she had power over her mistress; because, with the loss of the drops of blood, she became weak and powerless. When, then, she would mount again upon the horse Falada, the Maid said, "No, Falada belongs to me; you must get upon this horse;" and she was forced to

THE GOOSE-GIRL

yield. Then the servant bade her take off her royal clothes, and put on her common ones instead; and, lastly, she made the Princess promise and swear by the open sky that she would say nought of what had passed at the King's palace; for if she had not so sworn she would have been murdered. But Falada observed all that passed with great attention.

Now was the servant mounted upon Falada, and the rightful Princess upon a sorry hack; and in that way they travelled on till they came to the King's palace. On their arrival there were great rejoicings, and the young Prince, running towards them, lifted the servant off her horse, supposing that she was the true bride; and she was led up the steps in state, while the real Princess had to stop below. Just then the old King chanced to look out of his window, and saw her standing in the court, and he remarked how delicate and beautiful she was; and, going to the royal apartments, he inquired there of the bride who it was she had brought with her, and left below in the courtyard.

"Only a girl whom I brought with me for company," said the bride. "Give the wench some work to do, that she may not grow idle."

The old King, however, had no work for her, and knew of nothing; until at last he said, "Ah! there is a boy who keeps the geese: she can help him." This youth was called Conrad, and the true bride was set to keep geese with him.

Soon after this, the false bride said to her betrothed, "Dearest, will you grant me a favour?" "Yes," said he, "with the greatest pleasure." "Then let the knacker be summoned, that he may cut off the head of the horse on which I rode hither, for it has angered me on the way." In reality she feared lest the horse might tell how she had used the rightful Princess, and she was glad when it was decided that Falada should die. This came to the ears of the Princess, and she promised secretly to the knacker to give him a piece of gold, if he would show her a kindness, which was that he would nail the head of Falada over a certain large and gloomy arch, through which she had to pass daily with the geese, so that then she might still see, as she had been accustomed, her old steed. The knacker promised, and, after killing the horse, nailed the head in the place which was pointed out, over the door of the arch.

Early in the morning, when she and Conrad drove the geese through the arch, she said in passing,—

"Ah, Falada, that you should hang there!"

and the Head replied,—

"Ah, Princess, that you should pass here!
If thy mother knew thy fate,
Then her heart would surely break!"

Then she drove on through the town to a field; and when they arrived on the meadow, she sat down and unloosened her hair, which was of pure gold; and its shining appearance so charmed Conrad, that he endeavoured to pull out a couple of locks. So she sang,—

"Blow, blow, thou wind,
Blow Conrad's hat away;
Its rolling do not stay
Till I have combed my hair,
And tied it up behind."

Immediately there came a strong wind, which took Conrad's hat quite off his head, and led him a rare dance all over the meadows; so that when he returned, what with combing and curling, the Princess had rearranged her hair, so that he could not catch a loose lock. This made Conrad very angry, and he would not speak to her; so that all day long they tended their geese in silence, and at evening they went home.

The following morning they passed again under the gloomy arch, and the true Princess said,—

"Ah, Falada, that you should hang there!"

and Falada replied,—

> "Ah, Princess, that you should pass here!
> If thy mother knew thy fate,
> Then her heart would surely break!"

Afterwards, when they got into the meadow, Conrad tried again to snatch one of her golden locks; but she sang immediately,—

> "Blow, blow, thou wind,
> Blow Conrad's hat away;
> Its rolling do not stay
> Till I have combed my hair,
> And tied it up behind."

So the wind blew, and carried the hat so far away, that by the time Conrad had caught it again, her hair was all combed out, and not a single one loose; so they tended the geese till evening as before.

After they returned home, Conrad went to the old King, and declared he would no longer keep geese with the servant.

"Why not?" asked the old King.

"Oh! she vexes me the whole day long," said Conrad; and then the King bade him relate all that had happened. So Conrad did, and told how, in the morning, when they passed through a certain archway, she spoke to a horse's head, which was nailed up over the door, and said,—

> "Ah, Falada, that you should hang there!"

and it replied,—

> "Ah, Princess, that you should pass here.
> If thy mother knew thy fate,
> Then her heart would surely break!"

and, further, when they arrived in the meadow, how she caused the wind to blow his hat off, so that he had to run after it ever so far.

When he had finished his tale, the old King ordered him to drive the geese out again the next morning; and he himself, when morning came, stationed himself behind the gloomy archway, and heard the servant talk to the head of Falada. Then he followed them also into the fields, and hid himself in a thicket by the meadow; and there he saw with his own eyes the Goose Girl and boy drive in their geese; and after awhile, she sat down, and, unloosening her hair, which shone like gold, began to sing the old rhyme,—

> "Blow, blow, thou wind,
> Blow Conrad's hat away;
> Its rolling do not stay
> Till I have combed my hair,
> And tied it up behind."

Then the King felt a breeze come, which took off Conrad's hat, so that he had to run a long way after it; while the Goose Girl combed out her hair, and put it back in proper trim, before his return. All this the King observed, and then went home unremarked; and when the Goose Girl returned at evening, he called her aside, and asked her what it all meant. "That I dare not tell you, nor any other man," replied she; "for I have sworn by the free sky not to speak of my griefs, else had I lost my life."

The King pressed her to say what it was, and left her no peace about it; but still she refused. So at last he said, "If you will not tell me, tell your griefs to this fireplace;" and he went away. Then she crept into the fireplace, and began to weep and groan; and soon she relieved her heart by telling her tale. "Here sit I," she said, forsaken by all the world, and yet I am a King's daughter; and a false servant has exercised some charm over me, whereby I was compelled to lay aside my royal clothes; and she has also taken my place at the bridegroom's side, and I am forced to perform the common duties of a Goose Girl. Oh, if my mother knew this, her heart would break with grief!"

The old King, meanwhile, stood outside by the chimney, and listened to what she said; and when she had finished, he came in, and called her away from the fireplace. Then her royal clothes were put on, and it was a wonder to see how beautiful she was; and the old King, calling his son, showed him that it was a false bride whom he had taken, who was only a servant-girl; but the true bride stood there as a Goose Girl. The young King was glad indeed at heart when he saw her beauty and virtue; and a great feast was announced, to which all people and good friends were invited. On a raised platform sat the bridegroom, with the Princess on one side, and the servant-girl on the other. But the latter was dazzled, and recognised her mistress no longer in her shining dress. When they had finished their feasting, and were beginning to be gay, the old King set a riddle to the servant-girl: What such a one were worthy of who had, in such and such a manner, deceived her masters; and he related all that had happened to the true bride. The servant-girl replied, "Such a one deserves nothing better than to be put into a cask, stuck all round with sharp nails, and then by two horses to be dragged through street after street till the wretch be killed."

"Thou art the woman, then!" exclaimed the King; "thou has proclaimed thine own punishment, and it shall be strictly fulfilled."

The sentence was immediately carried into effect, and afterwards the young King married his rightful bride, and together they ruled their kingdom long in peace and happiness.

The Poor Man and the Rich Man

IN olden times, when the good angels walked the earth in the form of men, it happened that one of them, while he was wandering about, very tired, saw night coming upon him before he had found a shelter. But there stood on the road close by two houses opposite to one another, one of which was large and handsome, while the other appeared miserably poor. The former belonged to a Rich Man, and the other to a Poor Man; so that the Angel thought he could lodge with the former, because it would be less burdensome to him than to the other to entertain a guest. Accordingly he knocked at the door, and the Rich Man, opening the window, asked the stranger what he sought. The Angel replied, "I seek a night's lodging." Then the Rich Man scanned the stranger from head to foot, and perceiving that he wore ragged clothes, and seemed like one who had not much money in his pocket, he shook his head, and said, "I cannot take you in; my rooms are full of herbs and seeds; and should I shelter every one who knocks at my door, I might soon take the beggar's staff into my own hand. Seek a welcome elsewhere."

So saying, he shut his window to, and left the good Angel, who immediately turned his back upon him, and went over to the little house. Here he had scarcely knocked, when the door was opened, and the Poor Man bade the wanderer welcome, and said, "Stop here this night with me; it is quite dark, and to-day you can go no farther." This reception pleased the Angel much, and he walked in; and the wife of the Poor Man also bade him welcome, and, holding out her hand, said, "Make yourself at home; and though it is not much that we have, we will give it to you with all our heart." Then she placed some potatoes on the fire, and, while they roasted, she milked her goat for something to drink with them. When the table was laid, the good Angel sat down and ate with them; and the rude fare tasted well, because they who partook of it had happy faces. After they had finished, and bed-time came, the wife called her husband aside, and said to him, "Let us sleep to-night on straw, my dear, that this poor wanderer may have our bed whereon to rest himself; for he has been walking all day long, and is doubtless very tired."

"With all my heart," replied her husband; "I will offer it to him:" and, going up to the Angel, he begged him, if he pleased, to lay in their bed that he might rest his limbs thoroughly. The good Angel at first refused to take the bed of his host, but at last he yielded to their entreaties, and lay down, while they made a straw couch upon the ground. The next morning they arose early, and cooked their guests a breakfast of the best that they had, and when the sun shone through the window he got up too, and, after eating with them, prepared to set out again. When he stood in the doorway he turned round, and said to his hosts, "Because you are so compassionate and pious, you may wish three times, and I will grant each time what you desire."

The poor man replied, "Ah, what else can I wish than eternal happiness, and that we two, so long as we live, may have health, and strength, and our necessary daily bread? For the third thing I know not what to wish for."

"Will you not wish for a new house in place of this old one?" asked the Angel.

"Oh, yes!" said the man; "if I might keep on this spot, so would it be welcome."

Then the good Angel fulfilled his wishes, and changed their old house into a new one; and giving them once more his blessing, went out of the house.

It was already broad daylight when the Rich Man arose, and, looking out of his window, saw a new handsome house of red brick where formerly an old hut had stood. The sight made him open his eyes, and he called his wife up, and asked, "Tell me what has happened: yesterday evening an old miserable hut stood opposite, and to-day there is a fine new house! Run out, and hear how this has happened!"

The wife went and asked the Poor Man, who related that the evening before a wanderer had come, seeking a night's lodging, and that in the morning he had taken his leave, and granted them three wishes – eternal happiness, health and food during their lives, and instead of their old hut a fine new house. When he had finished his tale, the wife of the Rich Man ran home and told her husband all that had passed, and he exclaimed, "Ah! had I only known it! the stranger had been here before, and would have passed the night with us, but I sent him away."

"Hasten, then," returned his wife, "mount your horse, and perhaps you may overtake the man, and then you must ask three wishes for yourself also."

The Rich Man followed this advice, and soon overtook the good Angel. He spoke softly and glibly, begging that the Angel would not take it ill that he had not let him in at first, for that he had gone to seek the key of the house-door, and meanwhile he had gone away, but if the Angel came back the same way he would be glad if he would call again. The Angel promised that he would come on his return, and the Rich Man then asked if he might not wish thrice as his neighbour had been allowed. "Yes," said the Angel, "you may certainly, but it will not be good for you, and it were better you did not wish."

But the Rich Man thought he might easily obtain something which would tend to his happiness, if he only knew that it would be fulfilled; and so the Angel at length said, "Ride home, and the three wishes which you shall make shall be answered."

The Rich Man had now what he desired, and, as he rode homewards, began to consider what he should wish. While he thought, he let his rein fall loose, and his horse presently began to jump, that he was jerked about, and so much so that he fix his mind on nothing. He patted his horse on the neck, and said, "Be quiet, Bess!" but it only began fresh friskings, so that at last he became savage, and cried quite impatiently, "I wish you might break your neck!" No sooner had he said so, than down it fell upon the ground, and never moved again, and thus the first wish was fulfilled. But the Rich Man, being covetous by nature, would not leave the saddle behind, and so, cutting it off, he slung it over his back, and went onwards on foot. "You have still two wishes," thought he to himself, and so was comforted; and as he slowly passed over the sandy common the sun scorched him terribly, for it was midday, and he soon became vexed and passionate; moreover, the saddle hurt his back; and, besides, he had not yet decided what to wish for. "If I should wish for all the treasures and riches in the world," said he to himself, "hereafter something or other will occur to me, I know beforehand, but I will so manage that nothing at all shall remain for me to wish for." Then he sighed, and continued, "Yes, if I had been the clownish peasant who had also three wishes, and knowing how to help himself chose first much beer, then as much beer as he could drink, and for the third a cask of beer more."

Many times he thought he knew what to wish, but soon it appeared too little. Then it came into his thoughts how well his wife was situated, sitting at home in a cool room, and appropriately dressed. This idea angered him uncommonly, and, without knowing it, he said aloud, "I wish she were sitting upon this saddle, and could not get off it, instead of its being slipping about on my back."

As soon as these words were out of his mouth, the saddle disappeared from his back, and he perceived that his second wish had passed its fulfilment. Now he became very hot, and began to run, intending to lock himself up in his room, and consider there something great for his last wish. But when he arrived and opened the house-door, he found his wife sitting upon the saddle in the middle of the room, and crying and shrieking because she could not get off. So he said to her, "Be contented, I will wish for all the riches in the world, only keep sitting there."

But his wife shook her head, saying, "Of what use are all the riches of the world to me, if I sit upon this saddle? You have wished me on it, and you must also wish me off."

So, whether he liked it or not, he was forced to utter his third wish, that his wife might be freed from the saddle, and immediately it was done. Thus the Rich Man gained nothing from his wishes but vexation, trouble, scolding, and a lost horse; but the poor couple lived contented and pious to their lives' end.

The Young Giant

A CERTAIN countryman had a son no bigger than a thumb when he
was born, and even in after years he grew not a bit. One morning,
when the man was going forth to plough, the little fellow said,
"Father, I will go with you." "Will you though?" replied he. "You
had better stop where you are of use: you would only get lost along
with me."

Then Thumbling began to cry, and would not stop till his Father
at last put him in his pocket and took him with him. When they got
into the fields the Father took his son out and set him in a fresh
furrow. Presently, over the mountains, came a great Giant towards
them. "Do you see that great monster coming to fetch you?" asked
the man of his son, thinking so to frighten him; but scarcely had he
spoken, when the Giant, making a couple of strides with his long
legs, reached the furrow, and took little Thumbling out without
speaking a word, and carried him away with him. The Father stood

by, and from terror could not utter a sound; and he thought he had lost his son for ever.

The Giant, however, carried Thumbling home, and fed him so heartily, that he grew big and strong like a young giant. After the lapse of two years the Giant took the youth into the forest to try his strength, and said to him, "Now, cut down a switch for yourself." The young one was now so strong that he pulled a little tree by the roots out of the ground; but this was not enough for the Giant, who took him back and fed him two years longer. When they tried again the youth was so strong that he could break down an old tree; but still this was not enough for the old Giant, who took him home again and fed him for another two years. At the end of that time they again visited the forest, and when the old Giant said, "Now, pluck up a good stick for me," the youth tore out of the ground the thickest oak tree there was, as if it were merely a joke. "Now you have done enough," cried the Giant; "you have learnt everything." And with these words he conducted him back to the same field from whence he had fetched him. His Father was there walking behind his plough, and the young Giant went up to him and said, "Do you see, Father, what a man your son has grown?" But the Father was frightened, and said, "No, you are not my son; I know nothing about you."

"Really and truly I am your son, though," said the young Giant. "Let me work here, I can plough as well and even better than you." But the Peasant persisted, "No, no, you are not my son, you cannot plough; come, be off with you!"

But at length, being afraid of the great fellow, he let go the plough, and, stepping back, stationed himself on one side, near the edge. Then the youth took the plough and pressed with one hand upon it, but so powerfully, that it cut deeply into the ground, and the Peasant called out, "If you must plough, do not press so heavily, or your work will be badly done." At this the young Giant unharnessed the horse and drew the plough himself, first saying to the Peasant, "Go you home, Father, and let Mother cook a large dish of victuals; meanwhile I will just plough over this field."

The Father, accordingly, went home, and ordered his wife to get dinner ready; but the son not only ploughed over the whole field, which was a usual two day's job, but also harrowed it perfectly, making use of two harrows. As soon as that was done he went into the forest and tore up two oak-trees, which he laid across his shoulders, and then, fixing them before and behind the two harrows, he carried them all home like a bundle of straw, driving the horse also before him. When he went into the courtyard his Mother did not recognise him, and asked, "Who is that frightful big man?"

"That is our son," replied the husband. "No, no!" said she; "our son was never like him; we never had such a great child; ours was a very little thing." And, so saying, she ordered him to go away. The young Giant, however, was silent; and, driving the horse into the stable, he gave it beans and hay, and all that it needed. This done, he went into the kitchen, sat himself down upon the dresser, and said, "Mother, I want my dinner very much; is it not nearly ready?"

"Yes," said she, and brought two great dishes full of victuals, which would have satisfied herself and her husband for eight days at the least; but the young Giant quickly devoured all, and then inquired if they could not give him more. His Mother told him no, that was all they had. "That was only a taste, then," said he; "I must have more;" and this speech so frightened the woman, that, not daring to oppose him, she went and fetched a large fish-kettle, which she filled and put on the fire, and, as soon as it was ready, bore its contents to the young Giant. "At length," said he, "at length, comes a good bit;" but when he had eaten it all his hunger was even then not satisfied. "Ah, Father," said he, "I perceive quite well that I shall never get enough here; but if you will procure me a bar of iron, so strong that I cannot break it across my knee, I will go away into the world."

The Peasant was glad to hear this, and, harnessing his two horses to the wagoon, he fetched from the smith's a bar of iron as thick as his horses could drag. This the young Giant tried across his knee, and snap! he broke it like a twig, and threw it away. Then the Father harnessed four horses to the waggon, and brought back a bar as heavy as the four beasts could draw. This the son also broke in halves as soon as he tried it with his knee, and threw it away, saying, "Father, that is of no use; you must harness more, and fetch me a still stronger bar yet." So he harnessed now eight horses to the waggon, and fetched a bar as thick and heavy as they could carry; but when the young man took it he broke it just as easily as the two former ones, saying, "Ah, my Father, I see you cannot procure me such a bar as I need, and, therefore, I will not stop with you any longer!"

So he went away and announced himself as a smith wanting work, and soon he arrived at a village wherein dwelt a Smith, who was a very avaricious man, coveting the goods of everybody, and wishing to keep all for himself, and the young Giant asked him if he needed an assistant. The Smith looked at him and thought, "Ah, here is a brave fellow who will beat a good stroke and deserve his bread!" and so he nodded assent to the question, and inquired how much wages he would require. "Oh, very little will do for me," was the reply; "only every fourteen days, when you pay the other workmen their wages, I will give you two strokes over the shoulders, which you must endure." To this the Smith readily consented, for he imagined he should thereby save money. The next morning the new workman had to be tried, and, as soon as he gave the first blow to the red-hot bar which the Master brought, it split quite in halves and flew a long way off, while the anvil was driven so far into the ground, that neither of them could pull it up again. The Smith flew into a tremendous passion, and cried out, "Ah, you are of no use to me; you strike much too hard! but what will you have for this one stroke?" The youth said, "I will only give you a slight blow, nothing further;" and, so saying, he raised his foot and gave the Smith a kick, which sent him flying over four stacks of hay. Then he looked out the thickest iron bar he could find in the smithy, and, using it for a walking stick, trudged off.

After travelling a short distance he came to a large farm, and there asked the Bailiff whether he needed a head-servant. "Yes," he replied, "I want one, and you seem a likely fellow to do what you profess; pray what amount of wages do you ask for a year?" The young Giant made the same answer as before, that he wanted no other privilege than to be allowed to give him three strokes, which he must endure. To this the Bailiff consented, and thought he had made a capital bargain.

The next morning men had to go and fetch wood, and when they were all ready they found the head-servant still lying in bed. They called to him, "Get up, it is time; we have to fetch wood, and you must go with us!" "Oh, go away!" he replied, quite sleepy, "go away! I will yet get there before any of you."

So they went then to the Bailiff, and told him the head-servant was still lying in bed, and would not get up after the wood. The Bailiff bade them wake him once more and tell him to harness the horses; but when they did so the head-servant only cried out as before, "Go away, I will come presently and be there before you." With these words he turned over again and slept two hours longer, and then, raising himself up from the feathers, he first fetched two measures full of herbs and cooked a broth with them, which he ate very leisurely, and when he had finished he yoked the horses to and went after the wood. Now not far from the forest was a narrow valley, through which he must pass, and so, first leading his waggon on, he made the horses stand still on the other side, and then, going back, he made with trees and shrubs such a huge barrier across the way that no horse could pass through. When he came out of the valley again, the other servants were just passing by on their way home with loaded waggons, and he told them to drive forward, for he would yet overtake them and reach home first. So saying he walked on a little way, and, presently tearing up two of the largest trees on the spot, he threw them on his waggon and turned it round. When he came to the barrier he found the others standing before it, unable to get through. "There," said he, "do you not see you might have waited for me at first? you would have got home just as quickly, and had an hour's more sleep into the bargain." So saying he tried to drive on himself, but his horses could not force the barrier down, and he at length unharnessed and laid them a-top of the trees, and then, taking the pole of the waggon under his own arm, he pressed on through everything, making the trees bend down like feathers. As soon as he reached the other side he called to the others, "There, you see, after all, I am through sooner than you!" and then, driving on, he left them standing there lost in wonder. But no sooner had he reached the courtyard, than, taking one tree in his hand, he showed it to the Bailiff, and asked him whether it was not a good stock of wood; and the Bailiff, turning to his wife, said, "This slave is a good fellow; for, if he does sleep a long time, he yet reaches home sooner than the others."

The young Giant after this served the Bailiff a year, and when that was past, and the other slaves received their wages, he thought it was time he took his own. But the Bailiff was much distressed about the strokes he had to receive, and he begged the head-servant to forego them, for he would rather himself change places with him, and let him be Bailiff, than take them. "No, no!" said the servant, "I will not be Bailiff. I am head-servant, and shall remain so; but still I will divide the conditions."

The poor Bailiff offered him what he desired; but nothing helped; the servant answered "No" to all offers; and at length, not knowing how to manage, he requested fourteen days' respite to consider the matter.

To this the servant consented, and the Bailiff summoned all his secretaries to advise him what to do. For a length of time they consulted, and agreed together that nobody's life was safe from the young Giant, who knocked men down, as if they were gnats. At length they made a decision, which was, that the man should be asked to step into a pond and wash himself, and it was their intention that when he was there they should roll upon his head one of the millstones, so as to bury him for ever from the light of day. This advice pleased the Bailiff, and the servant stepped into the pond, and as soon as he was below water they threw down the largest millstone, and thought they had cracked his head in two; but, instead, he called out, "Hunt those hens away from the pond-side; they keep throwing the corn into my eyes, so that I cannot see!" So the Bailiff made noises, as if he were chasing the fowls away, and soon the servant reappeared, and as soon as he was out of the water he said, "See what a fine necklace I found at the bottom!" and when they looked they found he had put the millstone round his neck! The young Giant now demanded his reward, but the Bailiff asked for another fourteen days' consideration; and when the secretaries were summoned they advised him to send the servant into the Enchanted Mill to grind corn there for a night, as no one had ever yet come out alive from the place. The proposal pleased the Bailiff, and, calling the servant to him the same evening, he bade him fetch eight measures of corn, which he was to grind during the night, for they were in want of it. The servant went at once, and put two measures in his right pocket, two in his left, and four in a sack, which he slung over his shoulders, so that half of its contents rested on his back and half on his breast. Thus laden he went to the Enchanted Mill, where the Miller told him he might grind very well indeed by day, but at night the mill was enchanted, and whoever went into it at that time was always found dead in the morning. The young Giant told him, however, he should get safely through, and bade him hasten away and remark what passed. Thereupon he went into the mill and shot out the corn, and about eleven o'clock he sat himself down on a bench in the kitchen. He had not been there very long before all at once the door opened, and an immense table entered, upon which wine and meat, and every delicacy, were placed, and seemingly there was no one who brought it in. Next, all the chairs ranged themselves round the table, but no guests appeared; till presently he saw fingers which carved with the knives and forks, and laid pieces upon the plates; and at length, being hungry himself at the sight of food, he sat down to table and took his share of the good things. As soon as he had satisfied himself, and the others had emptied their plates, all the lights were put out at once, and this he heard done clearly, and when it was quite dark he felt something like a box on the ears. He called out, "If that is done again, I shall give it back!" and when he felt a second box on the ears he struck out himself. And so it went on all night through: he took nothing without a return, and gave blows right and left until daybreak, when all ceased.

In the morning the Miller came, and was surprised to find him still living; but the young Giant told him, "I have eaten and satisfied myself, and received boxes on the ears, and I have also given them." The Miller was much pleased, and declared he had rescued his mill, and would willingly have given him any money as a reward. But the young Giant would not have any money, and, taking his meal-sack upon his shoulders, he returned home, and told the Bailiff he wished now to have his promised reward. The Bailiff was terribly frightened when he heard this, and knew not what to do with himself, walking up and down the room till the sweat ran off his brow in great drops. At last he opened his window for some fresh air, and while he stood there the young Giant gave him such a kick, that he flew through the window away so high in the air that nobody could see him. When he was out of sight the young Giant said to the Bailiff's wife, "If your husband does not return, you must take the other stroke!" She cried out, "No, no! I cannot endure it!" and opened the other window to make her escape, while the sweat stood upon her brow in great drops. The young Giant, as soon as he saw her at the window, gave her a kick, which sent her much higher up than her husband, for she was lighter in weight.

Her husband then called to her, "Come down to me!" but she cried, "Come you to me, I cannot come to you!" And there they fluttered about in the breeze, and neither could get to the other, and, for all I know, there they flutter still; and the young Giant took his iron staff and travelled onwards.

Hans Married

THERE was once a young country chap called Hans, whose Uncle
wanted very much to marry him to a rich wife, so he set him beside
the oven and let a good fire be lighted. Then he fetched a jug of milk
and a large piece of white bread, and gave Hans a shining newly-
coined penny, saying, "Hans, keep this penny safely, and break your
white bread into this milk; and mind you stop here, and do not stir
from your stool till I return."

"Yes," said Hans, "I will faithfully do all you require."

Then the Uncle went and drew on a pair of old spotted breeches,
and, walking to the next village, called on a rich farmer's daughter,
and asked her whether she would marry his nephew Hans, assuring
her that he was a prudent and clever young man, who could not fail
to please her. The girl's covetous father, however, asked, "How is he
situated with regard to property? Has he the wherewithal to live?"

"My dear friend," said the Uncle, "my nephew is a warm youth, and has not only a nice penny in hand, but plenty to eat and drink. He can count too, quite as many specks" (meaning money) "as I;" and, so he spoke, he slapped his hand upon his spotted breeches. "Will you," he continued, "take the trouble to go with me, and in an hour's time you shall see everything as I have said?"

The offer appeared so advantageous to the covetous Farmer that he would not let it slip, and therefore said, "If it is so, I have nothing more to say against the wedding."

So the ceremony was performed on an appointed day, and afterwards the young wife wished to go into the fields and view the property of her husband. Hans drew his spotted smock first over his Sunday clothes, saying to his bride, "I do not wish to spoil my best things!" This done, they went together into the fields, and wherever a vine-stock was planted on the road, or the meadows and fields divided, Hans pointed with his finger there, and then laid it on one great spot or another on his smock, and said, "This spot is mine and thine too, my dear! Do just look at it." Hans meant by this, not that his wife should gape at the broad fields, but that she should look at his smock, which was really his own!

"Did you then go to the wedding?" "Yes! I was there in full toggery. My head-piece was of snow, and there came the sun and melted it; my clothes were of worsted, and I walked through thorns, so that they were torn off; my shoes were of glass, and I stepped upon a stone, and they cracked and fell to pieces."

The Dwarfs

THERE was once upon a time a rich King who had three daughters, who all day long were accustomed to walk in the gardens of their father's palace. The King was a great admirer of every species of tree, but of one in particular it was said that whoever should pluck off a single apple would sink a hundred feet into the ground. Now, when harvest came, the apples on this tree were as red as blood, and the three Princesses went every day under the tree to see if any of the fruit had fallen; but the wind did not blow any down, and the branches were so overloaded that they hung almost on the ground. At last the youngest of the three daughters took such a fancy to the fruit that she said to her sisters, "Our father loves us so much he will never cause us to disappear underground; he only meant that judgment for strangers;" and so saying, she plucked an apple, and, jumping before her sisters, invited them also to taste it. So the three sisters shared it between them; but as soon as they had eaten it they all sank down below the earth, so far that no bird could scratch them up.

By-and-by, when it became noon, the King wanted his daughters, but they were nowhere to be found, though the servants searched all over the house and gardens. At length, when he could hear nothing about them, the King caused it to be proclaimed throughout the country, that whoever should bring back the Princesses should receive one of them as a bride. Thereupon numbers of young men travelled about on land and sea to find the maidens; for every one was desirous to regain them, they were so amiable and pretty. Amongst others there went out three young Huntsmen, who, after travelling about eight days, came to a large castle, wherein every room was splendidly furnished; and in one room they found a large table, and on it was spread all manner of delicate food, and everything was still so warm that it smoked; yet nowhere did they hear or see any human being. Here they waited half the day, while the meats still smoked before them, till at length they became very hungry, and, sitting down, they ate what they liked, and afterwards agreed together that one should remain in the castle while the two others sought the Princesses; and, to decide the matter, they drew lots; and it fell to the share of the eldest to stop on the spot. The next day, accordingly, the two younger Brothers took their departure, while the eldest remained in the castle; and about noon a little Dwarf entered, and brought in some pieces of roast meat, which he cut in pieces, and then handed them; and while he held it to the young Huntsman he let one piece fall, and the Dwarf asked him to be good enough to pick it up again. So he bent down to do so, and immediately the Dwarf jumped on him, and caught him by the hair, and beat him roughly. The next day the second brother remained at home, but he fared no better; and, when the two others returned, the eldest asked him how he had passed the day. "Oh! badly enough, I can tell you," he replied; and the two Brothers told each other of what had befallen them; but they said nothing to their youngest Brother, for fear he should refuse to have any part in the matter. So the third day he remained at home, and the Dwarf entered as usual with the meat, and, letting one piece fall, requested the youth to pick it up. But he said to the Dwarf, "What! can you not pick that up yourself? If you had the trouble of earning your daily bread you would be glad enough, but now you are not worth what you eat!"

This answer made the Dwarf very angry; but the youth gripped hold of him, and gave him such a shake that he exclaimed, "Stop, stop! and let me go, and I will tell you where the King's daughters are."

When the youth heard this he let him drop, and the little mannikin said he was an underground Dwarf, and there were more than a thousand like him; and if any one went with him he could show him where the Princesses were living: that he knew the place, which was a deep well, where no water entered. The Dwarf told him further that he knew his Brothers would not act honourably to him, and, therefore, if he would rescue the King's daughters he must go alone, and must take with him a great basket wherein to let himself down, and go armed with his forester's knife; and below he would find three rooms, in each of which would sit a Princess, guarded by dragons with many heads, all of which heads he must cut off. As soon as the Dwarf had said all this he disappeared; and about evening the two Brothers returned, and asked the youngest how he had passed the time. "Oh! very well, indeed," he replied; "and about noon a Dwarf came in, who cut up the meat, and let one piece fall, which he asked me to pick up; but I refused; and, as he flew into a passion, I gave him a shake, and presently he told me where to find the Princesses."

This tale sorely vexed the other Brothers, who turned blue with suppressed rage; but the next morning they all went up the hill, and drew lots who should descend first into the basket. The lot fell, as before, to the eldest, and he went down, taking a bell with him, which when he rang they were to pull him up as fast as they could. So after he had been down a little while he rang his bell furiously; and, as soon as he was drawn up, the second Brother took his place and went down; but he quickly rang to be pulled up again. The turn now came to the youngest Brother, who allowed himself to be let down to the very bottom, and there, getting out of the basket, he marched boldly up to the first door, with his drawn knife in his hand. There he heard the dragons snoring loudly; and, on his carefully opening the door, he saw one of the Princesses sitting within, with the dragon's nine heads on her lap. He raised his knife and cut these heads off; and immediately the Princess jumped up and hugged and kissed him, and fell upon his neck, and then gave him her golden necklace for a reward. Next he went after the second Princess, who had a dragon with seven heads by her side: he also freed her, and then went to the youngest, who was guarded by a four-headed dragon. This beast he also destroyed; and then the three Sisters embraced and kissed him so much that at last he clashed the bell very hard, so that those above might hear. When the basket came down he set each Princess in by turns, and let them be drawn up; but, as it descended for him, he remembered the Dwarf's saying that his Brothers would be faithless to him. So he picked up a huge stone, and laid it in the basket, and just as the false Brothers had drawn it half-way up they cut the cord at the top, and the basket with the stone in it fell plump to the bottom. By this means they thought they had rid themselves of their Brother; and they made the three Princesses promise that they would tell their father it was they who had delivered them; and then they went home to the King and demanded the Princesses for their wives. But meanwhile the youngest Brother wandered about sadly in the three chambers, and thought he should have to die there, when all at onnçe he perceived on the walls a flute, and he thought to himself, "Ah! what good can this be here? What is there to make one merry?" He kicked, too, the dragons' heads, saying, "And what good are you to me? you cannot help me!" Up and down, to and fro, many times he walked, so often, indeed, the floor was worn smooth.

By-and-by other thoughts came into his head, and, seizing the flute, he blew a little on it; and, behold, ever so many little Dwarfs instantly appeared! He blew a little longer, and with every note a fresh one came, till at last the room was quite filled with them. Then all of them asked what his wishes were, and he told them that he wanted to be up above the earth again, and in the clear daylight. Immediately each Dwarf seized a hair of his head, and away they flew up the well with him till they landed him at the top. As soon as ever he was safe on his legs again, he set out for the royal palace, and arrived about the time the weddings of the Princesses were to be celebrated. So he hurried up to the room where the King sat with his three daughters; and as soon as he entered they were so overcome that they fainted away. This made the King very angry; and he ordered the new-comer to be put in prison, for he thought he had done his children some injury; but as soon as they recovered themselves they begged their father to set him at liberty. But he asked them their reason; and when they said they dare not tell him, he bade them tell their story to the oven; and meantime he went outside and listened at the door. When the King had heard all, he caused the two traitorous Brothers to be hanged; but he gave his youngest daughter in marriage to the true deliverer.

And to their wedding I went in a pair of glass shoes, and, kicking against the wall, broke them all to pieces.

The King of the Golden Mountain

A CERTAIN merchant had two children, a boy and a girl, who, at the time our tale begins, were both so little that they could not run alone. This merchant had just sent away two richly laden vessels in which he had embarked all his property, and, while he hoped to gain much money by their voyage, the news came that both ships had sunk to the bottom of the sea. Thus, instead of a rich merchant, he became quite a poor man, and he had nothing left but a field near the town where he dwelt, and therein, to divert his thoughts for a while from his loss, he went to walk. While he paced to and fro, there suddenly appeared a little Black Dwarf, who asked him the reason of his sorrowful looks, and what it was he took so much to heart?

"If you are able to help me," said the Merchant, "I will tell you."

"Who knows," replied the Dwarf, "whether I can or not?"

So then the Merchant told him what had happened; how all his wealth was sunk at the bottom of the sea, and nothing remained to him but his one field.

"Do not grieve yourself any longer," said the Dwarf; "for, if you will promise to bring me here in twelve years whatever first rubs itself against your leg on your return home, you shall have all the money you can require." The Merchant thought it would be his dog who would meet him first, for he remembered not, just then, his children, so he gave the little black Man his word and honour to the bargain, and returned to his home.

Just as he came within sight of the house his little Boy saw him, and was so glad that he toddled up to him and clasped him by the knees. The Father was frightened, for his promise occurred to him, and he knew now what he had sworn to; but still, as he found no money in his coffers, he imagined it was only a joke on the part of the Dwarf. A month afterwards, however, he went on his land to seek for anything he could find to sell, and there he saw a great heap of gold. Now was he again prosperous, and bought and sold and became a great merchant, as he had been before. Meanwhile his Boy grew up clever and sensible, and the nearer he came to the age of twelve years the sadder became his Father, till people could see the traces of his anguish in his countenance. One day the Son asked him what was amiss; the Father would not tell him at first, but at last he related how he had sold him without knowing it to a little Black Dwarf for a heap of money, and how he had set his seal and name to the bargain, so that when twelve years had passed he must deliver him up. "My Father," answered the Son, "do not be sorry about such a matter; all will yet go well, for the Dwarf can have no power over me."

After this the Son caused himself to be blessed by a Priest, and, when the hour came, he and his Father went together to the field, and the Son drew a circle within which they both placed themselves.

Presently came the Black Dwarf, and asked, "Have you brought with you what you promised?" The Father was silent; but the Son replied, "What do you want here?"

"I came to speak with your Father, and not with you," said the Dwarf.

"You have deceived and betrayed my Father," said the Son; "give up the paper you extorted from him."

"No! I will not surrender my rights!" replied the Dwarf.

Then they consulted together for some time, and at last they agreed that the Son, because he would not obey the Dwarf, and did not any longer belong to his Father, should place himself in an open boat which laid upon the waters, and then that his Father should give the vessel a push that it might float whither it would. The Son, therefore, took leave of his Father, and set himself in the boat, which the Father thereupon pushed off; but, unhappily, the boat turned bottom upwards with the force of the shock, and the Father was forced to return home with the belief that his Son was dead, which grieved him sorely.

But the boat did not entirely sink, but floated quietly away with the Youth clinging to it, till at length it touched on an unknown land and remained there. The Youth then scrambled on shore, and saw, just opposite, a fine castle, towards which he hurried. As soon as he entered, he found that it was an enchanted palace, and he walked through all the rooms, and found them all empty, till he came to the last, in which he discovered a snake curling itself round and round. This snake, however, was an enchanted Maiden, who was overjoyed to see the Youth enter, and she said to him, "Are you come to deliver me? For twelve years have I waited for you, for this kingdom is enchanted, and you must free it from the spell."

"How can I do that?" he asked.

"This night," she replied, "twelve Black Dwarfs will come, laden with chains; and they will ask you what you do here; but, mind, give them no answer, and let them do what they will to you. They will torment you, beat and poke you about, but let all this happen without a word on your part, and then for twelve years they must be off again. The second night twelve others will come, and the third night four-and-twenty, and these last will cut off your head; but at midnight their power passes away, and if you restrain yourself till then, and never speak a word, I am saved. Afterwards I will come to you with a flask which contains the water of life, and with this I will sprinkle you, that you shall regain your breath, and be as healthy and well as before."

"I will save you willingly," he replied.

Now everything happened as the Snake said. The Black Dwarfs failed to compel him to speak, and the third night the Maiden became disenchanted, and came with the water of life, as she had said, to the Youth, and restored him to life. Then the beautiful Princess fell around his neck, and kissed him, and through all the castle there was joy and gladness. Soon their wedding was celebrated, and the Merchant's Son became the King of the Golden Mountain.

The happy pair lived in great contentment, and in course of time the Queen bore a son, and when eight years more had passed over their heads, the King bethought himself of his Father, and his heart was so touched with the recollection that he wished to revisit him. The Queen would not at first hear about such a thing, but he talked about it so often that at length she was obliged to consent, and said, "I know the journey will cause misfortune to me." At his departure she gave him a wishing-ring, and said, "Take this ring and wear it on your finger, and then, wherever you wish to be there you will find yourself; but this you must promise me, that you will not wish me to leave here to visit your Father's house."

The King promised, and, putting the ring on his finger, he wished himself before the town where his Father dwelt. At the same moment he found himself there, and tried to go into the town; but as he came to the gate the guards would not let him pass, because he wore clothes so peculiar, and so rich and magnificent. Thereupon he climbed up a hill where a shepherd was watching sheep, and with him he changed clothes, and thus passed into the town unquestioned in the rough smock. When he came to his Father's house he was not recognised, and the Merchant would not believe it was his son, but said he certainly once had a son, but that he had been dead some years. Still, because he saw he was a poor thirsty shepherd, he willingly gave him a plate of food. At last the Youth asked his parents, "Do you know of any mark on my body whereby you will recognise me, for indeed I am your true son!"

"Yes," said the Mother; "our son had a mole-spot under his arm."

Instantly he drew his shirt back from his arm, and there they saw the mole-spot, so that they no longer doubted that he was their son. Then he told them that he was King of the Golden Mountain, and had a beautiful Princess for a wife, and a child seven years old. But the Merchant laughed at his son, saying, "Never can this be true! Here is a fine King indeed, who comes here in ragged shepherd's smock!"

This made the Son very angry; and, without consideration, he turned round his ring, and wished both his child and wife were with him. In a moment they appeared; but the Queen wept, and complained that he had broken his promise, and made her unlucky. The King told her he had done it without thought and with no bad intention; and she appeared to be reconciled, but, in reality, she had evil in her heart.

After a while he took her to the field, out of the town, and showed her the water where his boat had been overturned, and there, feeling tired, he said to her, "I am weary; so rest yourself a while, and I will lay my head in your lap and go to sleep." He did so, and the Queen waited quietly till he was sound asleep, and then she drew the ring off his finger, and carefully laid his head on the ground. Thereupon she took her child in her arms, and wished herself back in her kingdom. When, then, the King awoke, he found himself all alone, his wife and child gone, and the ring from his finger too. "Home to your parents," said he to himself, "you cannot go; they will say you are a magician; so you must travel about till you come again to your kingdom." With these thoughts he took courage, and by-and-by came to a mountain, before which three Giants stood, and contended with each other, because they knew not how to share their paternal inheritance. As soon as they saw the young man passing by, they called to him, and said, "Come! little men have often wise heads: you shall divide our patrimony."

Now this inheritance consisted, firstly, of a sword, which if one

took into his hand, and said, "Heads off all round, but not mine!"
instantly every head near lay on the ground; secondly, of a cloak
which rendered its wearer invisible; and, thirdly, of a pair of boots
which were capable of taking their wearer wherever he wished. The
youth, therefore, said, "Give me these three things, that I may prove
them whether they are in good order or not." So they gave him the
cloak, and as soon as he put it on he became invisible, in the form of
a fly. He soon took his old form again, and said, "The cloak is good:
now give me the sword." "Oh, no!" said the Giants, "we do not give
you that; for if you should say, 'Heads off all round, but not mine!'
all our heads would fall off, and you alone would have one." Still
they gave it him on condition that he should prove it on a tree. This
he did, and the sword cut the trunk in two as if it were a straw. Then
he wished to have the boots, but the Giants said, "No, we do not give
them away; for, if you should pull them on, and wish yourself on the
summit of this mountain, we may stand here without anything!" But
the Youth said he would not do that, and so they gave him the boots:
and, as he had now all three things, he though of nothing but his wife
and child; and he said, "Ah! were I upon the Golden Mountain!"
Immediately he disappeared from the sight of the Giants, and thus
divided their inheritance. As he came near his castle he heard great
rejoicings, and the notes of flutes and fiddles, and the people told
him that his consort was about to celebrate her wedding with
another husband. This put him in a passion, and he exclaimed, "The
false wretch! she has deceived and left me while I slept!" Then he put
on the cloak, and rendered himself invisible while he entered the
castle, and in the hall he saw a large table spread out with costly
delicacies, and guests eating and drinking, singing and laughing. In
the middle sat the Queen, dressed in royal clothes, upon a
magnificent throne, with a crown upon her head. The true King
placed himself behind her; but nobody saw him; and when they
placed meat upon her plate he took it up and ate it himself; and each
glass of wine which was handed to her he drank out, and so it went
on: neither plate nor glass stayed in its place, each one disappeared
in a moment. This disturbed the Queen very much, and put her to

shame, so that at length she got up, and went to her own chamber to weep; but here also he followed her. There she called out, "Is this the devil who persecutes me? or did my deliverer never come?" At these words he struck her on the cheek, and cried, "Did thy deliverer never come? He is beside thee, thou traitress! Have I deserved this of thee?" Then he rendered himself visible again, and, going into the hall, he cried, "The wedding is over! the true King is come!" Then the kings, princes, and councillors, who were assembled, mocked him and jeered him; but he gave them short answers, and asked, "Will you be off or not?" Then they tried to catch and imprison him; but he drew his sword, and said "Heads off all round, but not mine!" So all their heads rolled down the hill, and he was left master alone, and became once more King of the Golden Mountain.

The Raven

ONCE upon a time there was a Queen whose daughter at the time this story begins was yet a child in arms, and one day she was so naughty that, spite of all her mother said, she would not be quiet. At last the Queen lost all patience, and, because the ravens were then flying about the palace, she opened the window and said, "I wish you were a raven, and could fly away, and then I should have some peace!" Scarcely had she said the words when the child changed into a raven, and flew away out of her arms through the window into a dark forest, where she remained a long time, and the parents heard nothing about her.

Some little time afterwards a man, while travelling along, found himself in this wood, and there he heard the Raven cry, and he followed the sound. As he came near, the Raven said to him, "I am a princess by birth, and am bewitched; but you can deliver me from the charm."

"What can I do, then?" he asked.

"Go on further into the wood," she replied, "and you will find a house wherein sits an old woman, who will offer you meat and drink; but do not venture to take anything, for if you do you will fall into a deep sleep, and fail to free me. In the garden behind this house is a large heap of tan, whereon you may stand and wait for me. For three days I shall come at two o'clock, in a carriage drawn, the first time, by four white horses, then by four red, and lastly by four black; and if you are asleep when I come you will not rescue me; so you must mind to keep awake."

The man promised to do all that she desired; but the Raven said, "Ah! but I know well you will not deliver me, for you will take something from the old woman." The man promised again he would not touch either meat or drink, and then he went on, and when he came to the house and entered, the old woman met him, and said to him, "Poor man, how weary you look! come, and refresh yourself with these dishes." But he said, "No, I will neither eat nor drink." Still she pressed him, saying, "Well, if you will not eat, take a draught of wine; one glass is nothing." So the man allowed himself to be persuaded, and drank a little, and by-and-by, when midnight came, he went out into the garden, on to the tan heap, and waited for the Raven. But while he stood there he became all at once very tired, and could not shake off the feeling, so he lay down a bit, without venturing to sleep. However, he had scarcely stretched himself out when his eyes closed of themselves, and he soon began to snore, and was so very fast asleep that nothing on earth could have awakened him. About two o'clock came the Raven, drawn by four white horses, and as she came along she felt assured she should find the man asleep; and so it was: as soon as she came into the garden, she saw him lying on the tan-heap fast asleep. She alighted from her carriage, went up to him, shook him, and shouted to him; but he did not awake. The next night, at twelve, the old woman came, and brought the man food and drink, but he would take nothing, till she pressed him so long and left him no rest till at last he took a long ,draught out of the glass of wine. About two o'clock he began again to watch upon the heap of tan for the Raven, but, as before, he soon felt so weary that his legs would not support him, and he was forced to lie down, and he fell into a deep sleep. When the Raven, therefore, came with her four red horses, she was in great distress, for she had a presentiment of finding the man asleep, as she did; and all her efforts to awaken him were in vain. The next day the old woman scolded the man and said, "What will happen if you neither eat nor drink? you will die?" "I dare not, and will not, eat and drink," replied the man. Nevertheless, the old woman set the dishes before him, and, the savour of them was so nice, he could not resist, and he made a hearty meal, and afterwards, when the time came, he went out into the garden, and there waited for the Princess upon the tan-heap. Soon he felt more weary than he had ever been before, and he lay down, and went as fast asleep as a stone. About two o'clock came the Raven, drawn by four black horses, and the coach also was black, and all the harness. She was already in tears, for she knew, as she drove along, she should find the man asleep; and so he was. She shook him and called to him, but in vain; she could not awaken him. So she laid by him a loaf of bread, a joint of meat, and a bottle of wine, of which he might take as much as he would, without lessening ,the quantity. Then she drew a golden ring off her finger, and put it on his finger, and on it her name was engraven. Lastly, she laid beside him a letter, wherein was stated what was given to him; and further it said, "I see well thou wilt never save me here; but, if thou yet desire to do so, come to the Golden Castle of Stromberg; it is in thy power." And as soon as she had done all this she placed herself in her carriage again, and was driven to that castle.

By-and-by the man awoke and saw what had happened, and he was sad at heart, for he thought, "Now she has gone away, and I have not saved her." Then his eyes lighted upon the things she had left, and he read the letter which contained the account of them. Soon he arose and would have marched at once to the Golden Castle of Stromberg, but he recollected he did not know where it was. For some time he wandered about the world, and at length he came to a large forest, wherein for fourteen days he walked to and fro, and could not get out. One day, as evening came on, he felt tired and lay down in a thicket and went to sleep. The next day he walked still further, and lay down at night beneath another thicket; but there he heard such a howling and groaning that he could not sleep. When the time came that people put out their lights he saw a lamp glimmering, towards which he made his way, and there he came to a house before which stood a Giant. But he thought to himself, "If I go in, and the Giant see me, my life is scarce worth counting on;" and with this idea he waited a long while before he entered. At last he ventured, and as soon as the Giant saw him he cried, "It is well that you have come, for I have eaten nothing for a long time, and you will serve for my supper."

"Let that be!" said the man; "I am not at all willing to be roasted; but, if you want to eat, I have enough here to satisfy you!"

"Well, if that is true," said the Giant, "you may rest quietly: I only meant to eat you because I had nothing else!" Thereupon they went in and sat down to table, and the man produced bread and meat and wine. "This pleases me well enough," said the Giant; and he ate to his heart's content. By-and-by the man asked him, "Can you tell me where the Golden Castle of Stromberg is situate?"

"I will look at my map," replied the Giant, "whereon are laid down all the cities, villages, and houses hereabouts." So saying, he fetched the map, which he kept in another room, and looked for the castle, but it was nowhere to be found. "It does not matter," said the Giant: "I have a still larger map upstairs in a closet;" but when they looked over that the name was not to be found there either. The man would then have proceeded further, but the Giant begged him to stop a couple of days, until his brother returned who was gone to seek for something to eat. As soon as the brother came home, they asked him after the Golden Castle of Stromberg; but he would not talk about anything till he had satisfied his hunger, and then he mounted with them to his chamber, and there they searched all over the map for the castle, without success; so then they fetched other maps, and did not leave off looking till at last they found the place; but it was many thousand miles away from where they were. "Now, how can I get there?" asked the man.

"I have two hours to spare," said the Giant, "and in that time I will carry you near the castle, but I must then return at once and feed the child we have." So the Giant took the man within about a hundred miles of the castle, and there set him down, and told him he could easily go the rest of the way by himself. So saying, he turned homewards; but the man journeyed on day and night, till at length he arrived in sight of the Golden Castle of Stromberg. Now, this castle stood upon a glass mountain, and he could see the Princess riding round in her carriage, and then go into the gate. At this sight he felt very glad, and began to mount up to the place, but every step he took he slipped back again. When, therefore, he perceived he could not reach the Princess he became very sorrowful, and said to himself, "I will stop here, and wait upon her." So he built himself a hut, and for a whole year lived in it, every day seeing the Princess driving about up above while he was unable to reach her.

One day he perceived from his hut three robbers beating one another, and he called to them. "God be with you!" They ceased at the voice, but when they saw nobody, they began again to knock each other about, so that it was quite dangerous. Then he called to them a second time, "God be with you!" They ceased at the word, looked about, but saw nobody, and they began to beat each other again; and so the man exclaimed for the third time, "God be with you!" and went out and asked the three combatants what they wanted. The first said he had found a stick which opened every door against which it was struck; the second had found a cloak which rendered its wearer invisible; but the third had caught a horse upon which any one could ride up the glass mountain. Now, they could not agree whether they should keep company with one another, or should separate; so the man said, "These three things I will exchange with you; money certainly I have not, but other things which are more valuable. Still, I must first have a trial, that I may see if you have spoken the truth." So they let him mount the horse, and hung the cloak around him, and put the stick into his hand, and when they had given him all he was invisible to them. Then he gave them heavy blows upon the shoulders, and exclaiming, "Now, you bear-hunters, now you have your deserts; be content therewith!" he rode up the glass mountain, and as he arrived before the castle door, he found it closed. He, therefore, tapped upon it with his stick, and immediately it flew open, and he entered and mounted the stairs which led to the room where the Princess sat with a golden cup full of wine before her. She could not see him, because he wore the cloak, and as he came close to her chair, he drew off the ring which she had given him, and threw it into the cup of wine, so that it rang against the side. Then she exclaimed, "That is my ring, and the man must also be here who will deliver me!" and she made a search for him all over the castle; but he had gone out meanwhile, and now sat on his horse outside the door with the cloak thrown off. As soon, therefore, as she went out at the door she saw him, and cried for joy, and the man dismounting from his horse, took her in his arms, and the Princess kissed him and said, "Now you have indeed saved me, and to-morrow we will be married!"

Old Hildebrand

ONCE upon a time there lived an old Farmer, and his Daughter with him, whom the Parson of the village, having once seen, took a great fancy to; and he thought he should be very happy if he could manage one day to have a long talk with her alone. To this the Daughter had no objection, and the Parson one day said to her, "Oh! my dear maiden, hear what I have to say: I will tell you how to manage, that we may have a whole day all to ourselves. About the middle of this week do you lie in bed one morning, and tell your father you are very ill, and groan and sigh very badly, and keep that up all the week. Then, on Sunday, when I come to deliver my sermon, I will preach that whoever has at home a sick child, a sick husband, a sick wife, a sick father or mother, a sick sister or brother, or any other relative, and shall make a journey to the Bell Mountain in Wales, such an one's sick child, sick husband or wife, sick father or mother, sick sister or brother, or any other relative, shall become well on the instant!"

"Oh! that I will do for you," said the girl; and thereupon, about the middle of the week, she laid a-bed, and, spite of all her Father brought or did for her, she groaned and sighed till the Sunday, as if she were full of pain. On Sunday the daughter said to her Father, "Oh! I am really so miserably ill, I feel as if I should die; but once before my end I should like to hear the Parson again, and hear the sermon which he will deliver to-day."

"Ah! my child," replied the Farmer, "you must not do that; you would be all the worse for it if you got up. But never mind; I will go to church, and pay great attention to the sermon, and afterwards come and tell you all the Parson said."

"Ah! very well," said the Daughter; "but mind you are very attentive, and tell me everything."

So away went the Farmer to church; and, after the Parson had chanted and read all the service, he got into the pulpit and began his sermon. In the course of it he said, "If any one here has a sick child, a sick husband or a sick wife, a sick father or mother, a sick brother or a sick sister, or any other relative, and shall go to the Bell Mountain in Wales, such a one's sick child, sick husband or wife, sick father or mother, sick sister or brother, or any other relative, shall regain health immediately; especially if he take with him a cross and some laurel leaves which I will give him after service." Then was nobody quicker than the Farmer in going to the Parson after service for his laurel leaves and cross; and as soon as he had received them, he hurried home; and almost before he got to the door he called out, "Come, my dear daughter, you will soon be well. The Parson has preached to-day that whosoever having a sick child, a sick husband or wife, a sick mother or father, a sick brother or a sick sister, or any other person, shall go to the Bell Mountain, with a cross and laurel leaves given him by the Parson, his sick child, sick husband or wife, sick father or mother, sick sister or brother, or any other relative, shall recover immediately. Now, the laurel leaves and cross I have received from the Parson, and I shall set out immediately on the journey, that you may be the sooner in good health." So saying, he set out; but scarcely had he gone, when the Daughter got up, and very soon afterwards in stepped the Parson. Here we will leave them a bit, while we follow the Farmer in his wanderings. As we have said, he had set out at once, that he might reach the Bell Mountain the quicker; and on his way his Cousin met him, who was an egg-merchant, and was just come home from market, having sold his eggs.

"Good day to you," said the Cousin; "whither are you going?"

"To Wales, Cousin," he replied; "my daughter is very ill; and the Parson said yesterday in his sermon that whoever having at home a sick child, a sick husband or wife, a sick father or a sick mother, a sick brother, sister, or any other relation, should then make a journey to the Bell Mountain in Wales carrying in his hand some laurel and a cross, blessed and given by the Parson – whoever should do this, then that his sick child, sick mother, or sick father, husband or wife, sick brother or sick sister, or any other relative, would immediately be restored to health. So this laurel and cross I have received from the Priest, and now I am hastening to the mountain."

"But hold, Cousin, stop!" said the other to the Farmer, "are you so simple as to believe that? Why, how do you know that the Parson may not perchance wish to have a comfortable talk with your daughter alone, and therefore has contrived this tale to take you away from home?"

"Mercy on us!" said the Farmer, "if I did but know whether that were true or not!"

"Well, you soon can see," replied the Cousin; "just get into my cart, and I will drive you home, that you may satisfy yourself."

It was soon done; and as they drove nearer to the house they heard the sounds of merriment. There had the Farmer's daughter gathered the best of everything out of the farmyard and garden, and made all manner of savoury dishes, and the Parson was there to partake of them. So the Cousin knocked at the door, and the Maiden inquired who was there.

"It is only me, Cousin," replied he; "will you give me a night's lodging? I have just sold my eggs in the market, and I meant to have got home to-night, but it is so dark already that I dare not go."

"You have come at a very unlucky moment, Cousin," replied the Farmer's Daughter; "but since you are quite alone, you may come in and set yourself down in the chimney-corner."

So the egg-merchant, carrying his basket, in which the Farmer was concealed, came in and sat down where he was bid, while the Parson and the Daughter made themselves very merry together over their meal. Presently the Parson said, "You can sing, I think, my dear; just give us a bit of a song."

"Well," said she, "I could sing once when I was very young; but now I have forgotten how, and it is almost all lost to me."

"Never mind; do just try!" entreated the Parson. So the Farmer's Daughter began:—

> "Oh! well have I sent my father away
> To the mountains in Wales so high!"

and then the Parson joined in,—

> "And there he shall stop for a year and a day;
> And merry the time will pass by."

Presently the Cousin within struck up (but here I must tell you the Farmer's name was Hildebrand),—

> "Hearest thou that, my Hildebrand dear?
> Why sitt'st thou so quiet, so near, so near?"

And directly the Farmer made answer,—

> "Oh! more of your singing I never can stand!
> And out this basket I must get my hand!"

With these words, he jumped up from the basket, and bundled the Parson out of the house.

The Three Birds

MANY years ago there lived up among the hills in our country some pretty Kings, who every day went out hunting, and had their palaces high above everybody else. One day when one of them had come forth from his castle with his Huntsmen there were three Girls who were tending their cows, and, as they saw the King pass by with his people, the eldest of them, pointing to the King, called out to her companions, "Hilloa! hilloa! if I had any I would have him." Then the two Girls on the other side of the hill exclaimed, each pointing to the two men nearest the King, the one with her right hand, the other with her left, "Hilloa! hilloa! if I had any I would have him." Now these two were the King's Ministers. The King, who heard all that was said, as soon as he returned from the hunt, ordered the three Maidens to be fetched, and asked them what they had meant in the morning by what they said on the mountains. This question, however, they would not answer, and at last the King inquired of the eldest if she would have him for a husband. To this she said yes; and her two Sisters were then asked in marriage by the Ministers, for they were all three beautiful and fair, especially the King's wife, who had flaxen hair.

Now the two Sisters had no children at first, and, as the King had to undertake a long journey, he invited them to come and stay with the Queen. During his absence the Queen bore a child, who had a red forehead, and was, besides, very pretty. The two Sisters, however, agreed together they would throw the child into the mill-pond, and as they did so a little Bird flew up into the air, which sang,—

> "Ready to die
> And for ever to quit
> These lilies and flowers,
> Brave boy, are you fit?"

When the two Sisters heard this they wer very much alarmed, and made all the haste they could home. Afterwards, when the King returned, they told him that the Queen had borne a dead child; but the King only replied, "What God wills I must bear." Meanwhile a Fisherman had fished the little Boy up out of the water while it still breathed, and, as his wife had no children of her own, they brought it up. A year after the King again went on a journey, and in his absence another Boy was born, which the two Sisters stole away as before and threw into the water. Just as they did so a Bird flew up as at the first time and sang,—

> "Ready to die
> And for ever to quit
> These lilies and flowers,
> Little boy, are you fit?"

When the King returned they told the same tale as before about the Queen; but he merely replied, "What God wills I must bear." However, the Fisherman had again luckily rescued the child, whom he brought up with his brother.

Some time passed before the King journeyed again, but during his absence a child was born, and this time it was a little Girl, which the false Sisters also threw into the river, and the little Bird instantly flew up, singing,—

"Ready to die
And for ever to quit
These lilies and flowers,
Little maid, are you fit?"

Afterwards, when the King returned, he was told the same tale as before, and this made him so angry that he caused the Queen to be put in prison, where she was kept for many years.

During that time the Children grew up; but when the eldest went out to fish, the other boys would not let him come near, and said, "Go your own way, you foundling!" This made him very sad, and he asked the Fisherman who he was, and the Fisherman told him how he had fished him and his brother and sister all out of the water in his net. The eldest boy resolved thereupon that he would go in search of their Father; but the Fisherman was very unwilling to part with him. At length he consented, and the Boy set out, and after travelling for several days came to an immense piece of water, by which stood a Woman fishing.

"Good day, mother," said the Boy.

"Thank you, my lad," she replied.

"You will sit there a good long time before you catch any fish," said the Boy.

"And you will seek a long while before you find your father," returned the Woman. "And pray how do you mean to cross this water?" "Heaven alone knows!" he replied; and thereupon the old Woman took him on her back and carried him across, and there he searched everywhere, but could never find his Father.

A year after his departure his Brother made up his mind to go in search of him, and he also, coming to the same great water, found the old Woman, with whom he held the same conversation, and was likewise carried across as his Brother had been. The Sister was now left alone at home, but she became so restless and dispirited at her brothers' absence that she set out herself in search of them. On her way she came, as they had done, to the great piece of water, and found there the same old Woman, to whom she said, "Good day, mother." "Thank you, my child," was the reply. "God bless your fishing!" said the Girl. As soon as the old Woman heard this she became very friendly, and after carrying the maiden across the water she gave her a staff, and said, "Now, go straight along on this path, my daughter, and when you come to a great black Dog you must take care neither to laugh at it nor kick it, but pass it by quietly. Then you will come to a large castle, upon whose threshold you must let the staff fall, and then go straight through it to a fountain on the other side of the castle. This fountain will be in a stream, wherein stands also a tree, on which there will hang a bird in a cage, which you must take off. Then take also a glass of water from the fountain, and return with these the same way exactly as you came. On the threshold pick up your staff again, and when you pass the Dog the second time hit it in the face, and then come straight back to me." The Maiden found everything just as the old Woman said, and at the back of the castle she found also her two Brothers, who had been seeking half through the world. So they went together and came to the place where the black Dog lay, whose face they knocked, and immediately the Dog became a handsome Prince, and accompanied them to the great water. There still stood the old Woman, who was very glad to see them return, and carried them all across the water. This done, she disappeared, for she was now released from her labours. The Brothers and Sister, however, returned to the Fisherman, and all were made happy on seeing each other again; but the Bird they hung upon the wall in his cage. The second Brother, however, could not rest at home, and soon he took his cross-bow and went to the hunt. When he got tired he took out his flute and played a tune, which the King, who was also hunting, heard, and coming up to the youth, inquired who had given him leave to hunt there. "Nobody," he replied.

"To whom do you belong, then?" asked the King.

"I am the Fisherman's son," was the reply.

"But he has no children," said the King.

"If you will not believe me," said the Youth, "come and see."

So the King went to the Fisherman, who told him all that had taken place; and the Bird on the wall began to sing,—

> "The mother sits lonely
> In prison fast kept,
> And these are her children
> Stolen away while she slept,
> By the false-hearted sisters,
> Who, the children to kill,
> In the deep waters threw them,
> By the side of the Mill."

This frightened them all, and the King took the Bird, the Fisherman, and the three Children with him to the castle, and ordered the prison to be opened, and brought his Wife out, who at first was very ill and weak after her long confinement. So her daughter gave her some of the water she had procured at the fountain, and that made her quite well again as soon as she had drunk it. Afterwards the two false Sisters were burnt, and the Daughter of the King married the handsome Prince: and so all were made happy and lived to a good old age.

The Water of Life

ONCE upon a time there was a King who was so ill that everybody despaired of his life, and his three sons were very sorry, and went out into the palace gardens to weep. There they met an old man, who asked the cause of their grief, and they told him their Father was so ill that he must die, for nothing could save him. The old Man said, "I know a means of saving him: if he drinks of the water of life it will restore him to health, but it is very difficult to find."

"I will soon find it," said the eldest Son, and, going to the sick King, he begged his permission to set out in search of the water of life, which alone could save him. "No; the danger is too great," said the King; "I prefer to die." Nevertheless the Son begged and entreated so long that the King consented and the Prince went away, thinking in his own heart, "If I bring this water I am the dearest to my Father, and I shall inherit his kingdom."

After he had ridden a long way he met a Dwarf on the road, who asked him. "Whither away so quickly?"

"You stupid dandyprat," replied the Prince proudly, "why should I tell you that?" and he rode off. But the little Man was angry and he wished an evil thing, so that, soon after, the Prince came into a narrow mountain-pass, and the further he rode the narrower it grew, till at last it was so close that he could get no further; but neither could he turn his horse round, nor dismount, and he sat there like one amazed. Meanwhile the sick King waited a long while for him, but he did not come; and the second Son asked leave to go too and seek the water, for he thought to himself, "If my Brother is dead the kingdom comes to me." At first the King refused to spare him; but he gave way, and the Prince set out on the same road as the elder one had taken, and met also the same Dwarf, who stopped him and asked him, "Whither ride you so hastily?" "Little dandyprat," replied the Prince, "what do you want to know for?" and he rode off without looking round. The Dwarf, however, enchanted him, and it happened to him as it had to his Brother: he came to a defile where he could move neither forwards nor backwards. Such is the fate of all haughty people.

Now, when the second Son did not return, the youngest begged leave to go and fetch the water, and the King was obliged at last to give his consent. When he met the Dwarf, and was asked whither he was going so hurriedly, he stopped and replied, "I seek the water of life, for my Father is sick unto death." "Do you know where to find it?" asked the Dwarf. "No," replied the Prince. "Since you have behaved yourself as you ought," said the Dwarf, "and not haughtily like your false Brothers, I will give you information and show you where you may obtain the water of life. It flows from a fountain in the court of an enchanted castle, into which you can never penetrate if I do not give you an iron rod and two loaves of bread. With the rod knock thrice at the iron door of the castle, and it will spring open. Within lie two lions with open jaws, but if you throw down to each a loaf of bread they will be quiet. Then hasten and fetch some of the water of life before it strikes twelve, for then the door will shut again, and you will be imprisoned."

THE WATER OF LIFE

The Prince thanked the Dwarf, and, taking the rod and bread, he set out on his journey, and as he arrived at the castle he found it as the Dwarf had said. At the third knock the door sprang open; and, when he had stilled the Lions with the bread, he walked into a fine large hall, where sat several enchanted Princes, from whose fingers he drew off the rings, and he also took away with him a sword and some bread which lay there. A little further he came to a room wherein stood a beautiful maiden, who was so pleased to see him that she kissed him and said he had freed her, and should have her whole kingdom, and if he came in another year their wedding should be celebrated. Then she told him where the fountain of the water of life was placed, and he hastened away lest it should strike twelve ere he gained it. He came next into a room where a fine clean covered bed stood, and, being tired, he laid down to rest himself a bit. But he went to sleep, and when he awoke it struck the quarter to twelve, and the sound made him hurry to the fountain, from which he took some water in a cup which stood near. This done, he hastened to the door, and was scarcely out before it struck twelve, and the door swung to so heavily that it carried away a piece of his heel.

But he was very glad, in spite of this, that he had procured the water, and he journeyed homewards, and passed again where the Dwarf stood. When the Dwarf saw the sword and bread which he had brought away he declared he had done well, for with the sword he could destroy whole armies: but the bread was worth nothing. Now, the Prince was not willing to return home to his Father without his Brothers, and so he said to the Dwarf, "Dear Dwarf, can you tell me where my Brothers are? they went out before me in search of the water of life, and did not return." "They are stuck fast between two mountains," replied the Dwarf; "because they were so haughty, I enchanted them there."

Then the Prince begged for their release, till at last the Dwarf brought them out; but he warned the youngest to beware of them, for they had evil in their hearts.

When his Brothers came he was very glad, and he related to them all that had happened to him; how he had found the water of life and brought away a cup full of it; and how he had rescued a beautiful Princess, who for a whole year was going to wait for him, and then he was to return to be married to her, and receive a rich kingdom. After this tale the three Brothers rode away together, and soon entered a province where there were war and famine raging, and the King thought he should perish, so great was his necessity. The youngest Prince went to this King and gave him the bread, with which he fed and satisfied his whole people; and then the Prince gave him the sword, wherewith he defeated and slew all his enemies, and regained peace and quiet. This effected, the Prince took back the bread and sword, and rode on further with his Brothers, and by-and-by they came to two other provinces where also war and famine were destroying the people. To each King the Prince lent his bread and sword, and so saved three kingdoms. After this they went on board a ship to pass over the sea which separated them from home, and during the voyage the two elder Brothers said to one another, "Our Brother has found the water of life and we have not; therefore our Father will give the kingdom which belongs to us to him, and our fortune will be taken away." Indulging these thoughts they became so envious that they consulted together how they should kill him, and one day waiting till he was fast asleep, they poured the water out of his cup and took it for themselves, while they filled his up with bitter salt-water. As soon as they arrived at home the youngest Brother took his cup to the sick King, that he might drink out of it and regain his health. But scarcely had he drunk a very little of the water when he became worse than before, for it was as bitter as wormwood. While the King lay in this state, the two elder Princess came, and accused their Brother of poisoning their Father; but they had brought the right water, and they handed it to the King. Scarcely had he drunk a little out of the cup when the King felt his sickness leave him, and soon he was as strong and healthy as in his young days. The two Brothers now went to the youngest Prince, mocking him, and saying, "You certainly found the water of life; but you had the trouble and we had the reward; you should have been more cautious and kept your eyes open, for we took your cup while you were asleep on the sea; and, moreover, in a year one of us intends to fetch your Princess. Beware, however, that you betray us not; the King will not believe you, and if you say a single word your life will be lost; but if you remain silent you are safe." The old King, nevertheless, was very angry with his youngest Son, who had conspired, as he believed, against his life. He caused his court to be assembled, and sentence was given to the effect that the Prince should be secretly shot; and once as he rode out hunting, unsuspicious of any evil, the Huntsman was sent with him to perform the deed. By-and-by, when they were alone in the wood, the Huntsman seemed so sad that the Prince asked him what ailed him. The Huntsman replied, "I cannot and yet must tell you." "Tell me boldly what it is," said the Prince, "I will forgive you." "Ah! it is no other than that I must shoot you, for so has the King ordered me," said the Huntsman with a deep sigh.

The Prince was frightened, and said, "Let me live, dear Huntsman, let me live! I will give you my royal coat and you shall give me yours in exchange." To this the Huntsman readily assented, for he felt unable to shoot the Prince, and after they had exchanged their clothing the Huntsman returned home, and the Prince went deeper into the wood.

A short time afterwards three wagons laden with gold and precious stones came to the King's palace for his youngest Son. They were sent by the three Kings in token of gratitude for the sword which had defeated their enemies, and the bread which had nourished their people. At this arrival the old King said to himself, "Perhaps, after all, my Son was guiltless;" and he lamented to his courtiers that he had let his Son be killed. But the Huntsman cried out, "He lives yet! for I could not find it in my heart to fulfil your commands;" and he told the King how it had happened. The King felt as if a stone had been removed from his heart, and he caused it to be proclaimed everywhere throughout his dominions that his Son might return and would again be taken into favour.

Meanwhile the Princess had caused a road to be made up to her castle of pure shining gold, and she told her attendants that whoever should ride straight up this road would be the right person, and one whom they might admit into the castle; but, on the contrary, whoever should ride up not on the road, but by the side, they were ordered on no account to admit, for he was not the right person. When, therefore, the time came round which the Princess had mentioned to the youngest Prince, the eldest Brother thought he would hasten to her castle and announce himself as her deliverer, that he might gain her as a bride and the kingdom besides. So he rode away, and when he came in front of the castle and saw the fine golden road he thought it would be a shame to ride thereon, and so he turned to the left hand and rode up out of the road. But as he came up to the door the guards told him he was not the right person, and he must ride back again. Soon afterwards the second Prince also set out, and he, likewise, when he came to the golden road, and his horse set its fore-feet upon it, thought it would be a pity to travel upon it, and so he turned aside to the right hand and went up. When he came to the gate the guards refused him admittance, and told him he was not the person expected, and so he had to return homewards. The youngest Prince, who had all this time been wandering about in the forest, had also remembered that the year was up, and soon after his Brothers' departure he appeared before the castle and rode up straight on the golden road, for he was so deeply engaged in thinking of his beloved Princess that he did not observe it. As soon as he arrived at the door it was opened, and the Princess received him with joy, saying he was her deliverer and the lord of her dominions. Soon after their wedding was celebrated, and when it was over the Princess told her husband that his Father had forgiven him and desired to see him. Thereupon he rode to the old King's palace, and told him how his Brothers had betrayed him while he slept, and had sworn him to silence. When the King heard this he would have punished the false Brothers, but they had prudently taken themselves off in a ship, and they never returned home afterwards.

The Peasant's Wise Daughter

THERE was once a time a poor Peasant, who had no land, but merely a little cottage, and an only Daughter, who one day said to him, "We must ask the King for a piece of waste land."

Now, when the King heard of their poverty, he presented them with a corner of a field, which the man and his daughter tilled, and prepared to sow in it corn and seeds. As they turned the land about they found a mortar of pure gold, and the Peasant said to his daughter, "Since his Majesty the King has been so gracious to us as to present us with this acre, we ought to give him this treasure."

But to this the Daughter would not agree, saying, "If we have the mortar, and not the pestle, we must procure the pestle for it; therefore be silent."

However, the Father would not obey her, but took the mortar to the King, and said he had found it while tilling the ground, and asked the King if he would accept the offering. The King took it, and asked if he had found nothing more. "No," replied the Peasant. "Then," said the King, "you must procure the pestle for it." The Peasant said they had not found that; but it was of no use, he might as well have spoken to the wind, and he was ordered to be put in prison until he discovered it. The keepers had to bring him daily bread and water, which is all one gets in prison, and when they did so they heard the man always lamenting, "Had I but obeyed my daughter! had I obeyed my daughter!" So these keepers went and told the King that the man was always crying, "Had I obeyed my daughter!" and would neither eat nor drink. His Majesty commanded them to bring the prisoner before him, and then he asked him why he was always crying out in this manner, and what his Daughter had said.

"She told me," said the man, "not to bring the mortar to you before I had found the pestle."

"What! have you such a wise daughter? let her come hither at once!" said the King. So the girl came, and the King asked her if she were so wise as was said, for he would propose a riddle, which if she solved he would then marry her. "What is that which is unclothed and yet is not naked, that moves along and yet neither rides nor walks, and that goes not in the road nor out of it?"

The girl said she would do her best, and went away and pulled off all her clothes, so that she was not clothed; then she took a large fishing-net, and set herself in it, and wrapped it round her, so she was not naked; then she bought an ass, and bound the net to its tail, so dragged her along, and thus she neither rode nor walked. The ass, too, had to trail her along in a rut, so that she was neither in the road nor out of it, for only her big toes touched the ground. Now, as the King saw her coming towards him, he said she had solved the riddle, and fulfilled all the conditions. Then he let her father out of prison, and made the daughter his bride, and committed to her all the royal possessions.

Several years had passed away, when once, as the King was walking on parade, it happened that several peasants, who had sold wood, stopped before the palace with their waggons: some of them had oxen yoked and some horses, and one peasant had three horses, one of which was a young foal, which ran away, and laid itself down between two oxen who were in front of a waggon. Soon the peasants grouped together and began to quarrel, wrangle, and dispute with each other: the peasant with the oxen would keep the foal, saying that it belonged to him, while the peasant with the horses denied it, and said the foal was his, for his horses went with it. The quarrel was brought before the King, and he gave judgement that the foal should keep where it was, and so it passed into possession of the man with the oxen to whom it did not belong. So the other went away weeping and lamenting for his foal; but he had heard that the Queen was a very kind woman, because she had herself been born of peasant folk, so he went to her and asked her to help him that he might regain his own foal. The Queen said she would do so, and if he would promise not to betray her she would tell him how. Early in the morning when the King was on the watch-parade he was to place himself in the midst of the path by which he must pass, and take a large fish-net, and pretend to fish and shake the net about over the terrace as if it were full of fish. She told him, also, what to answer if the King asked any questions; and the next day, accordingly, he stood there fishing in a dry place. When the King came by, and saw him, he sent his page to ask who the simpleton was, and what he was about. The peasant merely replied, "I am fishing."

The page asked how he could fish where there was no water; and the man replied, "So well as two oxen can bear a foal, so well can I fish in a dry place."

With this answer the page left him, and told it to the King, who bade the peasant come before him and asked him from whom he had the answer he made, for it could not be from himself. The man refused to tell, and replied to every question, "God forbid! I had it from myself." At last they laid him upon a heap of straw, and beat him and tortured him so long till at last he confessed that he had the answer from the Queen. As soon as the King returned home afterwards, he said to his wife, "Why are you so false to me? I will no longer have you about me; your time is over; go away to whence you came – to your peasant's hut."

He gave her leave, however, to take with her what she considered dearest and best to herself, and the Queen said, "Yes, dearest husband I will do as you bid me," and she fell upon his breast and kissed him, and said she would take her leave. But first she made a strong sleeping-mixture to pledge him in, and the King took a long draught, but she drank only a little. Soon he fell into a deep sleep, and when she perceived it was so, she called a servant, and, wrapping a fine white linen napkin over her lord's face, she caused him to be laid in a carriage, and drawn to the cottage from whence she first came. There she laid him in a bed, where he slept a night and a day, and when he awoke he looked round him amazed, and called for a servant, but none answered the call. At last came his wife to the bed, and said, "My dear lord and King, you commanded me to take out of the castle whatever I thought dearest and best, and, because I had nothing dearer or better than you, I have brought you with me here."

At these words tears came into the King's eyes, and he said, "Dear wife, you shall be mine and I will be thine!" and so he took her back again to the palace; and there they are living still in the full enjoyment of health and happiness, for aught I know to the contrary.

Doctor Know-All

A LONG time ago there lived a peasant named "Crab," who one day drove into a certain city his cart laden with a bundle of faggots, drawn by two oxen. He soon found a purchaser for his wood in the person of a learned Doctor, who bought it for two dollars, and, while the money was being counted out, the Peasant, peeping in at the door, saw how comfortably his customer was eating and drinking; and the thought thereupon came into his head that he would like to be a professor too. So he waited a little while, and at last mustered courage to ask whether he could not be a Doctor. "Oh, yes," replied the Doctor, "that can soon be managed!"

"What must I do?" asked the Peasant.

"First of all, buy an A B C book, one which has a cock-a-doodle-doo for a frontispiece; secondly, sell your cart and oxen, and turn them into money to buy good clothes with, and what else belongs to a Doctor's appearance; lastly, let a sign be painted, with the words, 'I am the Doctor Know-All,' and nail that over your house door."

The Countryman did all that he was told, and after he had practised a little time, but not to much purpose, a certain very wealthy Baron had some money stolen from him. Mention was made to the Baron of Doctor Know-All who dwelt in such a village, and who would be sure to know where the money was gone. As soon as the Baron heard of him, he ordered his horses into his carriage and drove to the place where the Doctor lived. The Baron inquired if he were the Doctor Know-All, and he replying "Yes," the Baron said he must return with him and discover his money.

"Very well," replied the Doctor; "but my wife Gertrude must accompany me."

To this the Baron agreed, and, all being seated in the carriage, away they drove back again. When they arrived at the house a splendid collation was on the table, of which the Doctor was invited to partake. "Certainly," said he, "but my wife Gertrude too;" and he sat down with her at the bottom of the table. As soon as the first servant entered with a dish of delicate soup, the Doctor poked his wife, saying, "He is the first!" meaning he was the first who had brought in meat. But the servant imagined he meant to say, "He is the first thief!" and because he really was so, he felt very much disturbed, and told his comrades in the kitchen, "The Doctor knows all; we shall come off badly, for he has said I am the first!" When the second servant heard this he felt afraid to go; but he was obliged, and, as soon as he entered the room with the dish, the man poked his wife again, and said, "Gertrude, that is the second!" This frightened the servant so much that he left the room as soon as possible; and the third servant who entered fared no better, for the Doctor said to his wife, "That is the third!" The fourth servant had to bring in a covered dish, and the Baron said to the Doctor he must show his powers by telling truly what was in the dish. Now, there were crabs in it, and the Doctor looked at the dish for some minutes, considering how to get out of the scrape. At last he cried out, "Oh, poor *Crab* that I am!" When the Baron heard this he exclaimed,

"Good! he knows it! he knows, too, where my money is."

The servant, however, was terribly frightened; and he winked to the Doctor to follow him out. When he had done so he found all four servants there who had stolen the money, and were now so eager to get off that they offered him a large sum if he would not betray them; for if he did their necks would be in danger. They led him also to the place where the money lay hid, and the Doctor was so pleased that he gave them the required promise, and then returned to the house, where he sat down again at table, and, producing his book, said, "I will now look in my book, Baron, and discover the place where the money lies." A fifth servant, who had had a share in the robbery, wished to hear if the Doctor knew more, and so he crept up the chimney to listen. Below sat the Countryman, turning the leaves of his book backwards and forwards, forwards and backwards, looking for the cock-a-doodle-doo. However, he could not find it, and he at length exclaimed, "You must come out, for I know you are in it!" This made the servant up the chimney believe he meant him, and down he slipped, and came out, crying, "The man knows all, the man knows all!"

Then Doctor Know-All showed the Baron where the money lay; but he said nothing about who had stolen it, so that from both sides he received a large sum of money as a reward, and, moreover, he became a very celebrated character.

The Two Wanderers

IT IS certain that hills and valleys never meet; but it often happens on the earth that her children, both the good and the wicked, cross each other's path continually. So it once occurred that a Shoemaker and a Tailor fell together during their travels. Now, the Tailor was a merry little fellow, always making the best of everything; and, as he saw the Shoemaker approaching from the opposite road, and remarked by his knapsack what trade he was, he began a little mocking rhyme, singing—

> "Stitch, stitch away with your needle,
> Pull away hard with your thread,
> Rub it with wax to the right and the left,
> And knock the old peg on the head!"

The Shoemaker, however, could not take a joke, and pulled a long face, as if he had been drinking vinegar, while he seemed inclined to

THE TWO WANDERERS

lay hold of the Tailor by the collar. But the latter began to laugh, and handed his bottle to the other, saying, "It is not ill-meant; just drink and wash down the gall." The Shoemaker thereupon took a long pull, and immediately the gathering storm vanished; and, as he gave the Tailor back his bottle, he said, "I should have spoken to you roughly, but one talks better after a great drinking than after long thirst. Shall we travel together now?" "Right willingly," answered the Tailor, "if you have but a mind to go into some large town where work is not wanting to those who seek it." "That is just the place I should like," rejoined the Shoemaker; "in a little nest there is nothing to be earned, and the people in the country would rather go barefoot than buy shoes." So they wandered away, setting always one foot before the other, like a weasel in the snow.

Time enough had both our heroes, but little either to bite or break. When they came to the first town, they went round requesting work, and, because the Tailor looked so fresh and merry, and had such red cheeks, every one gave him what he could spare to do, and, moreover, he was so lucky, that the master's daughters, behind the shop-door, would give him a kiss as he passed. So it happened that, when he met again with his companion, his bundle was the better filled of the two. The fretful Shoemaker drew a sour face, and thought, "The greater the rogue the better the luck;" but the other began to laugh and sing, and shared all that he received with his comrade. For, if only a couple of groschen jingled in his pocket, he would out with them, throw them on the table with such force, that the glasses danced, and cry out, "Lightly earned, lightly spent!"

After they had wandered about for some time, they came to a large forest, through which the road passed to the royal city; but there were two ways, one of which was seven days long, and the other only two, but neither of the travellers knew which was the shorter. They therefore sat down under an oak-tree, to consult how they should manage, and for how many days they could take bread with them. The Shoemaker said, "One must provide for further than one goes, so I will take with me bread for seven days."

"What!" cried the Tailor, "carry bread for seven days on your back like a beast of burden, so that you can't look round? I shall commit myself to God and care for nothing. The money which I have in my pocket is as good in summer as in winter, but the bread will get dry, and musty beside, in this hot weather. Why should we not find the right way? Bread for two days, and luck with it!" Thereupon each one bought his own bread, and then they started in the forest to try their fortune.

It was as quiet and still as a church. Not a breath of wind was stirring, not a brook bubbling, a bird singing, nor even a sunbeam shining through the thick leaves. The Shoemaker spoke never a word, for the heavy bread pressed upon his back so sorely, that the sweat ran down over his morose and dark countenance. The Tailor, on the other hand, was as merry as a lark, jumping about, whistling through straws, or singing songs. Thus two days passed; but on the third, when no end was to be found to the forest, the Tailor's heart fell a bit, for he had eaten all his bread; still he did not lose courage, but put his trust in God and his own luck. The third evening he laid down under a tree hungry, and awoke the next morning not less so. The fourth day was just the same, and when the Shoemaker sat down on an uprooted tree, and devoured his midday meal, nothing remained to the Tailor but to look on. He begged once a bit of bread, but the other laughed in his face, and said, "You are always so merry, and now you can try for once in your life how a man feels when he is sad: birds which sing too early in the morning are caught by the hawk in the evening." In short, he was without pity for his companion. The fifth morning, however, the poor Tailor could not stand upright, and could scarcely speak from faintness: his cheeks, besides, were quite white, and his eyes red. Then the Shoemaker said to him, "I will give you to-day a piece of bread, but I must put out your right eye for it."

The unhappy Tailor, who still wished to preserve his life, could not help himself: he wept once with both eyes, and then the Shoemaker, who had a heart of stone, put out his right eye with a needle. Then the poor fellow recollected what his mother had once said to him when he had been eating in the store-room, "One may eat too much, but one must also suffer for it." As soon as he had swallowed his dearly-purchased bread he got upon his legs again, forgot his misfortune, and comforted himself by reflecting that he had still one eye left to see with. But on the sixth day hunger again tormented him, and his heart began to fall in. When evening came he sunk down under a tree, and on the seventh morning he could not rise himself from faintness, for death sat on his neck. The Shoemaker said, "I will yet show you mercy and give you a piece of bread, but as a recompense I must put out your left eye." The Tailor, remembering his past sinfulness, begged pardon of God, and then said to his companion, "Do what you will, I will bear what I must; but remember that our God watches every action, and that an hour will come when the wicked deeds shall be punished which you have practised upon me, and which I have never deserved. In prosperous days I shared with you what I had. My business is one which requires stitch for stitch. If I have no longer sight, I can sew no more, and must go begging. Let me not, when I am blind, lie here all alone, or I will perish."

The Shoemaker, however, had driven all thoughts about God out of his heart, and he took the knife and put out the left eye of his comrade. Then he gave him a piece of bread to eat, reached him a stick, and led him behind him.

As the sun was setting they got out of the forest, and before them in a field stood a gallows. The Shoemaker led the blind Tailor to it, left him lying there, and went his way. From weariness, pain, and hunger, the poor fellow slept the whole night long, and when he awoke at daybreak he knew not where he was. Upon the gallows hung two poor sinners, and upon each of their heads sat a Crow, one of which said to the other, "Brother, are you awake?" "Yes, I am," replied the second. "Then I will tell you something," said the first Crow. "The dew which has fallen over us this night from the gallows will give sight to him who needs it if he but washes himself with it. If the blind knew this, how many there are who would once more be able to see, who now think it impossible!"

When the Tailor heard this he took his handkerchief, spread it on the grass, and as soon as it was soaked with dew he washed his eyeballs therewith. Immediately the words of the Crow were fulfilled, and he saw as clearly as ever. In a short while afterwards the Tailor saw the sun rise over the mountains, and before him in the distance lay the King's city, with its magnificent gates and hundred towers, over which the spires and pinnacles began to glisten in the sunbeams. He discerned every leaf upon the trees, every bird which flew by, and the gnats which danced in the air. He took a needle out of his pocket, and, when he found he could pass the needle through the eye as easily as ever, his heart leaped for joy. He threw himself upon his knees and thanked God for the mercy shown to him, and while he said his morning devotions he did not forget to pray for the two poor sinners who swung to and fro in the wind like the pendulum of a clock. Afterwards he took his bundle upon his back, and, forgetting his past sorrows and troubles, he jogged along singing and whistling.

The first thing he met was a brown Filly, which was running about in the fields at liberty. The Tailor caught it by its mane, and would have swung himself on its back to ride into the city, but the Filly begged for its liberty, saying, "I am still too young; even a light Tailor like you would break my back; let me run about till I am stronger; a time, perhaps, will come, when I can reward you."

"Run away, then," replied the Tailor; "I see you are still a romp!" and with these words he gave it a cut with a switch, which made it lift its hind-legs for joy, and spring away over a hedge and ditch into a field.

But the Tailor had eaten nothing since the previous day, and he thought to himself, "The sun certainly fills my eyes, but the bread does not fill my mouth. The first thing which meets me now must suffer, if it be at all eatable." Just then a Stork came walking very seriously over the meadow. "Stop, stop!" cried the Tailor, catching it by the leg, "I don't know if you are fit to eat, but my hunger will not admit of choice; so I must chop off your head and roast you." "Do it not," answered the Stork; "I am a sacred bird, to whom nobody offers an injury, and I bring great profit to man. Leave me alone, and then I can recompense you at some future time." "Be off, Cousin Longlegs," said the Tailor; and the Stork, raising itself from the ground, flew gracefully away, with its long legs hanging downwards. "What will come of this?" said the Tailor to himself; "my hunger grows ever stronger, and my stomach yet more empty: what next crosses my path is lost." As he spoke he saw a pair of young Ducks swimming upon a pond. "You have come just when you were called," cried he, and, seizing one by the neck, he was about to twist it round, when an old bird, which was hid among the reeds, began to quack loudly, and swam with open bill up to the Tailor, begging him pitifully to spare her dear child. "Think what your poor mother would say if one fetched you away and put an end to your life!" "Be quiet!" replied the good-natured Tailor, "you shall have your child again;" and he put the prisoner back into the water.

As soon as he turned round again he perceived the old hollow tree, and the wild bees flying in and out. "Here at last I shall find the reward of my good deed," said the Tailor; "the honey will refresh me." But scarcely had he spoken when the Queen Bee flew out, and thus addressed him, "If you touch my people, and disturb my nest, out stings shall pierce your skin like ten thousand red-hot needles. Leave us in peace and go your own way, and perhaps at a future time you shall receive a reward for it."

The Tailor perceived at once that nothing was to be had there. "Three empty dishes and nothing in the fourth is a bad meal," thought he to himself; and, trudging on, he soon got into the city, where, as it was about noon, he found a dinner ready cooked in the inn, and gladly sat down to table. When he was satisfied he determined to go and seek work, and, as he walked around the city, he soon found a master, who gave him a good welcome. Since, however, he knew his business thoroughly, it very soon happened that he became quite famed, and everybody would have his new coat made by the little Tailor. Every day added to his consequence, and he said to himself, "I can get no higher in my art, and yet every day trade gets brisker." At length he was appointed court tailor.

But how things do turn out! The same day his former comrade

was made court shoemaker; and when he saw the Tailor, and remarked that his eyes were as bright and good as ever, his conscience pricked him. But he thought to himself, "Before he revenges himself on me I must lay a snare for him." Now, he who digs a pit for another often falls into it himself. In the evening, when the Shoemaker had left off work, and it was become quite dark, he slipped up to the King, and whispered, "May it please your Majesty, this Tailor is a high-minded fellow and has boasted that he can procure again the crown which has been lost so long."

"That would please me much!" replied the King; "but let the Tailor come here to-morrow." When he came the King ordered him to find the crown again, or to leave the city for ever. "Oho! oho!" thought the Tailor; "a rogue gives more than he has. If the crusty old King desires from me what no man can produce, I will not wait till morning, but this very day make my escape out of the town." So thinking he tied together his bundle, and marched out of the gate; but it grieved him sorely to give up his business, and to turn his back upon the city wherein he had been so fortunate. Soon he came to the pond where he had made acquaintance with the ducks, and there sat the old one whose children he had spared by the shore, pluming herself with her bill. She recognised him, and asked why he hung his head so. "You will not wonder," he replied, "when you hear what has happened;" and he told her his story. "If that be all," said the Duck, "we can assist you. The crown has fallen into the water, and lies at the bottom, whence we will soon fetch it. Meanwhile spread your handkerchief out on the shore." With these words the Duck dived down with her twelve young ones, and in five minutes they were up again, carrying the crown, which, resting on the old bird's wings, was borne up by the bills of the twelve ducklings who swam around. They came to the shore and laid the crown on the handkerchief. You could not believe how beautiful it was; for when the sun shone on it it glittered like a hundred carbuncles. The Tailor tied it up in his handkerchief and carried it to the King, who was so much pleased, that he gave its finder a chain of gold to hang round his neck.

When the Shoemaker found his first plan had failed he contrived a second, and, stepping before the King, said, "May it please your Majesty, the Tailor has grown so high-minded again, he boasts he can model in wax the whole castle, and all that is in it, fixed and unfixed, indoors and outdoors." The King thereupon caused the Tailor to be summoned, and ordered him to model in wax the whole castle, and everything inside and outside; and if he did not complete it, or even omitted one nail upon the wall, he should be kept prisoner underground all his lifetime. The Tailor thought to himself, "It comes harder and harder upon me; no man can do that!" and, throwing his bundle over his shoulder, he walked out at the gate. When he came to the hollow tree he sat down and hung his head in despair. The Bees came flying out, and the Queen asked if he had a stiff neck, because he kept his head in such a position. "Oh, no!" he replied: "something else oppresses me!" and he related what the King had demanded of him. The Bees, thereupon, began to hum and buzz together, and the Queen said to the Tailor, "Go home now, but return in the morning, and bring a great napkin with you, and about this hour all will be ready." So he returned home, and the Bees flew to the Royal Palace, right in at the open window, crept into every corner, and observed all the things in the most minute manner. Then they flew back and formed a castle in wax with great speed, so that it was ready by the evening. The next morning the Tailor came, and there stood the whole beautiful building, with not a nail upon the wall, or a tile upon the roof omitted, but all was delicately white, and moreover, as sweet as sugar. The Tailor wrapped it carefully in his cloth and took it to the King, who could not sufficiently admire it, and gave him a house made of stone as a reward.

The Shoemaker, however, was not satisfied, and went again to the King, and said, "May it please your Majesty, it has come to the ears of the Tailor that no water springs in the castle-yard; and he has, therefore, boasted that it shall gush up in the middle clear as crystal." The King ordered the Tailor to be summoned, and told him that if a stream of water was not running the following morning, as he had said, the executioner should make him a head shorter in that very court. The poor Tailor did not think very long, but rushed out of the gate, and, as he remembered his life was in danger, tears rolled down his cheeks. Whilst he sat thus, full of grief, the Filly came jumping towards him, to which he had once given liberty, and which had become a fine brown horse. "Now is the hour come," it said to the Tailor, "when I can reward your kindness. I know already what you need, and will soon assist you; but now sit upon my back, which could carry two like you." The Tailor's heart came again, and he vaulted into the saddle, and the horse carried him full speed into the town, and straight to the castle yard. There it coursed thrice round as quick as lightning, and at the third time fell down. At the same moment a fearful noise was heard, and a piece out of the ground of the court sprang up into the air like a ball, and bounded away far over the Castle; and at the same time a stream of water, as high as the man and his horse, and as clear as crystal, played up and down like a fountain, and the sunbeams danced on it. As soon as the King saw this he was astounded, and went up and embraced the Tailor before all his court.

But this fortune did not last long. The King had daughters enough, and each one prettier than the other, but no son at all.

Now the wicked Shoemaker went for the fourth time to the King, and said, "May it please your Majesty, the Tailor is as high-minded as ever. Now he has boasted that, if he might, he could bring the King a son down from the air." Thereupon the King ordered the Tailor to be summoned, and said, "If you bring me a son within nine days, you shall have my eldest daughter as a wife." "The reward is immense," thought the Tailor; "and one may as well have it as another; but now the cherries hang too high for me, and if I climb after them the branches will break beneath me, and I shall fall down." So thinking, he went home, set himself with his legs crossed under him upon his work-table, and considered what he should do. "It is of no use," he cried at length; "I must be off, I cannot rest in peace here!" So he tied up his bundle and hurried out of the door; but just as he arrived upon the meadow, he perceived his old friend the Stork, who, like a world-wise man, walked up and down, a while stood still, and considered a frog nearer, and at length snapped it up. The Stork came up and greeted him. "I see," said it, "you have your bundle upon your back; why have you left the city?" The Tailor told the Stork what the King had commanded of him, and how, as he could not do it, he was grieving at his ill-luck. "Do not let your grey hairs grow on that account!" replied the Stork, "I will assist you out of your trouble! Sometimes already I have brought infants into the city; and I can also fetch a little prince out of the spring. Go home and keep quiet. In nine days return to the Royal Palace, and I will come thither also."

The Tailor went home, and on the right day went to the Palace. In a short time the Stork came flying through the air, and knocked at the window. The Tailor opened it, and cousin Longlegs marched gravely in, and, with stately steps, passed over the marble floors, carrying in his beak a child, as beautiful to look at as an angel, and already stretching out his hands towards the Queen. The Stork laid it upon her lap, and she embraced and kissed it, almost beside herself with joy. Before he flew away, he took a knapsack off his shoulder and handed it to the Queen; and therein were dates and coloured bonbons, which were divided among the Princesses. But the eldest received none, because she took instead the merry young Tailor as husband. "It seems to me," said the Tailor, "as if I had won a great game. My mother rightly said, 'He who trusts in God and his own fortune, will never go amiss.' "

The Shoemaker had to make the shoes in which the Tailor danced at the wedding, and as soon as he had done them he was ordered to leave the city. The road from thence to the forest led him past the gallows; and, from rage, disappointment, and weariness with the heat of the day, he threw himself on the ground beneath it. As soon as he had closed his eyes and prepared to go to sleep, the two Crows flew down from the heads of the two criminals, and with loud cries pecked out the Shoemaker's eyes. Insane with rage and pain he ran into the forest, and there he must have perished; for nobody has seen or heard anything of the wicked Shoemaker since.

The Spirit in the Bottle

THERE was once upon a time a poor Woodcutter who worked from morning till quite late at night, and after doing so for a very long time he managed to save some money, and said to his Son, "You are my only child, and so this money, which I have earned by the hard sweat of my brow, shall be spent on your education. Do you learn something useful whereby you may support me in my old age, when my limbs become so stiff that I am obliged to sit still at home."

Thereupon the son went to a great school, and was very industrious, so that he became much noticed for it; and there he remained a long time. After he had gone through a long course of study, but still had not learnt all that was to be learnt, the store of money which his Father had earned was exhausted, and he was obliged to return home again.

"Ah! I can give you no more," said the Father, sadly, "for in these dear times I can scarcely earn enough for my daily bread."

"Make yourself easy on that point, my dear Father," replied the Son, "if it is God's will, be sure it is all for the best: I will suit myself to the times."

Afterwards, when the Father was about to go to the forest to earn something by chopping and clearing, his Son said, "I will accompany you and help you." "Ah, but, my son," said the Father, "that will be a hard matter for you, who have never been used to such hard work; you must not attempt it; besides, I have only one axe, and no money either to buy another."

"Go, then, and ask your neighbour to lend you one, till I shall have earned enough to buy one for myself," replied the Son.

So the Father borrowed an axe of his neighbour, and the next morning, at break of day, they went together to the forest. The Son assisted his Father, and was very lively and merry over his work, and about noon, when the sun stood right over their heads, the Father proposed to rest for a while, and eat their dinner, and then, after that, they would be able to work all the better. The Son, however, taking his share of bread, said, "Do you rest here, Father; I am not tired; and I will go a little way into the forest, and look for birds' nests."

"Oh, you silly fellow!" said the Father, "what do you want to run about for? You will make yourself so tired, you will not be able to raise your arm: keep quiet a bit and sit down here with me."

But the young man would not do so, but went off among the trees, eating his bread, and peeping about among the bushes for any nest he could find. To and fro he walked a long way, and presently came to an immense oak-tree, which was certainly many hundred years old, and could not have been spanned round by any five men. He stopped still to look at this tree, thinking that many a bird's nest must be built within it, and while he did so he suddenly heard, as he thought, a voice. He listened, and soon heard again a half-smothered cry of "Let me out! let me out!" He looked around, but could see nothing; still the voice appeared to come, as it were, from the ground. So he called, "Where are you?" and the Voice replied, "Here I stick, among the roots of the oak-tree: let me out! let me out!" The Scholar, therefore, began to search at the foot of the tree, where the roots spread, and at last, in a little hollow, he found a glass bottle. He picked it up, and, holding it to the light, he perceived a thing, in shape like a frog, which kept jumping up and down. "Let me out! let me out!" cried the thing again; and the Scholar, thinking no evil, drew out the stopper of the bottle. Immediately a Spirit sprang out, and began to grow and grow so fast, that in a very few moments he stood before the Scholar like a frightful giant, half the size of the tree. "Do you know," he cried, with a voice like thunder, "do you know what your reward is for letting me out of the glass bottle?"

"No," replied the Scholar, without fear; "how should I?"

"Then I will tell you," cried the Spirit: "I must break your neck!"

"You should have told me that before," returned the Scholar, "and then you should have stuck where you were; but my head will stick on my shoulders in spite of you, for there are several people's opinions to be asked yet about that matter."

"Keep your people out of my way," rejoined the Spirit, "but your deserved reward you must receive. Do you suppose I have been shut up so long out of mercy? No; it was for my punishment: I am the mighty Mercury, and whoever lets me out, his neck must I break."

"Softly, softly!" said the Scholar, "that is quicker said than done; I must first know really that you were in the bottle, and that you are truly a spirit; if I see you return into the bottle, I will believe, and then you may do with me what you please."

Full of pride, the Spirit answered, "That is an easy matter;" and drawing himself together, he became as thin as he had been at first, and soon crept through the same opening back again into the bottle. Scarcely was he completely in when the Scholar put the stopper back into the neck, and threw the bottle down among the oak tree roots at the old place. So the Spirit was deceived.

After this the Scholar would have gone back to his Father, but the Spirit cried lamentably, "Oh, let me out! do let me out!"

"No," replied the Scholar, "not a second time: he who tried to take away my life once, I shall not let out in a hurry, when I have got him safe again."

"If you will free me," pleaded the Spirit, "I will give you as much as will serve you for your lifetime."

"No, no!" rejoined the Scholar, "you will deceive me as you did at first."

"You are fighting against your own fortune," replied the Spirit; "I will do you no harm, but reward you richly."

"Well, I will hazard it," thought the Scholar to himself; "perhaps he will keep his word, and do me no injury;" and, so thinking, he took the stopper out of the bottle again, and the Spirit sprang out as before, stretched himself up, and became as big as a giant.

"Now you shall have your reward," said the Spirit, reaching the Scholar a little piece of rag in shape like a plaster. "If you apply one end of this to a wound it shall heal directly, and if you touch with the other steel or iron, either will be changed into silver."

"That I must try first," said the Scholar; and, going to a tree, he tore off a piece of the bark with his axe, and then touched it with the one end of the rag, and immediately the wound closed up as if nothing had been done. "Now it is all right," said the Scholar, "now we can separate." Then the Spirit thanked him for releasing him, and the Scholar thanked the Spirit for his present, and went back to his Father.

"Where have you been roaming to?" asked the father; "why, you have quite forgotten your work. I said rightly that you would do nothing of this kind well."

"Be contented, Father; I will make up the time," said the Son.

"Yes, you will make it up, truly," broke in the Father, angrily, "without an axe!"

"Now see, father, I will cut down that tree at one blow!" and, so saying, the son took his rag, rubbed the axe with it, and gave a powerful blow, but because the axe was changed into silver the edge turned up. "Ah, father, do you see what an axe you have given me! it has no edge at all!" said the Son.

The Father was frightened, and said, "Ah! what have you done? Now I must pay for the axe, and I know not how; for it is the one which I borrowed for your work."

"Don't be angry; I will soon pay for the axe," said the Son; but the Father exclaimed, "Why, you simpleton, how will you do that? you have nothing but what I give you: this is some student's trick which is stuck in your head, but of wood-cutting you know nothing at all!"

After a pause, the Scholar said, "Father, I can work no more; let us make holiday now."

"Eh? what?" was the answer; "do you think I can keep my hands in my pockets as you do? I must get on, but you may go home." The Son replied, he did not know the way, as it was his first time of being in the forest, and at last he persuaded his Father to accompany him home, his wrath being passed away. When they arrived at their house, the Father told his Son to go and sell the axe which was damaged, and the rest he must earn in order to pay his neighbour for it. So the Son took the axe, and carried it to a Goldsmith in the city, who, after proving it, laid it in his scales, and said, "It is worth four hundred dollars, and so much I have not by me in the house."

"Give me what you have," said the Scholar, "and I will trust you the remainder." The Goldsmith gave him three hundred dollars and left the other as a debt, and thereupon the Scholar went home, and said to his Father, "Go, ask the neighbour what he will have for his axe; for I have got some money."

"I know already," answered the Father; "one dollar six groschen is the price."

"Then give him two dollars and twelve groschen; that it double, and enough: see, here, I have money in abundance!" and he gave his Father one hundred dollars, saying, "You shall never want now! live at your ease."

"My goodness!" said the man, "where have you procured this money?"

The Son told his Father all that had happened, and how he had made such a capital catch by trusting his luck. With the rest of the money, however, he returned to the university, and learnt all that he could; and afterwards, because he could heal all wounds with his plaster he became the most celebrated surgeon in the whole world.

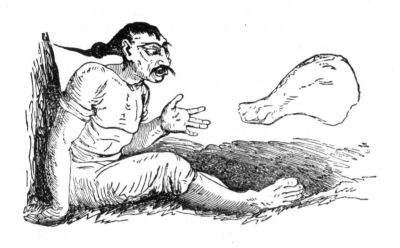

The Experienced Huntsman

THERE was once upon a time a young Lad, who, after he had learnt the trade of a locksmith, told his Father he wished to go and seek his fortune in the world. "Well," said the Father, "very well, I am content;" and gave him money for the journey. So he set off, looking about for work; but after a while he determined to follow his trade no longer, for he had got tired of it, and wished to learn the art of hunting. While he was in this mood he met a Huntsman, dressed in green, who asked him whence he came, and whither he would go. The Youth told him he was a locksmith, but his business did not suit him any longer, and he had a wish to learn how to shoot, if he would take him as a pupil. "Oh, yes!" replied the other, "come with me." The Youth accompanied him, and for several years abode with him while he learnt the art of hunting. Afterwards he wished to leave, but the Huntsman gave him no further reward than an air-gun, which had the property of missing nothing at which it was fired. With this gift he went off, and by-and-by came to a very large forest, to which he could find no end the first day, so he perched himself upon a lofty tree where the wild beasts could not reach him. Towards midnight it seemed to him that a light was glimmering at a distance, and he peeped through the boughs in order to mark more exactly where it was. Then, taking his hat he threw it in that direction that it might serve as a guide for him when he had descended the tree; and as soon as he was down, he ran after his hat, and, putting it on again, he walked straight ahead. The further he went the larger the light appeared; and when he came nearly up to it, he discovered that it was caused by a great fire, round which three Giants were sitting, watching the roasting of an ox, which hung on a spit above it. Just at that moment one of the Giants said he would taste and see if the meat were done enough; and, tearing a piece off, he was going to put it into his mouth, when the Huntsman shot it clean out of his hand. "Now, then," cried the Giant, "the wind blows the meat out of my hand!" And, taking another piece, he was about to bite it when the Huntsman shot that out of his hand. Thereupon he gave the Giant next to him a box on the ear, saying angrily, "Why do you snatch my piece away?" "I did not take it away," replied the other; "it was some sharpshooter who shot it away." So the Giant took a third piece, but that also he could not hold, for the Huntsman shot it away. "This must be a good shot," cried all the Giants; "a man who can shoot away the food from one's mouth would be very useful to us." And then, speaking louder they called to him, "Come, you sharpshooter, sit down by our fire, and eat till you are satisfied, and we will do you no harm; but if you don't come, and we have to fetch you, you will be lost."

At these words, the Huntsman stepped up to the fire, and said he was an experienced Huntsman, so much so, that whatever he aimed at, he shot, without ever missing. The Giants said, that if he would go with them he should be well treated; and they told him, besides, that out of the forest there was a large piece of water, on the other side of which was a tower, wherein dwelt a beautiful Princess, whom

THE EXPERIENCED HUNTSMAN

they desired to possess. The Huntsman said he would willingly fetch her; and they further told him, that outside the tower lay a little dog, which would begin to bark as soon as it saw any one approach, and immediately it did so, everybody would wake up in the royal palace; and it was on that account they had never been able to enter, and therefore he must first shoot the dog. To this the Huntsman assented, declaring it was mere play; and soon afterwards he went on board a ship, and sailed over the water; and, as he neared the land, the little dog came running down and would have barked, but he, aiming with his air-gun, shot it dead. As soon as the Giants saw this done, they were very glad, and thought they had the Princess for certain; but the Huntsman told them to remain where they were until he called them, for he must see how it was to be accomplished. He went into the castle, and found everybody as still as mice, for they were fast asleep; and as he entered the first room he saw a sabre hanging up made of pure silver, and ornamented with a golden star and the King's name. Below it stood a table, whereon laid a sealed letter, which he broke open, and read that whoever possessed the sabre could bring to life whomever it passed. The Huntsman took the sabre down from the wall, and, hanging it around him, walked on till he came to a room where the King's daughter lay asleep. She was so beautiful that he stood still and looked at her, holding his breath while he thought, "How dare I deliver this innocent maiden into the power of these Giants, with their evil intentions?" He peeped about, and under the bed espied a pair of slippers; on the right one was marked the King's name with a star, and on the left his Daughter's, also with a star. She had also a large handkerchief over her, woven of silk and gold, having on the right side her father's name, and on the left her own, all done in golden threads. So the Huntsman took a knife and cut off the right corner, and then he took the slipper with the King's name in it, and put them both in his knapsack. All the while the Princess remained quite passive; and, as she was wrapped up in a sheet, the Huntsman cut off a piece of that, as well as the handkerchief, and put it in his knapsack with the others. All these things he did without touching her, and afterwards went away without noise. When he got outside he found the three Giants who were waiting in expectation that he would bring the Princess with him. He shouted to them to come in, for the Maiden was already in his power, but he could not open the door, and therefore they must creep through a hole which was in the wall. The first Giant came, and, as soon as he poked his head through the hole, the Huntsman seized him by the hair, and chopped his head off with the sabre. Then he pulled the body through, and called to the second, whose head he chopped off likewise, and then the third Giant shared the same fate. As soon as this was done he cut out the tongue of each and put it in his knapsack, rejoicing to think he had freed the Princess from her enemies. He resolved next to visit his Father, and show him what he had done, and afterwards to travel again about the world; "for," said he "the fortune which God apportions to me will reach me anywhere!"

Meanwhile the King of the castle, when he awoke, had perceived the three Giants lying dead in the hall, and, going into his daughter's apartment, he awoke her, and inquired who it was that had destroyed the Giants. "I know not, dear father," she replied; "I have been sleeping." But when she arose, and wished to put on her slippers, she found the one for the right foot missing; and her handkerchief also wanted the right-hand corner, which had been cut off, as well as a piece out of the sheet. The King thereupon caused the whole court to be assembled, soldiers and every one, and then put the question, who had freed his daughter, and put to death the Giants? Now, the King had a captain, a one-eyed and ugly man, who said he had done it. The old King, therefore, declared that, since it was he, he must marry the Princess. But as soon as he said so the Princess exclaimed, "Rather than marry him, dear father, I will wander over the world as far as my feet will carry me!" The King replied she might do as she pleased; but if she would not marry the man she must take off her royal clothes, and put on peasant's clothes to travel in, and, also, she must go to a potter and begin business in the earthenware trade. So the King's daughter drew off her royal clothes, and went to a potter, from whom she hired a crate of earthenware, and promised that if she had sold them by the evening she would pay for them. The King commanded her to sit at a certain corner of the market, across which he ordered that several waggons should be driven, so as to crush in pieces all the crockery. By-and-by, therefore, when the Princess had stationed herself in the appointed place, the waggons came driving past, and smashed her goods. Thereupon she began to cry, saying, "Ah, heaven! how am I to pay the potter?" But the King hoped by this means to have compelled his daughter to marry the captain: instead of which she went to the potter and asked if he would trust her with another crate. He refused till she should pay for the former one; and so the Princess was forced to go crying and groaning to her father, that she wished to wander into the wide world. The King said, "I will cause a cottage to be built in the middle of the wood, wherein you shall sit all your lifetime, and cook for anybody who comes, but without taking money for it." When the house was ready, a sign was hung over the door, on which was inscribed —

"Gratis to-day: To-morrow, payment."

There she sat for a long time, while it was talked about in the world around, that a maiden sat in a cottage in the wood, and cooked gratis, as was stated on a sign over the door. This the Huntsman heard, and he thought to himself, "This is good news for me, who am so poor, and have no money." So he took his air-gun and knapsack, in which he kept all the memorials he had brought away from the castle; and, going into the forest, came soon to the cottage where was written up —

"Gratis to-day: To-morrow, payment."

Now, he had the sword buckled round him which he had used to execute the three Giants; and he stepped into the cottage and ordered something to eat. The Princess asked him whence he came and whither he was going; and he replied, "I am wandering about the world." She asked next where he procured his sword, on which she perceived her father's name. "Are you the daughter of the King?" he inquired; and, as she nodded assent, he said, "With this sword I have cut off the heads of three Giants!" and he held up the three tongues for a token, together with the slipper, and the pieces which he had cut off the handkerchief and sheet. The Princess was glad indeed to see these things, and told the Huntsman it was he who had saved her. Then they went to the King; and the Princess led him to her chamber, and declared that it was the Huntsman who had delivered her from the three Giants. The King at first would not believe; but as soon as he was shown the tokens he could no longer doubt; and, in order to show his pleasure and his gratitude, he promised his daughter to the Huntsman as his wife, which pleased the Princess very much. Afterwards the King ordered a grand banquet, whereat the Huntsman appeared as a distinguished stranger. When they sat down to table, the Captain took his place on the left hand of the King's Daughter, and the Huntsman, whom the former believed to be a visitor of rank, on the right. When they had finished eating and drinking, the old King told the Captain he would propound a question, which he must answer, and it was this: "If one should say he had killed three Giants, and was asked, therefore, where the tongues of the Giants were, and should then go to seek them and find none, how would he explain that?" "By saying that they had none!" replied the Captain. "Not so!" said the King; "every creature has a tongue; therefore, what should such a one deserve for his answer?" "To be torn in pieces!" said the Captain boldly.

"You have pronounced your own sentence!" said the King to the Captain; who was first imprisoned, and afterwards torn in four pieces. But the Huntsman was married to the King's daughter; and, after the wedding, he invited his father and mother to live with him; and, after the old King's death, the Huntsman ascended the throne.

Bearskin

THERE was once upon a time a young fellow who enlisted for a soldier, and became so brave and courageous that he was always in the front ranks when it rained blue beans.* As long as the war lasted all went well, but when peace was concluded he received his discharge, and the captain told him he might go where he liked. His parents meanwhile had died, and as he had no longer any home to go to he paid a visit to his brothers, and asked them to give him shelter until war broke out again. His brothers, however, were hard-hearted, and said, "What could we do with you? we could make nothing of you; see to what you have brought yourself;" and so turned a deaf ear. The poor Soldier had nothing but his musket left; so he mounted this on his shoulder and set out on tramp. By-and-by

* Small shot

he came to a great heath with nothing on it but a circle of trees, under which he sat down, sorrowfully considering his fate. "I have no money," thought he; "I have learnt nothing but soldiering, and now, since peace is concluded, there is no need of me. I see well enough I shall have to starve." All at once he heard a rustling, and as he looked round he perceived a stranger standing before him, dressed in a grey coat, who looked very stately, but had an ugly cloven foot. "I know quite well what you need," said this being; "gold and other possessions you shall have, as much as you can spend; but first I must know whether you are a coward or not, that I may not spend my money foolishly."

"A soldier and a coward!" replied the other, "that cannot be; you may put me to any proof."

"Well, then," replied the stranger, "look behind you."

The Soldier turned and saw a huge bear, which eyed him very ferociously. "Oho!" cried he, "I will tickle your nose for you, that you shall no longer be able to grumble;" and, raising his musket, he shot the bear in the forehead, so that he tumbled in a heap upon the ground, and did not stir afterwards. Thereupon the stranger said, "I see quite well that you are not wanting in courage; but there is yet one condition which you must fulfil." "If it does not interfere with my future happiness," said the Soldier, who had remarked who it was that addressed him; "if it does not interfere with that, I shall not hesitate."

"That you must see about yourself!" said the stranger. "For the next seven years you must not wash yourself, nor comb your hair or beard, neither must you cut your nails nor say one pater-noster. Then I will give you this coat and mantle, which you must wear during these seven years; and if you die within that time you are mine, but if you live you are rich, and free all your life long."

The Soldier reflected for a while on his great necessities, and, remembering how often he had braved death, he at length consented, and ventured to accept the offer. Thereupon the Evil One pulled off the grey coat, handed it to the soldier, and said, "If you at any time search in the pocket of your coat when you have it on, you will always find your hand full of money." Then also he pulled off the skin of the bear, and said, "That shall be your cloak and your bed; you must sleep on it, and not dare to lie in any other bed, and on this account you shall be called Bearskin." Immediately the Evil One disappeared.

The Soldier now put on the coat, and dipped his hands into the pockets, to assure himself of the reality of the transaction. Then he hung the bearskin around himself, and went about the world chuckling at his good luck, and buying whatever suited his fancy which money could purchase. For the first year his appearance was not very remarkable, but in the second he began to look quite a monster. His hair covered almost all his face, his beard appeared like a piece of dirty cloth, his nails were claws, and his countenance was so covered with dirt that one might have grown cresses upon it if one had sown seed! Whoever looked at him ran away; but, because he gave the poor in every place gold coin, they prayed that he might not die during the seven years; and, because he paid liberally everywhere, he found a night's lodging without difficulty. In the fourth year he came to an inn where the landlord would not take him in, and refused even to give him a place in his stables, lest the horses should be frightened and become restive. However, when Bearskin put his hand into his pocket and drew it out full of gold ducats the landlord yielded the point, and gave him a place in the outbuildings, but not till he had promised that he would not show himself, for fear the inn should gain a bad name.

While Bearskin sat by himself in the evening, wishing for his heart that the seven years were over, he heard in the corner a loud groan. Now, the old Soldier had a compassionate heart, so he opened the door and saw an old man weeping violently and wringing his hands. Bearskin stepped nearer, but the old man jumped up and tried to escape; but when he recognised a human voice he let himself be persuaded, and by kind words and soothings on the part of the old Soldier he at length disclosed the cause of his distress. His property had dwindled away by degrees, and he and his daughters would have to starve, for he was so poor that he had not the money to pay the host, and would therefore be put into prison.

"If you have no care except that," replied Bearskin, "I have money enough;" and, causing the landlord to be called, he paid him, and put a purse full of gold besides into the pocket of the old man. The latter, when he saw himself released from his troubles, knew not how to be sufficiently grateful, and said to the Soldier, "Come with me, my daughters are all wonders of beauty, so choose one of them for a wife. When they hear what you have done for me they will not refuse you. You appear certainly an uncommon man, but they will soon put you to rights."

This speech pleased Bearskin, and he went with the old man. As soon as the eldest daughter saw him, she was so terrified at his countenance that she shrieked out and ran away. The second one stopped and looked at him from head to foot; but at last she said, "How can I take a husband who has not a bit of human countenance? The grizzly bear would have pleased me better who came to see us once, and gave himself out as a man, for he wore a hussar's hat, and had white gloves on besides."

But the youngest daughter said, "Dear father, this must be a good man who has assisted you out of your troubles; if you have promised him a bride for the service your word must be kept."

It was a pity the man's face was covered with dirt and hair, else one would have seen how glad at heart these words made him. Bearskin took a ring off his finger, broke it in two, and, giving the youngest daughter one half, he kept the other for himself. On her half he wrote his name, and on his own he wrote hers, and begged her to preserve it carefully. Thereupon he took leave, saying, "For three years longer I must wander about; if I come back again, then we will celebrate out wedding; but if I do not, you are free, for I shall be dead. But pray to God that he will preserve my life."

When he was gone the poor bride clothed herself in black, and whenever she thought of her bridegroom burst into tears. From her sisters she received nothing but scorn and mocking. "Pay great attention when he shakes your hand," said the eldest, "and you will see his beautiful claws!" "Take care!" said the second, "bears are fond of sweets, and if you please him he will eat you up, perhaps!" "You must mind and do his will," continued the eldest, "or he will begin growling!" And the second daughter said further, "But the wedding will certainly be merry, for bears dance well!" The bride kept silence, and would not be drawn from her purpose by all these taunts; and meanwhile Bearskin wandered about in the world, doing good where he could, and giving liberally to the poor, for which they prayed heartily for him. At length the last day of the seven years approached, and Bearskin went and sat down again on the heath, beneath the circle of trees. In a very short time the wind whistled, and the Evil One presently stood before him and looked at him with a vexed face. He threw the Soldier his old coat and demanded his grey one back. "We have not got so far as that yet," replied Bearskin; "you must clean me first." Then the Evil One had, whether he liked it or no, to fetch water, wash the old Soldier, comb his hair out, and cut his nails. This done, he appeared again like a brave warrior, and indeed was much handsomer than before.

As soon as the Evil One had disappeared, Bearskin became quite light-hearted; and going into the nearest town he bought a fine velvet coat, and hired a carriage drawn by four white horses, in which he was driven to the house of his bride. Nobody knew him; the father took him for some celebrated general, and led him into the room where his daughters were. He was compelled to sit down between the two eldest, and they offered him wine, and heaped his plate with the choicest morsels; for they thought they had never seen any one so handsome before. But the bride sat opposite to him dressed in black, neither opening her eyes nor speaking a word. At length the Soldier asked the father if he would give him one of his daughters to wife, and immediately the two elder sisters arose, and ran to their chambers to dress themselves out in their most becoming clothes, for each thought she should be chosen. Meanwhile the stranger, as soon as he found himself alone with his bride, pulled out the half of the ring and threw it into a cup of wine, which he handed across the table. She took it, and as soon as she had drunk it and seen the half ring lying at the bottom her heart beat rapidly, and she produced the other half, which she wore round her neck on a riband. She held them together, and they joined each other exactly, and the stranger said, "I am your bridegroom, whom you first saw as Bearskin; but through God's mercy I have regained my human form, and am myself once more." With these words he embraced and kissed her; and at the same time the two eldest sisters entered in full costume. As soon as they saw that the very handsome man had fallen to the share of their youngest sister, and heard that he was the same as "Bearskin," they ran out of the house full of rage and jealousy.

The Wren and the Bear

ONE summer's day the Bear and the Wolf were walking in the forest, and the Bear heard a bird singing very sweetly, and said, "Brother Wolf, what kind of bird is that which is singing so delightfully?"

"That is the King of the birds, before whom we must do reverence," replied the Wolf; but it was only the Wren.

"If that be so," said the Bear, "I should like to see his royal palace; come, lead me to it." "That cannot be as you like," replied the Wolf, "you must wait till the Queen returns." Soon afterwards the Queen arrived with some food in her bill, and the King too, to feed their young ones, and the Bear would have gone off to see them, but the Wolf, pulling his ear, said, "No, you must wait till the Queen and the King are both off again."

So after observing well the situation of the nest the two tramped off, but the Bear had no rest, for he wished still to see the royal palace, and after a short delay he set off to it again. He found the King and Queen absent, and, peeping into the nest, he saw five or six young birds lying in it. "Is that the royal palace?" exclaimed the Bear; "that is a miserable palace! you are no King's children, but dishonourable young brats." "No, no, that we are not!" burst out the little Wrens together in a great passion, for to them this speech was addressed. "No, no, we are born of honourable parents, and you, Mr Bear, shall make your words good!" At this speech the Bear and the Wolf were much frightened and ran back to their holes; but the little Wrens kept up an unceasing clamour till their parents' return. As soon as they came back with food in their mouths the little birds began, "We will none of us touch a fly's leg, but will starve rather, until you decide whether we are honourable children or not, for the Bear has been here and insulted us!"

"Be quiet," replied the King, "and that shall soon be settled;" and thereupon he flew with his Queen to the residence of the Bear, and called to him from the entrance, "Old grumbler, why have you insulted my children? That shall cost you dear, for we will decide the matter by a pitched battle."

War having thus been declared against the Bear, all the four-footed beasts were summoned, the ox, the ass, the cow, the goat, the stag, and every animal on the face of the earth. The Wren, on the other hand, summoned every flying thing; not only the birds, great and small, but also the gnat, the hornet, the bee, and the flies.

When the time arrived for the commencement of the war, the Wren King sent out spies to see who was appointed commander-in-chief of the enemy. The Gnat was the most cunning of all the army, and he therefore buzzed away into the forest where the enemy was encamped, and alighted on a leaf of the tree beneath which the watchword was given out. There stood the Bear and called the Fox to him, and said, "You are the most crafty of animals, so you must be general, and lead us on." "Well," said the Fox, "but what sign shall we appoint?" Nobody knew. Then the Fox said, "I have a fine long bushy tail, which looks like a red feather at a distance; if I hold this tail straight up all is going well and you must march after me; but if I suffer it to hang down, run away as fast as you can." As soon as the Gnat heard all this she flew home and told the Wren King everything to a hair.

When the day arrived for the battle to begin, the four-footed beasts all came running along to the field, shaking the earth with their roaring and bellowing. The Wren King also came with his army, whirring and buzzing and humming, enough to terrify any one out of his senses. Then the Wren King sent the Hornet forward to settle upon the Fox's tail and sting it with all his power. As soon as the Fox felt the first sting he drew up his hind-leg with the pain, still carrying, however, his tail as high in the air as before; at the second sting he was obliged to drop it a little bit; but at the third he could no longer bear the pain, but was forced to drop his tail between his legs. As soon as the other Beasts saw this, they thought all was lost, and began to run each one to his own hole; so the Birds won the battle without difficulty.

When all was over the Wren King and the Queen flew home to their children, and cried out, "Rejoice! rejoice! we have won the battle; now eat and drink as much as you please."

The young Wrens, however, said, "Still we will not eat till the Bear has come to our nest and begged pardon, and admitted that we are honourable children."

So the Wren King flew back to the cave of the Bear, and called out, "Old grumbler, you must come to the nest and beg pardon of my children for calling them dishonourable, else your ribs shall be crushed in your body!"

In great terror the Bear crept out and begged pardon, and afterwards the young Wrens, being now made happy in their minds, settled down to eating and drinking; and I am afraid they made themselves tipsy, for they kept up their merriment till it was very late.

The Sweet Soup

ONCE upon a time there was a poor but pious little Girl, who lived alone with her mother, and when my story begins they had nothing in the house to eat. So the child went out into the forest, and there she met with an old Woman, who already knew her distress, and who presented her with a pot which had this power: – if one said to it, "Boil, little pot!" it would cook sweet soup; and when one said, "Stop, little pot!" it would immediately cease to boil. The little Girl took the pot home to her mother, and now their poverty and distresses were at an end, for they could have sweet broth as often as they pleased. One day, however, the little girl went out, and in her absence the mother said, "Boil, little pot!" So it began to cook, and she soon ate all she wished; but when she wanted to have the pot stop, she found she did not know the word. Away, therefore, the pot boiled and very quickly was over the edge; and as it boiled and boiled the kitchen presently became full, then the house, and the next house, and soon the whole street. It seemed likely to satisfy all the world, for, though there was the greatest necessity to do so, nobody knew how to stop it. At last, when only a very small cottage of all the village was left unfilled with soup, the child returned, and said at once, "Stop, little pot!" Immediately it ceased to boil; but whoever wishes to enter the village must eat his way through the soup!!!

The Faithful Beasts

THERE was once a Man who had not a great deal of money, but with the little he had he wandered into the wide world. Soon he came to a village where the boys were running together screaming and laughing, and he asked them what was the matter. "Oh!" replied they, "we have got a mouse which we are going to teach to dance: only see what a beautiful sport it is; how it will skip round!" The Man, however, pitied the poor Mouse, and said, "Let it escape, my boys, and I will give you money." So he gave them some coppers, and they let the poor animal loose, which ran as fast as it could into a hole close by. After this the Man went on and came to another village, where the boys had a Monkey, which they forced to dance and tumble, and laughed at without letting the poor thing have any rest. To these also the Man gave money that they might release the Monkey; and by-and-by, coming to a third village, he saw the boys making a Bear in chains dance and stand upright, and if he growled they seemed all the better pleased. This animal's liberty the Man also purchased, and the Bear, very glad to find himself on his four feet again, tramped away.

The Man, however, with these purchases spent all his money, and he found he had not a copper farthing even left in his pocket. So he said to himself, "The King has much in his treasure-chamber which he does not want: of hunger I cannot die; I must take some of this money, and then when I become rich I can replace it." With these thoughts he managed to get into the treasure-chamber and took a little from the heaps, but as he was slipping out he was seized by the King's guards. They said he was a thief, and took him before the justice, who sentenced him, as he had done a criminal act, to be put in a chest on the water. The lid of the chest was full of holes whereby he might obtain air, and, besides, a jug of water and a loaf of bread were put in with him. While he was floating about in great distress of mind, he heard something gnawing and scratching at the lock of his chest, and all at once it gave way and up flew the lid. Then he saw the Mouse and the Monkey and the Bear standing by, and found it was they who had opened the chest because he had helped them; but they did not know how to proceed next, so they held a consultation together. In the meanwhile a white Stone rolled by into the water, in shape like a round egg. "That has come in the very nick of time," said the Bear, "for it is a wonderful stone, which whoever owns he can wish himself in whatever place he desires."

The Man, therefore, picked up the Stone, and as he held it in hand he wished himself in a castle with a garden and stables. Scarcely had he done so when he found himself in a castle with a garden and stables just to his mind, and everything was so beautiful and nice that he could not admire it enough.

After a time some merchants came by that way, and, as they passed, one called to the others, "See what a noble castle stands here, where, lately, when we were here before, there was nothing but dreary sand." Their curiosity was therefore aroused, and they entered the castle and inquired of the Man how he had managed to build the place so quickly. "I did not do it," said he, "but my wonderful Stone." "What kind of a stone can it be?" inquired the merchant; and, going in, the Man fetched it and showed it to them. The sight of it pleased them so much that they inquired if it were not for sale, and offered him all their beautiful goods in exchange. The goods took the Man's fancy, and, his heart being fickle and hankering after new things, he suffered himself to be persuaded and thought the beautiful things were worth more than his Stone, so he gave it away to them in exchange. But scarcely had he given it out of his hands when all his fortune vanished, and he found himself again in his floating chest on the water with nothing but his jug of water and loaf of bread. The faithful beasts, the Mouse, Monkey, and Bear, as soon as they saw his misfortune, came again to help him, but they could not manage to unfasten the lock, because it was much stronger than the former one. Thereupon the Bear said, "We must procure the wonderful Stone again, or our work is useless." Now, the merchants had stopped at the castle and lived there constantly, so the three faithful animals went away together, and when they arrived in the neighbourhood the Bear said the Mouse must peep through the keyhole and see what was going on, for since he was small no one would notice him. The Mouse consented and went, but soon returned, saying, "It is useless, I have peeped in, but the Stone hangs on a red riband below the mirror, and above and below sit two great cats with fiery eyes to watch it." Then the others said, "Never mind, go back again and wait till the master goes to bed and falls asleep, then do you slip in through the hole and creep on to the bed, and twitch his nose and bite off one of his whiskers." So the Mouse crept in and did as she was told, and the master, waking up, rubbed his nose in a passion, and exclaimed, "The cats are worth nothing! they let the mice in who bite the very hair off my head!" And, so saying, he hunted them all away, and the Mouse won her game.

The next night, as soon as the master was sound asleep, the Mouse crept in again, and nibbled and gnawed at the riband until it broke in halves, and down fell the Stone, which she then pushed out under the door. But this latter matter was very difficult for the poor Mouse to manage, and she called to the Monkey, who drew it quite out with his long paws. It was an easy matter for him, and he carried the Stone down to the water side accompanied by the others. When they got there the Monkey asked how they were to get at the chest. "Oh," replied the Bear, "that is soon done; I will swim into the water, and you, Monkey, shall sit upon my back, holding fast with your hands while you carry the Stone in your mouth; you, Mouse, can sit in my right ear." They all did as the Bear suggested, and he swam off down the river, but very soon he felt uneasy at the silence, and soon began to chatter, saying, "Do you hear, Mr Monkey, we are brave fellows, don't you think?" But the Monkey did not answer a word. "Is that manners?" said the Bear again. "Will you not give your comrade an answer? crabbed fellow is he who makes no reply." Then the Monkey could no longer restrain himself, and letting the Stone fall into the water, he cried out, "You stupid fellow, how could I answer you with the Stone in my mouth? Now it is lost, and all through your fault."

"Do not be angry," said the Bear; "we will soon recover it." Thereupon they consulted together, and summoned all the frogs and other creatures living in the water, and said to them, "There is a powerful enemy coming against you; but make haste and procure us the stones as quickly as possible, and we will then build a wall to protect you."

These words frightened the water animals, and they brought up stones on all sides, and at last came a fat old frog waddling along who had the wonderful Stone in her mouth, hanging by a piece of red riband. Then the Bear was glad, and, relieving the frog of her burden, he politely said it was all right, they might go home again now, and so took a short leave. After this the three beasts swam to the Man in the chest, and, breaking the lid in by the aid of stones, they found they had come just in the nick of time, for he had just finished his jug of water and loaf of bread, and was almost starved. However, as soon as the Man had taken the wonderful Stone in his hand he wished himself quite well and back in the castle with the garden and stables. Immediately it was so, and there he and his three faithful beasts dwelt together, happy and contented, to the end of their days.

The Three Army Surgeons

THREE Army Surgeons were once on their travels, confident that they had learnt their profession perfectly; and one day they arrived at an inn where they wished to pass the night. The landlord asked them whence they came and whither they were going; and one of them replied that they were travelling about in search of employment for their talents. "In what do your talents consist?" inquired the landlord. The first said he could cut off his hand, and in the morning put it on again without difficulty; the second said he could take out his eyes, and in the morning replace them without injury; and the third declared he could take out his own heart and put it back again.

"Can you do these things?" said the landlord: "then indeed you are well taught." But they had a salve which healed whatever it touched; and the bottle which contained it was always carried carefully with them. So the one cut off his hand, another took out his eyes, and the third cut out his heart, as they had said, and gave them on a dish to the landlord, who delivered them to the servant to put them by in a cupboard till the morning. Now this servant had a sweetheart on the sly, who was a soldier; and he, coming in, wanted something to eat. As soon as the landlord and the Three Surgeons had gone to bed, the maid opened the cupboard and fetched her lover something; but in her hurry she forgot to shut the door again, and sat down to table with the soldier, and they made themselves merry. While she sat thus, apprehending no misfortune, the cat came slipping in, and, seeing the cupboard door open, snatched the hand, heart and eyes of the Three Surgeons, and ran away with them. As soon as the Soldier had finished, the maid went to put the dish away in the cupboard, and then perceived that the plate which her master had given into her care was gone. She was terribly frightened and exclaimed, "Oh! what will become of me? the hand is gone, the heart is gone, and the eyes too; how shall I manage in the morning?" "Be quiet," said her sweetheart, "I will help you out of your difficulty; on the gallows outside hangs a thief, whose hand I can cut off; which was it?" "The right," said she, and gave him a sharp knife, with which he went and cut off the right hand of the criminal, and brought it in. Then he caught the cat and took out her eyes; but what was to be done for the heart? "Did you not kill a pig to-day and put the carcass in the cellar?" asked the soldier. "Yes," said the maid. "Then that. is just the thing," returned the soldier; "go and fetch the heart from it." The servant did so, and they placed all three on the plate and put them in the cupboard, and then her sweetheart having taken leave, the maid went to bed.

On the morrow when the three Army Surgeons were up, they bade the servant fetch the plate on which lay the hand, heart, and eyes. She brought it from the cupboard, and the first man spread the hand with his salve, and immediately it joined as if it had grown there. The second took up the cat's eyes and placed them in his head, while the third put the pig's heart where his own came from. The landlord meanwhile stood by, wondering at their learning, and saying he would never have believed them had he not seen what they did. Afterwards they paid their bill and went away.

They had not gone far before he with the pig's heart began to run about and snuff in every corner after the manner of swine. The others tried to hold him by the coat, but it was of no use, he would run about among the thickest brush-wood. The second Surgeon all this while kept rubbing his eyes and could not make out what was amiss. "What have I done?" said he to his comrades. "These are not my eyes, I cannot see; you must lead me, or I shall fall." So they travelled till evening with great trouble to themselves, when they came to another inn. They stepped into the parlour, and there in the corner sat a rich man at a table counting his money. The Surgeon with the thief's hand went up to him and peered at him, and as soon as his back was turned, made a grasp at the gold and took a handful. "For shame, comrade," cried the others; "you must not steal; what are you doing?" "Oh, how can I help myself!" he asked. "My hand is drawn to it, and I must take it whether I will or not!" Soon after this they went to bed, and it was so dark that one could not see his hand before his eyes. All at once the Surgeon with the cat's eyes woke up, and disturbing the others, cried out, "See, see, how the white mice are running about in the room!" The two others thereupon raised their heads, but they could see nothing. "It is evident to me now," said the first Surgeon, "that we have not got our own, we must go back to the landlord who deceived us."

The following morning they rode back to the first inn, and told the landlord they had not received their own things again, for one had got a thief's hand, another a pig's heart, and the third a cat's eyes. The landlord thereupon went to call the servant-maid, but she had escaped out of the backdoor as soon as she saw the Surgeons coming, and did not return. The three now threatened to set fire to the house if the landlord did not give them a large sum of money, and the poor man was compelled to give them all he could scrape together, with which they went away. But although they had enough to last them their lifetime, each would rather have had his own hand, heart, or eyes, than all the money in the world.

Three little Tales about Toads

I

ONCE upon a time there was a little Girl, whose mother gave her every day at noon a little basin of milk and bread, which she used to eat, sitting outside the house in the court. Once when she began to eat, there came a little Toad out of a crack in the wall, which put its head into the milk, and drank some. The Child was pleased with this; and the next day, and every day when she sat there with her basin, and the Toad did not make its appearance, she used to call it thus:—

> "Toadie, Toadie, quickly come;
> Hither come, my pet;
> And you shall have a little crumb
> And milk before you set!"

At these words the Toad would run and squat itself down to its feast. It showed itself grateful, too, for it always brought the child something out of its secret treasure – shining stones, pearls, or golden toys – but the Toad would only drink milk, and not touch the bread; so once the Child took its little spoon, and tapped the Toad gently on the head, saying, "Eat some bread, too, pet!" The mother, standing in the kitchen, heard the Child speaking to something, and when she saw it tap the Toad with its spoon she ran out with a faggot of wood and killed the good creature.

From that time a change came over the Child. So long as the Toad had played with it, it had grown strong and hearty, but now its red cheeks vanished, and it became quite thin. Soon the death-bird began to scream in the forest, and the red-breasts collected leaves and twigs for a crown of death; and by-and-by the poor little Child lay on a bier.

II

An orphan Child was sitting and spinning on the city wall, and saw a Toad come out of an opening beneath the wall. The Child quickly spread out its blue cotton handkerchief near itself, so that the Toad might be obliged to walk over it; and, as the child hoped, rest upon it. As soon as the Toad saw what was done, it turned round, and came again, bringing a little golden crown, which it laid down on the handkerchief, and then returned to its hole. The little

Girl took up the crown, which was spun of delicate threads of gold, and glittered in the sun, and put it out of sight; so the Toad, when it came again, could not see it.

Thereupon the poor Toad crept up to the wall, and beat its little head against it, till it lost all its strength, and fell down dead. Now, if the Child had left the crown where it was laid, the Toad would have brought more treasures out of its hole.

III

"Huhu, huhu!" cried a Toad.

"Come hither," said a Child to it. When the Toad came, the Child asked,

"Have you seen my sister, Red-stocking, this morning?"

"No, no; not I!" croaked the Toad: "how should I? huhu, huhu!"

And the Toad hopped away.

The Valiant Tailor

THERE was once upon a time an excessively proud Princess, who proposed a puzzle to every one who came courting her; and he who did not solve it was sent away with ridicule and scorn. This conduct was talked about everywhere, and it was said that whoever was lucky enough to guess the riddle would have the Princess for a wife. About that time it happened that three Tailors came in company to the town where the Princess dwelt, and the two elder of them were confident, when they heard the report, that they should without doubt be successful, since they had made so many fine and good stitches. The third Tailor was an idle, good-for-nothing fellow, who did not understand his own trade; but still he likewise was sure of his own powers of guessing a riddle. The two others, however, would fain have persuaded him to stop at home; but he was obstinate, and said he would go, for he had set his heart upon it; and thereupon he marched off as if the whole world belonged to him.

The three Tailors presented themselves before the Princess, and told her they were come to solve her riddle, for they were the only proper people, since each of them had an understanding so fine that one could thread a needle with it! "Then," said the Princess, "it is this: I have a hair upon my head of two colours: which are they?"

"If that is all," said the first man, "it is black and white like the cloth which is called pepper and salt."

"Wrong!" said the Princess; "now, second man, try!"

"It is not black and white, but brown and red," said he, "like my father's holiday coat."

"Wrong again!" cried the Princess; "now try, third man; who I see will be sure to guess rightly!"

The little Tailor stepped forward, bold as brass, and said, "The Princess has a gold and silver hair on her head, and those are the two colours."

When the Princess heard this she turned pale, and very nearly fell down to the ground with fright, for the Tailor had guessed her riddle, which she believed nobody in the world could have solved. As soon as she recovered herself, she said to the Tailor, "That is not all you have to do; in the stable below lies a Bear, with which you must pass the night; and if you are alive when I come in the morning I will marry you."

The little Tailor readily consented, exclaiming, "Bravely ventured is half won!" But the Princess thought herself quite safe, for as yet the Bear had spared no one who came within reach of its paws.

As soon as evening came the little Tailor was taken to the place where the bear lay; and, as soon as he entered the stable, the beast made a spring at him. "Softly, softly!" cried the Tailor, "I must teach you manners!" And out of his pockets he took some nuts, which he cracked between his teeth quite unconcernedly. As soon as the Bear saw this he took a fancy to have some nuts also; and the Tailor gave him a handful out of his pocket; not of nuts, but of pebbles. The Bear put them into his mouth, but he could not crack them, try all he might. "What a blockhead I am!" he cried to himself; "I can't crack a few nuts! Will you crack them for me?" said he to the Tailor. "What a fellow you are!" exclaimed the Tailor; "with such a big mouth as that, and can't crack a small nut!" With these words he cunningly substituted a nut for the pebble which the Bear handed him, and soon cracked it.

"I must try once more!" said the Bear; "it seems an easy matter to manage! And he bit and bit with all his strength, but, as you may believe, all to no purpose. When the Beast was tired, the little Tailor produced a fiddle out of his coat, and played a tune upon it, which as soon as the Bear heard, he began to dance in spite of himself. In a little while he stopped and asked the Tailor whether it was easy to learn the art of fiddling. "Easy as child's play!" said the Tailor; "you lay you left fingers on the strings, and with the right hold the bow; and then away it goes. Merrily, merrily, hop-su-sa, oi-val-lera!"

"Oh! well, if that is fiddling," cried the Bear, "I may as well learn that, and then I can dance as often as I like. What do you think? Will you give me instruction?"

"With all my heart!" replied the Tailor, "if you are clever enough; but let me see your claws, they are frightfully long, and I must cut them a bit!" By chance a vice was lying in one corner, on which the Bear laid his paws, and the Tailor screwed them fast. "Now wait till I come with the scissors," said he; and, leaving the Bear groaning and growling, he laid himself down in a corner on a bundle of straw, and went to sleep.

Meanwhile the Princess was rejoicing to think she had got rid of the Tailor; and especially when she heard the Bear growling, for she thought it was with satisfaction for his prey. In the morning accordingly she went down to the stable; but as soon as she looked in she saw the Tailor as fresh and lively as a fish in water. She was much alarmed, but it was of no use, for her word had been openly pledged to the marriage; and the King her father ordered a carriage to be brought, in which she and the Tailor went away to the church to the wedding. Just as they had set off the two other Tailors, who were very envious of their brother's fortune, went into the stable and released the Bear, who immediately ran after the carriage which contained the bridal party. The Princess heard the beast growling and groaning, and became very much frightened, and cried to the Tailor, "Oh, the Bear is behind, coming to fetch you away!" The Tailor was up in a minute, stood on his head, put his feet out of the window, and cried to the Bear, "Do you see this vice? if you do not go away you shall have a taste of it!" The Bear considered him a minute, and then turned tail and ran back; while the Tailor drove on to church with the Princess, and made her his wife. And very happy they were after the marriage, as merry as larks; and to the end of their lives they lived in contentment.

The Poor Miller's Son and the Cat

ONCE upon a time there lived in a mill an old Miller who had neither wife nor children, but three apprentices instead; and after they had been with him several years, he said to them one day, "I am old, and shall retire from business soon; do you all go out, and whichever of you brings me home the best horse, to him will I give the mill, and, moreover, he shall attend me in my last illness."

The third of the apprentices was a small lad despised by the others and so much so, that they did not intend that he should ever have the mill, even after them. But all three went out together, and as soon as they got away from the village the two eldest brothers said to the stupid Hans, "You may as well remain here; in all your lifetime you will never find a horse." Nevertheless Hans went with them, and when night came on they arrived at a hollow where they lay down to sleep. The two clever brothers waited till Hans was fast asleep, and then they got up and walked off, leaving Hans snoring. Now they thought they had done a very clever thing, but we shall see how they fared. By-and-by the sun arose and awoke Hans, who, when he found himself lying in a deep hollow, peeped all around him, and exclaimed, "Oh, Heavens! where have I got to?" He soon got up and scrambled out of the hollow into the forest, thinking to himself, "Here am I all alone, what shall I do to get at a horse?" While he ruminated, a little tortoiseshell Cat came up, and asked in a most friendly manner, "Where are you going, Hans?" "Ah! you can help me," said Hans. "Yes, I know very well what you wish," replied the Cat; "you want a fine horse: come with me, and for seven years be my faithful servant, and then I will give you a handsomer steed than you ever saw."

"Well," thought Hans to himself, "this is a wonderful Cat! but still I may as well see if this will be true."

So the Cat took him into its enchanted castle, where there were many other Cats who waited upon it, jumping quickly up and down the steps, and bustling about in first-rate style. In the evening when they sat down to table three cats had to play music; one played the violincello, a second the violin, and a third blew a trumpet so loudly that its cheeks seemed as if they would burst. When they had finished dinner the table was drawn away, and the Cat said, "Now, Hans, come and dance with me." "No, no," replied he, "I cannot dance with a Cat! I never learned how!"

"Then take him to bed," cried the Cat to its attendants; and they lighted him at once to his sleeping apartment, where one drew off his shoes, another his stockings, while a third blew out the light. The following morning the servant-cats made their appearance again, and helped him out of bed: one drew on his stockings, another buckled on his garters, a third fetched his shoes, a fourth washed his face, and a fifth wiped it with her tail. "That was done well and gently," said Hans to the last. But all day long Hans had to cut wood for the Cat, and for that purpose he received an axe of silver and wedges and saws of the same metal, while the mallet was made of copper.

Here Hans remained making himself useful. Every day he had good eating and drinking, but he saw nobody except the tortoiseshell Cat and her attendants. One day the Cat said to him, "Go and mow my meadow and dry the grass well;" and she gave him a scythe made of silver and a whetstone of gold, which she bade him bring back safe. Hans went off and did what he was told; and, when it was finished, he took home the scythe, whetstone, and hay, and asked the Cat if she would not give him a reward? "No," said the Cat, "you must first do several things for me. Here are beans of silver, binding clamps, joists, and all that is necessary, all of silver, and of these you must first build me a small house." Hans built it, and when it was done he reminded the Cat he had still no horse, although his seven years had passed like half the time. The Cat asked him whether he wished to see her horses? "Yes," said Hans. So they went out of the house, and as they opened the door there stood twelve horses, very proud creatures, pawing the ground impatiently. Hans was glad enough to see them, but as soon as he looked at them for a minute the Cat gave him his dinner, and said, "Go home; I shall not give you your horse with you, but in three days I will come to you and bring it with me." So Hans walked off, and the cats showed him the way to the mill; but, as they had not furnished him with new clothes, he was forced to go in his old ragged ones, which he had taken with him, and which during the seven years had become much too short for him. When he arrived at home, he found the two other apprentices had preceded him, and each had brought a horse; but the one was blind and the other lame. "Where is your horse, Hans?" inquired they. "It will follow me in three days," he replied. At this they laughed, and cried, "Yes, Hans, and when it does come it will be something wonderful, no doubt." Hans then went into the parlour, but the old Miller said he should not sit at table because he was so ragged and dirty; they would be ashamed of him if any one came in. So they gave him something to eat out-of-doors, and when bedtime came the two brothers refused Hans a share of the bed, and he was obliged to creep into the goose-house and stretch himself upon some hard straw. The next morning was the third day mentioned by the Cat, and as soon as Hans was up there came a carriage drawn by six horses, which shone from their sleek condition, and a servant besides, who led a seventh horse, which was for the poor Miller's boy. Out of the carriage stepped a beautiful Princess, who went into the mill, and she was the tortoiseshell Cat whom poor Hans had served for seven years. She asked the Miller where the mill-boy, her little slave, was, and he answered, "We could not take him into the mill, he was so ragged and dirty; he lies now in the goose-house." The Princess bade him fetch Hans, but before he could come the poor fellow had to draw together his smock-frock in order to cover himself. Then the servant drew forth some elegant clothes, and after washing Hans put them on, so that no king could have looked more handsome. Thereupon the Princess desired to see the horses which the other apprentices had brought home, and one was blind and the other lame. When she had seen them she ordered her servant to bring the horse he had in his keeping, and as soon as the Miller saw it he declared that such an animal had never before been in his farmyard. "It belongs to the youngest apprentice," said the Princess, "And the mill too," rejoined the Miller; but the Princess said he might keep that and the horse as well for himself. With these words she placed her faithful Hans in the carriage with her and drove away. They went first to the little house which Hans had built with the silver tools, and which had become a noble castle, wherein everything was of gold and silver. There the Princess married him, and he was so very rich that he had enough for all his life.

Hans the Hedgehog

ONCE upon a time there was a Farmer who had quite enough of money and property to live upon, but rich as he was he lacked one piece of fortune; he had no children. Ofttimes when he went to market with the other farmers they laughed at him and asked why he had no children? At length he flew into a passion, and when he came home he said, "I will have a child, and it shall be a hedgehog." Soon after this speech a child was born to him, which was like a hedgehog in the upper part of its body, and formed as a boy below, and when his wife saw it she was frightened, and cried, "See what you have wished for!" So the man said, "It cannot be helped now, and it must be christened, but we can procure no godfather for it." "We cannot call him anything else than 'Hans the Hedgehog,' " said the wife; and when the priest baptized him he said, "On account of his spikes he can sleep in no common cradle." So behind the stove a little straw was laid, upon which the child slept, and there he kept for eight years, till his father grew tired of him and wished he might die. However, the child did not, but remained in a torpid state, and one day the Farmer resolved to go to a fair which was to be held in the neighbouring town. He asked his wife what he should bring home, and she told him "a little piece of meat and a couple of rolls of bread for the housekeeping." Then he asked the servant, and she requested a couple of pots and a pair of stockings. Lastly he asked Hans what he liked, and the child replied, "Bring me, father, a bagpipe." Accordingly, when the Farmer returned home he brought his wife the meat and bread, his servant the pots and stockings, and Hans the Hedgehog the bagpipe. As soon as Hans received his gift he said, "Father, go to the smithy, and let the Cock be bridled, that I may ride away upon it and never return."

The father was glad to be freed from his son, and caused the Cock to be harnessed, and as soon as it was ready Hans the Hedgehog set himself upon it and rode away, taking with him a Boar and an Ass, which he meant to tend in the forest. But in the forest the Cock flew to the top of a lofty tree with him on its back, and there he watched the Boar and Ass for many years until there were many of them, and all the time his father knew nothing of him. While Hans sat on the tree-top he played upon his bagpipe and made beautiful music; and once a King came riding past who had lost his way in the forest, and chanced to hear him. He wondered at the sound, and sent his servants to inquire from whence the music proceeded. They looked about, but saw only a little animal upon a tree which seemed like a cock, and had a hedgehog upon its back which made the music. The King told them to ask why it sat there, and if it knew the way to his kingdom. Then Hans the Hedgehog came down from the tree, and said he would show the way if the King would promise him in writing what first met him in the royal court on his return. The King thought to himself, Hans the Hedgehog understands nothing, and I can write what I please, and so taking pen and ink he wrote something, and when he had done Hans showed him the road, and he arrived happily at home. But his daughter, seeing him at a distance, was so full of joy that she ran to meet her father and kissed him. Then he remembered Hans the Hedgehog, and told her what had happened to him, and how he had promised to a wonderful animal whatever met him first, and how this animal sat upon a cock and played music. However, he had written he should not have the first, for Hans the Hedgehog could not read what was written. Thereupon the Princess was glad, and said it was well done, for she could not have been given up to such a creature.

Meanwhile Hans the Hedgehog still tended his flocks and herds and was very merry, sitting up in his tree and blowing his bagpipe. Now it happened that another King came travelling by with his attendants and courtiers, who had also lost himself and knew not how to get home, because the forest was so immense. All at once he heard the music at a distance, and said to his servant, "Go and see at once what that is." So the servant went under the tree and saw the cock perched upon it and the hedgehog on its back, and he asked what he did up there. "I am watching my flocks and herds; but what is your desire?" was the reply. The servant said they had lost their way, and could not find their kingdom, if he did not show them the road. Then Hans the Hedgehog climbed down the tree with his cock, and told the old King he would point out the path if he would give to him certainly whatever should meet him first before his royal palace. The King said "Yes," and subscribed to it with his own hand that he should have it. When this was done Hans rode before the King on his cock, and showed him the road, whereby he quickly arrived in safety in his own kingdom. As soon as he approached his court, there was great rejoicing, and his only child, a daughter, who was very beautiful, ran to meet him, embraced and kissed him in her great joy at seeing her dear father return home again. She inquired also where he had stayed so long in the world, and he told her of all his wanderings, and how he had feared he should not get back at all because he had lost his way in such a large forest, where a creature half like a hedgehog and half like a man sat upon a cock in a high tree and made beautiful music. He told her also how this animal had come down from the tree and showed him the road on condition that he gave him whatever first met him in his royal palace on his return home; and she was the first, and that made him grieve. His daughter after a while promised to go with the animal when he came, out of love to her dear father.

Meanwhile Hans the Hedgehog tended his swine, and so many pigs were born that they filled the whole forest. Then Hans would stay no longer in the woods, and sent his father word he should clear all the stables in the village, for he was coming with such great herds that whoever wished might kill from them. At this news the father was grieved, for he thought his son had been dead long since. Soon after, Hans came riding upon his cock, and driving before him his herds into the village to be killed, when there was such a slaughtering and shrieking you might have heard it eight miles off! Hans the Hedgehog did not stay long: he paid another visit to the smithy to have his cock rebridled, then off he started again, while his father rejoiced that he should never see him again.

Hans the Hedgehog rode to the first kingdom we before mentioned, and there the King had ordered that if any one came riding upon a cock, and carrying with him a bagpipe, all should shoot at him, cut at him, and kill him, that he might not enter the castle. When, therefore, Hans the Hedgehog came riding along they pressed round him with bayonets, but he flew high up into the air over the gate to the window of the palace and, there alighting, called the King to give him what he had promised or he would kill both him and his daughter. Then the King spoke kindly to his child and begged her to go away, that her life and his might be saved. At last she consented, turning very pale however, and her father gave her a carriage drawn by six white horses, and servants, money and plate besides. She set herself in it, and Hans the Hedgehog by her side, with his cock and bagpipe. Then they took leave and drove away, while the King thought he should never see them again; and it happened just as he imagined, for as soon as they had gone a little way out of the city Hans the Hedgehog pulled off the Princess's shawl and pricked her with his quills, saying, "That is your reward for falsehood! go away! I will have nothing to do with you!" With these words he hunted her home, and to her end she was despised.

Hans the Hedgehog rode away next upon his cock with his bagpipes in his hand to the second kingdom to which he had directed its King. This King had ordered that, if any one like Hans the Hedgehog came riding to the gate, the guards should present arms, admit him freely, shout Viva! and conduct him to the palace. As soon as the Princess saw the animal coming she was at first frightened, because it appeared so curious, but as soon as she recollected her promise she became reconciled. She welcomed Hans the Hedgehog, and was married to him, and afterwards they dined at the royal table, sitting side by side, and eating and drinking together. When evening came on and bedtime, the Princess said she was afraid of her husband's spikes, but he said she need not fear, he would do her no harm. Then he told the old King to appoint four men who should watch before the chamber-door and keep up a great fire; and when he entered and prepared to go to bed, he would creep out of his hedgehog skin and lay it down before the bed. When he had so done, the men must run in, snatch up the skin, and throw it in the fire, and keep it there till it was quite consumed.

Afterwards, when the clock struck twelve, Hans the Hedgehog entered his room, stripped off his skin, and laid it down by the bed. Immediately the four men ran in, snatched it up, and threw it into the fire, and as soon as it was consumed Hans was freed, and lay in the bed in a proper human form, but coal-black as if he was burnt. Thereupon the King sent to his physician, who washed the young Prince with a precious balsam which made his skin white, so that he became quite a handsome youth. As soon as the Princess saw this she jumped for joy; and the following morning they arose gladly, and were married again in due form and with great feasting; and afterwards Hans the Hedgehog received the kingdom from the hands of the old King.

When several years had passed away the young King went with his bride to his father's house, and told him he was his son. The Farmer, however, declared he had no children. He had once, he said, had one who was covered with spikes like a hedgehog, but he had wandered away into the world. Then the King made himself known to his father, and showed that he was really his son; and the Farmer rejoiced greatly, and returned with him to his kingdom.

The Child's Grave

THERE was once a Mother who had a little Boy, seven years old, so pretty and good that no one saw him without loving him; and she, especially, loved him with her whole heart. One day it happened that he suddenly fell sick, and by-and-by the good God took him to himself; and the poor Mother was so grieved that she would not be comforted, but cried day and night. Soon after his burial the Child appeared one night in the place where during his lifetime he had been wont to sit and play; and while his Mother wept he wept too, and at daybreak disappeared. When, however, the Mother still lamented his death, and cried without ceasing, he appeared again one night in the white shroud in which he was laid in his coffin, and with the garland of flowers round his head. He sat down at the foot of his Mother on the bed, and said to her, "Ah! my Mother, cease to weep, else can I not sleep in my coffin, for my shroud is moistened continually with your tears which fall upon it!"

The Mother thereupon was frightened, and dried her tears: and the next night the Child appeared once more, holding a light in his hand. "See, my dear Mother!" he said, "see, my shroud is dry now, and I can rest in my grave!"

After this the Mother sorrowed no more, but bore her loss with patience and trust in God; while her Child peacefully slept in his narrow grave.

The Two Kings' Children

ONCE upon a time there was a King who had a little boy, of whom it was foretold that when he was sixteen years old he would be killed by a stag. Just when he had reached this age, he went out hunting with the royal huntsman, and, during the chase, the Prince wandered away from his companions and soon perceived a fine stag, which he took a fancy to shoot. He pursued it a long way without success, until the stag ran into a little hollow, where it changed itself into a tall, thin man, who said to the Prince, "Now all is well; I have caught you at last; often have I followed you with silent footsteps, but never till this time could I catch you." So saying, the man took the Prince with him, and rowed him over a wide lake, till they came to a royal palace, where they sat down at a table and partook of a meal together. When they had finished, the King said, "I have three daughters, the eldest of whom you must watch this night, sitting from nine o'clock in the evening till morning; and every time the clock strikes, I shall come and call gently, and, if you give me no answers, in the morning you shall die; but, if you reply readily each time, you shall have my daughter to wife."

When the young Prince was led into the chamber he saw a great stone image there, to which the Princess said, "When my father comes at nine, and every hour afterwards, do you give an answer when he speaks instead of the Prince." The stone image nodded its head, at first rapidly, and the gradually slower, till it stopped altogether. The next morning the King told the Prince he had performed his work well, but he could not yet give up his daughter, and he must watch this night the second one, and after that he would consider about giving him his eldest daughter to wife. "Again," said he, "I shall come every hour, and call gently, that you may answer; but if you do not answer, your blood shall flow as a punishment!"

With this they went up to the second daughter's chamber, and there stood a much larger image, which the Princess bade to answer when the King called. The large stone image thereupon nodded its head, as the other had done, first in quick time, and gradually slower, till it stood still. The Prince laid down upon the threshold and went to sleep, with his head resting upon his arm, and the next morning the King said again, "I cannot now give up my daughter, although you have performed what I required; so this night you must watch my youngest child, and then I will consider if you can

THE TWO KINGS' CHILDREN

have my second daughter to wife; again I shall come every hour, and call, and, if you reply, well and good; but if not, your blood must flow in satisfaction!"

They ascended to the youngest Princess's room, and there was a much taller and larger image, twice as big as the other two, to which this Princess also said, "Answer, if my father calls." The tall image nodded its head for half-an-hour and then ceased, while the King's son laid down upon the threshold, as before, and went to sleep. The following morning the King said he had certainly watched well, but still he could not give him his daughter till he had first removed a certain huge forest, which, if he had effected by the evening of that day, he would consider the matter. Then he gave him a glass axe, a glass wedge, and a glass mallet, with which the Prince began his work; but at the first stroke the axe broke in halves, and at the first blow both the wedge and the mallet were shivered to pieces. Thereupon he was so troubled, believing that he should be put to death, that he sat down and wept. And, as it was just noonday, the King said to his daughters, "One of you must take him something to eat." "No, no," said the two eldest, "we will not; let the one he watched last wait upon him." So the youngest Princess had to carry the Prince his meal, and when she got to the forest she asked him how he got on. "Alas," said the youth, "everything goes ill!" The Princess pressed him to eat a bit before he went on, but he refused, saying, "No; I must die, and I am resolved I will eat no more." At length he was over-persuaded and did eat what she brought. When he had finished, she made him play at ball with her; and soon he fell asleep from weariness. Then she took her handkerchief, and tied a knot in the end, with which she knocked three times upon the ground, and cried, "Earthmen, come up!" Immediately ever so many little Dwarfs made their appearance, and inquired of the Princess what she wanted. "In three hours from this time," said she, "this forest must be cleared away, and all the timber piled up in heaps."

The earthmen collected all their forces and set to work, and in three hours all was completed, and they summoned the Princess to see, who thereupon rapped upon the ground again, crying, "Earthmen, go home!" and all disappeared at once. Then she awoke the Prince, who was overjoyed to see what was done; but she bade him not return till it struck six. At that time he came back, and the King inquired if he had done his work. "Yes," answered the Prince, "I have cleared away the forest." Afterwards they sat down to supper, and the King then told the Prince he could not yet give him any of his daughters to wife till he had performed another work. This was to clear out a deep ditch and fill it with water, so that it should look as clear as a mirror, and, besides, be full of all sorts of fish. The next morning accordingly the King gave him a glass spade, and said the ditch must be ready at six o'clock. The Prince began to dig at once, but as soon as he struck the spade into the ground it broke in two, as the hatchet had done the day before. He was sore troubled, for he knew not what to do, and waited till noonday, when the youngest Princess again brought him his dinner, and asked how he got on. "Alas!" said he, hiding his face in his hands, "the same ill-luck has befallen me." The Princess tried to comfort him, saying that he would think differently when he had eaten and rested. Still he refused, declaring that he should die, and would eat no more. At last she persuaded him to sit down, and when he had finished he fell asleep, being weary with care. And while he was snoring the Princess took out her handkerchief and rapped on the ground, as before, thrice, while she called, "Earthmen, come up!" They appeared at once, and asked her business. "In three hours from this time you must clear this ditch, and make it as clear as crystal, and, besides, all sorts of fish must be within it."

The earthmen thereupon collected all their strength, and worked so hard that in two hours it was all ready. When they had done they told the Princess her command was obeyed; and she, rapping thrice on the earth as before, said, "Return home, then, earthmen!" They all disappeared at once, and she awoke the Prince, who saw that the ditch was ready. Then the Princess returned home, and bade him not come till six o'clock, at which hour he arrived, and the King asked him whether the ditch were ready. "Yes," he replied. "That is well," said the King; but at supper he again declared that he could not give up his daughter till he had done another thing. "What, then, is that?" asked the Prince. "There is a great hill," replied the King, "whereupon are several crags of rock, which must all be demolished; and, instead thereof, you must build up a fine castle, which must be stronger than one can imagine, and, besides, filled with every necessary appurtenance." The following morning the King gave him a glass pickaxe and bore, and told him the work must be ready by six o'clock. At the first stroke with the pickaxe the pieces flew far and wide, and he had only the handle left in his hands, and the bore would make no impression. At these misfortunes he was quite disheartened, and sat down to wait and see if his mistress would assist him. At noonday she came as before, bringing him somewhat to eat, and he ran up to her and told her all his troubles. First she made him eat and go to sleep as before, and then she wrapped thrice as before with her knotted handkerchief on the ground, crying, "Come up, little earthmen!" They made their appearance at once, and asked her wishes. And she told them that, in three hours from that time, they must remove all the rocks which were on the hill, and build in their stead a noble castle, finer than any one had ever seen, and filled, moreover, with all the necessary appurtenances. The Dwarfs fetched their tools and worked away, and in the three hours they completed everything. They told the Princess when they had finished, and she, rapping on the ground as before three times with her knotted handkerchief, cried, "Earthmen, go home!" and immediately they all disappeared. Then she awoke the Prince; and they were merry together as birds in the air, and when six o'clock struck they went home together. The King asked, "Is that castle ready, too?" "Yes," was the reply. Afterwards, when they sat down to table, the King said to the Prince, "I cannot give you my youngest daughter till you have asked her two sisters." This speech saddened both the Princess and the Prince, who knew not what to do. But at night he came to her, and they escaped together; but on the way the Princess looked back and saw her father pursuing them. "Alas!" she cried, "what shall we do? my father is behind us, and will overtake us; I will change you into a thorn-bush, and myself into a rose, and always rest in your protection."

So when the father came to the spot he found only a thorn-bush and a rose, which he was going to pull off, when the thorns pricked his finger, and sent him home again. On his return his wife asked him why he had not brought them with him, and he told her he had followed them till he had lost sight of them, and when he came to the spot he found only a thorn and a rose. "You should have broken the rose-bud off, and the thorn-bush would have followed of itself!" exclaimed his wife. Thereupon he went away to fetch the rose, but in the meantime the two had escaped farther away from the field where he left them, and the King was obliged to follow them. The Princess peeped behind her, and, seeing her father coming, cried, "Ah! now what shall we do? I will transform you into a church, and myself into the parson, and mount in the pulpit to preach." So when the King came to the spot, he found a church and a parson preaching in the pulpit, so he stopped and heard the sermon, and then returned home. The Queen asked if he had brought the fugitive, and he replied no: he had followed them to the spot where he thought they were, and had seen only a church, in the pulpit of which a parson was delivering a sermon. "You should have brought the parson with you," said the wife; "the church must have followed also; but now I must go myself, for it is useless to send you." Just as she was getting near the church, the Princess, peeping round, saw her mother coming, and exclaimed, "This is worse luck than all, for here comes mother; I will change you into a pond and myself into a fish." So when the Queen came to the place she found a large pond, and in the midst of it a fish swimming about and leaping out of the water merrily. The Queen tried to catch the fish, but she could not manage it, and so she drank up the whole pond, but it soon filled again, and she found that she could not succeed. So she turned to go home, but first she gave her daughter three walnuts, and said, "With these you can help yourself if you are in necessity."

The young people journeyed on again, and in about an hour's time they came in sight of the castle where the Prince formerly dwelt,

close by which was a village. The Prince, as they approached the
place, said to his companion, "Stop here, my dearest, while I go up
to the castle and bring down carriages and servants to meet you."

As soon as he arrived at the castle there was great rejoicing at his
return, and he told them his bride was waiting for him down in the
village below while he went to bring a carriage. The servants soon
harnessed the horses, and placed themselves behind the carriage; but
the Prince, before he got in, kissed his mother, and as soon as he had
done so he forgot all that had happened and all that he was about.
The Queen Mother then commanded the horses to be taken out of
the carriage and all went back into the house.

Meanwhile the Princess remained below in the village waiting and
waiting to be fetched, but nobody came, and by-and-by she hired
herself to the miller, whose mill belonged to the castle, and there, by
the water, she sat all day long washing linen. One morning the Queen
came by the stream while she was taking an airing, and saw the
maiden sitting there. "What a fine girl that is!" she exclaimed; "she
pleases me well!" but the Queen passed on and thought no more
about her. So the maiden remained a long while with the miller, till
the time came that the Queen had found a bride from a far distant
country for her son. When his bride came a great number of people
were invited to celebrate her arrival, and the maiden asked leave of
her master to go too. On the wedding-day she opened one of the
three nuts her mother had given her, and in it she found a very
beautiful dress, which she put on, and went into the church and took
a place near the altar. Presently the bride and bridegroom entered
and placed themselves before the altar, but, just as the priest was
about to bless them, the bride, peeping on one side, saw the maiden
with the beautiful dress, and thereupon refused to be married unless
she was dressed the same. So all the train had to return home, and
the strange lady was asked if she would lend her dress. No! and
neither would she sell it for any money; but there was one condition
on which she would part with it. This was, that she should be allowed
to sleep one night before the door of the Prince's chamber. This was
granted; but the servants gave their master a sleeping-draught, so

that he did not hear a word of the maiden's plaints, and there she lay all night long endeavouring to remind him how she had cut down the wood for him, filled up the ditch, built the castle, changed him into a thorn-bush, a church, and lastly, a pond, and yet he had forsaken her. But the Prince heard nothing, and the next morning the bride put on the dress, and they went again to church. Then the same events took place as the day before, and the maiden had leave to sleep again in return for her dress. This time the Prince did not take his draught, and he heard all her complaint and was very much troubled. The next morning he went to the maiden and begged her forgiveness for all his forgetfulness. The true bride then drew out and cracked her third nut, and the dress which laid in it was so beautiful, that all the boys and girls ran after, and strewed flowers in the path of the bride. So the Prince and Princess were happily married; but the old Queen and the envious bride were forced to run away.

The Thief among Thorns

THERE was once upon a time a rich man, who had a servant so honest and industrious that he was every morning the first up, and every evening the last to come in; and, besides, whenever there was a difficult job to be done, which nobody else would undertake, this servant always volunteered his assistance. Moreover, he never complained, but was contented with everything, and happy under all circumstances. When his year of service was up, his master gave him no reward, for he thought to himself, that will be the cleverest way, and, by saving his wage, I shall keep my man quietly in my service. The servant said nothing, but did his work during the second year as well as the first; but still he received nothing for it, so he made himself happy about the matter, and remained a year.

When this third year was also past, the master considered, and put his hand in his pocket, but drew nothing out; so the servant said, "I have served you honestly for three years, master, be so good as to give me what I deserve; for I wish to leave, and look about me a bit in the world."

"Yes, my good fellow," replied the covetous old man; "you have served me industriously, and, therefore, you shall be cheerfully rewarded." With these words he dipped his hand into his pocket, and drew out three farthings, which he gave the servant, saying, "There, you have a farthing for each year, which is a much more bountiful and liberal reward than you would have received from most masters!"

The honest servant, who understood very little about money, jinked his capital, and thought, "Ah! now I have a pocketful of money, so why need I plague myself any longer with hard work!" So off he walked, skipping and jumping about from one side of the road to the other, full of joy. Presently he came to some bushes, out of which a little man stepped and called out, "Whither away, merry brother? I see you do not carry much burden in the way of cares." "Why should I be sad?" replied the Servant; "I have enough; the wages of three years are rattling in my pocket."

"How much is your treasure?" inquired the Dwarf.

"How much? three farthings, honestly counted out," said the Servant.

"Well," said the Dwarf, "I am a poor needy man, give me your three farthings; I can work no longer, but you are young, and can earn your bread easily."

Now, because the Servant had a compassionate heart, he pitied the old man, and handed him the three farthings, saying, "In the name of God take them, and I shall not want."

Thereupon the little man said, "Because I see you have a good heart I promise you three wishes, one for each farthing, and all shall be fufilled."

"Aha?" exclaimed the servant, "you are one who can blow black and blue! Well, then, if it is to be so, I wish, first, for a gun, which shall bring down all I aim at; secondly, a fiddle, which shall make all who hear it dance; thirdly, that whatever request I make to any one, it shall not be in their power to refuse me."

"All this you shall have," said the Dwarf; and diving into his pocket he produced a fiddle and gun, as soon as you could think, all in readiness, as if they had been ordered long ago. These he gave to the Servant, and then said to him, "Whatever you may ask, shall no man in the world be able to refuse." With that he disappeared.

"What more can you desire now, my heart?" said the Servant to himself, and walked merrily onwards. Soon he met a thief with a purse of gold, who was standing listening to the song of a bird which hung high up upon a tree. "What a wonder," he was exclaiming, "that such a small creature should have such an immense voice! if it were only mine! Oh, that I could strew some salt upon its tail!"

"If that is all," broke in the Servant, "the bird shall soon be down;" and aiming with his gun he pulled the trigger, and down it fell in the middle of a thorn-bush. "Go, you rogue, and fetch the bird out!" said he to the thief.

"Leave out the rogue, my master," returned the other; "before the dog comes I will fetch out the bird, because you killed it so well." So saying, the thief went down on his hands and knees and crawled into the bush; and while he stuck fast among the thorns, the good Servant felt so roguishly inclined, that he took up his fiddle and began to play. At the same moment the thief was upon his legs, and began to dance about, while the more the Servant played the better went the dance. But the thorns tore his shabby coat, combed out his beard, and pricked and stuck all over his body. "My master," cried the thief, "what is your fiddling to me? leave the fiddle alone; I do not want to dance."

But the Servant did not pay any attention, and said to the thief, while he played anew, so that the poor man jumped higher than ever, and the rags of his clothes hung about the bushes, "You have fleeced people enough in your time, and now the thorny hedge shall give you a turn." "Oh, woe's me!" cried the thief; "I will give the master what he desires, if only he leaves off fiddling – a purse of gold." "If you are so liberal," said the Servant, "I will stop my music; but this I must say to your credit, that you dance as if you had been bred to it;" and thereupon taking the purse he went his way.

The thief stood still and watched him out of sight, and then he began to abuse him with all his might. "You miserable musician, you beer-tippler! wait, if I do but catch you alone, I will hunt you till the soles of your shoes fall off! you ragamuffin, you farthingsworth!" And so he went on calling him all the names he could lay his tongue to. As soon as he had regained his breath he ran into the town to the justice, pretending to be an honest merchant. "My lord judge," he said, "I have a sorry tale to tell: see how a rascally man has used me on the public highway, robbed and beaten me! a stone on the ground might pity me; my clothes all torn, my body scratched and wounded all over, poverty come upon me with the loss of my purse, besides several ducats, one piece more valuable than all the others; for Heaven's sake let the man be put in prison!"

"Was it a soldier," inquired the judge, "who has thus cut you with his sabre?" "God forbid!" cried the thief; "it was no sword the rogue had, but he carried a gun upon his shoulder, and a fiddle slung round his neck; the evil wretch is easily known."

So the judge sent his people out after the man, and they soon found the Servant whom they drove slowly before them, when they found the purse upon him. As soon as he was set before the judge he said, "I have not touched this man, nor taken his money; for he gave it to me of his own freewill, because he wished me to cease my fiddling which he could not endure."

"Heaven defend us!" cried the thief, "he tells lies as fast as he can catch the flies upon the wall."

The judge also would not believe his tale, and said, "This is a bad defence, for no one would do as you say." Thereupon, because the robbery had been committed on the public road, he sentenced the good Servant to be hanged. As he was led thither the thief began again to abuse him, crying out, "You bearskin! you dog of a fiddler! now you shall receive your well-earned reward!" But the Servant walked quietly with the hangman to the gallows, and upon the last step of the ladder he turned round and said to the judge, "Grant me one request before I die."

"Yes, if you do not ask your life," said the judge.

"Not life do I request, but that you will allow me to play one tune upon my fiddle, for a last favour," replied the Servant.

The thief raised a great cry of "Murder! murder! for God's sake do not allow it!" "Why should I not grant him this short enjoyment?" asked the judge: "it is almost all over with him, and he shall have this last favour." (However, he could not have refused the request which the Servant had made.)

Then the thief exclaimed, "Oh! woe's me! hold me fast, tie me fast!" while the Servant, taking his fiddle from his neck, began to screw up, and no sooner had he given the first scrape, than the judge, his clerk, and the hangman began to make steps, and the rope fell out of the hand of him who was going to bind the thief. At the second scrape, all raised their legs, and the hangman let loose the good Servant and prepared for the dance. At the third scrape all began to dance and caper about; the judge and the thief being first performers. And as he continued to play, all joined in the dance, and even the people who had gathered in the market out of curiosity, old and young, fat and thin, one with another. The dogs, likewise, as they came by, got up on their hind legs and capered about; and the longer he played the higher sprang the dancers, till they toppled down over each other on their heads, and began to shriek terribly. At length the judge cried, quite of breath, "I will give you your life if you will stop fiddling." The good Servant thereupon had compassion, and dismounting the ladder he hung his fiddle round his neck again. Then he stepped up to the thief, who lay upon the ground panting for breath, and said,

"You rascal, tell me, now, whence you got the money, or I will take my fiddle and begin again." "I stole it, I stole it!" cried the thief; "but you have honestly earned it." Upon this the judge caused the thief to be hung on the gallows, while the good Servant went on his way rejoicing in his happy escape.

The Flail which came from the Clouds

A COUNTRYMAN once drove his plough with a pair of oxen, and when he came about the middle of his fields the horns of his two beasts began to grow, and grow, till they were so high that when he went home he could not get them into the stable-door. By good luck just then a Butcher passed by, to whom he gave up his beasts, and struck a bargain, that he should take to the Butcher a measure-full of turnip-seed, for every grain of which the Butcher should give him a Brabant dollar. That is what you may call a good bargain! The countryman went home, and came again, carrying on his back a measure of seed, out of which he dropped one grain on the way. The Butcher, however, reckoned out for every seed a Brabant dollar; and had not the Countryman lost one he would have received a dollar more. Meanwhile the seed which he dropped on the road had grown up to a fine tree, reaching into the clouds. So the Countryman thought to himself he might as well see what the people in the clouds were about. Up he climbed, and at the top he found a field with some people thrashing oats; but while he was looking at them he felt the tree shake beneath him, and, peeping downwards, he perceived that some one was on the point of chopping down the tree at the roots. "If I am thrown down," said the Countryman to himself, "I shall have a bad fall;" and, quite bewildered, he could think of nothing else to save himself than to make a rope with the oat straw, which laid about in heaps. He then seized hold of a hatchet and flail which were near him, and let himself down by his straw rope. He fell into a deep, deep hole in the earth, and found it very lucky that he had brought the hatchet with him; for with it he cut steps, and so mounted again into the broad daylight, bringing with him the flail for a sign of the truth of his tale, which nobody, on that account, was able to doubt!

There is a wonderful adventure!!!

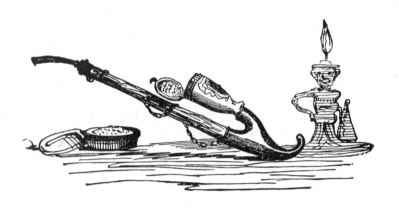

The Blue Light

THERE was once upon a time a Soldier, who had served his King faithfully for many years; but when the war came to a close, the Soldier, on account of his many wounds, was disabled, and the King said to him, "You may go home, for I no longer need you: but you will not receive any more pay, for I have no money but for those who render me a service for it." The Soldier did not know where to earn a livelihood, and, full of care, he walked on the whole day ignorant whither he went, till about night he came to a large forest. Through the darkness which covered everything he saw a light, and, approaching it, he found a hut wherein dwelt a Witch. "Please give me a night's lodging, and something to eat and drink, or I shall perish," said he to the old woman. "Oho! who gives anything to a worn-out Soldier?" she replied; "still out of compassion I will take you in, if you will do what I desire." The Soldier asked what she wished, and she told him she wanted her garden dug over. To this he willingly consented, and the following day, accordingly, he worked with all his strength, but could not get his work finished by the evening. "I see very well," said the Witch, "that you cannot get further today, so I will shelter you another night; and in return you shall fetch me a pile of faggots to-morrow, and chop them small." The Soldier worked all day long at this job, but as he did not finish till quite the evening, the Witch again proposed that he should stop the night. "You shall have but a very little work to-morrow," said she; "I want you to fetch me out of a half-dry well behind my house my blue light which floats there without ever going out." The next morning, accordingly, the old Witch led him to the well, and let him down into it in a basket. He soon found the blue light, and made a sign to be drawn up; and as soon as he reached the top, the old woman tried to snatch the blue light out of his hand. "No, no!" cried the Soldier, perceiving her wicked intentions, "no, no, I don't give up the light till both my feet stand on dry ground." The Witch flew into a passion when he said so, and letting him fall down into the well again, went away.

The poor Soldier fell without injury on the soft mud, and the blue light kept burning: but to what use? he saw well that he should not escape death. For a while he sat there in great trouble, and at length searching in his pocket, he took out his tobacco-pipe, which was only half-smoked out. "This shall be my last consolation," said he to himself and lighting the pipe at the blue light, he began to puff. As soon, now, as the smoke began to ascent, a little black man suddenly stood before the Soldier, and asked, "Master, what are your commands?"

"What are my commands? repeated the astonished Soldier. "I must do all you desire," replied the Dwarf. "That is well," said the Soldier; "then help me first out of this well." The Dwarf, thereupon, took him by the hand and led him through a subterraneous passage out of the well, while he carried the blue light with him. On the way he showed the Soldier the concealed treasure of the Witch, of which he took as much as he could carry; and as soon as they were out of the ground he bade the Dwarf fetch the old Witch, and take her before the judge. In a very short time she was brought riding on a wild cat, which made a fearful noise, and ran as swiftly as the wind; and the Dwarf, taking them before the Judge, quickly returned to his master, with the news that the Witch was hung on the gallows. "Master, what else have you to command?" inquired the Dwarf. "Nothing further at present," replied the Soldier, "and now you can go home, only be at hand when I summon you again."

"All that is necessary for that," said the Dwarf, "is, that you should light your pipe at the blue lamp, and immediately I shall present myself." With these words the little man disappeared.

Then the Soldier returned to the city from whence he first came, and, going to the head inn, ordered some fine clothes, and bade the landlord furnish him a room in the most expensive style. As soon as it was ready, the Soldier took possession of it, and summoned the Black Dwarf, to whom he said, "The King of this city I served formerly for many years faithfully, but he sent me away to suffer hunger, and now I will take my revenge."

"What shall I do then?" inquired the Dwarf. "Late in the evening, when the King's daughter is asleep, you must fetch her out of her bed, and bring her here to wait upon me as my maid-servant."

The Dwarf expostulated with the Soldier, but to no purpose, telling him that though it would be an easy matter for him to bring her, it might cause him danger if it were found out. Accordingly, when twelve o'clock struck, the Dwarf appeared with the Princess. "Aha! you are there," cried the Soldier to the Princess; "come, fetch your brush and sweep the room." When she had done that, he called her to his seat, and, stretching his feet out, bade her pull off his boots. This she did, and, as he threw the boots in her face, she was obliged to go and wash herself. But all was done by her with eyes half shut, without complaint or resistance; and at the first crow of the cock the Dwarf carried her back again to bed in the royal castle.

The next morning when the Princess arose she went to her father, and told him what a curious dream she had had. "I was carried," she said, "through the streets with lightning speed, and taken into the room of a soldier, whom I waited upon as his maid, even sweeping the room and polishing his boots. But it was only a dream, and yet I am as tired as if I had really done all this work."

"The dream may have been real," said the King, "and so I will give you this piece of advice. To-night, fill your pocket with peas, and make a hole in it, so that if you are fetched again, they will drop through as you go along, and leave a trace on the road."

While the King spoke this the Dwarf was standing by and overheard all he said; and at night he strewed peas in every street, so that those dropped by the Princess, as he carried her along, were no guide afterwards. The poor maiden had again to do all sorts of hard work till the first cock-crow, when the Dwarf took her home to bed.

The next morning the King sent out his servants to seek traces of his daughter's journey: but it was all in vain, for in every street the children were picking up the peas and saying, "It has rained peas during the night."

"We must think of some other plan," said the King, when his servants returned unsuccessful; and he advised his daughter to keep her shoes on when she went to bed; and then, if she were carried off, she must leave one behind in the room whither she was taken, and in the morning it should be searched after. But the Black Dwarf again overheard the plan, and counselled the Soldier not to have the Princess that evening, for there was no remedy for the stratagem her father had planned. The Soldier, however, would be obeyed, although the finding of the shoe would be a serious offence: and the poor Princess was obliged again to work like any servant; but she managed to conceal one of her shoes beneath the bed before she was taken back to the palace.

The following morning the King ordered the whole city to be searched for his daughter's shoe, and it was discovered in the room of the Soldier, who, however, at the entreaty of the Dwarf, had slipped out of the door. He was soon caught and thrown into prison, but, unfortunately, he had left behind his best possessions – the blue light and his gold, and had only a single ducat with him in his pocket. While he stood at the window of his cell, laden with chains, he perceived one of his old comrades passing by. So he knocked at the bars, and beckoned his comrade, whom he asked to go to the inn, and bring back a bundle which he had left behind, and he should receive a ducat for the service. The man ran away and soon returned with the wished-for bundle. As soon, then, as the Soldier was alone, he lighted up his pipe and summoned up the Dwarf. "Be not afraid," said the black mannikin; "go whither you are led, and let everything happen as it may, only take with you the blue light."

The next day the Soldier was brought up to be tried, and although he had done no great wrong, he was condemned to death by the judge. When he was led out for execution, he begged a last favour of the King. "What is it?" asked the King. "Permit me to smoke one pipe before I die." "You may smoke three if you please," said the King; "but do not expect me to spare your life." Thereupon the Soldier drew out his pipe and lighted it at the blue light; and before a couple of wreaths of smoke had ascended the Black Dwarf appeared, holding a little cudgel in his hand, and asked, "What are your commands, master?" "Knock down, first, the unjust judge, and his constables, and do not spare the King even, who has treated me so shabbily." The little Black Dwarf commenced wielding his cudgel, and at every blow down went a man, who never ventured to rise again. The King was terribly frightened when he saw this, and begged for mercy, but the Soldier only pardoned him on condition of his giving him his daughter to wife, and his kingdom to rule; and to this the unhappy King consented, for he had no choice.

The Seven Swabians

THERE were once Seven Swabians in company, the first of whom was named Schulz, the second Jacky, the third Marli, the fourth Jergli, the fifth Michael, the sixth Hans, and the seventh Veitli; and they all were travelling in search of adventures, and for the performance of mighty deeds. In order that they might not be without protection, they thought fit to carry along with them a very long and strong pole. Upon this they all seven held, and in front the boldest and most courageous man, who was Schulz, walked, while the others followed behind, and Veitli was last.

One day in July, after they had travelled some distance, and had nearly entered the village where they intended to pass the night, it happened that just as they came to a large meadow a hornet or dragonfly flew out from behind a bush and hummed about the travellers in a warlike manner. Schulz was frightened and almost let go the pole, and the perspiration stood all over his body from terror.

"Listen, listen!" he cried to his companions; "I hear a trumpeting!" Jacky, who was last but one in the row, and had got I know not what into his nose, exclaimed, "Something certainly is at hand, for I can smell brimstone and powder!" At these words Schulz sprang over a hedge in a trice in his haste to escape, and, happening to alight on the prongs of a rake which was left in the field by the haymakers, the handle sprung up and gave him an awkward blow on the forehead. "Oh! oh! oh! woe is me!" cried Schulz; "take me prisoner, I give myself up, I surrender!" The six others thereupon jumped over the hedge too, and cried likewise, "We surrender if you surrender! we surrender if you surrender!"

At length, when they found no enemy came to bind and take them away, they saw they were deceived, and in order that the tale might not be told of them among the villagers, and they get laughed at and mocked, they took an oath among themselves never to say anything about it unless any one of them should open his mouth unawares.

After this adventure they went further, but the second danger they met with must not be compared with the first. For after several days had elapsed their road chanced to lead them through an unploughed field where a hare was lying asleep in the sun, with his ears pricked up to catch every sound, and his large glossy eyes wide open. The Seven Swabians were terribly frightened at the sight of this frightful ferocious animal, and they took counsel together what would be the least dangerous plan to adopt. For if they fled away it was to be feared that the monster would pursue them and cut them to pieces. So the resolved to stand and have a great battle; for, said they, "Bravely dared is half won!" All seven, therefore, grasped hold of their spear, Schulz being foremost and Veitli hindmost. But Schulz wanted to have the spear himself, whereupon Veitli flew into a passion and broke away.

Then the rest advanced together upon the dragon, but first Schulz crossed himself devoutly and invoked the assistance of Heaven. Then he marched on, but as he approached the enemy he felt very fearful and cried in great terror, "Han! hurlehau! han! hauhel!" This awoke the hare, who sprang away quite frightened, and when Schulz saw it flee, he jumped for joy and shouted,—

> "Zounds, Veitli, what fools we are!
> The monster after all is but a hare!"

After they had recovered their fright the Seven Swabians sought new adventures, and by-and-by they arrived at the River Moselle, a smooth and deep water, over which there are not many bridges; but one must cross in boats to the other side. The Seven Swabians, however, were ignorant of this, and they therefore shouted to a man who was working on the other side of the river and asked him how they were to cross. But the man did not understand what they said on account of the distance and his ignorance of their language, and so he asked in his dialect "Wat? wat?" With this Schulz imagined the man said, "Wade, wade through the stream;" and, being foremost on the bank, he jumped into the river and began to walk across. Soon he got out of his depth and sank in the deep driving current; but his hat was carried by the wind to the opposite shore. As it reached there a frog perched himself on it, and croaked, "Wat! wat! wat!" This noise the six other Swabians, who then reached the bank, heard, and they said to each other, "Listen! does not Schulz call us? Well, if he could wade across we can also." With these words each one jumped into the river, but they also all sank; and so it happened that the frog caused the death of six Swabians, for nobody has heard of or seen them ever since.

The Three Journeymen

THERE were once three Journeymen, who agreed together to travel in company, and always work in the same town. But one season they could find no master to employ them, so that by degrees they became quite ragged, and had nothing to live upon. They asked each other what they should do; and one proposed that they should not stop any longer where they were, but wander about; and when they came to a town where no work was to be had, they should separate, first making an agreement with the landlord of their inn, that he would receive their letters, so that each might know where his companions were. This plan appeared the best they could adopt, and they set out on their travels. On the road a well-dressed man met them, who inquired of them who they were. "We are Journeymen," said they, "in search of work, and hitherto we have been successful; but when we are no longer fortunate we mean to separate."

"There is no necessity for that," said the stranger; "if you only do what I tell you, you shall not want for money or work; for you may even become great lords, and ride in your own carriages."

"If it does not injure our souls and happiness," said one, "we will readily do what you wish."

"No; I have no claim upon you," replied the man; "of that sort, at least."

The other Journeyman, meanwhile, had observed the stranger's feet; and when he saw one was a horse's hoof and the other a human foot, he would have nothing to do with the agreement at first. But the Evil One said it was not their souls, but some other man's, which he wanted; and so being reassured, the three Journeymen consented to the agreement. The Evil One then told them that what he desired was, that the first man should answer to every question, "All three of us;" the second, "For money;" and the third should cry, "That is right." This they were to say on all occasions, but any other word they must not speak, on pain of losing all their money again; but so long as they obeyed the instructions, their pockets would always be full of money. For a beginning the Evil One gave them as much as they could carry, and bade them go into such and such a city, and stop at such and such an inn. They entered the appointed place, and the landlord came towards them and asked if they wished for something to eat. The first man replied, "All three of us," "Yes," said the landlord, "that is what I mean." "For money," said the second man. "That is understood." "That is right," said the third. "Yes, that *is* right," repeated the Landlord.

Soon a plentiful meal was spread before them, and they were well waited on; and as soon as they had finished the Landlord brought in his bill, and laid it before the three companions. "All three of us," said the first; "For money," said the second; and the third repeated, "That is right." "You are quite right, sirs," said the Landlord, "all three of you must pay; and without the money I cannot entertain you." Thereupon they counted out more money than was asked, and the guests who were looking on said to each other, "These people must be mad!" "Yes; they do not appear quite sane," said the

Landlord: but still they remained in his house, speaking no other words than "All three of us. For money; That is right." Nevertheless they saw and knew all that was going on: and one day it chanced that a great merchant came, bringing with him a great deal of money, to the inn. He said to the Landlord, "Take care of my gold, or these three foolish Journeymen may steal it from me." The Landlord did so, and as he carried the saddle-bags into his room he felt that they were heavy with gold. So he put the three Journeymen into a lower room, and the merchant into the best room by himself. At midnight, when the Landlord thought everybody was asleep, he went, accompanied by his wife, into the rich merchant's chamber, and killed him by a stroke with an axe. The murder committed, they went to bed again; and when daylight came they made a great uproar, for the merchant was found dead, lying in pools of blood. All the inmates of the inn were collected, and the Landlord declared the murder had been committed by the three Journeymen. This the other lodgers confirmed, saying no one else could have done it; and when the three Journeymen were called, and asked if they had done the deed, the first replied, "All three of us;" the second, "For money;" and the third said, "That is right!"

"Now hear them," said the Landlord, "they confess it themselves." Thereupon the three were taken and thrown into prison; and while they lay there they perceived that it was a serious matter for them. But by night the Evil One came, and said to them, "Keep up your courage for one day, and despair not of your fortune, for not a hair of you shall be injured."

The following morning they were taken before the judge, and asked by him, "Are you the murderers?" "All three of us," replied the first. "Why did you kill the merchant?" asked the judge, secondly. "For money," was the reply. "You wretched men," exclaimed the judge, "have you repented of your crime since?" "That is right," said the third Journeyman. Then the judge ordered them to be led away to die, for they had confessed their crime, and were hardened about it.

So the three companions were led away, and the Landlord had to

accompany them, being the accuser. Just as they were seized by the
hangman and led up to the scaffold, where the executioner stood
with a sharp sword, all at once a coach appeared drawn by four
blood-red foxes, who went so fast that fire flew out of the stones,
while from the window of the coach some one beckoned with a white
handkerchief. The executioner said, "There comes a pardon!" and
from the coach a voice was heard shouting, "Pardon, pardon!"
Presently out of the coach the Evil One stepped, dressed as a
distinguished lord, and said to the three prisoners, "You are
innocent, you may speak now and state what you saw and heard."
Thereupon the first Journeyman said, "We did not kill the
merchant, the murderer stands there" (pointing to the Landlord),
"and for a proof to this go into his cellar, and you will find many
other bodies of those he has destroyed."

The judge, therefore, sent his guards, and they found the cellar as
the man described, and the Landlord was consequently taken, and
his head was struck off. The Evil One then said to the three
Journeymen, "You are free, and will have money all your life, for I
have got that for which I bargained."

Ferdinand the Faithful and Ferdinand the Unfaithful

ONCE upon a time there lived a certain Man and his Wife who as long as they were in prosperous circumstances were blessed with no children, but as soon as poverty came upon them a little boy was born to them. They were now so poor that they could get no one to stand godfather to their child, and the man determined he would go to another town and seek one. On his way he met a poor man, who inquired whither he was going, and he told him he was in search of some one to be sponsor to his son. "Oh!" said the poor man, "you are in distress, and I also! I will be godfather to your child, although I am too poor to give him any gift; go tell your wife and let her come to the church with the child." As soon as they got there the beggar said the name of the boy should be Ferdinand the Faithful; and so he was baptized.

FERDINAND THE FAITHFUL AND FERDINAND THE UNFAITHFUL

When they came away from the church the beggar said to the Mother, "I cannot go with you because I have nothing to give you, nor you to me; but take this key, and let your husband take care of it till your boy is fourteen years old; and at that age he must go up the hill, and he will there come to a castle to which this key belongs, and whatever is in the castle shall be his."

When the boy reached the age of seven, he was once playing with other children, and they teased him and said he had received no present from his godfather as they had all done. Thereupon the boy went to his father and asked him whether what they said was true. "Oh! no," replied the father, "your godfather left a key for you which unlocks a castle which you will find up the hill." The boy went up, but no castle was to be seen or heard of; but by-and-by, when another seven years had passed, he went up again, and there saw the castle. As soon as he unlocked it he found a horse in a stable, and this so pleased him that he mounted it and rode back to his father, saying, "Now I have got a steed, I will travel."

So he went off, and on the roadside he found a shepherd whom he thought at first of taking with him, but he resolved not to do so, and rode on. But as he passed, the man called, "Ferdinand the Faithful, take me with you." So he went back and took him up behind him. After they had ridden a little way the came to a lake on the shore of which a fish was lying gasping in agony. "Ah! my good fish," cried Ferdinand, "I must help you back into the water;" and, taking it up, he threw it in, and the Fish called out as it fell into the water, "Now since you have assisted me when I was in trouble I will also help you; take this reed pipe, and when you are in need blow thereon, and I will come; and if you chance to fall into the water I will help you out." After this Ferdinand rode on, and by-and-by he asked his companion whither he would go. "To the nearest place; but what is your name?" "Ferdinand the Faithful." "Indeed," replied the other; "then your name is like mine, for I am called Ferdinand the Unfaithful." So they rode on to the nearest place and stopped at the first inn.

Now, it was unfortunate that Ferdinand the Unfaithful came

there, for he knew all manner of evil tricks. There was at this inn a maiden, fair-faced and clear-eyed, who took a liking to Ferdinand the Faithful as soon as he came, because he was handsome and cheerful, and she asked him where he was going. When he had told her he was travelling about, she advised him to stop where he was, for the King needed good servants and couriers, and he was just the sort of man for him. At first he refused to hear about the matter, and said he must go on; so the maiden went herself to the King and said she knew of a good servant. The King bade her bring him before him; and as he had a horse which he said he could not part with on any account, the King made him his courier. As soon then as Ferdinand the Unfaithful heard of this, he asked the maiden if she could not assist him also; and, willing to oblige both, she went to the King and got him a place in the royal household also.

A morning or two after their arrival the King awoke groaning and lamenting that his dear bride was not with him. As soon as Ferdinand the Unfaithful heard this, he went to the King (because all along he had a spite against Ferdinand the Faithful) and advised him to send a messenger after her. "You have a courier," he said; "why not send him off to fetch her back? and if he does not bring her let his head pay the forfeit?" Thereupon the King summoned Ferdinand the Faithful, and ordered him on pain of death to bring back his beloved bride from the place where she was.

Ferdinand went into the stable to his favourite horse, and began to groan and weep. "Oh! what an unlucky man am I!" The Horse thereupon began to speak, and asked him what was the matter? Ferdinand was astonished to hear the horse speak, and exclaimed, "What, Schummel, can you talk? Know, then, that I have to fetch the King's bride, and know not where to go." Schummel replied, "Go you to the King, and tell him that if he will give you what you ask, you will fetch his bride; but it must be a shipful of meat and another full of bread, for there are giants across the lake where you must go, and would eat you if you brought no meat, and there are birds also who would peck out your eyes if you took no bread."

Ferdinand went and told the King, who caused all the butchers to kill and dress meat, and all the bakers to make loaves, with which two ships were filled. As soon as these were ready, Schummel said to Ferdinand, "Now take me with you in the ship, and set sail, and when we come to the Giants say to them,

> " 'Peace be with you, Giants dear,
> For I have brought you, never fear,
> A good supply of fleshly cheer!'

"And when the Birds come, say,

> " 'Peace be with you, Ravens dear,
> For I have brought you, never fear,
> A good supply of baker's cheer!'

"With these words they will be satisfied, and leave you, and when you come to the castle the Giants will help you; and two of them will go with you to where the Princess sleeps, whom the King wants. You must not awaken her, but the Giants must take her up in her bed, and carry her to the ship."

All this happened precisely as the Horse said, and Ferdinand the Faithful gave the Giants and the Birds what he had brought with him, and thereupon the Giants were satisfied, and brought the Princess to the King. As soon as she came, she said she must have her letters, which were left behind in the castle, and the King ordered Ferdinand the Faithful to fetch them on pain of death.

Ferdinand went again into the stable, and told his horse what duty he had to perform, and Schummel advised him to load the ships as before and sail to the castle. This he did, and the Giants and Birds were satisfied a second time; and when they arrived at the castle, Schummel told Ferdinand where the sleeping chamber of the Princess was, and he went up and fetched the packet of letters. On their way back Ferdinand unluckily dropped the letters into the water, and Schummel said, "Alas! alas! I cannot help you now!" Then Ferdinand bethought himself of his reed pipe, and began to blow it, and presently the Fish which he had formerly saved made its appearance, carrying in its mouth the letters, which it delivered to its preserver. After this they brought home the letters safely to the palace where the wedding was about to be held.

Now, the Queen did not love the King much, because he had a small nose, but she took a great fancy to Ferdinand the Faithful. And once, when all the court was assembled, the Queen said she knew some curious arts. She could cut off a person's head, and put it on again, without doing him any harm. When Ferdinand the Unfaithful heard this, he suggested that she should make the experiment on Ferdinand the Faithful. And so, after a while, she did; and after cutting off his head, put it on again, and it healed up, so that only a red mark was visible round the neck. "Where did you learn to do that, my child?" asked the King. "Oh, I understand it well enough," she replied; "shall I experiment on you?" The King consented, but when she had cut off his head she would not put it on again; and after the lapse of some time she married Ferdinand the Faithful.

Now he rode again upon his horse Schummel; and one day it told him to ride thrice up the hill; and, as soon as he had done so, the horse was disenchanted and stood up a handsome Prince.

The Shoes which were Danced to Pieces

THERE was once upon a time a King, who had twelve daughters, every one of whom was prettier than her sisters. They slept together in one room, where their beds all stood in a row, and in the evening, as soon as they were gone to sleep, the King shut the door and bolted it. One morning, when he opened the door as usual, he perceived that their shoes were danced to pieces, and nobody could tell how it happened. The King, therefore, caused it to be proclaimed that whoever could discover where they had danced in the night should receive one of them to wife, and become King at his death; but whoever should attempt to do it, and after three nights and days fail, must lose his life. In a short time a Prince came and offered himself to undertake the task. He was well received, and at night led to a room which adjoined the bed chamber of the Princesses. There he was to watch whither they went to dance; and, in order that they might not slip out secretly to another place, their room door was left open for him to see. But the Prince soon felt a mist steal over his eyes, and he went to sleep; and when he awoke in the morning he found the Princesses had all been dancing as usual, for their shoes stood there with holes in the soles. The second and third night it happened just the same; and on the morrow the Prince lost his head without mercy. Afterwards came many more and attempted the task, but they all lost their lives.

One day it chanced that a poor Soldier, who had a wound which prevented him from serving, came upon the road which led to the city where the King dwelt. There he met an old woman, who asked him whither he was going. "I do not know myself altogether," he replied; "but I had an idea of going to the place where the Princesses dance their shoes to pieces, to find out the mystery, and so become King." "That is not difficult," said the old woman, "if you do not drink the wine which will be brought to you in the evening, but feign to be asleep." With these words she gave him a cloak, and told him that if he put it on his shoulders he would become invisible and be able to follow the Princesses. As soon as the Soldier had received this good advice, he plucked up courage and presented himself before the King as a suitor. He was as well received as the others had been, and was dressed in princely clothes. When evening came he was led to his sleeping-room, and, as he was about to go to bed, the eldest Princess came and brought him a cup of wine, but he had fastened a bag under his throat into which he poured the wine, and drank none.

Then he laid himself down, and in a short time began to snore as if he were in a deep sleep, while the twelve sisters laughed to one another, saying, "He might have spared himself the trouble!" In a few minutes they arose, opened cupboards, closets and drawers, and pulled out a variety of beautiful clothes. As soon as they were dressed they looked at themselves in the glass, and presently began to dance; but the yougest sister said, "I know not how you are enjoying yourselves, but my heart sickens as if some misfortune were about to fall upon us!" "What a goose you are!" cried the eldest sister, "you are always fearing something; have you forgotten how many kings' sons have already lost their lives? why, if I had not given this Soldier his sleeping-draught, the simpleton could not even then

THE SHOES WHICH WERE DANCED TO PIECES

have kept his eyes open!" As they were now quite ready, they first looked at the Soldier and satisfied themselves all was right, for he kept his eyes shut and did not move a bit; and then the eldest sister knocking on her bed it sank down in the ground, and the twelve Princesses followed it through the opening, the eldest one going first. The Soldier, having observed everything all the while, put on his invisible cloak, and descended with the youngest sister. About the middle of the steps down he trod on her cloak, and she exclaimed, much frightened, "Who is that who holds my cloak?" "Don't be so silly," said the eldest sister; "you caught it on some nail or other, that is all." So they went completely down, and at the bottom was a wonderful avenue of trees, whose leaves were all silver, and shone and glittered. The Soldier thought to himself he would take one branch for a token, and broke it off, when a tremendous crack sounded as from the tree. "It is not all right!" cried the youngest; "did you not hear the crack?" "That is a shot of welcome!" said the eldest, "because we have been so lucky." Then they passed into another avenue where the leaves were of gold, and then into a further one where they shone like diamonds. From both he broke off a twig, and each time the youngest Princess shrieked with terror, while the eldest ones declared they were merely guns of welcome. So they went further and came to a lake, on which were twelve little boats, and in each boat a handsome Prince, who each took one sister, and the old Soldier sat down in the boat where the youngest one was. "I know not how it is," said the Prince, "but the boat seems much heavier than usual, and I am obliged to use all my strength to row it along." "Perhaps that proceeds from the warmth of the weather," said the Princess; "I am myself much more heated than usual." On the other side of this water stood a noble castle, which was well lighted, and one could hear the music of horns and fiddles within. Towards this they rowed, went in, and each Prince danced with his own partner, while the Soldier danced among them all invisible; and whenever a glass of wine was handed to one or the other he drank it out, so that it was empty when held to the lips; and the youngest sister again felt very uneasy, but her sister bade her hold her tongue. Here they danced till three in the morning at which hour, because their shoes were in holes, they were compelled to desist. The Princes rowed them back again over the water, but this time the Soldier sat down with the eldest Princess. On the shore they took leave of the Princes and promised to return the following morning. When they came back to the steps, the Soldier ran up first, and laid down again in his bed; and when the twelve sisters came up, weary and sleepy, he snored so loudly that they all listened, and cried, "How much safer could we be?" Then they took off their fine clothes, and locked them up, and, putting their dancing-shoes under the bed, they lay down to sleep. The next morning the Soldier said nothing, wishing to see more of this wonderful affair, and so the second and third nights passed like the first; the Princesses danced each time till their shoes were in holes, and the Soldier, for an additional token of his story, brought away a cup with him from the ball-room. When the time arrived for him to answer, he first concealed the twigs and cup about him, and then went before the King, while the twelve Princesses stood behind the door, and listened to all that was said. "Where have my daughters danced during the night?" asked the King. "With twelve Princes in a subterranean castle," he replied; and, relating everything as it had occurred, he produced his witnesses in the three twigs and the cup. The King then summoned his daughters, and asked them if the Soldier had spoken the truth. They were obliged to confess he had; and the King asked him which he would have for a wife. "I am no longer young," he replied, "and so it had better be the eldest." Thereupon the wedding was celebrated the self-same day, and the kingdom appointed to him at the old King's death. But the Princes were again bewitched in as many days as they had danced nights with the twelve Princesses.

The Bright Sun brings on the Day

A TAILOR'S journeyman was tramping about the country in search of work, but none could he find; and his poverty became so great that he had not a farthing to spend. Just at that time he met a Jew on the road, and, deaf to the voice of conscience, he went up to him, because he thought he had money, and seizing him cried out, "Give me your money, or I will take your life!" "Spare my life!" entreated the Jew, "for I have no more money than eight farthings." But the Tailor said, "You have money, and I will have it out;" and he beat the poor Jew till he was almost dead. But before he expired, the Jew cried, "The bright sun brings on the day;" and died immediately. The Tailor, thereupon, searched the pockets of his victim, and found nothing but the eight farthings which the Jew had mentioned. So he took up the body and threw it away among the bushes, and then went further in search of work. After he had travelled a long distance, he came to a city, where he was engaged by a Master Tailor, who had a pretty daughter, whom he married and lived with in great happiness. When some years had passed, and the journeyman and his wife had two children, the old father and mother died, and the young people had to keep house for themselves. One morning, as the husband was sitting at the table by the window, his wife brought him his coffee; and, just as he had poured it into the saucer to drink, the bright sun shone in on it at the open window, and danced on the opposite wall in circles. Thereupon the Tailor jumped up and cried, "It would bring on the day, but it cannot!" "Dear husband, what do you mean – what is it?" asked his wife. "That I dare not tell you," he replied. His wife, however teased him, and spoke so very affectionately to him, saying, she would tell nothing about it, till at last he told her that, many years ago, when he was travelling about for work, and had no money, he had killed a Jew, whose last words had been, "The bright sun brings on the day." That morning the sun had danced on the wall, but without continuing there, and that had reminded him of the Jew's words, but he begged his wife to say nothing of the matter to any one. As soon, however, as he had sat down to work, his wife went to her cousin and betrayed the secret to her, making her promise to tell nobody. In three days' time however, the cousin told some one else, and so it went on till the whole town knew it; and the Tailor was taken before the judge and condemned. Thus, the bright sun brought on the day.

The Prince who was Afraid of Nothing

ONCE upon a time there was a King's Son, who felt too much dissatisfied to stay at home any longer; and, as he feared nobody, he thought he would travel about the world, where there was plenty of time and space for him to meet with wonderful things. So he took leave of his parents and set out, walking straight onwards by day and night; for it was all one to him whither the road might lead. Presently it chanced that he came to a Giant's house, and, being weary, he sat down before his door to rest. He soon began to look about him, and saw in the courtyard bowls and ninepins as big as men, which formed the playthings of the Giant. In a little while he took a fancy to play; and, setting up the ninepins, he bowled at them with the balls, and as each one fell down he shouted for joy and pleasure. The Giant heard the noise, and, stretching his head out of the window, he saw a man no bigger than ordinary mortals playing with his balls.

"You worm!" cried the Giant, "what are you meddling with my balls for? who gave you strength to do that?" The King's Son looked around, up and down, and soon saw the Giant, to whom he replied, "You simpleton, do you think you alone have strength of arm? I can do anything I wish." The Giant thereupon came down, and looked on in astonishment at the bowling; but soon he said, "Child of man, if you are of that race, go and fetch me an apple from the tree of life."

"What do you want with it?" inquired the Prince.

"I do not require the apple for myself," said the Giant; "but I have a wife who longs for it. I have already gone far into the world, but cannot find the tree."

"I will soon find it," replied the Prince; "and I know not what shall prevent me from bringing away an apple."

"Do you think, then, it is such an easy matter?" said the Giant; "the garden wherein the tree stands is surrounded with an iron railing, and before this railing lie wild beasts one after the other, keeping watch, that nobody may enter."

"They will soon let me in," said the Prince.

"Yes, you may enter the garden and see the apples hanging on the tree," replied the Giant; "but still they are not thine; for on the tree is a ring, through which one must push his hand before he can reach the fruit to pluck it, and this has never yet been successfully performed."

"Then I shall be the first lucky one," said the Prince; and, taking leave of the Giant, he went over fields and through woods, up hill and down dale, till at last he came to the wonderful garden. The beasts lay around it in a circle, but they were all sunk in a deep sleep, and did not awake even when he stepped across them; and, climbing over the railing, he entered the garden. In the middle of this garden stood the tree of life, with the red apples glistening on the boughs. The Prince climbed up the trunk of the tree, and, as he reached his hand up to the fruit, he saw a ring hanging down, through which he thrust his hand without difficulty and broke off an apple. The ring slid down and closed tight upon his arm, and immediately he felt, as it were, a stream of fresh strength infused into his veins. When he had descended the tree again with the apple, he would not clamber over the railing to get out of the garden, but went to the great gate, and, giving it a shake, it sprang open with a crash. Then he went out, and the lion which had before lain at the door jumped up and followed him, not in rage and anger, but submissively as his master.

The Prince took the promised apple to the Giant, and said to him, "See, I have fetched it without trouble." The Giant was very glad to have his wish fulfilled so soon, and hastened to his wife to give her the apple which she had longed for. The wife was a beautiful young maiden, who, when she saw the ring was not on the Giant's arm, said, "I do not believe that you obtained it yourself, or else the ring would be on your arm." "I have only to go home and fetch it," replied the Giant; for he imagined it would be an easy matter to take the ring from the Prince by force, if he would not give it up willingly. So he went and demanded the ring, but the Prince would not part with it. "Where the apple is the ring must be too," said the Giant, "and, if you are not willing to give it to me, we must fight for it."

For a long time they wrestled and fought, but the Giant could not master the Prince, who was strengthened by the ring. So he bethought himself of a stratagem, and said to his opponent, "I am quite hot with fighting, and you are hot too; let us plunge into the stream and cool ourselves before we begin again." The Prince did not detect the false pretence, and, going to the river, he pulled off his clothes, together with the ring, and plunged in. Immediately he had done so, the Giant snatched up the ring and ran away with it; but the lion, who had perceived the thievish trick, pursued the Giant, and tearing the ring out of his hand brought it back to his master. Then the Giant hid himself behind a tree, and, when the Prince was busy drawing on his clothes again, he suddenly came behind, and, knocking him over, put out both his eyes.

Now the poor Prince was blind, and knew not how to help himself; and presently the Giant came, and, leading him by the hand, conducted him to the edge of a precipice. There he left the Prince standing, thinking to himself, "A couple of steps further and he will be a dead man, and the ring will fall into my hands." But the faithful liòn had not deserted his master, but kept tight hold of his clothes, and drew him back by degrees from the edge. Afterwards, when the Giant came to plunder the dead, he found his stratagem had failed. "Is this weak man, then, not to be destroyed?" exclaimed the Giant wrathfully; and, catching hold of the Prince's hand, he led him by quite another path to a frightful abyss; but here also the faithful lion accompanied his master, and saved him from the danger. As soon as they were come to the edge, the Giant let go of the Prince's hand, and thought he would soon walk over; but the lion gave the Giant himself a push, so that he fell into the abyss and was dashed to pieces.

The faithful beast then pulled his master away from the danger, and led him to a tree, near which a clear stream ran along. Here the lion made his master sit down, and began to sprinkle the water in his face with his tail. Scarcely had a couple of drops touched his eyeballs, when he immediately received his sight, and observed a little bird which flew by and settled on the branch of a tree. Then it flew down and bathed itself in the stream, and soon flew away again among the trees; for it had regained its sight, which was lost. Here the Prince recognised the providence of God, and, bathing himself in the stream, he washed his face; and when he came out of the water he found he could see as well as ever he had done in his life.

The Prince thereupon returned thanks to God for his great goodness, and travelled, accompanied by his lion, further a-field. It chanced next that he came to a castle which was enchanted, and at its door stood a young maiden of fine stature and appearance, but quite black. She addressed the Prince, saying, "Ah! could you save me from the wicked enchanter who has power over me?" "What shall I do to accomplish that?" asked the Prince. "You must pass three nights in the court of this enchanted castle," replied the maiden; "but during that time no fear must enter your heart. If you are troubled most horribly, and yet you bear it without complaint, I am saved, for they dare not take your life."

"I am not afraid," said the Prince; "with God's aid, I will try my fortune." And so saying, he went joyfully into the hall of the castle, and when it was dark sat down and waited the issue. Till midnight all was still, and then began a mighty uproar, for out of every corner and chink came evil spirits. They appeared not to observe the Prince, for they sat down in the middle of the room, and, making a fire, presently began to play. When one of them lost, he said, "It is not right, there is somebody here who does not belong to us, and it is his fault that I have lost." "Come and join us, you there behind the stove!" cried the others. All the while the screaming was so awful that nobody could have heard it without terror; but the Prince remained quite quiet and had no fear. At last all the evil spirits jumped over and upon him, and there was so many of them that he could not protect himself. They pulled him down on the ground, shook him, pricked him, beat him, and tormented him; but he uttered no cry. Towards morning they disappeared; but the Prince was so wearied that he could scarcely move his limbs. Soon the sun began to shine, and then appeared the black maiden, who carried in her hand a bottle containing the water of life. With this water she washed the Prince's face; and immediately all his strength returned and he was as vigorous as ever. "One night," said she to him, "you have luckily passed through; but there are yet two more to try you." So saying, she went away, and the Prince observed that her feet had become white again.

The next night the evil spirits came, and renewed their gambols; tumbling upon and over the poor Prince, as the night before, till his whole body was full of wounds. Nevertheless he bore it all; and when day broke they were forced to quit him; and the maiden again appeared and healed him with the water of life. As she went away he observed with joy that her arms had become white as far as the tips of her fingers. Now he had only one more night to pass; but that was the worst of the three; for when the crew of evil spirits came, and saw him there, they shouted, "What! are you here still? You shall be tormented now till your breath is almost gone." Thereupon they beat and knocked him about, threw him here and there, pulled his arms and legs as if they would tear them off; but he endured it all, and made no outcry. When the spirits left the Prince he lay quite helpless and unable to stir; and he could not even open his eyes wide enough to see the black maiden, who at daybreak came in with the water of life. Then all at once his aches and pains left him, and he felt quite refreshed and strong as if he were just awake; and when he opened his eyes he saw the maiden standing by him, with a snow-white skin, and a face as fair as the bright daylight! "Arise," said she, "and wave your sword thrice over the threshold; and then all will be saved!" As soon as the Prince did this, the whole castle was freed from its enchantment; and the maiden became what she really was, a rich Princess. Presently the servants entered and said the table was laid in the great hall, and the meat placed upon it. So the Prince and Princess sat down and dined together, and in the evening the wedding was celebrated with great magnificence and rejoicing.

The Idle Spinner

In a certain village lived a Man and his Wife, who was such a very idle woman that she would do no work at all scarcely; for what her husband gave her to spin she did very slowly, and then would not take the trouble to wind it, so that it lay on the ground ravelled and shackled. Whenever her husband scolded her she was always beforehand with an excuse, and used to say, "Why, how can I wind without a reel? you must go and fetch me one from the wood first." "Well, if that is all," said her husband one day, "if that is all, I will go and find you one." As soon as he said this, the Woman began to be afraid that if he found a piece of wood he would make a reel from it, and she would have to wind up what was ravelled and begin afresh. She therefore considered awhile what she should do, and then the lucky thought came to run into the forest secretly after her husband. She found him in the act of cutting a branch off, for the purpose of trimming it; and so, slipping in among the brushwood where he could not see her, she began to sing—

> "He that cuts a reel shall die,
> And he that winds shall perish."

The Man listened, laid down his axe, and wondered what the voice meant. At last he said, "Ah! well! what should it be? it was nothing but some fancy in my head, about which I need not fear!" So saying, he seized his axe and began again; but the voice sang as before—

> "He that cuts a reel shall die,
> And he that winds shall perish."

The Man stopped again, and began to feel very uncomfortable and frightened; but he soon took courage, and began to chop again. At the same time the voice cried again—

> "He that cuts a reel shall die,
> And he that winds shall perish."

This time he was too frightened to do anything more, and hastily leaving the tree, he set out homewards. Meanwhile his Wife, by a bypath, and by means of great exertion, reached home before him; and when he arrived she looked as innocent as if nothing had happened, and inquired of her husband if he had brought a good reel? "No, no!" he said; "I can see very well that it is of no use; winding won't do!" and then, after telling her all that had happened, he ceased to scold her for her idleness.

But only for a while, for soon the disorder in his house began to vex him again. "Wife, wife!" he said, "it is surely a shame that you leave your thread in that ravel." "Well, do you know what to do?" said she; "since we can get no reel, do you lie down on the floor, and I will stand above you, and then you must throw the thread up to me, and I will send it back to you, and so we will make a skein." "Ah! yes, that will do," said the Man; and they pursued this plan, and as soon as the skein was ready he talked of its being boiled. This aggravated the woman again, and she bethought herself of some new plot, while she consented to do as he proposed. Early in the morning, accordingly, she got up, made a fire, and putting on the kettle, put a lump of tow into it instead of the skein of thread, and left it to soak. This done, she went to her husband, who was still in bed, and said to him, "I have to go out now, but do you get up at once and see after the thread which is in the kettle over the fire; and mind you are very attentive to it, for if by chance the cock should crow before you look at it the thread will all turn to tow."

The husband thereupon got up at once, and stopped for no further directions, but, running as quick as he could into the kitchen, he looked into the kettle, and grew pale with affright; the thread was already changed into tow. After this the poor man was as still as a mouse, for he believed it was his fault that the thread was spoiled; and for the future he dared say nothing about thread and spinning.

But I must confess that after all the Woman was indeed an idle, slovenly wife.

The Three Brothers

THERE was once a Man whose family consisted of three sons, and his property only of the house in which he dwelt. Now, each of the sons wished to have the house at the death of their father; but they were all so dear to him that he knew not what to do for fear of offending the one or the other. He would have sold the house and shared the money, but it had been so long in his family he did not like to do that. All at once he thought of a plan, and said to his sons, "Go into the world, and each of you learn a trade, and he who makes the best masterpiece shall have my house."

With this plan the sons were contented, and the eldest became a Farrier, the second a Barber, and the third a Fencing-master. They appointed a time when they should all return, and went away; and it so chanced that each happened with a clever master, with whom he could learn his trade in the best manner. The Smith had to shoe the

King's horses, and thought he must undoubtedly receive the house. The Barber shaved many distinguished lords, and made sure of getting the house on that account. The Fencing-master got many a blow, but he bit his lip and showed no concern; for he feared if he flinched at any stroke the house would never become his. By-and-by the time came round when they returned home to their father; but they none of them knew how they should find occasion to show their proficiency, and so they all consulted together. While they sat in consultation, a hare came running across the field where they were. "Ah! he comes as if he were called!" cried the Barber; and, taking his soap and basin, he made a lather; and as soon as the hare came up he seized him, and shaved off his mustachios as he ran along, without cutting him in the least, or taking off any unnecessary hairs. "That pleases me very well!" said the Father; " and if the others do not do better the house is yours." In a very short time a carriage, with a traveller in it, came rolling by at full speed. "Now you shall see, father, what I can do!" cried the Farrier; and, seizing the horse's feet as he galloped along, he pulled off the shoes, and shod him again without stopping him. "You are a clever fellow!" cried the Father; "you have done your work quite as well as your brother, and I shall not know to whom to give the house." "Let me show you something!" said the third brother; and, as it just then luckily began to rain, he drew his sword and waved it so quickly above his head that not a drop fell upon him; and when the rain came faster, and at length so fast that it was as if one were emptying pails out of heaven, he swung the sword quicker and quicker in circles above his head, so that he kept himself as dry as if he had been under a roof. As soon as the Father saw this he was astonished, and said to his son, "You have performed the best masterpiece, the house is yours."

The two other brothers were contented with this decision; and, because they all loved one another, they all three remained in the house driving their several trades; and as they were so clever, and were so advanced in their arts, they earned much money. Thus they lived happily together till their old age, and when one fell sick and died his brothers grieved so for his loss, that they fell sick also and died.

THE THREE BROTHERS

Then, because they all three had been so clever in their several trades, and had loved one another so much, they were laid together in the same grave.

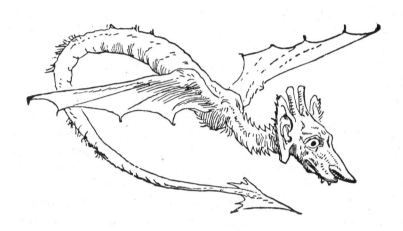

The Evil Spirit and his Grandmother

THERE was once upon a time a mighty war, and the king of a certain country had many Soldiers engaged in it; but he gave them such very small pay that they had scarce enough to live upon. At length three of the Soldiers agreed to run away, and one of them asked the others what they should do; for, supposing they were caught again, they would be hung upon the gallows. "Do you see yon great corn-field?" said the other, "there we will conceal ourselves, and nobody will find us; for the army will not dare to come there, and to-morrow they will march on." So they crept into the corn; but the army did not move, but remained encamped in the same place. The three Soldiers were obliged, therefore, to pass two days and two nights in the corn, and they became so hungry they thought they must die; but it was *certain* death if they returned to the army. They said to one another, "What avails our deserting? we shall now certainly perish miserably from hunger." While they were talking a great fiery Dragon came flying over their heads, and, alighting near the spot where they were, asked why they had concealed themselves. "We are three Soldiers," they replied, "and have deserted because our pay was so small; and now we shall die from hunger if we stay here, or be hung on the gallows if we return."

"If you will serve me seven years," said the Dragon, "I will carry you through the midst of the army, so that no one shall observe you."

"We have no choice, and so must consent to your proposal," replied the Soldiers. The Dragon thereupon caught them up by his claws, and carried them through the air, over the heads of their comrades, and presently set them down. Now, this Dragon was the Evil Spirit; and he gave the Soldiers a whip each, and then said, "If you crack this well, as much money as you require will instantly appear before you; and you can then live like lords, keep your own horses and carriages; but at the end of seven years you will be mine." With these words he handed them a book in which they had to write their names, while the Evil Spirit told them he would give them one chance when the time was up of escaping his power by answering a riddle which he would propose. Then the Dragon flew away from them; and the three Soldiers each cracked their whips, and cracked their whips for as much money as they required, with which they bought fine clothes, and travelled about like gentlemen. Wherever they went they lived in the greatest splendour, driving and riding about, and eating and drinking to their hearts' content; but no bad action could be laid to their charge. The time passed quickly by; and as the end of the seven years approached, two of the three Soldiers became very unhappy and dispirited; but the third treated the matter very lightly, saying, "Fear nothing, my brothers! I have got a plan in my head, and I will solve the riddle." Soon afterwards they went into the fields, where they sat down, and two of them made very wry faces. Presently an old Woman came by, and asked them why they were so sorrowful. "Alas!" said they, "alas! what does it signify? you cannot help us." "Who knows that?" she replied; "confide your griefs to me." So they told her they had become the servants of the Evil One, nearly seven years back, and thereby they came into possession of money as fast as they liked; but they had signed the deed, and if they could not guess a riddle which he would propose to them they were lost. "If you wish to be helped, "replied the old Woman, "one of you must go into the forest, and there he will find a rock overthrown, and made into the form of a hut; into this he must enter, and there he will meet with help." The two low-spirited Soldiers thought this would not help them; but the merry one got up, and, going into the forest, came soon to the rocky cave. In this place sat a very old Woman, who was Grandmother to the Evil Spirit; and she asked the Soldier when he entered, whence he came, and what his business was. He told her everything that had happened; and because his manners pleased her she took compassion on him, and said she could assist him. Thereupon she raised a large stone, under which was the cellar, wherein she bade the Soldier conceal himself, and he would hear all that transpired. "Only sit still and keep very quiet," said she, "and then when the Dragon returns I will ask him about the puzzle, and you must mind what answers he makes." About twelve o'clock at night the Dragon flew in, and desired his dinner. His Grandmother, therefore, covered the table with food and drink, and they ate and drank together till they were satisfied. Then she asked him what success he had met with that day, and how many souls had he secured? "Things did not go well to-day," replied the Dragon; "but yet I have caught three Soldiers safe enough." "Ah! three Soldiers!" said the old Woman; "and I suppose you have set them something to do, that they may not escape you." "They are mine, they are mine!" cried the Evil One, gleefully; "for I have set them a riddle which they will never guess."

"What is this riddle?" asked his Grandmother.

"I will tell you!" replied her Grandson.

"In the great North Sea lies a dead sea-cat, that shall be their roast meat; the rib of a whale shall be their silver spoon; and an old hollow horse's hoof shall be their wine-glass." As soon as the Dragon had said this he went to bed, and the old Woman raised the stone and let out the Soldier. "Have you attended perfectly to all that was said?" inquired the old Woman. "Yes," he replied, "I know well enough how to help myself now."

Then he had to slip secretly out of the window, and by another road regain his companions with all the haste he could. He told them how carefully the old Grandmother had overreached the Dragon, and had laid bare to him the solution of the riddle. When he had finished his story the two other Soldiers recovered their spirits; and, all taking their whips, flogged for themselves so much money that it lay in heaps all around them.

, Not long after this the seven years came to an end, and the Evil Spirit made his appearance with the book, and, pointing to their signatures, said to the Soldiers, "Now I will take you into my dominions, and there you shall have a meal; but, if you can tell me what meat you shall have, you shall be at liberty to go where you like and keep your whips."

"In the great North Sea lies a dead sea-cat, and that shall be the roast meat," replied the first Soldier.

The Evil Spirit was very much put out with this ready answer; hemmed and hawed, and asked the second man what should be the spoon? "The rib of a whale shall be the silver spoon!" replied the second Soldier.

The Evil Spirit now drew a longer face than before, began to grumble and swear, and asked the third Soldier, "Do you know what your wine-glass will be?"

"An old horse's hoof!" he replied.

At this reply the Evil Spirit flew away with a loud outcry, for he had no longer any power over the three Soldiers, who, taking up their whips, procured all the money they wanted, and thereon lived happily and contentedly to a good old age.

The Four Accomplished Brothers

ONCE upon a time there was a Man who had four sons, and when they were grown up young men he told them one day that they must push their own way in the world, for he had nothing to give them, and so they must go among strangers and each learn a different trade, till they were perfect. The four Brothers, therefore, took their walking staffs, and, after bidding their father good-bye, set out from their own door. After they had travelled some distance, they came to a point where four cross-roads met. "Here we must separate," said the eldest Brother; "but in four years' time we will meet again in this place, and recount our several fortunes."

Each Brother, therefore, went his way; and soon the eldest met a man who inquired of him his business and destination. "I wish to learn a trade!" he replied. "Then come with me!" said the man, "and become a Thief." "No!" replied the other; "that is not an honourable employment; and, besides, the end of that song is that one gets used like the clapper in a bell." "Oh, you need not fear the gallows!" said the Thief. "I will teach you so that nobody shall ever be able to catch you, or find any trace of you." Thereupon the man let himself be persuaded, and became, under the other's teaching, such an accomplished Thief that nothing was safe which he set his mind on having.

Meanwhile the second brother had met a man who had asked the very same questions as the first one did; and, when he was told what the business was, he invited the youth to become a Star-gazer. "There is nothing better than that," he said, "for nothing is hid from you." The third brother was taken in hand by a Huntsman, and received such capital instructions in all the branches of the art of shooting that he became quite a renowned marksman. On leaving, his master presented him with a gun, which he said would never miss, for whatever he aimed at it was sure to hit. The youngest brother had meanwhile met a Tailor, and was asked whether he would not like that trade. "I am not so sure about that," replied the youth; "for the sitting cross-legged from morning to night, the continual stitching backwards and forwards of the needle, and a tailor's goose, are not altogether to my mind." "There, there!" cried the man, "you are talking about what you do not understand; you will learn quite a different sort of tailoring with me, and one which is very honourable in its way, besides being easy and handsome." The youth was over-persuaded with these representations, and, accompanying his new friend, he learnt the tailoring trade from its very basis. At leaving, his master gave him a needle, and told him that he could sew together with that whatever he pleased, even if it were as tender as an egg-shell or as hard as steel, and not even a seam would be perceivable to any one after he had done it.

When the four years had passed over, the four Brothers arrived all together at the same time at the cross-ways, and, after embracing and kissing each other, returned home to their Father. "Ah!" he cried, when he saw them come in, "so the wind has blown you back again!" and thereupon they related all their adventures, and said they had each learnt a trade. While they were telling their tales they sat under a great tree, and, as soon as they had done, their father said he would now put their accomplishments to the test. So he looked up, and then said to his second son, "At the top of this tree, between two boughs, there is a bullfinch's nest; now tell me how many eggs there are in it." The Star-gazer took his glass, and, looking through it, said there were five eggs. "Fetch the nest down without disturbing the mother bird, who is sitting on the eggs," said the Father then to his eldest son. The clever Thief climbed up the tree, and took the five eggs from underneath the body of the bird without disturbing or frightening her, and brought them to his Father. The Father took them, and laying one at each corner of a table placed the fifth in the middle, and told the Huntsman to cut them all in halves at one shot. He aimed his gun, and at the first trial the five eggs were shot as his Father wished – and surely he must have a good charge of powder who shoots round a corner. "Now it is your turn," said the old Man to his other son; "do you sew the egg-shells together, and also the young birds which were in them, in such a manner that the shot may not appear to have injured them." The Tailor produced his needle, and soon did what was expected of him, and, when he had finished, the Thief had to carry the eggs back to the nest, and lay them again under the bird without being perceived by it. This he did, and the old bird hatched her eggs in a couple of days afterwards, and the young ones had a red streak round their neck where the Tailor had joined them together.

When his sons had done all these wonderful things, the Father said to them, "Well, you have certainly used your time well, and learnt what is very useful, and for this I must praise you in green clover, as the saying goes; but I cannot tell which of you ought to have the preference, and so that must be left to be seen when an opportunity occurs of displaying your talents publicly."   .

Not long after this a great lamentation was made in the country because the King's daughter had been carried away by a Dragon. Her father was overcome with grief all day and night long, and caused it to be proclaimed that whoever should rescue the Princess should have her for his wife. The four Brothers thereupon thought this was the opportunity they needed, and agreed to go together and deliver the Princess, and show their talents. "I will soon discover where she is!" cried the Star-gazer, and, peeping through his telescope, he said, "I can see her already; she is on a rock in the midst of the sea far away from here, and watched by the Dragon." Then he went to the King, and requested a ship for himself and his Brothers, in which they sailed over the sea till they came near the rock. The Princess observed their arrival, but the Dragon was fast asleep, with his head in her lap. "I dare not shoot!" said the Hunter, when he saw them, "for fear I should kill the Princess as well as the Dragon." "Then I will try my remedy!" said the Thief; and, slipping away, he stole the Princess out of the power of the Dragon, but so lightly and cunningly that the monster noticed nothing, but snored on. Full of joy, they hurried with her down to the ship, and steered away to the open sea; but the Dragon, soon awaking, missed the Princess, and came flying through the air full of rage in pursuit of her. Just as he was hovering above the ship, and was about to alight on it, the Huntsman took aim, fired, and shot the beast through the heart. The Dragon fell, but in his fall he crushed the whole ship to pieces, because of his great size and weight. Luckily they saved a couple of planks, and on these the four Brothers and the Princess floated about. They were now in a great strait, but the Tailor with his wonderful needle sewed together the two planks with great stitches, and then collected the remaining pieces of the ship. These he sewed together so cleverly that in a short time the whole vessel was as tight and complete as before, and they sailed home in her without further accident!

As soon as the King saw his dear daughter again he was very glad, and said to the four Brothers, "One of you shall have my daughter to wife, but which you must settle amongst yourselves."

Thereupon a tremendous quarrel took place between them, for each pressed his own claims. The Star-gazer declared that if he had not seen the Princess all their doings would have been of no use, and so she was his. But the Thief exclaimed, "Of what use would your seeing have been if I had not stolen her away from the Dragon? the Princess is mine!" "But you would have been all torn in pieces by the Dragon had not my ball reached his heart!" interrupted the Huntsman; "and so she must be mine." "That is all very fine!" said the Tailor; "but if it had not been for my sewing the ship together again you would have been all drowned! no, the Princess is mine!" When they had all spoken thus, the King decided the question by saying: "You have all an equal claim; but since you cannot all have the Princess, not one of you shall have her, but I will give each of you instead the half of a province as a reward."

This decision pleased the Brothers, who said, "Yes, it will be better so, for then we shall remain united." Thereupon each received half the revenue of a province, as the King said; and in the enjoyment of this they lived happily with their Father to the end of their lives.

·The Donkey Cabbages

ONCE upon a time there was a young Sportsman who was out in search of game. He had an honest and merry heart, and whistled as he went along; and by-and-by he met an ugly old Woman, who spoke to him and said, "Good day, my good huntsman; you are merry and well fed, but I am suffering from hunger and thirst; give me an alms, I pray you." The Sportsman pitied the poor woman, and, putting his hand in his pocket, gave her what he could afford. As soon as he had done so, he was walking on; but the Woman stopped him, and said to him, "Listen to what I have to say; for your good-heartedness I will make you a present; go now straight along this road, and soon you will come to a tree whereon sit nine birds, quarrelling over a cloak which one will have. Aim at them with your gun, and shoot in the midst of them; then, not only the mantle will drop, but also one of the birds will fall down dead. Take the cloak with you; it is a wishing-cloak, which if you put on your shoulders, you have only to wish yourself where you would be, and at the moment you will be there. Take out also the heart of the dead bird, and swallow it whole, and then every morning when you arise you will find a gold piece under your pillow."

The Huntsman thanked the wise woman, and thought to himself, "These indeed are good gifts, if they turn out as is promised." He had not gone a hundred yards from the spot before he heard a great chirping and rustling among the trees, and, looking up, he saw on one of them a bevy of birds, who were plucking at a cloth with their bills and claws, tearing it among them, for each one wanted it for itself. "Now, this is wonderful!" cried the Sportsman; "it is come to pass just as the old woman promised!" and, lifting his gun to his shoulder, he shot at the birds, who all flew away but one, which fell dead with the cloak over which they had been disputing. Then the Huntsman did as the old Wife had said; he cut out the heart of the bird and swallowed it whole, but the cloak he took home with him.

The next morning, when he awoke he remembered the promise, and, lifting his pillow up, he found under it a bright, shining piece of gold. The morrow morning it was the same, and so it went on: every day he got up he found another piece. Soon he collected a heap of gold, and thought, "What use is all this gold to me if I stay at home? I will go away and look about the world."

THE DONKEY CABBAGES

So he took leave of his parents, and, hanging around him his belt and pouch, he set out on his travels. One day it chanced that he passed through a thick forest, and as he came to the end of it he saw in the distance before him a magnificent castle. At one window of it stood an old Woman, with a wonderfully beautiful Maiden by her side, looking out. But this old lady was a Witch, and said to her daughter, "Here comes one out of the forest who has a wonderful treasure in his body, which we must have; for, my beloved daughter, it is more fit for us than for him: it is a bird's heart, and whoever possesses it finds a gold piece every morning under his pillow." She further told her daughter how it was to be procured, and what she was to do; and threatened her, if she did not obey, to visit her with some misfortune. As soon as the Huntsman approached he perceived the Maiden, and said to himself, "I am weary enough with travelling about, so I will now rest, and turn into this fine castle, for I have money enough." But the real reason was the beautiful face which he saw at the windows.

He entered the house, and was hospitably received and courteously entertained; and soon it came to pass that he was so in love with the daughter of the Witch that he could think of nothing else, and followed her with his eyes everywhere, willing to do all she wished. Then the old Woman said, "Now we must get the bird's heart, for he will not miss it when it is gone!" She concocted, therefore, a drink; and when it was ready she put it into a cup and gave it to her daughter, who had to hand it to the Huntsman, and say, "Now, dearest, drink to me!" He took the cup, and as soon as he had swallowed the draught the heart fell out of his mouth. The Maiden carried it secretly away, and then swallowed it, for the old Woman wanted it herself. Every after the Huntsman no longer found gold pieces under his pillow, for they lay now beneath the Maiden's head, and the old Witch fetched them every morning. But he never troubled himself about the matter, and was content so long as he passed his time with the Maiden.

Soon the old Witch began to say to her daughter, "We have the bird's heart, but not the cloak, which we ought also to have." This the Maiden would fain have left him, since he had lost his riches; but the old mother flew into a passion, and said, "This cloak is a wonderful thing, and such as is seldom found in the world, and I must and will have it!" With these words she beat her daughter, and vowed, if she did not obey her, to do her some injury. The daughter, therefore, at the bidding of her mother, placed herself at the window one day, and looked sadly at the far distance. "Why stand you so sorrowfully there?" asked the Huntsman. "Ah, my treasure!" she replied, "over there lies the granite mountain, where grow precious stones, and when I think about them I become quite sad, for I long so for them; but who can get them? only the birds which fly to and fro; no man ever can."

"Is that all you have to complain of?" said the Huntsman; "then I will soon remove that grief from your heart."

Thereupon he put her under his cloak, and wished himself over the granite mountain; and in a moment they were set down in the place. There glittered the precious stones on all sides, so that it was a pleasure to see them; and they collected the most costly ones together. But now the Witch had caused by her arts a great drowsiness to come over the poor Huntsman, and he said to the Maiden, "We will sit down and rest awhile, for I am so tired I cannot keep upon my feet." So they sat down, and he laid his head in her lap and went to sleep; and while he slept the Maiden took the cloak from his shoulder and threw it over her own back, and then, gathering up the precious stones, she wished herself home again.

By-and-by the Huntsman awoke, and found that his mistress had deceived him, and left him alone on the wild mountain. "Alas!" he cried, "what faithlessness there is in the world!" and he remained lost in care and anxiety, ignorant what to do.

The mountain belonged to some rough and mighty Giants, who dwelt upon it and earned their living there; and in a short time the Huntsman perceived three of them striding towards him. He laid himself down and feigned to be in a deep sleep, and presently the three Giants came striding along, and the first kicked him with his foot and exclaimed, "What earthworm is this lying here?" "Tread him to death!" said the second Giant. But the third said, contemptuously, "That is not worth while; let him alone, he cannot remain here, and if he climbs higher up the hill the clouds will take him and carry him away." After this conversation they went away; but the Huntsman had noted all they said, and as soon as they were gone he got up and climbed to the top of the mountain. After he had sat there a little while a cloud came sweeping by, which caught him up and carried him floating through the air. Then it began to sink down over a large walled-in vegetable garden, where, among cabbages and other herbs, he fell softly to the ground. Then the Huntsman looked round, and said, "If I had only something to eat, for with the distance I have travelled I am very hungry; but here I cannot see a single apple, berry or fruit of any kind; everywhere nothing but cabbages." At length he thought that out of necessity he would eat a salad, which, although it had not a delicate flavour, would yet refresh him. Thereupon he looked out for a good head of cabbage, and ate thereof; but he had scarcely tasted a couple of bites before he felt a wondrous change come over him, and found himself quite transformed. From his body grew four legs, a thick head and two long ears; and he perceived with anguish that he was changed into a donkey! Still, however, his appetite was not appeased, and because the cabbage tasted well now to his animal appetite, he ate with greater pleasure. At last he tasted a different kind, and immediately he felt another change come over him, and his human form returned.

The Huntsman now lay down and slept with weariness; and when he awoke in the morning he broke off a head of the bad and one of the good cabbages, and thought to himself, "These shall help me to my own again and punish the faithless one." With these words he concealed the cabbages about him, and, clambering over the wall, he set out to search for the castle of his love. He luckily discovered it when he had journeyed only a couple of days, and, quickly browning his face, so that his own mother would not have recognised him he went into the castle and begged a night's lodging. "I am so tired," he said, "I can go no further." The Witch asked him who he was, and what was his business; and he told her he was one of the King's messengers, and had been sent to seek the most delicate cabbage which grew upon the earth. "I have been successful," said he, "and have the herb with me; but the heat of the sun is so strong that the tender leaves threaten to wither, and I know not if I can carry it further."

As soon as the old Woman heard of this precious cabbage, she became very agreeable, and begged the Huntsman to allow her to taste the vegetable. "Why not?" he replied; "I have got two cabbages with me, and will give you one;" and, opening his sack, he handed her the bad herb. The Witch, suspecting nothing wrong, took the cabbage into the kitchen to cook it, for her mouth watered for the unknown delicacy. As soon as it was ready she could not wait until it was put on the table, but snatched a part of it, and put it into her mouth. Scarcely had she swallowed it when she lost her human form, and ran like a donkey into the stable-yard. Presently the servant went into the kitchen and saw the cabbage ready dressed, which she took up to carry in-doors; but, according to old custom, she tasted it on the way to the parlour. Immediately the charm began to work, and she became a donkey, and ran away to the other; while the dish fell on the ground, and its contents were spilled. The messenger meanwhile sat with the Maiden, and when the cabbage did not come she took a fancy to have some also, and wondered where it was. The Huntsman thought, "The cabbage has begun to work;" and said to the Maiden, "I will go into the kitchen and see what has happened." As soon as he went down he saw the two donkeys running about the court, and the cabbage lying on the floor. "All right!" cried he; "two have received their share!" and, picking up the rest of the cabbage, he laid it on a dish and took it to the Maiden. "I have brought you this delicate dish myself," said he, "that you may not have to wait longer." Thereupon she ate some of it, and soon, like the rest, lost her human form, and ran as a donkey round the court.

Afterwards, when the Huntsman had washed his face, so that the changed ones might recognise him, he went down into the court, and said to the three, "Now you shall be rewarded for your inconstancy!" He bound them all three together with a rope, and drove them away to a mill. There he knocked at the window, and the Miller, putting his head out, asked him what his wishes were. "I have three unruly animals here," he said, "whom I cannot keep any longer. Will you take them off me, and give them food and work, and treat them as I will tell you; because, if so, you shall have what you wish for so doing?"

"Why not?" replied the Miller; "but how shall I treat them?" The Huntsman told him that the old donkey, which was the Witch, must be given daily three beatings and one meal only; that the youngest, which was the Servant, should receive one beating and three meals; but the other, which was the Maiden, no blows, but three meals; for he could not make up his mind to cause her pain. Thereupon the Huntsman returned to the castle, in which he found all that he wanted. After three days came the Miller, and told him he wished to mention that the donkey for whom he had ordered only one meal and three beatings was dead. "The two others," he said further, "are certainly not dead, for they eat their three meals a-day, but they are so weak and ill they cannot last very long." At this relation the Huntsman pitied the poor beasts, and told the Miller to drive them up again. As soon as they came he gave them a piece of the good cabbage to eat, and in a few minutes their human form returned. Then the beautiful Maiden fell on her knees before him, and said, "Oh, my dear Huntsman, pardon me for the wrong I did you, for it was not of my own free will, but because my mother compelled me, that I acted so; then and now I love you with my whole heart. Your wishing-cloak hangs in yon closet, and the heart of the bird I will bring to you again."

When she had thus spoken the Huntsman pardoned her freely, and begged her to keep the heart, for he meant to make her his bride. Soon afterwards the marriage was performed, and they lived happily together to the end of their lives.

Little One-Eye, Little Two-Eyes, and Little Three-Eyes

ONCE upon a time there was a Woman, who had three daughters, the eldest of whom was named One-Eye, because she had but a single eye, and that placed in the middle of her forehead; the second was called Two-Eyes, because she was like other mortals; and the third, Three-Eyes, because she had three eyes, and one of them in the centre of her forehead, like her eldest sister. But, because the second sister had nothing out of the common in her appearance, she was looked down upon by her sisters, and despised by her mother. "You are no better than common folks," they would say to her; "you do not belong to us;" and then they would push her about, give her coarse clothing, and nothing else to eat but their leavings, besides numerous other insults as occasion offered.

Once it happened that Two-Eyes had to go into the forest to tend the goat; and she went very hungry, because her sisters had given her very little to eat that morning. She sat down upon a hillock, and cried so much that her tears flowed almost like rivers out of her eyes! By-and-by she looked up, and saw a Woman standing by, who asked, "Why are you weeping, Two-Eyes?" "Because I have two eyes like ordinary people," replied the maiden, "and therefore my mother and sisters dislike me, push me into corners, throw me their old clothes, and give me nothing to eat but what they leave. To-day they have given me so little that I am still hungry." "Dry your eyes, then, now," said the wise Woman; "I will tell you something which shall prevent you from being hungry again. You must say to your goat:—

> "Little kid, milk
> Table, appear!"

and immediately a nicely-filled table will stand before you, with delicate food upon it, of which you can eat as much as you please. And when you are satisfied, and have done with the table, you must say:—

> "Little kid, milk
> Table, depart!"

and it will disappear directly." With these words the wise Woman went away, and little Two-Eyes thought to herself she would try at once if what the Woman said were true, for she felt very hungry indeed.

> "Little kid, milk
> Table, appear!"

said the maiden, and immediately a table covered with a white cloth stood before her, with a knife and fork, and silver spoon; and the most delicate dishes were ranged in order upon it, and everything was warm as if they had been just taken away from the fire. Two-Eyes said a short grace, and then began to eat; and when she had finished she pronounced the words which the wise Woman had told her:—

> "Little kid, milk
> Table, depart!"

and directly the table and all that was on it quickly disappeared. "This is capital housekeeping," said the maiden, in high glee; and at evening she went home with her goat, and found an earthen dish which her sisters had left her filled with their pickings. She did not touch it; and the next morning she went off again without taking the meagre breakfast which was left out for her. The first and second time she did this the sisters thought nothing of it; but when she did the same the third morning their attention was roused, and they said, "All is not right with Two-Eyes; for she has left her meals twice, and has touched nothing of what was left for her; she must have found some other way of living." So they determined that One-Eye should go with the maiden when she drove the goat to the meadow, and pay attention to what passed, and observe whether any one brought her to eat or to drink.

When Two-Eyes, therefore, was about to set off, One-Eye told her she was going with her to see whether she took proper care of the goat and fed her sufficiently. Two-Eyes, however, divined her sister's object, and drove the goat where the grass was finest, and then said, "Come, One-Eye, let us sit down, and I will sing to you." So One-Eye sat down, for she was quite tired with her unusual walk and the heat of the sun.

"Are you awake or asleep, One-Eye?
Are you awake or asleep?"

sang Two-Eyes, until her sister really went to sleep. As soon as she was quite sound, the maiden had her table out, and ate and drank all she needed; and by the time One-Eye awoke again the table had disappeared, and the maiden said to her sister, "Come, we will go home now; while you have been sleeping the goat might have run about all over the world." So they went home, and after Two-Eyes had left her meal untouched, the mother inquired of One-Eye what she had seen, and she was obliged to confess that she had been asleep.

The following morning the mother told Three-Eyes that she must go out and watch Two-Eyes, and see who brought her food, for it was certain that someone must. So Three-Eyes told her sister that she was going to accompany her that morning to see if she took care of the goat and fed her well; but Two-Eyes saw through her design, and drove the goat again to the best feeding-place. Then she asked her sister to sit down and she would sing to her, and Three-Eyes did so, for she was very tired with her long walk in the heat of the sun. Then Two-Eyes began to sing as before:—

> "Are you awake, Three-Eyes?"

but, instead of continuing as she should have done,

> "Are you asleep, Three-Eyes?"

she said by mistake,

> "Are you asleep, *Two*-Eyes?"

and so went on singing:—

> "Are you awake, Three-Eyes?
> Are you asleep, Two-Eyes?"

By-and-by Three-Eyes closed two of her eyes, and went to sleep with them; but the third eye, which was not spoken to, kept open. Three-Eyes, however, cunningly shut it too, and feigned to be asleep, while she was really watching; and soon Two-Eyes, thinking all safe, repeated the words:—

> "Little kid, milk
> Table, appear!"

and as soon as she was satisfied she said the old words:—

> "Little kid, milk
> Table, depart!"

Three-Eyes watched all these proceedings; and presently Two-Eyes came and awoke her, saying, "Ah, sister! you are a good watcher; but come, let us go home now." When they reached home Two-Eyes again ate nothing; and her sister told her mother she knew now why the haughty hussy would not eat their victuals. "When she is out in the meadow," said her sister, "she says,

> 'Little kid, milk
> Table, appear!'

and directly a table comes up laid out with meat and wine, and everything of the best, much better than we have; and as soon as she has had enough she says:—

> 'Little kid, milk
> Table, depart!'

and all goes away directly, as I clearly saw. Certainly she did put to sleep two of my eyes; but the one in the middle of my forehead luckily kept awake!"

"Will you have better things than us?" cried the envious mother; "then you shall lose the chance;" and, so saying, she took a carving-knife and killed the goat dead.

As soon as Two-Eyes saw this she went out very sorrowful to the old spot and sat down where she had sat before to weep bitterly. All at once the wise Woman stood in front of her again, and asked why she was crying. "Must I not cry," replied she, "when the goat which used to furnish me every day with a dinner, according to your promise, has been killed by my mother, and I am again suffering hunger and thirst?" "Two-Eyes," said the wise Woman, "I will give you a piece of advice. Beg your sisters to give you the entrails of the goat, and bury them in the earth before the house-door, and your fortune will be made." So saying she disappeared, and Two-Eyes went home, and said to her sisters, "Dear sisters, do give me some part of the slain kid; I desire nothing else – let me have the entrails." The sisters laughed and readily gave them to her; and she buried them secretly before the threshold of the door, as the wise Woman had bidden her.

The following morning they found in front of the house a wonderfully beautiful tree, with leaves of silver and fruits of gold hanging from the boughs, than which nothing more splendid could be seen in the world. The two elder sisters were quite ignorant how the tree came where it stood; but Two-Eyes perceived that it was produced by the goat's entrails, for it stood on the exact spot where she had buried them. As soon as the mother saw it she told One-Eye to break off some of the fruit. One-Eye went up to the tree, and pulled a bough towards her, to pluck off the fruit; but the bough flew back again directly out of her hands; and so it did every time she took hold of it, till she was forced to give up, for she could not obtain a single golden apple in spite of all her endeavours. Then the mother said to Three-Eyes, "Do you climb up, for you can see better with your three eyes than your sister with her one." Three-Eyes, however, was not more fortunate than her sister, for the golden apples flew back as soon as she touched them. At last the mother got so impatient that she climbed the tree herself; but she met with no more success than either of their daughters, and grasped the air only when she thought she had the fruit. Two-Eyes now thought she would try, and said to her sisters, "Let me get up, perhaps I may be successful." "Oh, you are very likely indeed," said they, "with your two eyes: you will see well, no doubt!" So Two-Eyes climbed the tree, and, directly she touched the boughs, the golden apples fell into her hands, so that she plucked them as fast as she could, and filled her apron before she went down. Her mother took them off her, but returned her no thanks; and the two sisters, instead of treating Two-Eyes better than they had done, were only the more envious of her, because she alone could gather the fruits, – in fact, they treated her worse.

One morning, not long after the springing up of the apple-tree, the three sisters were all standing together beneath it, when in the distance a young Knight was seen riding towards them. "Make haste, Two-Eyes!" exclaimed the two elder sisters; "make haste, and creep out of our way, that we may not be ashamed of you;" and so saying they put over her in great haste an empty cask which stood near, and which covered the golden apples as well, which she had just been plucking off. Soon the Knight came up to the tree, and the sisters saw he was a very handsome man, for he stopped to admire the fine silver leaves and golden fruit, and presently asked to whom the tree belonged, for he should like to have a branch off it. One-Eye and Three-Eyes replied that the tree belonged to them; and they tried to pluck a branch off for the Knight. They had their trouble for nothing, however, for the boughs and fruits flew back as soon as they touched them. "This is very wonderful," cried the Knight, "that this tree should belong to you, and yet you cannot pluck the fruit!" The sisters, however, maintained that it was theirs; but while they spoke Two-Eyes rolled a golden apple from underneath the cask, so that it travelled to the feet of the Knight, for she was angry, because her eldest sisters had not spoken the truth. When he saw the apple he was astonished, and asked where it came from; and One-Eye and Three-Eyes said they had another sister, but they dared not let her be seen, because she had only two eyes, like common folk! The Knight, however, would see her, and called, "Two-Eyes, come here!" and soon she made her appearance from under the cask. The Knight was bewildered at her great beauty, and said, "You, Two-Eyes, can surely break off a bough of this tree for me?" "Yes," she replied, "that I will, for it is my property;" and climbing up, she easily broke off a branch with silver leaves and golden fruit, which she handed to the Knight. "What can I give you in return, Two-Eyes?" asked the Knight. "Alas! if you will take me with you I shall be happy, for now I suffer hunger and thirst, and am in trouble and grief from early morning to late evening: take me, and save me!" Thereupon the Knight raised Two-Eyes upon his saddle, and took her home to his father's castle. There he gave her beautiful clothes, and all she wished for to eat or to drink; and afterwards, because his love for her had become so great, he married her, and a very happy wedding they had.

Her two sisters meanwhile were very jealous when Two-Eyes was carried off by the Knight; but they consoled themselves by saying,

"The wonderful tree remains still for us; and even if we cannot get at the fruit, everybody that passes will stop to look at it, and then come and praise it to us. Who knows where our wheat may bloom?" The morning after this speech, however, the tree disappeared, and with it all their hopes; but when Two-Eyes that same day looked out of her chamber window, behold, the tree stood before it, and there it remained!

For a long time after this occurrence Two-Eyes live in the enjoyment of the great happiness; and one morning two poor women came to the palace and begged an alms. Two-Eyes, after looking narrowly at their faces, recognised her two sisters, One-Eye and Three-Eyes, who had come to such great poverty that they were forced to wander about, begging their bread from day to day. Two-Eyes, however, bade them welcome, invited them in, and took care of them, till they both repented of the evil which they had done to their sister in the days of their childhood.

The Three Black Princesses

OSTENDIEN was besieged by an enemy, who would not raise the siege unless he received six hundred dollars. So they made it known by the drummers that whoever could get them together should be Burgomaster. There was a poor Fisherman who fished in the sea with his Son, and the enemy came and took his Son prisoner, and gave him six hundred dollars for him. So the father went and gave them to the great men in the town; and the enemy marched off, and the Fisherman became Burgomaster. Then it was cried about that whoever did not say Mr Burgomaster should be hanged.

The Son got out of the enemy's clutches again, and came to a great forest on a high mountain. The mountain opened, and he went into a great enchanted castle, wherein the chairs, tables, and benches were all hung with black. There came three Princesses, who were dressed all in black, and only had a little bit of white on their faces; they told him not to be afraid, they would not do anything to him, and that he could release them. He said he should be glad enough to do so if he only knew how to set about it. They said that for a whole year he must not speak to them, nor even look at them: whatever he wanted he only had to ask for, and when they might answer him they would do so. When he had been there some time, he said he should like to go and see his father. So they said, "Very well;" and that he should have this bag of gold, and put on these clothes, and must be back again in eight days.

Then he was lifted up, and was in Ostendien directly. He could not find his father any more in the fishing-hut, and asked the people where the poor Fisherman had got to? but they told him he must not say that, or he would come to the gallows. He then arrived at his father's, and said, "Fisherman, how did you come to this?" Then he answered, "You must not say that, for if the great men of the town knew it you would come to the gallows." But he would not leave off, so he was taken to the gallows; and when he got there he said, "Oh, gentlemen, pray give me leave to go to the old fishing-hut!" Then he put on his old smock, and went back to the gentlemen and said, "Do you see now; am I not the son of a poor fisherman? In this dress I earned the daily bread for my father and mother." Then they knew him again, and begged his pardon, and took him home; and he told them all about what had happened to him; that he had got into a great forest on a high mountain; that the mountain opened, and that he had gone into an enchanted castle, where everything was black, and three Princesses had come, who were all black, except a little bit of white in the face. They had told him not to be afraid, and that he could release them.

Then his Mother said, "That cannot be right; you must take a hallowed kettle with you, and drop some scalding water into their faces."

He went back again and he shuddered from fear, and dropped some water into their faces while they were asleep, and they all turned half white. The three Princesses jumped up, and said, "Accursed dog, our blood shall cry for vengeance! now there is no one born in the world, and no one will be born, who can release us. We have three brothers locked in seven chains, and they shall tear you to pieces." Then there was a crash through the whole castle, and he jumped out of a window and broke his leg; and the castle sank into the ground again, and the mountain closed, and nobody knew where it had been.

The Six Servants

A LONG time ago lived an old Queen, who was also an enchantress; and her daughter was the most beautiful creature under the sun. But the old woman was ever thinking how to entice men, in order to kill them, and every suitor, therefore, who came was compelled, before he could marry the daughter, to answer a riddle which the Queen proposed, and which was always so puzzling that it could not be solved; and the unfortunate lover was thereupon forced to kneel down and have his head struck off. Many and many a poor youth had been thus destroyed, for the maiden was very pretty; and still another King's son was found who made up his mind to brave the danger. He had heard of the great beauty of the Princess, and he prayed his father to let him go and win her. "Never!" replied the King; "if you go away, you go to die!" At this answer the son felt very ill, and so continued for seven years nigh unto death's door, for no physician could do him any good. At last, when the old King saw all hope was gone, he said to his son, "Go now and try your fortune, for I know not how else to restore you!" As soon as the Prince heard the word he jumped up from his bed, and felt new strength and vigour return to him while he made ready for his journey.

Soon he set off, and as he rode along across a common he saw at a distance something lying on the ground like a bundle of hay; but, as he approached nearer, he discovered that it was a Man who had stretched himself on the earth, and was as big as a little hill! The fellow waited till the Prince came up, and then said to him, rising as he spoke, "If you need any one take me into your service!"

"What shall I do with such an uncouth fellow as you?" asked the Prince.

"That matters not," replied the Man; "were I a thousand times so clumsy, if I can render you a service."

"Very well, perhaps I shall need you," said the Prince; "come with me." So Fatty accompanied his new master, and presently they met with another Man, who was also lying on the ground, with his ear close to the grass. "What are you doing there?" asked the Prince.

"I am listening," he replied.

"And to what are you listening so attentively?" pursued the Prince.

"I am listening to what is going on in the world around," said the Man, "for nothing escapes my hearing; I can even hear the grass growing."

"Tell me then," said the Prince, "tell me what is passing at the court of the old Queen, who has such a beautiful daughter."

"I hear," replied the Man, "the whistling of the sword which is about to cut off the head of an unsuccessful wooer."

"Follow me, I can find a use for you," said the Prince to the

Listener; and so the three now journeyed together. Presently they came to a spot where were lying two feet and part of two legs, but they could not see the continuation of them till they had walked a good stretch further, and then they came to the body, and at length to the head. "Halloa!" cried the Prince, "what a length you are!"

"Oh!" replied Long-Legs, "not so much of that! why, if I stretch my limbs out as far as I can, I am a thousand times as long, and taller than the highest mountain on the earth; but, if you take me, I am ready to serve you."

The Prince accepted his offer, and, as they went along, they came to a man who had his eyes bandaged up. "Have you blood-shot eyes," inquired the Prince, "that you bind your eyes up in that way?"

"No!" replied the Man; "but I dare not take away the bandage, for whatever I look at splits in two, so powerful is my sight; nevertheless, if I am of use, I will accompany you."

Thereupon the Prince accepted also the services of this Man; and, as they went on, they found another fellow, who, although he was lying on the ground in the scorching heat of the sun, trembled and shivered so that not a limb in his body stood still. "What makes you freeze, when the sun shines like this?" asked the Prince.

"Alas! my nature is quite different from anything else!" replied the Man; "the hotter it is the colder I feel, and the frost penetrates all my bones; while the colder it is the hotter I feel; so that I cannot touch ice for the heat of my body, nor yet go near the fire for fear I should freeze it!"

"You are a wonderful fellow!" said the Prince; come with me, and perhaps I may need you." So the Man followed with the rest; and they came next to a Man who was stretching his neck to such a length that he could see over all the neighbouring hills. "What are you looking at so eagerly?" asked the Prince.

"I have such clear eyes," replied the Man, "that I can see over all the forests, fields, valleys, and hills; in fact, quite round the world."

"Come with me, then," said the Prince, "for I have need of a companion like you."

The Prince now pursued his way with his six servants to the city where the old Queen dwelt. When he arrived he would not tell his name, but told the witch if she would give him her daughter, he would do all she desired. The old Enchantress was delighted to have such a handsome young man fall into her clutches, and told him she would set him three tasks, and if he performed them all, the Princess should become his wife.

"What is the first, then?" asked the Prince.

"You must fetch for me a ring which I have let fall into the Red Sea," said the Queen. Then the Prince returned home to his servants, and said to them, "The first task is no easy one; it is to fetch a ring out of the Red Sea; but let us consult together."

"I will see where it lies," said he with the clear eyes; and looking down into the water, he continued, "there it hangs on a pointed stone!"

"If I could but see it I would fetch it up," said Long-Arms. "It that all?" said Fatty, and, lying down on the bank, he held his mouth open to the water, and the stream ran in as if into a pit, till at length the whole sea was as dry as a meadow. Long-Arms, thereupon, bent down a little, and fetched out the ring, to the great joy of the Prince, who carried it to the old Witch. She was mightily astonished, but confessed it was the right ring. "The first task you have performed, happily," she said; "but now comes the second. Do you see those three hundred oxen grazing on the meadows before my palace? all those you must consume, flesh, bones and skins, and horns; then in my cellar are three hundred casks of wine, which must all be drunk out by you; and if you leave a single hair of any of the oxen, or one drop of the wine, you will lose your life."

"May I invite any guests to the banquet," asked the Prince, "for no dinner is worth having without?" The old woman smiled grimly, but told him he might have one guest for company, but no more.

Thereupon the Prince returned again to his servants, and told them what the task was; and then he invited Fatty to be his guest. He came, and quickly consumed the three hundred oxen, flesh and bones, skin and horns, while he made as if it were only a good breakfast. Next he drank all the wine out of every cask, without so much as using a glass, but draining them all to the very dregs. As soon as the meal was over the Prince went and told the Queen he had performed the second task. She was much astonished, and said no one had ever before got so far as that; but she determined that the Prince should not escape her, for she felt confident he would lose his head about the third task. "This evening," said she, I will bring my daughter into your room, and you shall hold her round with one arm; but mind you do not fall asleep while you sit there, for at twelve o'clock I shall come, and if my daughter is not with you then you are lost." "This task is easy," thought the Prince to himself; "I shall certainly keep my eyes open." Still he called his servants together, and told them what the old woman had said. "Who knows," said he, "what craftiness may be behind? foresight is necessary; do you keep watch, that nobody passes out of the chamber during the night."

As soon as night came the old Queen brought the Princess to the Prince, and then Long-Arms coiled himself in a circle round the pair, and Fatty placed himself in the doorway, so that not a living soul could enter the room. So there the two sat, and the maiden spoke not a word, but the moon shone through the window upon her face, so that the Prince could see her great beauty. He did nothing but look at her, was full of happiness and love, and felt no weariness at all. This lasted till eleven o'clock, and then the old Witch threw a charm over all, so that they fell asleep, and at the same moment the maiden was carried off.

Till a quarter to twelve the three slept soundly, but then the charm lost its strength, and they all awoke again. "Oh, what a terrible misfortune!" cried the Prince as soon as he awoke, "I am lost!" The faithful servants also began to complain; but the Listener said, "Be quiet, and I will hear where she is!" He listened a moment, and then said, "The Princess is sitting three hundred miles from hence, inside a cave, bewailing her fate. You alone can help us, Long-Arms; if you set to the task you will be there in a couple of strides." "Certainly!" said Long-Arms; "but Sharp-Eyes must also go with us to pierce the rock." Then he hoisted Sharp-Eyes upon his back, and in a moment, while one could scarcely turn his hand round, they were before the enchanted rock. Immediately Sharp-Eyes removed his bandage, and, looking round, the rocky cave was shattered into a thousand pieces. Then Long-Arms took the Princess out of the ruins and carried her home first, and, immediately returning for his companion, they were all seated, rejoicing at their fortunate escape, before the clock struck twelve.

As soon as it did strike, the old Enchantress slipped into the room, smiling horribly, for she thought her daughter was safe enough in the rocky cave, and the Prince was hers. But when she perceived her daughter in the arms of the Prince she was terrified, and exclaimed, "Here is one that can do more than I can!" She dared not, however, deny her promise, and the maiden was therefore betrothed to the Prince. But the old Woman whispered in her daughter's ear, "Shame upon you that you listened to common folks, and dared not to choose a husband after your own wishes!"

With these words the pround heart of the Princess was inflamed, and she thought of revenge; and accordingly, the following day, she caused three hundred bundles of faggots to be heaped together, and then said to the Prince, "The three tasks were soon performed; but still I will not marry you until some one shall be found who will sit upon the fire of these faggots and endure it." She thought none of his servants would be burnt for their master; and so that, because out of love for her he would himself sit upon the pile, she would be freed from him. But the servants said that Frosty had done nothing as yet, though they all had, and so they placed him on the top of the pile of wood. The fire was immediately kindled, and burnt for three days, until all the wood was consumed; but when the flames ceased, there stood Frosty in the midst of the ashes, shivering like an aspen-leaf, and declaring that he never before experienced such a frost, and must have perished if it had continued longer.

After this no further excuse could be made, and the beautiful Princess was obliged to take the unknown stranger as her husband. But just as they were going to church the old Queen declared again that she could not bear the shame, and she sent her guards after the wedding-party with orders, at all risks, to bring back her daughter.

The Listener, however, had kept his ears open, and he discovered the secret designs of the old Witch. "What shall we do?" asked he of Fatty; but the latter was equal to the occasion, and, spitting behind him once or twice a drop or two of the sea-water which he had formerly drunk, there was formed a great lake, in which the Queen's guards were caught and drowned. The Queen as soon as she saw this catastrophe, despatched her mounted guards; but the Listener heard the rattlings of their trappings, and unbound the eyes of their fellow-servant, whose look, as soon as he directed it upon the approaching enemy, shivered them like glass. The bridal party now passed on undisturbed; and, as soon as the blessing had been pronounced over the new-married pair, the six servants took their leave, saying to their former master, "Your wishes are fulfilled, and you no longer require us; we will, therefore, journey on and seek our fortunes elsewhere."

Now, about half a mile from the Queen's palace was a village before which a swineherd was tending his drove of pigs; and, as the Prince and Princess passed by it, the former said to his wife, "Do you know who I really am? I am no King's son, but a swineherd, and this man here with the drove is my father; we two must, therefore, get out and assist him!" So saying, he dismounted with her from the carriage, and they went together into the inn; and he ordered the host to carry away secretly during the night the royal clothes belonging to his wife. Accordingly, when morning came; the poor Princess had nothing to wear; but the hostess gave her an old gown and a pair of old slippers, and of these things made a great favour, telling her that she certainly would not have lent them to her had not her husband begged for them!

The Princess now began really to believe that her husband was a swineherd, and with him she tended the drove, and thought it was a punishment for her pride and ambition. This continued for eight days, and then she could bear it no longer, for her feet were wounded all over. Just at that time two persons came to her, and asked if she knew who her husband was. "Yes, he is a swineherd," she replied, "and is just now gone to drive a little trade with a few ribands and laces."

"Come with us now, and we will take you to him," said the two strangers to the Princess; and they took her into the palace, where her husband stood arrayed in his royal robes in the great hall. She did not, however, recognise him until he fell on her neck, and said to her, "I have suffered so much for you, that it was only right that you should also suffer for me!" and with these words he kissed her lovingly. Soon afterwards their wedding was celebrated with due form, and with so much grandeur that I who tell this story would like to have been there to see!

The Old Woman in the Wood

ONCE upon a time a poor Servant Girl was travelling with her boxes through a wood, and just as she got to the middle of it she found herself in the power of a ferocious band of robbers. All at once they sprang out of the brushwood, and came towards her; but she jumped out of her cart in terror, and hid herself behind a tree. As soon as the robbers had disappeared with their booty she came from her hiding-place, and saw her great misfortune. She began to cry bitterly, and said to herself, "What shall I do now, a poor girl like me; I cannot find my way out of the wood; nobody lives here, and I must perish with hunger?" She looked about for a road, but could not find one; and when evening came she sat down under a tree, and, commending herself to God, determined to remain where she was, whatever might happen. She had not sat there a long while before a little White Pigeon came flying towards her, carrying in his beak a small golden key. The bird put the key into the Girl's hand, and said, "Do you see yon great tree? within it is a cupboard, which is opened with this key, and there you will find food enough, so that you need not suffer hunger any longer." The Girl went to the tree, and, unlocking it, found pure milk in a jug, and white bread fit to break into it; and of these she made a good meal. When she had finished, she said to herself, "At home now the cocks and hens are gone to roost, and I am so tired I should like to go to bed myself." In a moment the Pigeon flew up, bringing another gold key in his bill, and said, "Do you see yon tree? open it and you will find a bed within!" She opened it, and there stood the little white bed; and, after saying her prayers and asking God's protection during the night, she went to sleep. In the morning the Pigeon came for the third time, bringing another key, with which he told the Girl to open a certain tree, and there she would find plenty of clothes. When she did so, she found dresses of all kinds ornamented with gold and precious stones, as beautiful as any princess could desire. And here in this spot the Maiden dwelt for a time; while the Pigeon every day brought her what she needed; and it was a very quiet and peaceful life.

One day, however, the Pigeon came and asked the Maiden whether she would do an act of love for him. "With all my heart!" was her reply. "I wish you then," said the Pigeon, "to come with me to a little cottage, and to go into it, and there on the hearth you will see an old Woman, who will say, 'Good Day!' But for my sake give her no answer, let her do what she will; but go past her right hand, and you will see a door which you must open, and pass into a room, where upon a table will lie a number of rings of all descriptions, and among them several with glittering stones; but leave them alone, and look out a plain one which will be there, and bring it to me as quickly as possible."

THE OLD WOMAN IN THE WOOD

The Maiden thereupon went to the cottage, and stepped in; and there sat an old Woman who made a great face when she saw her, but said, "Good day, my child!" The Maiden made no answer, but went towards the door. "Whither are you going?" cried the old Woman, "that is my house, and nobody shall enter it unless I wish!" and she tried to detain the Maiden by catching hold of her dress. But she silently loosened herself, and went into the room, and saw the heap of rings upon the table, which glittered and shone before her eyes. She threw them aside and searched for the plain ring, but could not find it; and while she searched she saw the old Woman slip in and take up a bird-cage, with which she made off. So the Maid pursued her, and took the bird-cage away from her. As she looked at it she saw the ring in the bill of the bird which was in it. She took the ring and ran home, joyfully expecting the White Pigeon would come and fetch the ring, but he did not. So she leaned herself back against her tree and waited for the bird; but presently the tree became as it were weak and yielding, and its branches began to droop. All at once the boughs bent round, and became two arms; and as the Maiden turned round, the tree became a handsome man, who embraced and kissed her, saying, "You have saved me out of the power of the old Woman, who is an evil witch. She changed me into a tree a long while ago, and every day I became a White Pigeon for a couple of hours; but so long as she had possession of the ring I could not regain my human form." Thereupon his servants and horses recovered also from the enchantment, for they likewise had been changed into trees; and once more they accompanied their master to his kingdom (for he was a King's son), and there he married the Maiden, and they lived happily ever afterwards.

The White and the Black Bride

ONE fine day a Woman, accompanied by her Daughter and Step-daughter, were walking over the fields in search of food. Presently they met a poor Man, who asked them, "Which is the way to the village?" "If you want to know," replied the Mother, "find it yourself!" and her daughter continued, "If you have a mind to go right, you had better take a guide with you!" But the Step-daughter said, "Poor man! I will show you; come with me."

Thereupon the Beggar, who was an Angel in disguise, turned his back upon the Mother and Daughter, and wished they might become as black as night and as ugly as owls. But to the other poor Girl the Angel was kind, and went with her till they approached the village, when he gave her a blessing, and said, "Choose now three things, and they shall be given you." "I would wish, then, to be as beautiful and spotless as the sun;" and, as she spoke, her skin became as white and fair as a sunbeam. "I would like next to have a purse of money which should never be empty!" and, this also the Angel gave her, saying, "Forget not what is best." "For the third thing," said the Maiden, "I desire to inherit a place in the kingdom of heaven after my death." This also was promised, and then the good Angel disappeared.

By-and-by the Step-mother and Daughter returned home; but as soon as they perceived their own black skins, and ugly faces, and saw the pureness and brightness of the other Girl's face, evil thoughts entered their hearts, and they thought how they could injure her. Now the Girl had a brother, Reginald, whom she loved very dearly, and to him she told all that had happened. "Dear sister," said he to her, "I will paint your portrait, that I may always have you before me; for my love for you is so great I wish never to part with you." "Then let no one ever see it, I beg you," said the Sister. So he painted the portrait, and hung it up in his room at the royal palace, for he was Coachman to the King; and every day he used to stand before it and bless God for his goodness to his Sister. Just at that time, however, the King, his master, had lost his wife, who was such a beautiful woman that nobody had ever seen her equal; and the King was consequently in very deep grief. Now, the Coachman's fellow-servants had remarked how he was accustomed every day to stand before a certain picture, and they grew jealous of him, and mentioned it to the King. The King ordered the portrait to be brought to him; and when he saw the likeness to his dear wife, only the Girl was still more beautiful, his sorrows broke out afresh. He summoned the Coachman, and asked whom the picture represented; and when his servant told him it was his Sister, he determined to make her his bride; and, giving the Coachman a carriage and horses and beautiful clothes, he sent him away to fetch his Sister. As soon as Reginald arrived with his message his Sister rejoiced; but the black one was jealous at the other's good fortune, vexed herself above measure, and said to her Mother, "Of what use now are all our arts, since they have never brought me such luck as this?" "Be quiet!" said the old Woman; "I will turn it to you;" and then, through her witchcraft, she caused a half-blindness to come over the Coachman's eyes, and took away the hearing of her white Daughter-in-law. After this they got into the carriage together; first the Bride, in her beautiful princely robes, and then the Stepmother with her Daughter, while Reginald sat on the box to drive. When they had gone a short distance the Coachman said,

> "Now cover yourself, my sister dear,
> That the wind may not come too near, too near!
> That the rain may not against you beat,
> And make you unfit the King to greet!"

"What does my dear brother say?" asked the Bride. "Oh," said the old Mother, "he says you are to take off your fine golden dress and give it to your sister." She drew if off as she was bid and gave it to her Sister, receiving in exchange an old grey cloak. Then they drove on, and presently the Coachman sang again,

> "Now cover yourself, my sister dear,
> That the wind may not come too near, too near!
> That the rain may not against you beat,
> And make you unfit the King to meet!"

"What does my dear brother say?" asked the Bride again. "He says," said the old Woman, "that you must take off your golden hood, and give it to your sister!" The Bride therefore handed it to her without a word, and placed it on her black hair, and presently the Coachman sang the same words a third time,

> "Now cover yourself, my sister dear,
> That the wind may not come too near, too near!
> That the rain may not against you beat,
> And make you unfit the King to greet!"

The Bride asked once more, "What does my brother say this time?" "Alas!" cried the old Stepmother, "he told you to look out of the carriage and see the palace in the distance." Just as she spoke they were passing over a bridge under which ran a deep river; and so when the Bride stood up to look out her Mother and Sister pushed her out of the carriage, and she fell into the water. At the same moment that she sank a snow-white Swan made its appearance on the surface of the stream, and swam down it. But of all these proceedings the Brother had observed and known nothing till he had driven up to the palace. There he took the black Sister to the King, and presented her as the original of his portrait, for he really thought she was so because his eyes could see nothing but the glitter of the golden dress. But the King was terribly enraged when he saw the ugliness of his proposed bride, and he ordered the Coachman to be flung into a pit full of vipers and snakes. The old Witch, however, contrived to deceive the King, and blinded his eyes so much through her arts, that he received her and her black Daughter, and at length was really married to the latter.

One evening afterwards, when the black Bride was sitting on the King's lap, a white Swan came to the gutter in the kitchen, and, swimming in, said to the Cookmaid,

"Make a good fire I pray, I pray!
That I my feathers may dry!"

So the Maid made up a roaring fire on the hearth, and the Swan placed herself before it, and smoothed her feathers down with her bill. While she did so, she asked,

"What does my brother Reginald?"

The Cookmaid answered,

"He lies buried in the ground,
With vipers all round!"

Then the Swan asked,

"What does the black Witch in this house?"

And the Cookmaid answered,

"She sits by the fire as still as a mouse!"

"Heaven have mercy upon her!"

cried the Swan, and thereupon swam out of the gutter-hole. But the following night she came again and asked the same questions, and also the third night, and after that the Kitchenmaid could keep the matter to herself no longer, and therefore went and told the King everything. The King, however, wished to see the truth of the tale for himself, and so he watched the fourth evening, and when the Swan stretched its neck through the gutter-hole he raised his sword and cut off the bird's head. Immediately the Swan was changed into a beautiful Maiden, and she appeared exactly like the portrait which her Brother had painted of her. The King thereupon was greatly rejoiced, and ordered princely clothes to be brought to the Maiden, in which she arrayed herself. Then she told the King how she had been betrayed by stratagem and cunning, and had been thrown into the river, where she had received the form of a Swan. When she had told all this, she begged, as the first favour, that her Brother should be released from the vipers' pit; and, as soon as the King had done that, he went into the chamber of the old Witch, and asked her what such a person would deserve who should do such things, and told her the tale which the Princess had just related. Now, the old Witch was so blind that she did not perceive what was behind, and replied that such a one would deserved to be placed in a cask stuck all over with nails, and then drawn by a horse, which should be harnessed to it, all through the streets. But in saying this she had pronounced her own fate, for the King ordered her to be so treated, together with her Daughter. Afterwards the King married the beautiful white Bride, and rewarded the faithful brother, whom he placed in a situation of power and influence.

The Man of Iron

ONCE upon a time there was a King, who possessed a great wood, which lay behind his castle, and wherein it was his pleasure to hunt. One day it happened that one of his huntsmen, who had gone into this wood in the morning, did not return as usual. The next day, therefore the King despatched two others to seek him; but they likewise never reappeared; and so the King then ordered all his huntsmen to make themselves ready to scour the whole forest in search of their missing companions. But, after they had set out, not one of them ever returned again, nor even a single dog out of the whole pack that accompanied them. After this occurrence an edict was issued that nobody should venture into the forest; and from that day a profound stillness and deep solitude crept over the whole forest, and one saw nothing but owls and eagles, which now and then flew out. This lasted a long time, till once came a strange

Huntsman to the King, and, begging an audience, said he was ready to go into the dangerous forest. The King would not at first give his consent, saying, "I am afraid it will fare no better with you than with the others, and that you will never return;" but the Huntsman replied, "I will dare the danger, for I know nothing of fear."

Thereupon the Huntsman entered the forest with his dog, and in a few minutes the hound, espying a wild animal on the road, pursued it; but it had scarcely gone a couple of yards before it fell into a deep pool, out of which a naked arm stretched itself, and catching the dog, drew it down beneath the water. As soon as the Huntsman saw this he went back and fetched three men, who came with pails to bale out the water. When they came to the bottom they found a Wild Man, whose body was brown, like rusty iron, and his hair hung over his face down to his knees. They bound him with cords and led him away to the King, who caused an immense iron cage to be fixed in the courtyard, and forbade any one, on pain of death, to open the door of the cage, of which the Queen had to keep the key in her charge. After this time anybody could go with safety into the forest.

Now the King had a son eight years old, who was once playing in the courtyard, and during his play his ball accidentally rolled into the iron cage. He ran up to it and demanded his ball of the prisoner. "Not till you open my door," replied the man. "No, that I cannot," said the Boy, "for my father the King has forbidden it;" and so saying he ran away. But the next morning he came again and demanded his golden ball. "Open my door," said the Wild Man; but the Boy refused. The third morning the King went out a-hunting, and presently the Boy went again to the cage, and said, "Even if I would open the door, I have not got the key to do it." "It lies under your mother's pillow," said the Wild Man, "and you can get it if you like." So the Boy casting all other thoughts to the winds but his wish to have his ball, ran and fetched the key. The door swung heavily, and the Boy jammed his finger, but soon it opened, and the Wild Man, giving him the golden ball, stepped out and hurried off. At this the Boy became alarmed, and cried, and called after the Man, "Wild Man, do not go away, or I shall be beaten!" The Man turned round,

THE MAN OF IRON

and raising the Boy up, set him upon his shoulders and walked into the forest with hasty strides. As soon afterwards the King returned, he remarked the empty cage, and asked the Queen what had happened. She called her Boy but no one answered, and the King sent out people over the fields to search for him; but they returned empty-handed. Then he easily guessed what had really happened, and great grief was shown at the royal court.

Meanwhile, as soon as the Wild Man had reached his old haunts, he set the Boy down off his shoulders, and said to him, "Your father and mother you will never see again; but I will keep you with me, for you delivered me, and therefore I pity you. If you do all that I tell you, you will be well treated, for I have enough treasure and money; in fact, more than any one else in the world." That evening the Iron Man let the Boy sleep on some moss, and the next morning he took him to the pool, and said, "See you, this golden water is bright and clear as crystal; hereby you must sit, and watch that nothing falls into it, or it will be dishonoured. Every evening I will come, and see if you have obeyed my commands." So the Boy sat down on the bank of the pool; but by-and-by, while he watched, such a sudden pain seized one of his fingers, that he plunged it into the water to cool it. He quickly drew it out again, but lo! it was quite golden, and in spite of all his pains he could not rub off the gold again. In the evening came the Iron man, and after looking at the Boy, he asked, "What has happened to my pool?" "Nothing, nothing!" replied the Boy, holding his finger behind him, that it might not be seen. But the man said, "You have dipped your finger into the water; this time, however, I will overlook it, only take care it does not happen again."

The next day the Boy resumed his post at the first daybreak; but in the course of a little while his finger ached again, and this time he put it to his head, and unluckily pulled off a hair, which fell into the water. He took it out again very quickly; but it had changed into gold, and by-and-by the Iron Man returned, already conscious of what had occurred. "You have let a hair fall into the pool," he said to the Boy; "but once more I will overlook your fault, only, if it happens again, the pool will be dishonoured, and you can remain with me no longer."

The Boy took his usual seat again on the third morning, and did not once move his finger, in spite of the pain. The time, however, passed so slowly, that he fell to looking at his face reflected in the mirror of the waters; and, while he bent down to do so, his long hair fell down from his shoulders into the pool. In a great hurry he raised his head again; but already his locks were turned to gold, and shone in the sun. You may imagine how frightened the poor Boy was! He took his pocket-handkerchief and bound it round his head, so that no one might see his hair; but as soon as the Iron Man returned he said to him, "Untie your handkerchief,!" for he knew what had happened. Then the golden hair fell down on the Boy's shoulders, and he tried to excuse himself but in vain. "You have not stood the proof," said the Iron Man, "and must remain here no longer. Go forth into the world, and there you will see how poverty fares; but, because your heart is innocent, and I mean well towards you, I will grant you this one favour – when you are in trouble come to this forest, call my name, and I will come out and help you. My power is great, and I have gold and silver in abundance."

So the young prince had to leave the forest, and travelled over many rough and smooth roads, till he came at length to a large town. There he sought work, but without success, for he had learnt nothing which was of use, and at last he went to the King's palace itself and inquired if they could take him in. The court servants were unaware of any vacancy which he could fill, but because he seemed well favoured they allowed him to remain. Soon afterwards, the Cook took him into his service, and told him he might fetch wood and water for the fire and sweep up the ashes. One day, however, as no one else was at hand, the Prince had to carry in a dish to the royal table, but, because he would not allow his golden hair to be seen, he entered the room with his cap on his head. "If you come to the royal table," exclaimed the King when he saw him, "you must pull off your cap!" "Ah, your majesty," replied the Prince, "I dare not, for I have a bad disease on my head!" Thereupon the King ordered the Cook into his presence, and scolded him because he had taken such a youth into his service, and further commanded him to discharge him. But the Cook pitied the poor lad, and changed him with the Gardener's Boy.

Now the Prince had to plant and sow, to dig and rake, in spite of all weathers, for he must bear the wind and rain. One day in summer, as he was working along in the garden, he took off his cap to cool his head in the breeze, and the sun shone so upon his hair, that the golden locks glittered, and their brightness became reflected in the mirror in the chamber of the King's daughter. She jumped up to see what it was, and perceiving the Gardener's Boy, called him, to bring her a nosegay of flowers. In a great hurry he put on his cap and plucked some wild flowers, which he arranged together. But, as he was going up the steps with them to the Princess, the Gardener met him, and said, "How can you take the Princess such a nosegay of bad flowers? go back and fetch the rarest and most beautiful." "Oh, no!" said the Boy, "the wild flowers bloom the longest and will please the best." So he went up to the chamber, and there the Princess said to him, "Take off your cap; it is not becoming of you to wear it here!"

The Boy, however, replied, he dared not remove it, because his head was too ugly to look at, but she seized his cap and pulled it off, and his golden hair fell down over his shoulders, most beautiful to see! The Boy would have run away, but the Princess detained him and gave him a handful of ducats. Then he left her and took her money to the Gardener, whom he told to give it to his children to play with, for he despised money. The following day the Princess called him again to give her a bouquet of wild flowers, and when he entered with them she snatched again at his cap, but this time he held it fast with both hands, and would not let it go. She gave him still another handful of ducats, but he would not keep them, but gave them to the Gardener's children for playthings. The third day it was just the same: the Princess could not get his cap, and he would not keep her ducats.

Not long after these events the country was drawn into a war, and the King collected all his people, for he knew not whether he should be able to make a stand against the enemy, who was very powerful, and led an immense army. Amongst others, the Gardener's Boy asked for a horse, saying he was grown up and ready to take his part in the fight. The others, however, laughed at him, and said, "When we are gone we will leave behind a horse for you, but take care of yourself!" So, as soon as the rest had set out, the young Prince went into the stable, and found there a horse, which was lame, and clicked its feet together. Nevertheless, he mounted it, and rode away to the gloomy forest, and as soon as he arrived there he called, "Iron Man! Iron Man!" in such a loud voice, that the trees re-echoed it. Soon the Wild Man appeared, and asked, "What do you desire?" "I desire a strong horse, for I am going to battle," said the Youth. "That you shall have, and more than you desire," said the Iron Man; and diving in among the trees, a Page suddenly made his appearance, holding a horse so fiery and mettlesome, that he was scarcely to be touched. Behind the steed followed a troop of warriors, all clad in iron, with swords, which glittered in the sun. The Youth, thereupon, delivered up his three-legged horse to the Page, and, mounting the other, rode off at the head of his troop. Just as he reached the field of battle he found the greater part of the King's army already slain, and the rest were on the point of yielding. The Youth, therefore, charged at once with his iron troop, like a storm of hail, against the enemy, and they cut down all who opposed them. The enemy turned and fled, but the young Prince pursued and cut to pieces all the fugitives, so that not one man was left. Then, instead of leading his troop before the King, he rode back with them to the forest, and summoned the Iron Man. "What do you desire now?" he inquired.

"Take back all these soldiers and your steed, and restore me my three-legged horse." All this was done as he desired, and he rode home on his limping animal. When the King arrived afterwards, his Daughter greeted him, and congratulated him on his victory. "I do not deserve it," he said; "the victory was owing to a strange knight who came to our aid with his troop." His Daughter inquired then who he was; but the King told her he did not know, for he had pursued the enemy and had not returned again. The Princess afterwards inquired of the Gardener respecting his Boy, and he laughed, and said he had just returned home on his three-legged steed; while the others had laughed at him, saying, "Here comes our Hop-a-day-Hop!" They asked also behind what hedge he had hid himself, and he replied, "I have done the best I could, and without me you would have fared badly." And for this speech the poor Boy was still more mocked.

Some time after this the King said to his Daughter, "I will cause a great festival to be held, which shall last three days, and you shall throw a golden apple, for which, perhaps, the unknown Knight will contend."

As soon as the proclamation was made, the young Prince went to the forest, and called for the Iron Man. "What do you desire?" he asked. "That I may catch the golden apple!"

"It is all the same as if you had it now," said the Iron Man; "but you shall have a red suit of armour for the occasion, and ride there upon a proud fox-coloured horse."

When the appointed day came the youth ranged himself along with the other knights, and was not recognised by any one. Presently the Princess stepped forward and threw up the golden apple, which nobody could catch but the Red Knight, who coursed away as soon as he obtained it. The second day the Iron Man dressed the youth as a White Knight, and gave him a grey horse; and again he caught the apple, and he alone. The King was angry when the Knight ran away with the prize, and said, "That is not right; he must appear before me and declare his name." Then he ordered, if the Knight who had caught the apple did not return the next day, some one should pursue him; and, if he would not return willingly, cut him to pieces. The third day the Prince received from the Iron Man a black coat of armour and a black steed, and caught again the apple when it was thrown. When he rode away the King's people pursued him, and one came so near him that he wounded the Black Knight with the point of his sword. Still he escaped them, but his horse jumped so violently, that the helmet fell off the Knight's head, and his golden hair was seen. The knights thereupon rode back and told the King.

The day following these sports the Princess inquired of the Gardener after his Boy. "He is working in the Garden," he replied;

"the wonderful fellow has also been to the festival, and yesterday evening he returned home and gave my children three golden apples which he won there." When the King knew of this he caused the Youth to be brought before him, and he appeared as usual with his cap on his head. But the Princess went up to him and took it off; and then his golden hair fell down over his shoulders, and he appeared so handsome, that every one was astonished. "Are you the knight who appeared each day at the festival, and always in a different colour, and won the three golden apples?" asked the King. "Yes," he replied, "and these are the apples," and, so saying he took them out of his pocket and handed them to the King. "If you desire any other proof," he continued, "I will show you the wound which your people gave me as I rode away; but I am also the Knight who won the victory for you over your enemy."

"If you can do such deeds," said the King, "you are no Gardener's Boy; tell me, who is your father?"

"My father is a mighty King, and of gold I have not only my desire, but more even than can be imagined," said the Young Prince.

"I own," said the King, "that I am indebted to you; can I do anything to show it?"

"Yes, if you give me your daughter to wife!" replied the Youth. The Princess laughed, and said, "He makes no roundabout tale; but I saw long ago that he was no Gardener's Boy from his golden hair;" and with these words she went and kissed him.

By-and-by the wedding was celebrated, and to it came the Prince's father and mother, who had long ago given up their son for dead, and lost all hope of seeing him again.

While they sat at the bridal-feast, all at once music was heard, and, the doors opening, a proud King entered, attended by a long train. He went up to the Prince, and embraced him, and said, "I am the Iron Man, whom you saved from his wild nature; all the treasures which belong to me are henceforth your property!"

The Fair Catherine and Pif-Paf Poltrie

"GOOD-DAY, Father Hollenthe. How do you do?" "Very well, I thank you, Pif-paf Poltrie." "May I marry your daughter?" "Oh, yes! if the mother Malcho (Milk-Cow), the brother Hohenstolz (High and Mighty), the sister Kâsetraut (Cheese-maker), and the fair Catherine, are willing, it may be so."

"Where is, then, the mother Malcho?"

"In the stable, milking the cow."

"Good-day, mother Malcho. How do you do?" "Very well, I thank you, Pif-paf Poltrie." "May I marry your daughter?" "Oh, yes, if the father Hollenthe, the brother Hohenstolz, the sister Kâsetraut, and the fair Catherine, are willing, it may be so."

"Where is, then, the brother Hohenstolz?"

"In the yard, chopping up the wood."

"Good-day, brother Hohenstolz. How are you?" "Very well, I thank you, Pif-paf Poltrie." "May I marry your sister?" "Oh, yes! if the father Hollenthe, the mother Malcho, the sister Kâsetraut, and the fair Catherine, are willing, it may be so."

"Where is then, the sister Kâsetraut?"

"In the garden, cutting the cabbages."

"Good-day, sister Kâsetraut. How do you do?" "Very well, I thank you, Pif-paf Poltrie." "May I marry your sister?" "Oh, yes! if the father Hollenthe, the mother Malcho, the brother Hohenstolz, and the fair Catherine, are willing, it may be so."

"Where is, then, the fair Catherine?"

"In her chamber, counting out her pennies."

"Good-day, fair Catherine. How do you do?" "Very well, I thank you, Pif-paf Poltrie." "Will you be my bride?" "Oh, yes! if the father Hollenthe, the mother Malcho, the brother Hohenstolz, and the sister Kâsetraut, are willing, so am I."

"How much money have you, fair Catherine?"

"Fourteen pennies in bare money, two and a half farthings owing to me, half a pound of dried apples, a handful of prunes, and a handful of roots; and don't you call that a capital dowry?"

"Pif-paf Poltrie, what trade are you? are you a tailor?" Better still!" "A shoemaker?" "Better still!" "A ploughman?" "Better still!" "A joiner?" "Better still!" "A smith?" "Better still!" "A miller?" "Better still!" "Perhaps a broom-binder?" "Yes, so am I; now, is not that a pretty trade?"

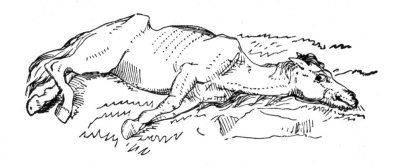

The Fox and the Horse

THERE was once a Farmer who had a Horse which served him faithfully till he was too old to work any longer, and then his master would not give him anything to eat, but said, "I cannot really find any use for you now, but still I mean you well, and so, if you will show yourself strong enough to bring home a Lion, I will requite you! but now you must make yourself scarce in this stable!" So saying, the Farmer drove the poor horse out; and he went with drooping head towards the forest to shelter himself there from the weather. In among the trees he met a Fox, who asked him why he looked so careworn and walked so downcast.

"Alas!" said the Horse, "avarice and fidelity dwell not in the same house together; my master has forgotten all the services which I have rendered him for so many years, and, because I am unable now to work any longer, he will not give me any fodder, but has driven me out of the stable."

"Without any hope?" inquired the Fox.

"The hope is slight enough," replied the Horse; "he said that if I could manage to bring him back a Lion he would receive me; but he knows well I cannot do that."

"Then I will help you," replied the Fox; "now lay down and stretch yourself out, and do not stir, so that you may appear dead."

The Horse, accordingly, did as he was bid, and the Fox went to the Lion, whose den was not very far off, and said to him, "Near here lies a dead Horse; come with me and you may make a capital meal." The Lion accompanied the Fox, and when they came to the Horse the Fox said, "Hist! listen to what I am about to say; you can have this at your convenience: I will bind it to you by the tail, and you shall then drag it away to your den, and devour it at your leisure." This advice pleased the Lion, and, in order that the Fox might knot the Horse's tail fast to him, he stood with his back towards it quite still. The Fox, however, cunningly tied the Lion's legs together with the hairs of the Horse's tail, and pulled and knotted all so carefully that no strength could have divided it. As soon as his work was finished the Fox tapped the Horse on the shoulder, and cried, "Drag, my friend, drag!" The Horse jumped up at once and drew the Lion away with him. The beast soon began to roar, so that all the birds in the forest flew away in terror, but the Horse let him roar while he quietly dragged him to his master's door. Now, when the Farmer saw this proof of the fidelity of his Horse, he thought better of his former resolution, and said to the faithful animal, "You shall remain with me now, and live at your ease." And so the good Horse had good meals and good treatment till he died.

The Iron Stove

IN the days when wishing was having, a certain King's Son was enchanted by an old Witch, and obliged to sit in a great iron stove which stood in a wood! There he passed many years, for nobody could release him; till one day a Princess who had lost herself, and could not find her way back to her father's kingdom, came at last, after nine day's wandering, to the spot where the iron stove stood. As she approached it, she heard a voice say, "Whence comest thou, and whither goest thou?" "I have lost the road to my father's kingdom, and am unable to find my home!" she replied. "I will help you, and that in a short time," said the voice from the iron stove, "if you will consent to what I desire; I am the child of a far greater King than your father, and am willing to marry you."

The Princess was frightened at this proposal, and exclaimed, "What can I do with an iron stove?" but, nevertheless, as she was anxious to get home, she consented to what he should wish. Then the Prince told her that she must return after she had been home, and bring with her a knife to cut a hole in the stove; and then he gave her such minute directions as to her road that in two hours she reached her father's palace. There was great joy there when the Princess returned, and the old King fell on her neck and kissed her; but she was sore troubled, and said, "Alas! my dear father, how things have happened! I should never have reached home out of the great wild wood, had it not been for an iron stove, to which I have therefore promised to return to save it and marry it."

The King was so frightened when he heard this, that he fell into a swoon; for she was his only daughter. When he recovered, they resolved that the miller's daughter, a very pretty girl, should take her place; and so she was led to the spot, furnished with a knife, and told to scrape a hole in the iron stove. For four-and-twenty hours she scraped and scraped; but without making the least bit of a hole; and when day broke, the voice out of the stove exclaimed, "It seems to me like daylight." "Yes," replied the girl, "it seems so to me too, and methinks I hear the clapping of my father's mill." "Oh then, you are the miller's daughter," said the voice again; "well, you may go home, and send the Princess to me."

The girl therefore returned, and told the King the stove would not have her, but his daughter, which frightened the King again, and made the Princess weep. But the King had also in his service a swine-herd's daughter, prettier still than the miller's, to whom he offered a piece of gold if she would go instead of the Princess to the iron stove. Thereupon, this girl went away, and scraped for four-and-twenty hours on the iron without producing any impression; and when day broke, a voice out of the stove exclaimed, "It seems to me like daylight." "Yes, it is so," said the girl; "for I hear my father's horn."

"You are then the swine-herd's daughter," said the voice; "go straight back, and tell the Princess who sent you, that it must be as I said; and therefore, if she does not come to me, everything in the old kingdom shall fall to pieces, and not one stone left upon another anywhere."

THE IRON STOVE

As soon as the Princess heard this, she began to cry; but it was of no use, for her promise must be kept. So she took leave of her father; and carrying a knife with her, set out towards the iron stove in the wood. As soon as she reached it she began to scrape the iron; and before two hours had passed, she had already made a small hole. Through this she peeped, and beheld inside the stove a handsome Prince, whose dress all glittered with gold and precious stones; and she immediately fell in love with him. So she scraped away faster than before, and soon had made a hole so large that the Prince could get out. "You are mine, and I am thine," he said, as soon as he stood on the earth; "you are my bride, because you have saved me." Then he wanted to take her at once to his father's kingdom; but she begged that she might once more go back to her father, to take leave of him. The Prince consented to this; but said she must not speak more than three words, and immediately return. Thereupon the Princess went home; but alas! she said many more than three words; and the iron stove consequently disappeared, and was carried far away over many icy mountains and snowy valleys; but without the Prince, who was saved, and no longer shut up in his former prison. By-and-by the Princess took leave of her father; and taking some gold with her, but not much, she went back into the wood, and sought for the iron stove, but could find it nowhere. For nine days she searched; and then her hunger became so great, that she knew not how to help herself, and thought she must perish. When evening came she climbed up a little tree, for she feared the wild beasts which night would bring forth; and just as midnight approached she saw a little light at a distance. "Ah, there I may find help," thought she, and getting down, she went towards the light, saying a prayer as she walked along. Soon she came to a little hut, around which much grass grew; and before the door stood a heap of wood. "Ah, how came you here?" thought she to herself, as she peeped through the window and saw nothing but fat little toads; and a table already covered with meat and wine, and plates and dishes made of silver. She took courage and knocked; and immediately a Toad exclaimed:—

"Little Toad, with crooked leg;
Open quick the door, I beg,
And see who stands without?"

As soon as these words were spoken, a little Toad came running up, and opened the door; and the Princess walked in. They all bade her welcome, and told her to sit down; and then asked her whence she came, and whither she was going. She told the Toads all that had happened, and how, because she had overstepped the mark in speaking more than three words, the stove had disappeared as well as the Prince; and now she was about to search over hill and valley till she found him. When she had told her tale, the old Toad cried out:—

"Little Toad, with crooked leg;
Quickly fetch for me, I beg,
The basket hanging on the peg."

So the little Toad went and brought the basket to the old one, who laid it down, and caused meat and drink to be given to the Princess; and after that showed her a beautiful neat bed, made of silk and velvet, in which, under God's protection, she slept soundly. As soon as day broke the Princess arose; and the old Toad gave her three needles out of the bag, to take with her, for they would be of use, since she would have to pass over a mountain of glass, three sharp swords, and a big lake before she would regain her lover. The old Toad gave her besides the three needles, a ploughwheel and three nuts; and with these the Princess set out on her way; and by-and-by approached the glass mountain, which was so smooth that she used the three needles as steps for her feet, and so reached the top. When she came to the other side, she placed the three needles in a secure place; and soon coming to the three swords, she rolled over them by means of her ploughwheel. At last she came to the great lake; and when she had passed that, she found herself near a fine large castle. Into this she entered; and offered herself as a servant, saying she was a poor girl; but had, a little while back, rescued a King's son out of an iron stove, which stood in the forest. After some delay she was hired as a kitchen-maid, at a very small wage; and soon found out that the Prince had an intention to marry another lady, because he supposed his former favourite was long since dead. One evening when she had washed and made herself neat, she felt in her pocket, and found the three nuts which the old Toad had given her. One of them she cracked, and instead of a kernel found a fine royal dress, which, when the Bride heard of, she said she must have, for it was no dress for a servant-maid. But the Princess said she would not sell it but on one condition, which was, that she should be allowed to pass a night by the chamber of the Prince. This request was granted, because the Bride was so anxious to have the dress, since she had none like it; and when evening came she told her lover that the silly girl wanted to pass the night near his room. "If you are contented, so am I," he replied; but she gave him a glass of wine, in which she put a sleeping draught. In consequence, he slept so soundly, that the poor Princes could not awake him, although she cried the whole night, and kept repeating, "I saved you in the wild forest, and rescued you out of the iron stove; I have sought you, and travelled over a mountain of glass, and over three sharp swords, and across a wide lake, before I found you; and still you will not hear me!" The servants, however, who slept in the ante-room, heard the complaint, and told the King of it the following morning. That evening after the Princess had washed and cleaned herself, she cracked open the second nut and found in it a still more beautiful dress than the former; so that the Bride declared she must have it. But it was not to be purchased except on the same condition as the first; and the Prince allowed her to sleep where she had before. The Bride, however, gave the Prince another sleeping draught; and he slept too soundly to hear the poor Princess complaining and crying as before: "I saved you in the wild forest, and rescued you out of the iron stove; I have sought you, and travelled over a mountain of glass, and over three sharp swords, and across a wide lake, before I found you; and still you will not hear me!" The servants, however, in the ante-room, heard the crying again; and told the Prince of it the next morning.

On the same evening, the poor scullery-maid broke her third nut; and produced a dress starred with gold, which the Bride declared she must have at any price; and the maid petitioned for the same privilege as before. But the Prince poured out this time the sleeping-draught; and therefore, when the Princess began to cry, "Alas! my dear treasure, have you forgotten how I saved you in the great wild wood, and rescued you out of the iron stove?" the Prince heard her, and jumping up, exclaimed, "You are right, I am thine, and you are mine." Thereupon while the night lasted, he got into a carriage with the Princess; first taking away the clothes of the false Bride, that she might not follow them. When they came to the lake, they rowed over very quickly, and passed the three sharp swords again by means of the ploughwheel. Soon they crossed the glass mountain by the aid of the three needles; and arrived at last at the little old house, which, as soon as they entered, was changed into a noble castle. At the same moment all the Toads were disenchanted and returned to their natural positions; for they were the sons of the King of the country. So the wedding was performed, and the Prince and Princess remained in the castle; for it was much larger than that of her father. However, because the old King grieved at his daughter's continual absence, they went and lived with him and joined the government of the two kingdoms in one; and so for many years they reigned in happiness and prosperity.

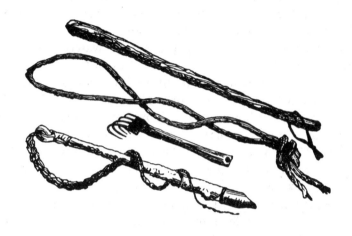

Going out a-Travelling

ONCE upon a time there was a poor Woman who had a Son so very fond of travelling that his mother used to say to him, "Where can you ride, when you have no money to take with you?" "I can help myself well," said the Son; "and all day long I will say, 'Not much, not much, not much!'"

So he travelled a whole day and kept saying, "Not much, not much, not much!" By-and-by he came to a Fisherman, to whom he said, "God help you, not much!" "How say you, fellow?" cried the Fisherman, "not much!" When he drew out the net there were very few fish, and taking up a stick he beat the Youth, saying, "Have you never seen me thrash?" "What shall I say, then?" asked the Youth. "A good catch, a good catch, a good catch!"

Thereupon the Youth walked a whole day long, crying, "A good catch!" till he came to a gallows, where they were about to hang up a poor Criminal. "Good morning!" said the Youth, "a good catch, a good catch!" "What do you say, fellow?" said the Criminal, "shall there not be a bad man in the world? is one not enough?" So saying he went up the ladder. "What shall I say then?" asked the Youth. "You should say, 'God comfort a poor soul!'"

The next day accordingly the Youth walked all day long, repeating "God comfort a poor soul!" Presently he came to a grave, whereby stood a Knacker about to kill an old horse. "Good morning! God comfort the poor soul!" said the Youth. "What do you say, you silly fellow?" said the Knacker, giving the Youth a blow on the ear, so that he could scarce see out of his eyes. "What shall I say, then?" "You should say, 'There lies a carcass in its grave!'"

So all the next day the Youth went on, saying, "There lies a carcass in its grave!" Presently he met a waggon full of people, "Good morning! there lies a carcass in its grave!" said the Youth. As he spoke the waggon fell into the grave, and the driver, jumping off, gave the Youth a cut with his whip, and drove him home to his Mother.

And all his life long afterwards he never went out a-travelling.

The Little Lamb and the Little Fish

ONCE upon a time there were a Brother and Sister who loved one another very much. Their own mother was dead, but they had a Stepmother who was very unkind to them, and did them privately all the injury she could. One day it happened that the two were playing with other children on the meadow before their house, in the middle of which was a pond which ran past one side of the house. Round this the children used to run, joining hands and singing,—

> "Eneke, Beneke, let me go,
> And I will give my bird to you;
> The bird shall fetch of straw a bunch,
> And that the cow shall have to munch;
> The cow shall give me milk so sweet,
> And that I'll to the baker take,
> Who with it shall a small cake bake;
> The cake the cat shall have to eat,

> And for it catch a mouse for me,
> Which I will turn to sausage meat,
> And cut it all to pieces!"

While they sang they ran round and round, and upon whom the word "pieces" fell he had to run away, and the other must pursue him and catch him. The old Stepmother stood at her window and watched the game, which vexed her very much; but, as she understood witches' arts, she wished that both of the children might be changed, the one into a Lamb and the other into a Fish. Thereupon the Brother swam round the pond in the form of a Fish, and the Sister trotted to and fro on the meadow, sorrowful and unhappy, and would not eat nor touch a single blade of grass. Thus a long time passed, till one day foreign strangers came to the castle on a visit. "Now is a good opportunity!" thought the Stepmother, and called the cook, and bade him fetch the Lamb out of the meadow, for there was nothing else for the visitors. The cook went for the Lamb, and, leading into the kitchen, tied it by the foot, that it might suffer patiently. While he went for his knife, and was sharpening it on the grindstone, to kill the poor animal with, a little Fish swam up the gutter to the sink, and looked at him. But this Fish was the Brother, and he had seen the cook carry away his Lamb, and had swam from the pond to the house. When the Lamb saw him she cried,—

> "Ah! my brother in the pond,
> Woe is in my heart so fond!
> The cook is sharpening now his knife
> To take away my tender life!"

The Fish replied:—

> "Ah! my sister; woe is me,
> That I am far away from thee!
> Swimming in this deep, deep sea!"

When the cook heard the Lamb speaking, and observed the sorrowful words which she said to the Fish, he was frightened, for he thought it could not be a natural animal, but had been bewitched by the wicked woman in the house. So he said to the Lamb, "Be still, I will not kill you!" And with these words he fetched another lamb and dressed it for the guests. Then he took the Lamb to a good honest countrywoman, and told her all he had seen and heard. Now, this woman was in former days the nurse of the two children, and she conjectured what had really taken place, and went with them to a wise woman. This latter said a blessing over the Lamb and Fish, and thereby they regained their natural forms. Then the little Brother and Sister went into the forest and built for themselves a little cottage, in which they lived happily and contentedly, though alone.

Simeli-Mountain

ONCE upon a time there lived two Brothers, the one rich and the other poor. The rich man, however, gave nothing to the poor one, who earned a miserable living by trading in corn; and sometimes he was so badly off that he had no bread for his wife or children. Once he was trundling his barrow through the forest, and suddenly he perceived on one side of the road a great mountain, naked and uncultivated; and, because he had never observed it before, he stopped in astonishment. As he stood thus, twelve great Wild Men came up, and, thinking they were robbers, he pushed his barrow among the brushwood, and climbed up a tree to watch their proceedings. The twelve men went up to the mountain and exclaimed, "Semsi-Mountain, Semsi-Mountain, open!" Immediately the hill parted in two, and the twelve men entering, it closed again as soon as they had done so. In a little while the mountain opened, and the men came out, carrying heavy sacks on their shoulders, and as soon as they had all emerged into daylight, they said, "Semsi-Mountain, Semsi-Mountain, shut yourself up!" Then the hill closed directly, and there was no opening to be seen, and the twelve men went away. When they were out of sight the poor man descended from the tree, feeling curious to know what was hidden in the mountain. So he went up and said, "Semsi-Mountain, Semsi-Mountain, open!" It opened directly, and stepping in he found the hill was hollow and filled with gold and silver, and in the further part of it heaps of pearls and precious stones were accumulated like corn. The poor man did not know what to take, for there were so many treasures to choose from: at length he filled his pockets with gold and silver, and let alone the pearls and precious stones. As soon as he got outside again he said the words, "Semsi-Mountain, close up!" and immediately all appeared as if there was no opening to be made. He went home with his barrow, and had now no cares to trouble him, for with his gold he could buy bread and wine for his wife and children; and could afford to live freely and liberally, besides giving to the poor and doing good to everybody. But when his money came to an end he went to his brother, and borrowed a measure, with which he fetched more money, but touched none of the precious stones. A third time he borrowed this measure, but this time his brother's cupidity was excited, for the rich man had for a long time been dissatisfied with his property, and his already beautiful house, and he could not conceive where his Brother got so well paid, or what he did with the measure. So he bethought himself of a stratagem, and spread the bottom of the measure with pitch; and, when his Brother returned it to him, he found a gold piece sticking in it. Thereupon he went to his Brother, and asked him what he had measured with the measure. "Corns and beans," said the other. Then the rich man showed the gold piece, and threatened his Brother if he did not tell the truth to take him before the sheriff. The poor Brother, therefore, related all that had happened, and the rich man, harnessing his horses to his carriage, went away, determined to profit by the circumstance, and bring home greater treasures. As soon as he came to the mountain he called out, "Semsi-Mountain, Semsi-Mountain, open!" The hill opened immediately, and he went in. There lay all the treasures before him, and for a long while he stood considering what he should take. At length he seized the precious stones and took as much as he could carry; but when he wanted to leave the mountain he had forgotten its name, for his heart and mind were full of treasures which he had seen. "Simeli-Mountain, Simeli-Mountain, open!" he cried; but that was not the right name, and the mountain moved not, but remained closed. Soon he became terrified, but the longer he thought the more bewildered he became, and all his treasures availed nothing. In the evening, however, the mountain opened, and the twelve robbers came in, and as soon as they saw the rich man they laughed and exclaimed, "Ah! have we caught you at last, my bird? did you think we had not remarked your two previous visits, when we could not catch you? but this time you will not go out again."

"It was not me, but my Brother," cried the rich man; but his protestations were of no use, and beg as he might for his life they had no mercy, but cut off his head.

Snow-White and Rose-Red

THERE was once a poor Widow, who lived alone in her hut with her two children, who were called Snow-White and Rose-Red, because they were like the flowers which bloomed on two rose-bushes, which grew before the cottage. But they were two as pious, good, industrious, and amiable children, as any that were in the world, only Snow-White was more quiet and gentle than Rose-Red. For Rose-Red would run and jump about the meadows, seeking flowers, and catching butterflies, while Snow-White sat at home helping her Mother to keep house, or reading to her, if there were nothing else to do. The two children loved one another dearly, and always walked hand-in-hand when they went out together; and ever when they talked of it they agreed that they would never separate from each other, and that whatever one had the other should share. Often they ran deep into the forest and gathered wild berries; but no beast ever harmed them. For the hare would eat cauliflowers out of their hands, the fawn would graze at their side, the goats would frisk

SNOW-WHITE AND ROSE-RED

about them in play, and the birds remained perched on the boughs singing as if nobody were near. No accident ever befel them; and if they stayed late in the forest, and night came upon them, they used to lie down on the moss and sleep till morning; and because their mother knew they would do so, she felt no concern about them. One time when they had thus passed the night in the forest, and the dawn of morning awoke them, they saw a beautiful Child dressed in shining white sitting near their couch. She got up and looked at them kindly, but without saying anything went into the forest; and when the children looked round they saw that where they had slept was close to the edge of a pit, into which they would have certainly fallen had they walked a couple of steps further in the dark. Their mother told them the figure they had seen was doubtless, the good angel who watches over children.

Snow-White and Rose-Red kept their Mother's cottage so clean that it was a pleasure to enter it. Every morning in the summer-time Rose-Red would first put the house in order, and then gather a nosegay for her Mother, in which she always placed a bud from each rose-tree. Every winter's morning Snow-White would light the fire and put the kettle on to boil, and, although the kettle was made of copper, it yet shone like gold, because it was scoured so well. In the evenings, when the flakes of snow were falling, the mother would say, "Go, Snow-White, and bolt the door;" and then they used to sit down on the hearth, and the Mother would put on her spectacles and read out of a great book, while her children sat spinning. By their side, too, lay a little lamb, and on a perch behind them a little white dove reposed with her head under her wing.

One evening, when they were thus sitting comfortably together, there came a knock at the door, as if somebody wished to come in. "Make haste, Rose-Red," cried her Mother; "make haste and open the door; perhaps there is some traveller outside who needs shelter." So Rose-Red went and drew the bolt and opened the door, expecting to see some poor man outside; but, instead, a great fat bear poked his black head in. Rose-Red shrieked out and ran back, the little lamb bleated, the dove fluttered on her perch, and Snow-White hid herself behind her Mother's bed. The Bear, however, began to speak, and said, "Be not afraid, I will do you no harm; but I am half-frozen, and wish to come in and warm myself."

"Poor Bear!" cried the Mother; "come in and lie down before the fire; but take care you do not burn your skin;" and then she continued, "Come here, Rose-Red and Snow-White, the Bear will not harm you, he means honourably." So they both came back, and by degrees the lamb too and the dove overcame their fears and welcomed the rough visitor.

"You children!" said the Bear, before he entered, "come and knock the snow off my coat." And they fetched their brooms and swept him clean. Then he stretched himself before the fire and grumbled out his satisfaction, and in a little while the children became familiar enough to play tricks with the unwieldy animal. They pulled his long shaggy skin, set their feet upon his back and rolled him to and fro, and even ventured to beat him with a hazel-stick, laughing when he grumbled. The Bear bore all their tricks good-temperedly, and if they hit too hard he cried out,—

> "Leave me my life, you children,
> Snow-White and Rose-Red,
> Or you'll never wed."

When bedtime came and the others were gone, the Mother said to the Bear, "You may sleep here on the hearth if you like, and then you will be safely protected from the cold and bad weather."

As soon as day broke the two children let the Bear out again, and he trotted away over the snow, and ever afterwards he came every evening at a certain hour. He would lie down on the hearth and allow the children to play with him as much as they liked, till by degrees they became so accustomed to him, that the door was left unbolted till their black friend arrived. ·

But as soon as spring returned, and everything out of doors was green again, the Bear one morning told Snow-White that he must leave her, and could not return during the whole summer. "Where are you going, then, dear Bear?" asked Snow-White. "I am obliged to go into the forest and guard my treasures from the evil Dwarfs; for in winter, when the ground is hard, they are obliged to keep in their holes and cannot work through; but now, since the sun has thawed the earth and warmed it, the Dwarfs pierce through, and steal all they can find; and what has once passed into their hands, and gets concealed by them in their caves, is not easily brought to light." Snow-White, however, was very sad at the departure of the Bear, and opened the door so hesitatingly, that when he passed through it he left behind on the latch a piece of his hairy coat; and through the hole which was made in his coat Snow-White fancied she saw the glittering of gold, but she was not quite certain of it. The Bear, however, ran hastily away, and was soon hidden behind the trees.

Some time afterwards the Mother sent the children into the wood to gather sticks, and while doing so they came to a tree which was lying across the path, on the truck of which something kept bobbing up and down from the grass, and they could not imagine what it was. When they came nearer they saw a Dwarf, with an old wrinkled face and a snow-white beard a yard long. The end of this beard was fixed in a split of the tree, and the little man kept jumping about like a dog tied by a chain, for he did not know how to free himself. He glared at the Maidens with his red, fiery eyes, and exclaimed, "Why do you stand there? are you going to pass without offering me any assistance?" "What have you done, little man?" asked Rose-Red. "You stupid, gazing goose!" exclaimed he, "I wanted to have split the tree, in order to get a little wood for my kitchen, for the little food which we use is soon burnt up with great faggots, not like what you rough, greedy people devour! I had driven the wedge in properly, and everything was going on well, when the smooth wood flew up upwards, and the tree closed so suddenly together, that I could not draw my beautiful beard out; and here it sticks, and I cannot get away. There, don't laugh, you milk-faced things! are you dumb-founded?"

The children took all the pains they could to pull the Dwarf's beard out, but without success. "I will run and fetch some help," cried Rose-Red at length.

"Crack-brained sheep's-head that you are!" snarled the Dwarf; "what are you going to call other people for? You are two too many now for me; can you think of nothing else?"

"Don't be impatient," replied Snow-White; "I have thought of something;" and, pulling her scissors out of her pocket, she cut off the end of the beard. As soon as the Dwarf found himself at liberty, he snatched up his sack, which laid between the roots of the tree, filled with gold, and, throwing it over his shoulder, marched off, grumbling, and groaning, and crying, "Stupid people! to cut off a piece of my beautiful beard. Plague take you!" and away he went without once looking at the children.

Some time afterwards Snow-White and Rose-Red went a-fishing, and as they neared the pond they saw something like a great locust hopping about on the bank, as if going to jump into the water. They ran up and recognised the Dwarf. "What are you after?" asked Rose-Red; "you will fall into the water." "I am not quite such a simpleton as that," replied the Dwarf; "but do you not see this fish will pull me in?" The little man had been sitting there angling, and, unfortunately, the wind had entangled his beard with the fishing-line; and so when a great fish bit at the bait, the strength of the weak little fellow was not able to draw it out, and the fish had the best of the struggle. The Dwarf held on by the reeds and rushes which grew near, but to no purpose, for the fish pulled him where it liked, and he must soon have been drawn into the pond. Luckily just then the two Maidens arrived, and tried to release the beard of the Dwarf from the fishing-line, but both were too closely entangled for it to be done. So the Maiden pulled out her scissors again and cut off another piece of the beard. When the Dwarf saw this done he was in a great rage, and exclaimed, "You donkey! that is the way to disfigure my face. Was it not enough to cut it once, but you must now take away the best part of my fine beard? I dare not show myself again now to my own people. I wish you had run the soles off your boots before you had come here!" So saying, he took up a bag of pearls, which laid among the rushes, and, without speaking another word, slipped off and disappeared behind a stone.

Not many days after this adventure, it chanced that the Mother sent the two Maidens to the next town to buy thread, needles and pins, laces and ribbons. Their road passed over a common, on which, here and there, great pieces of rock were lying about. Just over their heads they saw a great bird flying round and round, and every now and then dropping lower and lower, till at last it flew down behind a rock. Immediately afterwards they heard a piercing shriek, and, running up, they saw with affright that the eagle had caught their old acquaintance the Dwarf, and was trying to carry him off. The compassionate children thereupon laid hold of the little man, and held him fast till the bird gave up the struggle and flew off. As soon, then, as the Dwarf had recovered from his fright, he exclaimed in his squeaking voice, "Could you not hold me more gently? You have seized my fine brown coat in such a manner, that it is all torn and full of holes, meddling and interfering rubbish that you are!" With these words he shouldered a bag filled with precious stones, and slipped away to his cave among the rocks.

The Maidens were now accustomed to his ingratitude, and so they walked on to the town and transacted their business there. Coming home they returned over the same common, and unawares walked up to a certain clean spot, on which the Dwarf had shaken out his bag of precious stones, thinking nobody was near. The sun was shining, and the bright stones glittered in its beams, and displayed such a variety of colours, that the two Maidens stopped to admire them.

"What are you standing there gaping for?" asked the Dwarf, while his face grew as red as copper with rage: he was continuing to abuse the poor Maidens, when a loud roaring noise was heard, and presently a great black Bear came rolling out of the forest. The Dwarf jumped up terrified, but he could not gain his retreat before the Bear overtook him. Thereupon he cried out, "Spare me, my dear Lord Bear! I will give you all my treasures. See these beautiful precious stones which lie here; only give me my life; for what have you to fear from a little weak fellow like me? you could not touch me with your big teeth. There are two wicked girls, take them; they would make nice morsels; as fat as young quails; eat them, for heaven's sake!"

The Bear, however, without troubling himself to speak, gave the bad-hearted Dwarf a single blow with his paw, and he never stirred after.

The Maidens were then going to run away, but the Bear called after them, "Snow-White and Rose-Red, fear not! Wait a bit and I will accompany you." They recognised his voice and stopped; and when the Bear came, his rough coat suddenly fell off, and he stood up a tall man, dressed entirely in gold. "I am a King's son," he said, "and was condemned by the wicked Dwarf, who stole all my treasures, to wander about in this forest in the form of a bear till his death released me. Now he has received his well-deserved punishment."

Then they went home, and Snow-White was married to the Prince, and Rose-Red to his brother, with whom they shared the immense treasure which the Dwarf had collected. The old Mother also lived for many years happily with her two children; and the rose-trees which had stood before the cottage were planted now before the palace, and produced every year beautiful red and white roses.

The Maid of Brakel

ONCE upon a time a Girl went from Brakel to the St Anne's chapel under the Hinne mountain; and as she would have liked to have a husband, and thought there was nobody else inside, she began to sing—

> "Oh, holy St Anne,
> Get me a husband as soon as you can;
> You know him quite well,
> He lives at the Suttmer gate
> Has a round yellow pate,
> You know him quite well."

The Sacristan, however, was standing behind the altar, and heard it all; and he called out in a very gruff voice, "You shan't have him; you shan't have him!"

The girl thought it was the little infant standing by the mother Anne that had called out; so she flew into a passion, and cried, "Pepperlepap, little stupid! hold your noise and let the mother speak!"

Knoist and his Three Sons

BETWEEN Werrol and Soist there lived a man, and his name was Knoist. He had three sons: the one was blind, the other was lame, and the third was stark naked. They once went into the fields, and there they saw a hare. The blind one shot it, the lame one caught it, and the naked one put it into his pocket. Then they came to a mighty big piece of water, on which there were three ships: the one floated, the other sank, and the third had no bottom in it. The one that had no bottom they all three got into. Then they came to a mighty great forest, and there was a great mighty tree: in the tree there was a mighty great chapel, in the chapel there was a wizened old Sacristan and a savage old Priest, and they were dealing out holy water with sticks.

"Happy is he
Who from holy water gets free."

The Turnip

ONCE upon a time there were two Brothers who had both served as soldiers, but one had got rich while the other remained poor. So the poor man, in order to help himself out of his difficulties, drew off his soldiering coat and turned ploughman. He dug and ploughed over his piece of land, and then sowed some turnip-seed. Soon the seed began to show itself above ground, and there grew one turnip immensely large and thick, which seemed as if it would never have done growing, but was the princess among turnips; and as there had never before been seen such a turnip, so there has never been such another since. At length it grew to such a size, that it filled of itself a whole cart, and two oxen were required to draw it; but the poor man knew not what to do with it, or whether it would be the making of his fortune, or just the contrary. At last he thought to himself that if he sold it he should not get very much for it; and as to eating it, why the ordinary-sized turnips would do as well; and so he resolved to take it to the King and offer it to him. So he laid in on a cart, and harnessing two oxen, took his turnip to court and presented it to the King. "What curious thing is this?" asked the King; "such a wonderful sight I have never before seen, though I have looked at some curiosities; pray from what seed was this grown? or are you a luck-child who have picked it up?"

"Oh, no," said the man, "I am no luck-child, but only a poor soldier, who, because he could not get enough to live on, has pulled off his uniform and turned ploughman. I have got a brother who is rich and well known to you, your majesty, but I, because I have nothing, am forgotten by all."

Thereupon the King took compassion on the poor Soldier, and said to him, "Your poverty shall be put an end to, and you shall receive so much from me that you shall be equal to your rich brother." So saying, the King presented the man with gold, land, flocks, and herds, and made him thereby so rich that his brother's property was not to be compared with his. When the latter heard what his brother had gained by a single turnip, he envied him, and resolved in his own mind how he could manage to happen with the like luck. He thought he would be much cleverer, and took to the King gold and horses as a present, thinking that he would receive a much handsomer present; since his brother had been treated so liberally for a mere turnip, what would not his generous present be requited with? The King received the present very graciously, and told the Soldier he could give him in return nothing richer or rarer than the magnificent turnip! So the wealthy Soldier was obliged to lay the turnip upon his carriage and drive it home with him. When he reached his house he knew not what to do with himself for vexation and rage, till by degrees wicked thoughts took possession of him, and he resolved to kill his brother. So he hired some murderers, whom he placed in ambush, and then, going to his brother, he said to him, "I know a secret treasure, my dear brother, which we will obtain and share together." The good brother was deceived by these words, and unsuspectingly accompanied the wicked one. But as they went along the murderers burst out upon them, and binding the good man prepared to hang him on a tree. But while they were about it a sudden shouting and laughing was heard at a distance, which frightened the assassins so much that they tumbled their prisoner head over heels into a sack, and suspended him on a bough, and then took flight. The Soldier, however, worked himself about in the sack till he got his head through a hole at the top, and then he perceived that the noise which had saved him was made by a Student, a young fellow who was singing and shouting snatches of songs as he walked along. As soon as this Student was just under the tree, the man in the sack called out, "I hope you are well at this lucky moment?" The Scholar looked about him and wondered where the voice came from, for he could see nobody; at last he said, "Who calls me?" "Raise your eyes, and you will see me sitting above here in wisdom's sack. In a short time I have learnt great things; in fact, this place beats all schools hollow! In a little while I shall have learnt everything, and then I shall descend and mix with my fellow-men. I understand astronomy and the signs of heaven, the motion of all the winds, the sand in the sea, the art of healing the sick, the virtue of every herb, birds and stones! Were you once in this place you would feel what a noble thing it is to sit in the sack of wisdom!"

When the Scholar heard all this he was astonished, and said, "Blessed be the hour in which I found you! can I also come a little while into the sack?"

"For a short time I will allow you to take my place in consideration of some reward and your fair speech; but you must first wait an hour, for there is one piece of learning which I have not yet fully mastered."

The Scholar accordingly sat down to wait, but the time appeared to him terribly long, and he soon began to pray to be allowed to take his place, because his thirst for wisdom was so great. The man in the sack at length pitied his impatience, and told him to let the sack down carefully by the rope which held it, and then he should get in. Thereupon the Scholar let him down, and, opening the mouth of the sack, delivered the man, and as soon as he had done so he got into the sack, and said, "Now pull me up quickly!"

"Stop, stop!" cried the other; "that is not quite right;" and laying hold of the Scholar by the shoulders he thrust him head downwards into the sack. Then he pulled the neck to, and, fastening the rope on, swung the sack up on the bough of the tree, while he exclaimed, "How do you feel now, my good fellow? do you find that wisdom comes with experience? Stay there quietly till you become wiser!"

With these words he mounted the Student's horse and rode off; but in an hour's time he sent somebody to release the poor Student from the sack.

The Little Ass

ONCE upon a time there lived a King and Queen, who were very rich, and possessed all they desired, but children. On this account the

Queen used to cry and groan all day long, saying, "I am like a barren field where nothing will grow!" At last her wishes and prayers were answered, and a child was born; but when the nurses took it they said it was a Little Ass, and not a human child. When the mother perceived this, she began to cry and groan again, for she would rather have had no child than a Little Ass, and she ordered them to throw the thing into the water, that it might feed the fishes. The King, however, said, "No! God gave it, and it shall be my son and heir, and at my death sit upon the throne, and wear the royal crown." So the Little Ass was taken care of and brought up well, while its ears grew to a good size, and were straight and well formed. Now, it was a frolicsome animal, and used to jump about, and, besides, it had a very great passion for music, so much so, that it went to a celebrated Musician, and said, "Teach me your art, that I may strike the lute as well as you." "Ah! my dear sir," replied the Musician, "that would be difficult; your fingers are not altogether made for the purpose; I am afraid you could not touch the strings."

The Ass, however, would not be put off, and, being determined to learn, he applied himself so strenuously and industriously that in the course of time he could play as well as the master himself. One day afterwards the young prince went out walking in a thoughtful mood, and, presently coming to a running brook, he looked in and saw his own figure reflected like an ass. The sight made him so sad that he wandered away from his home, attended but by one trusty friend. They travelled to and fro for many months, and at last came to a kingdom over which ruled an old King, who had an only but very beautiful daughter. "Here we will stay," said the Ass-prince; and knocking at the palace-door, he cried out, "Open, if you please! a visitor stands without who wishes to come in." The door was not opened, and so the Ass sat down on the steps and played his lute in the most charming way with his two fore-feet. At this the guard at the door opened his eyes very wide, and running to the King told him that a young Ass was at the door, who was playing the lute like a regular musician. "Let him come in, then," said the King. But, as soon as the Ass entered, all began to laugh at such a lute-player, and he was told to sit down and feed with the slaves at the lower end of the hall. This he would not do, but said, "I am no common animal, I am a distinguished Ass." "If you are so," said the others, "take your place with the soldiers." "No! I will sit by the King himself." said the Ass. The King laughed, but said good-naturedly, "Yes, it shall be so, as you desire; come up hither." By-and-by the King asked, "How does my daughter please you?" The Ass turned his head towards her, looked at her, and, nodding, said, "The Princess pleases me beyond measure, she is so beautiful as I have never seen any one before." "Well, then, you shall sit by her," said the King. "That is just right," said the Ass, and sitting down by her side, he ate and drank with her, for he knew how to conduct himself before company.

At this court the noble beast stayed many months; but soon he began to think, "Of what use is all this? I may as well return home:" and, hanging his head down, he went to the King and mentioned his wishes. But the King had become very partial to the Ass, and said, "What is the matter, my dear friend? you look as sour as a vinegar-cruet. Do stop with me, I will give you whatever you desire; do you want money?" "No," said the Ass, shaking his head. "Do you need treasures or jewels?" "No." "Will you have the half of my kingdom?" "Ah, no, no!" "I would I knew what would content you," cried the King; "will you have my beautiful daughter to wife?" "Oh, yes! that would please me well," replied the Ass, and his spirits returned at once, for it was the very thing he had wished. So thereupon a large and magnificent wedding was celebrated. At night, when the bride and bridegroom were about to go to their sleeping-apartment, the King took a fancy to know if he would retain his form or not, and so he bade a servant to conceal himself in his room. By-and-by, when they entered, the bridegroom bolted the door after him, and then, believing that he and his wife were alone, he threw off his Ass's skin, and stood up a handsome and well-formed man. "Now you see," said he to his bride, "who I am, and that I am not unworthy of you." She was of course in transports of joy to see the good change, and kissed him, and thenceforth loved him dearly. As soon as morning came over, he got up and put on again his skin, so that no one ever would have known what was concealed beneath it. Soon the old King came, and when he saw the Ass, he exclaimed, "Ah! what up already!" and then turning to his daughter, he said to her, "Alas! you are doubtless in grief, because you have not really a human husband." "Oh, no, dear father," she replied; "I love him as much as if he were the handsomest man possible, and I will comfort him all my life."

The King went away astonished; but the servant followed him and told him what had happened. "That never can be true," said the King. "Then watch yourself to-night, my lord King," answered the servant; "and you will see with your own eyes the truth of my words; but I would advise you to snatch away the skin and burn it, and then your son-in-law will be compelled to show himself in his true character." "Your advice is good," said the King; and in the middle of the night, when everybody was asleep, he slipped into the chamber of his son-in-law, and when he looked at the bed the moonbeams showed clearly that it was no Ass, but a fine young man who lay there, while by the side the skin had been thrown down on the floor. The King took the skin up and caused a great fire to be made, into which he threw it, and stood by till it was burnt to ashes. He was anxious still to see how the youth would behave when he discovered his loss, and so he stopped the rest of the night watching. At daybreak the youth arose, and looked about for his ass-skin; but he could find it nowhere. Then he was frightened, and cried out in sorrow and anguish, "Alas! I must make my escape!" but as he left the room, he found the King standing outside, who said, "Whither away, my son, in such a hurry? what do you intend? Remain here; you are too handsome a man to be readily parted with. I will give you now the government of half of my kingdom, and at my death you shall have the whole."

"So wish I that this good beginning may have a good ending," said the youth. "I will remain with you."

Thereupon the old King put half the kingdom under his care, and, when he died, about a year after, the whole government descended to the young King, and in another year he was called upon to rule the kingdom of his own father, who died and left it to him. And over these two countries he ruled so wisely that the people prospered, and his Queen and he were happy and contented.

The Little Shepherd Boy

ONCE upon a time there was a little Shepherd Boy who was famed far and wide for the wise answers which he gave to every question. Now the King of the country heard of this lad, but he would not believe what was said about him, so the Boy was ordered to come to court. When he arrived the King said to him, "If you can give me answers to each of the three questions which I will now put to you, I will bring you up as my own child, and you shall live here with me in my palace."

"What are these three questions?" asked the Boy.

"The first is, how many drops of water are there in the sea?"

"My Lord King," replied the Shepherd Boy, "let all the waters be stopped up on the earth, so that not one drop shall run into the sea before I count it, and then I will tell you how many drops there are in the sea!"

"The second question," said the King, "is, How many stars are there in the sky?"

"Give me a large sheet of paper," said the Boy; and then he made in it with a pin so many minute holes that they were far too numerous to see or to count, and dazzled the eyes of whomever looked at them. This done he said, "So many stars are there in the sky as there are holes in this paper: now count them." But nobody was able. Thereupon the King said, "The third question is, How many seconds are there in eternity?"

"In Lower Pomerania is situate the adamantine mountain, one mile in height, one mile in breadth, and one mile deep; and thither comes a bird once in every thousand years which rubs its beak against the hill, and, when the whole shall be rubbed away, then will the first second of eternity be gone by."

"You have answered the three questions like a sage," said the King, "and from henceforward you shall live with me in my palace, and I will treat you as my own child."

The Glass Coffin

NEVER tell a body that a tailor cannot travel far, and arrive at as high
an honour as he chooses. Nothing more is necessary than that he
should go to the right spot, and, what is of most consequence, that he
should have good luck.

Such a clever and nimble Tailor's lad went out once upon his
wanderings, and came to a great forest, in which, because he did not
know the road, he lost his way. Night overtook him, and there was
nothing else for him to do but to seek a bed in this frightful solitude.
He could have easily made a good bed on the soft moss, had he not
been afraid of the wild beasts, the thought of which disquieted him
so much that he resolved at length to pass the night on a tree. He
picked out a lofty oak, to the top of which he climbed, and thanked
heaven that he had brought his goose with him, so that the wind
which whistled among the trees could not blow him away. After he

had spent some hours in the darkness, not without trembling and shivering, he perceived at a short distance the glimmering of a candle, and thinking that it might be the habitation of some man, where he could find a better resting-place than on the boughs of his tree, he cautiously descended, and walked towards the light. Presently he came to a little hut, built of reeds and rushes, and, knocking boldly at the door, which opened of itself, he saw inside a very old, grey-headed man, dressed in a frock made of various-coloured rags. "Who are you, and what do you want?" asked this figure in a hoarse voice.

"I am a poor Tailor," he replied, "surprised by night in this forest, and I pray you earnestly to keep me in your hut till the morning." "Go your way," cried the Old Man peevishly; "I will have nothing to do with vagabonds, seek a welcome elsewhere;" and so saying he would have pushed the man out of the house. The Tailor, however, caught hold of his coat, and begged so earnestly, that the Old Man, who seemed much rougher than he really was, yielded at length, and took the Tailor into his hut, where he gave him something to eat, and then showed him a bed in a corner.

The weary Tailor needed no rocking, but slept soundly till morning, and even then he would not have got up had he not been aroused by a loud cry. A terrible screaming and moaning pierced through the thin walls of the cottage, and the Tailor, excited by an unusual courage, jumped up, and, drawing his clothes on hastily, went out. Then he saw near the cottage a great black beast and a pretty Goat engaged in a hot contest. They were butting at one another with so much fury that the ground trembled under their feet, and the air resounded with their cries. For some time it was uncertain which would gain the victory; but at last the Goat thrust his horns into his enemy's body with so much force that the latter fell to the ground with a fearful howl, and was soon despatched with a stroke or two more on the part of the Goat.

The Tailor, who had watched the fight with astonishment, was still standing by at its close, and as soon as the Goat perceived him, it rushed at him, and, catching him upon its horns before he could

escape, bolted away with him over hedge and ditch, hill and valley,
meadow and wood. He held fast to the horns with both hands (for he
had managed to get on the goat's back), and resigned himself to his
fate; but it came sooner than he expected, for at last the Goat
stopped before a ridge of rocks, and let the Tailor softly down to the
ground. More dead than alive, he lay for a long time before he
recovered his senses, and when he did so, the Goat, which had
remained by him all the time, thrust his horns with such force into a
seeming door in the rock that it split open. Flames of fire came out,
and presently a great smoke followed which hid the Goat from the
eyes of the Tailor, who now knew not what to do, nor where to turn
to get out of the wilderness. While he stood considering, a voice
came from the rock which said, "Step in hither without fear, and no
harm shall happen to you." The Tailor hesitated; but drawn by an
invisible power, he obeyed the voice, and, passing through the iron
door, he found himself in an immense hall, whose roof, walls, and
floor, were formed of bright and polished square stones, on each of
which characters unknown to him were engraved. He observed
everything with wonder, and was on the point of making his way out
again, when the voice said, "Step upon the stone which lies in the
middle of the hall, and there await your fate."

The Tailor's courage was up now, and he walked to the spot
indicated, and presently the stone gave way beneath him, and sank
slowly deeper and deeper. When it stopped, and the Tailor looked
about him, he saw another large chamber like the first in extent; but
there was much more to attract his attention and wonder. In the
walls were cut recesses, in which stood vessels of clear glass, some
filled with coloured fluids and others with a bluish smoke. On the
ground of the hall stood, opposite each other, two great glass chests,
which at once excited his wonder. He stepped up to them, and found
that one contained a handsome building similar to a castle, with
farm-buildings, stables, and outhouses attached, and surrounded by
all other necessaries. Everything was diminutive, but made so
delicately that it must have been executed with the greatest ingenuity
by a cunning workman. The Tailor could scarcely take his eyes away

from this curiosity, but the voice warned him to desist, and to look instead at what was contained in the other glass chest. To what a pitch was his wonder raised when he perceived in it a beautiful Maiden lying fast asleep, and enveloped from head to foot with her own yellow hair! Her eyes were fast closed, but the fresh colour of her cheeks, and the motion of a riband to and fro, which swayed with her breath, left no doubts as to her being alive. The Tailor looked at her with a beating heart, and all at once she opened her eyes and closed them again with a joyful cry. When she saw him, "Just heaven!" she exclaimed, "my liberty approaches! Quick, quick, help me out of my prison; push back the bolt of my glass cage, and I am free!"

The Tailor obeyed without trembling, and as soon as he raised the glass lid, the Maiden stepped out and hastened to one corner of the hall, where she wrapped herself in a large cloak. Then she sat down upon a stone, and, calling the young Tailor to her, gave him a friendly kiss and then said, "My long-desired deliverer! a gracious heaven has led you hither to put an end to my sorrows. On the same day that they end, your good fortune shall begin. You are my husband, chosen by heaven, and you shall spend your life in undisturbed peace, beloved by me, and endowed with all my earthly riches. Sit down, now, and hear the history of my misfortunes.

"I am the daughter of a rich Count. My parents died when I was yet in tender childhood, and delivered me as their last bequest to the care of my elder Brother, by whom I was to be educated. We loved each other dearly, and we were so of one mind in our ways of thinking and acting, that we both resolved to remain single, and live together to the end of our lives. In our house there was never any lack of company; neighbours and friends visited us constantly, and we exercised towards all the greatest possible hospitality. Thus it happened that one evening a Stranger rode into our castle-yard under the pretext of not being able to reach the next town, and requested shelter. We treated his request with our usual courtesy, and he entertained us for the rest of that evening with his conversations and relations of his various adventures. My Brother even took such a fancy to him that he pressed him to stay for a couple of days, to which he consented after some hesitation. Late at night we arose from table, and after the Stranger had been shown to his apartment, I hastened, weary as I was, to lay myself down on the soft feathers of my bed. I had scarcely dropped asleep when I heard the tones of a delicious strain of music. I could not conceive from whence it proceeded, and I resolved to summon my chamber-maid, who slept in the adjoining room. To my astonishment it seemed as if a mountain were laid upon my breast, and all power of speech was so taken away from me by some invisible means, that I was unable to utter a single word. Meanwhile, I saw, by the shining of the lamp, the Stranger step into my room through two doors which I supposed were fast closed. He approached me, and said that by the aid of enchantments which were at his service he had caused the notes of the music which had awakened me, and that now he was come at all risks to offer me his heart and hand. My indignation, however, at his enchantments was so great that I deigned no answer to him; and for a long time he remained immovable before me, apparently awaiting my favourable decision. As I continued silent, however, he declared passionately that he would revenge himself, and find some means to punish my haughtiness; and so saying he quitted my room. I passed the rest of the night in the greatest anxiety and did not sleep till morning, and then as soon as I awoke I hastened to my Brother to tell him of what had happened to me, but I found him not in his room, and the servants told me that he had ridden out to hunt with the Stranger at daybreak.

"This foreboded no good to me. I dressed myself quickly, caused my palfrey to be saddled, and rode, attended only by one servant, at full gallop into the forest. On our way the servant let his horse fall and broke his knees, so that he was unable to follow me; but I continued without a stoppage to hurry on, and in a few minutes I saw the Stranger, leading a Goat by a string, coming towards me. I asked him where he had left my Brother, and how he had come by the Goat, from whose large eyes tears were streaming. Instead of answering me he began to laugh loudly; and thereupon I became very angry, and, drawing a pistol, fired it at the monster; but the ball rebounded from his breast and pierced the head of my horse. I was thrown to the ground, and the Stranger murmured some words which deprived me of sensibility.

"When I recovered again the use of my faculties, I found myself enclosed in a glass coffin, in this subterraneous chamber. The black Magician appeared once more, and told me he had changed my Brother into a Goat, inclosed my castle with all its surrounding buildings in another glass case, and shut up my people in the form of smoke in glass bottles. If I were willing, he said, to fulfil his wishes now, nothing was easier for him than to put things in their previous position; he need only to open the cases and everything would return to its natural shape. I answered him, however, as little as before, and he disappeared, leaving me lying in my glass prison-house, where I presently fell into a deep sleep. Among the visions which then came across my dreams was the consoling one that a youth came and delivered me; and when I opened my eyes to-day, I saw you, and knew my dream was fulfilled. Help me now to complete what I then dreamed. The first thing is to raise this glass chest which contains my castle, and place it on that wide stone."

As soon as the stone was thus laden it began to rise, carrying with it the Maiden and the Tailor; and at length it passed through the floor of the upper room, and from thence they quickly came into the open air. Here the Maiden raised the lid of the case, and it was wonderful to see how, immediately, castle, farm-buildings, stables, etc., unfolded themselves, and grew with marvellous rapidity to their natural size. Thereupon the Maiden and the Tailor turned back into the subterraneous cave, and caused the stone to raise with them the bottles filled with smoke. Scarcely were they opened when the blue smoke pressed out and assumed the form of men, whom the Maiden recognised as her servants and attendants. Their joy at this recognition was still further increased when the Brother, whom the Enchanter had changed into a Goat, appeared, coming out of the wood in his natural form; and the Maiden, in the excess of her joy, gave her hand to the lucky Tailor on the very same day.

The Undutiful Son

ONCE upon a time a man and his wife were sitting before their house-door, with a roast fowl on a table between them, which they were going to eat together. Presently the man saw his old father coming, and he quickly snatched up the fowl and concealed it, because he grudged sharing it, even with his own parent. The old man came, had a draught of water, and then went away again. As soon as he was gone his son went to fetch the roast fowl again; but when he touched it he saw that it was changed into a toad, which sprang upon his face and squatted there, and would not go away. When any one tried to take it off, it spat out poison and seemed about to spring in the face, so that at length nobody dared to meddle with it. Now this toad the undutiful son was compelled to feed, lest it should feed on his flesh; and with this companion he moved wearily about from place to place, and had no rest anywhere in this world.

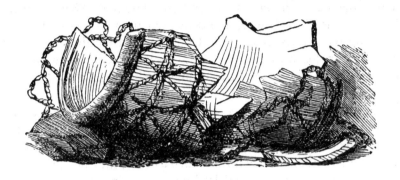

Lazy Harry

HARRY was a lazy fellow, and, although he had nothing further to do than to drive his goat daily to the meadow, he sighed continually when he reached home, after his day's work, and would say: "In truth it is a weary life this, and a troublesome job, year after year, to drive a goat into the field every day till the autumn comes. It were better if one could lie down and sleep; but no! one must always be watching lest the goat should injure the young trees, or creep through the hedge into some garden, and so get away. Now how can I obtain quiet and enjoy life?" Once he sat down to collect his thoughts and consider how he should free his shoulders from their burden. For a long time nothing came of his reflections, till all at once it flashed upon him as if a scale had fallen from his eyes. "I know what I will do," he cried; "I will marry fat Kate; she also has a goat, and she can drive out mine with hers, and so save me the trouble."

So thinking, Harry got up and set his weary legs in motion to cross over the road (for the distance was no further to the parents of fat

Kate) to offer himself as a husband for their industrious and virtuous daughter. The parents did not consider long; "Like and like agree together," thought they, and so consented. Thereupon fat Kate became Harry's wife, and drove out the two goats while her husband passed his time easily, troubling himself about no other labour than his own laziness! Only now and then he went out, because, as he said, he relished the quiet the better afterwards; and if he did not go out he lost all feeling for the rest.

Soon, however, fat Kate became no less lazy. "Dear Harry," said she one day, "why should we sour our lives without necessity, and harass the best part of our young days? Would it not be better if we gave our two goats, which now disturb us every morning in our best sleep, to our neighbour, and let him give us in return a bee-hive which we can place behind the house in a sunny place, and afterwards need trouble no more about it? The bees need no looking after, and have not to be driven every day into the meadow, for they will fly out and return home of themselves, and collect their honey without any interference on our part!"

"You have spoken like a wise woman," replied lazy Harry; "let us pursue your plan without delay; besides honey both tastes and nourishes better than goats' milk, and can be kept much longer!"

The neighbour willingly gave a bee-hive in exchange for the two goats, and certainly the bees did fly unceasingly from early morning till late in evening in and out of their hive, and filled it too with a store of the choicest honey, so that Harry was able to take out a large jar-full in the autumn.

This jar they placed on a board which was nailed to the wall in their sleeping-room; and as they feared it might be stolen from them, or that the mice might manage to get at it, fat Kate fetched a stout hazelstick and laid it by her bed, so that she could reach it without troubling herself to get up, and drive away by these means the uninvited guests.

Lazy Harry, however, would not leave his bed till noonday; "He who rises early wastes his possessions," he said. One morning when the bright daylight found him still in his bed, and he had just awakened from a long sleep, he said to his wife, "You women like sweets, and you have been stealing some of the honey; it were better, before you eat it all out, that we barter it away with some one for a goose." "But not before we have a boy to take care of it," replied the fat Kate. "Shall I distress myself about the young geese and waste my strength unnecessarily on their account?"

"Do you think," said Harry, "that a boy will take care of them? Now-a-days the children don't mind anybody, but act just as they think proper, because they fancy themselves wiser than their elders; just like that boy who instead of looking after the cow hunted three blackbirds."

"Oh," replied Kate, "he shall catch it if he does not do what I tell him. I will take a stick and give him no end of blows across the shoulders. See here, Harry," she cried, and caught up the stick which was laid to keep away the mice. "See here, I will lay on him like this." But unluckily, in raising the stick she hit the honey-jar, and threw it down on the bed. The jar was shivered to atoms, and the beautiful honey flowed all over the ground. "There lies our goose and goose boy," exclaimed Harry; "they will not want to be tended now. But still it is a lucky thing that the jar did not fall upon my head, so we have good reason to be contented with our fate." So saying, he looked among the broken fragments and discovered one in which some honey was still left. "This we will eat," said he to his wife, "and then rest a while longer after our fright, for what does it signify if we do lie a little later than usual in bed? the day is long enough!"

"Yes, yes," replied fat Kate, "the affair has happened at a very good time. Do you know, the snail was once invited to a wedding, but he tarried so long on the road, that he arrived at the christening instead. In front of the house he fell over the step, but all he said was, 'Hurrying is no good.'"

The Family Servants

"WHERE are you going to?" "To Walpe."

"I to Walpe, you to Walpe; so, so, together we go."

"Have you got a husband? how do you call your husband?"

"Cham." "My husband Cham, your husband Cham; I to Walpe, you to Walpe; so, so, together we go."

"Have you got a child? how do you call your child?"

"Grild." "My child Grild, your child Grild; my husband Cham, your husband Cham; I to Walpe, you to Walpe; so, so, together we go."

"Have you got a cradle? how do you call your cradle?"

"Hippodadle." "My cradle Hippodadle, your cradle Hippodadle; my child Grild, your child Grild; my husband Cham, your husband Cham; I to Walpe, you to Walpe; so, so, together we go."

"Have you got a man? how do you call your man?"

"Do-as-well-as-you-can." "My man Do-as-well-as-you-can, your man Do-as-well-as-you-can; my cradle Hippodadle, your cradle Hippodadle; my child Grild, your child Grild; my husband Cham, your husband Cham; I to Walpe, you to Walpe; so, so, together we go."

The Old Griffin

THERE was once a King, but where he reigned and how he was called I know nothing about. He had no son, only a Daughter, who was always ill, and no doctor could cure her; then it was prophesied to the King, that his Daughter would eat herself well with an apple. So he made it known all over the kingdom, whoever brought his Daughter some apples with which she should eat herself well should marry her and be King. Now, a Peasant, who had three sons, heard of it; and he said to the eldest, "Go to the garden, take a basketful of those beautiful apples with the red cheeks, and carry them to the court. Perhaps the King's Daughter will be able to eat herself well with them: and then you can marry her and be King." The chap did as he was bid, and took to the road. When he had walked a little while he met quite a little Iron Man, who asked him what he had in his basket. So Hele, for that was his name, said, "Frogs' legs!" The little man then said, "Well, so it shall be, and remain;" and then went on. At last Hele came to the castle, and had it announced that he had got some apples which would cure the Princess if she ate them. At that the King was mightily pleased, and had Hele in court. Oh, dear! when he opened it, instead of apples, he had frogs' legs in the basket, and they were kicking about still. The King got into a great rage, and had him kicked out of the castle. When he got home he told his Father how he had fared. Then the Father sent his next son, whose name was Saeme, but it went just the same with him as with Hele. The little Iron Man met him very soon, and asked him what he had in the basket, and Saeme said, "Sow-thistles;" and the little Man said, "Well, so it shall be, and remain." When he arrived at the King's castle, and said he had apples with which the King's Daughter could eat herself well, they would not let him in, and told him there had already been one who had made fools of them. But Saeme insisted he had really such apples; they should only let him in. At last they believed him, and took him before the King; but when he opened the basket he had nothing but sow-thistles. That annoyed the King most dreadfully, so that he had Saeme whipped out of the castle. When he got home he told them what had happened to him. Then came the youngest boy, whom they had always called stupid Jack, and asked the Father whether he, too, might go with apples. "Yes," said the Father, "you are just the right sort of fellow; if the clever ones can't succeed, what will you be able to do?" The boy did not believe it. "Well, Father, I will go too." "Get away, you stupid chap!" said the Father; "you must wait till you grow wiser;" and then turned his back upon him; but the boy tugged at his smock-frock behind, and said, "Now Father, I will go too." "Well, just as you like; go – you will be sure to come back," he answered in a spiteful way. The boy was beyond measure delighted, and jumped for joy. "Ay, there! act like a fool! You get stupider from one day to the next," said the Father. That did not affect Jack a bit, who would not be disturbed in his joy. As night soon came on, he thought he

THE OLD GRIFFIN

would wait the next morning; anyhow, he would not be able to get to court that day. He could not sleep that night in bed, and when he only slumbered a little he dreamed of beautiful maidens, of castles, gold, silver, and all that sort of thing. Early next morning he went his way and soon the Little Man in his iron dress met him and asked him what he had in the basket. "Apples," he answered, "with which the King's Daughter should eat herself well." "Well," said the Little Man, "such it shall be, and remain." But at court they would not let Jack in at all; for that there had been two who had said they brought apples, and one had frogs' legs, and the other sow-thistles. But Jack insisted tremendously he had no frogs' legs, but the most beautiful apples that grew in the kingdom. As he spoke so nicely the doorkeeper thought he could not be telling a lie, and let him in; and they did quite right too, for, when Jack uncovered the basket before the King, apples as yellow as gold came tumbling out. The King was delighted, and had some of them taken to his Daughter at once, and waited in anxious expectation until they should bring him word what effect they had. Not long after news is brought him; but what think you it was? It was the Daughter herself! As soon as she had ate of those apples she had jumped out of bed quite well. What the King's delight was cannot be described.

But now the King would not give Jack his daughter to marry, and said that he must first make him a boat that would swim better on land than in the water. Jack agreed to the condition and went home and told his adventures. So the Father sent Hele into the wood to make such a boat; he worked away diligently, and whistled the while. At midday, when the sun was at the highest, came the little Iron Man, and asked what he was making. "Wooden bowls," answered he. The little Man answered, "Well, so it shall be, and remain." In the evening Hele thought he had made the boat; but, when he was going to get into it it turned to wooden bowls. The next day Saeme went into the wood; but he met with exactly the same fate as his brother. On the third day stupid Jack went: he worked very hard, so that the wood resounded all through with his heavy blows, and he sang and whistled besides right merrily. The little man came to him at midday when it was the hottest, and asked him what he was making. "A boat that will swim better on dry land than in the water," he answered, "and that when he had done it he should marry the King's Daughter." "Well," said the little Man, "such a one it shall be, and remain." In the evening, when the sun was setting like a ball of gold, Jack made ready his boat and all things belonging to it, and rowed towards the castle; but the boat went as fast as the wind. The King saw it a long way off; but would not give Jack his Daughter yet, and said he must first take a hundred hares out grazing from early morning to late in the evening, and if one were missing he should not have his Daughter. Jack was quite contented, and the next day went out with his herd to the meadow, and kept a sharp look-out that none should stray away. Not many hours had passed when a Maid came from the castle, and said Jack was to give her a hare directly, as some visitors had arrived. But Jack saw through that well enough, and said he would not give her one; the King might treat his visitors to hare-pepper. But the Maid did not believe him, and at last set to scolding. So Jack said that if the King's Daughter came herself he would give her a hare. The Maid told them in the castle, and the King's Daughter did go herself. But in the meantime the little Man had come again to Jack and asked him what he was doing there. "Oh, he had got to watch a hundred hares so that none ran away, and then he might marry the King's Daughter, and be King." "Good!" said the little Man, "there's a whistle for you, and when one runs away only just whistle and he will come back again." When the King's Daughter came, Jack gave her a hare into her apron. But when she had got about a hundred steps off, Jack whistled, and the hare jumped out of the cloth, and jump, jump! was back to the herd directly. In the evening the hare-herd whistled again, and looked to see they were all right, and drove them to the castle. The King wondered how Jack had been able to take care of a hundred hares, so that none should run off: but he would not yet give him his Daughter so easily, but said he must first get him a feather from the Old Griffin's tail.

Jack started at once, and marched right briskly on. In the evening he arrived at a castle, where he asked for a night's lodging, for at that time there were no such things as hotels; and the master of the castle greeted him very civilly, and asked him where he was going to. Jack answered, "To the Old Griffin." "Oh, indeed! to the Old Griffin; they say he knows everything, and I have lost the key to an iron money-chest; perhaps you would be good enough to ask him where it is!" "Certainly," said Jack, "that I will." Early the next morning he started off again on his road, and arrived at another castle, where he again passed the night. When the people learned that he was going to the Old Griffin, they said a daughter was ill in the house; they had already tried every possible remedy, but without effect; would he be kind enough to ask Old Griffin what would cure her? Jack said he would do it with pleasure, and went on again. He arrived at a lake; and, instead of a ferry-boat, there was a big man who had to carry everybody over. The man asked him where he was bound for? "To the Old Griffin," said Jack. "When you get to him," said the Man, "just ask him why I am obliged to carry everybody over the water." "Yes, to be sure," said Jack; "goodness gracious! yes, willingly!" The Man then took him up on his shoulder, and carried him over. At last Jack arrived at the Old Griffin's house, and only found the wife at home – not Old Griffin. The woman asked him what he wanted, so he told her he must have a feather from Old Griffin's tail; and that in a castle they had lost the key to the money-chest, and he was to ask the Griffin where it was; and then, in another castle the daughter was ill, and he was to know what would make her well again; then not far from there was the water, and the man who was obliged to carry everybody over, and he should very much like to know why the man was obliged to carry everybody over. "But," said the Woman, "look you, my good friend, no Christian can speak with a Griffin; he eats them all up; but, if you like, you can reach out and pull a feather out of his tail; and as to those things that you want to know, I will ask him myself." Jack was quite satisfied with the arrangement, and got under the bed. In the evening Old Griffin came home, and when he stepped into the room he said, "Wife, I smell a Christian!" "Yes," said the Wife, "there has been one here to-day, but he went away again." So Old Griffin said no more. In the middle of the night, when Griffin was snoring away lustily, Jack reached up and pulled a feather out of his tail.

The Griffin jumped up suddenly, and cried, "Wife, I smell a Christian! and it was just as if someone had been plucking at my tail." The Wife said, "You have no doubt been dreaming. I have told you already that one has been here to-day, but that he went away again. He told me all sorts of things: that in one castle they had lost the key of the money-chest, and could not find it." "Oh, the fools!" exclaimed the Griffin; "the key lies in the wood-shed, behind the door, under a log of wood." "And, further, he said that in another castle the daughter was ill, and they knew no means to cure her." "Oh, the fools!" said the Griffin, "under the cellar stairs a toad has made its nest of her hair, and if she got the hair back again she would be well." "And then, again, he said, at a certain place there was a lake, and a man who was obliged to carry everybody over." "Oh, the fool!" said the Old Griffin, "if he were only to put somebody into the middle he need not carry any more over."

Early next morning the Old Griffin got up and went out, and Jack crept from under the bed with a beautiful feather, having heard what the Griffin had said about the key, the daughter, and the man. The Wife repeated it all to him so he should not forget, and then he started off towards home. He came to the man at the water first, and he asked him directly what the Griffin had said; but Jack said he must carry him over first, and then he would tell him. So he carried him over; and when they got there Jack told him he had only to put somebody into the middle and then he need carry no more. The man was delighted beyond measure, and told Jack that out of gratitude he should like to carry him over and back once more. But Jack said nay, he would save him the trouble; he was quite contented with him already, and then went on. Then he arrived at the castle where the daughter was ill; he took her on his shoulder, for she was not able to walk, and carried her down the cellar stairs, and then took the toad's nest from under the bottom step, and put it into the daughter's hand, and all at once she jumped off his shoulder, up the stairs before him, strong and well. Now the father and mother were delighted indeed, and made Jack presents of gold and silver, and whatever he wanted, they gave him. When Jack arrived at the other castle he went straight to the wood-shed, and found the key right enough behind the door, under the log of wood, and took it to the master. He was not a little pleased, and gave Jack in return a great deal of gold that was in the box, and all sorts of things besides, such as cows, and sheep, and goats. When Jack returned to the King with all these things, with the money, and gold, and silver, and the cows, sheep, and goats, the King asked him where ever he had come by it all. So Jack said the Old Griffin would give one as much as one liked. The King thought he could find a use for that sort of thing himself, and so started off to the Griffin; but when he got to the water he happened to be the first who arrived there since Jack, and the man put him in the middle and walked off, and the King was drowned.

So Jack married the King's Daughter and became King.

The Old Beggar-Woman

ONCE upon a time there was an old Woman, who begged as you may have seen other old women do; and when anybody gave her anything she would say, "God bless you!" Now this old Beggar-Woman went to a door, and before the fire stood a good-natured lad warming himself; and, as soon as he saw the poor Woman shivering outside, he said to her, "Come and warm yourself." She went in; but going too near the fire, her old rags began to burn before she was aware of it. The youth stood and looked at her; but should not he have extinguished the fire? Certainly; and if he had no water at hand, he should have caused water to flow out of his eyes; and so two charming little streams would have been given!

The Three Sluggards

A CERTAIN King had three Sons, all of whom he loved so much that he did not know which he should name to be King after him. When the day of his death approached, he called them to his bedside, and thus spoke to them: "Dear children, I have something on my mind which I wish to tell you; whichever of you is the laziest, he shall be King when I am dead."

"Then, father, the kingdom belongs to me," said the eldest Son; "for I am so lazy, that if I lie down to sleep, and tears come into my eyes, so that I cannot close them, I yet go to sleep without wiping them away!"

"The kingdom belongs to me," cried the second Son; "for I am so lazy that when I sit by the fire to warm myself, I allow my boots to scorch before I will draw away my feet."

But the third Son said, "The Kingdom is mine, father, for I am so lazy that were I about to be hanged, and even had I the rope round my neck, and any one should give me a sharp sword to cut it with, I should suffer myself to be swung off before I took the trouble to cut the rope."

As soon as the Father heard this he said to his youngest Son, "You have shown yourself the laziest of all, and you shall be King."

The Hen-Roost

ONCE upon a time there was an Enchanter who collected around him a great crowd of folks, before whom he performed his wonderful tricks. Among other things he caused an old hen to be brought in, which raised a heavy beam for a roosting-place, as thought it were as light as a feather. But there was a Girl standing by who had found a four-bladed leaf of shamrock, through which she became so wise that no trick could deceive her, and she saw the pretended beam was nothing but a straw. So she cried out, "Do you not see, you people, that it is no beam, but a straw which the hen is carrying?" Thereupon the enchantment vanished, and the gazers perceiving the truth, hunted the Enchanter away with scorn and ridicule.

Some time afterwards the Girl was to be married, and in a very smart dress she walked in great state over the fields which led to the church. All at once she came to a large swollen stream, over which there was no bridge or plank to cross by. Thereupon the Bride was in distress, but, holding her dress up, she tried to wade through the water. But just as she came about the middle of it a voice, which was that of the Enchanter, cried derisively, "Ah! where are your eyes, that you take this place for water?" At these words her eyes were opened, and she perceived that she stood holding up her dress in the middle of a field of corn-flowers. Then she, in her turn, got laughed at by the spectators; so the Enchanter turned the tables upon her.

The House in the Wood

THERE was a poor Wood-cutter, who lived with his Wife and three Daughters, in a little hut on the edge of a large forest. One morning, when he went out to his usual work, he said to his Wife, "Let my dinner be brought by our eldest Daughter, I shall not be ready to come home; and that she may not lose her way, I will take with me a bag of seeds and strew them on my path."

So when the sun was risen to the centre of the heavens, the Maiden set out on her way, carrying a jug of soup. But the field and wood-sparrows, the larks, blackbirds, goldfinches, and greenfinches, had many hours ago picked·up the seeds, so that the Maiden could find no trace of the way. So she walked on, trusting to fortune, till the sun set and night came on. The trees soon began to rustle in the darkness, the owls to hoot, and the girl began to feel frightened. All at once she perceived a light shining at a distance among the trees. "People must dwell there," she thought, "who will keep me during the night;" and she walked towards the light. In a short time she came to a cottage where the windows were all lighted up, and when she knocked at the door a hoarse voice called from within, "Come in." The girl opened the door and perceived a hoary Old Man sitting at a table with his face buried in his hands, and his white beard flowing down over the table on to the ground. On the hearth lay three animals, – a Hen, a Cock, and a brindled Cow. The girl told the Old Man her adventures, and begged for a night's lodging. The Man said:—

> "Pretty Hen, pretty Cock,
> And pretty brindled Cow,
> What have you to say to that?"

"Cluck!" said the animals: and as that meant they were satisfied, the Old Man said to the Maiden, "Here is abundance, and to spare; go now into the kitchen and cook some supper for us."

The girl found plenty of everything in the kitchen, and cooked a good meal, but thought nothing about the animals. When she had finished she carried a full dish into the room, and, sitting down opposite the Old Man, ate till she satisfied her hunger. When she had done, she said, "I am very tired; where is my bed, where I shall lie down and sleep?" The animals replied:—

THE HOUSE IN THE WOOD

"You have eaten with him,
You have drunk too with him;
And yet you have not thought of us;
Still you may pass the night here."

Thereupon the Old Man said, "Step down yon stair, and you will come to a room containing two beds, shake them up, and cover them with white sheets, and then I will come and lie down to sleep myself." The Maiden stepped down the stair, and as soon as she had shaken the beds up and covered them up afresh, she laid herself down in one bed, without waiting for the Old Man. But after some time the Old Man came, and, after looking at the girl with the light, shook his head when he saw she was fast asleep; and then, opening a trap-door, dropped her down into the cellar below.

Late in the evening the Wood-cutter arrived at home, and scolded his Wife because she had let him hunger all day long. "It is not my fault," she replied; "the girl was sent out with your dinner; she must have lost her way; but to-morrow she will return, no doubt." At daybreak the Wood-cutter got up to go into the forest, and desired that the second Daughter should bring him his meal this time. "I will take a bag of peas," he said; "they are larger than corn-seed; and the girl will therefore see them better, and not lose my track." At noonday, accordingly, the girl set out with her father's dinner; but the peas had all disappeared, for the wood-birds had picked them all up as they had on the day before, and not one was left. So the poor girl wandered about in the forest till it was quite dark, and then she also arrived at the Old Man's hut, was invited in, and begged food and a night's lodging. The Man of the white beard asked his animals again:—

"Pretty Hen, and pretty Cock,
And pretty brindled Cow,
What have you to say to that?"

They answered again, "Cluck!" and everything thereupon occurred the same as on the previous day. The girl cooked a good meal, ate and drank with the Old Man, but never once thought of the animals; and when she asked for her bed, they made answer:—

> "You have eaten with him,
> You have drunk too with him;
> And yet you have not thought of us;
> Still you may pass here the night!"

As soon as she was gone to sleep the Old Man came, and, after looking at her and shaking his head as before, dropped her into the cellar below.

Meanwhile the third morning arrived, and the Wood-cutter told his Wife to send their youngest child with his dinner: "For," said he, "she is always obedient and good; she will keep in the right path, and not run about like those idle hussies her sisters!"

But the Mother refused, and said, "Shall I lose my youngest child too?"

"Be not afraid of that," said her husband; "the girl will not miss her way, she is too steady and prudent; but for more precaution I will take beans to strew, they are larger still than peas, and will show her the way better."

But, by-and-by, when the girl went out with her basket on her arm, the wood-pigeons had eaten up all the beans, and she knew not which way to turn. She was full of trouble, and thought with grief, how her Father would want his dinner, and how her dear Mother would grieve when she did not return. At length, when it became quite dark, she also perceived the lighted cottage, and entering it, begged very politely to be allowed to pass the night there. The Old Man asked the animals a third time in the same words:—

> "Pretty Hen, pretty Cock,
> And pretty brindled Cow,
> What have you to say to that?"

"Cluck, cluck!" said they. Thereupon the Maiden stepped up to the fire, near which they lay, and fondled the pretty Hen and Cock, smoothing their plumage down with her hands, while she stroked the Cow between her horns. Afterwards, when she had got ready a good supper at the Old Man's request, and had placed the dishes on the table, she thought to herself, "I must not appease my hunger till I have fed these good creatures. There is an abundance in the kitchen, I will serve them first." Thus thinking she went and fetched some corn and strewed it before the fowls, and then she brought an armful of hay and gave it to the Cow. "Now, eat away, you good creatures," said she to them, "and when you are thirsty you shall have a nice fresh draught." So saying she brought in a pailfull of water; and the Hen and Cock perched themselves on its edge, put their beaks in, and then drew their heads up as birds do when drinking; the Cow also took a hearty draught. When the animals were thus fed, the Maiden sat down at table with the Old Man and ate what was left for her. In a short while the Hen and Cock began to fold their wings over their heads, and the brindled Cow blinked with both eyes. Then the Maiden asked, "Shall we not also take our rest?" The Old Man replied as before:—

> "Pretty Hen, pretty Cock,
> And pretty brindled Cow,
> What have you to say to that?"

"Cluck, cluck!" replied the animals, meaning,—

> "You have eaten with us,
> You have drunk too with us,
> You have thought of us kindly, too;
> And we wish you a good night's rest."

So the Maiden went down the stairs and shook up the feather-beds and laid on clean sheets, and when they were ready, the Old Man came and lay down in one, with his white beard stretching down to his feet. The girl then lay down in the other bed, first saying her prayers before she went to sleep.

She slept quietly till midnight, and at that hour there began such a tumult in the house that it awakened her. Presently it began to crack and rumble in every corner of the room, and the doors were slammed back against the wall, and then the beams groaned as if they were being riven away from their fastenings, and the stairs fell down, and at last it seemed as if the whole roof fell in. Soon after that all was quiet, but the Maiden took no harm, and went quietly off again to sleep. When, however, the bright light of the morning sun awoke her, what a sight met her eyes! She found herself lying in a large chamber, with everything around belonging to regal pomp. On the walls were represented gold flowers growing on a green silk ground; the bed was of ivory, and the curtains of red velvet, and on a stool close by was placed a pair of slippers ornamented with pearls. The Maiden thought it was all a dream; but presently in came three servants dressed in rich liveries, who asked her what were her commands. "Leave me," replied the Maiden; "I will get up at once and cook some breakfast for the Old Man, and also feed the pretty Hen, the pretty Cock, and the brindled Cow." She spoke thus because she thought the Old Man was already up; but when she looked round at his bed, she saw a stranger to her lying asleep in it. While she was looking at him, and saw that he was both young and handsome, he awoke, and starting up, said to the Maiden, "I am a King's son, who was long ago changed by a wicked Old Witch into the form of an Old Man, and condemned to live alone in the wood, with nobody to bear me company but my three servants in the form of a Hen, a Cock, and a brindled Cow. And the enchantment was not to end until a Maiden should come so kind-hearted, that she should behave as well to my animals as she did to me; and such a one you have been; and, therefore, this last midnight we were saved through you, and the old wooden hut has again become my royal palace."

When he had thus spoken the girl and he arose, and the Prince told his three servants to fetch to the palace the Father and Mother of the Maiden, that they might witness her marriage.

"But where are my two Sisters?" she asked. "I have put them in the cellar," replied the Prince, "and there they must remain till to-morrow morning, when they shall be led into the forest, and bound as servants to a collier, until they have reformed their tempers, and learnt not to let poor animals suffer hunger."

Love and Sorrow to Share

ONCE upon a time there was a Tailor so quarrelsome that his poor Wife could never get on with him, although she was both affectionate, pious, and industrious. He was discontented with whatever she did; and would not only mutter and scold, but even knock her about, and beat her. At last the Magistrate was told of his conduct, and the Tailor was summoned and put into prison till he should behave better. For a long time he was kept on bread and water, and at length released, after being admonished to beat his Wife no more, but to live with her in concord, and to share affection and sorrow, as it was fit that married people should do.

For some time all went on well; but soon the Tailor fell into his old habits, and grew more and more discontented and quarrelsome.

However, because he dared not beat his Wife, he would pull her hair instead; and one day she escaped from him and rushed out-of-doors. The Tailor pursued her with his yard-measure and shears in his hands, and as he did not gain on her steps he threw the measure and shears at her. The poor woman ran round their court, while her husband continued to throw the shears at her; and if he missed his aim he abused her, and if he hit her he laughed. He kept up this sport so long that the neighbours came to the assistance of his Wife, and he was taken again before the Magistrate and reminded of his promise. "My dear lord," replied the Tailor, "I have kept to what I promised; I have not beaten my Wife, but shared with her affection and sorrow."

"How can that be?" asked the Judge; "when she has now come a second time with these loud complaints of your conduct!"

"I have not beaten my Wife," reiterated the Tailor; "but all I did was to try and comb out her hair, because she looked so wild. But she ran away from me, and would not hear what I said; so then I pursued her, and in order to remind her of her duty, I threw at her what I chanced to have in my hand; I have also shared with her my love and my sorrow, for as often as I hit her she was made sorry and I was glad; and when I missed her she was glad and I was sorry!"

The Judge, however, was not satisfied with this answer, but sentenced him to a well-earned punishment!

Star Dollars

ONCE upon a time, there was a little Girl whose father and mother were dead; and she became so poor that she had no roof to shelter herself under, and no bed to sleep in; and at last she had nothing left but the clothes on her back, and a loaf of bread in her hand, which a compassionate body had given to her. But she was a good and pious little Girl, and when she found herself forsaken by all the world, she went out into the fields trusting on God. Soon she met a poor Man, who said to her, "Give me something to eat, for I am so hungry." She handed him the whole loaf; and, with a "God bless you!" walked on further. Next she met a little Girl crying very much, who said to her, "Pray give me something to cover my head with, for it is so cold!" So she took off her own bonnet, and gave it away. And in a little while she met another Child who had no cloak, and to her she gave her own cloak. Then she met another who had no dress on, and to this one she gave her own frock. By that time it was growing dark, and our little Girl entered a forest, and presently she met a fourth Maiden, who begged something, and to her she gave her petticoat; for, thought our heroine, "It is growing dark, and nobody will see me, I can give away this." And now she had scarcely anything left to cover herself; and just then some of the stars fell down in the form of silver dollars, and among them she found a petticoat of the finest linen! and in that she collected the star-money, which made her rich all the rest of her lifetime!

Lean Betty

VERY different from lazy Harry and fat Kate – who never troubled themselves to disturb their ease – was lean Betty. She busied herself from morning till night, and gave her husband, tall John, so much to do, that he was as heavily burdened as an ass which carries three sacks. But all was in vain; they had nothing, and they gained nothing, and one night when they went to bed, and could not move their limbs from weariness, they could not sleep for the thoughts that oppressed them. Lean Betty poked her husband in his side, and said to him, "Listen to me, long John! hear what I have thought. Suppose I should find a florin, and some one should give me a second, and then if I borrowed a third, and you gave me a fourth, with these four florins I would buy a young cow."

The husband was pleased with this plan; but he said, "I certainly do not know where I shall get the florin which I am to give you; but, however, supposing you get the money, and can buy a cow with it, you will do well if you follow out your plan. It pleases me to think," he continued, "that if the cow should produce a calf, I could then refresh myself often with a draught of milk!"

"The milk is not for you," returned the wife; "we must let the calf suck, that it may grow big and fat, and then we can sell it for a good price."

"Oh, certainly!" replied the husband; "but still we will take a little milk, for that can make no difference."

"Who ever taught you anything about cows?" said the wife angrily; "it may or may not do harm, but I will not have it done: and, although you may take all the pains you like, you shall not have a drop of milk. Do you think, you lanky John, that because you cannot satisfy yourself, you are going to make away with what it has cost me so much trouble to earn!"

"Hold your tongue, woman!" exclaimed the husband, "or I'll give you a box on the ear."

"What!" exclaimed she in return; "what, you will strike me, you whipper-snapper! you sneak! you lazy fellow!" And, so saying, she tried to catch hold of his hair; but long John, raising himself up, pinioned the thin arms of Betty to her side with one hand, and with the other he kept her head on the pillow, and let her abuse him as she liked, till she fell asleep tired out.

But whether when they awoke they quarrelled again, or went out to look for florins, or found them, I know nothing about!

The Bride-Choosing

THERE was once a young Shepherd who wished to get married; but although he knew three Sisters, each one was as pretty as the others, and the choice was therefore so difficult, that he did not know to which to give the preference. So he asked his Mother's advice; and she told him to invite all three of them to supper, and to place a cheese before them and observe how they cut it. The youth did so; and the first Sister ate her cheese, rind and all; the second cut off the rind so hastily, that she cut with it some of the good cheese and threw it all away; but the third Sister pared the rind off very carefully, neither too much nor too little. The Shepherd thereupon told all this to his Mother, and she said, "Take the youngest Sister to wife."

And he did so, and lived contentedly and happily with her all his life long.

The Stolen Farthings

ONCE upon a time a Father sat at table with his wife and children, and with them was a good Friend who had come on a visit. While they sat eating, it struck twelve, and then the Friend saw the door open, and a Child, pale as death, dressed in snow-white garments, come in. It did not look round or speak, but went straight into the next room. Soon it returned and went as silently out at the door again. The second and the third day it happened the same, and then the Friend asked the Father to whom the Child belonged which entered the house every day at noontime. "I have not seen it, nor do I know to whom it belongs," said the Father. So on the following day when the Child came the Friend pointed it out to the Father, but he could not see it, nor the Mother either, nor her children. Then the Friend got up, and, going to the chamber door, opened it a little and peeped in. There he saw the Child sitting on the ground, digging and picking industriously between the crevices of the boards; but as soon as it perceived the stranger it disappeared. The Friend now told the Father what he had seen, and described the child exactly, whereupon the Mother recognised his description, and said, "Ah! that is my dear Child who died four weeks ago." Then they broke up the boards of the room and found beneath them two Farthings which the Child had once received from his Mother to give to a poor man, but he had thought to himself, "One can buy biscuits with these," and so he had kept the Farthings and dropped them between the boards. And on that account he had no rest in his grave, and every mid-day he was compelled to come and seek for the Farthings.

So the parents gave the Farthings to a poor man, and the Child was never once seen again.

King Wren

In the olden times the birds had their own particular language, which each of them understood; now it sounded like a piping, now like a screeching, now like a whistling, and with some like music without words. Once it came into the heads of the birds that they would go no longer without a King, but would choose one among themselves. Only one bird, the Plover, was opposed to this plan;

"Free I have lived and free I will die!" he said, and so flew angrily away crying, "Where shall I rest? where shall I rest?" He flew on till he came to an unfrequented swamp, and there he stayed, and never showed himself again among his fellows.

The birds kept to their first resolution, and one fine May morning they all assembled together from the woods and fields. There were the Eagles and Finches, the Owls and the Crows, the Larks and the Sparrows; (need I name them all?) for even the Cuckoo came, and the Hoopoe, his coachman, so called because he always appears two days earlier; also a very small Bird who as yet had no name, mingled in the crowd. The Hen, who by chance had heard nothing of the affair, wondered at the immense assemblage. "Wat, wat, wat, is all this?" she quacked, but the Cock comforted his dear Hen by telling her what it all meant. It was determined that he should be King who could fly the highest, and thereupon a green Frog which sat among the bushes began to croak, "Natt, natt, natt, natt!" because it thought that there would be many tears shed on that account. But the Crow cried out, "Back, croaker! everything will be kept quiet."

It was next resolved that the trial should be made at once, because it was such a beautiful morning, and in order that no one might afterwards say, "I could easily have flown much higher, but the evening coming on prevented me."

At a given sign the whole assemblage mounted in the air, causing such an immense dust to rise from the field, that it seemed as if a black cloud was formed with the whirring, rustling, and beating of their wings. The small birds, however, soon fell back, for they could not fly very far, and so they alighted on the ground again. The larger birds kept it up longer, but none of them like the Eagle, who mounted so high that he almost touched the sun! Then he perceived that the others were not near him at all, and he thought to himself, "What need I to fly any higher? I am certainly the King!" and so saying, he began to fly downwards. When he alighted, the birds all exclaimed, "You must be our King, nobody has flown higher than you!"

"Except me!" cried the little fellow without a name, who had hidden himself among the feathers on the Eagle's back; and so saying he flew up high and higher still than the Eagle. When he had got as high as he possibly could, he folded his wings and dropped down again, exclaiming with his shrill voice, "I am King, I am King!"

"You our King!" replied the other birds in a rage, "you have gained it by means of craft and stratagem!" So they made another condition that he should be King who should fall deepest into the earth.

How the Goose swam cackling to land with her broad breast! How quickly the Cock grubbed up a hole! The Duck went the boldest to work, for she jumped into a grave, but in so doing sprained her foot, and waddled away to the nearest pond, crying, "Bad work, bad work!" But the Little Bird without a name found a mouse-hole into which it crept and called out in its shrill voice, "I am King, I am King!"

"You our King!" replied the other birds in a rage, "Do you think your cunning shall gain you anything?" and they resolved to keep the poor Bird in the hole and starve him out. Thereupon the Owl was set to keep watch during the night, and forbidden to let out his charge on pain of death! Then, because they were weary with so much flying, and the evening was come, the other birds went to bed with their wives and children, leaving the Owl standing alone by the mouse-hole, staring into it with both his eyes. By-and-by the Owl began to feel tired, and thought that one eye would do to watch that the evil thing did not escape, while he went to sleep with the other. Soon the Little Bird peeped out, and thought about escaping; but the Owl perceived him, and drove him back. Then the Owl began to close first one eye, and go to sleep with that, and then the other, and so intended to pass the whole night; but unluckily he once forgot to open the one eye when he shut the other, and so going to sleep with both he did not remark the Little Bird, who took advantage of this slip to make his escape.

From that time the Owl dared not any more suffer himself to be seen by day, for fear the other birds should pursue him, and maltreat him. He flies now only during the night, and persecutes mice, because they make such, to him, unfortunate holes! The Little Bird, too, did not like to venture among the others, lest he should be injured, or killed. He concealed himself in the hedges; and, when he thought himself quite safe, he called out, "I am King, I am King!" Therefore the other birds called him Hedge-King in scorn, and that means the Wren.

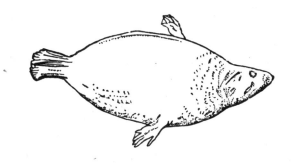

The Sole

THE Fishes once grew very discontented because no order was kept in their dominions. None turned aside for the others, but each swam right or left just as it pleased him, sometimes between those who wished to be together, or else pushing them to one side, and the stronger ones gave the weaker blows with their tails, which made them get out of the way as fast as they could, or else devoured them. "How nice it would be," thought the Fishes, "if we had a king who should exercise the power of judging between us!" And so at last they assembled together to choose a lord, who should be he who could swim the quickest and render help best to the weaker fishes.

So they laid themselves all in rank and file by the shore, and the Pike gave a signal with his tail, on which they started off. Like an arrow darted away the Pike, closely followed by the Herring, the Gudgeon, the Perch, and the Carp, and the rest. Even the Sole swam among them, hoping to gain the prize.

All at once a cry was heard, "The Herring is first, the Herring is first!" "Who is first?" asked the flat envious Sole in a vexed tone, "Who is first?"

"The Herring, the Herring!" was the reply.

"The nak-ed Herring, the nak-ed Herring!" said the Sole disdainfully. And since that time the Sole's mouth has become all on one side for a punishment.

The Duration of Life

WHEN the world was first created, it was appointed how many years each creature should exist. So the Ass came and inquired how long he was to live. "Thirty years," he was told, and then he was asked, "Is that sufficient?" "Alas!" replied the Ass, "that is a long time.

Think how many wearisome burdens I shall have to carry from morning till night; cornsacks to the mill, that others may eat bread, and I receive nothing but blows and kicks, and yet keep always active and obliging! Take away some of my years, I pray!"

So the Ass was pitied, and a life of only eighteen years appointed to him; whereupon he went gladly away, and the Dog then made his appearance, and asked the same. "How long do you wish to live?" was inquired of him; thirty years were too much for the Ass; but perhaps you will be satisfied." "Do you think so?" said the Dog; "remember how much I shall have to run; my feet will not last out; and then when I have lost my voice and cannot bark, and my teeth and cannot bite, what will there be for me to do but to crawl and howl from one corner to another?"

So the Dog's plea was allowed, and twelve years appointed for his age, after which he departed and made room for the Monkey. "You will live thirty years willingly, no doubt," was said to the Monkey; "you need not work like the Ass and the Dog, and therefore will always be well off."

"Alas! it should be so," said the Monkey; "but really it is very different. I must always be making comical faces for people to laugh at; and all the apples they give me to eat turn out sour ones. How often is sadness hidden by a joke! But thirty years I can never endure!"

Thereupon ten years were allowed to him.

Last of all, Man appeared, healthy and vigorous, and requested a time to be appointed to him, "You shall live thirty years," was the reply; "is that enough?" "What a short time!" exclaimed Man; "just when I shall have built myself a house, and lighted a fire upon my own hearth, and just when I shall have planted trees to bear me fruit in their season, and I am thinking of enjoying life, I must die! I pray let my life be lengthened!"

"The eighteen years of the Ass shall be added."

"That is not enough!" said Man.

"You shall have also twelve years of the Dog's life."

"Still too little!" replied Man.

"Well, then, you may have the ten years allowed to the Monkey; but you must desire no more."

Man was then obliged to leave, but he was not satisfied.

Thus Man lives seventy years. The first thirty are the days of his manhood, which pass quickly away; he is then healthy and vigorous, works with pleasure, and rejoices in his being. Then follow the eighteen years of the life of the Ass, which bring to him one burden after another; he must work for corn which nourishes others, and abuse and blame become the reward of his labours. Next come the twelve years of the Dog, during which Man has to sit in corners, grumbling because he has no longer any teeth to bite with. And when this time is up, then the ten years of the Monkey bring the close of the scene. Then Man becomes childish and foolish, and does strange things, which make him ridiculous in the eyes of children!

The Bittern and the Hoopoe

"Where do you find the best pasture for your flocks?" asked a Master of an old Cowherd.

"Here, Master, where the grass is neither too thick nor too scanty; else it is no use!"

"Why not?" asked the Master.

"Do you hear that moaning cry out on the meadow?" asked the Cowherd; "that is the Bittern, who was once a herdsman, and the Hoopoe also. I will tell you the tale:—

"The Bittern once kept his flocks on a flourishing green meadow, where flowers grew in great abundance, so that the cows became fat and mettlesome. But the Hoopoe drove his cattle to a high and barren hill, where the wind twisted the sand about, and his cows therefore grew thin and gained no strength. When evening came, and the flocks had to be driven home, the Bittern could not collect his cows, because they were so well fed, and they ran away from him. He called to them, 'Come here, pretty cows!' but in vain, they paid no attention to his words. The Hoopoe, on the contrary, could not get his cows upon their legs, they were become so weary and strengthless. 'Up, up! get up!' he cried; but it was no use, they remained lying on the sand. And so it always happens when one forgets moderation. And to this day, although they no longer keep flocks, the Bittern cries daily, 'Bunt herüm,' (here, pretty cow,) and the Hoopoe, 'Up! up! up!' "

Misfortune

WHEN misfortune pursues any one, it will find him out into whatever corner he may creep, or however far he may flee over the world.

Now, once upon a time, a certain man became so poor, that he had not a single faggot of wood left wherewith to light his fire. So, he went into the forest to fell a tree, but they were all too large and too strong; and he penetrated deeper among them till he found one which he thought would do. Just as he was about to raise his axe he perceived a pack of wolves, coming out of the brushwood, who howled dreadfully as they came nearer. The man threw away his axe, and ran till he came to a bridge. The deep water, however, had rotted the bridge; and so, just as he was about to run over it, it cracked and fell into the water. What was he to do now? If he stopped still, the wolves would overtake him and tear him to pieces; so, in his perplexity, he jumped into the water, but there, because he could not swim, he soon began to sink. By chance a couple of fishermen, who sat on the other bank, saw him; and one of them swam after him and brought him to shore. Then they laid him down beneath an old wall, to dry in the sunshine and regain his strength a bit. But, just as he recovered his senses, and tried to thank the fishermen for their help and to tell his tale, the wall fell upon him and crushed him!

The Owl

A COUPLE of hundred years ago, when people were not so wise and crafty as they are now-a-days, a curious circumstance occurred in a certain small town. By chance, one of the large Owls, which folk call Screech-Owls, came from a neighbouring forest, and took up its dwelling in a shed belonging to a citizen of the town, from whence it dared not come out except at night, for fear the other birds should raise a great outcry against it for disturbing their peace. One morning when the Stable-boy went into the shed to fetch some straw, he was frightened so dreadfully on perceiving the Owl, that he ran away, and told his Master that a horrible monster, such as he had never before seen in his lifetime, was sitting in one corner of the shed, and rolled its eyes round as if it would devour everything it could see. "I know you of old," replied his Master; "you have courage enough to chase a blackbird over the fields, but if you see a dead hen lying about, you want a stick laid on you before you will approach it. I must now go myself and see what sort of monster this is."

So saying, the Master set off and walked as bold as possible into the shed and peeped round. But as soon as he saw the curious and hideous creature with his own eyes he went into as great a panic as his servant. He made his escape with a couple of leaps and ran to his neighbours, whom he begged with tears in his eyes to come and assist him against an unknown and dangerous animal, or perhaps the whole town might be endangered if it should make its escape from the shed where it was concealed. Immediately there arose a great outcry and noise in the streets of the town, and the townsmen came armed with spikes, rakes, spades, and hatchets, as if they were going to attack an enemy. At last appeared the Mayor himself at the head of his councillors, and when they were all arranged in the market-place, they made their way to the shed and surrounded it on all sides. Then one of the bravest of the assemblage stepped before the others and entered the shed armed with a pole; but he came out again directly with a shriek, and looking as pale as death he ran off without saying a word. Two others next made the attempt, but they met with no better success; but at last a tall and very strong man, renowned for his deeds of valour, stepped forward and said, "With bare looking at the monster you will never drive him away; some determination must be used; but I see you are all playing the part of old women, and none of you will beard the enemy." So saying, he caused his body armour, his sword, and spear to be brought, and, equipping himself with these, prepared for the attack, while all the others praised his courage, although many of them feared for his life. The two doors of the shed were thrown open, and the warrior perceived the Owl perched in the middle of a large beam which ran across. He caused a ladder to be brought, and when it was fixed ready for him to mount, all called out to him to behave bravely, and reminded him of St George and the Dragon. He mounted the ladder, and as the Owl saw what his intentions were, and became frightened also by the cries of the people outside, who prevented its exit, it rolled its eyes, ruffled its feathers, snapped his beak, and screeched loudly. "Rush on it! rush on it!" exclaimed the crowd to the valiant Soldier. "If you stood where I do," he said, "you would not be so ready to shout." Then he mounted a stave higher on the ladder; but there he began to tremble, and at length he beat a retreat half fainting!

And now there was no one left who would venture to face the danger. "The monster," said the crowd, "has all but poisoned and wounded to death with his snapping and breathing, our strongest man, and shall we also venture our lives?" Thereupon, they consulted with one another what they should do to prevent ruin from involving the whole town. For a long time nothing satisfactory was proposed, till at last the Mayor hit upon a plan. "My idea is this," he said, "that out of the common course we purchase and make good to the owner this stable with all it contains, straw, hay, and corn, and then that the whole building, together with the fearful monster therein, be burnt to ashes, and so no one shall lose his life by this occurrence. There is no time to spare, and parsimony in this case would be badly exercised."

All the rest agreed to this proposal, and so the stable was set light to at the four corners, and the poor Owl miserably burnt to death!

The Nail

A TRADESMAN had once transacted a good day's business at a fair, disposed of all his goods, and filled his purse with gold and silver. He prepared afterwards to return, in order to reach home by the evening. So he strapped his portmanteau, with the money in it, upon his horse's back, and rode off. At noon he baited in a small town, and as he was about to set out again, the Stable-boy who brought his horse said to him, "Sir, a nail is wanting in the shoe on the left hind-foot of your animal."

"Let it be wanting," replied the Tradesman; "I am in a hurry and the iron will doubtless hold the six hours I have yet to travel."

Late in the afternoon he had to dismount again, and feed his horse and at this place also the Boy came and told him that a nail was wanting in one of the shoes, and asked him whether he should take the horse to a farrier. "No, no, let it be!" replied the Master; "it will last out the couple of hours that I have now to travel; I am in haste." So saying he rode off; but his horse soon began to limp, and from limping it came to stumbling, and presently the beast fell down and broke its leg. Thereupon the Tradesman had to leave his horse lying on the road, to unbuckle the portmanteau, and to walk home with it upon his shoulder, where he arrived at last late at night.

"And all this misfortune," said he to himself, is owing to the want of a nail. More haste the less speed!"

Strong Hans

THERE was once upon a time a man and his wife, who had but one child, and they lived in a solitary valley all alone. Once it happened that the woman went into the forest to collect firewood, and took with her the little Hans, who was just turned two years of age. It was the beginning of spring, and the child took great delight in the various flowers which were then blooming; and running from one to another, they strayed far into the forest. Suddenly two robbers jumped up out of a thicket, and seizing the mother and child, carried them deep into the black wood, where from year to year nobody ever penetrated. The poor woman begged the robbers earnestly to let her and her child go home; but their hearts were of stone, and they paid no attention to her weeping and prayers, but only used force to drive her on further. After they had thus travelled over two miles, through thorns and bushes, they came to a rock in which was a door, whereat the robbers knocked, and immediately it opened of itself. Then they had to pass through a long gloomy passage, and came at length to a great cave, lighted by a fire which was burning on the hearth. On the wall were hanging swords, sabres, and other weapons, which shone in the light; and in the middle of the cave was a black table, at which the four robbers sat down to play, and at the head sat the Captain. The latter, as soon as he saw the woman enter, came up to her and said, that if she were quiet and not passionate, they would do her no harm, but she would have to take care of their household; and if she kept everything in good order she would be well treated. So saying, he gave her something to eat, and showed her the bed where she was to sleep with her child.

The woman remained many years with these robbers, and Hans grew big and strong. His mother told him tales and taught him to read from an old book of chivalry, which she found in the cave. When Hans was nine years old, he made himself a staff out of the branch of a fir-tree, and hiding it behind the bed, he went and said to his mother, "Dear mother, do tell me who my father is; I must and will know." But his mother was silent, and would not tell him lest he should become homesick; besides, she knew the wicked robbers would not have allowed Hans to escape: nevertheless, it would have broken her heart had she thought Hans would never see his father again. That night, when the robbers returned from their day's plundering, Hans fetched out his cudgel, and placing himself before the Captain, said to him, "I must know now who is my father, and if you will not tell me I will knock you down!" But the Captain only laughed at him, and gave him a box on the ears, so that he rolled under the table. Hans soon got up, but held his tongue, thinking, "I will wait a year longer, and then try; perhaps I shall manage better."

So when the year was up, he fetched his cudgel again, sharpened its point, and congratulated himself that it was a trusty and strong weapon. At night the robbers returned, and began to drink wine, one bottle after another, till their heads dropped on the table. Then Hans took his cudgel, and stationing himself before the Captain, asked him again, "Who is my father?" The Captain dealt him a box on the ear by way of answer, which knocked him under the table; but Hans was soon up again, and beat the Captain and his comrades so forcibly about the legs and arms that they could not stir. The mother meanwhile remained in a corner, astonished at her son's bravery and strength; but as soon as he had finished his work, he came to her and said, "You see now that I am in earnest, so tell me who is my father." "Dear Hans," she replied, "let us go and seek till we find him."

So saying she robbed the Captain of the key of the outer door, and Hans, fetching a large meal-sack, crammed it full of gold, silver, and all the valuables he could find, and then threw it over his back. They left the cave; but imagine what was the astonishment of Hans, when he emerged from darkness into the light of day, and saw the green trees, the flowers, the birds, and the morning sun shining over all in the clear sky! He stood still and gazed all around him quite bewildered, till his mother began to look for the road to her home, where they happily arrived, after two hours' walking, and found it still in the solitary valley.

At the door sat the father, who wept for joy when he recognised his wife, and heard that Hans was his son, whom he had long ago believed to be dead. But Hans, although only twelve years of age, was already a head taller than his father; and they all went together into the house, where Hans put down his sack upon the chimney-corner. As soon as he did so, the house began to crack; and presently the chimney-seat gave way, and then the floor, so that the heavy sack fell quite down into the cellar. "Heaven protect us!" exclaimed the father. "What is that? Why, you have broken our house down!"

"Pray don't let your grey hairs grow on that account, my dear father," replied Hans; "there is in that sack much more than will build a house!"

So, soon after, the father and son began to erect a new cottage, and to buy cattle and land, and go to market. Hans ploughed their fields; and when he went behind the plough and pushed it through the soil, the oxen had no need to draw at all. The following spring, Hans said, "Father, bestow some money on me, and let me make an exceedingly heavy walking-stick, that I may go into strange lands." When this staff was ready, Hans left his father's house, and walked off, till he came to a large dense forest. There he heard something crackling and crashing, and looking around, saw a fir-tree, which was coiled round from top to bottom like a rope. And, as he lifted his eyes, he perceived a great fellow who had caught hold of the tree, and was twisting it round like a reed. "Hilloa!" cried Hans, "what are you doing there?" "I have plucked up two fir-stems," replied the fellow, "and am about to make a rope of them for my own use." "He has got some strength," thought Hans to himself: "I might find him useful." And then he called out, "Let them be and come with me." Thereupon the fellow descended the tree, and walked with Hans, than whom he was a head taller, though Hans was by no means little. "You shall be called 'Fir-Twister,'" said Hans to him. As they walked on they heard somebody knocking and hammering so hard, that at every blow the ground shook; and presently they came to a great rock, before which a giant was standing, knocking off great pieces with his fist. When Hans asked him what he was about, he replied, "When I want to go to sleep at night, there come bears, and wolves, and all creatures of that kind, who snuff and prowl around me and prevent me from sleeping, so now I want to build myself a house to rest in."

"Ah, very well, I can use you too," thought Hans; and said to the giant, "Come with me, leave your house-building, and you shall be called 'Rock-Splitter.'"

The man consented, and the three strode along through the forest, and wherever they came the wild beasts fled away from them, terrified. At evening time they came to an old deserted castle, into which they stepped, and laid down to sleep in the hall. The following morning Hans went into the garden, and found it quite a wilderness and full of thorns and weeds. As he walked about, a wild boar suddenly sprung out at him, but he gave it such a blow with his staff, that it fell down at his feet dead. So he threw it over his shoulder, and taking it home, put it on a spit to roast, and chuckled over the treat it would be. Afterwards, the three agreed that every day they should take it by turns – two to go out and hunt, and the third to remain at home and cook for each nine pounds of meat. The first day the Fir-Twister remained at hom; and Hans and the Rock-Splitter went out hunting. While the former was busy at home with his cooking, there came to the castle-gate a shrivelled up little old man, who asked for meat.

"Take yourself off, you sneak!" replied the cook; "you want no meat!" But scarcely had he said these words, than, to his great surprise, the little insignificant old man sprang upon him and thrashed him so with his fists, that he could not protect himself from the blows, but was at last forced to drop down, gasping for breath. The little man did not leave till he had fully wreaked his vengeance; but when the other two returned from hunting, the Fir-Twister said nothing to them of the old man or his blows, for he thought, when they remained at home, they might as well have a trial with the fellow; and the bare thought of it pleased him very much.

The following day, accordingly, the Rock-Splitter stopped at home, and it happened to him just as it had done to the Fir-Twister; the old man beat him unmercifully because he would give him no meat. When the others came home at evening, the Fir-Twister perceived at once what had happened; but both held their tongues, thinking that Hans should also taste of the supper.

Hans, whose turn it now was to stay at home, did his work in the kitchen as he thought fit, and just as he was about to polish the kettle, the little man came and demanded without ceremony a piece of meat. "This is a poor fellow," thought Hans; "I will give him some of my share, that the others may not come short;" and he handed him a piece of meat. The Dwarf soon devoured it, and demanded another piece, which the good-natured Hans gave him and said it was such a fine piece he ought to be contented with it. But the Dwarf asked a third time for more meat. "You ought to be ashamed of yourself," said Hans, and gave him nothing. Thereupon the ill-tempered Dwarf tried to spring on him, and serve him as he had done the Fir-Twister and the Rock-Splitter; but he had come at an unlucky moment, and Hans gave him a couple of blows which made the Dwarf jump down the castle steps. Hans would then have pursued him, but he was so tall that he actually fell over him, and when he got up again the Dwarf was off. Hans hurried after him into the forest, and saw him slip into a rocky hole; after which he returned home, first marking the place. But the two others, when they came back, wondered to see Hans so merry, and when he told them all that had passed in their absence, they also concealed no longer the tale of their adventures. Hans laughed at them, and said, "You are served quite right, you should not have been so grudging with your meat; but it is a shame that two such big fellows as you should have allowed yourselves to be beaten by a Dwarf."

After their dinner they took a basket and some cord, and all three went to the rocky hole, into which the Dwarf had crept, and let Hans down in the basket, staff in hand. As soon as he came to the bottom he found a door, on opening which he saw a Maiden more beautiful than I can describe, and near her sat the Dwarf, who grinned at Hans like a sea-cat. But the Maiden was bound by chains, and looked so sadly at Hans that he felt a great compassion for her, and thought to himself, "You must be delivered from the power of this wicked Dwarf;" and he gave the fellow a blow with his staff, which killed him outright. Immediately the chains fell off the Maiden, and Hans was enchanted with her beauty. She told him she was a Princess, whom a rebellious Count had stolen away from her home, and concealed in a cave, because she would not listen to his offers of marriage. The Dwarf had been placed there by the Count was watchman, and he had caused her daily vexation and trouble. Thereupon Hans placed the Maiden in the basket, and caused her to be drawn up; but when the basket came down again Hans would not trust his two companions, for he thought they had already shown themselves false in not telling about the Dwarf before, and nobody could tell what design they might have now. So he laid his staff in the basket, and it was very lucky he did so, for as soon as the basket was halfway up, the two men let it fall again, and Hans, had he been really in it, would have met with his death. But Hans now did not know how he should make his way out of the cave, and although he considered for a long while he could come to no decision. While he walked up and down he came again to the chamber where the Maiden had been sitting, and saw that the Dwarf had a ring on his finger which shone and glittered. This he pulled off and put on, and as soon as it pressed his finger, he heard suddenly some rustling over his head. He looked up, and saw two Spirits fluttering about in the air, who said he was their master, and they asked his wishes. Hans at first was quite astonished, but at last he said he wished to be borne up on the earth. In a moment they obeyed and he seemed as if he was flying up; but when they set him down on the ground, he saw nobody standing about, and when he went into the castle he could find nobody there either. The Fir-Twister and the Rock-Splitter had made their escape, and carried away with them the beautiful Maiden. Hans, however, pressed the ring, and the Spirits came at once, and said the two false comrades were gone off to sea. Hans thereupon hastened as fast as he could to the sea-shore, and there he perceived far out at sea the ship in which his perfidious friends had embarked. In his passionate haste he actually jumped into the sea, staff in hand, and began to swim; but the tremendous weight of his staff prevented him from keeping his head up. He was just beginning to sink when he bethought himself of his ring, and immediately the Spirits appeared, and carried him on board the ship with the speed of lightning. As soon as he was safely set down, Hans swung his staff round, and gave the wicked traitors their well-merited reward; after which he threw them into the sea! Then he steered the vessel home to the father and mother of the Princess, who had been in the greatest terror while in the hands of the two giants, and from whom he had happily saved her for the second time.

Soon afterwards Hans married the Princess, and their wedding was the occasion of the most splendid rejoicings.

The Sparrow and his Four Children

A SPARROW had four Young Ones in a swallow's nest, but just as they were fledged some naughty boys discovered the nest and pushed the birds out; but happily a slight breeze was blowing at the time, and bore them up. But the Old Sparrow was sorry because her Children were gone out into the world before she had warned them of its dangers or taught them good manners.

Now, in the spring-time a great many sparrows chanced to meet together in a field of corn, and among them the Old Sparrow happily met with his Young Ones, and took them home with him in great joy. "Ah! my dear children," he said to them, "what a trouble I have been in about you all the summer, while you faced the world without my advice: now hear my words, and attend to your father, and take care of yourselves, for little birds must needs meet great dangers."

Thereupon he asked his eldest Young One where he had been during the summer, and how he had kept himself. "I have been in a garden," he replied, "eating caterpillars and worms, till the cherries were ripe." "Ah! my dear son," replied the Old Bird, "bill-grubbing is not so bad, but there is great danger in it; therefore keep a good look-out, especially if people come into the garden carrying long green poles, which are nevertheless hollow and have a small hole at the top!"

"Yes, my dear father," replied the young Sparrow; "but what if a green leaf is stuck with wax over that little hole?" "Where have you so seen it?" inquired the father. "In a merchant's garden," was the reply. "Oh! my son," cried the Old Bird, "merchants are crafty people; truly you have been among the world's children, and have seen their cunning ways; take care now that you make a good use of what you have learnt, and do not be too confiding."

Then he asked the second Young One where he had been. "At court," he replied. "Sparrows and those sort of birds do not belong to such places as that," said the father; "at court there is much gold, velvet, silk, armour, harness, and such birds as hawks, falcons, and owls. Do you keep to the stables where they store the oats, or thrash out the corn, and then you can satisfy your wants with a daily supply of food." "Yes, father," said the son; "but if the boys weave their straw into knots and meshes, many a one may get hanged by them."

"Where have you seen that?" asked the Old Bird.

"At court, among the stable-boys."

"Ah! my son, stable-boys are bad boys! If you have been at court with the fine lords, and yet have left behind you no feathers, you have learnt carefully, and know how to behave yourself in the world: still keep a sharp watch, for the wolves often eat the cleverest dogs."

"And where have you sought your living?" asked the Old Bird of his third Young One. "On the highways and byways I have turned over tubs and ropes, and so now and then I have happened upon corn and barley-seed."

"That is, indeed, a fine subsistence," said the father; "but mind you observe the hedges, and see that no one bends down to pick up a stone; for if so, it is time for you to start."

"That is true," said the young Bird; "but what if one should carry little pebbles in his bosom or pocket before stone walls?"

"Where have you seen that?"

"With the miners, dear father," he replied; "for when they travel about they carry with them secretly stones to throw at people."

"Oh, miners, working people, curious people they! If you have been among them you have seen and experienced a great deal."

At last the father came to the youngest son, and said, "Ah! my dear Cacklenestle, you were always the weakest and most foolish; do you stop with me, the world has so many wicked and rough birds with sharp beaks and long claws, who attack and devour all the little birds: keep you with me, and let the worms and spiders on the trees and ground near us content you."

"Ah! my dear father, he who finds his own living without injury to others, he fares well, and no hawk, owl, eagle, or falcon, shall harm him; for at all times, and every morning and evening, he desires of God his daily food, – of God who is both the Creator and Protector of all the forest and village birds, and who also feeds the young ravens, and hears their cries, for without his will no sparrow nor starling falls to the ground."

"Where did you learn all this?" cried the Old Bird, astonished.

"When the breeze took me away," replied the Bird, "I came to a church, where I spent the summer in eating the flies and spiders off the windows, and there I heard the sermon preached, for the Father of all Sparrows nourished me through the summer, and kept me from all misfortune and fierce birds!"

"True, my dear son," said the Old Bird; "fly back to the church and keep the flies and the spiders from the windows. Also forget not to chirp to God like the ravens, and pray to the Creator daily, and so you will keep well, were the whole world full of wild knavish birds: for he who commends his affairs to God, endures all, prays, and is gentle and kind, keeps his faith strictly, and his conscience clear, him God will ever protect and defend."

The Shreds

ONCE upon a time there was a Maiden who was very pretty, but lazy and careless. When she used to spin, she was so impatient that, if there chanced to be a little knot in the thread, she snapped off a long bit with it and threw the pieces down on the ground near her. Now she had a Servant-Girl, who was industrious, and used to gather together the shreds of thread, clean them, and weave them, till she made herself a dress with them.

And a young Man had fallen in love with this lazy Maiden; and their wedding-day was appointed. On the evening before, the industrious Servant-Girl kept dancing about in her fine dress, till the Bride exclaimed,—

> "Ah! how the Girl does jump about,
> Dressed in my shreds and leavings!"

When the Bridegroom heard this, he asked the Bride what she meant, and she told him that the Maid had worked herself a dress with the shreds of thread which she had thrown away. As soon as the Bridegroom heard this, and saw the difference between the laziness of his intended and the industry of her Servant, he gave up the Mistress, and chose the Maid for his wife.

Death's Messengers

IN olden times a Giant was once wandering up and down a road, when suddenly an unknown man appeared in his path, and cried, "Stop! not a step further." "What, you stripling!" said the Giant, "why, I could crush you between my fingers; will you stand in my way? Who are you who speak so boldly?"

"I am Death," replied the stranger, "whom nobody opposes, and whose commands you must obey."

The Giant, however, refused, and began to wrestle with Death. It was a long and hasty battle, but at length the Giant got the best of it, and knocked Death down with his fist, so that he dropped like a stone. The Giant, thereupon, went his way, leaving Death vanquished and strengthless, so that he could not rise again. "What will be the consequence?" thought Death; "if I lie here in this corner nobody will die in the world, and it will soon get so full of human beings, that they will not be able to stir for one another." Just then, a Young Man came up the road, strong and healthy, singing a song, and looking well about him. As soon as he perceived the helpless beaten one, he went up to him, and compassionately raising him poured a draught of cordial out of his flask down his throat, and waited till strength returned. "Do you know," asked Death, when he had recovered a bit, "do you know who I am, whom you have thus helped on his legs again?"

"No," replied the Youth, "I know you not." "I am Death," he replied; "I spare no-one, and can take no excuse from you even. But, to show you that I am not ungrateful, I promise not to take you unawares; but I will send my messengers before I come and fetch you."

"Very well," said the Young Man, "that is a bargain, that I shall know when you are coming, and so long shall be safe from your visit."

With this understanding he pursued his way merrily, and lived in prosperity for some time. But youth and health will not remain for ever; soon came sicknesses and troubles to the Young Man, so that he complained by day and could get no rest at night. "I shall not die," he said to himself, "for Death must first send his messengers; but I wish these terrible days of illness were over!"

By-and-by he did get well again, and began to live as usual. One day somebody knocked at the window, and looking round he saw Death standing behind him, who said, "Follow me, the hour is come for your departure from the world."

"How so?" exclaimed the Man; "will you break the promise that you made to me to send your messengers before you come yourself? I have seen none."

"Be silent," replied Death; "have I not sent you one messenger after another? – did not fever come and seize you, shake you, and lay you prostrate? – did not a giddiness oppress your head? – had you not gout in all your limbs? – did not a singing noise injure your ears? – had not you lumbago in your back? – a film over your eyes? – Above all, did not my dear half-brother, Sleep, remind you of me every night when you laid down, as if you were already dead!"

The Man knew not what to reply to all this, and surrendering himself therefore to his fate he followed Death.

Master Cobblersawl

MASTER COBBLERSAWL was a small, meagre, but very active man, who had no rest in him. His face, whose only prominent feature was a turned-up nose, was seamed and deadly pale; his hair was grey and rough; his eyes small, but they peered right and left in a piercing way. He observed everything, found fault with everything, knew everything better, and did it better, than any one else, in his own estimation. When he walked in the streets he swung his two arms about in such a hasty fashion, that once he knocked the pail which a girl was carrying so high into the air that the water fell all over him. "Sheep's-head!" he exclaimed, shaking himself, "could you not see that I was following you?" By trade he was a shoemaker; and when he was at work, he pulled his thread out so hastily, that nobody went near him for fear of his elbows poking into their sides. No comrade remained with him longer than a month, for he had always something to remark upon in the best work. Either the stitches were not even, or one shoe was longer than the other, or one heel higher than the other, or the leather was not drawn sufficiently tight. "Wait," he would say to a young hand, "wait, and I will show you how one can whiten the skin!" and so saying, he would fetch a strap and lay it across the shoulders of his victim. He called everybody idle and lazy; but still he did not do much for himself, because he could not sit quiet two quarters of an hour together. If his wife got up early in the morning and lighted a fire, he would jump out of bed and run barefoot into the kitchen, crying out, "Do you want to burn the house down? there is a fire fit for any one to roast an ox at! Wood costs money."

If the maid, while standing at the washtub, laughed and repeated to herself what she had heard, he would scold her and say, "There stands a goose, chattering and forgetting her work with her gossip." "Of what use is that fresh soap? shameful waste and a disgraceful dirtiness, for she wants to spare her hands by not properly rubbing out the stains!" So saying, he would jump up and throw down a whole pailful of water, so as to set the kitchen a-swimming!

Once they were building a new house near him, and he ran to his window to look on. "There! they are using that red sandstone again which never dries," he said; "nobody in that house will be healthy. And see how quickly the fellows are laying on the stones. The mortar too is not properly mixed; gravel should be put in, not sand. I expect the house will fall some day on the heads of the owners." So saying, he sat down again, and did another stitch or so; but soon he sprang up, and throwing away his apron, "I will go and speak to those men myself." The carpenters were at work just then. "How is this?" he asked; "you are not cutting by line. Do you think the beams will lay straight? no, they will come all away from the joists." Then he snatched an axe out of the hand of one of the carpenters to show him how he should cut; and just then a waggon laden with clay chanced to be going past, so Master Cobblersawl threw away the axe, and cried to the peasant who was with it, "How inhuman you are! who would harness young horses to a heavily laden waggon? the poor beasts will fall down presently."

The peasant, however, gave him no answer, and so he went back to his workshop in a passion. Just as he was about to commence again the job which he had left, his apprentice handed him a shoe. "What is this, again?" exclaimed Master Cobblersawl; "have I not told you often and often not to stitch your shoes so wide. Who will buy a shoe like this with scarce any sole at all to it? I desire that you will follow my commands to the letter."

"Yes, master," replied the apprentice, "you may be in the right to say that the shoe is worth nothing, but it is the very same that you sewed, and were just now at work upon; for when you ran out you threw it under the table, and I picked it up. But an angel from heaven would not convince you that you were wrong."

A night or two afterwards Master Cobblersawl dreamed that he was dead and on the way to heaven. When he arrived there and knocked at the door, the Apostle Peter opened it to see who desired to enter. "Ah, is it you, Master Cobblersawl?" said the Saint, "I will let you in, certainly; but I warn you not to interfere with what you may observe in heaven, or it will be the worse for you."

"You might have spared yourself the trouble of saying that," replied Cobblersawl; "I know very well how to behave myself; and here, thank God, there is nothing to blame, as there is on earth." So saying, he stepped in and walked up and down over the wide expanse of heaven, looking about him right and left, and now and then shaking his head or muttering to himself. Presently he perceived two angels carrying a beam, the same which a certain one once had in his own eye when he perceived the mote in his brother's eye. But they

were carring the beam not longways but crossways and this caused
Master Cobblersawl to say to himself, "Did ever anybody see such
stupidity?" Still he held his tongue, thinking that after all it was no
matter whether the beam were carried straight or not, provided it did
not interfere with anybody. Soon afterwards he saw two angels
pouring water out of a spring into a tub which was full of holes, so
that the water escaped on all sides. They were watering the earth
with rain. "Alle Hagel!" exclaimed he suddenly; but recollecting
himself, he kept his opinions to himself, and thought, "Perhaps it is
mere pastime, and intended for a joke, so that one may do idle things
here in heaven as well as upon earth." So he went onwards and saw a
waggon stuck fast in a deep rut. "No wonder," said he to the person
in charge; "who would have filled it so extravagantly? what have you
there?"

"Pious wishes," replied the man; "I could not get with them into
the straight road; but fortunately I was able to push along as far as
here, and they will not let me stick fast now."

Just then an angel did really come and harnessed horses to the
waggon. "Quite right," thought Cobblesawl; "but two horses are
not enough to pull the waggon out: there must be four horses at the
least." Presently came a second angel, leading two more horses, but
he did not harness them before, but behind. Now this was too much
for Master Cobblersawl. "Tollpatsch!" he exclaimed aloud, "what
are you about? Did anybody ever as long as the world has stood pull
a waggon in that way up this road? You think you know better than I
in your conceited pride!" and he would have said more, but one of
the inhabitants of heaven caught him by the neck and shoved him
out of the place with a stern push. Just outside the gate Master
Cobblersawl turned his head round, and saw the waggon raised up
by four winged horses.

At the same moment he awoke. "Things are certainly somewhat
different in heaven to what they are on earth," he said to himself,
"and much may therefore be excused; but who could patiently see
two horses harnessed behind a waggon and two before? Certainly
they had wings, but I did not observe that at first. However, it is a

great absurdity that a horse with four good legs must have wings too! But I must get up, or else they will make further mistakes about that house. Still, after all, it is a very lucky thing that I am not dead!"

The Tale of Schlauraffenland

I WAS once in Schlauraffenland, which some folks call "Fools' Paradise," and there saw I Rome and the Lateran hanging by a silken thread, a footless man who outran a quick horse, and a sword sharp as a razor which formed a bridge. There I saw, too, a young ass with a silver nose, which was coursing two hares, and a lime tree full of foliage, whereon grew hot pancakes. There, too, I saw a clumsy old goat, which carried on its back a hundred cartloads of grease and sixty cartloads of salt. Is not that enough?

There, also, I saw a plough going without a horse or wheels, and a one-year-old child threw four mill-stones from Ratisbon to Treves, and from Treves away to Strasburg, and a hawk swam over the Rhine without difficulty! There, too, I heard fishes caught with one another's cries, and sweet honey flowed like water out of a deep valley up a high mountain!

There were also two crows which mowed a meadow, and I saw two flies building a bridge, and two doves tearing a wolf; two children who threw down two kids, and two frogs threshing corn with might and main!

There I saw two mice consecrate a bishop; two cats who scratched out a bear's tongue, and a snail who slew two lions. There stood a barber who shaved off his wife's beard, and two sucking children who rocked their mother in a cradle! There I saw two greyhounds dragging a mill out of the water, and an old horse-knacker who said it was all right; and in a stable stood four horses kneading dough with all their strength, and two goats which heated the oven, and a red cow put the bread into the oven. There, also, a cock crowed, "Cock-a-doodle-doo!"

"My tale is over! Cock-a-doodle-doo!"

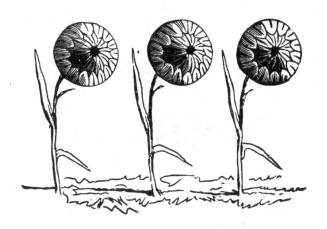

A Puzzling Tale

THREE Women were once changed into flowers, and grew in a field; but one was permitted to go home at night. So one time she said to her Husband, when day was dawning and she was about to return to her companions in the field and become a flower again: "This noontime come and break me off, and then I shall be released and be able to dwell with you in future," – and thus it happened.

But now the question is how the Husband knew his Wife; for all the flowers were alike, and had no difference at all between them. The answer is this: during the night which she passed at home with her Husband, the dew fell upon her two companions which were in the field; and so he knew his Wife, because there was no dew on her flower.

The Nix of the Mill-Pond

THERE was once upon a time a Miller who lived very happily with his Wife, for they were very well off, and their prosperity increased year by year. But misfortune comes by night. As their riches had grown, so they disappeared; and thus they melted away yearly till at last the Miller had only his mill, and that he could scarcely call his own property. He became very full of trouble over his losses; and when he lay down after his day's work he could get no rest, but tossed about in his bed, thinking and thinking. One morning he arose before daybreak, and went out into the open air, to consider some way of lightening his heart; and as he passed by the mill-dam the first ray of the sun shone forth, and he heard a rippling in the pond. He turned round and saw a beautiful Maiden raising herself slowly out of the water. Her long hair, which she had gathered behind her shoulders with her long fingers, fell down on both sides of her face, and covered her white bosom. The Miller saw at once that it was the Nix of the mill-pond, and he knew not from fear whether to stop or go away. The Nix solved his doubts by calling him by name in a gentle voice, and asking him why he was so sad. At first the Miller was dumb; but as she spoke so kindly to him, he took courage, and told her that he had once lived in riches and prosperity, but he was now so poor he knew not what to do.

"Rest quietly," said the Nix; "I will make you richer and happier than you were before; only you must promise me that you will give me what has just now been born in your house. "That can be nothing else than a puppy or a kitten," thought the Miller, and so promised the Nix what she desired. Thereupon she dived again under water, and the Miller hastened home to his mill in good spirits. He had almost reached it, when the Maid coming from it met him, and told him to rejoice, for his Wife had just borne him a little boy. The Miller started back, as if struck by lightning, for he at once perceived that the crafty Nix was aware of the fact, and had deceived him. He went into his Wife's room drooping his head; and when she inquired why he did not congratulate her on her happiness, he told her what had happened, and the promise which he had given to the Nix. "Of what use are wealth and good luck to me," he continued, "if I lose my child? but what can I do?" And none of the friends who came to congratulate him on the birth of a son and heir could give any advice.

Meanwhile the luck of the mill returned. What its Master undertook prospered; and it seemed as if chests and coffers filled themselves, for the money in the cupboard increased every night, till before many months had passed away, the Miller was much richer than before. He could not, however, feel any pleasure in the prospect, for his promise to the Nix weighed on his mind; and as often as he passed the pond, he feared lest she should rise and claim her debt. The Boy himself he would never allow to go near the water; but told him continually to beware of doing so, for if he should fall in, a hand would rise and draw him under. Still, as year after year passed away, and the Nix made no second appearance, the Miller began to lose his suspicions.

The Boy grew up a fine youth and was bound to a Huntsman to learn his art, which when he had thoroughly studied, the Lord of the village took him into his service. Now in this village there dwelt a beautiful and good Maiden, who took a fancy of the young Hunter, and when his Master perceived it, he presented him with a small cottage; and thereupon the two married, and lived happily and lovingly together.

One day the Hunter pursued a stag, and when the animal escaped from the forest into the open fields, he followed it, and at last struck it down with a shot from his gun. But he did not observe that he had come to the brink of the dangerous pond, and so when he had flayed his booty, he went to it to wash his hands free from the blood-stains. Scarcely had he touched it when the Nix arose, and, smilingly embracing him with her naked arms, drew him so quickly below the surface that the water rippled on without a bubble.

By-and-by, when evening came, and the Hunter did not return home, his Wife felt very anxious. She went out to seek him; and as he had often told her that he had to take care of the appearance of the Nix, and not venture too near the mill-pond, she suspected already what had happened. She hastened to the water; and as soon as she saw his gun lying on the bank, she could no longer doubt the misfortune which had befallen her. Wringing her hands with grief and terror, she called her beloved by name, but in vain; she hurried from one side of the pond to the other; she alternately entreated and scolded the Nix; but no answer followed – the surface of the water remained as smooth as a mirror, and only the half-crescent of the moon looked up at her fixedly.

The poor Wife could not leave the water. With quick and hasty steps, she walked round and round the pond without cessation, now silent, and now uttering a fearful shriek, and anon a smothered lament. At length her strength forsook her; and sinking to the earth she fell into a deep sleep, and soon a dream passed over her mind.

She thought she was sorrowfully climbing up between great blocks of stone; thorns and nettles pierced her feet, the rain beat in her face, and the wind disordered her long hair. But when she reached the top of the height, quite another aspect appeared. The sky was blue, the air balmy, the ground softly declined; and upon a green meadow, spangled with flowers, stood an elegant cottage. She thought she went up to it and opened the door, and saw an Old Woman with white hair sitting within, who beckoned to her kindly; and at that moment she awoke. The day was already dawning, and the poor Wife determined to follow out her dream. There was a hill close by her, and up this she ascended, and found the road as she had seen in her dream. On the other side stood the cottage, and in it an Old Woman, who kindly received her, and showed her a chair to sit down upon. "You must have suffered some misfortune to induce you to seek my solitary hut," said the Old Woman. The Wife related to her with tears what had happened; and the Old Woman replied, "Be comforted, I will help you. Here you have a golden comb; wait now till the rising of the full moon; and then go to the pond, and sit down on the bank, and comb your long black hair with it. When you have done, lie down on the bank, and you will see what happens."

The Wife returned, but the time passed very wearisomely till the rise of the moon. At length the shining orb appeared in the sky, and she went down to the pond, and, sitting on its bank, combed her long black hair with the golden comb, and then lay down on the shore to wait the issue. In a short time the waters began to bubble, and a wave rolling on to the bank carried away with it the comb as it receded. In as much time as was necessary for the sinking of the comb to the bottom, the waters parted, and the head of the Huntsman appeared.

He did not speak, but looked at his Wife sorrowfully; and at the same moment another wave rolled on and covered his head. All then disappeared, the water became as placid as before, and nothing was to be seen in it but the face of the moon.

The Wife turned back uncomforted, and her dreams again showed the Old Woman's hut. So a second time she travelled up the hill, and laid her complaint before the Old Woman, who this time gave her a golden flute, with directions to wait till the next full moon, and then to play a sweet tune upon the shore of the pond, and that finished, to lie down and wait the result as before.

The Wife did exactly as the Old Woman told her, and as soon as she laid the flute down, a bubbling took place in the water, and a rising wave carried away the flute. Then appeared not only the head but half of the body of the Man, and stretched out his arms towards his Wife; but at the same instant a wave came, and covering his head, drew him down again.

"Alas! how am I helped," cried the unhappy Wife, "if I see my Husband only to lose him?" Grief again overcame her; but in her dreams she visited again the Old Woman's hut. Accordingly she set out on the journey a third time, and received a spinning-wheel of gold from the Old Woman, who comforted her, and told her, "All is not yet complete; wait till the next full moon, and then sit down as before on the shore of the pond and spin your reel full, which done, lay it down near the water and await the result."

The Wife did everything exactly. As soon as the full moon came she carried her wheel to the shore and spun the reel full; but she had scarcely set it down against the water than the bubbles began to rise quicker than ever, and a huge wave dashing up carried away with it the spinning-wheel. Immediately afterwards the head and whole body of the Man arose, and he, springing quickly to the shore, caught his Wife by the hand and fled away with her. But they had gone but a little distance, when with a terrible rushing noise the whole pond overflowed its banks, and streamed away into the fields with overwhelming force. The fugitives perceived at once death before their eyes, and in her terror the poor Wife called upon the Old

Woman for help, and in a moment they were changed, the one into a Frog and the other into a Toad. The flood which then reached them could not kill them, but it tore them asunder and carried them far away. When the water subsided again, and the Toad and Frog touched dry ground their human forms returned, but neither knew where the other was, and both were among strange people who knew nothing of their country. High hills and deep valleys lay between them, and in order to earn a livelihood each had to tend sheep; and through many long years they fed their flocks in field and forest, grieving and longing for each other.

When once again spring had covered the earth with its first-fruits, it chanced that both drove their flocks out the same day, and towards the same point. The former Huntsman perceived on a distant peak of a hill a flock, and drove his sheep to the same place. Thus the two came together in a valley; but, without recognising each other, they were glad that they would have no longer to wander in solitude. From that day they drove their flocks together, and without speaking much, they felt a certain comfort steal over them. One evening when the full moon appeared in the heavens, and the flocks were resting, the Shepherd taking a flute from his pocket, played a soft and mournful air. As he finished, he saw that the Shepherdess was weeping bitterly, and he asked the reason.

"Alas! I remember," she replied, "how the full moon was shining as it is now, when I played that air upon a flute and the head of my beloved rose above the water."

The Shepherd looked at her as she spoke with an earnest gaze, and, as if a cloud had been taken away from his eyes, he recognised his dear Wife. At the same instant she remembered him, for the moon showed his face clearly; and I am sure no one needs to ask how happy they were, and how happy they remained.

The Presents of the Little Folk

A TAILOR and a Goldsmith were once wandering in company, and one evening, when the sun had sunk behind the hills, they heard the sound of distant music, which became clearer and clearer. The tones were uncommon, but so inspiriting, that, forgetting their weariness, the two walked on. The moon had risen, when they arrived at a hillock on which they perceived a number of little Men and Women, who had joined hands, and were whirling round in a dance with great spirit and delight, and singing thereto in the sweetest manner possible, and so making the music which the travellers had heard. In the middle sat an Old Man, taller than the others, who wore a parti-coloured coat and an iron-grey beard, so long that it reached down to his waist. The two stopped, full of wonder, and looked on at the dancers, when the Old Man beckoned to them to join in, while the circle opened readily to receive them. The Goldsmith, who was deformed, and like all other hunchbacks quick enough, stepped in but the tailor, feeling shy at first, held back, till, seeing how merry the circle was, he took heart and joined in too. The circle closed again directly, and the Little Folks began to sing and dance in the wildest manner, while the Old Man, taking a broad-bladed knife which hung at his girdle sharpened it, and when it was fit, looked round at the strangers. They became frightened, but they had no time to consider: for the Old Man, seizing the Goldsmith, and then the Tailor, shaved off both their beards and hair with the greatest despatch. Their terror, however, disappeared when the Old Man, having completed his work, tapped them both on the shoulder in a friendly manner, as much as to say, they had acted well in having endured his sport without resistance. Then he pointed with his finger towards a heap of coals which stood on one side, and showed them by signs, that they should fill their pockets with them. Both obeyed, though neither of them could see of what service the coals would be to them; and then they journeyed in quest of a night's lodging. Just as they came to the next valley, the clock of a neighbouring church struck twelve, and at the same moment the singing ceased, all disappeared, and the hill lay solitary in the moonshine.

The two wanderers found a shelter, and making a straw couch, each of them covered himself with his coat, but forgot, through weariness, to take the coals out of their pockets. A heavy weight pressed upon their limbs more than usual, and when they awoke in the morning and emptied their pockets, they could not trust their eyes when they saw that they were not filled with coals, but pure gold. Their hair and beard, too, had also grown during the night to their original length. They were now become quite rich, but the Goldsmith was half as rich again as the Tailor, because, impelled by his covetous nature, he had filled his pockets much fuller.

Now a miserly man, the more he possesses, desires yet an increase; and so it happened that the Goldsmith, after the lapse of a day or two, made a proposition to the Tailor to go and obtain more gold from the Old Man of the Mountain. The Tailor refused; saying, "I have enough, and am satisfied: now I am become a master-tradesman, and I will marry my object (as he called his sweetheart), and be a happy man." However, he stopped behind a day, in order to please his comrade. In the evening, the Goldsmith slung across his shoulder a couple of bags, that he might be well furnished, and then set out on his road to the hillock. He found the Little Folk singing and dancing, as on the previous night; and the Old Man, looking at him with a smile, treated him the same as before, and pointed to the heap of coals afterwards. The Goldsmith delayed no longer than was necessary to fill his pockets, and then returned home in high glee, and went to sleep, covered with his coat. "Although the gold does weigh heavily," said he to himself, "I will bear it patiently;" and so he went to sleep with the sweet belief of awaking in the morning a very wealthy man. Judge, therefore, what was his astonishment, when, on awaking and arising, he searched in his pockets, and drew out only black coals, and nothing besides. He consoled himself, however, for his disappointment, by reflecting that he still possessed the gold which he had taken on the previous night, but what was not his rage when he discovered that that also was become coal again; he beat his forehead with is coal-begrimed hands, and then found out that his whole head was bald and smooth as his chin! His mishaps were not yet ended; for he perceived that during the night, a similar hump to that on his back had made its appearance on his breast. He began to weep bitterly at this sight, for he recognised in it the punishment of his covetousness. The good Tailor, who then awoke, comforted the unhappy man as much as he could, and told him that since he had been his companion during his travels, he would share his treasure and remain with him.

The Tailor kept his word; but the poor Goldsmith had to carry all his lifetime two humps, and to cover his bald head with a wig.

The Goose-Girl at the Well

THERE was once upon a time a very very old Lady, who dwelt with her flock of geese in a waste place between two hills, where she had a small cottage. The common was surrounded by a large forest, into which this old Woman hobbled every morning on crutches. There she was very active, more than one could have believed considering her great age, in collecting grass for her geese; she gathered also all the wild fruit she could reach, and carried it home on her back. One would have thought so heavy a burden would have bowed her down to the ground, but she always reached home safe and sound. If any one met her, she greeted him kindly, and would say, "Good day to you, my dear countryman; what beautiful weather it is! Ah! you wonder how I get over the ground, but every one must bear his own burden!" People at last, however, grew afraid to meet her, and took a by-path; and if a father passed near with his children, he would say to them, "Take care of that old Woman; she has mischief behind her ears; she is a witch."

One morning a lively young fellow passed through the wood. The sun was shining brightly, the birds were singing, and a gentle breeze was blowing among the trees and made everything seem gay and pleasant. Still he had met nobody, till he suddenly perceived the old Woman kneeling on the ground, and cutting grass with a sickle. She had already placed a large heap in her handkerchief, and by her side stood two baskets, filled with apples and wild berries. "Ah! my good Woman," exclaimed the Youth, "how will you carry all that?" "I must carry it, my good master," she replied, "but rich people's children do not want to do such things. Will you not help me?" she continued, as the Youth remained by her; "you have a straight back yet, and young legs, it will be easy for you. My house is not far from here; it stands on the common beyond yon hill. How soon your legs could jump there!"

The Youth took compassion on the old Woman, and replied to her, "Certainly; my father is no peasant, but a rich Count; still that you may see it is not only the peasants who carry burdens, I will take your bundle."

"If you will try it," said the old Woman, "I shall be much obliged to you; but there are the apples and berries which you must carry too. It is but an hour's walk which you will have to take, but it will seem much less to you."

The Youth became a little thoughtful when he heard of an hour's journey, but the old Woman now would not let him off, but packed the handkerchief of grass on his back, and hung the two baskets on his arms. "See you, how light it is," said she. "No, it is not at all light," answered the young Count, making a rueful face: "the bundle weighs heavily as if it were full of big stones, and the apples and berries seem like lead; I can scarcely breathe."

So saying he would have liked to lay the bundle down again, but the old Woman would not permit it. "Just see," cried she in scorn, "the young Lord cannot convey what an old Woman like me has so often borne. You people are very ready with your fair words, but

THE GOOSE-GIRL AT THE WELL

when it comes to working, you are equally ready with your excuses. Why do you stand trembling there?" she continued; "come pick up your legs; nobody will take your bundle off again."

Now so long as the young Count walked on level ground, he managed pretty well, but when he came to the hill and began to ascend it, and the stones rolled under his feet as if they were alive, his strength began to fail. Drops of sweat stood upon his brow, and ran down his back, now hot and now cold. "My good woman," he exclaimed, "I can go no further till I have rested a while." "Not here, not here," answered the old Woman; "when we arrive at our destination you can rest, but now we must keep on; who knows what good it may do you!"

"You are shameless, you old Woman!" cried the Youth, trying to throw away the bundle, but he wearied himself in vain; it stuck as fast to his back as if it had grown there. He turned and twisted himself, but with no effect; he could not get rid of the bundle, and the old Woman only laughed at his exertions, and danced around him on her crutches. "Don't put yourself in a passion, my dear Lord," said she; "you are getting as red in the face as a turkey-cock. Bear your burden patiently; when we arrive at home, I will give you a good draught to refresh you." What could he do? He was obliged to bear his fate and follow patiently behind the old Woman, who appeared to become more and more active as his burden grew heavier. All at once she made a spring and jumped on the top of the bundle, where she sat down; and thin and withered as she was, her weight was yet more than that of the stoutest farm-servant. The Youth's knees trembled and shook, but if he did not keep onwards, the old Woman beat him with a strap and stinging nettles about the legs. Under this continual goading, he at last ascended the hill, and arrived at the old Woman's cottage, just when he was ready to drop. As soon as the geese perceived the old Woman they stretched out their wings and their necks, and ran towards her crying "Wulle! wulle!" Behind the flock walked a middle-aged Woman with a stick in her hand, who was big and strong, but as ugly as night. "My mother," said she to the old woman, "has something happened, that you have remained out so long?" "Never fear, my dear daughter," replied the old Woman; "nothing evil has met me, but in fact the young Count there has carried my bundle for me: only think, when I was tired, he took me also on his back! The road has not been too long either, for we have been merry, and made jokes on one another?" At length the old Woman ceased talking, and took the bundle off the youth's back, and the baskets from his arms, and then looking at him cheerfully she said to him, "Sit down on the bench by the door and rest yourself; you have honestly earned your reward, and it shall not be overlooked;" and turning to the Goose-Girl she continued, "Go into the house, my daughter; it is not correct that you should be alone with this young man; one ought not to pour oil on the fire, and he might fall in love with you."

The young Count did not know whether to laugh or cry. "Such a treasure!" he thought to himself. "Why, even if she were thirty years younger, my heart would not be touched!" Meanwhile the old Woman caressed and stroked her geese, as if they were children, and at last went into the house with her daughter. The Youth stretched himself on the bench beneath an apple-tree, where the breeze blew softly and gently; while around him was spread a green meadow, covered with primroses, wild thyme, and a thousand other flowers. In the middle of it flowed a clear stream, on which the sun shone; and the white geese kept passing up and down, or paddling in the water. "It is quite lovely here," he said to himself; "but I am so tired that I cannot keep my eyes open; so I will sleep awhile, provided that no wind comes and blows away my legs from my body, for they are as tender as tinder!"

After he had slept some time, the old Woman came and shook him till he awoke. "Stand up," she said; "you cannot stop here. Certainly I did treat you rather shabbily, but it has not cost you your life. Now I will give you your reward; it will be neither money nor property, but something better." With these words she placed in his hands a small book, cut out of a single emerald, saying, "Keep it well, and it will bring you good luck."

The Count thereupon jumped up, and felt himself quite strong and refreshed; so he thanked the old Woman for her present, and set off on his journey, without once looking back for the beautiful daughter. And when he had walked a considerable way he could still hear the loud cackling of the geese in the distance.

The young Count had to wander three days in the wilderness before he could find his way out, and then he came to a large city, where, because nobody knew him, he was led to the royal palace, where the King and Queen sat on their thrones. There the Count sank on one knee, and drawing forth the emerald book, laid it at the feet of the Queen. She bade him arise and hand the book to her; but scarcely had she opened it and looked at its contents, than she fell as if dead upon the ground. Thereupon the Count was seized by the King's servants, and would have been led off to prison, had not the Queen soon opened her eyes and begged him to be set at liberty, for she must speak with him privately, and therefore every one must leave the room.

As soon as the Queen was left alone, she began to weep bitterly, and to say, "What avails all this honour and pageantry which surrounds me, when every morning I give way to grief and sorrow! I once had three daughters, the youngest of whom was so beautiful that all the world thought her a wonder. She was like the shining of a sunbeam. If she cried, her tears were like pearls and gems falling from her eyes. When she was fifteen, her father caused her and her sisters to come before his throne; and you should have seen how the people opened their eyes when she came in, for it was like the appearance of the sun. The King then said to them, 'My daughters, I know not when my last day will arrive, and therefore to-day I will appoint what each shall do at my death. You all love me, but whoever of you loves me best shall have the best portion.' They each of them said they loved him best; and the King then asked them whether they could not express in words how much they loved him, and then he would be able to judge. So the eldest said she loved him as the sweetest sugar; the second that she loved her father as her smartest dress; but the youngest was silent. 'My dear child, how do you love me?' asked the King. 'I know not,' she replied; 'and I can compare my love with nothing.' Her farther, however, pressed her to say something, and at length she said, 'The most delicate food is tasteless to me without salt, and therefore I love you, father, like salt.' At this reply the King became very angry, and exclaimed, 'If you love me like salt you shall be rewarded with salt.' Thereupon he divided the kingdom between the two eldest daughters; but he caused a sack of salt to be bound on the shoulders of his youngest child, and two slaves had to lead her into the wild forest. We all wept and prayed for her to the King, but his anger was not to be turned away. How did she not weep when she left us, so that the whole path was strewn with the pearls which fell from her eyes! However, afterwards, the King did repent of his great harshness, and caused a search to be made in the forest for the poor child, but without success. And now, when I think how, perhaps, the wild beasts devoured her, I know not what to do for grief; but many a time I try to comfort myself with the idea that haply she is living still, concealed in some cave, or under the hospitable protection of some one who found her. But imagine my feelings when, on opening your emerald-book, I saw lying therein a pearl of the same kind as used to drop from my daughter's eyes, and then you may also conceive how my heart was moved at the sight. But now you shall tell me how you came by the pearl."

The young Count then told the Queen that he had received it from an old Woman, living in a wood which seemed to be haunted, and who appeared to be a witch; but of the Queen's child he had neither seen nor heard anything. The King and Queen came to the resolution to seek out this old Woman, for they thought where the pearl had been, there they should also obtain news of their daughter.

The old Woman sat in her house in the wilderness, spinning at her wheel. It was dark already, and a faggot, which burnt on the hearth below, gave a feeble light. All at once there was a noise outside; the geese were coming home from the meadow, and they cackled with all their might. Soon afterwards the daughter stepped in, but the old Woman scarcely thanked her, and only shook her head. The daughter sat down, and taking her wheel spun the thread as quickly as a young girl. Thus they sat for two hours, without speaking to one another, till at length something rattled at the window, and two fiery eyes glared in from the outside; it was an old night-owl, which screeched thrice; and then the old Woman, looking up from her work said, "Now is the time, my daughter, for you to go out, and do your work."

The daughter got up and went away over the meadows deep into a valley beyond. By-and-by, she came to a brook near which stood three oak-trees; and at the same time the moon arose round and full above the mountain, and shone so brightly, that one might have picked up a needle by its light. She drew off the mask which covered her face, and then bathing in the brook began to wash herself. As soon as she had done that, she dipped the mask also in the water, and then laid it again on the meadow to dry and bleach in the moonshine. But how was the Maiden changed! So much as you could never have fancied. Her golden hair fell down like sunbeams, and when she removed the cap which confined it, it covered her whole form. Only her eyes could be seen peeping through the trees like the stars in heaven, and her cheeks blooming like the soft red of the apple-blossoms.

But the fair Maiden was nevertheless sad; and she sat down and wept bitterly. One tear after another flowed from her eyes, and rolled to the ground between her locks; and thus sitting she would have remained for a long time had she not been disturbed by a rustling noise in the branches of one of the trees. She jumped up and sprang away like a fawn disturbed by the gun of the hunter; and at the same moment a black cloud obscured the moon, under cover of which the Maiden slipped on her old mask and disappeared like a light blown out by the wind. She ran home trembling like an aspen-leaf, and found the old Woman standing before the door: but when she was about to relate what had happened to her, the old Woman laughed, and said she knew already all about it. The old mother then led the Maiden into the room and lighted a fresh faggot; but instead of sitting down to her wheel, she fetched a broom and began to sweep and dust. "It must all be clean and respectable," said she to the

Maiden. "But mother," replied she, "why do you begin at this late hour? what is the matter?"

"Do you then know what hour it is?" inquired the old mother.

"Not quite midnight, but past eleven," returned the daughter.

"Do you not remember, then," continued the old Woman, "that to-day you have been with me three years? Your time is now expired; we can remain together no longer!"

"Alas! dear mother, you will not drive me out," said the Maiden in an alarmed tone; "where shall I go? I have neither home nor friends, and whither could I turn? I have ever done all you desired, and you have been satisfied with me; send me not away!" The old Woman would not however tell the Maiden what was coming, but said instead, "My dwelling is no longer here, but since the house and this room must be clean when I leave, hinder me not in my work, and cease to care on your own account; you shall find a roof under which to dwell, and with the reward which I shall give you, you will also be contented."

"But do tell me what is coming," entreated the Maiden.

"I tell you a second time, do not disturb me in my work. Speak not a word more, but go into your own room and pull off the mask from your face, and put on the beautiful dress which you wore when you came to me, and then remain where you are till I call you."

And now I must tell you what befell the King and Queen, who were preparing, when we last heard of them, to go in search of the old Woman in the wilderness. The Count was, first of all, despatched by night to the forest alone, and for two days he wandered before he found the right road. Along this he went till darkness overtook him, and then he climbed a tree to pass the night, for he feared he might lose his way in the dark. As soon as the moon rose he perceived a figure coming across the mountain, and although she had no rod in her hand, he could not doubt but that it was the Goose-Girl whom he had seen before at home with the old Woman. "Oho!" he exclaimed to himself; "here comes one witch, and when I have got her, I will soon catch the other!" But how astonished he was, when, on stepping up to the brook, she laid aside her mask, and washed herself, and he saw her golden hair fall down and cover her whole figure, and render her more beautiful than any one he had ever before seen! He scarcely ventured to breathe, but he stretched out his neck as far as he could from the foliage and looked at her with fixed eyes. Unfortunately, he bent over too far, and the bough cracked beneath his weight; and at the same instant the Maiden disappeared, favoured by a dark cloud, and when the moon appeared again, she was out of sight.

The young Count, however, made haste down from the tree and pursued the Maiden with hasty strides; but before he had gone very far, he perceived two figures wandering over the meadows in the twilight. They were the King and Queen, who had perceived at a distance the light in the old Woman's cottage and were hastening towards it. The Count told them what marvellous things he had witnessed by the brook, and they felt no doubt but that he had seen their lost daughter. Full of joy they journeyed on till they came to the cottage, around which lay the geese, with their heads under their wings, and none stirred at their approach. The three peeped in at the window and saw the old Woman spinning silently, without raising her eyes from her work, but simply nodding her head now and then. The room was as perfectly clean as if it had been inhabited by the Cloud-Men, who carry no dust on their feet; and for some minutes they observed the whole scene in silence; but at last plucking up courage they knocked at the window lightly. Thereupon the old Woman got up, and looking at them kindly as if she had expected them, called out, "Come in; I know who you are."

As soon as the King, Queen, and Count had entered the room, the old Woman said, "You might have spared yourselves this long journey if you had not driven out, for three long years in the forest, your child who was so affectionate and so beautiful. She has come to no harm, and for these three years past she has tended my geese; neither has she learnt any evil, but kept her heart pure and spotless. But you have been righteously punished by the sorrow and trouble which you have suffered." With these words she went to the chamber-door and called to the daughter to come out, and as soon as the Princess made her appearance, dressed in her silk gown, with her golden hair and bright eyes, it seemed like the entrance of an angel into the room.

She went up to her father and mother and fell on their necks and kissed them, which made them both cry with joy. But when she perceived the young Count standing by them, she blushed as red as a moss-rose without knowing wherefore.

"My dear child," said the King to her, "what shall I give you, for I have parted my kingdom already?"

"She needs nothing," said the old Woman, "for I present her with the tears which she has wept, which are in reality pearls more beautiful than any that can be found in the sea, and of more value than your entire kingdom. And for a further reward for her services to me I give her this house." As soon as the old Woman had said these words she disappeared, and immediately after a little knocking at the walls the house became a noble palace, and the room in which they stood a hall, in the midst of which a princely table was set out, with many servants hastening to and fro.

The story ends here, for my grandmother, who related it to me, had partly lost her memory, and so she had forgotten its conclusion. I believe, however, that the beautiful Princess was married to the young Count, and that they remained in the palace, and lived happily so long as God suffered them to remain on earth. But whether the snow-white geese whom the Princess had tended, were really men (nobody needs to be offended), whom the old Woman had taken to herself, and then restored to their natural form to wait as servants upon the young Queen, I cannot say, though I suspect it was so. This much is certain, that the old Woman was no witch, as people believed, but a wise woman, who had good intentions. Apparently, too, it was she who, at the birth of the Princess, had endowed her with the power to weep pearls instead of tears.

At this day, however, that does not happen, else would the poor soon become rich!

The Poor Boy in the Grave

THERE was once upon a time a poor Lad, whose father and mother were dead, so the Magistrate placed him in the house of a rich Farmer to be fed and brought up. But this Man, and his Wife too, had very bad dispositions; and with all their wealth they were avaricious and mean, and very angry when anyone took any of their bread. So the poor Boy, do what he might, received little to eat and many blows.

One day he was set to watch the hen and her chickens, and she ran through a hole in the paling, and a hawk just then flying by, pounced upon her, and carried her off to his roost. The Boy cried, "Thief, thief! stop, thief!" but to what end? the hawk kept his prey, and did not return. The Master hearing the noise came out, and perceived that his hen was gone, which put him in such a rage that he beat the Boy so much that, for a couple of days afterwards, he was unable to stir. Then the poor Lad had to watch the chickens, which was a harder task still, for where one ran the others followed. At last, thinking to make it sure, he tied all the chickens together by a string, so that the hawk could not take one. But what followed? After a couple of days he fell asleep from weariness with watching and with hunger, and then the hawk came and seized one of the chickens; and, because all the others were tied together to that one, he bore them all away and devoured them. Just then the Farmer came home, and perceived the misfortune which had happened, which angered him so much that he beat the Lad so unmercifully, that for several days he could not leave his bed.

When he was on his legs again, the Farmer said to him, "You are so stupid that I can no longer keep you as a watch, and, therefore, you shall be my errand-boy." So saying, he sent him to the Judge, to take him a basket of grapes, and a letter with them. On the way, hunger and thirst plagued the Lad so much that he ate two of the grape bunches. So when he took the basket to the Judge, and the latter had read the letter and counted the grapes, he said, "Two bunches are missing." The Boy then honestly confessed, that, driven by hunger and thirst, he had eaten two bunches; wherefore the Judge wrote a letter to the Farmer, and requested more grapes. These, also, the Boy had to carry, with a letter; and again, urged by great hunger and thirst, he devoured two bunches more. But before he went to the Judge, he took the letter out of the basket, and, laying it under a stone, put the stone over it, so that it could not be seen and betray him. The Judge, however, taxed him with the missing grapes. "Alas!" cried the Boy, "how did you know that? the letter could not tell you, for I had laid it previously under a stone." The Judge was forced to laugh at the simplicity of the Lad, but sent the Farmer a letter, in which he advised him to treat the Boy better, and not allow him to want meat or drink, or he might be taught the difference between justice and injustice.

"I will show you the difference at once!" said the hard-hearted Farmer, when he had read the letter; "if you will eat, you must also work; and if you do anything wrong, you must be recompensed with blows."

The following day he set the poor Boy a hard task, which was to cut a couple of bundles of straw for fodder for the horse. "And," said the Master, in a threatening tone; "I shall be back in five hours, and if the straw is not cut to chaff by that time, I will beat you till you cannot stir a limb."

With this speech the Farmer went to market with his Wife and servant, and left nothing behind for the Boy but a small piece of bread. He sat down at the machine, and began to cut the straw with all his strength, and, as he became hot, he drew off his coat and threw it aside on the straw. Then, in his terror, lest he should not get done in the time, he caught up, without noticing it, his own coat with a heap of straw, and cut it all to shreds. Too late he became aware of this misfortune, which he could not repair, and cried out, "Alas! now it is all up with me. The bad Master has not threatened in vain; when he comes back and sees what I have done, he will beat me to death. I would rather he took my life at once."

Now the Boy had once heard the Farmer's wife say that she had set a jar of poison under her bed, but she had only said so to keep away the sweet-tooths, for, in fact, it contained honey. The Boy, however, drew it out and ate the contents, and when he had done so, he thought to himself, "Ah! people have told me that death is bitter, but it tastes sweetly to me! No wonder that the mistress should so often wish for death." So thinking, he sat down on a stool to die; but instead of growing weaker, he felt really strengthened by the nourishing food. Soon he began to think, "This can be no poison, but I recollect the Farmer once said that in his clothes-chest was a bottle of fly-poison, which will certainly kill me." But this also was no poison, but Hungary wine. The Boy, however, fetched the bottle and drank it out, saying, "This death also tastes sweetly!" Soon the wine began to mount into his head, and to stupify him, so that he thought his death really was at hand. "I feel that I must die," he said; "I will go to the churchyard and seek a grave." He reeled out-of-doors as he spoke, and managed to reach the churchyard, where he dropped into a fresh-opened grave, and at the same time lost all consciousness. Never again in this world did the poor boy awake. The fumes of the hot wine, acted upon by the cold dews of evening, took away his life, and he remained in the grave wherein he had laid himself.

By-and-by, when the Farmer received the news of the death of his servant, he was frightened, because he feared he might be taken before the Judge, and his terror was so great that he fell to the earth in a swoon. His Wife, who was turning some butter in a pan over the fire, ran to his assistance, and in a moment the grease caught fire and soon communicated with the whole house, which was burnt to ashes in a few hours.

Then the years during which the Farmer and his Wife lived afterwards were spent by them in misery and poverty.

The Giant and the Tailor

A CERTAIN Tailor, who was a large boaster but very small performer, took it once into his head to go and look about him in the world. As soon as he could, he left his workshop, and travelled away over hills and valleys, now on this, and now on that; but still onwards. After he had gone some way, he perceived in the distance a steep mountain, and behind it a lofty tower, which rose from the midst of a wild dense forest. "Good gracious!" cried the Tailor, "what is this?" and driven by his curiosity, he went rapidly towards the place. But he opened his mouth and eyes wide enough when he got nearer; for the tower had legs, and sprang in a trice over the steep hill, and stood up a mighty giant before the Tailor. "What are you about here, you puny fly-legs?" asked the Giant in a voice which rumbled on all sides like thunder. "I am trying to earn a piece of bread in this forest," whispered the Tailor.

"Well, then, it is time you entered my service," said the Giant fiercely.

"If it must be so, why not?" said the Tailor, humbly; "but what will you give me?" "What wage shall you have?" repeated the Giant contemptuously; "listen and I will tell you: every year, three hundred and sixty-five days, and one besides, if it be leap-year. Is that right?"

"Quite," said the Tailor; but thought to himself, "one must cut according to his cloth; I will seek to make myself free very soon."

"Go, little rascal, and fetch me a glass of water," cried the Giant. "Why not the whole well, and its spring too?" said the Tailor, but fetched as he was bid. "What! the well and its spring too?" bellowed the Giant, who was rather cowardly and weak, and so began to be afraid, thinking to himself, "This fellow can do more than roast apples; he has a heap of courage. I must take care, or he will be too much of a servant for me!" So, when the Tailor returned with the water, the Giant sent him to fetch a couple of bundles of faggots from the forest, and bring them home. "Why not the whole forest at one stroke, every tree, young and old, knotty and smooth?" asked the Tailor, and went away. "What! the whole forest, and the well, too, and its spring!" murmured the frightened Giant in his beard; and he began to be still more afraid, and believed that the Tailor was too great a man for him, and not fit for his servant. However, when the Tailor returned with his load of faggots, the Giant told him to shoot two or three wild boars for their supper. "Why not rather a thousand at one shot, and the rest afterwards?" cried the boaster.

"What, what!" gasped the cowardly giant, terribly frightened. "Oh, well! that is enough for to-day, you may go to sleep now!"

The poor Giant, however, was so very much afraid of the little Tailor, that he could not close his eyes all the night, but tossed about thinking how to get rid of his servant, whom he regarded as an enchanter conspiring against his life. With time comes counsel. The following morning the Giant and the Dwarf went together to a marsh where a great many willow-trees were growing. When they got there the Giant said, "Sit yourself on one of these willow rods, Tailor; on my life I only wish to see if you are in a condition to bend it down."

The boasting Tailor climbed the tree, and perched himself on a bough, and then, holding his breath, he made himself heavy enough thereby to hand the tree down. Soon, however, he had to take breath again, and immediately, having been unfortunate enough to come without his goose in his pocket, the bough flew up, and to the great joy of the Giant, carried with it the Tailor so high into the air that he went out of sight. And whether he has since fallen down again, or is yet flying about in the air, I am unable to tell you satisfactorily.

The Hare and the Hedgehog

This tale, my young readers, will seem to you to be quite false; but still it *must* be true, for my Grandfather, who used to tell it to me, would wind up by saying, "All this is true, my son, else it would never have been told to me." The tale runs thus:—

It was a fine summer's morning, just before harvest-time; the buckwheat was in flower, and the sun was shining brightly in the heaven above; a breeze was blowing over the fields, where the larks were singing; and along the paths the people were going to church dressed in their best. Every creature seemed contented, even the Hedgehog, who stood before his door singing as he best could a joyful song in praise of the fine morning. Indoors, meanwhile, his Wife was washing and drying the kitchen, before going into the fields for a walk to see how the crops were getting on. She was such a long while, however, about her work, that Mr Hedgehog would wait no longer, and trotted off by himself. He had not walked any very long distance before he came to a small thicket, near a field of cabbages, and there he espied a Hare, who he guessed had come on a similar errand to himself; namely, to devour a few fine heads. As soon as Mr Hedgehog saw the Hare, he wished him a good morning; but the latter, who was in his way a high-minded creature, turned a very fierce and haughty look upon the Hedgehog, and made no reply to his greeting. He asked, instead, in a very majestic tone, how he came to be walking abroad at such an early hour. "I am taking a walk," replied the Hedgehog. "A walk!" repeated the Hare, in an ironical tone, "methinks you might employ your legs about some thing better!"

This answer vexed the Hedgehog most dreadfully, for he could have borne anything better than to be quizzed about his legs, because they were naturally short, and from no fault of his own. However, he said to the Hare, "Well, you need not be so proud; pray what can you do with those legs of yours?" "That is my affair," replied the Hare. "I expect, if you would venture a trial, that I should beat you in a race," said the Hedgehog.

"You are laughing! you, with your short legs!" said the Hare, contemptuously. "But still, since you have such a particular wish, I have no objection to try. What shall the wager be?"

"A gold louis d'or and a bottle of brandy," replied the Hedgehog.

"Done!" said the Hare, "and it may as well come off at once."

"No! not in such great haste if you please," said the Hedgehog; "I am not quite ready yet; I must first go home and freshen up a bit. Within half-an-hour I will return to this place."

Thereupon the Hedgehog hurried off, leaving the Hare very merry. On his way home, the former thought to himself, "Mr Hare is very haughty and high-minded, but withal he is very stupid; and although he thinks to beat me with his long legs, I will find a way to defeat him." So, as soon as the Hedgehog reached home, he told his Wife to dress herself at once to go into the field with him.

"What is the matter?" asked his Wife. "I have made a wager with the Hare, for a louis d'or and a bottle of brandy, to run a race with him, and you must be witness."

"My goodness, man! are you in your senses?" said the Wife; "do you know what you are about. How can you expect to run so fast as the Hare?"

"Hold your tongue, Wife! that is my affair. Don't you reason about men's business. March, and get ready to come with me."

As soon then as the Hedgehog's Wife was ready they set out together; and on the way he said, "Now attend to what I say. On the long field yonder, we shall decide our bet. The Hare is to run on the one side of the hedge and I on the other, and so all you have to do is to stop at one end of the hedge, and then when the Hare arrives on the other side at the same point, you must call out, 'I am here already.'"

They soon came to the fields, and the Hedgehog stationed himself at one end of the hedge, and his Wife at the other end; and as soon as they had taken their places the Hare arrived. "Are you ready to start?" asked the Hare. "Yes," answered the Hedgehog, and each took his place. "Off once, off twice, three times and off!" cried the Hare, and ran up the field like a whirlwind; while the Hedgehog only took three steps and then returned to his place.

The Hare soon arrived at his goal, as he ran all the way at top-speed: but before he could reach it, the Hedgehog's Wife on the other side called out, "I am here already!" The Hare was thunderstruck to hear this said, for he thought it was really his opponent, since there was no difference in the appearance of the Hedgehog and his Wife. "This will not do!" thought the Hare to himself; but presently he called out, "Once, twice, and off again;" and away he went as fast as possible, leaving the Hedgehog quietly sitting in her place. "I am here before you," cried Mr Hedgehog, as soon as the Hare approached. "What! again?" exclaimed the Hare in a rage; and added, "Will you dare another trial?" "Oh! as many as you like; do not be afraid on my account," said Mr Hedgehog, courteously.

So the Hare then ran backwards and forwards three-and-seventy times; but each time the Hedgehogs had the advantage of him, for either Mr or Mrs shouted before he could reach the goal, "Here I am already!"

The four-and-seventieth time, the hare was unable to run any more. In the middle of the course he stopped and dropped down quite exhausted, and there he lay motionless for some time. But the Hedgehog took the louis d'or and bottle of brandy which he had won, and went composedly home with his Wife.

The True Bride

ONCE upon a time there lived a Girl, young and pretty, who lost her Mother at an early age, and her stepmother behaved very cruelly to her. Although she sometimes had to do work beyond her years, she was left to herself, and forced to do, unpitied, more than her strength would allow. She could not by any means touch the heart of the wicked woman, who was always discontented and unsatisfied. The more industriously she worked the more was laid upon her, and the Stepmother was always contriving how to inflict an additional burden, and make her daughter's life more intolerable.

One day the Stepmother said to the Girl, "Here are twelve pounds of quills for you to strip, and remember if you are not ready with them by this evening you will get a good beating. Do you think you are to idle all day?" The poor Girl set to work, while the tears rolled fast down her cheeks, for she saw that it was impossible to finish her work by the time. Every now and then as the heap of feathers before her increased, she sighed and clasped her hands, and then, recollecting herself, stripped the quills quicker than before. Once she put her elbows on the table, and burying her face in her hands, exclaimed, "Alas! then, is there nobody on earth who will pity me?" As she spoke she heard a soft voice reply, "Comfort yourself, my child; I am come to help you." The Girl looked up and saw an Old Woman standing by her side, who took her hand, and said to her, "Trust me, and tell me what are your troubles." Encouraged by her kind voice, the Girl told the Old Woman of her sad life, how one burden was heaped upon another until she could make no end even with the most unremitting labour. She told her also of the beating promised by her Stepmother if she did not finish the feathers that evening. Her tears began to flow again as she concluded her tale, but the Old Woman said to her, "Dry your tears and rest yourself while I go on with your work." The Girl lay down upon a bed and went to sleep; and the Old Woman sat down at the table, and made such short work with her thin fingers that the twelve pounds of feathers were soon ready. When the girl awoke she found a great heap of snow-white feathers before her, and everything in the room put in order, but the Old Woman had disappeared. So the Girl thanked God, and waited till evening, when the Stepmother, coming into the room, was astonished to see the work finished. "Do you not see, simpleton," she cried, "what one can do when one is industrious? But was there nothing else that you could have begun, instead of sitting there with your hands in your lap?" and she went out muttering, "The Girl can eat more than bread; I must set her some harder job."

The next morning, accordingly, she called the Girl and gave her a spoon saying, "Take this, and empty the pond at the bottom of the garden with it, and mind, you know what will follow if you have not finished by the evening." The Girl took the spoon, and perceived that it had a hole in it, and even if there had not been she never could have emptied the pond in time. However she fell on her knees by the side of the water and began to scoop it out. Soon the Old Woman appeared again, and as soon as she heard the cause of the Girl's grief, she said to her, "Well, never mind; do you go and lay down in yon thicket, and let me do your work." The Girl did as she was bid, and the good Old Woman, when she was alone, only touched the pond, and immediately all the water ascended in the form of vapour and mingled with the clouds. The pond was then completely dry, and when the sun set, the Girl awoke, and saw nothing the fishes skipping about in the mud. So she went and told her Stepmother she had done her work. "You ought to have been ready long ago," she said, pale with rage, and turned away to think of some fresh device.

The next morning she said to the Girl, "You must build me a fine palace in yon plain, and get it ready by the evening." The poor Maiden was terrified when she heard this, and asked, "How can I possibly complete such a work?" "I will take no refusal," screamed the Stepmother: "if you can empty a pond with a spoon with a hole in it, you can also build a palace. And I require it done to-day, and should it be wanting in one kitchen or cellar you will catch what you well deserve."

So saying, she drove the Girl out-of-doors, who went on till she came to the valley where the stones lay piled up; but they were all so heavy that she could not move the very smallest of them. The poor Maiden sat down and cried, but hoped still the good Old Woman would come to her assistance. In a short time she did make her appearance, and bade the Maiden go and sleep in the shade while she erected the castle for her, in which she told her she might dwell when she was happy. As soon as the Old Woman was alone she touched the stones, and immediately they raised themselves and formed the walls as if giants were building. Then the scaffolding raised itself, and it seemed as if countless hands were laying stone upon stone. The tiles were laid on in order on the roofs by invisible hands, and by noonday a large weathercock, in the shape of a figure with a turning wand, appeared on the summit of the tower. The interior of the castle was also completed by the evening – how the Old Woman did it, I know not – but the walls of the various rooms were hung with silk and velvet, and highly ornamented chairs were also placed in them, and richly-carved armchairs by marble tables, while crystal chandeliers hung in the halls, and mirrored themselves in the smooth walls; green parrots also were there in golden cages, and many other peculiar birds, which sang charmingly; and about everything there was a magnificence as if a king were to inhabit the palace.

The sun was just about to sink when the Maiden awoke and perceived the light of a thousand lamps shining from the castle. With hasty steps she entered it through the open door, passing up a flight of steps covered with red cloth, and adorned with flowers on the gilt balustrade. As soon as she entered the room, and saw its magnificence, she stood aghast; and how long she might have remained so I know not, had she not thought of her Stepmother. "Ah!" said she to herself, "perhaps if she were established here she would be contented, and harass me no more." With this thought she ran to her Stepmother and pointed to the finished palace. "I will go and see it," said she, and hastened off; but as soon as she entered the hall she was forced to cover her eyes for fear of being blinded by the glare of the lamps.

"You see, now," she said to the Maiden, "how easily it is done; I wish I had set you something harder to do!" and then, going into every room, she peered about in all corners to find out something that was wanting, but she could not. "Now we will go up-stairs," said she, with an envious look at the Maiden; "I must also inspect the kitchens and cellars, and if there is anything forgotten, you shall suffer for it." There was a fire, however, burning on the hearth, the meat cooking in the pots, nippers and scales hanging on the wall, and the bright copper utensils ranged in rows. Nothing was wanting, not even the coal-scuttle or the water-pails! "Where is the door to the cellar?" exclaimed the old woman, after she had looked all round. "I warn you; you will catch it, if it is not well filled with wine-casks!" So saying, she raised the trap-door herself and went down the steps; but before she got down very far the heavy door fell upon her. The Maiden heard a cry, and raised the door up as quickly as she could to render assistance, but before she reached the bottom of the stairs, she found the old woman lying dead upon them. The noble castle belonged now to the Maiden, who dwelt there all alone, and felt quite bewildered with her good fortune. For in every closet the most beautiful dresses were hung upon the walls, with their trains, powdered with gold and silver, or with pearls and precious stones; and, moreover, she had not a wish which was not immediately fulfilled. Soon the fame of her beauty and riches went abroad through the whole world, and every day suitors introduced themselves to her presence, but none of them pleased her. At length, however, came a young Prince, who touched her heart, and to whom she betrothed herself. Now, in the castle garden stood a green linden-tree, under which they were one day sitting engaged in conversation. "I will go home and obtain my father's consent to our marriage," said the young Prince to his companion; "wait here for me under this tree, for I shall be back in a few hours." The Maiden kissed him first on his left cheek, and said, "Keep true to me, and let nobody kiss you on this cheek, till you return. I will wait for you here."

So she remained under the tree until the sun went down, but the Prince did not return; and although she waited three days afterwards, from morning till evening, he came not. When the fourth day passed with the same result, the Maiden thought that some misfortune had fallen upon him, and she resolved to go out and search for him till she found him. So she packed up three of her most beautiful dresses; the one powdered with stars of gold, the second with silver moons, and the third with golden suns; she took also a handful of jewels in a handkerchief, and, thus furnished, began her travels. At every place she came to she inquired after her betrothed lover, but nobody had seen him or knew him. So she wandered on, far and wide, over the world, but with no result; and at last, in despair, she hired herself to a farmer as a Shepherdess, and concealed her clothes and jewels under a stone.

Thus she lived for a couple of years, tending her flocks in sadness, and ever thinking of her beloved Prince. At this time she possessed a calf, which would feed out of her hands, and if she said to it the following rhyme, it would kneel down while she stroked it:—

> "Little calf, little calf, kneel you down,
> Forget not your Mistress, deary!
> Like the King's son, who his sweetheart left
> Under the linden dreary."

When two years had passed, a report was spread everywhere, that the King's daughter was about to be married. Now, the road to the city passed through the village where the Maiden dwelt, and so it happened that one day as she was watching her flocks, the Bridegroom of the Princess passed by. He was sitting proudly upon his horse and did not observe the Shepherdess, who recognised him at once as her former lover. The shock was, as it were, like a sharp knife thrust into her heart. "Alas!" she cried, "I thought he was true to me, but he has, indeed, forgotten me."

The next day he rode by her again: as he passed she sang—

> "Little calf, little calf, kneel you down,
> Forget not your Mistress, deary!
> Like the King's son who his sweetheart left
> Under the linden dreary."

The Prince looked round when he heard the voice, and stopped his horse. He looked earnestly at the face of the Shepherdess, and pressed his hand to his forehead, as if trying to recollect something; but in a minute or two, he rode on and disappeared. "Alas! alas!" cried the Maiden, "he knows me no longer!"

Soon after this occurrence, a great festival of three days' duration was appointed to be held at the royal court, and all the King's subjects were invited to it. "Now I will make a last trial," thought the Maiden; and on the evening of the first day she went to the stone under which she had buried her treasures. She drew out the dress adorned with the golden suns, and, putting it on, bedecked herself also with the jewels. Her hair, which till now she had hidden under a cap, she allowed to fall down in its natural curls, and, thus apparelled, she went to the city unperceived in the dusky twilight. As soon, however, as she entered the well-lighted ball-room, all were struck with her beauty, but nobody knew who she was. The Prince went up to her, but did not recognise her; and after he had danced with her, her manners so enchanted him, that he altogether slighted the other bride. As soon as the ball was over, she disappeared in the crowd, and, hastening back to the village, put on her shepherd's dress before the day broke.

The second evening she took out the dress with the silver moons, and adorned her hair with a crescent of precious stones. As soon as she appeared in the ball-room all eyes were turned on her, and the Prince, intoxicated with love, danced with her alone, quite forgetful of any other person. Before she went away, he made her promise to come again on the following evening.

When she thus appeared for the third time, she wore her star dress, which glittered with every step she took, not to mention her girdle and head-dress, which were stars of diamonds. The Prince took her arm as soon as she entered the room, and asked her whom she was, "For," said he, "it seems to me as if I had known you before."

"Have you forgotten what I did when you parted from me?" asked the Maiden, at the same time kissing him on his left cheek. As soon as she did this, a mist, as it were, fell from his eyes, and he recognised his true Bride. "Come," he said, "I must remain here no longer;" and taking her by the hand, he led her out to his carriage. As if the wind were pulling, the horses galloped to the wonderful castle, whose windows were already lighted up, and shone to a long distance. As the carriage passed beneath the linden-tree, innumerable glow-worms swarmed among the boughs, so that the leaves were shaken and sent down their fragrance. On the castle steps bloomed the flowers, and from the aviaries came the songs of many rare birds; but in the hall the whole court stood assembled, and the priests to celebrate the marriage of the young Prince and the True Bride.

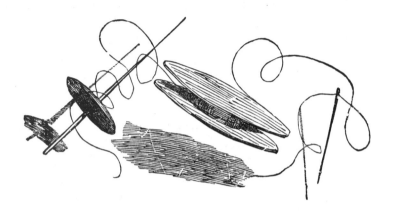

The Spindle, the Shuttle, and the Needle

THERE was once upon a time a little Girl whose father and mother died when she was quite young. At the end of the village where she lived, her Godmother dwelt in a small cottage, maintaining herself by spinning, weaving, and sewing, and she took the poor child to maintain, teaching her to work and educating her piously. Just when the girl had reached the age of fifteen, the Godmother fell ill, and calling her to her bedside said to her, "My dear daughter, I feel my end approaching. I leave you this cottage, where you will be protected from wind and weather, and also this Spindle, Shuttle, and Needle, with which you may earn your living." With these words she laid her hands on the Girl's head and blessed her, saying, "So long as you remember God, everything will prosper with you." Soon afterwards the good Godmother closed her eyes in death, and when she was carried to the grave, the poor Maiden followed the coffin, weeping bitterly, to pay her the last respect.

The little Girl now lived alone in her cottage, industriously spinning, weaving and sewing, and upon everything that she did rested the blessing of God. It seemed as if the flax in her room increased by itself; and when she wove a piece of cloth or tapestry, or hemmed a shirt she always found a purchaser readily, who paid her so handsomely, that she had enough for herself and could spare a little for others who were poorer.

Now about this time the Son of the King of this country was looking about him for a bride, and as he was not allowed to marry a poor wife, he would not have a rich one. So he said, "She shall be my bride who is at once the richest and the poorest." When he came to the village where the Maiden dwelt, he asked, as was his custom, who was the richest and poorest maiden in the place. The people first named the richest, and then told him that the poorest was the Maiden who dwelt in the cottage at the end of the village. The young Prince therefore went first to the rich Maiden, and found her sitting before her door in full dress; but as soon as she saw him approaching, she got up and made him a very low curtsey. He looked at her once, and then, without speaking a word, rode away to the house of the poor Maiden, whom he found not standing at the door, but sitting in her kitchen. He stopped his horse and, looking through the window into the kitchen, perceived how brightly the sun shone into it, and how industriously the girl herself was engaged at her Spinning-wheel. She looked up, but as soon as she saw the Prince peeping at her, she blushed as red as a rose, and looked down again, industriously turning her wheel round. Whether the thread just then was quite even or not, I know not, but she spun on till the Prince rode away. Then she stepped to the window and opened it, saying, "It is so hot in this kitchen!" but she remained at the window looking out as long as she could see the white feathers upon the Prince's hat.

After this she sat down again to her work, and presently a sentence came into her head which her Godmother had often repeated whilst she was working. She sang:—

> "Spindle, Spindle, out with you,
> And bring a wooer home."

Scarcely had she spoken the words when the Spindle sprang from her hands and out of the door, and as she sprang up and looked after it, she saw it merrily dancing along over the field, leaving a golden thread behind it. In a short time it was out of sight, and then the Maiden, having no other Spindle, took the Shuttle in her hand and began to weave.

Meanwhile the Spindle still danced on, and as the thread came to an end it reached the King's son. "What do I see?" exclaimed he; "the Spindle showing me the way?" and turning his horse's head round, he rode back guided by the golden thread. At the same time the Girl sitting at work, sang:—

> "Shuttle, Shuttle, out with you,
> And bring a wooer home."

Immediately it sprang out of her hands and through the door, before which it began to weave a carpet more beautiful than was ever before seen. On both borders were represented roses and lilies blooming and in the middle, on the golden ground, green vine-branches; hares and rabbits, too, were represented jumping about, and fawns and does rubbing their heads against trees, on whose boughs were sitting pretty birds, who wanted nothing but the gift of song. And all this pattern the Shuttle wove so quickly that it seemed to grow by itself.

But, because the Shuttle had run away, the Maiden sat down to her sewing; and while she stitched her work she sang:—

> "Needle, Needle, sharp and fine,
> Fit the house for wooer mine."

As soon as she had said this, the Needle flew out of her fingers, and sprang all about the room like a flash of lightning. It seemed as if invisible spirits were at work, for in a few minutes the table and bench were covered with green cloths, the chairs with velvet, and on the walls were hung silken curtains. And scarcely had the Needle put the last stitch to them when the Maiden saw through the window the white feathers on the hat of the Prince, who was coming towards her cottage drawn by the golden thread of the Spindle. As soon as he approached the door he dismounted, and walked upon the carpet into the cottage, and as soon as he entered the room there stood the Maiden in her shabby clothes glowing like a rose in a bush.

"You are the poorest, and yet the richest Maiden," said the Prince to her; "come with me, and you shall be my Bride."

She said nothing, but held out her hand, which the Prince took, and giving her a kiss, he led her out of the cottage and seated her behind him on his horse. He took her to the King's castle, where the wedding was performed with great magnificence, and afterwards the Spindle, the Shuttle, and the Needle, were placed in the treasure-chamber and held in great esteem.

The Master-Thief

AN old man and his Wife were, many years ago, sitting one day before their miserable hut, resting for a while from their work. All at once a handsome carriage, drawn by four black steeds, drew up at

THE MASTER-THIEF

the door, and out of it stepped a well-dressed Man. The Peasant got up and asked the seeming Lord what he wanted, and how he could serve him. The stranger offering his hand to the Peasant, said, "I desire nothing more than to enjoy a homely repast with you. Cook some potatoes in you usual fashion, and when they are ready I will sit down at your table and eat them."

The Peasant laughed, and replied, "You are some Count, or Prince, or perhaps some Archduke; distinguished Lords like you have often such fancies; but your will shall be done."

The Peasant's Wife thereupon went into the kitchen, and began to wash the potatoes, peel them, and make them into dumplings, as they were used to prepare them. While she thus proceeded with her work the Peasant invited the Lord to come and look round his garden, which yet yielded a little produce. Now, in the garden he had dug holes, in order to set trees.

"Have you no children to help you in your work?" asked the Stranger.

"No!" replied the Peasant; "but I once had a son, but he wandered out into the world a long while ago. He was a wild youth, and very spirited, and so, instead of learning anything, he was always up to some tricks; at last he ran away from me, and I have heard nothing of him since."

As the Man spoke he took a young tree, and placing it in one of the holes, planted a pole besides it. Then, as he filled in the soil, and pressed it down, he tied the stem at the bottom, middle, and top to the pole, with a straw band.

"But tell me," suddenly said the Stranger, "why you do not bind the crooked, knotty stem in yon corner, which is almost bent to the ground, likewise to a pole that it may grow straight?"

"My Lord," replied the Peasant, with a laugh, "you talk as you know; one may easily see that you understand nothing of gardening. Yon tree is old and knotted by age, and nobody could make it straight again. Trees should be trained while they are young." "So it is with your son," said the Stranger; "had you trained him when he was young in right ways, he would not have run away; now, he will also grow hardened and knotted."

"Truly, it is long since he went away," replied the old Man, "but perhaps he is changed."

"Would you know him again if he came back?" asked the Stranger abruptly.

"Not by his face, indeed," replied the Peasant; "but he has a mark upon him, a mole upon his shoulder as large as a bean."

At these words the Stranger drew off his coat, and, baring his shoulder, showed his father the mole.

"You are indeed my son," said the old Man, and all his love returned for his child; "but yet, how can you be my son? you have became a great Lord, rolling in riches and abundance; by what path have you arrived at this?"

"Alas! my Father," replied the Son, "the young tree was bound to no pole, and grew crooked; now is it too old to become straight again. How have I gained this, you ask; I have been a Thief. But do not be frightened; I am a Master-Thief. Neither locks nor bolts avail against me; whatever I wish for is mine. Think not that I steal like a common thief; no, I only take from the abundance of the rich. The poor are safe, for I rather give to them than take from them. So also I touch not what I can obtain without craft or skill."

"Alas! my son," replied the old Man, "I can have no pleasure in this; a thief is a thief, whether clever or not, and, I warn you, comes not to any good end." So saying, he led him to his Mother, and when she heard that he was her son she wept for joy, but when she was also told that he had become a thief, two rivers, as it were, of tears flowed from her eyes. At length she said, "He is still my son, although become a Master-Thief, and mine eyes have seen him once more."

The three then sat down to table, and he ate again with his parents the coarse fare which he had not tasted for so long. During the meal the old Peasant said to his son, "If our master, the Count of the castle above there, knew who you were, and what you were doing, he would not, methinks, take you in his arms and rock you, as he once did at your christening; he would rather cause you to be hung on the gallows."

"Do not be afraid, my dear Father, he will do nothing to me; I understand my trade too well. To-day even I will go to him."

So when it was evening, the Master-Thief got into his carriage and drove to the castle, where the Count received him with courtesy, because he took him for some noble personage. But when the Stranger disclosed his real character, the Count turned pale, and sat in silence for some time. At last he said, "Since you are my godson, I will forego justice for mercy, and show forbearance to you. But because you profess to be a Master-Thief, I will put your art to the proof, and if then you fail, you must keep your wedding with the hangman's daughter, and the cawing of the rooks shall be the music to celebrate it."

"My lord Count," replied the Master-Thief, "think of three as difficult tasks as you can, and if I do not fulfil my pretentions, do with me as you will."

The Count considered for some minutes, and then said, "For the first task you shall steal out of its stable my favourite horse; for the second you shall take away from my wife and me, when we are asleep, the counterpane under which we lie, without our knowledge, and also the ring off my wife's finger. For the third, and last task, you shall steal out of the church the parson and the clerk. Now mark all this well, for your neck depends upon its due performance."

Thereupon the Master-Thief went to the nearest town, and there purchased the old clothes of a country-wife, and put them on. Then he dyed his face a deep brown, and fashioned wrinkles on it so that nobody could have recognised him. Lastly, he filled a small cask with old Hungary wine, in which he mixed a powerful sleeping drug. Then, laying the cask in a basket which he carried upon his shoulder, he walked with wavering and tottering steps to the castle of the Count. It was quite dark when he arrived there, and so, sitting down upon a stone in the courtyard, he began to cough like an asthmatic old woman, and rubbed his hands together as if they were cold. Now, before the door of the stables, Soldiers were lying round a fire, and one of them remarking the old Woman, called to her to come nearer and warm herself. The seeming old Woman tottered up to the group, and taking her basket from her head, sat down near them.

"What have you got in your basket, old Woman?" cried one. "A good taste of wine," she replied; "I maintain myself by trading with it; for some money and your fair words I will give you a glassful." "Come along, then," returned the Soldier; but as soon as he had drunk what was given him, he said, "Ah! this wine is very good; I would rather have two glasses than one!" and so he took a second glass, and then his comrades followed his example.

"Holloa, there!" exclaimed one of the soldiers to another inside in the stable, "here is an old Woman with some wine so good, that it will warm your chest more than all the fire." As he spoke, she carried her cask into the stable, and saw there three Soldiers; one of whom sat on the saddled horse. Another had the bridle in his hand, and a third held on by the tail. The old Woman served out to them the wine as long as it lasted, and then its effects began to show themselves. He who had the bridle let it drop from his hand, and, sinking to the ground, soon began to snore; the other let go the tail and fell asleep, snoring louder than the other; and the soldier who was sitting on the horse bent his head upon its neck, and so fell asleep, and snored like the noise of a smith's bellows. The Soldiers outside, also, had long before fallen asleep, and were lying motionless as stones round their fire. When the Master-Thief saw himself so favoured, he gave to him who held the bridle a rope in his hand, and to the other who held the tail, a wisp of straw; but what to do with him who sat upon the horse's back puzzled him. He could not throw him off, for that would have awakened him, and he would have called for help, so he was obliged to adopt a stratagem. He unbuckled the saddle girths, and knotted fast to the saddle a couple of ropes, which passed through rings in the wall. This done, he drew the sleeping rider, saddle and all, up in the air, and then made the ropes secure to the posts of the stable. He next unchained the horse, but before he led him over the stone floor of the yard, he wrapped his hoofs round with old rags, so that they might not make any noise which could awaken the watchers. Then he led his prize out cautiously, and swinging himself upon his back rode off in haste.

As soon as the day broke, the Master-Thief returned to the castle, mounted on the stolen steed. The Count was up already, and looking out of his window.

"Good morning, sir Count," said the Thief; "here is your horse, which I have luckily taken from his stable. Look around, and see your soldiers lying in the yard fast asleep; and if you go into the stable you will find them equally well occupied there."

The Count was forced to laugh, and said, "Well, for once you have succeeded; but this second time you will not come off so easily. And, I warn you, if you meet me as a Thief, I shall treat you as a Thief."

By-and-by night came, and the Countess went to bed, with her wedding-ring held fast in her closed hand. "All the doors are locked and bolted," said the Count, "and I shall keep awake and watch for this Thief, that, if he makes his appearance at the window, I may shoot him."

The Master-Thief, however, went in the dark to the gallows, and cutting down from the rope a poor criminal who had been hung there that day, carried him on his back to the castle. There he placed a ladder up to the sleeping-chamber of the Count, and hoisting the dead man upon his shoulders, began to mount. As soon as he had got so high that the head of the dead man was on a level with the window, the Count, concealed by the curtain, pointed a pistol at it and fired. Immediately the Master-Thief pitched the corpse over, and then, rapidly descending the ladder, concealed himself in a corner. The night was bright, with a clear moonshine, and the Master-Thief plainly saw the Count descend the ladder, and bear the dead man away into the garden, where he began to dig a hole in which to bury him. "Now is the lucky moment!" said the Thief to himself; and slipping from his hiding-place, he ran up the ladder, and entered the sleeping-room. "Dear wife," he began, imitating the Count's voice, "the Thief is dead, but he is nevertheless my godson, and more of a rogue than a criminal; I do not wish, therefore, to put his family to shame, for I pity his poor parents. I wish, therefore, before daybreak, to bury him in the garden, that the affair may be kept quiet. Give me the bed-covering, that I may wrap his body in it, and bury him decently."

The Countess gave him the counterpane readily, and as she did so, the Thief continued, "Do you know, I have a fit of magnanimity; give me your ring; since this unfortunate fellow has perilled his life for it, I will bury it with him."

The Countess did not wish to disoblige the Count, and so, drawing off her ring, though unwillingly, she handed it to him. Thereupon the Thief made off with both his prizes, and luckily reached his home before the Count had finished his grave-digging.

You may fancy what a long face the Count pulled the next morning when the Master-Thief brought him the bed-covering and the ring. "Are you a wizard?" he said to him. "Who has fetched you out of the grave, in which I myself laid you, and who has brought you to life again?"

"You did not bury me," replied the Thief, "but a poor criminal from the gallows;" and then he related circumstantially all that had occurred, so that the Count was compelled to believe that he was a clever and crafty fellow.

"But your tasks are not ended yet," said the Count; "you have still the third to do, and if you do not manage that all your former work will be useless."

The Master-Thief laughed, but made no answer; and when night came he went to the village-church with a long sack on his back, a bundle under his arm, and a lantern in his hand. In the sack he had some crabs, and in the bundle some short wax-lights. When he got into the churchyard he stopped and took a crab from his sack, and fixing one of his wax-lights upon its back he placed it on the ground and made it crawl about. Then he took out a second, and a third, and so on, till he had emptied the sack. After that he put on a long black cloak, like a monk's gown, and fastened a grey beard with wax to his chin. Then, being thus completely disguised, he took the sack in which the crabs had been, and, going into the church, proceeded up the chancel. At the same moment the steeple-clock struck twelve, and as soon as the last stroke had rung, the Master-Thief began to cry with a clear, loud voice, "Hear, all you sinners! hear, hear! the end of the world is come, the eternal day is near; hear, hear! Whoever will go to heaven with me, let him creep into this sack. I am Peter, who opens and shuts the gate of heaven. See out there in the churchyard the dead wandering about, collecting their bones together. Come, come, come, and creep into the sack, for the world passes away."

His words resounded through the whole village; but the Parson and Clerk, who lived close to the Church, first understood what he said; and when they perceived the lights wandering about in the churchyard, they believed that something uncommon was happening, and went into the church. They listened for a while to the preacher; and at length the Clerk nudged the Parson, and said to him, "It would not be a bad plan if we made use of this opportunity, before the dawning of the eternal day, to get to heaven in an easy way."

"Oh, certainly!" replied the Parson, "that is exactly what I think; if you desire it, we will forthwith enter on the journey."

"Yes!" said the Clerk; "but you have the precedence, Mr Parson; I will follow you."

So the Parson mounted the chancel steps, and crept into the sack which the Master-Thief held open, closely followed by the Clerk. Immediately the Thief drew the neck of the sack tight, and, swinging it round, dragged it down the steps, and so often as the heads of the poor fellows in it knocked against the floor, he cried to them, "Ah, now we are going over the mountains!" When they were out of the church he dragged them in the same manner through the village, and called the puddles which the sack went into "the clouds." By-and-by they came to the castle, and as he dragged the sack up the steps he named them as those which led to the gate of heaven, and said he, "We shall soon be in the entrance-court now." As soon as he got to the top, he pushed the sack into the dove-cote; and when the doves fluttered about he told the Parson and the Clerk to listen to the angels fluttering their wings. Then he pushed the bolt to and went away.

The next morning the Master-Thief presented himself before the Count, and told him that he had performed the third task, and drawn the Parson and Clerk out of the church. "Where have you left them then?" asked the Count.

"They are lying in a sack in the dove-cote," said the Thief, "and fancy themselves in heaven."

The Count went himself and saw that the Thief had spoken the truth; but he freed the poor men from their imprisonment. After he had done so, he said to the Thief, "You are indeed an arch-thief, and have won your wager. For this time you may escape with a whole skin, but take care to keep away from my provinces; for if you venture again into my power, you shall be elevated on the gallows."

The Master-Thief then took his leave; and after he had said good-bye to his parents, he went away to a distant country, and nobody has seen or heard of him since.

The Robber and his Sons

ONCE upon a time there lived in a large forest a Robber and his band, who concealed themselves in caves and clefts of rocks; and when any princes, nobles, or rich merchants, passed near them, they started out and robbed them of their money and other property. But in course of time the head Robber grew old; and then he took an aversion to his employment, and repented of the many bad actions he had done. He determined, therefore, to lead a better life, like an honest man, doing good wherever he could. People wondered to see him change so quickly, but they were nevertheless glad of it. Now, he had three Sons, whom, when they had grown up, he called to him, and bade them choose what trade or profession they would be, that they might earn their living honestly. The Sons consulted with one another, and then answered, "The apple falls not far from its tree; we will maintain ourselves as you did, we will become Robbers. A business whereat we must work from morning till night, and yet earn a scanty living and little gains, does not please us at all."

"Alas! my dear children," replied the Father, "why will you not live quietly, and be content with little? Honest gains last the longest. Robbery is a wicked and godless trade, which leads to bad endings; in the riches which you may acquire, you will have no peace, for that I know from my own experience. I tell you again it has an evil ending; the jug is taken once too often to the well, and gets broken; you will be caught at last and hung on the gallows."

His Sons, however, paid no attention to his warnings, but remained unconvinced. So the three youths resolved to make a trial, and because they knew that the Queen had a fine horse of great value in her stables, they determined to steal it. They were aware that the horse ate no other fodder than a tender kind of grass, which grew in a certain marshy wood. Thither they went and cut some of this grass, which they made into a large bundle, and in the middle thereof the two elder brothers hid the younger so cleverly, that he could not be seen. This bundle they carried to the market, and the Queen's stable-keeper purchased it, caused it to be carried to the stable of the horse, and there thrown down. As soon as midnight came, and everybody was fast asleep, the boy made his way out of the bundle of grass, and, untying the horse, bridled it with its golden bridle, and laid across it the cloth picked out with gold, which formed the saddle, and the bells which hung from it he stopped with wax, that they might not make any sound. This done, he opened the stable door and rode away in great haste back to his brothers. The watchmen in the town, however, remarked the thief, and pursued him; and catching him, together with his brothers, they took all three prisoners, and carried them off to gaol.

The next morning they were taken before the Queen, and when she saw how young they were, she made inquiries about their parentage, and learnt that they were the three sons of an old Robber, who had changed his mode of life, and was now living an obedient subject. She caused them to be taken back to prison, and asked the Father if he would release his Sons. The Old Man said, "My Sons are not worthy of a penny being spent to release them."

"You are a well-known and notable Robber," replied the Queen to him; "tell me the most remarkable adventure which you have met with in your life, and I will release your Sons."

Thus bidden, the old Robber replied, "My lady Queen, hear my tale of an occurrence which frightened me more than fire or water. While travelling about, I learnt that in a wild wooded ravine between two hills, twenty miles distant from any human habitation, there dwelt a Giant in possession of an immense treasure of many thousand pieces of gold and silver. So I selected from my companions as many as a hundred men, and we set out together to the place. It was a long and toilsome road among rocks and precipices, and when we came to the spot, to our great joy we did not find the Giant at home, so we took as much as we could carry of the gold and silver. Just as we were making our way home with this treasure, and fancied ourselves quite safe, we were unawares surrounded and taken prisoners by the Giant, who was accompanied by nine others. They divided us amongst them, each taking ten, and I with nine others fell to the lot of the Giant from whom we had taken the treasure. He bound our hands behind our backs and carried us like sheep to a rocky cave, and when we offered to ransom ourselves with money or property, he replied, 'I do not want your treasures; I shall keep you and devour you, for that is what I reckon upon.' So saying, he felt of us all, and, singling out one, said, 'This is the fattest of you all, and I will make a beginning with him.' Then he struck him down, and putting his flesh in morsels into a kettle full of water, he set it on the fire till it was boiled through, and afterwards made his meal of it. Thus every day he devoured one of us, and because I was the leanest, I was the last. So when my nine companions were devoured, I bethought myself of a stratagem to escape my turn, and at length I said to the Giant, 'I see you have bad eyes, and suffer with pain in your face; I am a physician, and well experienced in my profession, and therefore if you will spare my life, I will heal your eyes.'

"He promised me my life if I were able to do what I said, and gave me everything that I asked for. I put oil in a vessel and mixed it with sulphur, pitch, salt, arsenic, and other destructive ingredients, and then I put it over the fire, as if I were preparing a plaster for his eyes. As soon then as the oil boiled I caused the Giant to lie down, and I then poured over his eyes, head and body, the whole contents of the vessel, so that he fully lost his sight, and the whole skin of his body was blistered and burnt. With a fearful howl he jumped up, threw himself then on the ground again, and wallowed here and there, uttering dreadful cries, and roaring like a bull or lion. Then again, springing up in his rage, he caught up a large club which was lying on the ground, and ran all over the cave striking now against the floor and then on the walls, thinking each time to hit me. I could not escape, for the cave was everywhere surrounded with high walls, and the doors were closed with iron bolts. I jumped from one corner to the other, and at last, because I knew not what else to do, I mounted by a ladder to the roof and hung thereon by both hands. There I remained a day and a night, and then, because I could bear it no longer, I climbed down again and mixed with the sheep. There I was obliged to be very active and always run between the Giant's legs with the flock that he might not notice me. At length, I found in one corner of the sheepfold a ram's skin, and managed to draw it on so well that the beast's horns came where my head was. Now the Giant was accustomed when the sheep were going to the meadows to make them run between his legs, by which means he counted them, and also picked out the fattest one, whom he caught and cooked for his dinner. On this occasion I thought I should easily escape by pressing through his legs as the sheep did; but he caught me, and finding me heavy, said, 'You are fat, and shall fill my belly to-day.' I gave one leap and sprang out of his hands, and he caught me again. I escaped a second time, but he caught me again; and seven times I thus alternately eluded and fell into his grasp. Then he flew into a passion and said to me, 'You may run away, and may the wolves devour you, for you have fooled me enough!' As soon as I was outside the cave I threw off the skin which disguised me, and shouted in a mocking tone to him that I had escaped him in spite of all. While I did so he drew a ring from his finger and held it out to me, saying, 'Take this ring as a pledge from me; you have well deserved it. It would not be becoming either, that so crafty and clever a man should go unrewarded by me.' I took the gold ring and put it on my finger, not knowing that it was enchanted, and that it compelled me to utter, whether I wished or not, the words, 'Here I am! here I am!' In consequence of this the Giant was made aware where I was, and pursued me into the forest. But there, because he was blind, he ran every moment against some roots or trunks of trees, and fell down like an immense rock. Each time, however, he quickly raised himself, and, as he had such long legs, and could make such enormous strides, he gained on me very soon, while I still cried, without cessation, 'Here I am! here I am!' I was well aware that the ring was the cause of my exclamations, and I tried to draw it off, but without success. At last, as there was no other resource, I bit off my finger with my own teeth, and, at the same time, I ceased to cry, 'Here I am!' and so luckily escaped the Giant. Certainly I thus lost one of my fingers, but I preserved my life by doing so."

Here the Robber broke off and said to the Queen, "Madam, if it please you, I have told you this adventure to ransom one of my Sons; and now, to liberate the second, I will narrate what further happened to me:—

"As soon as I had escaped from the Giant, I wandered about the wilderness totally unable to tell which way to turn. I climbed to the tops of the firs, and up all the hills, but wherever I looked, far and wide, there was no house, nor field, nor a single trace of human habitation: the whole country was one terrible wilderness. From mountains, which reached up to heaven, I reached valleys which were only to be compared with abysses. I encountered lions, bears, buffaloes, zebras, poisonous snakes, and fearful reptiles; I saw two wild uncouth men, people with horns and beaks, so frightful, that I shudder even now when I think of them. I hurried on and on, impelled by hunger and thirst, though I feared every minute I should sink with exhaustion. At last, just as the sun was going down, I came to a high mountain, from whence I saw in a deserted valley a column of smoke rising, as it were, from a baker's oven. I ran out as quickly as I could down the mountain in the direction of the smoke, and when I got below I saw three dead men hanging on the bough of a tree. The sight terrified me, for I supposed I had fallen into the power of some other Giant, and I feared for my life. However, taking courage, I went on, and soon came to a cottage whose door stood wide open; and by the fire on the hearth, sat a woman with her child. I entered, greeted her, and asked her why she sat there alone, and where her husband was; I asked, too, if it were far from any human habitation. She told me, in reply, that any country where there were men's dwellings was at a very great distance; and she related, with tears in her eyes how, on the previous night, the wild men of the wood had entered her house and stolen her away with her child from the side of her husband, and carried her to this wilderness. She said, too, that that morning the monsters, before going out, had commanded her to kill and dress her own child, that they might devour it on their return. As soon as I had heard this tale I felt great pity for the poor woman and her child, and resolved to rescue them from their situation. So I ran away to the tree, on which hung the three thieves, and, taking down the middle one, who was the stoutest, carried him into the house. I cut him to pieces and told the woman to give them to the robbers to eat. Her child I concealed in a hollow tree, and then I hid myself behind the house, where I could see when the wild men arrived, and if it were necessary, hasten to the relief of the woman. As soon as the sun set the three Giants came down from the mountain; they were fearful objects to look at, being similar to apes in their stature and figure. They were dragging behind them a dead body, but I could not see what it was. As soon as they entered the house, they lighted a large fire, and, tearing the body to pieces with their teeth, devoured it uncooked. After that they took the kettle, in which was cooked the flesh of the thief, off the fire, and divided the pieces among them for their supper. As soon as they had done, one of them, who appeared to be the head, asked the woman if what they had eaten was the flesh of her child. She said 'Yes.' And then the monster said, 'I believe that you have concealed your child, and given us to eat one of the thieves off the tree.' So saying, he told his companions to run off and bring him a piece of the flesh of each of the three thieves that he might assure himself they were all there. As soon as I heard this I ran and hung myself by the hands between the two thieves on the rope which had been round the neck of the third. When the monsters came, they cut a piece of flesh from the side of each of us, and I endured the pain without suffering any cry to escape me. I have even now the scar for a witness of the truth of the tale."

Here the Robber again ceased, and told the Queen that what he had said was intended as a ransom for his second Son, and for the third he would narrate the conclusion of his tale. Then he went on thus:—

"As soon as the wild people had gone away with these three pieces of flesh, I let myself down again and bound up my wound as well as I could with strips of my shirt, but I could not stop the blood, which streamed down me still. I paid no attention to that, however, but kept thinking still how to perform my promise of saving the woman and her child. I hastened back, therefore, to my concealment, and listened to what was passing in the cottage. I could scarcely keep my attention fixed, however, for I felt so much pain from my wound, and, besides, I was quite worn out with hunger and thirst. I observed, nevertheless, the Giant trying the three pieces of flesh which were brought to him, and when he took up the third, which was mine, he exclaimed to his three comrades, 'Run at once and fetch me the middle thief, for his flesh seems to me the best flavoured!' As soon as I heard this I hurried to the gallows and suspended myself again by the rope between the two thieves. Soon the monsters came, and pulling me down, dragged me over the thorns and stones to the house, where they threw me on the floor. Then, sharpening their knives, they prepared to slay and devour me, but just as they were about to begin, there suddenly rolled such a clap of thunder, accompanied by lightning, over the house, that the monsters themselves trembled and paused in their work. The thunder and lightning continued and the rain fell in torrents, while the wind blew as if the whole cottage would be swept away. In the midst of the noise and confusion the monsters fled out of the cottage through the window and roof and left me lying on the ground. The storm lasted for three hours, and then daylight appeared, and soon the sun shone out. I got up, and seeking the woman and her child, we left the ruined hut, and for fourteen days wandered about the wilderness, subsisting on nothing but roots, herbs, and berries, which grew on our path. At length we arrived in a civilised country, and I found the husband and the wife, whose joy you may easily imagine on the return of his wife and child."

Here the Robber ended his tale, and as soon as he had concluded, the Queen said to him, "You have atoned for much evil by your restoration of this poor woman to her husband, and, therefore, I now liberate your three Sons."

Wise Hans

How happy is the man, and how well his affairs go on at home, who has a wise boy who listens to every word that is said to him, and then goes and acts according to his own discretion! Such a wise Hans was once sent by his Master to look for a lost cow. He remained a long while absent; but the Master thought, "My trusty Hans spares himself no trouble in his work!" When, however, a still longer time had elapsed, and the Boy did not return, his Master began to fear something had happened, so he made himself ready to go in search of him. He looked about for a long while, and at length found Hans running up and down in a wide field. "Now, my good Hans," cried his Master when he had overtaken him, "have you found the cow which I sent you after?"

"No, Master," he replied, "I have not found the cow, for I have not looked for it."

"What have you been looking for, then, Hans?" asked the Master.

"Something better, and I have found it, too, luckily."

"What is it, Hans?"

"Three Blackbirds," answered the Boy.

"And where are they?" continued his Master.

"One I hear, the second I see, and the third I am hunting," said the Boy.

Take now example by this; do not trouble yourself with your Master's business or his orders; but do rather whatever may please you at the moment, and then you will be reckoned as fine a fellow as this wise Hans.

The Countryman and the Evil Spirit

ONCE there lived a bold and cunning Countryman, whose tricks are too numerous to be told entire; but one of the best tales is that showing how he managed to over-reach an Evil Spirit and make a fool of him.

It was growing quite dusky one day, when, having ploughed over his fields, he was preparing to return home. Just then he perceived in the middle of his field a heap of red-hot coals, and as he approached it, full of wonder, he observed a little Black Spirit sitting on the top. "You are sitting upon some treasure?" said the Countryman, inquiringly. "Yes, indeed," replied the Spirit; "a treasure containing more gold and silver than you ever saw in your life."

"Then the treasure belongs to me, because it lies on my field," said the Countryman, boldly.

"It shall be thine," replied the Spirit, "if you give me for the next two years half the produce of your land. Of gold I have more than enough, and I wish for some of the fruits of the earth."

To this bargain the Countryman agreed; but first stipulated that to avoid dispute in the division of the produce, what was above ground should belong to the Spirit, and what was beneath the surface to himself. To this, the Spirit readily consented, but the crafty Countryman sowed turnip-seed. So when the harvest time arrived, the Spirit appeared to claim his fruits; but he found nothing but withered yellow stalks, while the Countryman contentedly dug up his turnips. "For once you have got the advantage of me," exclaimed the angry Spirit, "but it shall not happen so again; mine is what grows under the ground, and your what grows above it." "Very well, I am satisfied," said the Countryman; and when sowing time came round. he put maize seed in the ground instead of turnips. The corn ripened in due course, and then the Spirit appeared to fetch away his crops. Just before he came, the Countryman had cut and carried all his corn, and so when the Evil Spirit arrived he found nothing else but stubble, and thereupon he hurried off in a terrible rage. "So must one toss foxes in blankets!" cried the Countryman when the Evil Spirit was gone, and went and fetched the treasure.

The Lying Tale

I WILL tell you something. I saw two roast hens flying; they flew quickly, and had their heads to the sky and their tails to the ground! I saw an anvil and a mill-stone swimming over the Rhine, but slowly and lightly, and a frog sat and ate a plough-share at Whitsuntide on the ice. There were three fellows wished to catch a hare, and went upon crutches and stilts; the one was deaf, the second blind, and the third dumb, and the fourth could not stir a foot. Do you wish to know how that happened? The blind man saw the hare coursing over the fields, the dumb man called to the lame one, and he caught the hare by the neck.

There were some fellows who wished to sail on dry land, and they spread the sail, and were carried over the meadows; but when they attempted to get up a high mountain they were miserably drowned. A crab was hunting a hare, and high upon the roof lay a cow which had climbed there. In this land flies are as big as goats.

Pray open the window that these lies may escape.

The Drummer

ONE evening a young Drummer was walking all alone on the sea-shore, and as he went along he perceived three pieces of linen lying on the sand. "What fine linen!" said he; and, picking up one of the pieces, he put it in his pocket and went home, thinking no more of his discovery. By-and-by he went to bed, and just as he was about to fall asleep, he fancied he heard someone call his name. He listened, and presently distinguished a gentle voice, calling, "Drummer, Drummer! awake!" He could see nothing, for it was quite dark; but he felt, as it were, something flitting to and fro over his bed. "What do you want?" he asked at length. "Give me back my shirt," replied the voice, "which you found yesterday on the sea-shore."

"You shall have it again if you tell me who you are."

"Alas! I am the Daughter of a mighty King; but I have fallen into the power of a Witch, who has confined me on the glass mountain. Every day I am allowed to bathe with my two sisters in the sea; but I cannot fly away again without my shirt. Yester-eve my sisters escaped as usual, but I was obliged to stay behind, so I beg you to give me my shirt again."

"Rest happy, poor child," replied the Drummer, "I will readily give it back;" and, feeling for it in his pocket, he handed it to her. She hastily snatched it, and would have hurried away, but the Drummer exclaimed, "Wait a moment, perhaps I can help you!"

"That you may do," said the voice, "if you climb up the glass mountain and free me from the Witch; but you cannot get there, nor yet ascend, were you to try."

"Where there's a will there's a way," said the Drummer. "I pity you, and I fear nothing; but I do not know the way to the glass mountain."

"The path lies through the large forest, where the Giants are," said the child; "more I dare not tell you;" and, so saying, she flew away.

At break of day the Drummer arose, and, hanging his drum round him, walked straight away without fear into the forest. After he had traversed some distance without perceiving any Giant, he thought to himself he would awake the sleeper; and so, steadying his drum, he beat a roll upon it, which disturbed all the birds so much, that they flew off. In a few minutes a Giant raised himself from the ground, where he had been lying asleep on the grass, and his height was that of a fir-tree. "You wretched wight!" he exclaimed, "what are you drumming here for, awaking me out of my best sleep?"

"I am drumming," he replied, "to show the way to the many thousands who follow me."

"What do they want here in my forest?" asked the Giant.

"They are coming to make a path through, and rid it of such monsters as you," said the Drummer.

"Oho? I shall tread them down like ants."

"Do you fancy you will be able to do anything against them?" said the Drummer. "Why, if you bend down to catch any of them, others will jump upon your back; and then when you lie down to sleep, they will come from every bush and creep upon you. And each one has a steel hammer in his girdle, with which he means to beat out your brains."

The Giant was terribly frightened to hear all this, and he thought to himself, "If I meddle with these crafty people they will do me some injury. I can strangle wolves and bears, but these earthworms I cannot guard against." Then, speaking aloud, he said, "Here you little fellow, I promise for the future to leave you and your comrades in peace; and if you have a wish tell it to me, for I will do anything to please you."

"Well, then," replied the Drummer, "you have got long legs, and run quicker than I, so carry me to·the glass mountain, and I will beat a retreat-march to my companions, so that for this time you shall not be disturbed."

"Come hither, you worm," said the Giant, "set yourself on my shoulder, and I will bear you whither you desire."

The Giant took him up, and the Drummer began to beat with all his might and main. "That is the sign," thought the Giant, "for the others to go back." After a while a second Giant started up on the road, and took the Drummer from the shoulders of the first, and put him in his button-hole. The Drummer took hold of the button, which was as big as a plate, to hold on by, and looked round in high spirits. By-and-by they met with a third Giant, who took him out of the button-hole and placed him on the rim of his hat. Here the Drummer walked round and round observing the country; and, perceiving in the blue distance a mountain, he supposed it to be the glass mountain, and so it was. The Giant took only a couple more strides and arrived at the foot of the mountain, where he set down the Drummer. The latter desired to be taken to the summit, but the Giant only shook his head and went away, muttering something in his beard.

So there the poor Drummer was left standing before the mountain, which was as high as if three hills had been placed upon each other, and, withal, as smooth as a mirror, so that he knew not how he should ascend it. He began to climb, but it was in vain, he slipped back every step. "Oh that I were a bird!" he exclaimed; "but of what use was wishing? wings never grew for that." While he ruminated, he saw at a little distance two men hotly quarrelling. He went up to them and found that their dispute related to a saddle, which lay on the ground before them, and for the possession of which they were contending. "What fools you are," he exclaimed, "to quarrel about a saddle, for which you have no horse!"

"The saddle is worth fighting about," replied one, for whoever sits upon it, may wish himself where he will, and may even go to the end of the world if he so desire. The saddle belongs to us in common; but it is now my turn to ride, and this other will not let me."

"I will soon end your quarrel!" exclaimed the Drummer, walking a few steps forward, and planting a white wand in the ground; "run both of you to that point, and whoever gets there first shall ride first."

The two men started off at once, but they had scarcely gone two steps when the Drummer sat himself hastily down on their saddle, and, wishing himself on the top of the glass mountain, was there before one could turn his hand round. On the summit was a large plain, whereon stood an old stone mansion, and before its door a fish-pond, and behind, a dark wood. The Drummer saw neither man nor beast, all was still, but the noise of the wind among the trees; while, close above his head, the clouds were rolling along. He stepped up to the door of the house and knocked thrice, and after the third time, an old Woman, with red eyes and a brown face, opened it. She had spectacles upon her nose, and looked at him very sharply before she asked what his business was.

"Entrance, a night's lodging, and provisions," replied the Drummer boldly.

"That you shall have, if you promise to perform three tasks!" said she.

"And why not?" he replied, "I am not afraid of work, be it ever so hard!"

So the old Woman let him come in, and gave him supper, and afterwards a good bed.

The next morning when the Drummer arose, the old Woman

handed him a thimble off her withered finger, and said, "Now, go to work and empty the pond out there with this thimble, but you must finish it before night; and, besides that, you must take out all the fishes, and range them according to their species upon the bank."

"That is a queer job!" said the Drummer; but, going to the pond, he began to thimble out the water. He worked all the morning, but what could he do with a single thimble, if he had kept at work for a thousand years? When noonday came he stopped and sat down; for, as he thought, "It is no use, and all the same whether I work or not." Just then a Girl came from the house, and brought him a basket of provisions. "What do you want," she asked, "that you sit there so sorrowful?"

The Drummer looked up, and, seeing that the speaker was very beautiful, he replied, "Alas! I cannot perform the first task, and how I shall do the others, I cannot tell! I have come here to seek a King's daughter, who lives hereabouts, but I have not found her, and I must go further."

"Stop here!" said the Girl, "I will assist you out of your trouble. You are tired, so lay your head in my lap and go to sleep; when you awake again the work will be done!"

The Drummer needed not twice telling; and, as soon as his eyes were closed, the Maiden pressed a wishing-ring, which she had, and said, "Out water, out fishes." Immediately the water rose in the air like a white vapour, and rolled away with the other clouds; while the fishes all jumped out, and arranged themselves on the banks according to their size and species.

By-and-by the Drummer awoke, and saw, to his astonishment, the work completed. "One of the fishes," said the Maiden, "does not lie with his companions, but quite alone; and so, when the old Woman comes this evening and sees all that is done she will ask why this fish is left out, and you must take it up and throw it in her face, saying, 'That is for you, old Witch.'"

So when it was evening the old Woman came and asked the question, and he immediately threw the fish in her face. She did not appear to notice it, but only looked silently and maliciously at him.

The next morning she said to him, "You got off too easily yesterday, I must give you a harder task; to-day you must cut down all my trees, split the wood into faggots, and range them in bundles, and all must be ready by night." With these words she gave him an axe, a mallet, and two wedges; but the first was made of lead, and the others of tin. When, therefore, he began to chop, the axe doubled quite up, while the mallet and wedges stuck together. He knew not what to do; but at noon the Maiden came again with his dinner and comforted him. "Lay your head in my lap," said she, "and when you awake the work will be done." Thereupon she turned her wishing-ring, and at the same moment the whole forest fell down with a crash, the timber split itself, and laid itself together in heaps, as if innumerable giants were at work. As soon as the Drummer awoke, the Maiden said to him, "See, here is all your wood properly cut and stacked, with the exception of one bough which, if the old Woman, when she comes this evening, asks the reason of, give her a blow with it, and say, 'That is for thee, old Witch.' "

Accordingly, when the old Woman came, she said, "See, how easy the work is; but for whom is this bough left out?"

"For you, old Witch!" he replied, giving her a blow. But she appeared not to feel it, and, laughing fiendishly said to him, "To-morrow you shall lay all the wood in one pile, and kindle and burn it."

At daybreak he arose again and began to work; but how could a single man pile up a whole forest? The work proceeded very slowly. The Maiden, however, did not forget him in his troubles, and brought him as usual his midday meal, after eating which he laid his head in her lap and slept. On his awaking he found the whole pile burning in one immense flame, whose tongues of fire reached up to heaven. "Attend to me," said the Maiden to him; "when the Witch comes she will demand something singular, but do what she desires without fear, and you will take no harm; but if you are afraid, the fire will catch and consume you. Lastly, when you have fulfilled her demands, take her with both hands and throw her into the midst of the flames."

Thereupon the Maiden left him, and presently the old Woman slipped in, crying, "Hu! hu! how I freeze! but there is fire to warm me and my old bones; that is well; but," she continued, turning to the Drummer, "there is a log which will not burn, fetch it out for me; come if you do that, you shall be free and go where you will, only be brisk."

The Drummer plunged into the flames without a moment's consideration; but they did him no harm, not even singeing a single hair. He bore the faggot off and laid it beside the old Witch; but as soon as it touched the earth it changed into the beautiful Maiden, who had delivered him from his troubles, and he perceived at once by her silken shining robes that she was the King's daughter. The old Woman laughed fiendishly again, and exclaimed, "Do you think you have her? not yet, not yet!" And, so saying, she would have seized the Maiden; but the Drummer, catching her with both his hands, threw her into the middle of the burning pile, and the flames closed in around her, as if rejoicing in the destruction of such a Witch.

When this was done the Maiden looked at the Drummer, and, seeing that he was a handsome youth, and that he had ventured his life to save hers, she held out her hand to him, and said, "You have dared a great deal for me, and I must do something for you; promise me to be true and faithful, and you shall be my husband. For wealth we shall not want; we have enough here in the treasure which the old Witch has gathered together."

Thereupon she led him into the house and showed him chests upon chests, which were filled with treasures. They left the gold and silver, and took nothing but diamonds and pearls; and then, as they no longer wished to remain on the glass mountain, the Drummer proposed that they should descend on the wishing-saddle. "The old saddle does not please me," said the Maiden, "and I need only turn the ring on my finger and we shall be at home."

"Well, then, wish ourselves at the city gate," replied the Drummer; and in the twinkling of an eye they were there. "I will go and take the news to my parents first," said the Drummer; "wait here for me, for I shall soon be back."

"Ah! I pray you, then, take care not to kiss your parents when you arrive on the right cheek, else will you forget everything, and I shall be left here all alone in this field." "How can I forget you?" said he, and promised her faithfully to return in a very short time. When he entered his father's house nobody knew him, he was so altered, for the three days which he had imagined he had spent on the glass mountain were three long years. He soon recalled himself to their remembrance, and his parents hung round his neck, so that, moved by affection, he entirely forgot the Maiden's injunctions, and kissed them on both cheeks. Every thought concerning the Princess at once faded from his mind, and, emptying his pockets, he laid handfuls of precious stones upon the table. The parents could not tell what to do with so much wealth, till at length they built a noble castle, surrounded by gardens, woods, and meadows, and fit for a prince to inhabit. When it was done the mother of the Drummer said to him, "I have looked out for a wife for you, and you shall be married in three days' time."

Now, the Drummer was quite content with all that his Parents proposed; but the poor Princess was very disconsolate. For a long time after he first left her she waited for him in the fields; but when evening fell she believed that he had kissed his Parents on the right cheek, and forgotten all about her. Her heart was full of grief, and she wished herself in some solitary forest that she might not return to her father's court. Every evening she went to the city and passed by the Drummer's house, but although he saw her many times he never recognised her. At last she heard one day the people talking of the wedding of the Drummer, and she thereupon resolved to make a trial if she could regain his love. As soon as the first festival-day was appointed, she turned her wishing-ring, saying, "A dress as shining as the sun." Immediately the dress lay before her, and seemed as if wove out of the purest sunbeams! Then, as soon as the guests had assembled, she slipped into the hall, and everybody admired her beautiful dress; but most of all the bride elect, who had a passion for fine dresses, and went up to her and asked if she would sell it. "Not for money," she replied; "but for the privilege of sleeping for one night next to the chamber of the bridegroom."

The Bride elect could not resist her wish for the dress, and so she consented; but first of all she mixed in the sleeping draught of the Bridegroom a strong potion, which prevented him from being awakened. By-and-by, when all was quiet, the Princess crept to the chamber-door, and, opening it slightly, called gently,—

> "Drummer, Drummer, O list to me,
> Forget not what I did for thee;
> Think of the mountain of glass so high,
> Think of the Witch and her cruelty;
> Think of my plighted troth with thee:
> Drummer! Drummer! O list to me!"

She cried all in vain, the Drummer did not awake, and when day dawned the Princess was forced to leave. The second evening she turned her wishing-ring, and said, "A dress as silvery as the moon." As soon as she had spoken it lay before her; and when she appeared in it at the ball, the Bride elect wished to have it as well as the other, and the Princess gave it to her for the privilege of passing another night next the chamber of the Bridegroom. And everything passed as on the first night.

The servants in the house, however, had overheard the plaint of the strange Maiden, and they told the Bridegroom about it. They told him, also, that it was not possible for him to hear anything about what was said because of the potion, which was put into his sleeping-draught.

The third evening the Princess turned the ring and wished for a dress as glittering as the stars. As soon as she appeared in the ball-room thus arrayed, the Bride elect was enchanted with its beauty, and declared rapturously, "I must and will have it." The Maiden gave it up, like the former, for a night's sleep next the Bridegroom's chamber. This time he did not drink his wine as usual, but poured it out behind the bed; and so, when all the house was quiet, he heard a gentle voice repeating,—

"Drummer, Drummer, O list to me,
Forget not what I did for thee;
Think of the mountain of glass so high,
Think of the Witch and her cruelty;
Think of my plighted troth with thee:
Drummer! Drummer! O list to me!"

All at once his memory returned, and he exclaimed, "Alas! alas! how could I have treated you so heartlessly? but the kisses which I gave my parents on the right cheek, in the excess of my joy, they have bewildered me." He jumped up, and, taking the Princess by the hand led her to the bedside of his Parents. "This is my true Bride," said he; "and if I marry the other I shall do a grievous wrong." When the Parents heard all that had happened, they gave their consent, and thereupon the lights in the hall were rekindled, the drums and trumpets refetched, the friends and visitors invited to come again, and the true wedding was celebrated with great pomp and happiness.

But the second Bride received the three splendid dresses, and was as well contented as if she had been married!

The Ears of Wheat

AGES upon ages ago, when the angels used to wander on earth, the fruitfulness of the ground was much greater than it is now. Then the Ears of Wheat bore, not fifty or sixty-fold, but four times five-hundred-fold. Then the corn grew from the bottom of the stalk to the top; and so long as the stalk was, so long were the Ears. But as men always do in the midst of their abundance, they forgot the blessing which came from God, and became idle and selfish.

One day a Woman went to a corn-field, and her little Child who accompanied her fell into a puddle and soiled her frock. The Mother tore off a handful of Wheat-ears and cleaned her Daughter's dress with them. Just then an Angel passed by, and saw her. He became very angry, and declared to her that henceforth the Wheat-stalks should no longer produce Ears, for, said he, "You mortals are not worthy of heaven's gifts." The bystanders who heard him, fell on their knees, weeping and praying him to leave the Wheat-stalks alone, if not for themselves, yet for the poor fowls, who must otherwise perish with hunger. The Angel pitied their distress and granted part of their prayer; and from that day the Ears of Wheat have grown as they do now.

The Grave-Mound

ONCE upon a time a rich Farmer was standing in his yard, looking out over his fields and gardens, where the corn was growing quite yellow, and the trees hanging down with fruit. The produce of the previous year lay in his granaries, and its weight was so great that the beams could scarcely support it. Next he went into his stables, and there stood stall-fed oxen, fat cows, and sleek horses. Lastly, he went back to his kitchen and his parlour, where stood the iron chests in which his gold was contained. Whilst he stood meditating upon his riches he heard suddenly a knock close to him. It was not the door of his house, but at his heart. He listened, and heard a voice which said to him, "Have you done good with your wealth? have you cared for the troubles of the poor? have you shared your bread with the hungry? have you been contented with what you possess, or have you desired more?" His heart replied without delay, "I have been hard and unmerciful to all; I have done good to no one; when a poor man has come to my door I have turned away my eyes; nor have I concerned myself about a God, but thought only how to increase my riches, and had all that heaven covered been mine, I should not even then have been satisfied!" As soon as these answers had passed through his mind, he became terribly frightened; and his knees trembled so much that he was forced to sit down. Then a second knock was heard by him, but this time is was not at his heart, but at the door. It was his neighbour, a poor Man, who had a great many children, more than he could satisfy. "I know that my neighbour is rich," the poor fellow had thought to himself; "but he is also very stingy: I do not believe that he will help me, but my children cry so for bread, I will venture it!" When the Rich Man answered the knock, the Poor Man said to him, "You are not accustomed, I know, to give readily to the poor; but I stand here like one whose head is nearly under water; my children are hungry, lend me four measures of meal?"

The Rich Man looked at him for some time, and soon the first sunbeam of compassion began to melt the ice of his selfishness. "I will not lend you four measures," he replied; "but I will give you eight measures, on one condition!"

"What is that?" asked the Poor Man.

"When I am dead, you must watch three nights by my grave."

This condition caused the Poor Man much secret uneasiness; still on account of the necessity in which he was, he consented; and promising all, he carried the corn home with him.

It seemed as if the Rich Man had a presentiment of what was to happen, for after three days he suddenly fell dead on the ground; nobody knew the cause of his decease, but no suspicion was excited. After he was buried, the Poor Man remembered his agreement, from which he wished he could have released himself; but he thought,

"The man behaved very compassionately to me, and I satisfied my children's hunger with his corn; and besides, I promised, and must perform."

As soon, then, as night fell, he went to the churchyard and sat down on a grave-mound. All was still, only the moon was shining on the hillocks, and many times an owl flew by, making her doleful cries. As soon as the sun again rose, the Poor Man returned home wearied out; and in due time passed the second night in similar quiet. But on the third evening he felt a peculiar terror; it seemed as if something stood before him. As soon as he got out he perceived a man on the wall of the churchyard, whom he had never seen before. He was by no means young, for his face was full of wrinkles; but his eyes shone with a bright light. He was quite enveloped by a large cloak, and only his large jack-boots were to be seen. "What are you seeking here?" asked the Peasant; "are you not afraid of the lone churchyard?"

"I fear nothing and desire nothing," replied the Man. "I am like the youth who travelled to learn what shivering meant, and wearied himself in so doing, but still received a Princess for his wife, and great riches; but I have always been poor; I am nothing but a discharged Soldier, and want to pass the night here, because I have no other shelter."

"If you have no fear, then," said the Peasant, "remain with me, and assist me to watch this grassy mound."

"Keeping guard is part of the Soldier's business," replied the stranger; "so whatever meets us here, whether bad or good, we will bear in common."

To this the Peasant assented, and the pair sat down by the grassy mound. Everything was quiet till midnight; and then all at once a cutting sound was heard in the air, and the two watchers perceived an Evil Spirit standing before them. "Away, you rascals!" he cried, "away! the man who lies in this grave belongs to me; I am come to fetch him, and if you do not take yourselves off I will break your necks." "Captain with the red feather!" replied the Soldier, "you are not my captain; I need not obey you; and to fear I have never learnt. Go your way! we shall stop here."

When the Soldier had spoken this, the Evil Spirit began to think to himself that perhaps he could manage the two watchers better by offering them money; and so, moderating his tune, he asked civilly whether they would not be satisfied to go home on the receipt of a purse of gold.

"That deserves consideration," said the Soldier; "but we shall not be sufficiently rewarded with one purseful of gold: if, however, you will give us as much as will fill one of my jack-boots, we will leave the field to you and go away."

"I have not so much with me," replied the Evil Spirit; "but I will fetch it. In the neighbouring town lives a banker, who is an intimate friend of mine, and he will readily lend me all I require."

So saying, the Spirit disappeared; and as soon as he was gone, the Soldier, drawing off his left boot, said to his companion, "Ah! now see how we will pull the nose of this coal-burner; only give me your knife, cousin."

He first cut off the sole and then set the boot upright in the long grass on the edge of a half-dug grave, near the one they were watching. "That is well done," he said: "now the chimney-sweeper may come as soon as he likes."

The pair sat down again to watch, and in a short time the Spirit returned, carrying a bag of gold in his hand.

"Shoot it in!" said the Soldier, raising the boot up a little as he approached; "but that lot will not be enough." The Spirit emptied the bag; but the gold fell through the boot of course, so that there remained nothing in it. "Stupid Spirit!" exclaimed the Soldier; "it is nothing at all, did I not tell you so? You must return and fetch more." Shaking his head, the Spirit went and returned in an hour with a much larger bag under his arm. "Shoot it in!" said the Soldier again, "but I doubt there is still not enough." The gold clinked as it fell, but the boot was still empty, and the Spirit himself looking in with fiery eyes, convinced himself of the fact. "You have shamefully big calves!" exclaimed the Spirit, making a wry face.

"Did you think," answered the Soldier, "that I had hoofs like you? Since when have you been so illiberal! Come, make haste and fetch some more gold, or our bargain will be at an end."

The Evil Spirit trotted off a third time, and after some long while returned with a sack upon his shoulders which nearly bent him double. He shot its contents quickly into the boot, but still it remained as empty as before. Thereupon he flew into a dreadful passion, and tried to snatch the boot out of the ground; but at the same moment the first dawn of daylight appeared, and the sun began to rise, so that the Evil Spirit was forced to fly away with loud shrieks. And the body of the Rich Man thenceforth rested in peace.

The Peasant would have shared the gold which the Spirit had left behind him; but the Soldier said, "No! give to the poor what should belong to me, and I will return with you to your cottage, and there we will spend the remainder of our days in quiet happiness, so long as it shall please God to spare us."

Old Rinkrank

THERE was once a King who had a Daughter; and he had a glass mountain built, and said that whoever could run over it without tumbling should have this daughter for his wife. Then there was one who was so fond of the King's Daughter that he asked the King whether he might not marry her. "Yes," said the King, "if you can run over the mountain without tumbling, then you shall have her." The King's Daughter said she would run over with him, so that she might hold him up if he were going to fall; so they ran over together, but when they got up to the middle the King's Daughter slipped and fell, and the glass mountain opened itself, and she tumbled right into it. Her Sweetheart couldn't see a bit where she had gone through, for the mountain had closed again directly. Then he fretted and cried so much, and the King too was so wretched, that he had the mountain broken down again, thinking he would get his Daughter out again; but they could never find the place where she had tumbled through. In the meantime the King's Daughter had got quite deep into the ground, in a great cave. There, there came to her an old fellow with a tremendous long grey beard, and he told her that if she would be his servant and do all he bade her, she should remain alive; if not he would make away with her. So she did all he told her. In the morning he took his ladder out of his pocket and placed it against the mountain, and climbed up out of it. Then he pulled the ladder up after him. She had then to cook his dinner, to make his bed, and to do all his work; and when he came home again he always brought great heaps of gold and silver with him.

Now, when she had been many years with him, and had already grown quite old, he called her Mother Mansrot, and she had to call him Old Rinkrank. One day, when he was out again, she made his bed, and washed his dishes, and then she shut up all the doors and windows quite close; but there was a little loophole, through which the light shone into the house, and that she left open. When old Rinkrank came home again he knocked at his door, and called out, "Open the door for me." "Nay, Old Rinkrank," said she; "I shan't open the door." Then he said:

> "Here stand I, poor Rinkrank,
>   Upon my seventeen long shanks;
>   Mother Mansrot, wash my dishes!"

"I have already washed your dishes," said she. Then he said again:

> "Here stand I, poor Rinkrank,
>   Upon my seventeen long shanks;
>   Mother Mansrot, make my bed!

"I have already made your bed," said she. Then he said again:

> "Here stand I, poor Rinkrank,
>   Upon my seventeen long shanks;
>   Mother Mansrot, open the door!"

Then he ran all round about the house, and saw that the little loophole was open, so he thought, "I will just look in there, to see what she is about that she won't open the door for me." So he went and tried to look in, but he couldn't get his head through on account of his long beard; so he poked his beard through the loophole first, and when he had got it quite through Mother Mansrot ran up, and fastened the trap-door with a band which she had tied to it, and so the beard was fastened in quite tight. Then he began to scream most miserably, it hurt him so; and he begged and prayed she would let him loose; but she said not before he gave her the ladder on which he climbed out of the mountain. Then, whether he willed or not, he was obliged to say where the ladder was. So she tied a very long band to the trap-door, and placed the ladder against the mountain, and climbed up out of it; and when she was at the top she pulled the trap-door open. She went then to her father and narrated all that had happened to her. The King was greatly rejoiced; and her Sweetheart was there still; so they went and dug up the mountain, and found old Rinkrank with all his gold and silver. Then the King had old Rinkrank killed, and took home all his silver and gold. And the King's Daughter married her old Sweetheart, and they lived right merrily in splendour and happiness.

The Ball of Crystal

THERE was once upon a time an Enchantress who had three sons, who loved one another dearly, but yet their mother would not trust them, and was always suspecting that they would rob her of her power; so she changed the eldest into an Eagle, and condemned him to dwell on the tops of a rocky chain of mountains, where one might see him many times wheeling round and round in the air in great circles. The second brother she changed into a Whale, and he dwelt in the deep sea, where one might see him now and then throwing up a huge stream of water. These two could retake their human form for two hours a-day. The third son, however, fearing that he might be changed into some wild beast, bear or lion, secretly took his departure, for he had heard that in the Castle of the Golden Sun sat an enchanted Princess awaiting a deliverer. Many a youth had felt bound to venture his life in her cause, but already had three-and-twenty met with horrible deaths, and only one remained to tell the dreadful tale. Our hero drove away all fear from his mind, and resolved to search out this wonderful castle. For a very long time he had wandered about, when one day he unexpectedly arrived in a large forest, from which he could not get out. He perceived, however, in the distance, two Giants, who beckoned him with their hands. He went towards them, and they told him that they were fighting for the possession of a hat; but, as they were both equally strong, neither could gain the mastery, and they wished, therefore, to leave the decision to him, since men of his size were generally very wise and crafty.

"What can induce you to fight for an old hat?" asked the Youth.

"You do not know the wonderful properties which belong to it." answered the Giants; "it is a wishing hat, and whoever wears it may go instantly whither he wishes."

"Give me the hat," said the Youth; "I will go a short way, and if you both run as if for a wager, and whoever comes up to me first shall have the hat." With these words he put the hat on and walked off; but, beginning to think of the Princess, he forgot the Giants, and walked on and on. All at once he heaved a sigh from the bottom of his heart, and exclaimed, "Ah! that I were near the Castle of the Golden Sun." Scarcely had the words passed his lips when he found himself standing on a high mountain before the very place. He entered the castle by the door and passed through all the rooms till he came to the last, where he found the Princess. But how startled he was when he saw her! Her face was full of wrinkles, her eyes were sunk deep in her head, and her hair was red. "Are you the King's Daughter of whose beauty all the world talks?" asked the Youth. "Alas!" she replied, "this is not my form; the eyes of mortal men can only see me in this hateful guise; but that you may know how beautiful is the reality, look in this mirror which cannot err, that will show you my face as it is in reality." She gave him a mirror, and he beheld in it the portrait of the most beautiful Maiden the earth could contain, and over her cheeks he could even see the tears of sorrow rolling. "How can I save you?" he asked; "no danger will appal me."

The Princess replied, "He who can obtain possession of the Crystal Ball, and hold it before the Enchanter, will thereby break his power, and I shall return to my original shape. But, alas! already many a one has met death for me, and I shall grieve for your youthful blood if you dare these great perils."

"Nothing can keep me from the attempt," said the Youth; "but what must I do?"

"You shall know all," said the Princess: "if you descend the mountain on which this castle stands you will find a wild Ox, with which you must fight; and if you are lucky enough to kill it, a Fiery Bird will rise from its carcass, in whose body is a red-hot egg, the yolk of which forms the Crystal Ball. This Bird will not drop the egg till it is compelled; but if it falls to the ground it will burn and consume whatever is near it, and then the iron will melt, and with it the Crystal Ball, and all your trouble will be futile."

The Youth, thereupon, descended to the bottom of the mountain, where he saw the Ox, who commenced as soon as he appeared to bellow and run at him. After a long fight the Youth plunged his sword into its body, so that it fell dead to the ground. At the same instant the Fiery Bird rose from the carcass, and was about to fly away, when the Eagle, the brother of the Youth, who was just then passing over the spot swooped down and struck the Bird towards the sea, so that in its endeavours to escape it let fall the egg. The egg, however, did not fall into the sea, but on the roof of a fisherman's hut which stood on the shore. The roof began to burn, for the egg instantly blazed up; but at the moment, immense waves dashed out of the sea, and, rolling quite over the hut, extinguished the fire. It was the other brother, the Whale, who had caused this, having luckily swum there at the right time. As soon as the fire was out, the Youth searched for the egg, and found it very quickly; it was not quite molten, but the shell was so cracked by the sudden cooling of the cold sea-water, that he managed easily to extract the Crystal Ball.

The Youth took it at once to show to the Enchanter, who, as soon as he saw it, said, "My power is destroyed, and you are henceforth King of the Castle of the Golden Sun. Your brothers, also, can now return to their human forms."

The Youth then hastened to the Princess, and as soon as he entered the room her former beauty returned in all its glory, and they both exchanged rings with great joy, which means to say, I suppose, that they married and were very happy.

Jungfrau Maleen

THERE was once upon a time a King's Son, who went a-wooing the Daughter of another mighty King, and her name was Jungfrau Maleen. Her father, however, refused his permission to the match, because he wished her to marry some one else. But they both still loved one another so dearly, that Jungfrau Maleen told her father she could not and would not marry any one except this Prince. When she said so, he father flew into a great passion, and caused a gloomy tower to be built, into which no ray of either sun or moon could penetrate. When it was completed he said to his Daughter, "For seven years you shall sit therein; and at the end of that period I will come and see if your stubborn disposition is conquered." Meat and drink sufficient for these seven years were carried into the tower, and then the Princess and her Maid were led into it, and bricked up, so that earth and heaven were shut out from them. They were quite in darkness, and knew no difference between day and night. The Prince often came to the outside of the tower and called their names, but they heard nothing, for no sound could penetrate through the thick walls. What could they do, then, except weep and lament their fate! So time passed by; and, by the decreasing of their food and drink, they perceived that the end of their imprisonment was approaching. They imagined that their release was at hand; but no sound of a hammer was to be heard, nor were any stones picked out of the wall, and it seemed as if the King had forgotten them. So when they had sufficient food left for only a few days, and the prospect of a miserable death stared them in the face, Jungfrau Maleen said to her companion, "It is time now that we should try to break through the wall."

So saying she took their bread-knife, and picked and scraped away the mortar round one stone; and when she was tired, the Maid assisted her. After a long time they succeeded in taking out one stone, then a second, and a third, and thus, after three days' labour, a ray of light illuminated their cell; and then they made the opening so large that they could peep through it. The heaven was blue and a fresh breeze came in their faces, but how mournful looked everything around! The castle of the King lay in ruins; the towns and villages, as far as the eye could reach, were burnt to the ground; the fields far and near were laid waste; and not one human being was to be seen. Soon the opening in the wall was so large that they could pass through it; and the Maiden first jumping out, her Mistress followed her. But where were they to turn? Enemies had depopulated the whole kingdom, and driven away or slain the King, with all his subjects. The pair therefore wandered on and on, seeking some other country; but nowhere could they find a shelter, or any man to give them bread to eat, and their hunger compelled them to eat the burnt roots of nettles.

However, after much weary travelling, they did at last come to cultivated land, and there, at every house, they offered their services; but nobody would take them in, or show them any pity. At last they arrived at a large city, and went to the King's palace; but there, also, they were on the point of being turned back, when the cook told them they might stop and serve as kitchen-maids if they liked.

Now the son of this King was the very same who was betrothed to Jungfrau Maleen, and his father had engaged him to another maiden, who was as wickedly disposed in her heart as she was ugly in her looks. When the two travellers arrived, the wedding-day had been already appointed, and the bride was come, but she had shut herself up in her room, and would not be seen, because of her ugliness, and Jungfrau Maleen was ordered to take in her meals. When the day came that the betrothed couple should go to church, the bride elect was so ashamed of her ugliness that she feared she should be laughed at, and derided by the common people if she showed herself to them. So she said to Jungfrau Maleen, "A great piece of luck is presented to you, for I have hurt my foot and cannot walk at all on the road; so you shall put on my bridal clothes, and take my place; a greater honour could not have fallen to your share."

Jungfrau Maleen, however, refused, and said, "I desire no honour that does not belong to me;" and she would not be tempted even with gold. At last the bride elect exclaimed passionately, "If you do not obey me, it shall cost you your life. I have only to say one word, and your head will lie at my feet."

Jungfrau Maleen was now forced to comply, and she arrayed herself in the bridal clothes and ornaments. As soon as she appeared in the royal apartments all were astonished at her great beauty, and the King told his son she was the bride whom he had chosen for him, and it was time now to go to church. The Prince was astonished, and thought to himself, "She looks like my Jungfrau Maleen, and I almost believe it is she; but no! she is dead, or shut up in the tower." He took the Maiden by the hand, and led her to the church, and on the road they passed a nettle-bush, whereupon the bride sang in a strange language—

"Nettle-bush! oh, nettle-bush!
Have you forgot the day
When I cooked your juicy roots,
My hunger sharp to stay?"

"What did you say then?" asked the Prince. "Nothing! I was only thinking of Jungfrau Maleen," replied the seeming Bride. He marvelled that she should know her, but he said nothing, and when they came to the church steps she sang—

"Church steps, break not, I pray,
The true Bride comes not to-day."

"What did you say?" asked the Prince. "Nothing," she replied, as before: "I was but thinking of Jungfrau Maleen."

"Do you know that Maiden, then?" asked the Prince. "No, how should I? I have only heard of her," said she; and when they passed through the church-door she sang—

"Church door, crack not, I pray,
The true Bride comes not to-day."

"What did you say?" asked the Prince a third time. "Alas! I was only thinking of Jungfrau Maleen," she said. Then he drew out a costly chain and fastened it around her neck, and thereupon they walked into the church, and the priest, joining their hands together at the altar, married them in due form. The ceremony over, the Bridegroom led back the Bride, but she never spoke a single word all the way home. As soon as they arrived at the palace, she hastened into the Bride's chamber, and, laying aside her beautiful clothes and ornaments, she put on her grey kirtle, but kept the chain round her neck, which she had received from the Bridegroom.

When night came, and it was time for the Bride to be ushered into the Bridegroom's chamber, the ugly Maiden let fall her veil over her features, that the deceit might not be discovered. As soon as they were alone, the Bridegroom asked her, "What did you say to that nettle-bush which we passed on the road?"

"To what nettle-bush?" she asked, "I spoke to no nettle-bush!"
"If you did not, you are not my real Bride," said he. Thereupon
she left the room, and, seeking Jungfrau Maleen, asked her what she
had said to the nettle-bush. She sang the words over—

> "Nettle-bush! oh, nettle-bush!
> Have you forgot the day
> When I cooked your juicy roots,
> My hunger sharp to stay?"

And as soon as she had done, the Bride ran back to the room and
repeated them to the Prince. "But what did you say to the church-
steps as we passed up them?" he inquired. "To the church-steps!"
she echoed in surprise; "I spoke to none." "Then you are not the
right Bride!" said the Bridegroom again. "I will go and ask my Maid
what my thoughts were," said the Bride; and, seeking Jungfrau
Maleen, she inquired of her what she had said. The Maid repeated
the words—

> "Church-steps, break not, I pray,
> The true Bride comes not to-day."

"That shall cost you your life!" exclaimed the Bride; but, hastening
back to the chamber, she told the Prince the words which she had
just heard. "But what did you say to the church-door?" he inquired
next. "To the church-door!" she replied; "I spoke to no church-
door."

"Then you are not the right Bride," said the Prince. Thereupon
away she went a third time to Jungfrau Maleen, and inquired what
she had said. The Maid repeated the words—

> "Church door, crack not, I pray,
> The true Bride comes not to-day."

"Your neck shall be broken for saying so!" exclaimed the Bride in
a rage; but, hastening back to the chamber, she repeated the words
she had just heard to the Bridegroom.

"But where have you put the chain I gave you at the church-door?" asked the Prince.

"What chain? You gave me no chain!" exclaimed the Bride. "But I hung it round your neck myself, and fastened it myself; and if you do not remember that you are not the right Bride." With that he tore the veil from her face, and when he saw her extreme ugliness, he exclaimed, springing away from her, "Who are you? whence come you?"

"I am your betrothed Bride," she replied; "but, because I feared the people would mock me if I showed myself to them, I ordered our Kitchen-Girl to put on my dresses, and go to church in my place."

"Where is the Girl then, now? Go and fetch her immediately," said the Prince.

She went out and told the other servants that the Kitchen-Girl was an enchantress, and that they must drag her away from the court and cut off her head. The servants soon caught the Maiden, and would have done as they were told; but she cried so loudly for help, that the Prince heard her voice, and hastening out of his room, gave orders for the Maiden's instant release. Lights were immediately brought, and then the Prince perceived round the Maiden's neck the gold chain which he had given her at the church-door.

"You are the true Bride who went to church with me!" he exclaimed; "come with me now!" As soon as they were alone, he said to her, "On the way to church you named Jungfrau Maleen, who was once betrothed to me. Now, if I thought it possible, I should say that you were that Maiden, for you are so like to her."

"I am Jungfrau Maleen!" she replied; "and for seven long years have I been shut up in darkness; hunger and thirst, too, I have suffered; and in poverty and distress have I lived ever since; but on this day the sun shines again. I did, indeed, accompany you to church, and it was to me that you were married."

So the Prince recovered his true Bride, Jungfrau Maleen, and with her lived happily for many long years.

But the false Bride had her head cut off.

The Boots made of Buffalo-Leather

A SOLDIER who is afraid of nothing, cares for nothing. Now such a one had received his discharge, and because he had learnt no trade, he could earn no money; and so he wandered about hither and thither, begging alms of good people. Over his shoulders hung an old weatherproof cloak, and he had still left a pair of Buffalo-leather Boots. One day, thus equipped, he went on walking through the fields without attending to the guide-posts, and at last he came to an immense forest. He did not know where he was, but he saw a man sitting upon the trunk of a tree, who was well dressed in a green huntsman's coat. The Soldier held out his hand to him, and then laying himself down on the grass, stretched out his legs. "I see you have a pair of fine shining boots on," said he to the Huntsman; "but if you had to walk about as much as I, they would not last you very long. Look at mine! they are made of Buffalo-leather, and although they have served me a long time, they would still go through thick and thin." The Huntsman made no answer; and after a while the Soldier got up and said, "I can stop here no longer; hunger urges me forward; but pray, Brother Thin-Boots, where does this path lead to?" "I do not know myself," replied the Huntsman; "I have lost myself in this forest." "Then you are in the same plight as I," returned the Soldier; "like and like please one another; we will remain together and seek the way." The Huntsman only laughed, but they set out together, and kept on till nightfall. "We shall not get out of this forest to-night," exclaimed the Soldier at last; "but I can see a light glimmering in the distance, where they will give us something to eat." It was a stone cottage, and when they knocked at the door, an old Woman opened it. "We are seeking a night's lodging," said the Soldier to her, "and some fodder for our stomachs, for mine is as empty as my purse."

"You cannot stop here," answered the old Woman; "this is a robber's house, and you will be wise if you go away before they return, or you will lost."

"It cannot be worse," said the Soldier; "for two days I have not eaten a morsel; and so it is all one to me whether I perish in this house or out in the forest. I shall come in and risk it!"

The Huntsman did not wish to follow, but the Soldier, drawing his arm within his own, drew him in, saying, "Come, comrade, we will suffer together!"

The old Woman pitied them, and told them to creep behind the stove, and then when the robbers were satisfied and slept she would give them something to eat. Scarcely had they hid snugly in the corner, than in came the twelve robbers; and placing themselves round the table, demanded their supper with harsh language. The old Woman soon brought in an immense dish of baked meat, and the robbers prepared to fall to. Soon the smell of the savoury mess ascended the Soldier's nose, and he said to the Huntsman, "I can hold out no longer, I must sit down at the table and take a share!" "You will lose your life!" whispered the Huntsman, holding him fast by the arm. The Soldier began to cough loudly, and as soon as the

THE BOOTS MADE OF BUFFALO LEATHER

robbers heard this, they threw aside their knives and forks, and rising hastily from the table discovered the pair behind the stove. "Aha, you rascals!" they called; "what are you sitting there in that corner for? Are you sent as spies? Just wait a bit, and you shall learn how to fly on a bare branch!" "Oh! have some manners, if you please?" returned the Soldier; "give us something to eat first, and afterwards you shall do what you like with us!" The robbers were astonished to hear such bold words, and the Captain said, "Good! I see you are not afraid; eat you shall, but afterwards you shall die." "We shall see!" muttered the Soldier; and sitting down at the table, he began to cut and eat in earnest. "Brother Thin-Boots," he exclaimed to the Huntsman, "come and eat; you are hungry as well as I, and a better joint than this you could not have at home." The Huntsman, however, refused; and the robbers looking at the Soldier, said to one another, "This fellow makes no ceremony." When he had done eating, he asked for something to drink, saying, "Well! the meat was good enough; now let us have a good draught of wine." The Captain happened to be in a good humour, and so he told the old Woman to fetch a bottle of the very best wine out of the cellar. When it was brought, the Soldier drew out the cork so that it made a great noise; and then going to the Huntsman he whispered to him, "Pay attention, my brother, and you shall see a grand wonder; I will now drink the health of the whole company!" So saying, he swung the bottle over the heads of the robbers, at the same time shouting out, "You shall all live, but with your mouths open and your right hands uplifted!" Scarcely were the words out of his mouth, than the robbers all sat motionless as if they were made of stone, their mouths open and their right arms stretched out. "I see," said the Huntsman to the Soldier, "you can play any other trick you please; but, come now, let us go home." "Oh, no, Brother Thin-Shoes!" replied the Soldier, "that were too early to march away; we have beaten the enemy and now we must take the booty. Come now, eat and drink what you like." So they stopped there three days, and every day the old Woman had to fetch up fresh wine. The fourth day the Soldier said to his companion, "It is time now to break the spell, but that we may have a short march the old Woman shall show us the nearest road."

As soon as they arrived at the town the Soldier went to his old comrades, and told them that he had found in the forest a nest of thieves, and if they wished he would show them where. They agreed to go, and the Soldier persuaded the Huntsman to accompany him again, and see how the robbers behaved when they were caught. So first he placed the soldiers round the robbers in a circle, and then drinking a draught of wine out of the bottle, he swung it over them and exclaimed, "You shall all live." In a moment they had the power of motion again, but they were soon thrown down and bound hand and foot with ropes. Then they were thrown like sacks upon a waggon, and the Soldier bade his comrades drive it away to the prison. But the Huntsman, taking aside one of the soldiers, gave him a commission and sent him off to the town. They walked on, and by-and-by, as they approached the town, the Soldier perceived an immense crowd of men rushing out at the gates, hurrahing loudly and waving green branches of trees in the air. He soon saw that it was the body-guards of the King who were approaching them; and turning to the Huntsman he asked, "What does this mean?" "Do you not know," he replied, "that the King has been absent from his kingdom for a length of time? To-day he returns, and these are coming out to meet him." "But where is the King? I do not see him," said the Soldier. "Here he is," answered the Huntsman; "I am the King, and I caused my return to be proclaimed." With these words he opened his hunting-coat and showed his royal dress. The Soldier was frightened, and falling on his knees he begged the King's pardon for having treated him so unceremoniously, and called him by such names. The King, however, holding out his hand, said to him, "You are a brave Soldier, and have saved my life; you shall suffer poverty no longer; I will care for you, and if at any time you want a piece of meat as good as we had in the forest, come to my palace and dine with me. But before you drink healths you must ask my permission."

The Golden Key

ONE winter, when a deep snow was lying on the ground, a poor Boy had to go out in a sledge to fetch wood. As soon as he had collected together a sufficient quantity, he thought that before he returned home he would make a fire to warm himself at, because his limbs were so frozen. So sweeping the snow away, he made a clear space, and presently found a small gold key. As soon as he picked it up, he began to think that where there was a key there must also be a lock; and digging in the earth he found a small iron chest. "I hope the key will fit," thought he to himself; "there are certainly great treasures in this box!" He looked all over it, but could not find any key hole; till at last he did discover one, which was, however, so small, that it could scarcely be seen. He tried the key, and behold! it fitted exactly. Then he turned it once round, and now we must wait until he has quite unlocked it, and lifted the lid up, and then we shall learn what wonderful treasures were in the chest!

The Legend of Saint Joseph in the Forest

THERE was once upon a time a Mother who had three Daughters, the eldest of whom was stupid and bad-tempered; the second, however, was much better, though she, too, had her faults; but the youngest was a pious, good child. The Mother was odd in her tastes, for she loved the eldest the most, and could not endure her youngest Daughter; and therefore she often sent the poor girl out into the forest, where she hoped to be rid from her, hoping that she would wander about so as to lose herself. Her guardian angel however, (and such a one watches over every good child), did not forsake her, but led her always along the right road. Once the angel seemed to have forsaken her, and the Child wandered on by herself. She walked on till evening, and then saw a light burning in the distance.

She went up to it, and found a little cottage, and knocking at the door it opened, and she came to a second door, where she knocked again. An old man, with a snow-white beard and a venerable countenance, opened it, and he was no other than St. Joseph. In a friendly voice he said, "Come in, dear Child; sit down on my stool by the fire and warm yourself; I will fetch you some clear water if you are thirsty, but I have nothing for you to eat but a couple of roots, and those you must scrape and cook for yourself." With these words St. Joseph handed her the roots, and, carefully peeling them, she took up a small saucepan and put them in. The she added to them some water and the bread which her Mother had given her, and put them over the fire till they were boiled down to a soup. When it was done, St. Joseph said, "I am so hungry, give me some of your broth to eat." This the Girl very willingly did, and gave him more than she took for herself. Still, however, with God's blessing, she had quite sufficient. As soon as they had finished their supper, St. Joseph said, "It is time now to go to bed, but as I have only one bed, do you lie down in that, and I will make my bed of straw." "No, no," she replied; "keep you your own bed, the straw is tender enough for me." St. Joseph, however, would carry her to the bed, and there laying her down, she went to sleep as soon as she had said her prayers. The next morning, when she awoke, she would have said, "Good morning!" to St. Joseph, but she could nowhere see him. She arose and looked for him, but she could not find him in any corner; and while she searched she perceived hanging behind the door a sack full of money, on which it was written that it was for the Maiden who had slept there that night. She took the sack, and jumping merrily along under its weight, took it to her Mother, who was obliged for once to be satisfied with her youngest Daughter.

The following day the second Daughter also took a fancy to go into the forest, and her Mother gave her a much larger pancake and a piece of bread. It happened to her the same as it had done to her Sister. Towards evening she came to the cottage where St. Joseph lived, and he told her to make herself some soup. As soon as it was ready he said as before, "I pray you give me some of that to eat, for I am so hungry." The child told him to eat with her; and when afterwards he proposed to give her his bed and lie himself on the straw, she said to him, "Share the bed with me, there is room enough for us both!" But St. Joseph laid her down in the bed by herself and slept on the straw, and by the next morning, when she awoke, he had disappeared. Behind the door she found a small bag of gold, as long as her hand, and on it was written that it was for the Maiden who had slept there that night. She took the bag and hastened home to her Mother, but she kept secretly two pieces of gold for herself.

Now the eldest Sister became covetous, and the next morning she prepared to go to the forest. Her Mother gave her several pancakes, as many as she liked, and not only bread, but cheese. About evening she arrived, like her Sisters, at the cottage of St. Joseph, and found him there. She was also bidden to cook her soup, and when it was ready St. Joseph said, "I am so hungry, give me some of your soup to eat." But the Maiden replied, "Wait until I am satisfied, and then what I leave you shall have." So she went on eating till she had nearly finished, and S. Joseph had only the scrapings of the basin. The good old man, however, offered her his bed, and said he would lie on the straw, and this kindness she took as if it were her due, and she let the Saint lie down on his hard couch. The next morning, when she awoke, he had disappeared, but she cared nothing about that, and thought only of the bag of gold, which she expected to find behind the door. She certainly did see something lying there, but because she could not exactly tell what it was, she bent herself down so that her nose touched it. It stuck to her nose, and when she stood up and looked at herself she found to her terror that it was a second nose growing from the first! She began to howl and shriek, but to what purpose? she could not help seeing her nose, because it was so long. She ran out of the house with a loud cry, and ran on till she met St. Joseph, and as soon as she saw him she fell down on her knees and begged him to take away the second nose. Out of pity for her, he did at last remove it and gave her two pennies. As soon as she reached home her Mother met her at the door, and asked her what she had received. She told a lie, and answered, "A great sack full of money, but I lost it on the way." "Lost it!" repeated the Mother, "then let us look for it again;" and catching her Daughter's hand, she dragged her back to search. At first she wept and would not go, but at length she consented, and on they went. At every step they took snakes and lizards started up, so many that they could not guard them off; and soon one stuck its fangs into the breast of the Daughter and she fell dead; and then another pierced the foot of the Mother because she had not brought her Child up better.

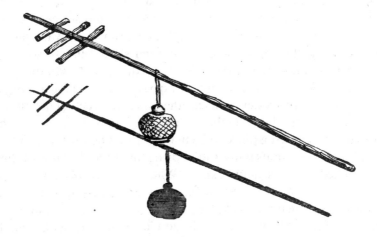

Humility and Poverty lead to Heaven

ONCE upon a time there was a King's Son, who went into the fields sad and thoughtful. He looked up at the sky, which was so beautifully blue and clear, and said with a sigh, "Ah! how happy must they be who are in heaven." At the same moment he perceived a grey old Man, who was walking the same way, and he asked him the question how he could go to heaven. "Through humility and poverty," answered the old Man. "Put on my old clothes, and wander about the world for seven years to learn what misery is: take no money with you, but when you are hungry, beg a piece of bread of charitable people, and thus you will approach gradually the gate of heaven."

Thus advised, the Prince drew off his fine clothing, and putting on instead the Beggar's rags, he went forth into the world, and endured much misery. He took only the scantiest meals, spoke never a word, but prayed daily to God, to take him, if he pleased, to heaven. When seven years had passed, he returned to his father's house, but nobody recognised him. He told the servants to go and tell his parents that he was returned; but the servants would not believe him, and only laughed at his pretensions. "Then go and tell my brothers," said he, "that they may come to me, for I should like to see them once again." This request they also refused; but at length one went and told the King's children, but they troubled not their heads about it. Then he wrote a letter to his mother, and depicted all his misery, but said nothing about his being her son. The Queen, pitying his misfortunes, caused a place to be made for him below the staircase, and there two servants daily had to bring him food. But one of them was wicked at heart, and asked, "What shall the Beggar do with good food?" and so he kept it for himself, or gave it to the dogs, while he took the poor weak, half-starved Prince nothing but water. The other servant, however, was honest, and took him daily what he received for him. It was only a little, but still enough to sustain life for a long while; and with it he was quite content, though he grew weaker and weaker. But when his illness increased, he desired to receive the last rites of the church, and while the service was performing, all at once every bell in the city and the country round tolled. As soon as the service was over, the Priest went to the poor Beggar, and found him lying dead, holding in one hand a rose, and in the other a lily; and near him lay a paper, whereon was written his history.

And after he was buried, there grew on one side of his grave a rose, and on the other side a lily.

The Three Green Twigs

ONCE upon a time there lived a Hermit at the foot of a mountain near the forest, who spent his time in prayer and good works, and each evening he carried up the hill a pail of water as an act of penitence. Many a beast refreshed himself from this pail, and many a flower also was revived, for on the height blew continually a hot wind, which dried the air and the earth. The wild fowls also, who avoided human beings, would circle down near the water and dip their long beaks into it. And because the Hermit was so pious, unseen an Angel always accompanied him up the hill, counting his steps, and bringing him, when the work was done, a meal, like as was done to that Prophet who, at God's command, was fed by the ravens. Thus the Hermit grew older and more pious every day; and once it happened that as he ascended the hill, he saw at a distance a poor sinner led to the gallows. As he looked he said, "Now is he judged rightly!" and as soon as he had so said the Angel left him and brought him no food that evening. He grew frightened, and tried in his heart to think how he had offended God; but he could remember nothing. He ceased to eat or drink, and throwing himself on the earth, prayed all day and night long. Once, as he was bitterly weeping in the forest, he heard a little Bird singing clearly and beautifully, and the sound so disturbed him that he exclaimed, "Alas! you sing merrily, because you are happy; but I would that you could tell me wherein I have offended God that I might do penance, and so my heart become glad again!" Presently the Bird spoke, "You did wrong because you condemned a poor criminal whom you saw led to the gallows, and therefore was God angry, because to him alone belongs the right of judgement. Still, if you are penitent and confess your sins, God will yet pardon you." At the moment the Bird finished speaking the Angel stood once more beside the Hermit, and giving a withered branch, said to him, "You shall carry this till Three Green Twigs spring from it; and at night when you sleep you must always place it beneath your head. Your bread you must beg from door to door, and you must not remain in any house more than one night. This is the penance which God imposes on you."

So the hermit took the dry branch and went back to the world which he had not seen for so long. He ate and drank nothing but what was given to him at the door of charitable people, although at many houses his prayer was refused, and many a door was shut against him, and thus he often passed whole days without a crumb of bread. One day he had thus passed, door after door was shut against him, and nobody would give him anything, or shelter him for the night; so he went into the wood and found a tumble-down cottage, in which an old Woman was sitting. He went in and said to her, "Pray shelter me this night, my good Woman." She replied, "No, I dare not, even if I would; I have three sons, wild and wicked, who, if they come home from their plundering and find you here, will kill us both." "Let me stop, nevertheless," entreated the Hermit: "they will do nothing to either you or me." So the old Woman took compassion on him and bade him sit down. He laid himself down in a corner with the dry branch under his head, and when the old

Woman observed this she inquired the reason, and he told her that he carried it as a penance, and was forced to use it every night for his pillow. "I have offended God," he said, "because when I saw a poor criminal led to the gallows, I said that justice was done to him." The old Woman began to weep bitterly as he finished his tale, and exclaimed, "Alas! if God so punishes for a single word, how will he judge my sons when they appear before him!"

At midnight the Robbers came home shouting and laughing. They lighted a fire, and as the blaze lit up the cottage they saw the old Man lying in one corner. In a rage they started up and asked their Mother, "Who is this man? Have we not forbidden you ever to allow any one to enter our house?"

"Let him be, he is only a poor sinner doing penance for his sins," pleaded the Mother. "What has he done?" asked the Robbers; and, turning to the old Man, they said, "Tell us your crimes." So the Hermit lifted himself up, and related how he had sinned by saying a few words, for which God was very angry with him, and had made him do penance. As he finished his tale the hearts of the Three Brothers were powerfully affected, and they were so frightened with the remembrance of their daily lives that they began to repent with heartfelt sorrow. Meanwhile, the old Hermit having thus turned the three sinners from their evil ways, laid down to sleep. In the morning he was found dead, and from the dry branch which formed his pillow Three Green Twigs had burst forth.

And by this it was known that God had fully pardoned him.

The Old Widow

In a certain large town there once lived an Old Widow, who sat every
evening alone in her room, thinking how, one by one, she had lost
and buried her husband, her two sons, and all her relations and
friends, so that now she was quite alone in the world. Her heart grew
very sorrowful with these thoughts; but the loss of her two sons
troubled her the most, and she wept for them very bitterly. She sat
quite still, lost in thought, and all at once she heard the bell ringing
for early prayers in the church. She wondered how she could have
passed all the night in sorrowing; but lighting her lantern she went to
the church. As she entered she saw it was already lit up: but not as
usual with tapers, but a glimmering light shone through the whole
building. It was already filled with worshippers, and every seat was
occupied, so that when the Poor Widow went to her accustomed
place, she found it already filled. As she looked round at the people,
she perceived that they were her deceased relations, who sat there in

their old every-day dresses; but with pale countenances. They neither spoke nor sang, but a gentle whisper and hum floated through the church. Presently an Aunt of the Poor Widow got up and said to her, "Look towards the altar, and you will see your two sons." She looked and saw her two children, the one hanging on the gallows, and the other broken on the wheel. "See," continued the Aunt, "thus would it have happened to them, had life been given to them, instead of their being mercifully taken by God when they were innocent children." With trembling steps the Old Widow went home, and on her knees thanked God that he had dealt so much better with her than her heart had imagined. But on the third day she laid down on her bed and died.

The Rose

THERE was once a poor Woman who had two Children, and the youngest went every day into the forest to fetch wood. Once, when it had strayed far away looking for branches, a little, but strong and healthy Child came to it and helped it to pick up wood, and carried the bundles up to the house; but then in less than a moment he was gone. The Child told its mother of this; but she would not believe it. At last the Child brought home a Rose, and told its mother that the beautiful Child had given it, and had said that when the Rose was in full bloom then he would come again. The Mother put the Rose into water. One morning the Child did not get out of bed, and the mother went to it and found it dead; but it lay looking quite happy and pleased, and the Rose that morning was in full bloom.

THE END